THE
SAVIOR'S
SISTER

JENNA MORECI

THE SAVIOR'S SISTER

Book 2 of The Savior's Series

Copyright © Jenna Moreci 2020

First edition: September 2020

Library of Congress Control Number: 2020908590

For inquiries, please direct all mailed correspondence to:
PO Box 475
San Carlos, CA 94070
USA

ISBN: 978-0-9997352-4-4 (hardback)

ISBN: 978-0-9997352-5-1 (paperback)

ISBN: 978-0-9997352-6-8 (ebook)

www.JennaMoreci.com

Edited by Kimberly Cannon

Book Cover by Damonza

THE
SAVIOR'S
SISTER

JENNA MORECI

ALSO BY JENNA MORECI

～

THE SAVIOR'S CHAMPION

Book 1 of The Savior's Series

THE BETRAYAL

"Leila's turn!"

Leila stared up at the mural, ignoring Her sisters. Spots of pink, gold, and icy blue covered the ceiling, a piece She had seen a hundred times yet never ceased to captivate Her.

"Let's play palace." Cosima giggled, her red curls bouncing. "I want to be the queen!"

Delphi rolled her eyes. "You picked last."

"You can be my servant and braid my hair!"

"It's *Leila's* turn, stupid," Delphi said.

Leila's gaze didn't leave the mural—a vision of the realm's first Savior, Her violet eyes, Her glowing skin. *My great, great, great grandmother...or something.*

A flurry of men in colorful tunics headed into the atrium, led by a royal in a red drape and a black eye patch, a crown of silver prongs nestled amid his curls. He sat at the dining table, and Leila's shoulders curled.

Father.

"Leila?" Delphi nudged Her shoulder. "Pick something." Instead She gazed at the floor, twirling the lining of Her dress between Her fingers. Maybe he wouldn't notice Her. Maybe if She was quiet—

"Leila," Her father shouted. "Come."

She hesitated, then flinched when he snapped his fingers, springing to Her feet and skittering his way. She stopped a pace or two from his side, Her throat catching. He took Her hand, wrenching Her closer.

"You're certain of the time?" His gaze was locked on the page before him. "We can't afford delays."

"The entire event has been arranged down to the second, Your Highness."

His grip hardened, and color pricked at Leila's skin, spilling from his palm to Hers. Looking up at the muraled ceiling, She hoped to see the same shades of pink, or gold, or icy blue. To feel them.

Murky grey. She never saw pretty colors in Her father.

"And what of the people?" Her father said. "I don't want them getting close."

"A path will be cleared for you and Her Holiness." His page glanced over a lengthy scroll. "Guards will line the walkway. No one will be permitted through."

"It's Her first public appearance. They'll be absolutely uncivilized."

"There will be much celebration, but no one gets through, I assure you." The page smiled at Leila, bowing his head. "Is this acceptable, Your Holiness?"

"Y—" She stuttered, then raised Her voice. "Yes."

"Ixion," Her father barked.

A portly Senator had entered the room, stopping at the sound of his name. Leila's father flagged him over. "You weren't at today's meeting."

"I'm resigning." Squaring his shoulders, Ixion approached the table. "From this day forth, I relinquish my title in the Thessian Senate."

"Care to tell us why?" Her father said.

"We can discuss privately."

"Anything you have to say can be shared here."

Ixion eyed the surrounding men. "I'm...uncomfortable with recent arrangements."

"Arrangements you yourself have championed for a number of years."

"Circumstances have changed."

Ixion glowered, but Leila's father offered nothing—no words, no reaction. He turned to the others. "Did you know outside his work in politics, Ixion is a recreational chemist? Creates peculiar concoctions, some with very powerful and often dangerous effects."

Ixion's face paled. "Your Highness—"

"Were you hoping to keep this to yourself? I do aim to respect the privacy of my Senators. Then again, you've resigned your post, haven't you."

Clearing his throat, Ixion nodded. "I could reconsider."

"Smart man."

Bowing, the Senator plodded off, meek and wounded. Her father was good at that—getting people to do as he ordered. The sign of a true Sovereign, many said. Perhaps people expected Leila to be like him one day. Poised. Powerful. She hung Her head.

A man with thinning black hair and a hooked nose appeared in the corridor, capturing Her father's attention. "Romulus, a word in my chamber?" Her father waved the others away, then turned to Leila. "Go."

He released his grip on Her, and She sucked in a full breath. Still, She didn't move, Her eyes on his back as he disappeared from view.

Small hands slapped against Her shoulder blades.

"Leila's it!" Cosima said.

Leila spun around as Her two sisters fled the atrium in a fit of laughter. "Hey!" She tore after them, but She was so small, and Her sisters had those long legs. "Wait! That's not fair!"

Delphi and Cosima peeled around a faraway corner, nearly toppling over.

Leila growled. She never won this game. "It's not fair! Stop!"

Her eyes locked onto the last place She had seen them. *Run faster*, but Her feet couldn't catch up to Her thoughts. She squinted, focusing long and hard on that corner. *Catch up.*

Light flooded Her vision, and a second later She stumbled around the corner.

Leila staggered to a halt, Her gaze darting to the corridor behind Her—the stretch She had cleared in an instant. *How did I do that?* It was impossible...until She remembered the flash of light.

The mark of Her power.

She looked down at Her glowing hands. Heat pulsed through them, burning with a power She had known Her whole life. And now that power had expanded.

The atrium. Her vision went white, Her body warm, and suddenly the muraled ceiling loomed above Her yet again. She clasped Her hands over Her mouth, containing a squeal. *A new trick.* Delphi and Cosima may have had those long legs, but they couldn't hop from room to room.

She appeared in the bathhouse, then the courtyard, transported by the sheer will of Her thoughts. Her excitement turned into wild glee, and She closed Her eyes, imagining the comfort of Her bed. Light consumed Her, harsh and fiery, and when She opened Her eyes, She stood in Her bedchamber.

Leila spun in a circle, reveling in Her latest discovery. She turned to Her mirrored wardrobe, greeted by Her flushed, grinning reflection, along with the faces of two women. Women who weren't in the room. Who weren't even of this world, at least not any longer. *Another trick.* She knew this one well.

Panting, She planted Her hands on the mirror. "Mummies."

Both women smiled at Her—one with Leila's white skin, the other with deep brown features. A mother She had never met, and one She had loved.

Leila's gaze danced across Her room. Her chamber opened up to a vast garden, and far beyond it stood a large, stone wall—the edge of the fortress.

Travel past the fortress.

Nothing. Leila remained rooted to the floor, no sudden voyage. She turned to Her mothers. "I can't? But why?"

Her mothers didn't answer. They never did.

"I'm going to show Delphi."

Their faces vanished behind streaks of white. She was back in the atrium. Empty. Then the gallery. No one. She tried the grand staircase; servants walked by, and She hid behind a column. *Delphi has to see it first.* Another surge of light, but still no sign of Her sister. Closing Her eyes, She dissolved within Her power, traveling to another corridor.

Her father's chamber stood ahead, sending Her rigid. Holding Her breath, She tiptoed past it.

4

"You're certain everything's secure? I need this to work."

"All possible complications have been prepared for."

"You said that last time."

Two voices fired off within the chamber—Her father and Romulus, tense and heated. But it was the severity of Her father's words that struck Her, and the way his colors seeped straight beneath the door, the murky grey now a blazing red.

He was angry.

"One more time." Her father's footsteps echoed as he paced the floor. "Let's run through it one more time."

"Your Highness—"

"I need Her *gone*," he spat. "I should be ruling, not playing *father*."

Father. An insult, as if speaking it had left a foul taste in his mouth. She glanced across the corridor—no servants, no staff—then pressed Her ear to the door.

"The moment draws near." Romulus's voice was strong and assured. "Tomorrow, Leila will be killed, and Thessen will be under your complete domain."

Her heart shot into Her throat.

"The plan," Her father said.

"We take Her into the commons, present Her to the adoring crowd," Romulus rattled off. "Our man shoots. She dies in the arms of Her grieving father before plenty of witnesses. A rebel has already been located. He'll take the fall."

Silence. Her father paced.

"I can kill the girl myself, Your Highness. We didn't have to recruit outside."

"You killed my wife, and look what that got me. A damn child. No, I'm leaving this to someone who knows what they're doing." Her father let out a deep sigh. "Everything would have been so much simpler if we'd ended Her as an infant."

Leila clutched Her dress, cowering beneath his words.

"The blame would point to you," Romulus said. "Your wife and daughter, dead under suspicious circumstances, and so quickly—"

"I'm not *stupid*," Her father hissed. "I know this." He grumbled under his breath. "All this work. End the wife, end the nanny, end the girl. Toma still opposes?"

"As do Ixion and Gelanor. They think the people will speculate given the similar nature of Her mother's passing. They argue for more distance."

"Gelanor and Toma can be convinced. Get rid of Ixion. Discreetly."

"Yes, Your Highness."

"And what of you?" The pacing stopped. "What are your thoughts?"

"I think the throne has been calling your name for some time now."

Leila pulled away. *My chamber.* Another white flash, and again She stood in front of Her mirrored wardrobe and those two faces.

Kind.

Sad.

Her gaze panned between them. Glowing skin, ebony skin. Blue eyes, brown eyes. *End the wife. End the nanny.*

Leila would die next.

Her father's words rang in Her ears, and panic latched onto Her. She wept in Her chamber until Her cheeks were raw and red, Her thoughts wavering between mourning and madness.

How do I stop this?

A shaky breath. She had to calm Herself. Wiping Her nose, She stared at Her mothers in the mirror—two dead women. She wouldn't share their fate.

One day She would be like him. Poised. Powerful. Today was that day. It had to be.

Light surged within Her.

Romulus's chamber.

Brown walls, an emerald rug, a simple wooden desk. In the corner sat a familiar little girl with thin blonde hair and large blue-green eyes.

This was who She was looking for.

Leila stood before the girl, hands shaking at Her sides. *I can't.*

She stifled a whimper. She had no other choice.

"I know you don't understand." Her voice trembled. "But I have to."

She wasn't sure how long She waited for him. Time had lost significance, Her insides tearing at the seams—the stripping of Her innocence. The torment became consuming, flushing out all second thoughts, all hesitations. Perhaps a part of Her was dying, but something else was growing in its place. Something else was newly born.

Romulus appeared, lurching to a stop. The blonde girl sat cross-legged on the rug, and Leila sat behind her, brushing her hair.

"Your Holiness." He glanced across the room. "How did You—?"

"Doesn't she look pretty?" Leila said.

Romulus didn't respond, his lips parted.

"Are you going to ignore The Savior when She speaks to you?"

He cleared his throat. "She looks very pretty, Your Holiness."

"She's My age, isn't she? Her mummy died pushing her from her belly. You share no blood, but you call her kin. You loved her mummy as your own."

Romulus said nothing.

"She's different." Leila pointed to the girl's forehead. "Here. Hasn't spoken a word. You're not even sure she knows who you are." She looked him in the eyes. "She doesn't."

"How do You know this?"

"I know lots about her. I know lots of things."

One brush, two. Leila tightened Her grip, digging Her nails into the woodgrain. "Why do you hide her away? Is it because you're scared of My father?"

Romulus didn't answer, his tension palpable—a swampy green.

"You shouldn't be scared of him. You should be scared of Me."

"Your Holiness—"

"You killed My mother." Leila stared down at the girl's hair, Her vision clouded with tears. "Father doesn't want Me. He's going to kill Me too."

"Your Holiness, please...what do You want?"

"I want to kill her, like you killed My mother." She looked up at him with an unblinking gaze. "You took from Me. Tell Me why I shouldn't take from you?"

"This isn't You. You're...You're just a child—"

"I am no child. I am *The Savior*," She hissed.

Her insides ignited, lit with a fire that threatened to burn through Her flesh. Her light had never felt this severe before. This enraged.

"I can kill her right now. Or I can take care of her. Give her the life you can't."

Romulus swallowed. "I'll do anything."

"My appearance tomorrow. Make it go away."

"Your Holiness, I'm not sure how—"

Leila grabbed a fistful of the girl's hair, and his eyes widened. "Yes, of course, whatever You say. It's just, the Sovereign will need a reason—"

"Find one."

Sweat beaded along his forehead. "There's opposition to the plan. I can sway him in that direction."

Leila's jaw tightened. "Then what?"

"What do You mean?"

"If I live, what's to become of Me?"

"We hold You captive," he said. "In the fortress. Dismantle Your authority. Your father retains control, and You are reduced to...a symbol. An empty title."

Leila stared at the floor. The life She knew was gone in an instant, leaving Her with nothing but Her blackening insides.

"Do it."

"Yes, Your Holiness." Romulus cleared his throat. "And my granddaughter?"

"She joins My court in the morning." Hopping to Her feet, She took the girl's hand. "Come, Pippa. You're My sister now."

The two scurried to the door. Leila looked over Her shoulder, leveling Her eyes on the man behind Her, hatred bubbling within the heart of a child.

Except She wasn't a child. Not anymore.

"You work for Me now."

THE SENATORS

"**G**row."

Heat pulsed from Her body, seeping into the ground beneath Her. Everything around Her was warm—the dry summer air, the harsh rays of the sun—but nothing compared to the light within Her. She was always warm. She couldn't escape it.

"Be alive. Be well." She breathed in. "Grow."

As Her light poured into the dirt, She sifted Her fingers through the grass, taking in its response—vitality. A soupy blackness lingered deep underground, waiting to snake its way to the surface.

"Settle down now. Back to where you came from."

A pounding sounded at the door far behind Her. "Leila?" Delphi called out.

Leila sighed. "I'm busy."

"Everyone's waiting for You. Have You forgotten Your meeting?"

"I'm blessing the realm," She shouted.

"Then bless it quickly."

She groaned. "Give Me a moment."

One last pulse of light, and She propped Herself upright. A sea of color stretched ahead—an elaborate garden filled with manicured trees, mosaicked pots, and flowers of all kinds. Wiping the grass from Her naked body, She hopped to Her feet and headed up the steps, past the white pillars and black velvet curtains, and into Her bedchamber.

A stately bed with crimson throws, tall walls lined in gold molding, speckled tiles along the floor. Hers was the most lavish chamber in the palace, certainly the only one with a private garden. She threw open Her wardrobe and pulled on a lavender dress, its braided straps settling on Her shoulders, the neckline hanging low between Her breasts, then tied a pair of tanned leather sandals onto Her feet. Sticking Her leg out from one of the slits in Her dress, She buckled a blade to Her thigh—the final piece of Her ensemble, one She never went without.

Leila closed the mirrored doors of Her wardrobe and studied Her reflection, combing Her locks into place. Two other faces reflected back at Her—a woman with strawberry blonde hair and icy eyes, another with hair like ink and a sable gaze.

Leila cracked a smile. "Hello, Mothers."

She bounded through the chamber door, met with a pair of blue-green eyes.

"Good morning!"

Pippa threw her arms around Her, knocking Her off balance. Leila pulled back, patting down the flyaways of Pippa's blonde hair and giving her pale cheeks a pinch. Delphi stood at her side, her long black braids hanging over the front of her shoulders. God, she looked so much like her mother, especially those sable eyes.

"Took You long enough," she scoffed.

Taking Pippa's hand, Leila nodded at the corridor ahead. "Walk and talk?"

The three sisters made their way through the palace. Marble busts lined the walls, stained glass windows cast rainbows along the floor, and vaulted ceilings loomed high overhead, rendering them mere specks amid the majesty. The palace was as grand as it was vast, its enormity eclipsed only by the fortress surrounding it; gardens and vineyards peppered the royal dwellings, encircled by a tall stone wall. Beyond it lay Thessen, the realm Leila was to govern and rule.

The realm She had never seen.

The girls headed into the heart of the palace. Servants bowed, but Leila paid them little mind, occupied with more pressing thoughts.

Delphi squeezed Her arm. "You know what You're going to say?"

"Every word," Leila whispered.

"Really sell it. Lay it on nice and thick."

Leila snorted. "I know what I'm doing."

"You can't fault my worry. Weakness has never been Your strong suit."

"I'm not going with weakness. I'm going with anger."

Delphi's eyes lit up. "Oh. Much better. That's completely in character, they'll never suspect a thing."

Another woman wafted their way, and every male gaze in sight followed. Cosima—Leila's third and final sister, arguably the most enchanting. Pippa had delicate features and wide-set eyes, while Delphi was a vision of regality with rich brown skin and elegant curves. But Cosima commanded attention in every room she entered—her skin was like porcelain, her eyes apple-green, and her hair came down in fiery red waves, landing just shy of her full, enviable breasts. A dazzling smile sprang to her lips, and Leila could've sworn the room became brighter.

"Good morning, doves." Cosima nestled alongside them. "What are we whispering about?"

"The meeting," Delphi said. "She's on Her way."

"Ah, yes. How exciting."

The atrium opened up ahead—the largest, most lavish room in the palace, but today it was a cluttered mess. Baskets of ribbons were strewn across the massive dining table, and servants zigzagged through the space, wrapping garlands around the marble columns and hanging stars from the chandeliers.

"For Your birthday tomorrow," Cosima said.

Her voice hardly registered. Leila stopped in Her tracks, eyes locked on the opposite end of the room where a man stood reading over a scroll. "Who is *that*?"

Delphi followed the path of Her gaze and shrugged. "Some guard."

He was surely more god than guard, miles tall with sculpted arms. Shaggy, golden-blond hair danced across his brow, catching the light of the sun like a halo. It was rare to see young men in the palace, especially men who were this striking.

"I've never seen him before," Leila said. "I mean... I'm certain I've *never* seen him before."

"Oh, that's Asher." Cosima leaned in closer, speaking in hushed tones. "He's new—recruited from the border, just took his vow yesterday. You know how your father is: *more soldiers, more guards.*" Cosima eyed the man over. "Divine, isn't he?"

Asher. He gnawed at his bottom lip, focused on whatever he was reading, and a tremor ran through Leila. *God, if I could be that lip.*

Cosima chuckled. "You little minx, look at You! You're flushed!"

Leila scowled. "I most certainly am not."

"Oh stop it, no one can blame You. The man's a work of art." She eyed him up and down. "He's lovely too. Would You like to meet him?"

"What?" Leila snapped. "No. Definitely not."

"We haven't the time," Delphi said.

"Nonsense." Cosima grabbed Leila's wrist. "Asher, dove, look who I've found!"

Leila's eyes widened. "Cosima—"

Cosima ignored Her, dragging Her down the corridor. "Asher, have you had the pleasure of meeting Leila?"

Asher glanced between the two women. "No, I don't believe so."

Leila's throat caught. Tan skin, broad shoulders, and honey-brown eyes gazing straight into Hers. *Say something.* She mustered a smile. "Hello."

An infinite silence followed. Cosima let out a laugh. "Well, don't be rude, shake his hand."

She shoved Leila, sending Her staggering over the polished tiles, straight into a stretch of sunlight.

Oh, shit.

The glaring heat beat down on Her, and in turn every exposed inch of Her flesh was radiant.

Glowing.

"Oh my God." Asher stumbled backward. "You're..."

The words never came. His eyes rolled into the back of his skull, and he collapsed to the floor with a hard smack.

Gasps sounded across the atrium, and Leila cringed. *Not again.*

"Oh dear, I hadn't anticipated that," Cosima murmured.

Servants circled, gaping at the glowing woman and the man sprawled at Her feet. *How many times must this happen before it stops being humiliating?*

"Should we get a healer?" A servant said. "I can summon Diccus—"

"No, it's all right." Leila squatted beside the fallen guard. "I'll take care of it."

Delphi sighed. "Your meeting..."

"I'll take care of it." Leila looked her hard in the eye. "This is My duty."

She turned to Asher, pulling his eyelid open only for it to snap shut. *Out like a snuffed torch.* Tilting his head, She combed through his golden mane—no blood, no cracked skull. Blips of pain stung Her fingertips, traveling from his battered head to Her hand. Concussed. An easy fix. She planted Her palm on his forehead.

"Rouse his senses," She whispered. "Ease the ache. Bring him back."

Her hand went from warm to hot, burning in a way She was accustomed to. Light flooded from Her touch, flowing through him in waves, and the traces of his pain began to fade.

Asher stirred, and Leila dropped Her palm, revealing a bright white handprint beaming from his forehead.

"What is...?" He winced. "What happened?" His eyes fluttered open, settling on the woman hovering over him.

Still Leila. Still glowing.

"Oh my God," he said. "You're... You're—"

"The Savior." Cosima jutted her head into his line of sight. "The holy gift of Thessen. She's blessed you with Her divine light. Isn't that marvelous?"

Asher stared up at Leila in shock, then scrambled along the floor, kneeling before Her. "Apologies, Your Holiness—"

She stood. "It's Leila."

"I didn't mean to..." He wrinkled his nose. "Did I faint?"

"Yes, you did. It's quite common, actually—"

"How unseemly. Please forgive my weakness, I meant no offense."

"You don't have to—"

"It's an honor to serve You, Your Holiness," he said. "I took an oath to devote my life to Your safety and to the safety of Your palace. My body is Your shield."

My body is Your shield. She could think of better uses for it. "That's nice," She muttered.

Asher rose to his feet, staring at Her with a look of awe. Of disconnect. "Apologies for my lack of decorum. I am humbled to have met You, Your Holiness."

A frown fought its way across Her face. "Please, call Me Leila."

"Of course, Your Holiness. Good day, Your Holiness."

He shuffled off, ignorant to the bright white eyesore on his forehead.

"He's nice," Pippa said. "We should keep him."

Cosima chuckled. "Well, *You* created quite a scene, didn't You?"

"Yes, She did." Delphi scowled. "Who could've possibly predicted such a thing?"

Cosima ignored her, sighing. "Leila, if I've told You once, I've told You a thousand times: If You want a man's affection, You mustn't be so intimidating."

"I wasn't seeking his *affection*," Leila spat. "I was simply introducing myself."

"You're sure? You seemed rather taken. At least until, You know..." Cosima's gaze traveled to the spot where Asher fell. "Boom."

"You're wrong."

"Well, You would know best." Smiling, Cosima cupped Leila's cheeks. "You look beautiful, by the way. My sweet sister. Such a gift, You are."

She flitted off, leaving Leila glowing on the outside, muted within. *A gift.* Many made such claims—that Leila was divine, that Her light was a gift from God—but in moments like these, being *The Savior* was more burden than blessing.

Leila wasn't the only Savior to have graced the realm. The first was born centuries ago during a time of plague, a beacon of hope with striking eyes and ivory skin that glowed the moment it caught the sun. The light of Her body was strong enough to leave a person faint, but its true power manifested in the realm around Her. Desert lands flourished, crops sprouting from the arid sands, and the people were healed, free of disease and suffering. With this girl's birth came a cleansing, and the people gave to Her the title She had earned: Her Holiness, Ruler of Thessen.

Their Savior.

As the realm grew in prosperity, so did the royal line. The Savior birthed a daughter of equal power, who birthed a daughter as well, and each girl was welcomed with a beautiful fortress, loyal servants, and a court of sisters elected to grow alongside Her. The bloodline thrived, a succession of rulers with celestial flesh, piercing eyes, and an array of magical gifts, namely Their divine, healing light.

Like the Saviors before Her, Leila made the palace Her home, was bathed in riches, was appointed three sisters, Her faithful court. Still, Her reign was unique. She was the first to remain hidden within Her fortress. She was the first to be a mystery to Her people.

She was the first birthed from a corpse.

Delphi poked into Leila's line of vision, nodding at the path Cosima had taken. "She did that on purpose, You know."

Leila shook the debacle from Her mind. "We have more important concerns."

The women continued through the palace, stopping just shy of a large black door. Delphi turned toward Her. "You're sure You're prepared?"

"I am."

"Me too!" Pippa said.

Leila sighed. "Little duckling, I know you want to come along, but this meeting is just for The Savior. You understand, yes?"

Pippa pouted. "All right."

Delphi grabbed Leila's hands, squeezing them. "For Your realm."

Leila nodded. "For Mother."

She opened the door and headed inside.

Stark white walls, pitch-black floor, a domed ceiling—everything about the Senate room was severe. A map of the realm covered one of the walls, and a large, round table loomed ahead, encircled by nine men.

I hate you.

"Leila." The man seated across from Her scowled. "How kind of You to finally join us."

Her eyes bore through him—the red drape across his bare chest, the glower on his face.

Brontes. She hated him most of all.

Leila made Her way to the table, not once breaking his gaze. Their hair was the same deep brown, just shy of black, but Leila's was long and sleek, while Brontes's was flecked with grey. Brontes was large and brawny with bronze skin, while Leila had always been small and slender, Her skin ghostly in the shade, aglow in the sun. Then there were the eyes; Leila's were amber-gold in the shadows, but in the light they were wild flames. Brontes's didn't look anything like that, and he only had the one, his left socket hidden behind a thick black patch.

My nose is different. I have that freckle above my cheek. Never mind She had his full lips, that Her cheekbones sat high just as his did. Leila always looked for differences. Anything that told Her She was nothing like him.

She tore Her gaze from Brontes, eyeing the other men. Phanes. Erebus. Qar. The palace Senators, eight in total—and several empty seats.

"No Toma, I see?" She said. "Are we to start without him?"

"He's been missing for three days," Brontes muttered.

"Is that right? Another man gone? Well, we're better off for it. I never cared much for him anyway." She took Her seat. "Shall we begin?"

Brontes grumbled under his breath, "Who calls this meeting?"

"I do," Leila said.

"Second," Kastor added.

"First order of business: your retirement." Leila clasped Her hands together. "Tomorrow's My twentieth birthday. I'm of age. I haven't a need for you any longer."

The men glanced at one another, silent. Simon cleared his throat. "Your Holiness, with all due respect, we've discussed this at length many times over. The position we hold is binding."

"And I've told you *at length* that come My twentieth birthday, I will be severing whatever it is that *binds* us together," Leila said.

"Your Holiness, the law states we are to serve You indefinitely."

"The law you yourselves have written. How convenient."

Another man, his tawny skin weathered with age, offered a smile.

"Your Holiness, allow me to speak on behalf of the others when I say we understand Your opposition. You are a grown woman, and what a woman You've become." He glanced at Brontes, bowing his head. "But Your father, our righteous Sovereign, nominated us for a reason. The burden You carry is heavy. It is our duty to lighten it, for no purpose other than to benefit our One True Savior."

Gelanor—the Vault Keeper, easily the most well-spoken Senator of the bunch. The king of discourse. The master of bullshit.

"Your mother, God rest Her soul, was to teach You the art of governing," Gelanor said. "And as She is not here with us—a very sad turn of events indeed—we have taken it upon ourselves to aid Your hand."

Leila's lips pursed. *Bullshit.*

"So alas, in Your mother's departure, You have inherited this merry lot." He opened his arms wide. "Consider us Your surrogates."

Leila let out a laugh. "My surrogates? Is that right? Tell Me, are you going to whip out your tit and have Me suck it dry, *Mother?*"

"Leila, You vulgar shit, still Your tongue," Brontes snapped.

"I will not sit tolerantly while you lie to My face under the guise of duty. Tomorrow, I am of age. I *demand* My crown."

"For God's sake, You have a crown," he scoffed. "You have a whole collection."

"It is My purpose to govern. It is My birthright to lead—"

"You're *not* governing Thessen. Not now, not ever."

"Why?"

"Because You're incapable," he spat. "This outburst of Yours has proven that."

Leila glared at Her father, wishing Her eyes would tear through him.

"Who motions to keep the law as it stands?" he said.

"I do."

"Second."

Brontes cast Leila a glower. "The law remains."

She looked away, unable to stomach his gaze any longer. "Well then, it seems you all can continue to handle Thessen's affairs, and I will continue to do absolutely nothing. How free I feel, with My *burdens* lifted. They seem nonexistent, in fact."

An old, round Senator with plump, pink cheeks and unkempt white hair cut in. "Oh, that's not true, Your Holiness. Your duties are vast." He fiddled nervously with his sapphire drape. "Why, You bless the realm each day. Such a taxing process, I'm sure. The realm is eternally grateful."

Wembleton. The Master of Ceremonies. Another ass.

"Second order of business: the Sovereign's Tournament." Leila crossed Her arms. "That won't be happening."

Brontes groaned. "For the love of God..."

Wembleton's face dropped. "Your Holiness, it's tradition."

"Isn't tradition ours to break?" Leila said. "After all, we're not following the *tradition* of having The Savior lead Her realm. We're not following the *tradition* of allowing The Savior to leave Her fortress—"

Gelanor gasped. "Your mother was murdered in the streets of Thessen. Surely You must know we keep You here for Your own safety."

Leila resisted the urge to roll Her eyes. "With all these traditions abandoned, what's one more? Why not break tradition and nullify My tournament?"

"*My* tournament," Brontes said. "It's called *the Sovereign's Tournament*, is it not?"

"Yes, to find *My* husband." Leila shrugged. "Something I'm not particularly interested in."

Wembleton shook his head. "Your Holiness, You say that now, but when You meet these men, I assure You—"

"Perhaps I'm not interested in men at all. Maybe I like women. Developed a taste for cunt and tits."

"Enough!" Brontes slammed his fist against the table. "You are out of line!"

"The Sovereign's Tournament is a disgrace to Thessen. A bloodbath passed as spectacle, turns men into animals and The Savior into a prize. I will not have it—"

"You will if I say so."

"I am The Savior. My word—"

"Means *nothing*," Brontes hissed. "Haven't You learned, precious daughter? You hold no power. So be as insufferable as You'd like, but know it accomplishes nothing, same as always."

The room fell silent, all eyes on Leila.

"Tomorrow is Your birthday. The next day is the pool, and the day that follows will mark the start of the Sovereign's Tournament as planned." Brontes leaned forward. "And You will shut Your mouth and take it, do You understand me?"

I hate you. The words took shape in Her throat, begging for release.

"See? Isn't that so much better than Your ranting?" Brontes glanced around the table. "Who motions to end today's meeting?"

"I do."

"Second."

"Today's Senate meeting is terminated." Brontes flashed one last look of disdain Leila's way. "And what a waste of time it was."

The room filled with mutterings, some about Leila's candor, though most of it was riddled with those three heinous words: the Sovereign's Tournament. Thirty days of violence, all in the search of Leila's Champion. *My husband.*

"Your Holiness?"

A lean man with wrinkled copper skin, black-and-white hair balding at the crown, and a hooked nose hovered beside Her. "A word alone? To solidify terms for the tournament."

Romulus. Frowning, She mumbled under Her breath, "Fine."

The others filed from the room. Romulus trudged to the door, shutting it before turning Her way. "And what exactly was the point of all that?"

"I have My reasons," She muttered.

"They think You're weak now. Helpless, even."

"Then it seems My meeting served its purpose."

He faltered. "You have a plan."

Leila didn't bother responding, studying the ends of Her hair. "What of the tournament?"

"It is as You suspected. Brontes moves against You."

"Against Me how?"

"You know how. He's already taken Your power. But he wants the glory, always has. The people only worship him if You're gone."

A weight dropped in Her gut. "He's made the call. I am to die."

"The Sovereign's Tournament will mark Your assassination."

She sat calm and stoic, but rage bellowed within Her, screaming for action.

"The Senate?"

"All complicit," he said. "The guards, the soldiers—they know nothing of his plan, but they are loyal to Your father. They will aid him, knowingly or not."

"By what means?"

"Pardon?"

"The assassination. What is his strategy? How am I to be killed?"

Romulus wavered. "I don't know."

"You lie to Me."

"He scatters the information. No one man knows everything, it's how he retains his control."

Leila bit down on Her lip. "Give Me a name."

"Your Holiness—"

"A *name*."

Romulus tensed. "Gelanor."

"The Vault Keeper."

"He's met with Brontes several times recently. There's been discussion of a large transfer of funds. He'll know the most of anyone."

"And that slow trickle?"

"Still nothing," Romulus said. "No one knows where the coin is going."

Leila sat still, sorting through the mess in Her mind. "The tournament is to have a Proctor, yes? Someone who oversees the competitors?" Romulus nodded, and Her eyes narrowed. "*You* will be that Proctor. Make it so."

"I doubt I'll be his choice—"

"*Make it so.*"

Romulus's nostrils flared. "Yes, Your Holiness."

Leila rose from Her seat, making Her way to the door. "Well then, I suppose I have to pay Gelanor a visit."

"A brief request that I imagine will fall on deaf ears," Romulus called out behind Her. "Consider mercy for these men."

"Mercy? For the men who plan My assassination?"

"They're foolish. Influenced by greed. And they greatly fear Your father."

"You're right. They are foolish. They fear the wrong person." Her hands curled into fists. "No mercy. If they want blood, I will give it to them."

She threw open the door and was met with two faces—one wearing a wild grin, the other fierce and focused. Leila glanced between Pippa and Delphi, gesturing at the corridor ahead. "Walk and talk."

The two hurried alongside Her, Pippa taking Her hand while Delphi leaned over Her shoulder. "How'd it go?"

"As expected," Leila said.

"What now?"

Leila looked her in the eye. "Gelanor."

"Gelanor." Pippa giggled. "He's fat."

"Pippa, it's not polite to tease people for their shapes and sizes." Leila turned to Delphi. "I'm going now."

"You think he'll be there already?" Delphi said.

"Doesn't matter. I'll wait."

"It's that urgent?"

Leila's shoulders stiffened. "It's what we thought."

Delphi wavered, swallowing the lump in her throat. "To his chamber then."

"Meet Me there."

Delphi nodded. "I'll wait outside. Clear the area."

The women parted ways. Leila ventured through one corridor, another, studying the passing staff out of the corner of Her eye. Quickening Her pace, She headed into an adjacent hallway—empty— and Her destination materialized in Her thoughts.

Gelanor's chamber.

The corridor burst into rays of light, leaving Her weightless. Soon the light faded, revealing brown walls, an umber rug—and Gelanor.

He sat on his bed with his back to Her, tugging feverishly at his cock. Cringing, She cleared Her throat.

Gelanor looked over his shoulder, then jumped. "Mother of—"

"You can finish, if you'd like."

The old man fumbled to put his bits away. "Your Holiness..."

"Apologies for the interruption. I honestly didn't expect to find you here so soon. Figured you'd be occupied with more important matters." She watched him pull up his pants. "But apparently not."

"What are You doing here?" he stammered. "How did... How did You get in?"

"The same way I've gotten in each time before."

"Before?"

"I've been through this chamber many times."

Gelanor's expression turned bleak. "What do You want?"

Leila slid Her hand into the slit of Her dress, pulling Her blade from its place on Her thigh. "You and I are going to have a conversation."

Wide-eyed, Gelanor sprang for the window with the energy of a man half his age. Leila flung Her blade at him, launching it straight into his shoulder.

Wailing, he toppled face-first to the floor.

Leila hovered over him, unimpressed. "Calm yourself. There are much more painful spots, I assure you." She ripped the blade from his shoulder and waited for his cries to die. "Are you ready for that conversation?"

When Gelanor said nothing, She held Her blade low, making sure he caught sight of its bloody edge. His eyes widened. "Yes, we can talk. Just don't—"

"Hurt you? I'll try My best." She tugged at his arm, trying and failing to get him standing, then cocked Her head at a nearby chair. "Sit."

With a whimper, Gelanor pulled himself up. Once he was seated, Leila yanked his sheets from his bed, twisting them like rope and wrapping them around his ankles.

"Oh my God."

Her head perked up. "Is there a problem, Senator?"

Gelanor went quiet, and Leila continued Her work, tying his legs to the legs of the chair, his wrists to the armrests.

"It's You," Gelanor said. "All the Senators gone missing... It's You."

"How very astute you are."

"I don't understand. You're just...*killing* us? One by one?"

"It seems you understand perfectly."

"Have You gone *mad*?"

"Well, it's not as though you've left Me any choice," She scoffed. "You've imprisoned Me in My own home, have taken all My authority, and now that you've properly picked Me apart, you wait for Me to die—hover over My body like a flock of vultures. And on top of that, you leave Me with no political means of disbanding you all. You're here to stay, and I have no say in the matter. If I can't cast you out through legal means, then surely I must cast you out through death."

Gelanor didn't speak, his eyes darting between Leila and Her blade.

"I imagine you're wishing you had revoked that law earlier today," She said.

"I can do that for You. We can go right now—"

"Oh, that won't be necessary. I think I prefer it this way, to be honest."

His eyes narrowed into slits. "You twisted *bitch*."

"*I'm* twisted? *Me?*" She laughed. "You conspired to kill My mother. You conspired to kill Me when I was just a child. And now you plan My death yet again. You long to steal My realm from My line, and you do it all at the expense of My people—people who are healthy and prosperous because of Me. And *I'm* the twisted one for burying My blade into your throats? You understand, My duty, My birthright, is to purge this realm of sickness and evil. And I have found the foulest evils in My very own palace. In people like you."

"It'll never work, whatever You're doing. Brontes's network is vast, his plan extensive—far beyond what You know, what I know—"

"Of course. Why do you think *he's* still alive?"

"You are *The Savior*," he said. "A woman of light and purity. Not of...murder."

"Senator, I was born in death. You and your men made it so."

The Senator went silent, his mouth hanging open stupidly.

"You're going to answer a few questions for Me," She said.

"If You're to kill me, why should I answer anything?"

Leila slammed Her blade into the Senator's hand, nailing it to its armrest. He howled in agony, but Leila was immune to the sound. To the blood.

"A large sum of coin has been transferred from the vault. Where is it going?"

The man moaned, squirming in his restraints, but he said nothing. She ripped the blade from his hand, sending him reeling again. "Where is My *coin?*"

"How do You know any of this? You're not permitted in the vault."

"For My own good, yes? You know, if I was allowed to access My own coin, I wouldn't be standing here. Do you see the trouble you've put upon yourself?"

Tears dribbled down Gelanor's face. She tapped Her foot. "The coin. Where is it going?"

Silence.

She thrust Her blade toward his other hand.

"Wait!"

The steel tip grazed his wrinkled flesh. Her eyes panned to his.

"Three men," he said. "He's using the coin to pay three men."

"Who?"

"I don't know, but they're of an...unsavory disposition. He aims for them to move against you. In the tournament, somehow."

"Somehow?"

"I don't know his methods, I just know..." He sucked in a shallow breath. "I just know what I've already said. There's three of them, they're working within the Sovereign's Tournament...and none of it's good for You."

Tendrils of swampy-green oozed from his flesh, filling the space around him—the color of his terror.

"There's been a slow trickle of coin leaving the vault for some time now," She said. "Where's it going?"

He faltered. "I don't know."

"You're the Vault Keeper. You expect Me to believe that?"

"Brontes is handling those funds exclusively. He won't talk. It's very... It's very private, he says."

"Are you lying to me?"

"*No,*" he spat. "Your Holiness, no, I swear it."

She lunged forward, grabbing his face hard and tight.

"Your Holiness, please, I've told You all I know," he said. "All of it. I'm utterly useless to You now. Have mercy. I'll put this treachery behind me, I swear it."

She tightened Her grip, and putrid green spilled from his pores. Each emotion carried a color, and his, like every other man of his kind, was repulsive. She studied his rotten hue—the fear of a man who had played his cards. Who had nothing left to give.

"Please, I've told You everything," he stammered. "I'm useless."

Leila hesitated, then dropped Her hand. "I believe you."

He let out a relieved breath. "Thank You, Your Holiness. Thank You."

She slammed Her blade into his throat.

Blood poured from his neck, saturating the front of his tunic. As his life drifted away with the river of red, his eyes locked with Hers.

Leila frowned. "Oh, don't give Me that look. After all, you *are* useless to Me."

His stare went vacant, his body an empty vessel. Yanking Her blade from his flesh, Leila called over Her shoulder.

"Delphi, I've made another mess. Help Me clean it up, would you?"

2

THE BIRTHDAY

"**H**appy birthday, Your Holiness!"

Leila nodded at the servant and hurried up the marble steps. Purple ribbons wrapped the staircase bannisters, and ornamental gold stars hung from the ceiling. The palace looked lovely, as it did on each of Her birthdays, but this year the opulence was off-putting.

"Happy birthday!"

Another nod, and She abandoned the stairs, heading down one of the many corridors. More smiles, more kind wishes. She should've felt honored, but instead She wondered who was celebrating Her life and who was anticipating Her death.

A door appeared before Her, and She shoved it open. "Cosima, I..."

She staggered to a halt. Two bodies entwined, naked save for a sheet shared between them. Cosima's fair skin and fiery hair were instantly discernable, as were those tan arms and that shaggy, golden-blond mane.

"Oh God."

Asher's lips tore from Cosima's. "Your Holiness." Stumbling from the bed, he clutched a sheet to his nethers and kneeled. "Apologies for the improper circumstances."

Cosima laughed. "Oh, Asher, it's just Leila. She doesn't mind."

"I didn't know You were coming," he said.

"It's fine," Leila muttered.

"If I had known—"

"Just go."

"Of course, Your Holiness." He grabbed his clothes from the floor. "Good day, Your Holiness." He rushed away, leaving Leila with a glimpse of his bare ass before he slammed the door.

"Did You see that?" Cosima chuckled. "He just scampered off with one of my bed sheets. What a loon, I swear. What are You doing here, anyhow?"

"You summoned Me."

"Is that right? Oh my, I completely forgot. I can't even remember the reason for it, I feel so foolish. The matter must've slipped my mind in the heat of the moment."

Leila said nothing, Her cheeks burning.

"Are You all right?"

"I'm fine," Leila mumbled.

"You're not upset, are You? About me and Asher. You said You weren't seeking his affection. I assumed You wouldn't mind."

Her gut coiled. "I'm not upset."

"I assure You, it was just the one time. Well, a few times in one night, but never again."

"I said I'm fine."

Cosima smiled. "Of course, what was I thinking? You're not the type for such dramatics. You're bigger than that. A true woman."

The knot in Leila's gut pulled tighter, and She headed for the door.

"Leila?"

She glanced over Her shoulder, met by Her sister's smile.

"Happy birthday, dove."

Leila left without a word, holding Her chin high with a confidence that felt fraudulent. She reached a chamber a short distance away, where Delphi was curled up along the cool blue linens of her bed reading over a scroll.

"You're alone? That's unusual." Leila's voice broke once She spotted feet poking out from beneath the room divider. "Oh. Spoke too soon."

"Leila!" A servant girl popped out from behind the divider, still tying her dress into place. "Happy birthday!"

Leila mustered a smile. "Thank you, Shae."

"You're twenty! A grown woman!" Shae squealed, pinching Leila's cheeks. "Today is going to be the best day. We're all so excited for You." She headed for the door. "I'm off now. Happy birthday!"

As Shae disappeared, Leila turned to Delphi. "I thought she liked men."

"She was feeling curious. Who am I to deny her self-exploration?" Delphi smirked. "Aren't You supposed to be with Cosima?"

Sighing, Leila flopped down onto the bed. "She was occupied. Had that new guard, Asher, all good and naked."

"You're serious? The little cunt."

"Delphi..."

"I mean it. She's always been a bit uppish, but I swear she gets more and more cunty with age."

"She can bed whom she pleases."

Delphi rolled her eyes. "Please, You must see the intention. There are plenty of guards in this fortress, but she chose Asher, the exact man who made Your bits tingle. She did it to spite You."

"Well, it didn't work. I hadn't the slightest interest in him. No *tingle* whatsoever."

"Your saving face only does her favors."

"She's family."

"By title," Delphi said. "When was the last time she actually *behaved* as family?"

Leila's stomach churned. She sat upright, idly playing with the ends of Her hair.

"Well, we don't need her anyhow." Delphi plastered on a smile. "Do You want to discuss Your birthday?" When Leila didn't answer, Delphi tensed. "Your father then."

"He moves against me. Through the tournament."

"It's confirmed?"

Leila scowled. "Three men of an *unsavory disposition* were hired. I'm assuming he's placing them in the tournament. They'll likely compete for Me."

"And then?"

"And then...I die."

A red fog filled the space between them, bleeding from Delphi's flesh. Anger. *At least she doesn't pity Me.*

"Have You given any additional thought to killing Your father?"

Leila sighed. "Delphi, we can't."

"I know, I'm just rather fond of the idea."

"His network reaches far past what we know. If we cut off the head of the beast, another will grow in its place to strike Me down. Until we uncover all his allies, he lives."

"Well then, onto more pressing matters," Delphi said. "These three men—You think they're coming to do the deed? Stab stab, and You're dead?

"I can't think of any other explanation."

"So we watch them. Keep them close." She pointed her scroll Leila's way. "You're positioning Rom to be the Proctor, yes?"

"Already in the works."

"Good. Then we'll have eyes and ears on the inside."

"It's not enough. I need someone I can trust implicitly."

"Then I'll join him. Think of a reason to mingle amongst the men. Be Your spy." Delphi's eyes brightened. "What if I act as a servant? Get the men pretty for You. Women always babble when they're being made beautiful. I'm sure men are the same."

Leila didn't answer, and Delphi furrowed her brow. "Do You not want me down there? In the labyrinth?"

"No, it's not that..." Leila's voice trailed off, Her mind turning over Her sister's words—and words She Herself hadn't spoken, still gestating in Her thoughts. Romulus wasn't enough. Delphi wasn't enough.

I need to be in the labyrinth.

The door crept open, and a man poked his head inside. "Your Holiness?"

Leila flagged him over, and he bowed before walking in. Wavy black hair spilled down to his shoulders, his golden-brown skin splashed with freckles across his arms, his face, even his plump lips. He was clearly of Leila's age, yet boyish—his frame was tall and slender, his hands fidgety, and his large, chestnut eyes gaped at Her in reverence.

She frowned. "Can I help you?"

He shook himself, bowing again. "Apologies for the intrusion."

"I'm sorry, but...who are you?"

"Hylas. Page to the Sovereign." He bowed for a third time. "His former went missing inexplicably, so I'm told."

"Is that so? I hadn't any idea."

"Your Holiness, I hate to bother, but we've yet to receive Your preferences for the pool." Hylas rambled words that sounded rehearsed. "Tomorrow, the men of Thessen and beyond will line up for miles for the chance to compete in Your tournament. The pool will determine who among them is worthy. We're required to procure a variety of men, but some will be catered to Your tastes. So..." he unrolled a scroll, preparing to write, "...Your preferences?"

"I have no preferences."

He faltered. "But...this is Your future husband. Surely You have preferences."

"I'm sure the girls will sort it out on their own."

Hylas shifted from foot to foot. "Apologies, but I can't leave without Your answer."

Leila sighed. "All right then. I want a robust man with a body like marble, an ass tight enough to shatter a diamond, and a cock the length of a cucumber. A pillar. No, a *tower*." She nodded at his scroll. "Are you getting this?"

Hylas's face flushed. Clearing his throat, he scribbled across his parchment. "A...tower?"

"Of course. How could I possibly settle for less? Will that be all?"

With a quick bow, Hylas dashed for the door, throwing it shut behind him.

Delphi frowned. "He thinks You're serious."

"Doesn't matter. I won't be choosing a man anyway. Let them waste away searching for the cucumber cock." Leila wrinkled Her nose. "Is that big for a cock? Cucumber length? Oh, why am I even asking you..."

"Brontes will see these requests."

"Oh good, I hope to see his face when he does."

Leila chuckled, while Delphi gazed at the spot where Hylas once stood. "I'll track him down. Tell him to find some nice men for You. Give him Your real preferences."

"Why would you do that?"

"What about creative types? Intellectuals? I'll tell him to look out for those."

"So they can die in the tournament? That's just cruel."

Delphi kept quiet, a single eyebrow raised.

"Why are you looking at Me like that?" Leila said.

"You're not at all curious about the tournament? About these men?"

"You mean the ones coming to kill Me?"

"I mean the ones coming to *marry* You," Delphi said. "Or at least try to."

Leila laughed. "Oh, the idiots. No, not particularly."

"Leila—"

"They compete for a woman they've never met simply because She's *The Savior*." She played with the folds of Her dress. "It's foolish. Offensive, really. They come because they marvel at My title, not...Me."

"They'll marvel at You once they meet You. You are quite *marvelous*, after all."

"Have you lost sight of things? Brontes moves against Me."

"I know that."

"He killed our mothers."

"And there's nothing I want more than for him to rot. Except to see You happy." Delphi scooted closer, taking Her hand. "You're the last of my family, and I cannot watch You waste away in misery forever."

"And you think a cock would rectify all things."

"Not a cock. Just a companion."

Leila smiled. "I have you."

"A companion with a cock."

Groaning, Leila rolled Her eyes. "Delphi—"

"One for You to play with."

"God..."

"On Your fifteenth birthday, I found You crying in Your chamber. You said You feared You'd be a child forever. That You longed to kiss a boy, yet there was no one for You to kiss. And when a boy did come this way, he wasn't permitted to kiss You, or court You, or see You as

31

anything other than untouchable." Delphi gave Leila's hand a squeeze. "Cosima and I were already having our fun, and You were certain You'd be left behind. So I stayed up all night assuring You Your time would come. And *then* I explained to You the magic of two fingers strategically placed—"

"I was there, Delphi. I remember."

"You have twenty men coming to the palace for the sole purpose of winning Your affection. Surely it's crossed Your mind that this is an opportunity to partake in the one pleasure You've been denied Your entire life."

Leila glowered. "Seventeen men. You forget, three are coming to kill Me." She threw Her arms into the air. "But to hell with My assassination, let's put all our attention into finding that cock for Me to play with."

"Leila—"

"There are more important things."

"Of course," Delphi said. "But if You can heal the realm and slit the throat of a traitor in the same afternoon, why can't You reclaim Your power and kiss a man in the same tournament?"

The chamber door flew open, and a bevy of servant girls exploded into the room. "Happy birthday!"

Four grinning faces surrounded Leila, yanking Her from the bed.

"You're twenty!"

"You're positively glowing!"

"She's always glowing."

"Shut up, Nyx."

The servants dragged Her from Delphi's chamber, pulling Her down the corridor, the stairs, then into a periwinkle room lined in pillars, its pearlescent floor punctuated by a pool. The royal bathhouse. There was another like it for the rest of the palace to use, but this one was for Leila alone. She stood at the pool's edge as the girls peeled off Her dress, then tiptoed into the water, taking a seat on the bench.

Light beamed through the pool in ripples. Her submerged skin always set the water aglow, but the servants didn't react, accustomed to Her power to the point of apathy. She liked that about them—that Nyx, Hemera, Damaris, and Faun regarded Her as slightly-less-than-holy.

Faun hovered beside the pool, juggling a handful of colorful vials. "What'll it be today? Lavender? Vanilla?"

Hemera swatted her arm. "Do vanilla, it matches Her skin!"

"It's *Her* choice, dummy," Nyx scoffed.

"Vanilla is wonderful, thank you," Leila said.

The girls prepped Her bath, a flurry of bustling bodies in flowing white dresses. Faun was the eldest at twenty-one years with deep olive skin, long brown hair, and freckles dotting her nose and cheeks, though her most distinct feature were the black tattoos swirling down her arms all the way to her fingers. Damaris was plump with dark red locks, the soft pink of her skin a direct contrast to her cornflower eyes. And Nyx and Hemera were the youngest, identical twins just eighteen years old with the same golden skin, sharp features, and upturned, chestnut eyes. The only dissonance between them was their ebony hair; Hemera's was long with bangs, while Nyx's locks were short, falling over her ears.

Hemera rang out a hand rag. "I swear, I've been waiting for tonight for months. Years, even."

"Please, no one cares about tonight."

"Nyx, you bitch!" Hemera said. "It's Her birthday."

"Yes, and in two days the tournament begins. That's what everyone's been waiting for. You know I'm right."

Leila swallowed a groan. *Just one moment without mention of the tournament, that's all I ask.*

"You won't be seeing us tomorrow." Damaris lathered up Leila's leg. "Mousumi has us working the pool, same as all the other girls."

Leila frowned. "Apologies. That sounds dreadful."

"Oh, not at all," Damaris said. "I'm actually quite excited."

"Is that right?" Faun smirked. "Our untouched flower, eager to feast her eyes on Thessen's finest, unattached and as naked as the day they were born."

"*Naked?*" Damaris glanced between the girls. "No one said they were going to be naked."

"It'll be grand," Hemera said. "Hundreds of handsome men in the buff."

"And ugly men. And fat men. And hairy men," Nyx muttered.

33

"What about You, Leila?" Hemera looked up from her work and smiled. "Are You excited? You must be."

Vulgarities filled Leila's mouth, so She opted not to answer.

"Leila, Your hair is so beautiful." Hemera sighed, brushing Her long locks. "The envy of us all, I swear it."

"Pretty soon You'll have Your pick of men to brush Your hair," Faun said. "Play with Your hair... *Pull* Your hair."

"Faun!" Hemera squealed.

"You all were thinking it. I'm just saying it."

"Did You submit Your preferences?" Damaris took a seat behind Leila, massaging Her shoulders. "I'm just dying to know what The Savior desires."

"She asked for a massive cock!" Nyx said. "Hylas showed me! I saw it!"

Damaris gasped. "He showed you?"

"Well, I made him."

"A large cock?" Hemera giggled into her hands. "Leila, I never would've guessed You were such a minx!"

"She's not a minx. She's playing games." Scowling, Faun dropped her rag. "Leila, why didn't You submit Your true preferences?"

"I have no preferences," She said.

"You still fight the tournament? Even with it just days away?"

"Why would You fight the tournament?" Hemera scoffed. "I would *die* to have one of my own."

"Can you imagine?" Damaris kneaded Leila's back. "Twenty gorgeous men throwing themselves at you. It's like a dream."

"It's not My dream," Leila muttered.

"Well then, if You find the prospect so repugnant, why don't You let one of us take Your place, hm?" Faun chuckled. "We'll slip on Your glowing skin, wear Your flaming eyes, and play Savior for thirty days." She cast Leila a critical look. "Women of sound mind would kill for such a burden, You know."

"Your Holiness."

Leila jumped, sending a wave splashing onto the tiles. The servant keeper appeared at the pool's edge, about thirty years old with tawny skin, a statuesque figure, and thick, black curls tied at her nape. Her large, dark eyes scanned the unrolled scroll in her hands, her presence alone enough to render the girls silent.

"A word while You're freshened up?"

Leila nodded. "Of course, Mousumi."

Mousumi didn't bother looking Her way, still reading her parchment. "The schedule for Your birthday feast has been finalized. We require Your approval. After Your bath, You're to meet with Cecily for Your fitting. It seems she's chosen a red dress—a royal color for a royal occasion. Is this acceptable?"

"Yes, that sounds lovely."

She scribbled along her scroll. "Once all is prepared, Your court will be ushered into the atrium, followed by the Sovereign and then Yourself."

"Bring the Sovereign in first," Leila said. "Then the court. Then Me."

Mousumi's eyes lifted from the parchment. "Your father will see that as an affront. That the court holds title over him."

"Bring him in first."

Mousumi went back to scribbling, her nostrils flared. "The feast will be served, then Your gifts will be presented. The Sovereign's page will note Your gratitude and deliver Your thanks to the proper patrons."

"The page?" Damaris said. "Surely that's the scribe's job."

"The scribe retired his post," Mousumi muttered.

"Another?" Damaris glanced between the girls. "I swear, everyone's leaving."

"All friends of the Sovereign too." Nyx raised her eyebrows. "Bet you he's picking them off."

"*Quiet*. That's the Sovereign you speak of." Hemera splashed her sister. "Father of *Her Holiness*."

"I take no offense," Leila said.

Mousumi cleared her throat. "Does the schedule suit You, Your Holiness?"

"It's fine." Leila smiled. "Thank you."

"Right." Bowing, Mousumi rolled her scroll and headed off.

Hemera exhaled. "Thank God she's gone. I swear, she's so stiff."

Nyx shoved her arm. "Watch your words, she's our keeper."

"I think she's all right," Damaris said.

35

Hemera scoffed. "Don't lie, she's as frigid as a Kovahrian winter."

Leila flashed them a frown. "Be kind, ladies."

"Don't pretend You haven't noticed." Faun laughed. "She's not even nice to You."

Their chatter faded as Leila's thoughts churned. The tournament was fast approaching, and She still hadn't a proper plan. But amid Her nagging worries were the words of Her servants, gently prodding at Her mind.

Let one of us take Your place.

The girls finished their work, and Leila soon found Herself surrounded by the dusty rose walls of Her dressing room. The rays of the setting sun filtered through the window, bouncing off crystal and gold ornaments. Chairs lined with pink silk cushions littered the space, along with tables covered in perfume and jewelry.

"You seem sad. Is something troubling You?"

The woman spoke in soothing tones, but her gaze didn't leave her stitching. Cecily was the palace fitter, a servant of station, and every dress Leila wore passed through her hands first. She was older than most of the others at thirty-seven years, with fluffy brown curls, honey-hazel eyes, and sandy skin—a warm look to match her presence, though everything about this day felt cold.

"I'm just thinking," Leila said.

"It's the tournament, isn't it?" Cecily stitched the seam along Leila's hip. "You don't like it."

Leila's gaze shot toward her, and Cecily offered a smile. "Everyone knows." Pocketing her thread, she pulled out a fragrant vial. "Is it the lack of control? The fact that Your husband is chosen through challenges as opposed to Your will?" She pressed her perfumed fingertips to Leila's wrists. "Or is it something else?"

"It's many things."

"I understand. Love is scary enough without danger thrown into the mix. Whose idea was that, anyhow? It's a bit silly, I think."

Cecily shuffled off to one of the tables, looping several strands of jewelry around her wrist. She returned to Leila's side, stopping short at the sight of Her frown. "Oh, child, I know it's overwhelming, but try to see the good in this. You are to be presented with the finest men in

Thessen." She draped a string of jewels across Leila's neck. "I have faith this tournament is exactly what You need."

Leila nearly scoffed aloud, but She kept Her mouth shut.

"Almost done, child." Cecily's face flushed. "I suppose I should stop calling You that. You're a grown woman now. But You'll always be small to me. I can't help it."

A sliver of warmth crept through Leila, thawing Her. "I don't mind."

Cecily circled a table stacked with crowns, some intricately beaded, others made of gold-plated flowers, stopping in front of a crown of sharp, golden spikes—Leila's favorite. Prompted by Leila's nod, she placed the crown on Her head.

"Look at You." She steered Leila toward a mirror. "What do You think?"

A flowing red dress draped Her like a river of blood, pulled across one shoulder and cinched at Her waist. Topaz and rubies hung from Her throat, with rows of matching bands and bracelets stacked on Her arms and wrists. But the crown stole Her focus, sharp and severe: *"The rays of the sun,"* Her servants would say, though Leila saw blades. For once, an authentic smile graced Her lips.

"You've outdone yourself."

"You make my work easy," Cecily cooed.

Leila took one last look at Her reflection—the vision of a queen. Then, perhaps for the thousandth time, the tournament floated through her thoughts.

The vision of a queen, with none of the control.

She left the dressing room, attempting to still Her mind. The royal parlor appeared, its walls covered in burgundy tapestries, the furnishings ornate and bejeweled.

Pippa spun toward Her in a swirl of fine yellow linen, her usually disheveled hair tied up in a bun. "You look like a princess!"

"Like a *queen*." Cosima, wearing a layered dress the color of rose wine, pulled Her into an embrace. "Look at You! You take my breath away."

Memories of Cosima's naked flesh pressed to Asher filled Leila's mind, and She squirmed out of her grasp. Delphi stood at Her side, a beauty in mint green and lapis, but Leila was more interested in the two chalices of wine she carried. "When's our entrance?" She snatched up a chalice. "I want to get this over with."

"Brontes was just seated." Delphi raised an eyebrow. "I see You switched the order. Feeling mischievous, are we?"

Wembleton tromped into the parlor, wearing a rich gold tunic and too many colorful drapes. Leila took a generous gulp of wine, hoping to blur the sight of him.

"Your Holiness, congratulations to You on this special occasion. Your celebration awaits." Wembleton waited for Leila to respond, and when She didn't, he turned to Her sisters. "Ladies, are we ready?"

The court lined up in front of a set of golden doors—the entrance to the atrium. As the doors opened, Wembleton waddled out, his arms wide. "Ladies and gentlemen, join me in welcoming The Savior's court."

One by one, Leila's sisters waltzed away, and a weight dropped in Her gut. She hated this part.

"And now, please stand in attention for Her Holiness, our One True Savior."

The screeching of chairs sliding along the polished floor sent Leila rigid. After downing the last of Her wine, She headed through the doorway.

The atrium was lavish on a normal day, but on Her birthday, it was a sight to behold. The ceiling overflowed with splendor, with red and purple ribbons spiraling downward and golden stars dangling from string. Garlands of lilies wrapped the marble columns; shining gold place settings spotted the infinitely long dining table, spilling with food and drink; and rows of beautifully dressed people—Her palace staff in their finest garb—stood in silence, watching Her. Waiting.

She stopped at Her seat at the head of the table, a crimson throne boasting rays, gold as the sun. Her sisters waited by their seats alongside Her, their heads bowed in reverence, and the sight of it stung. She had always despised events like these—grand feasts, festivities for *The One True Savior*. They served as a reminder that She stood on a pedestal above all others, and She stood on that pedestal alone.

Taking Her seat, She nodded for the others to do the same. Only Wembleton remained standing, his chalice in hand. "Ladies and gentlemen, tonight we celebrate Her Holiness on this, Her coming of age. Let us pay tribute to Her glory, for it is Her light that unites us, that fills our bellies and gives us shelter, that keeps our great realm whole and pure." He turned Her way. "This feast is not a gift from us to You. No, it is a gift from You to all of us. And for that, we thank You. Truly. Humbly."

Leila dug Her nails into the table, sickened by the stale stench of his lies.

"For all that You are and all that You do, we devote our lives to Your service." Wembleton raised his chalice high. "Blessed be The Savior!"

"*Blessed be The Savior*," the others said in unison. Leila barely lifted Her chalice before taking a swig, longing to saturate Her insides. Music wafted through the space, and the people dug into the feast, laughing and indulging in the opulence. It seemed everyone was content with the night ahead. Except Leila.

And Her father.

He sat at the opposite end of the table, a crown of gold-plated leaves on his head, layers of maroon drapes adorning his bare chest. Perhaps he looked handsome, but it was hard to see past his hideous glower.

The spread of food thinned, the faces around Her reddening with inebriation. Hylas entered the atrium, a scroll and reed in hand. He cleared his throat, again, then once more until the room finally fell silent. "Presenting the gifts to Leila Tūs Salvatíraas, Her Holiness, our One True Savior, on this, Her coming of age."

Guards in silver chest plates marched into the atrium carrying armfuls of goods—black garnets from the realm of Ethyua, peach trees from the farmers' union—and with each lot Leila recited Her gratitude. "Tell the Monarch of Ethyua I'm in awe of his jewels. Extend to him My deepest thanks. Tell the farmers I'm delighted. Peaches are My favorite." All the while She stared at Her father, who stared at Her all the same, and Her rage burned deeper, charring Her insides.

"From Her sister, Delphinium Tūs Salvatíraas of The Savior's court," Hylas announced. "'The Warrior's Chant,' a poem by Karti, delivered in its original form."

Leila spun away from Her father, gaping at the scroll delivered to Her hands. "Delphi!" She gasped, unrolling the aged parchment. "Oh My God, this is My—"

39

"Favorite. I know," Delphi said.

"Look—he misspelled sanguinary."

"Poor bastard, bet he never heard the end of that."

As Leila scanned the faded ink, Delphi hovered over Her shoulder. "The ending's my favorite. '*Lo, he set his foes aflame, turned their flesh to rot and ash, and ne'er was he questioned. Cross a warrior, and be burned.*'"

Glancing sidelong at Brontes, Leila gave Her sister a squeeze. "Thank you so much."

Delphi whispered into Her ear, "May all who cross You burn."

"From Her sister, Cosima Tūs Salvatíraas of The Savior's court," Hylas said. "A piece formed by the elite glassworkers of Trogolia."

Guards plucked the scroll from Leila's hands, replacing it with a palm-sized ornament.

"I saw it and instantly thought of You," Cosima said. "I know how much you adore Your garden."

Leila rotated the piece in Her hands—a crystal rose, its clear petals reflecting all the colors of the rainbow. "Thank you. It's beautiful."

"Not nearly as beautiful as You." Cosima snatched the rose away, taking Leila's hands. "Precious dove, I'd do anything for You. You know that, yes?"

I'd do anything for You. But Cosima and Asher were still naked in Leila's mind, and her words lost all meaning, fading away like the flush of her pale skin.

Pale skin. Leila froze, studying Her sister—painted lips, shiny red waves, and milky flesh that could rival Her own. Leila was fairer in comparison, but the shade was similar, passable as the same to the untrained eye. *Eyes.* Cosima's apple-green irises weren't particularly unusual, but they were striking, and perhaps that was all that mattered.

"Are You all right?" Cosima asked.

Leila shook Herself. "Apologies. Too much wine."

Chuckling, Cosima flagged a servant, having Leila's chalice promptly refilled. "No such thing."

Pippa's gift was next to arrive—a circlet of jeweled violets. No doubt Cecily had assisted. Leila gave Her sister a firm hug, though Her mind remained on Cosima.

Pale skin. Striking eyes.

"From beyond the fortress," Hylas said, "a gift from Petros Elia, the principal artist of Thessen. An original painting to add to Your collection."

Leila's back shot straight. She rose from Her seat as two guards marched into the atrium, a large, framed canvas held between them.

The room fell silent. Leila inspected the painting up close, extending Her hand to touch it but stopping short. She couldn't, no, that felt wrong. Instead Her eyes danced over the piece: a vibrant sky spotted with soft clouds, tall green trees, thatched cottages. In its center stood a woman with icy eyes, strawberry blonde locks, and light pouring from Her body—a woman Leila knew well, if only by Her reflection.

"What is it called?"

Hylas read over his scroll. "Mother."

A pang shot through Her. Flowers with long white petals and spots of pink were painted at Her mother's feet, and Leila smiled at the sight. "Lilies."

"It says here they were Your mother's—"

"Favorite. Yes, they were." Her eyes didn't leave the canvas, taking in the sea of brilliant hues. She rarely saw these colors in people. Only in paintings.

"For Your gratitude?" Hylas said.

A painting by Petros Elia. The *Petros Elia.*

"Your Holiness—"

"Tell him it's beautiful," Leila said. "Tell him I said it's truly beautiful."

"As You wish."

"Tell him I extend My deepest gratitude. Tell him it moves Me. Tell him I love it."

"As You—"

"I *love* it. Make sure to emphasize that. He needs to know unequivocally."

"He heard You," Brontes barked.

Leila shot him a glare, turning back to Hylas. "Emphasize it. Don't forget."

"She's finished." Brontes flagged the guards. "Take it away."

Her stomach sank as the guards marched off with Her painting.

"This concludes the presentation of the gifts." Hylas bowed. "Gratitude to everyone for honoring Her Holiness."

"And what of the Sovereign?" Delphi said. "Is there no gift for his daughter on Her most anticipated of birthdays?"

Brontes didn't waver, his one eye locked on Leila. "My gift arrives tonight. Expect it at Your chamber, Your Holiness."

The feast continued in all its reverential glory, but Leila had grown tired of it. Once Her father's gaze left Hers, She slipped away, taking in a full breath. *Freedom*—but not quite. Making certain She was alone, She glanced over Her shoulder before allowing the most freeing vision to overtake Her.

The watchtower.

Light pierced Her eyes, fading to harsh grey stone and a vast black sky.

Leila leaned against the sill and stared out into the night. The watchtower was Her most treasured sanctuary. The conditions were haggard, but She didn't care about the crumbling walls, the dust on the floor. She came for the evening air, the solitude, and more than anything the view. The entire realm lay before Her, its towns lit with specks of light, its rolling hills sprinkled with cottages. A meager escape from the confines of Her palace.

Thessen. She strained Her eyes, focusing on the hillside, but predictably, nothing happened. *The town. The village. The well.* She tried to see Herself there, to summon Her light, but She remained in Her tower same as always.

"Are You trying to leave?"

Delphi sauntered up to Leila's side, gazing out at the realm with Her. Sighing, Leila dragged Her fingertip along the rough stone. "I try every night. My power is constantly evolving, who's to say it won't work one day?"

"No progress?"

"The farthest I've gotten is the wall."

"Still can't travel to places You've never been before, I take it?"

Leila growled. "Such a pain. What good are gifts if they come with limitations?"

"I think Your shadow walking serves You well. Certainly gives You a strategic advantage, since Brontes knows nothing of it. Our little secret, yes?"

Leila mustered a smile. "I like that you call it that. *Shadow walking.* Makes it sound mysterious."

Her eyes made their way back to the realm, and Her smile died.

"One day You'll be able to leave," Delphi said. "We both will. When it's safe."

"I can't remember the last time I felt safe."

"You will walk the streets of Thessen, and the people will weep in adoration."

Leila said nothing, tracing Her finger along the sill, drawing invisible circles.

"Everything will be rectified. This tournament doesn't mark Your end, it marks Your beginning." Delphi came in closer. "Everything will work out as it should."

"I should've made moves sooner," Leila muttered. "I should've disarmed the Senate years ago."

"No one can blame You for being reluctant."

"But now it's all happening. And there's so much left to do."

"Leila, You were a *child* when You learned of Your father's treachery. Girls of the same age were playing with dolls, yet You began studying politics, training to protect Yourself." Delphi leaned in closer. "Today is not Your coming of age. You and I know full well You became a woman long ago. You are strong, You are capable, but more than anything, You are *prepared*."

Leila didn't waver, and Delphi's shoulders slumped. "Nothing? Even after all that? I thought I was quite eloquent. I'm giving You my best material, You know."

"It's funny. I'm The Savior, yet I haven't saved much of anyone, have I?"

"Andreas broke his arm, and You mended it in just two days. Eos, she had that terrible cyst, and Rosealie, when she struggled with childbirth."

"Ah yes, the palace staff. I've helped those within the walls of this fortress, and no one else."

"You bless the land every day," Delphi maintained. "The whole of Thessen reaps Your harvests. You've told me time and again a sickness lingers beneath our soil, yet You alone keep it at bay. People are well because of You."

"Because of Me, The Savior locked in a cage."

"Leila—"

"I've saved nothing," Leila said. "And I'm starting to lose track of the men I've killed."

"Is that what this is about? You hate Yourself for circumstances beyond Your control?"

"Nothing is supposed to be beyond My control," Leila grumbled.

"You're doing what You can with what's been given to You. You're a warrior. A *survivor*."

"A killer. I kill people, Delphi."

"You rid the realm of corruption, as The Savior should. You protect Your people whether they know it or not." Delphi glowered. "I swear, first You're upset for not making moves sooner, now You call Yourself a killer. If You're going to condemn Yourself, at least pick one or the other."

A heavy silence wedged between them, and Delphi sighed. "Apologies. You're frustrated. I understand..."

"It's all right," Leila muttered. "I'd just like to be alone, that's all."

"I know. But You've been summoned."

"By who?"

"Romulus." Delphi nodded at the stairwell. "He's waiting in the east wing."

"Alone?"

"Of course."

Leila rolled Her eyes. "Fucking hell."

The east wing. Delphi disappeared behind rays of white, and in her place stood a marble bust on a pedestal. The east wing materialized around Leila—cream walls, amber-brown tiles, and Romulus lingering a ways away.

He walked through the space, gesturing for Her to follow, and Leila quickly reached his side. Glancing across the corridor, he spoke out of the corner of his mouth. "I couldn't do it. I couldn't secure the Proctorship."

"You failed?"

"Brontes went another way."

"Which way?"

He hesitated. "Simon."

"Simon's to be the Proctor?" Romulus nodded, and Leila growled. "I'll correct this. The work never ends, not even on My birthday."

Romulus veered down another passage, while Leila continued along the stretch of sameness. Conflicted emotions battled in Her gut, but She forced them down, trying instead to see only Brontes's glare and their unspoken war.

To Simon's chamber.

"Your Holiness?"

Leila spun around, meeting a golden mane and dumbfounded gaze. "Good God, Asher, you scared the shit out of Me."

Asher was considerably more clothed than the last time She saw him, decorated in silver armor with a spear in hand, but his eyes were lit with the same vacant awe. "Apologies, Your Holiness, I didn't intend to startle You, nor to force such language from Your tongue."

"Oh yes, these virtuous lips of Mine burn at the taste of foul words," Leila scoffed.

"Really? Is that so?"

Rolling Her eyes, Leila continued on Her way. "Good night, Asher."

"Wait." He stepped forward. "Your Holiness, I was actually looking for You."

"You were?"

"I waited at Your chamber for some time, but You never showed," he said.

"For what purpose?"

"Your birthday gift. From the Sovereign."

"Oh." She folded Her arms. "Well, go on then. Hand it over."

"It's me. I'm the birthday gift."

"...You're My birthday gift."

"That's right."

She eyed him up and down. "I don't...understand..."

"From this night forward, I'm to be Your personal guard." He held his chin high. "Each evening I will stand watch outside Your chamber.

Should anyone try to disturb You or God forbid seek You harm, they will be met by my vow and my spear."

Leila faltered. "*You're* My personal guard?"

"Yes." Asher smiled.

"So I'll be seeing your face...in front of My chamber...every night."

"Yes, exactly."

Groaning, Leila rubbed Her temples. "God."

"Is something wrong, Your Holiness?"

"Oh, not at all. Today's My twentieth birthday, and My father has gifted Me a nanny."

"It's for Your protection," Asher said. "The tournament begins soon. Eventually the competitors will be within these walls. The Sovereign's concerned for Your safety."

"I'm sure he is. And let Me guess, you're to report My whereabouts to him?"

"Exactly." Asher nodded at the corridor ahead. "Are You headed to Your chamber now?"

Leila spoke through gritted teeth. "Of course. I can't think of any other place I'd be headed at this hour."

Asher held out his arm. "I'll walk You."

Reluctantly, Leila linked Her arm with his and trudged along at his side. His skin against Hers was soft, warm, and a little repellent, as visions of him entangled in Cosima's sheets swam through Her mind. Her gold chamber door appeared before them, and Asher grinned as if he was pleased with himself.

Yes, Asher, you walked Me to My chamber. Such a heroic feat, how ever did you manage?

He turned to Her, displaying the door. "Here we are."

Leila forced a smile. "Well then, I suppose you can report to My concerned father that I'm turning in tonight. All this celebrating has left Me worn."

"Of course, Your Holiness. Pleasant evening, and happy birthday."

Her smile faded. "It's Leila, you know. My name. It's Leila."

"It's a lovely name, Your Holiness."

Another vacant gaze, but Leila didn't hold it for long, taking to Her chamber. With a huff, She peeled off Her jewelry, Her crown, until She stood unencumbered. Ready. Her mothers watched from Her wardrobe.

"It's My birthday," Leila whispered.

Their sad gazes spoke for them, adding a sting to go with Her sickness.

"Please forgive Me."

She closed Her eyes, and Her body filled with heat.

Simon's chamber.

When Her eyes opened, She was in another room entirely, and a gangly man stood paces away.

Simon gasped. "Your Holiness."

Leila squared Her shoulders, staring long and hard at the Senator— the man abetting Her end. She pulled Her blade from the sheath on Her thigh.

"Have a seat."

3

THE POOL

Grow.

Hot summer air filled Leila's lungs as Her light bled into the ground. It wasn't often She was able to bless the realm without interruption, but this morning had been particularly uneventful —thanks to the pool.

Fuck the pool.

She shook the thought from Her mind. The blackness beneath the soil reached toward Her, tirelessly longing for release, but She was more than used to forcing it down. Everything about that morning was effortless—there were no meetings, no staff summoning Her, no Senators to manage.

Because of the pool.

"For God's sake," Leila groaned, Her light dulled by Her sour mood. Pool or none, She had other matters to tend to, so She hoisted Herself from the grass and scampered to Her chamber. After slipping Her dress over Her head, She strapped Her blade into place, stopping to wipe a spot of dried blood from its edge. Her gaze floated up to the mirrored wardrobe where Her mothers waited, their lips pursed.

"Oh, don't look at Me like that. You know I haven't a choice."

With Her nose in the air, She left Her chamber, letting the door swing shut behind Her.

"Good morning, Your Holiness." Asher stood beside Her door, a proud smile on his face.

She glowered. "It's Leila."

Still frowning, She continued on Her way, winding through a maze of corridors. Cream walls and potted trees blurred in Her periphery, but there was nothing else. No people. Delphi's door appeared, and She held Her breath.

Let's get this over with.

The door flew open, and a servant dashed out.

"Your Holiness," She panted, tying Her dress into place.

Leila watched her dart away before heading into the chamber, where Delphi lay across her bed in a turquoise dress.

"Nessa was in quite the hurry," Leila said.

"She's late for the pool." Delphi winked. "My mistake."

Leila flopped down beside her. "God, the pool. Don't remind Me."

"You should know, the turnout has surpassed all expectations." Delphi rolled onto her stomach, scooting closer to Leila. "Have you ever seen the palace so empty? Nearly all Your servants were called in for assistance."

"All this fuss so seventeen men can be slaughtered for no good reason."

"Or maybe we'll thwart Your father once and for all, and You can still have Your happy ending with Your handsome Champion. Can you imagine? Hundreds of tents are stationed outside the Ceres Fountain, and the love of Your life could be standing inside one of them this very instant."

Leila rolled Her eyes. "Don't make Me sick."

"He's likely naked and humiliated, but still—"

"I have a plan."

Delphi sat upright. "You have a plan?"

"It came to Me last night. Perhaps sooner. I've been musing over it for a while, I just needed to put the pieces together."

"Well, go on then."

Leila situated Herself across from Her sister and took in a steady breath. "Three men were hired by Brontes. They'll join the tournament, no doubt try to kill Me. No matter the steps we take, I'm in jeopardy. I am their mark."

"Right. We know this."

"But what if I wasn't The Savior?"

Delphi faltered. "But... You are The Savior."

"I don't have to be. Brontes has kept Me locked in this fortress My entire life. Perhaps for once My imprisonment can be of some use to Me."

"I don't follow."

"No one knows who I am." Leila gripped the folds of Her dress. "They don't know what I look like. They don't know My name. So if twenty men were to compete in the tournament, and a woman were to stand before them and call herself The Savior... Well, they'd have to believe her, right? Even if that woman wasn't Me."

Delphi furrowed her brow. "Are You suggesting we enlist a...fake Savior? A *decoy* Savior?"

"Yes, exactly."

"Are You mad?" Delphi spat.

"It's a solid plan. With My title hidden, I can continue My efforts against Brontes without having to look over My shoulder any more than I do now. We afford ourselves some safety, and meanwhile the men compete none the wiser."

"That's all well and good, but there are so many things left to be considered."

"Name them. I promise you, I've considered them all."

Delphi crossed her arms. "All right, here's an obvious one: Who?"

"Who what?"

"Who's our *new Savior*? Or do You happen to know of another woman made of magical light that I'm unaware of?"

"Cosima."

Delphi's eyes widened. "*Cosima?*"

"She's perfect. Beautiful, eloquent. Her eyes are striking, her skin is fair."

"But does it glow?"

"The labyrinth is underground," Leila said. "There's no sunlight in those parts. When she makes her visits, no one will be expecting a glow of any kind."

"And what about the last two weeks of the tournament? They're held in the palace. Above ground. *Beneath the sun.*"

"We'll find ways around it. Close the shades. Plan her appearances in the evening. There are a million things—"

"You and Your father look alike," Delphi cut in. "There's a resemblance. For God's sake, You have the same hair. You don't think the men will question it?"

"Cosima is *stunning*. Men *worship* her." Leila's voice became hard. "They'd be more than happy to compete for her, willing to turn a blind eye to any red flag."

Delphi scowled. "What of Brontes? You think he'll just allow this little switch to happen?"

"He doesn't need to know."

"*How* will he not know?"

"Do you actually expect Brontes to involve himself in this tournament? As The Savior, I'm required to attend most of the challenges. My father can hardly tolerate being in the same room as Me." A pang ripped through Leila, but She held firm. "Brontes may pull the strings, but he won't bore himself with the formalities."

"You hide your identity for thirty days, and all the while Brontes remains oblivious?"

"I've been shadow walking through this fortress for years, and he hasn't a clue."

Delphi crossed her arms. "All right then, say all of this is true. The switch is made. The men compete for Cosima. Brontes suspects nothing. What will You be doing while all this is happening? Hiding like a scared little girl?"

"Of course not," Leila said. "The tournament is to be my assassination. I need to study these three men and stop it from happening."

Delphi arched an eyebrow. "And You'll do that how?"

"By going into the labyrinth."

"Leila!"

"What?"

"You hide Your title to protect Yourself, then venture into the very place that puts You in harm's way," Delphi said.

"Yes, but I'll be entering the labyrinth as someone else. Not as The Savior."

"Who?"

"A member of Her court." Leila raised Her chin. "I'll be The Savior's sister. Like you."

"And what reason would *The Savior's sister* have to visit the labyrinth? Did You just wander down there? Tell me, oh loyal *sister*, what is Your purpose?"

Shit. Her mind went blank, and She glanced across Delphi's chamber, searching for an answer amid the framed paintings, the wooden wardrobe, the tonics. *Tonics.* The back shelf boasted jars of herbs and physics—mementoes of Delphi's late mother, each with its own healing property.

"A healer." Leila spun toward Delphi. "I heal people, don't I?"

Delphi let out a laugh. "Oh, I see. You're going to use Your divine light to heal these men, and none of them will ever suspect You're The Savior. A fine plan."

"It'll work. I know what I'm doing."

"It's dangerous. This whole thing... There are too many risks."

"I have no other options." Leila's voice came out sharp. "Three men are coming to this fortress with the intention of killing Me. How does it benefit Me to sit here on display wearing My title like a target?"

"And You think Cosima would be happy to wear the target instead?"

"How many years did we play together, and she insisted on being queen? She covets My crown. You know it as well as I do. Perhaps we can put her malice to use."

Delphi fell silent, and Leila leaned in closer. "I know there are dangers. But I am already in danger. I am to *die*."

Still Delphi didn't respond, visibly conflicted. Lit with resolve, Leila spoke firmly. "Cosima will play the role of Savior. I'm certain I can convince her. And while she entertains the men, I will visit the labyrinth, locate the assassins, and have them killed before they can kill Me. I will *ruin* Brontes's plan, and I will ruin *Brontes*. But none of this works unless I can exist within the tournament as someone else. As anyone but The Savior."

"A last resort." Delphi looked Her in the eyes. "I will accept this as a last resort."

"Delphi—"

"Promise me You'll consider other options. I'm still willing to spy for You."

"Two spies are better than one."

"Leila—"

"I'll consider other options."

Delphi exhaled. "Thank you."

A last resort. It wasn't quite victory, but it was close enough.

Delphi shook her head, and Leila scowled. "What?"

"If You go with this plan," she said, "it'll be much harder to find a man."

Leila groaned. "No more of this, I swear."

"Your cunt will turn rank, just like Your mood—"

"If it's so important to you, I'll find one through some other means. The world is filled with men. I have plenty of options."

A knock sounded at the door, and Hylas poked his head in. "Your Holiness?"

Leila flagged him over, and he bowed. "Apologies for the interruption, but there's a meeting in the Senate room."

"A meeting?" Leila said. "When?"

"Now, Your Holiness."

"I didn't see it on the schedule."

"Changes were made due to unforeseen circumstances."

Visions of Her blade ripping through Simon's throat flashed through Her thoughts. "I see. I'll be right there."

With one last bow, Hylas dipped from the room, leaving the two sisters alone.

"You know, Hylas just proved My point." Leila turned to Delphi. "He's a young man right here in this very palace. I could very well wind up with him."

Delphi laughed. "You could, could You?"

"Sure." She eyed the spot where he had stood. "He's handsome...in a sweet way."

"Isn't he? And You know, the two of You have so much in common."

"Is that right?"

"Oh yes, you're both of age, you both enjoy the arts, you both like men—"

"Dammit," Leila grumbled.

Chuckling, Delphi nudged Her shoulder. "Go on then, *Your Holiness.* Go address these *unforeseen circumstances*." She hopped to her feet. "I'll be at the pool. Maybe I can find a few men who suit You in case You change Your mind."

"I won't."

Delphi waved Her away, waltzing from the room and leaving Leila on Her own. With a grunt, Leila picked Herself up and headed through the palace. Soon the Senate table loomed before Her, circled by seven faces—some cross, others nervous, though one in particular was its usual vision of contempt.

"Senators." Leila turned to Her father. "Brontes."

"If You're not going to address me as *Father*, You can at least call me by my title, *Daughter,*" he growled.

"Would someone care to tell Me the purpose of all this?" She took Her place at the table, studying the empty seats. "Or perhaps we should wait for the others to show."

"That, Your Holiness, is the exact reason for this meeting." Kastor gestured around the table. "Everyone's here."

"But there's only six of you." Leila sneered at Her father. "And *Brontes*, of course."

"Simon and Gelanor are missing," Kastor said.

"You're certain? For how long?"

"No one's seen Gelanor since our last meeting."

"Is that right?" Leila's eyes widened. "What a mystery."

"And Simon's been absent since Your birthday feast," Wembleton added.

"But that was just last night. Have you checked his chamber? I imagine he's just sick from the wine. It was quite strong. Even I felt a bit fuddled. I opted to turn in early, in fact." Leila flashed Brontes a smirk. "My *birthday gift* can attest to that."

"We're not here for speculation. We're here to redistribute duties," he said. "It's too soon to assume foul play—"

"Foul play?" Leila gasped. "In this very palace? You think so? My word..."

Brontes's one eye narrowed. "But the Sovereign's Tournament begins tomorrow, and all relevant commitments need to be resolved immediately. Simon was to proctor the tournament, and his position must be filled at once."

"If I may interject, I'm sure you recall our conversation from the other day." Romulus turned to the others. "I've expressed to his Highness my interest in proctoring the tournament. I humbly conceded in favor of his judgment, but now that the position is available once again, let it be known my offer still stands."

A smug laugh sounded from across the table. Phanes leaned back in his seat, stroking his patchy beard while giving Romulus a critical once-over.

"Is something funny?" Romulus's face was unchanging, though his tone carried his scorn. "Have I told a joke without knowing it?"

"I just find it odd you'd volunteer for such a position." Phanes chuckled. "Proctoring the Sovereign's Tournament. When Simon was chosen, I assumed it was a punishment. No sane man longs to spend his days in the labyrinth."

"A sane man may not long for it, but a man of duty makes sacrifices for those he serves." Romulus glanced at Brontes, bowing his head. "Are we not here to serve your daughter? To ensure the tournament unfolds in a manner worthy of Her *glory*?"

Brontes stared at Leila, his gaze venomous. "Shall we bring it to a vote?"

"All those in favor of Romulus holding the role of Proctor?" Wembleton said.

Arms shot overhead, though Phanes barely lifted his from the table. Brontes scanned the room, stopping at Leila, Her hands folded in Her lap.

"You don't vote, *Daughter*?"

"I haven't an opinion."

Brontes glowered. "Seven votes in favor, one abstention. Romulus is now Proctor of the Sovereign's Tournament. Allow me to personally commend your sense of duty. May the rest of you learn from his example."

Phanes's nostrils flared as if he smelled something rotten, and Leila basked in his offense. Everything about him repelled Her—his wavy tangles of carob-brown hair, his thin mustache, the gold chains hanging down his sculpted bronze chest. He was younger than most of the others, perhaps in his late thirties, but he carried himself with the hubris of a man far more seasoned.

Meeting Her prying gaze, he smiled and blew a wretched kiss.

"Next item." Brontes rustled through a stack of parchment. "The pool."

Leila nearly winced. *The damn pool.*

"Turnout is steady," Romulus said. "Two men have already been selected."

"Are the allowances prepared?"

Kastor cleared his throat. "Gelanor set the sums aside before his... parting. But guards are prepared to distribute the funds tomorrow morn." He glanced over a scroll. "Fifty thousand coin for each family."

"Fifty thousand?" Leila spoke before She could stop Herself. "That's over double the allowance of the last tournament. More than any tournament in history."

Brontes let out a grunt. "Inflation rates."

"Inflation isn't *that* high."

"Your Holiness, Your competitors will be battling grave dangers in the pursuit of Your affection," Wembleton said. "Surely their families ought to be honored for releasing their sons for such a heroic endeavor."

Leila scowled. "Honored? Do you mean incentivized?"

"There is no incentive greater than the love of The Savior. And such a generous allowance is in keeping with Your father's pious reputation." Kastor leaned in closer to Her, offering a smile that matched his soft, low voice. "There's no need to be wary. I assure You, You are more than worth it."

Leila looked him in the eyes, wishing the Senator's hazel gaze wasn't so gentle, that his handsome face matched his ugly insides. Kastor was the youngest of them all—thirty or so—with long black hair, a short, groomed beard, and copper skin chiseled and carved. His act was more convincing than the others, nearly enough to make him seem warm, as if he wasn't abetting Her end. But he was.

Leila turned away. "Well then, if that's all—"

"Actually, Your Holiness, there are other matters to discuss," Wembleton said. "Namely tomorrow's commencement ceremony."

Leila faltered. "The commencement ceremony?"

"For the tournament." Wembleton beamed. "The ceremony marks its grand introduction, and it's imperative that all things run smoothly. Thus, if I could humbly steal a moment of Your time so we can discuss the formalities, the decorum, Your entrance—"

Leila's stomach clenched. "My entrance?"

"Of course. You're the most esteemed guest of the ceremony. The people of Thessen will be overjoyed to finally lay their eyes upon their Queen—"

"I won't be attending," Leila said.

Wembleton's face dropped. "Come again?"

"I won't be attending the ceremony."

All eyes panned to Leila, but She held firm. Come tomorrow, She was anyone but The Savior, and no ceremony was going to ruin that.

Brontes's jaw tightened. "Do not play games with us. I haven't the patience."

"I'm not going. No need to trouble yourself with My entrance, because I won't be making one."

"Your Holiness, You've expressed such disdain over Your confinement," Wembleton said. "Don't You see, this is Your opportunity to finally reveal Yourself to Your people."

"Perhaps another time."

"This isn't a negotiation," Brontes growled. "A royal is required to attend—"

"Then *you* go, Your *Highness*." Leila met his glare with Her own. "This is *your* tournament after all. Isn't that what you said?"

"You're going to that ceremony. You will sit with Wembleton, and You will make Your plans—"

"Wembleton, let it be on record that My father will be attending the ceremony in My stead."

"Enough—"

"While the Sovereign is in full dictatorship of *his* tournament, there is no law that states he can force The Savior's hand," Leila said. "You can search the scrolls, but trust Me when I say I have them memorized. And it seems you haven't the time to change the laws yourself, as the lot of you have done so many times before."

"One more word, and I swear—"

"You've made it clear this tournament is yours to control. But you cannot control My participation. If a royal must attend tomorrow's ceremony, that royal will be you, because it most certainly will not be Me."

Brontes's lips curled into a grimace. "You little bitch."

"My decision is final."

"I'm warning You—"

"I said I'm not going!" She barked.

Silence filled the space. Brontes's glare turned sinister, and color lifted from his flesh, swimming through the air.

Red.

Rage.

"A word alone with my daughter," he said.

Wembleton cleared his throat. "Who calls this meeting to—?"

"Now."

The Senators shot up from their seats and hurried from the room, leaving a heavy quiet. There was only Leila, Her father, and his seething red.

"Don't you have arrangements to make?" Her nerves stirred, but She played with Her hair, feigning indifference. "For your appearance at the ceremony?"

Brontes circled the table. "You dare to defy me? In front of my entire Senate?"

"It wasn't the entire Senate. Remember, Gelanor and Simon are missing."

"You humiliated me in front of my constituents."

"I was exercising My legal right. Perhaps if you were more educated in Thessian law, this humiliation would've been avoided."

Brontes stopped at Her side. "You raise Your voice to me, the Sovereign of Thessen, in his own Senate room."

Leila's knees wobbled, but She stood. "I can speak to you how I please. You are beneath Me."

His hand plunged into Her hair, grabbing a fistful and slamming Her against the table. Pain fired through Her cheek, a familiar ache, yet it never ceased to shock Her. He wrestled Her wrists behind Her back, pinning Her down.

"Am I still beneath You? From where I'm standing, it doesn't appear so."

Yanking Her from the table, He shoved Her against the wall, sending new aches splintering through Her.

"Where's that light of Yours?" he hissed. "All that power You boast of? Will it show itself? Will it stop me?"

Shadow walk. The urge was fierce, but She forced Herself still. She wouldn't reveal Her hand.

"You know, there was a time when You weren't such a wretched cunt," he said. "Whenever did that change?"

Leila spoke through gritted teeth. "I took after My dear father."

"You remember that nanny You had when You were young? Delphinium's mother. I've forgotten her name. She pulled Your wet body from Your mother's corpse. Brought You to this palace. You were an ugly shit, small and hairless, horrid to look at. She insisted I give You a name that carried meaning. So after some thought, I decided on Leila. *Darkness.* Because the day You arrived here was the darkest day of my life."

Another ache shot through Her, one She had known since She was a little girl.

"Years later, the name continues to suit You well," he said. "Because since that day, You've never ceased being a black cloud over this palace."

"So sorry to have burdened you, Father," Leila muttered.

"I don't blame You for hating this tournament. I actually admire Your foresight." He loosened his grip, running his fingers through Her hair. "How painful it must feel, knowing twenty men are about to come upon this fortress, and none of them will care for You. As soon as they make Your acquaintance, they'll see what I see." He brought his lips to Her ear. "A *mistake*. And not a single one of them could possibly bring themselves to love You."

Leila said nothing, festering in Her indignity.

"You're smart, my little Dark One, to see this. Gives You time to prepare for the hurt."

"Can I go now?"

Brontes released Her, sending Her staggering across the floor before charging from the room.

Leila headed through the palace, holding Her head high—a bitter lie. Perhaps Brontes was watching Her, reveling in his victory.

Don't let him win.

She rounded the corner, and tears flooded Her eyes. Her insides stirred, piqued and trembling, and soon the rest of Her followed suit, Her hands shaking at Her sides, Her feet walking, then running through the corridor, up the stairs. Shame, hurt, and humiliation bombarded Her, tearing holes in Her pride, but the burning of Her blackened insides filled Her with purpose.

As Leila barreled into the chamber, Cosima spun around, startled. "Leila, what a pleasant... Oh my God, are You all right?"

Don't let him win. Leila forced the tears aside.

"I need to ask for a favor."

❦ 4 ❦

THE COMMENCEMENT

T he roar of the audience was a whisper to Leila. Sitting on the watchtower sill, She observed the commencement ceremony from afar, taking in the theater. A man made his way through the arena, followed by another—ants from where She sat, small enough to crush.

"You're glowing. They can see You."

Delphi leaned against the sill at Her side, but Leila kept Her eyes on the arena. "No one's looking at Me."

A tiny Wembleton waved his arms, no doubt blathering with delight. The entire display was devoid of purpose, empty in a way that felt contagious, as if Leila had become hollow by association. Another man entered the arena, and the crowd howled louder, shrill with the adoring cries of women. He must've been a sight.

"They look handsome," Delphi said.

Leila shrugged. "You can hardly see them. They're specks."

"They look like handsome specks."

"They look like fools to Me."

The last competitor marched into the arena, and soon after a man joined Wembleton in the royal balcony.

Brontes. The vilest speck of them all.

A hush fell over the pews. Leila whispered to Delphi as if the people might hear Her. "What's happening?"

"How am I supposed to know? I'm right here beside You."

The cheering returned with abrupt force, and a gate within the arena clanked opened. The entrance to the labyrinth.

One by one, the men filed through the blackened portal and vanished from sight.

Leila flinched as the gate slammed shut. The crowd roared in approval, but She didn't share their joy. The tournament had begun, and so had the countdown to Her death.

"The competitors." Leila turned to Delphi. "I want their records. All of them."

The servants had gathered notes on each man, a worthwhile asset if Leila had any clue where to find them. They dashed from the watchtower and scoured the palace, searching for a distinct set of scrolls. After hours of darting from room to room, rifling through documents and poking through drawers, Delphi tiptoed from one of the servants' stations, her arms overflowing with parchment.

Leila threw open the door to Her study and darted inside. The room was once covered in pink and reserved for play, but She had long since filled it with darkness. The walls were a deep plum; the curtains, desk, and shelves were black; the only spot of brightness came from the rose silk couches. The sisters took root at a round ebony table, fanning out the scrolls, and from that point forward their eyes belonged to the men of the tournament.

The Brave. Age: 26. Hair: red. Eyes: blue.

The Intellect. Age: 23. Hair: black. Eyes: brown.

Leila flipped through each scroll, taking in man after man.

"Look at these names," Delphi said. "The Prince, the Jester, the *Dog.* Makes them sound more like characters than men."

"I think that's the point," Leila murmured, distaste lacing Her words.

The Regal. The Poet. Each competitor had been given a laurel—a useless title to wear with false pride—then further divided into categories. Savants, Stalwarts—She snorted upon reading of the Lords, men of *coin and beauty*. The final category sent Her eyes narrowing.

The Beasts. These were the men She was looking for.

"Are you memorizing *all* of them?" Delphi asked.

Leila's gaze didn't lift from the parchment. "Indeed I am."

"You're suddenly interested?"

"I need to study them. They're coming into *My* home. I need to be prepared."

"You don't trust them."

Leila scoffed. "Why should I?"

"I thought we were searching for the assassins."

"We are. But we can do two things at once, yes?"

"Well then, be sure to read thoroughly. You've got everything You'd care to know about them right at Your fingertips, down to the size of their cocks." Delphi winked. "That's the most important part of all."

The door crept open, and four faces poked into the room. "What are you doing?" Nyx asked.

"Reading up on cocks," Delphi said nonchalantly.

Faun's eyes locked onto the parchment. "Are those the competitors' records?"

Hemera shoved past the others. "Oh good, Leila's finally coming around! I knew She would."

Nyx, Faun, and Damaris followed her into the study, giggling over the scrolls. A groan rose in Leila's throat, but She forced it down, returning to Her work.

The Artist. Age: 21. Hair: brown. Eyes: black. She faltered. *Black?*

"One man, I swear, is fated for You." Damaris peered over Leila's shoulder. "You wouldn't believe it, he ran in right as the pool was closing, barefoot no less. And he just so happens to be the exact man for You."

"I heard one of the men made it in by his cock alone," Hemera said.

Faun gasped. "No!"

"Yes!" Hemera leaned in closer. "Shae said it was the largest she had seen all day. Practically had to fold it in half just to fit it in his pants."

"God, no more of this. All day yesterday it was *men, men, men.* I'm positively tired of them." Nyx gestured toward her sister. "Deal."

Hemera pulled two decks of cards from her pocket and laid them on

63

the table, sweeping Leila's scrolls aside, polluting Her workstation. *Oh, for God's sake...*

Damaris turned to Delphi and Leila. "Would the two of you like to play?"

"Don't invite Leila! She always wins."

Hemera swatted her sister's arm. "Nyx, She's The Savior!"

"The Savior who *always wins*."

"We're all right for now, thank you," Leila muttered.

The Prince. The Hunter. She brought the next scroll up to Her face, trying to block out all distractions.

"How was the ceremony?" Damaris asked. "Were they just as You pictured?"

Sighing, Leila dropped the parchment. "The ceremony was fine."

"She didn't go," Delphi said.

Hemera's eyes widened. "You didn't go to the ceremony?"

Faun crossed her arms. "Leila, more of this?"

"She was assisting me." Cosima waltzed into the room wearing sunny yellow and a bright smile. "The poor dove, I was feeling so ill this morning, and our little Leila was the only one who could help me. She sacrificed Her own ceremony for my well-being. I can never repay Her. Are these all the men I stole You away from?" She plucked one of the scrolls from the table and laughed. "Good God, have You read this? It's got the length of his cock and everything. This one's not impressive. Don't pick the Physician."

"Are You supposed to see these?" Damaris leafed through a few records. "I thought they were for staff only."

"What Mousumi doesn't know won't hurt her," Leila said.

"Your Holiness, a word..."

As if summoned by Her thoughts, Mousumi walked into the room, stopping at the sight of the scrolls. "Are those the competitors' records? Where did You get those?"

Leila grimaced. *Spoke too soon.*

"Don't look at us," Nyx said. "She had them out when we got here."

Mousumi scowled. "Your Holiness, it's against tournament regulation for The Savior to view these records."

"I'm almost finished. It'll only be a moment." Leila waved her away.

"It'll taint Your opinion of the men."

"Trust Me, My opinion has long been tainted."

"This is Your father's tournament. If he were to learn of this transgression, he'd be—"

"Pissed to shit, I'm sure you're right." Leila kept Her eyes on the scrolls. "So if we could keep this between the lot of us—"

"What's all this fuss about?" Cecily floated into the study. "Are those the competitors' records?"

Leila slumped in Her seat. "Never mind."

Cecily's face dropped. "Child, You can't look at those. It'll spoil the excitement of meeting them on Your own."

"Oh, it's all in good fun, let Her play," Cosima said.

"It feels like play now, but it'll pollute Her mind, I'm certain." Cecily marched to the table and began plucking up slips. "Come, let's gather them up."

Delphi ripped the scrolls from her hands, and the room erupted, the women arguing on top of one another. Blocking out the disarray, Leila focused on the scrolls—pages She had read a hundred times over, but something was missing. She breezed through them again: *the Cetus, the Noble,* man after man with his own moniker and category. Five Savants, five Stalwarts, five Lords—

Two Beasts.

"Wait!"

All eyes landed on Leila, who had stopped reading the scrolls and started counting them. "Seventeen." She went through the stack once more. "There's only seventeen scrolls. Where are the last three?"

Mousumi hesitated. "That should be all of them, Your Holiness."

Cecily spun toward her. "You *lost* them?"

"*I* didn't lose *anything.*"

Another fit filled the space, and Leila groaned. "*Ladies,* I'd like a moment alone with My sisters."

The servants glanced at one another before filing reluctantly from the room. As the door closed behind them, Leila turned to Delphi and Cosima, pressing Her finger into the stack of parchment. "The assassins. They're the ones missing. They have to be."

"They never entered the pool." Delphi's hands fell into her lap. "Of course."

"And we don't even know their laurels," Leila muttered.

Sighing, Cosima shook her head. "What troubled times. But if anyone can tackle such a predicament, it's You. And I'm thrilled to be of service." She hopped from her seat and headed for the door.

"Where are you going?" Delphi called out. "I thought you were *thrilled* to be of service."

"Were we not finished here?"

"It's fine. You can go," Leila said.

Once Cosima flitted from the room, Delphi turned to Leila, her lips pursed. "I'm still wary of this plan."

"Well, unless you voice another soon, it's the only one we've got." Leila flipped through the parchment, grimacing. *The Farmer. The Artist.* She shoved the stack away. *Useless.*

"The assassins..." Delphi drummed Her fingers along the table. "Have You any clue who they are?"

"Not a one."

"Perhaps Your little friend would know more."

Leila's head perked up. "I could ask."

The slightest smile formed on Delphi's lips, and Leila couldn't help but mirror the sentiment. Delphi's eyes panned to the mess on the table. "Oh hell, the girls left their cards."

"I'll take care of it." Leila shuffled the cards into stacks and dumped them into Her pocket, abandoning the room soon after.

Perhaps Your little friend would know. If anyone knew anything, it'd be him.

The atrium appeared, Leila's birthday ribbons intact. She zeroed in on a bowl of peaches in the center of the table, snatching up two before continuing through the palace. The door to the Senate room loomed ahead, and She slipped inside.

The room was empty. She walked past the round table, grabbing a scroll at random and plopping down onto the window seat. With rehearsed efficiency, She dug into one of Her peaches, Her eyes on the parchment, then slid Her foot along the floor, grazing the tiles until one of them shifted.

Found you.

She scooted the loose tile aside, revealing a hole plunging underground, and dropped Her uneaten peach into the abyss—a gift for Her friend—before kicking the tile back into place.

"Your Holiness."

Leila flinched as Wembleton appeared, his hands resting on his belly. "I didn't expect to find You here," he said.

Leila resisted the urge to glance down at the loose tile. Hopefully She'd receive a response soon. "I'm just reading up on..." She eyed Her decoy scroll, "...Thessen's history of coin and accounting."

"Fascinating literature."

"Isn't it?"

Wembleton forced a chuckle. "Well, I'm glad I've found You. I was tasked to report to You the day's results."

"Results?"

"Yes. Of the tournament."

Leila turned to the window behind Her. The sun was already setting, the day gone in an instant. She'd been too distracted to notice.

"As Master of Ceremonies, I'm required to announce the happenings of each day's events to Your great realm," Wembleton said. "And to You as well, naturally, as these men belong to You."

"They don't *belong* to Me, they're not...linens or jewels."

He cleared his throat. "The competitors spent their first day navigating the labyrinth, a perilous obstacle course indeed. Horrors awaited them deep underground, testing their bravery, reminding them to respect and obey—"

"I know what the labyrinth is."

His smile waned. "We can make these meetings brief. I'll just cover the basics: winners, losers, casualties—"

"Casualties?" The word hit Her like a fist. "Someone's died already?"

"Today, we honor the Jester, the Farmer, and the Benevolent, for they died as heroes in the Sovereign's Tournament."

"*Three men* died today?"

"Yes, Your Holiness."

Leila set aside Her peach and parchment, trying to digest

Wembleton's words. "Three men. On the first day." Her eyes narrowed. "How?"

"I beg Your pardon?"

"How did they die?"

"The most honorable of deaths," he said. "Fighting for Your affection."

"Tell Me *how*, Wembleton. That is an order."

Wembleton fussed with his flashy drapes. "The Jester was the first to...expire. He received an injury to the head."

"What kind of injury?"

"Your Holiness, these details are rather gruesome, and for a delicate woman such as Yourself—"

"Now."

Wembleton cowered. "It looked like repeated blows to the skull."

"Blows? What sort of obstacle would do something like that?"

Wembleton continued his fidgeting, his gaze darting to the window, the shelves. "I've been told it wasn't an obstacle, rather...a fist."

"You're telling me the Jester was beaten to death? By another competitor?"

"I'm sure he did it in the name of love."

Fire flooded Leila's veins. "Who was it?"

"I wasn't there, Your Holiness. The only witnesses are deep underground."

Leila clenched Her jaw. She didn't need confirmation. She already knew the answer. "The next death. How did it happen? And I require specifics."

Wembleton stared up at the ceiling. "The Farmer was...impaled through the mouth by a rather large thorn. It's possible he fell at a very unfortunate angle...or he could've been shoved."

"Shoved. Of course. And the final man?"

"Ah, the Benevolent was most certainly killed by an obstacle. He stumbled in its path and was crushed to death."

Leila raised an eyebrow. "He stumbled. Into an obstacle."

"Precisely."

Sighing, She rubbed Her temples. "Could he have been pushed?"

"Well..."

Leila's jaw tightened. "Wonderful. There are murderers in the labyrinth."

"Not murderers, fierce warriors. Fighting in the name of—"

"Love, yes, I heard you," She said.

"The remaining competitors are resting in the sanctuary. Tomorrow, they spend another day navigating the most glorious—"

"You're dismissed."

Wembleton scurried away, and for that Leila was grateful. The loose tile rattled under Her foot; Her gift sat beneath it, but there wasn't time to wait for an answer. Three men were dead, and the tournament had only just begun.

I'm going into the labyrinth.

Light burst through Her vision, and She stood in a familiar chamber staring at the setting sun through the window. Delphi lay across her bed flipping through scrolls, while Cosima and Pippa sat at her desk tinkering with a line of perfumes.

"I want to wear this one," Pippa said. "And this one. And this one..."

Delphi looked up from her parchment, starting. "Leila, You sneak." She laughed. "I do adore Your presence, but You'd be wise to avoid shadow walking into my chamber late in the day. I might be occupied, if You understand my meaning."

Leila ignored her, flinging her wardrobe open and digging through its contents. Delphi furrowed her brow. "What are You doing?"

"What's My schedule for the rest of the evening?"

"Free as a bird, why?"

"I'm going into the labyrinth, and I'm going now."

"*Now?*" Delphi stood. "Leila—"

"Three competitors were killed today." Leila pushed aside dresses, searching through them. "And not by obstacles. By *other men.*"

"You think it was the assassins?"

"I need to see them." Leila pulled a black cloak from the wardrobe. "I need to know what I'm up against."

"I'll come with You," Delphi said.

"If You require *The Savior* for this endeavor, I can tag along," Cosima added.

"Thank you both, but I'm certain it'd look rather odd if The Savior and Her entire court disappeared on the same evening. No, you stay behind. If anyone asks for Me, I'm...somewhere. Think of something." Throwing the cloak over Her shoulders, She spun toward Delphi. "Do you have a satchel I can borrow?"

Delphi nodded at her room divider where a brown servant's satchel was hanging. Snatching it up, Leila scanned the room. *What would a healer carry?* She shouldered past Cosima, knocking the line of perfumes into Her satchel.

Pippa frowned. "Those were mine!"

"Apologies, but Sister needs these."

"And why exactly does *Sister* need perfumes in the labyrinth?" Delphi said.

"I'm the Healer. These are my tonics."

"You think the men are stupid enough to fall for that?"

"They were stupid enough to enter, weren't they?" She looped the satchel over Her shoulder. "How do I look?"

"Lose the jewels."

"Oh. Right." Leila tore off Her armlets, then turned to Delphi's mirror. The long, black cloak concealed most of Her ghostly flesh, the satchel around Her plain, ordinary. Sure, Her indigo dress was lovely, but without the jewels it could perhaps pass as simple, maybe common. *How do common folk even dress?*

"All right. I suppose I'm ready."

"I'm ready too!" Pippa sprang to Leila's side.

Leila sighed. "Little duckling, you can't come with Me."

Pippa's face dropped. "Why not?"

"Because it's very dangerous."

"But I want to help. Everyone else is helping."

"That's kind of you, but—"

"I can help just like Delphi and Cosima. I can." Pippa's voice turned frantic. "I've been practicing my spelling. I know all the provinces of the realm in order. I know things. I can help just like them. Do You think I can't? I can, I promise."

Pippa's desperate gaze ripped Leila in two, leaving Her to glance around the room for assistance that never came. She spun toward Delphi. "Have you spoken to the servants? Do you know what the men have to eat?"

"Water."

"*Water?*" Leila pushed past the surprise, grabbing Pippa's hands. "Run to the kitchen and grab some treats. You'll see to it that the men are properly fed. It's a very important duty, the most important of all. Do you think you can handle it?"

Pippa flew from the room, nearly stumbling over her feet as she vanished.

Delphi eyed Leila over, visibly conflicted. "You're really doing this?"

"Yes."

"And I can't stop You."

"Why would you?" Cosima was slumped across the bed lazily glancing over Delphi's scrolls. "The whole thing is utterly gripping. Savior by day, *spy* by nightfall."

"So, let me try to understand this," Delphi said. "You're going down into the labyrinth in search of Your assassins. You're disguising Yourself as a sister to The Savior—"

"And a healer," Leila cut in. "That's the most important part."

Delphi scowled. "And You'll perpetuate this façade by...*blessing* the men?"

"*Blessing* them? Of course not; that would expose Me. No, I'm just going to touch them."

"Touch them."

"Yes, My touch is healing enough. It does more good than any healer could." Leila raised Her chin. "They're lucky to have Me."

"Right. So You'll touch them..." Delphi's gaze drifted to Leila's satchel, "...with Your perfume tonics."

"Yes."

Delphi cradled her face. "God..."

"It'll work. I'm certain."

Pippa rushed into the room, an olive-green cloak strewn over her back and a lumpy satchel in her arms. "I ran so fast. The fastest ever."

"Good girl." Leila peeked into the satchel—apples and bread, certainly an improvement from water. "Come, let's tidy you up."

She plucked a brush from Delphi's desk and ran it through Pippa's blonde tangles. It took a few strokes for the moment to become familiar. Visions of a much younger Pippa intruded into Her mind, a memory that shamed Her each time it returned.

With her locks properly tied, Pippa spun toward Leila, shimmying her shoulders beneath her cloak. "Did You notice? We match!"

As Pippa pranced toward the door, Leila forced the horrors from Her mind, grabbing hold of her sister. "No duckling, we're not going that way. Hold My hand."

The two women stood side by side, Pippa grinning while Leila was fiercely focused. Delphi glanced between them, gnawing at the inside of her cheek.

Leila frowned. "Oh, don't look so sour. It's not like I'm headed off to die."

The chamber morphed into rays of light, and a breeze wafted by, carrying the flowery scent of summer.

Pink and purple painted the sky, the sun barely discernible over the horizon. Leila stood in a lush field miles from the palace, a fleeting freedom—until She caught sight of the fortress wall looming far ahead. Armored guards marched alongside it, mere specks in the distance, though they stirred Her nerves regardless.

"Come." She gave Pippa a tug. "Before we're spotted."

The two rushed through the grass hand in hand. The approaching nightfall dimmed the glow of Leila's skin, but still She pulled Her cloak over Her chest, desperate to remain unseen. The whisper of applause sounded from beyond the wall as Wembleton announced the day's theatrics to the people.

Three men are dead, and people are cheering.

A gate punctuated the grass. Leila yanked at its lock, and when nothing happened, She stuck Her blade in the cylinder, rattling it until it opened. A grey stairwell plunged underground, and the light of the setting sun faded behind them as they reached their destination—a dead end, the path blocked by a wall of black, stacked bricks.

Pippa frowned. "We're stuck."

Leila's eyes pierced through the darkness, scanning the walls around Her. *There.* A spot of red in the center of a single brick, shaped like a crown. Leila pointed its way, and Pippa strained her eyes.

"Red paint?"

Leila wavered. "Yes. Just paint."

She slammed Her fist against the crown, and the wall in front of them split in two, shifting apart brick by brick.

Pippa gasped and clapped, but the majesty was lost on Leila. A wave of stench hit Her in the face. Must and decay. She plunged into the stink, holding tight to Pippa's now-clammy hand.

A wide tunnel made of black bricks stretched ahead of Her, lit by scant blazing torches. The space around them was empty and innocuous, but She didn't let that fool Her. She had been through the labyrinth many times before, had studied its passageways, but now the air had shifted. Death lurked within these walls.

"Little duckling, a word of warning," She said. "This place is very dangerous."

Pippa's gaze darted across the walls. "It's dark."

"It is, and that's why you mustn't stray from My sight, do you understand?"

Pippa offered a hasty nod. "It's smelly down here. Where are we going?"

"This place is called the labyrinth. It's filled with traps and trials." Leila kept Her voice soft as She scanned the darkness. "We're headed to the sanctuary. All the men who navigated this tunnel are waiting there."

"They're waiting all by themselves?"

"Yes, that's right."

Pippa frowned. "They must be lonely."

"Oh, they're not lonely. Romulus comes to visit them each day."

"Romulus." Pippa giggled. "He's grumpy. I like him."

A pang shot through Leila's gut, and She stared at the path ahead in silence.

"Are these the men who are in love with You?"

"They've come to seek My hand," Leila said. "To become the next Sovereign."

"They want to marry The Savior. And make Savior babies."

Pippa's words sent Leila to an abrupt stop. "That reminds me— when you're down here, no calling Me by My title. Savior, Your Holiness, none of that. I'm just Leila, is that understood?"

"Why?"

"Because calling Me *Leila* is one of your very important duties. Also..." Leila shifted Pippa's cloak, pressing Her hand to her décolletage, "...I'm blessing you with the gift of shadow walking."

"Magic! Oh, I'm so excited!"

"It's not for play. It's for your own protection." Leila's voice became stern. "These men here...they may look nice, but some of them are *very* bad."

"I like boys."

"I know that, but not all boys like us back." She looked Pippa in the eye. "If anyone tries to hurt you, close your eyes really tight and imagine My chamber, and *poof.* You'll be safe and sound, and I'll come right after you. Is that understood?"

Pippa nodded, and Leila's touch turned fiery. *Give her the gift. Let her walk in the shadows.* Power pulsed from Her palm in ripples of heat, growing, intensifying, then dying away. She dropped Her hand, shaking out Her wrist.

"It's done," She said. "Now no one can hurt you."

Pippa burst into a grey mist, disappearing from view. Materializing paces away, she giggled into her hands, then vanished into another cloud of ink, traveling farther and farther down the tunnel.

Leila sighed. "Pippa, that's not what it's for."

"Let's go meet the boys!" Pippa said. "We're all going to be friends!"

Leila rushed after her. Pippa's laughter echoed off the walls, but soon it was accompanied by voices—male. A spot of light appeared at the end of the tunnel, and Leila hastened Her stride, watching the light grow larger.

Blood caked the wall ahead of Her, dripping down the brick.

"Little duckling, come close." Leila ran to Pippa's side, pulling her into Her chest and pointing at the distant glow. "Do you see that?"

"Is that the sanctuary?"

Leila eyed the remains as they passed. Entrails were fixed deep into the brick, and She shuddered. She was used to death, but not the innards that came with it.

"Leila?"

"Yes, that's the sanctuary." She guided Pippa past the blood, shielding her. "Be a good duckling. Follow My lead."

"Yes, *Leila*." Pippa grinned. "I didn't say Your title. See?"

The tunnel ended just in front of them, giving way to a bleak room speckled with canvas tents, wooden benches, and water barrels. Bodies wove through the space, filling it with flesh.

Men.

Young, muscular, and shirtless, certainly more men in one spot than She had seen in Her lifetime, save for the guards. *Fuck the guards.* The moment was surreal, as if She alone had stumbled upon a mythical species. *A wild herd of men.*

"What the..."

The voice sounded from the back of the room. One by one, the men turned to stare at Her. Straightening Her back, She donned a stern look. "We come as ordered by The Savior. We're of Her court. We're here to assist."

"She can assist my cock."

Laughter bounced off the walls. Before Leila could react, Pippa tugged at Her sleeve, pouting. "You said *The Savior*. You said we weren't supposed to."

"I have different duties than you," Leila whispered. "Now go feed them, and don't forget..."

Pippa was gone before She could finish, darting into the mix without a care.

Leila stood alone at the head of the sanctuary, the path before Her both compelling and overwhelming. Squaring Her shoulders, She plowed ahead. *Find the assassins.* Three bloodthirsty Beasts should've been easy to spot, and She scanned the space, resolved—until a man walked past, eyeing Her over before wiping blood from his abdomen.

His hard, sculpted abdomen.

Focus. But another man strutted into Her path, giving Her ample view of his brawny back, and a chill traveled through Her that nearly sent Her convulsing. *Dear God, control Yourself. These men are filthy. They stink. They're bleeding!* But all such qualms disappeared once chiseled flesh swept Her periphery. This man was easily the most godlike creature She'd ever seen, and She watched in awe as he ladled a helping of water, pouring it over his head and flipping his long, wet locks from his face.

A wall of muscle collided into Her, leaving Her pressed against a firm, sweaty chest. Her eyes widened. "Oh my God..."

"Apologies." The man offered a smile half-hidden behind a beard. "Nearly mowed you down, didn't I?"

Leila's gaze locked on his chest, its smattering of hair, the hands on his pecs. *Those are My hands. Oh My God, I'm touching him.*

"Be careful, Miss. Wouldn't want you to get hurt." He continued on through the space, but Leila stood paralyzed. *Contain Yourself. You're behaving like a fool.* But She could still feel his flesh against Her fingertips, and the memory sent Her heart pounding. *I touched his nipple.*

Leila cursed to Herself. *Your father conspires against You, yet You waste Your time entertaining base thoughts.* Her eyes narrowed, flitting across the sea of muscle. *Your assassins. Find them.* But She hadn't a clue what they looked like.

Shit.

A huddle of men whispered nearby, watching Her. She remembered the satchel hanging over Her shoulder jangling with perfumes. *You're the Healer. Get to healing.* She would find the assassins in time.

"Excuse me." She stopped at a man sitting on the floor. "May I have a look at your injuries?"

The man nodded, his gaze locked on the wall. Leila took a seat on the hard stone beside him, trying to get comfortable before accepting it was futile. He was handsome but not godlike, wearing the same black harem pants as all the others, his eyes vacant, his slender arms lined in gashes.

"Good God." She examined the lacerations up close. "How did you manage to get all these marks?"

The man let out a grunt. "Thorns."

"Thorns?"

"Big thorns. And lots of them."

Leila hesitated, then dug through Her satchel, not entirely sure what She was looking for. She pulled out a purple vial—lavender perfume, one of Her favorites—and pressed it to Her fingers, hoping the smell was somewhat medicinal, that Her behavior was convincing. All the while the man's gaze remained distant, as if his thoughts were far away.

"Apologies if this hurts. It'll only sting for a moment."

She pressed Her perfumed fingertips into the gashes, waiting for a reaction that never came. Her hands were warm as usual, radiating with power, but the man beside Her remained frozen.

She eyed his chest, focusing on a large, red lump. "What is—?"

"Spiders," he muttered. "Big ones. And lots of them."

Grimacing, She squeezed the lump, recoiling as it oozed. Each wound that followed received the same treatment—a reluctant draining, a dab of perfume—but no matter how much time passed, the man didn't say a word.

"You're awfully quiet, aren't you?"

Nothing. Against Her better judgment, She pressed Her hand to his flesh, taking the most tentative look inside. Flagrant shades of green bombarded Her.

He was afraid.

Find the assassins. But upon finishing with the last wound, She stayed put, eyeing the man's stony face: chestnut eyes, umber brown skin, coarse, black hair.

"You're the Intellect, right?"

He nodded, and She dug through Her pockets, fishing out two stacks of cards. "Here. To pass the time."

The Intellect stared down at the offering, reluctantly taking it from Her.

"It's a memory game. You lay the cards face down, flip one, and match it with its partner. If you draw an all-seeing eye, you move on to this stack"—she pointed to the second set of cards—"and solve a riddle. It's probably quite simple for someone of your station, but I suppose it's better than sitting here and staring at the wall. Maybe you can ask someone to play. Someone of an inviting nature."

His gaze met Hers for the first time. "Thank you."

"You didn't get those from me. Do you understand?"

He nodded, and Leila hopped to Her feet, walking off.

"I'm sorry," the Intellect called out behind Her.

Leila spun around. "For what?"

"For the way these men will undoubtedly treat you."

Her stomach sank, and She glanced across the sanctuary, the sea of flesh no longer enticing.

There wasn't time for apprehension. Drumming up Her courage, She marched up to the next man. "Excuse me."

A vibrant green gaze connected with Hers. "Why, hello there." Next came a white smile. "You have the loveliest eyes. Has anyone ever told you that?"

Leila's cheeks flushed. "I've come to look at your injuries."

"Oh, that's very kind of you. Please, sit."

Leila nestled beside him, at ease. *Clearly the Intellect was wrong. This man is delightful.* She tried to assess his wounds but instead lost Herself in his features. He was small in stature but lean and carved, with golden skin, a head full of shining black curls, and *God*, those emerald eyes. *The Cavalier.* She recognized him as if his scroll was right in front of Her.

"You're not quite as marked as the last man I saw."

"Then I count myself lucky," he said. "It was awfully precarious today. Three men were killed, you know."

This is it. This is Your opportunity. "Did you see who did it?" She dabbed at his injuries. "Who killed them?"

The Cavalier's gaze zigzagged the sanctuary. "That man, right there. He's hard to miss, wouldn't you agree?"

He stood like a monument, his massive frame an eyesore in the corner of the room. How She hadn't noticed him sooner, She couldn't say, but now She was taking in every detail: his wall of deep olive skin, his full-lipped scowl, the black stubble lining his head. She would've remembered a man like him from the records.

"Who is he?"

"The Giant," the Cavalier said. "You wouldn't believe what he did. I dare not speak it. It would only scare you."

"Tell me." The words came out sharper than She had intended. "I mean, I'm intrigued, is all."

He lowered his voice. "He shoved a man's face right into a giant thorn. And for no good reason. All the man did was defend The Savior's name. A kind, noble man, I'm sure—killed for honoring Her Holiness."

Leila's chest pinched. "What about the other two? Who killed them?"

Squinting, he scanned the room. "He's somewhere in here. An

ordinary fellow, not particularly fearsome to look at. I think he was called the Shepherd."

Leila tended to his wounds while eyeing the sanctuary, skeptical of each man who crossed Her gaze. *The Shepherd.* There had been no record bearing that laurel.

"I suppose all this is to be expected," the Cavalier continued. "Killing for love. For passion."

Pinpricks of color tickled Leila's fingers. Pink.

Pink?

She flattened Her palm against his ribs, and color swam through Her like rivers of sugar. She almost never saw pretty colors in people, certainly not pink. Pink was for affection. Pink was for lust.

"Men are so willing to stick their necks out for the sake of romance," he said. "Some say it's a flaw in our design, but I disagree. Life is meaningless without passion, after all."

What does this mean? The color danced from his pores, filling the space around them. *Is this for Me?* Leila's heart raced. *Don't just sit here, play along.*

"Well if you ask me, the whole thing's a mess." She rubbed Her perfumes across his skin. "Love isn't about brutality. It's about connection. This entire tournament would be better off if The Savior could just sit down with each man and perhaps get to know him as a person, not as some barbarian..."

Her voice trailed off once She took in his emerald gaze. He stared at the side of the room—at a lone man with a sinewy build—and Her excitement withered. The cloud of pink had become dense around them, but it wasn't for Her. It was for him.

The Cavalier's eyes darted back to Leila. "Were you saying something?"

"Just that I've finished." She grabbed Her satchel and stormed off.

Heat flooded Leila's face, and She fought to shake the humiliation. *You're not here for fun. You're here for the assassins.* The Giant still hovered in his corner, glaring at all who passed, and Her resolve became fierce.

Find the other two.

She stopped beside a man curled up on the floor. "Let's have a look at those injuries, shall we?"

She didn't wait for a response before plopping down beside him. This man certainly wasn't an assassin, as his cowering frame painted a less-than-fearsome picture. Scrapes covered his chest, and when She touched them, he jerked away.

"Mother of pearl!"

"Apologies," She mumbled.

As She pressed Her fingers to his skin, he flinched. "Apologies," She said, moving to a swollen spider bite, only for him to recoil. "Apologies." She reached for the bite a second time, and when he yanked away, She scowled. "If you keep jumping, I can't work."

"If you keep *hurting me*, I'll keep jumping," he spat.

The Poet. She recognized him by his fair skin and white-blond hair, but what truly gave him away were his violet eyes—or rather his one eye, as the other was hidden behind his hands.

"Did something happen to your eye?" She said.

"You'll just make it worse."

"Or I'll make it better. That's my job, after all."

The Poet shot Her a sideways glare before lowering his hands. Leila gasped.

"*Careful*," he grumbled.

His swollen eye was a raw shade of red, and his brow sat crooked on his face. *A broken socket.*

"It's a broken socket."

The voice startled Leila. A round, tawny face lingered behind Her, far too close for comfort. Black ringlets jutted from his head, and large, brown eyes stared into Hers, overflowing with criticism.

She glowered. "I can see that."

"Nothing in your satchel will fix it. The man requires treatment from a professional."

The Physician. It has to be him. Her scowl deepened. "*I* am the palace Healer. You question my competency?"

The Physician fell silent, and Leila turned to the Poet, nearly wincing at that horrid eye. "Who did this to you?"

"The Shepherd," the Physician said.

"Don't say his name," the Poet snapped. "He might hear!"

Leila lathered Her hand in a citrus scent and pressed it to his eye. "The Shepherd... Is he frightening?"

"He's the most terrible creature I've ever met." The Poet whimpered. "How the Sovereign gave him his blessing, I'll never understand."

"The Sovereign *blessed* him?"

"Today, at the ceremony," the Physician said. "The Sovereign chose his three blessed ones. Bestowed upon them his favor. Naturally he chose the fiercest warriors to protect The Savior."

Leila's shoulders tensed. "Was the Giant among them?"

"And the bloody Dragon. He may not have offed anyone, but mark my words, he will." The Poet lowered his voice to a whisper. "I don't care what the southerners say. You can't trust a man with that many tattoos. It's witchcraft."

With Her palm in place, Leila searched the sanctuary, locking onto a mess of inked flesh. A man paced beside the wall, his pale body covered in black, foreign text streaming from his neck down to his feet. His steel blue eyes panned the room as he walked, his ashy blond hair pulled back into a wet ponytail.

The Dragon. And he was *blessed* by the Sovereign. *The audacity.*

"I don't see how that'll solve anything."

The Physician's voice jolted Leila, ending Her trance. "Excuse me?"

"You're just pressing your hand against it. What good will that do?"

She nervously eyed Her hand—Her warm, healing touch. "I'm applying a soothing tonic."

"It smells like oranges." The Physician hovered close, breathing into Her ear. "I've seen no study suggesting that oranges produce any restorative properties."

"Oh God, is she making it worse?" The Poet glowered. "Do you even know what you're doing?"

"I know *exactly* what I'm doing. I've been a healer all my life."

"If you're going to treat his eye, you'll need a lot more than oranges," the Physician said. "I can show you a proper course of care if only you'd move."

"She's hurting me!" the Poet squealed.

"I'm saving *your eye*."

"I've treated many injuries such as this, and the first thing you ought to do—"

Leila spun toward the Physician. "Would *you* like to treat him?"

"I'm just being helpful. Shouldn't you be more appreciative?"

"That you're badgering me while I work? Oh, I appreciate it immensely. So much so that I think you should do the honors." She packed up Her satchel, flashing one last glare the Poet's way. "Do let me know how this works out for you."

Leila marched off, fuming. *I hate this place.* The stink of sweaty flesh had become unbearable, the muscle around Her grotesque, but none of that changed the fact that She had yet to fulfill Her purpose.

Find the Shepherd.

"Injures." She stopped at a circle of men. "Let's have a look."

A pair of wide eyes stared up at Her. "Do me first. This lump's killing me."

A second man laughed. "I'm sure you'd love for her to *do you first.*"

"Shut up, Neil."

"I'll go second or third, so long as she has a look at my lump as well."

A third man chuckled. "Dirty bastard."

Leila sat among them, ignoring their laughter. *Idiots.* Albeit handsome ones, perhaps the most stunning there. One was built like a warrior, large and robust with a heavy brow, though his impeccable grooming was far from soldierly. *The Regal.* His small, chartreuse eyes gave him away, as did his sun-kissed skin, his long blond locks. The next man was smaller and sleek with golden skin and decorative swirls carved into his sable hair. *The Noble.* She could tell by his eyes, a sky blue. Then there was the Adonis, the most tempting man She'd ever seen: hazel eyes, warm, olive skin, long waves of golden-brown hair, and a body so sculpted he could've been cut from stone.

"I still can't believe it." The Adonis pouted, numb to Leila's touch as She assessed his scrapes. "Not one look at The Savior. We didn't even get to see Her face."

The Regal scoffed. "Quit complaining. You've been at it all day."

"And I have every right. I'd at least like to know what I'm working with."

"What are you going to do? Chastise Her when you see Her?" The

Regal let out a hearty laugh. "Sling Her over your knee and give Her a spanking?"

The Adonis smirked. "I'd like that, actually. Maybe I will."

"You'd give Her the shock of Her life. I'll bet She's a spoiled thing, used to getting what She wants."

"Oh, I'll give Her plenty of what She wants."

Leila went rigid, Her hands freezing in their ministrations.

"Fuck what *She* wants," the Noble said. "If She's looking for a real man, then She's looking to serve."

The Regal's laughter climbed higher. *"Serve?"*

"Someone's daring." The Adonis elbowed him in the ribs. "You're toying with blasphemy."

"I'm stating facts. A true woman knows where She belongs: on Her back with Her legs spread wide."

Leila clamped down on Her lip, Her patience waning.

"You're all talk, I just know it." The Adonis shook his head, turning to the Regal. "He says it now, but when the time comes—"

"Piss off," the Noble said. "When the time comes I'll show The Savior who ought to be Champion."

"Please, you would never."

"I mean it. The moment I see Her, I swear to you, I'm dropping my trousers, whipping out the worm, and telling our Savior to get on Her knees and worship."

"Fucking pig," Leila grumbled.

The men fell silent, their eyes on Leila for the first time since Her arrival. "Did you hear that?" The Adonis glanced around the circle. "She called you a pig!"

The Noble smirked. "Is that because you're hungry for my sausage?"

The Regal laughed louder than ever. "You slay me every time, I swear."

"Are you feeling left out, Healer girl?" The Noble eyed Her up and down. "I'd be more than happy to practice with your mouth. Your plump lips would look grand wrapped around my cock."

Leila spun toward his friends. "You're perfectly content to hear him speak like this to a woman?"

The Regal waved Her away. "Calm yourself. It's all in fun."

"You're supposed to laugh," the Adonis said.

Leila packed up Her satchel. *"Hysterical."*

She barreled through the sanctuary, leaving their wounds to fester. *I hate them all.* Rage filled Her up like smoke, Her lungs surging, tears stinging Her eyes.

Leave. Please, just leave.

She stopped in Her tracks, taking in a deep breath. The tears retreated, and She curled her hands into fists, forcing the trembling at bay.

Find the Shepherd. Then She could leave.

"Injuries." She stopped in front of another man. "Show me."

A headful of messy hair was pointed Her way. The man's eyes slowly panned up to Hers. "Who are you?"

"The Healer," She barked. "Injuries. Show me."

He cocked his head at the space beside him, and She took a seat, inspecting his wounds: more of the same. She pointed to his slashed ribs. "Thorns?"

He nodded, and She moved to the lump on the side of his neck. "Spiders?"

Another nod, and She turned Her attention to his face. A split lip, a black eye—these wounds were different. The marks of a fight.

"Interesting..." She took his hands, bringing them in close. Torn, bloody knuckles. Definitely from a fight. She flipped them over, revealing his palms.

Stained with blood.

The Poet's shattered eye flashed through Her thoughts, as did his trembling voice. *Don't say his name.* Next came the Cavalier—*an ordinary fellow, not fearsome to look at.* Her heart pounded in Her throat.

This was the Shepherd.

"It was *you?*" She spat.

The man furrowed his brow. "What was me?"

"Picking fights with the competitors. Killing them off, for what? For sport? For *fun?*"

He faltered. *"Excuse* me?"

"Three men dead, and the tournament has only just begun." She leaned in closer, fighting the impulse to tear him apart. "It's repellent. It's *sickening*."

"Are you *mad?*"

"You're a disgrace to this competition. Do you realize that? You're a disgrace to this realm—"

"My best friend *died* today." He thrust his shredded knuckles in front of Her. "This?" He pointed at his black eye. "*This?* From fighting the man who *killed him*. Yes, three men are dead, and I didn't *touch* a single one of them."

Swirls of black clawed through his flesh, bursting free from his body and filling the air. The darkness hit Her in a wave, and Her rage faded behind his grief.

His misery.

Shame cut Her like a knife. "Apologies. I assumed wrong."

"Yes," he growled. "You did."

A strained quiet passed before She jolted awake, digging through Her satchel. She doused Her fingers in vanilla, resisting the urge to curse aloud. *You're a real bitch, You know that? Scolding a man in mourning. What is wrong with You?*

"I'm sorry to hear about your friend."

Pressing Her fingers into his gashed ribs, She filled his wounds with power, but his gaze remained distant.

"I suppose you don't like me very much anymore."

"Not particularly, no," he grumbled.

"It's all right." She offered a slight smile. "I'm a bit of an acquired taste."

"Vinegar, I imagine."

She sighed. "I deserved that." She poked Her head into his line of vision. "Now stop it."

The man went back to ignoring Her, and Leila went back to his injuries. Bronze skin slashed and marred, a mop of wavy brown hair damp with sweat, and large eyes so dark She could've sworn they were black. *Black eyes*. She cringed. *I accused the Artist of murder.*

His body went taut, his stare suddenly brimming with hate. She followed his gaze to a man sitting across the sanctuary, eyeing the collection of thin raised scars decorating his arm. Without hesitation, he dug a shard of brick into his flesh, drawing two bloody lines to match the others.

"What is he doing?" Leila said.

The Artist's voice came out hard. "It's a tally."

"Of what?"

"The people he's killed."

Leila spun toward him. "Is this the man who killed your friend?"

He didn't need to answer. His misery swirled with color, as rivers of red rage spilled from him like blood.

The man with the scars. He was the Shepherd.

"Don't look at him." The Artist grabbed Her wrist. "He's dangerous."

Leila held firm, watching the man without a hint of subtlety. The Cavalier was right; he wasn't fearsome to look at. He was handsome, in fact, with copper skin, sharp features, and short black hair, all utterly enticing—save for the scars littering his arms.

The marks of his kills.

"He doesn't scare me," Leila said.

The Shepherd glanced up from his work, his crystal blue eyes locking with Hers. She looked away, turning back to the Artist—his grip had tightened, his frame hard, as if he were Her shield. She faltered, then pulled free from his hold.

"He'll be penalized, yes?" he asked. "Killing is part of the tournament, I know this. But what he did? It isn't right. He murdered in cold blood for no reason at all."

"You're absolutely right. But I doubt he'll meet any punishment."

"How is that possible? Does The Savior not even care?"

"This has nothing to do with Her," She spat. She paused, containing Herself. "This tournament is led by the Sovereign exclusively. And I suspect today's events would leave him...pleased."

"*Pleased?*"

"You saw where his blessings lie."

"But that was before. Surely this changes things."

Leila gestured toward the Shepherd. "The man who killed your friend? He is a beast behaving as beasts do. Brontes knows this. And he pays no mind, because he's just like him. Beastly."

The Artist's expression went vacant. "You say this freely? Of the Sovereign?"

"I do."

"You're bold."

"I'm honest."

"Let me guess, he doesn't scare you either."

His words silenced Her. Busying Herself, She scrubbed the blood from his palms, warming his hands with Her light. Perhaps it would do more than heal, would calm him, but his black cloud lingered all the same.

"Your friend... Who was he?"

The Artist tensed. "Milo. The Benevolent."

"Milo." She thought back to the scrolls, trying to place his among the others before resigning Herself to platitudes. "He was a good man. He didn't deserve to die today."

"He had no business being here. He was a fool to enter."

"You're all fools," She said without thinking. "Everyone who enters is a fool."

Her shoulders stiffened, braced for another explosion, but the Artist merely cocked his head. "How do you figure?" he asked.

"What man in his right mind would risk almost certain death for a chance to marry a woman he's never met?"

"Come again?"

"I think I speak clearly."

He kept quiet for a long while. "Well, She's not just any woman."

"But isn't She? For all you know, She could be a real bore. Or a pain. Or a bitch."

"But...She's The Savior."

Leila's stomach sank. "Yes. And do you know anything else about Her?"

She didn't wait for an answer, packing Her satchel, eager to be rid of the sanctuary. "I believe I'm done. You should be feeling much better come morning." She eyed his torn knuckles. "At least as far as your wounds go."

Strings of black crawled back into Her vision. The Artist wasn't ignoring Her any longer—he was staring right at Her, his darkness enveloping them both. She cupped his cheek, giving him one last taste of Her light. Blips of his pain pricked Her fingers, and when he relaxed into Her touch, Her palm absorbed his ache.

"Tomorrow will be difficult. Dangerous." She hesitated. "Be careful."

She stood and headed through the sanctuary, worn and drained as though She'd survived a grueling battle. She hadn't expected the toll Her task would take—that She'd be leaving the labyrinth with a fraction of Her dignity.

Spotting Pippa, She hurried to her side. "Come, little duckling."

"But I'm having fun."

"I know, but it's time to go."

They walked through the sanctuary hand in hand, leaving Leila to eye the sea of muscle. *Idiots. All of them.* Then Her gaze floated to the Artist and his black cloud, and Her stomach twisted.

"Healer girl."

The Shepherd stood paces away with the Giant and Dragon, wearing a chilling smile. "What about us? Aren't you going to make us better?"

Leila tightened Her hold on Pippa. *The Giant. The Dragon. The Shepherd.* Three wicked creatures lined up in a row.

"You all look fine to me."

She left the sanctuary behind Her.

5

THE DUNGEON

"I'm going to kill them. I'm going to cut off their stones, and I'm going to kill them."

Leila paced Her bedchamber, Her hands wound into fists. Her thoughts overflowed with visions from the night before, namely those three heinous faces.

The Giant. The Dragon. The Shepherd.

Delphi sat on Leila's bed, watching as She paced. "They're assassins."

"Yes, and I'm going to *kill them*." Leila held Her chin high. "I'm going to assassinate My assassins."

"They're highly trained, I'm sure."

"What exactly are you implying?"

"Love, I know You're quite handy with a blade, but these men are older, larger, and have many kills under their belt. Meanwhile, Your kills have mostly consisted of aging men..." Delphi brought her thumb and index finger close together. "And You're about *this* big."

Leila pursed Her lips. "Oh, what do you know?" She turned on Her heel and continued pacing, practically stomping across the tiles.

"Have You heard back from Your little friend?"

Leila waved Delphi away. "Not yet. I'll check later. First, we plan the kill."

"Perhaps we should explore other options."

"What other options are there?"

"Maybe Your assassins fall in the tournament. The other competitors can take care of them."

Leila scoffed. "I am *much* more qualified than all of those men. *Combined.*"

"I take it You weren't impressed by them."

Leila snorted in response, falling back into Her steps.

"There were some who seemed promising," Delphi said. "Not a single one left a positive impression?"

"It's hard to feel positive when I've got My own death to prevent."

"I recall there being a Poet."

A groan tore from Leila's throat. "He was intolerable."

"What of the Intellect?"

"Are these the men you selected? How cruel of you to put them through this torture."

"That wasn't an answer."

"God, you're relentless."

Delphi folded her arms. "What of the Artist?"

Her words sent Leila to a hard stop. *The Artist.* She hadn't forgotten his face, and certainly not his miserable black cloud. "Poor thing. He'll likely die today."

A knock sounded at the door, and Hylas scurried inside, bowing. "Your Holiness, the Senate is waiting."

A scowl threatened to streak Her face, but She kept it at bay. Hylas bowed once more before leaving, and though She prepared to follow, every part of Her longed to stay put. She had enough horrid men to deal with.

"Worth it to go back down there?" Delphi asked. "In the labyrinth?"

God, no. Then swirls of darkness wafted through Leila's mind, followed by those large, black eyes.

"Maybe once or twice," She said. "Couldn't hurt."

With a deep breath, She threw open Her door and left Her chamber.

"Pleasant day, Your Holiness." Asher nodded.

She rolled Her eyes. "It's Leila."

She didn't look back at him, dwelling on the task ahead. It seemed like an especially twisted torture—spending Her morning plotting against Her demise, then sharing Her afternoon with the vultures who had set it into motion. The dreaded black door appeared, and She pushed it open, met with a flurry of male voices.

"Starting without Me, I see." She took a seat at the table. "How duplicitous. I'm not at all surprised."

"We were just discussing our service to You." Wembleton donned a smile. "Since Toma, Simon, and Gelanor have yet to resurface, naturally their responsibilities must be reallocated."

"What a puzzle. They're still missing?"

"Still missing," Brontes said. "Just like the competitors' records."

"Did you just compare three human lives to slips of parchment?" Leila tutted Her tongue. "What poor taste."

Brontes eyed Her for a long while before turning away. "We'll start with Gelanor's duties. It appears we need a new Keeper of the Vault. I propose Erebus."

Leila's gaze shot toward the Senator in question: a brute of a man, broad and layered in muscle. Black hair sat like a crown of curls on his head and lined his jaw in a short beard, and deep-set brown eyes scanned the room, penetrating. Sometimes he reminded Her of Her father; they were near enough in age, and his olive skin showed the same wear, but Brontes wore his royal drapes each day, while Erebus opted for a silver breastplate—a reminder of what he was capable of.

"Erebus?" She spun toward Brontes. "Are you mad?"

Brontes sighed. "You disapprove?"

"He's a soldier."

"You'd be wise not to demean him with such a base title. He is the strategos of Your army and a force on the battlefield."

"And how does any of that qualify him to handle coin?"

"Who would You propose, Your *Holiness*?"

Leila raised Her chin. "Me."

The room erupted in laughter—a reaction She had expected, but it boiled Her blood nonetheless. "It is My birthright, My duty, and above all else, *My coin*. How you can even offer up a creature like Erebus and claim him competent is beyond Me."

"A creature, You say?" Erebus's words sent the room to silence. His eyes locked with Hers, unblinking. "I believe You mean a monster. Don't think I shy from the title. You see, to stand in my way is to ask for death." He leaned forward, his voice low. "Do You stand in my way, Your Holiness?"

Leila was certain of Her carriage, that She held Herself with pride, but Her insides cowered.

"We'll bring it to a vote," Brontes said.

"This is not a democracy," Leila snapped.

"Those in favor of Her Holiness acting as Keeper of the Vault?"

Leila's arm shot up, but the others kept still, their hands folded in their laps.

"And those in favor of Erebus."

Each Senator raised his hand. She had known this would happen, but that didn't lessen the sting.

"So it is done." Brontes scribbled across a scroll, eyeing Leila sidelong. "Don't look so sullen. You have no one to blame for the humiliation but Yourself."

"With Erebus as Keeper of the Vault, You'll have plenty of time for matters better suited for You." Wembleton offered Her a smile. "Like blessing the realm. That is a duty of the utmost importance."

Phanes snickered, and Leila's eyes darted toward him, thinning into a glare.

"Next item. Toma's assignments: foreign relations..."

Her father droned on, his voice picking at Her nerves. She surveyed the room, searching for a distraction, then froze. In the distance, sitting on the tile floor, was a peach pit.

A message.

"Your Holiness?"

The voice roused Her. "Hm?"

"Do the terms suit You, Your Holiness?" Kastor said.

"Sure. Yes. They're fine."

Qar chuckled from across the table, twirling a golden ring around his little finger. "Her Holiness, an agreeable party. To what do we owe this rare occasion?"

"Oh, don't ride the girl too hard. I find Her protests most agreeable myself." Phanes offered Leila a wink. "Don't get too soft on us. I like You best when You bite."

The two men laughed while Qar tinkered with his ring, and Leila tasted bile.

"Next item." Brontes flipped through his stack of parchment. "The tournament. The competitors are spending the day in the labyrinth?"

"Yes, Your Highness," Romulus said. "They've entered the second stage."

"Predictions?"

"There will undoubtedly be casualties. The weakest will perish."

Black eyes appeared in Leila's thoughts, and Her stomach churned.

"Good. And the wedding?"

"Just finalizing the arrangements, Your Highness," Qar said.

Leila started. "Wedding? Whose wedding?"

"Yours," Brontes grumbled.

"The ceremony will be beautiful, Your Holiness," Qar added.

Leila sat in silence. *A wedding.* What was the purpose if She was to die?

"Aren't these plans premature?" She said. "I don't even have a suitor."

"You have twenty suitors, Your Holiness." Qar chuckled. "Well, seventeen as of yesterday."

"They hardly qualify. I don't even like any of them."

"Of course You do not like them, You have not yet met them." Qar's grin widened. "Regardless of how You feel now, Your future Champion navigates the labyrinth as we speak. Such a lucky man."

His words reeked of phoniness, a complement to his fussy appearance. His ebony skin gleamed, polished each day by servant girls, leaving not a hair on his head or his brows. The look was popular in Ethyua, and though he dressed in Thessian drapes and garbs, his homeland made itself known in his fluid accent and bevvy of jewels. Gems hung from his neck and jangled on his wrists, and on each of his fingers was a gold ring—his little pets, as he often stroked their sparkling stones.

"Anything further to discuss?" Brontes glanced around the table, stopping at Leila. "Anymore audacious requests from my dearest daughter?"

Obscenities filled Her mouth, but She swallowed them down, the peach pit a beacon in Her peripheral vision.

"Good." Brontes turned to the others. "Who motions to end today's meeting?"

"I do."

"Second."

The men filed through the door, buzzing past Her like insects. The space was empty, save for Leila.

And that peach pit.

She dashed across the room, swiping up the pit and settling on the window seat. She pounded Her heel into the wooden bench three times.

Three *thumps* sounded from beneath the floor.

Leila shot under the table, crawling between its legs and flipping the ruby throw rug. A wooden trapdoor sat in front of Her. She threw it open, plunging down the stone steps.

The air was thick with dust and pungent herbs. She had long since grown accustomed to it, same with the dirt floor, the stretch of barred cells. This was the palace dungeon—a myth, as it was supposedly destroyed centuries ago. An apothecary station sat against the wall, its wooden table covered in tins of spices, vials of elixirs, and small animals trapped in jars. Chains hung from the walls, and rods, whips, and pokers dangled from rusted hooks—all real, all sinister, and certainly not relics from ages past.

A mountain of a man stood in the farthest cell, watching Her. As She made Her way toward him, the mess of his body became clearer—the craters in his pale olive flesh, the scars cutting through him like canyons. His skin looked pieced together, unfinished, leaving him with scant patches of hair, one nipple, and eight-and-a-half fingers. Small grey eyes peered through the holes of a black leather mask covering his head.

Leila stopped in front of his cell. "Oh, take that silly thing off."

"Apologies, Your Holiness. It's a habit."

"Well, I can't imagine it's comfortable." She slipped between the narrow bars of his cell as he fiddled with the leather laces. He pulled the mask off, revealing a strong, whiskered jaw, an angular nose, and a head full of long hair, the color a blend of brown and ashy blond. It always struck Her, the dichotomy between his marred body and his untouched face.

"There." She stood on Her toes, reaching up high to pinch his cheeks. "Much better. I swear, you must've been the most handsome Beast to ever grace the Sovereign's Tournament." She paused, thinking. "Talos the..."

"Bronze," Talos said. "Thank You, Your Holiness."

Leila gestured toward his mask. "You know Brontes only makes you wear that thing because he's envious."

"He says it's to remind me. I am beneath man. I am to be faceless."

"Yes, well, Brontes says a lot of things that aren't true. My mother was very lucky to have you compete for Her affection."

"Thank You. I imagine You didn't come here to compliment me."

She sighed. "No. But I enjoy complimenting you all the same."

Her gaze drifted from Talos to the ceiling above—carved away at the corner, the loose tile barely visible—then down to the shackle wrapping his ankle, fastened to the wall with a lengthy chain. Conflicted emotion bubbled in Her gut.

"Has Brontes had any special meetings down here?" She said.

"Yes. With Your assassins."

"Tell Me everything."

Talos cocked his head at the lone bench at the back of his cell. "Sit with me?"

As he settled down on the wooden bench, Leila hopped up to a windowless sill carved into the wall, barely meeting his line of sight. "Start with the Dragon."

"Drake Toshkar," he said. "Thirty-five years old. Born in Kovahr, was shipped to the Outlands where he was sold into the service."

Leila's nose wrinkled. "My father put a *thirty-five*-year-old man in the competition? Disgusting."

"He paid for his freedom with blood. Became a mercenary. Kills for any power that can afford him."

"That's nearly twice My age. I know he doesn't intend to marry Me, but still." She shook Herself. "Apologies, I got distracted."

"He calls himself the Dragon as an ode to the Outlands."

"You know an awful lot about him."

"All dark circles know of the Dragon. His work is legendary." Talos gestured toward his chest. "His tattoos—they're an ancient protection spell, branded on his flesh by a witching tribe. He believes himself immortal."

"Well, we both know that's a crock of shit. What of the Giant?"

"Antaeus Argós. Twenty-five years old. An arena fighter, specializes in multiple styles and holds the most titles of all fighters still living. He craves the applause. The glory."

"An approval-seeking cunt," Leila scoffed. "Anything else you can tell Me about him?"

"He's stupid."

"How do you know this?"

"I've heard him speak."

She smiled. "Cheeky imp. You think we can use it against him?"

"Stupid men don't like to be reminded of the fact. They prefer blissful ignorance."

Leila chuckled, but the sound faded as the final assassin waltzed into Her mind. "What of the last one? The Shepherd."

"His name is Kaleo."

"Just Kaleo?"

"More commonly referred to as the Shepherd, both in and out of the tournament."

Leila sat quietly, waiting for him to continue. "And?"

"And that's all. He has no titles, no accolades. There are no legends bearing his name, no tales of glory." His voice was calm, a contradiction to his words. "He is a mystery. A man who doesn't exist."

"Oh, he exists. He marks his kills on his arms, you know. Wears them like trophies."

Talos stared off for a moment. "Makes sense."

"*That* makes sense to you?"

"A man who kills not for pride or reputation is a man who kills for pleasure."

She scowled. "A madman. Wonderful. Delphi doesn't think I can kill them."

Talos didn't respond.

"You don't think I can kill them either."

"You are very skilled, Your Holiness. My sharpest student. But these men are the best in all the realms."

"*Drake* and *Antaeus* are the best in all the realms. You don't know anything about Kaleo."

"Which means he's the most dangerous of them all."

Leila's scowl deepened. "Dammit. I was hoping this could be simple. Why can't *something* be simple?" She kneaded Her temples.

"Your Holiness, a warning," Talos said. "Brontes plans to involve Diccus in the challenges."

"I figured."

"He plans to involve me as well."

Sighing, She dropped Her hands. "I figured that too."

"I have no choice—"

"I know, Talos." She managed a weak smile. "I'm not upset."

"Do You have any requests? I don't know the part I play, but I can try to meet Your specifications."

"Can you kill My assassins?" She forced a laugh. "I'm kidding. I know you can't—not with Brontes lurking over your shoulder. No, no requests."

"He will have me hurt them. The men."

"They're doomed to die regardless. Brontes has already sealed their fates."

Talos nodded, leaving them with a pained silence.

"Is that all?" Leila fiddled with the folds of Her dress. "About the tournament. I hope it is. Not that I don't need the information, it's just...I hate talking about it. The tournament. I hate it so much."

"Yes, Your Holiness. That is all."

The strain didn't lift. Her mind was burdened, and though She had been fighting the weight of Her circumstances, everything was crashing down on Her.

Talos watched Her, his grey eyes expectant.

"How much time do we have?" She whispered.

"Enough."

"You don't think it's silly? That I'm too old now? I know I am."

"Stories grant escape, Little Light. For You and for myself."

Smiling, She nestled closer to him. "What was it like the first time you saw Her? I know you've told Me a hundred times already but...you know."

"I was a young man. A few years shy of Your age. Your mother visited the commons on occasion, but with the crowds, it was hard to see. But I saw Her then from a distance. Her glow. It was a great gift."

Leila strained to envision Her mother strolling through the commons—a hard sight to imagine, as She had never been through the realm Herself.

"The first time I saw Her up close was at the Commencement Ceremony," Talos said. "She came out in a red dress and a crown of golden flowers. She was the most beautiful woman I had ever seen. I'm sure the men at Your ceremony felt the same when they saw You."

"I didn't go to My ceremony..."

"I see."

"They can't know I'm The Savior. Because of Brontes's plan." She glanced his way. "I'm posing as palace staff. A healer."

"They will be awed by You all the same."

A hint of a smile crept across his face, but Leila didn't mirror the sentiment. All She could do was think of Her trip to the labyrinth, Her conversations with the men, and how none of them were awed by Her. Not even a little.

"What about the first time you spoke with Her?"

"An event of the tournament," he said. "The First Impressions. We were to each ask Her a question. I asked Her of Her favorite pastimes."

"That's a good question. I mean, I would be happy with it, if it were Me."

"She said She enjoyed dancing. Just as You enjoy art."

Looping Her arm through his, Leila wriggled Her hand into his palm, accustomed to their differences—that his arm was nearly the width of Her waist, that his hand swallowed Hers. "Do I remind you of Her?"

"You are small, but She was smaller. Your hair is different, as are Your eyes." He studied Her face. "You have Brontes's lips."

Leila's shoulders slumped, and he quickly added, "But You have Her skin. Her hands. The length of Your hair, the way it shines. Her smile. Her laugh."

His words brought Her a hint of comfort, though it faded when She gazed down at his shackled ankle. "I can try again. I've gotten quite good at picking locks."

"You've tried many times."

"What about a nice big mallet?"

"Only the key can open it." Talos repeated the same words he had spoken many times before. "Diccus has made it so."

"Whichever Savior thought it was a brilliant idea to bottle up Her magic and use it for things like *deadly labyrinths* and *enchanted locks* is a real bitch. Just because you *can* do something doesn't mean you should."

Talos said nothing, a helpless, heavy silence. Leila rested Her head on his shoulder. "When all is said and done, I will set you free. You'll always have a home here, but it will be no cell."

"Set Yourself free, Little Light. You are just as imprisoned as I am."

Door hinges creaked in the distance. "Diccus is coming," Talos whispered.

My chamber. Leila kissed him on the cheek, and the dungeon disappeared behind a blinding light.

Pillows bounced around Her as She flopped onto Her bed. Sitting upright, She stared at Her reflection in the doors of Her wardrobe.

"These men are the best in all the realms." A warning She ought to heed.

But soon the words became muddled, giving way to those three sinister faces, to the face of Her father.

She bolted from Her bed, throwing open the doors of Her wardrobe and snatching up Her satchel, Her cloak. Slamming the mirrors shut, She grabbed at the blade strapped to Her thigh, Her mind wrapped up in loathing and blood.

Light rose through Her body, taking Her to the lush fields of the fortress.

Instinct fueled Her, sending Her dashing through the grass and down the stone steps. The black bricks around Her dissolved, revealing a stone floor peppered with tents, water barrels, men. The three assassins were clustered together, a perfect target.

She stopped short. The herd of men had thinned.

Someone was missing.

Focus. But She was already counting faces, pairing them with laurels.

The Cavalier. The Intellect. She went through them once, twice. Three men were missing, and while logic said it didn't matter, Her nerves failed to listen. Her eyes swept the space again, and Her insides clenched. No mop of brown hair. No large black eyes.

The Artist was dead.

Sickness surged in Her belly, and She wilted beneath the firelight, Her hopes torn away at the roots.

A howl echoed off the walls, and She jumped. A mess of a man barreled into the sanctuary, lungs heaving, skin dripping with sweat—the Artist, worn and haggard but very much alive.

"Will one of you stupid fucks *help us?*" he spat.

A body hung from his shoulders, stuck with an arrow and covered in blood.

The Artist's eyes locked with Leila's, and he charged Her way, dropping to his knees. "Help him." He laid the bloodied man at Her feet. "*Now.*"

His words were sharp, an order from a man far below Her birth, yet She complied without hesitating. Crouching beside the bloodied man, She took in his drawn face, the arrow jutting from his flesh—a horrific sight, yet against all odds, he was alive.

"He's your competition...yet you saved his life." She stared up at the Artist. "Why?"

The Artist kept quiet save for his heavy breathing. God, he was a wreck, and no man would extend himself so severely without self-serving reason. Certainly none She'd ever known.

He stood and turned away. "Just do it."

Another order, and he was gone, weaving through the fast-forming crowd.

Men swarmed Her, but Leila was fixed on the Artist, Her eyes boring through the back of his head. He wasn't such a mess any longer; he was strong and bold—no, *gallant*, the blood on his ribs a mark of heroism, the sweat on his back inviting.

Appealing.

For God's sake, have some composure. You're embarrassing Yourself. But that didn't stop Her from staring at him, nor did it quell the rapid firing of Her heartbeat.

"Healer girl."

Two men hovered before Her, waiting—and the man with the arrow in his chest was still sprawled across the floor.

"Fuck, I'm going to die." He looked up at Her, speaking between shallow pants. "Am I going to die?"

Sleek black hair, sharp brown eyes, rich copper skin. This was the Prince, though the features described in his records were now streaked with red.

"His odds are hardly fair." The Physician sat beside Her, arms crossed matter-of-factly. "The arrow could've hit a number of organs, certainly a lung—"

"A *lung?*" The Prince's panting turned into gasps. "Oh God, I can't breathe."

"It didn't hit a lung." A third man turned to the Prince. Strong build, tanned skin, and a wiry brown beard. The Hunter. "Calm yourself, you're fine."

"The man needs a surgeon," the Physician said. "Not to mention proper tools. I imagine we need a scalpel, a hook, a bone drill—"

"A *bone drill?*" the Prince spat. "Why the fuck do we need a *bone drill?*"

"We don't need a bone drill." The Hunter shot the Physician a scowl. "Now's not the time for such words."

"I'm just saying, wounds such as this are quite precarious—"

"Are you going to treat him? Use your experience in this matter?"

"Well, I don't have any experience per se..."

"Then let the Healer work. That's what she's here for." The Hunter turned to Leila. "Right? You can manage this?"

All eyes panned Her way, the weight of their stares crippling. She glanced across the sanctuary at the three assassins, and a pang lurched in Her gut, pulling Her in their direction. *You're here for a reason.* But that reason had been abandoned the moment the Prince appeared at Her feet. This was Her purpose—the man sprawled before Her, slick with a feverish sweat—because She was the Healer.

Except She wasn't a healer, and She had no idea what She was doing.

Don't just sit here, do something. She planted Her hand over the wound, trying to assess the damage. The arrow was wedged between his pec and shoulder. *A survivable injury. Maybe. Hopefully. God, is it?*

Splinters of pain pierced Her palm, sharp like a blade. Like an arrowhead.

The surrounding madness faded, leaving Her with the Prince's pain —a keen ache, but no destruction. No fading life.

"It's a clean shot." She wiped Her bloody hand on Her cloak. "No vital organs."

The Physician wrinkled his nose. "How can you tell?"

"By the angle of the arrow," She lied. "Not to mention the depth of the shaft." She sat tall. "It's quite clear. Crystal, really."

"God, it hurts." The Prince glanced between the three faces above him. "Is someone going to fix this?"

The Physician snorted. "If you think *this* is fixable, you haven't yet come to terms with reality."

"Oh, will you just fuck off?" the Prince spat.

"Altair, if you have nothing of use to contribute, I suggest you leave," the Hunter said.

"*Leave?* But I'm a physician."

"You're here to compete." The Hunter nodded at Leila. "She's here to heal, appointed by The Savior Herself. Let her fulfill her role while you fulfill yours."

"But—"

"To question her is to question The Savior's authority."

"Well, I think The Savior would appreciate—"

"Piss off, you fat fuck, or I swear to God I'll rip this arrow from my chest and shove it up your ass," the Prince snapped.

The Physician froze, shocked and chagrined. Feebly, he tromped away.

With a sigh, the Hunter squeezed the Prince's shoulder. "Everything will be fine. You're in good hands." He turned to Leila. "Go on."

A lump caught in Her throat. This was not what She had signed up for. She stared down at the arrow and swallowed. *Do it. Just pull it out.* Cringing, She grabbed the arrow's shaft.

"Wait!" The Hunter's hand shot forward, stopping Her. He wavered, turning to the Prince. "Brother, cover your ears and count to one hundred."

The Prince furrowed his brow. "Why?"

THE SAVIOR'S SISTER

"Helps with the pain. Close your eyes while you're at it."

Wincing, the Prince struggled to cover his ears. After he was a ways into counting, the Hunter spun toward Leila. "You've never done this, have you?"

She faltered. "What makes you say that?"

"You can't just yank an arrow out of someone's chest."

"You can't?"

"Son of a bloody bitch fuck shit cunt!" The Prince dropped his hands. "It's not working. It hurts more. I think I'm dying."

"Keep going." The Hunter waited for him to resume his count. "We haven't much time. Do you know what you're doing?"

"Of course I know what I'm doing. I've healed plenty of wounds, mended injuries of all kinds, and I've never failed, not once." Leila's words lost their power, and She played with Her dress. "It's just, in this particular instance, I'm a bit out of my depth, as I've never actually removed an arrow from someone's body—"

"He's losing blood."

"I don't know what I'm doing," She said.

The Hunter cursed under his breath, and Leila winced. "Should we fetch the Physician?"

"God no, definitely not. I'll guide you." He gave the Prince a squeeze. "Brother, relax. I'm going to tell you exactly what our good Healer is doing while she does it. That way you can brace yourself."

"Brace myself? For what?"

The Hunter eyed Leila sidelong. "Our Healer is going to make an incision."

"An *incision?*" The Prince said. "There's already an incision, there's a hole in my chest with an arrow sticking out of it!"

"She's going to expand the wound."

"For what purpose?"

"Her fingers."

"Her *fingers?*" The Prince shook his head. "No, I refuse. I *fucking refuse.*"

"Brother—"

"No one is sticking their fingers in me!" The Prince thrashed on the

103

floor, blood pumping from his wound. "Not you, not her, not anyone! I will not have it!"

The Hunter grabbed his shoulders. "Keep still! You'll hurt yourself!"

Leila grabbed his arms only for him to yank himself free. Frantically, She glanced across the sanctuary. "Intellect, Cavalier! Hold him down!"

The Intellect dashed Her way, while the Cavalier hesitated, eyeing the hulking man beside him. "Can Enzo help?"

"*Now*," She growled.

The two men appeared at Her side, latching onto the Prince.

"Hold firm," the Hunter ordered.

The Prince was relentless, until a beast of a man loomed over him, grabbing him by the shoulders and slamming him down. The Prince glared at him. "Who the bloody fuck are *you*?"

"Do it now," the Hunter said.

Leila rummaged through Her cloak, snatching up Her blade. Cringing, She brought the tip to the Prince's chest, pressing it against the wound—

"No, wait, get away from me!"

—and dug Her blade into his flesh. It was the smallest incision, yet the moment chilled Her, the Prince's cries echoing in Her ears as She dragged the steel through his skin. Blood trickled down his chest, and when She dropped Her blade, Her only comfort was that he finally stopped screaming.

The Prince fought to slow his breathing. "Oh my God, that was awful. Is it over?"

"We've only just begun." The Hunter cast Leila a knowing glance. "The Healer needs to make sure the arrow hasn't struck bone. She's going to enter the wound—"

"Oh no no no, that is *not* happening." The Prince glared at Leila. "Don't you *dare* touch me."

The Hunter offered Her a nod—a hint of reassurance—and She plunged Her fingers into the wound.

Howls tore from the Prince's throat. Leila clamped down on Her lip, biting so hard She was sure She'd draw blood, all the while following the path of the arrow shaft. Something hard grazed Her fingertips—glassy and sharp, pointed at the tip.

"I found the arrowhead." She pulled Her fingers from the wound. "It's completely free, nowhere near bone."

"Good." The Hunter smiled at the Prince. "It's almost over, brother." As his gaze panned to Leila, his smile disappeared. "There's going to be a lot of blood."

A lot of blood. But there was already so much on his chest, the floor, Her hands.

Hands. Heat pulsed from Her open palms—Her light begging to be wielded. *You can't bless him. You'll expose Yourself.* But perhaps She wouldn't, not in these darkened conditions. *It's a foolish move.* But She was already digging through Her satchel, snatching up a vial of perfume and dousing Her palm.

"I'm ready."

The Hunter looked down at the Prince. "Are you ready, brother?"

"No, I am *not* ready!"

His words fell on deaf ears. The Hunter turned to Leila. "Remove the arrow."

Protests spewed from the Prince's lips, but Leila ignored him, staring at Her hands. *No one will suspect it. No one will know.* With gritted teeth, She grabbed hold of the arrow and slowly, gently pulled it from the Prince's chest.

Tearing flesh, agonized screams—each passing second was chaos, a cacophony of pain. The arrow popped from his body, blood gushing from the wound in torrents, and Leila planted Her hand over the injury.

Slow the bleeding. The blessing repeated in Her mind, traveling through Her with the surge of Her power, a steady flux of burning light.

"Hurry," the Hunter barked. "Close the wound!"

She didn't falter, pressing Her palm deeper into the injury.

"Close the wound—"

"*In a moment,*" She spat.

Mend the flesh. Slow the bleeding. The ensuing mayhem died around Her, leaving Her with the light filling the Prince's veins, heeding Her control.

The heat subsided, Her power still and calm. Leila pulled Her hand from his chest, revealing a soggy red wound that had ceased spilling over.

"Good God..." The Hunter examined the injury. "How did you do that?"

"It's the tonic." Wiping Her hands dry, She cocked Her head at the perfume vial. "Very effective. Simply needs a bit of time and pressure."

The Hunter plucked the vial from the floor, inspecting it. "It smells lovely. Not like any tonic I've ever heard of."

Leila snatched it from his grasp. "It's *special*."

"I was complimenting it, you know."

"Is she done?" The Prince's eyes fluttered open. "Is it over?"

"Yes, brother." The Hunter patted him on the shoulder. "You're fine now."

Relief washed over Leila, Her gaze drifting to the hole in the Prince's chest. *A foolish move.* But Her façade remained intact, and that was all that mattered.

"Fuck, I'm alive." The Prince exhaled. "I can't believe it. I'd pinch myself if I weren't so exhausted."

"You have our Healer girl to thank for that," the Hunter said. "And you can't forget the Artist. You'd still be floundering in the labyrinth if it wasn't for him."

The Prince wrinkled his nose. "Who's the Artist?"

Leila's eyes darted across the space, stopping at that unmistakable black cloud. The Artist sat on a bench engulfed in misery, but visions of him storming into the sanctuary replayed in Her mind, reigniting Her heartbeat.

"Can we go now?"

She flinched. She had forgotten about the Intellect, but there he sat staring right at Her, along with the Cavalier and whoever lingered at his side—a thick, sinewy man with a bald head and an unsettling slate gaze.

"Nonsense, the poor fellow's had such a trying day. Surely we ought to keep him company." The Cavalier nudged the burly man beside him. "Enzo here is from Kovahr. Realm of warriors, of all places, and he serves as a guard to the Queen herself. He has so many stories. I'm sure he'd love to share some."

The mound of muscle at the Cavalier's side kept quiet. His skin was nearly pale enough to rival Leila's, and his thin lips were pulled into a perpetual snarl, a contradiction to the pink fog encircling him—a perfect match to the Cavalier's. *So this is Enzo.* She nearly smiled, until She eyed the other men around Her—men with names She hadn't bothered to learn.

The Hunter laughed. "I think the story we're all eager to hear is how this man got himself into this mess in the first place."

The Prince flashed him a glare. "You think I did this to myself?"

"I think you pissed off the wrong man."

"The Dragon." The Intellect rolled his eyes. "This fool was taunting him throughout the entire obstacle."

"Fuck the Dragon. It was the damn Shepherd," the Prince grumbled.

Leila's head perked up. "Kaleo did this? Why?"

"Hell if I know," he said. "For his own bloody amusement, no doubt. But I'll tell you one thing—that man's a menace. I'm not one to shy from a challenge, but I'll be keeping my distance. Cross that man, and mark my words, it'll be your end."

Kaleo stood with his like-minded associates at the opposite end of the sanctuary, and the sheer sight of him rattled Her. *You came here to kill them. Assassins, of all people.* She abandoned the idea, as much as it wounded Her pride.

"Healer girl." The Hunter nodded in the Prince's direction. "A gentle reminder that our good man could use a dressing."

She rummaged through Her satchel knowing full well its contents were useless. "How careless of me, it appears I've left the bandages in my other satchel. Let me go fetch it. Intellect, didn't I hear you mention something about a card game?"

"Um..." The Intellect's eyes darted from side to side. "Yes, but—"

"Why don't you teach them how to play? Seems as though you could all use a distraction."

"Actually, I was hoping to turn in—"

"Play the game."

The Intellect studied Her hard stare before fishing the cards from his pocket. "So, it's fairly simple..."

While the men busied themselves with the cards, Leila headed off on Her errand. Perhaps it was for the best—She'd need plenty more supplies, as the Prince surely wouldn't be the only man to end up lying in Her lap.

The Artist.

She lurched to a stop. She ought to thank him. It was only proper. Nervous excitement surged within Her, and She spun toward his bench.

Nothing.

The Artist was gone, taking Her excitement with him. Deflated, She turned on Her heel and walked away.

✣ 6 ✣

THE FIRST IMPRESSIONS

Enzo, the Dog.
Raphael, the Intellect.
Caesar, the Regal.

Leila flipped from scroll to scroll, absorbing each name before Her. *Orion, the Hunter.* She read it once, twice, then moved on to the next, determined to ingrain them in Her mind. *Neil, the Noble.* She shuffled the stack, thumbing through the parchment before stopping at a single page.

Tobias. The Artist.

A glint flashed in Her peripheral vision. Delphi stared into Leila's mirrored wardrobe cinching her dress, a glowing handprint beaming from her chest.

"You really don't have to go down there," Leila said.

"Nonsense. Why should You get to have all the fun?" Delphi smiled over her shoulder. "Besides, I said I would. And I'm a considerably better judge of character."

Leila frowned. "You lie."

"Was Your last visit fruitful? Any new tidbits to share?"

The chaos of the previous evening invaded Her mind. "No. I got preoccupied."

"Gazing longingly at their beautiful flesh?"

Leila's frown deepened. "Just get them talking. Gather whatever information you can. Maybe one of them will be helpful."

"Sounds like someone's changed Her tune."

"We still know nothing about Kaleo, except that he's mad. What a shock. But he's dangerous, and I don't want you getting too close to him. Or the other two. But especially him."

"As You wish." Delphi plucked a silver cloak from Leila's wardrobe, glancing across the room. "What about you, *dove*? Have you nothing to contribute?"

Cosima lay across Leila's bed, fiddling with a string of emeralds. "Hm?"

"Any pearls of wisdom to aid against your sister's murder?"

"It seems the two of you have it covered," Cosima said. "You're positively marvelous at this."

Delphi's eyes narrowed, and Leila quickly cut in. "Our next step is to determine Brontes's plan. We know I'm to die, just not how, when, or where." She threaded a satchel over Delphi's shoulder. "So while you pretty them up—"

"Wait." Cosima dropped her jewels. "Are you bathing them?"

"I'm making them presentable," Delphi said. "That's the most reasonable cover we could agree upon."

Cosima held up a finger before scuttling from the room, returning with a bevvy of glass jars. "Here." She shoved the jars into Delphi's arms. "Use these."

Delphi inspected her new burden. "Oils?"

"Does wonders for the male physique. Just something to do while you're down there."

"You're giving me orders now?"

"I'm just saying, you're preparing them anyway, might as well do it right. We'll all enjoy it." Cosima gave Leila's waist a pinch before heading for the door. "See you at the First Impressions, doves."

As the door shut behind her, Delphi pursed her lips. "That woman is an oozing boil."

"Delphi..."

"You can hold out as much hope as You'd like, but Cosima's more cyst than sister."

A knot wound in Leila's stomach. She turned away, fiddling with the crystal rose on Her desk.

"All right, I'm ready." Delphi spun toward Leila, her cloak swirling in a circle. "Any additional instructions? Parting words?"

She was beautiful, the silver cloak shimmering against her rich brown skin. Such a vision belonged anywhere but the labyrinth. "Just be safe," Leila murmured.

"Anything else?"

A dark cloud swept through Her thoughts. "No."

Nodding, Delphi headed for the door, while those black swirls filled the corners of Leila's mind.

"Wait."

Delphi stopped, turning on her heel.

"There is one man..." Leila said.

A smirk crept across Delphi's lips. "Is there?"

"Brown hair, black eyes." Leila cleared Her throat. "His name is Tobias. The—"

"Artist. I remember."

"Help him."

"Help him?"

"See to it that he has an advantage of some kind," Leila said. "In as subtle of means as you can maintain."

"And what's triggered this decision?"

"He saved a man's life yesterday. I believe such action deserves recompense, don't you?"

"Interesting." Delphi's smile widened. "Didn't You expect him to die? Yet instead he comes out a hero. Who did he save?"

"Flynn. The Prince."

"A man above his birth? It seems our Artist is rather impressive, isn't he?"

Leila waved her away. "Oh, just go."

Chuckling, Delphi continued on her path.

"One more thing," Leila called out. "Be gentle. With Tobias, I mean.

His dear friend was brutally killed by Kaleo, of all people. He's in a delicate state, so...be gentle."

Delphi raised an eyebrow.

"I may have upset him when we first met."

"Ah. There it is." Delphi laughed, heading for the door. "Don't worry. I'll be gentle with Your Artist."

"*My* Artist?"

"Slip of the tongue. But I will say, if he saved a man's life in this *delicate* state of his, I can only imagine how admirable he is in full form."

Leila rolled Her eyes, then glanced over the handprint on Delphi's décolletage. "Don't forget. If at any moment you feel endangered—"

"Poof." Delphi threw the door open. "I'm gone." She glided away.

Leila stared at the door, racked with worry. Desperate to divert Her thoughts, She turned to Her desk, only to be met with the pile of records.

Tobias.

"Leila?"

The voice startled Her. Faun stood in the doorway, grinning. "It's time for Your bath. Today's the big day."

Leila shoved the scrolls into Her drawer and followed Faun from Her chamber.

"Pleasant day, Your Holiness," Asher chirped.

She growled. "My name is and will forever be Leila."

Soon the periwinkle walls of the bathhouse surrounded Her, and Her nakedness set the pool aglow. Her four favorite servants paid extra close attention to the softness of Her skin, the shine of Her hair, as Leila was to look especially beautiful.

Today was the First Impressions.

"You absolutely must tell us all about them," Hemera said.

Leila flinched, sending ripples through the pool. "Who?"

"The competitors. Who else?" Damaris chuckled, massaging Her tight shoulders. "You're finally meeting them, after all."

"I'm so excited." Hemera plopped down at the edge of the pool. "I bet they're all handsome. And noble. And kind. They must be."

Leila let out a snort and sank into the water, only for Nyx to yank at Her arms, hoisting Her upright. "Sit up straight, You'll wet Your hair."

"Is there anyone in particular You're excited to meet?"

A dark cloud slinked through Leila's thoughts. "No."

Damaris laughed. "Oh, these men will have a hard time impressing Her."

"Good." Faun winked. "They wanted a challenge, after all."

The grooming went on for much longer than usual, and hours of dressing followed. Once the whirlwind of silks settled, Leila headed to the labyrinth, nerves wrestling in Her gut.

Black bricks dissolved before Her, revealing a dreary room made of chipping stone. A long mirror in a florid gold frame leaned against the wall beside a rack of familiar cloaks. Her sisters waited expectantly, but Leila's eyes went straight to Cosima, her painted lips, and her emerald dress, the ideal fit for her curves.

"Cosima," Leila said. "You look beautiful."

"Thank You." She picked up the folds of her dress. "I thought this was well-suited for the occasion. It has a regal flair, don't You think?"

Leila took her in for a second longer before catching Her own reflection in the mirror. Violet draped Her figure, crisscrossing Her breasts and tying behind Her neck. Her long, dark hair was pulled into an elaborate braid and adorned in pearl pins, a perfect match to Her belt, Her bracelets. She nearly smiled, until She spotted Cosima in the mirror, eyeing Her jewels.

"Come." Leila beckoned her forward. "Let's get you situated."

Cosima glided to Her side, and Leila began stripping Her bracelets, threading them onto Her sister's wrists. Piece by piece, She peeled away the work of Her servants, and as Her body became barer, Cosima's became more embellished.

"So, dove, tell me, what's the plan for this meeting?" Cosima studied herself in the mirror, her eyes reflecting the light of Leila's jewels. "I'm vaguely aware of the formalities, but one can never be too prepared."

Leila kept Her gaze on Her work. "The competitors will join us shortly. Each will ask you a question, some attempt to gain your favor. All you have to do is answer as The Savior."

"Anything You'd like me to say? Or topics to avoid?"

"The fact that you're a fraud should probably remain unmentioned," Delphi said.

Leila shot her a sideways glare. "Use your best judgment. So long as the façade is kept, I am content."

"Of course. I just hope I live up to Your charm and grace. No one compares to The One True Savior. I'm honored to play the part."

Cosima's words were calm, loosening Leila's tense shoulders. She unlatched the belt from Her waist, fastening it around Her sister with care.

"Now tell me, what of Your power?"

Leila straightened. "My power?"

"Yes. Your magic," Cosima said.

"But you know all..." Leila cleared Her throat, "...most of My magic."

"I'm simply being prepared." Cosima's smile never wavered. "Naturally these men will be intrigued. What if they ask why I'm not glowing?"

"Tell them you only glow in the daylight." Delphi planted her hands on her hips. "The darkness is a precaution so they don't fall flat on their asses."

"But what if they ask how my light *works*?"

"Tell them it's none of their concern," Delphi said.

"Why would I say that?"

"Because it isn't!"

"It's fine." Leila sighed. "Let's just get through the day."

"Thank You," Cosima said. "Finally, a woman of reason."

Leila swallowed a groan. "The source of My power is My light. It fills My body with energy. *A divine illumination*—that's what the ancient scrolls call it. And everything in its path is strengthened. Renewed." She unraveled Her braid, combing the loose strands with Her fingers. "My light... It bleeds through Me. I can't help it. Just being near Me has its benefits. My touch is even better, like spoonfuls of tonic. And then there's My blessing. My consent to share My power."

Twirling a red curl around Her finger, Leila threaded a pearl pin into Her sister's hair. "Think of it this way. Your body is a barrel, and I'm filling you up with My light. And that light can perform a service for you. Whatever service I command. I can grant you one of My gifts, or restore you, heal your wounds from the inside."

Cosima nodded. "Is there anything else I should know?"

"What do you mean?"

"Your gifts. I imagine You have several. That shadow nonsense, for example."

"Shadow walking."

"Right. There has to be more You haven't shared." Her gaze brightened. "Say, what about Your eyes? They're utterly curious in the light, as if Your stare has been set ablaze. If Your glowing touch is so magical, certainly Your eyes must be the same."

Leila's muscles tightened, threatening to snap. She glanced at the mirror where Her mothers lingered in the reflection.

"Well then," Cosima prompted, "is there anything else?"

One mother gazed at Delphi in loving awe, while the other stared Leila hard in the eye, Her arms crossed as She shook Her head from side to side.

"No," Leila said. "That's it."

The wall ahead of them caved in, revealing a darkened portal with Romulus standing in its frame. "It's nearly time."

Cosima laughed. "What in the world are you wearing?"

Romulus glanced down at his drab grey robes, a far cry from his usual tunics. "My uniform."

"Cosima, be still." Leila planted a hand on Her sister's décolletage. "The viewing room is protected, but one can never be too safe. I'm giving you the gift of shadow walking."

Cosima's eyes lit up. "Marvelous."

"There will be killers in our midst. If you feel threatened at any moment, use the blessing to escape." The heat of Leila's palm died. "There. It's done."

"You can move things!" Pippa pulled a ribbon from her hair, sending it disappearing in a tiny grey cloud before reappearing in her opposite hand.

"I think we're ready." Leila turned to Romulus. "Bring them in."

His stare had softened, fixed on Pippa. He looked away. "It's not too late. You can reveal Yourself as The Savior. Devise another plan."

"Bring them *in*," Leila said.

Glowering, he left the room.

The court made final adjustments to their ensembles, while Leila paced the floor. Delphi glanced over Cosima's off-the-shoulder dress with a critical eye. "You'd be wise to cover yourself." She plucked an emerald cloak from the rack and threw it at Cosima. "The Savior has white, celestial flesh."

Cosima frowned. "Well, I'm certainly fair."

"And so is Leila. More so, in fact. Best not to fuel speculation, yes?" Delphi turned to Pippa, smiling. "You too, you little trickster. Come here." Pippa pranced to her side, standing somewhat still as Delphi clasped an olive cloak around her neck. She gave Pippa a pat on the bottom before turning Leila's way. "Your turn, love."

Leila trudged to her side, preoccupied over the task ahead as Delphi fastened the black cloak into place.

"Are You nervous?" Delphi asked.

"No." Leila's belly rumbled. "I mean, a little. About..." Her gaze floated toward Cosima, "...you know." She fiddled with Her hair, occupying Her restless hands. "How was your visit with the men?"

"We'll discuss it later." Delphi pulled Leila's hood over Her head. "But I will say, of all the prying questions the men threw my way, only one man asked if Her Holiness was kind. Would You like to guess who?"

Romulus's voice echoed through the portal. The First Impressions was nearly underway. "I'll enter first. The rest of you will follow." Leila spun toward Her other two sisters. "We all know our parts, yes?"

"Of course, dove," Cosima said. "We won't fail You."

"Thank you for doing this. You have no idea how much it means to Me."

Cosima's smile widened. "Anything for my beautiful sister."

"*Gentlemen, I give to you The Savior.*" Romulus's voice carried through the room, sending Leila taut. With a deep breath, She headed into the portal.

The tunnel was much shorter than She had hoped, quickly leading Her to the viewing room. Stone walls surrounded Her with traces of holy light bleeding through the crevices, illuminating the otherwise dreary space. Four thrones with black cushions and gold filigree sat ahead, and beyond them the air rippled like water. She was familiar with such shields, manipulations of magic from Saviors past, one of the few commendable examples of science paired with celestial power. Beyond the shield stood sixteen men, their shoulders low, chins high.

Bodies oiled.

Leila nearly started, unsettled by the glistening meat. Pippa and Delphi entered soon after, and She forced past the perversion, searching the men's faces for suspicion. Footsteps sounded, and Her stomach lurched when Cosima appeared.

Please let this work.

Cosima glided through the room, carrying herself with authority, regality. Stopping in front of her throne, she lowered her hood.

Leila stiffened. *What is she doing?* Cosima unclasped her cloak and set it aside, and every impulse within Leila fired off, mind swimming with worst case scenarios—with the weight of defeat before the ruse had begun.

"Kneel," Romulus spat.

All sixteen men dropped to one knee. The women took their seats, and while Her sisters were poised, Leila dug Her nails into Her armrests.

As Romulus opened his mouth to speak, Cosima's voice rang out instead.

"Please be seated."

The men sat along a stone bench, staring ahead with wide eyes and cocksure grins. They were captivated by Cosima, enough so to calm Leila's heartbeat.

"You have been blessed with the presence of The Savior. The One True Savior until Her divinity is passed. You may each ask Her one question of your choosing." Romulus nodded at the line of men. "We'll begin with the Poet."

Hansel. He was a mess, his busted eye wrapped in bandages and cheeks covered in bruises, but still he beamed with admiration. He and Cosima exchanged pleasantries, and he cleared his throat. "Is it true? Does Your skin glow?"

Leila nearly snorted. *That's his question? Of all things?*

"It does, in the sunlight." Cosima raised her hand, eyeing her pale flesh. "My body is filled with energy—a divine illumination. It can be quite stunning...though I do mean that literally. That's why I'm meeting you here, hidden from the sun's rays. It's best this way for now. The glow can be overwhelming for some."

Hansel bowed, a wonderstruck smile on his face. *Fifteen questions to go.* Hopefully each one went as smoothly.

"Physician," Romulus said. "Ask your question."

Altair. He looked just as antsy as Hansel, the sheen on his golden-brown skin surely more nervous sweat than oil.

"Your magic..." His voice came out soft and eager. "Can we see it?"

Leila glanced at Her sisters, astounded. *Of all the audacious requests...*

Romulus glowered. "Physician, you are to ask The Savior questions, not request performances—"

"It's all right," Cosima said. "I don't mind."

Leila spun toward Cosima, aghast. *Is she out of her mind?*

"Would you still like to see it?" Cosima asked. "My magic?"

What magic? You have no magic!

Smiling, Cosima slid her hands through her hair, pulling out one of Leila's pearl pins. She held it in her palm. "Open your hand for Me, dove."

Altair obeyed as if Cosima's order was of the utmost importance. The two stared at one another, Cosima's eyes narrowing with focus, while Leila clawed at Her armrests.

The pin burst into a grey cloud, reappearing in Altair's palm.

"A gift," Cosima said. "From Me to you."

The room gasped, while Leila let out a long breath. *The blessing.* She hadn't intended its use for parlor tricks, hadn't even considered the notion. She sank into Her chair, relief melting the tension in Her muscles.

"Regal." Romulus's voice echoed off the walls. "Your question."

The brawny blond Lord sat tall, a smug smile on his face. *Caesar.* She recalled his circle of swine and their lecherous jeers, and disdain oozed from Her pores.

"Good day, Your Holiness." He bowed. "I'm absolutely honored to make Your acquaintance. You're a beauty to behold—"

"The *question*," Romulus said.

"Well, the lot of us have just now seen some of Your magic, and what a fine act it was. But I'm curious, how exactly does Your magic work?"

Cosima studied her hands as if they carried purpose. "The source of My power is My holy light. It strengthens everything that crosses My path. Why, just being in My presence has its benefits. My touch alone is as good as a spoonful of tonic. But I can also bestow upon people a blessing. Think of it as My way of sharing My power. Your body is a barrel, and I'm filling you up with My light."

"Fascinating. What an answer, such poetry." Caesar glanced down the line at Hansel. "Better than anything this poor damsel could come up with, I'm sure."

Some of the men chuckled, but Leila sat still, silent. *Such poetry.*

Except those were Her words. Her poetry.

Romulus continued down the line, each question proving more insipid than the last. Beauty, magic—the topics were uninspired at best, yet She withered with each passing turn, wounded in a way She hadn't predicted. Before Her sat sixteen eligible men, and not a single one of them looked Her way.

Of course. That's the point. But no amount of logic lessened the burn.

None of them saw Her.

"Your Holiness, do You fancy Yourself a thief?"

All eyes shot straight to the Adonis—*Beau*, the most delectable meat slab of them all. He sat in the center of the line, his perfectly chiseled chin high.

Cosima wavered. "Pardon Me?"

"Adonis, *explain* yourself," Romulus hissed.

Beau smirked. "I only ask because it seems as though You've *stolen* my heart."

Leila let out a throaty sigh, rolling Her eyes into the back of Her skull. The task had already taken its toll, and all She could do was count the seconds.

A muffled snort sounded from across the room. At the end of the line sat a headful of brown locks, his chin bowed as he chuckled in his corner.

"Do you have something to contribute, Artist?" Romulus said.

Tobias's eyes darted between Romulus, Leila, and the other faces pointed his way. He cleared his throat, fighting a grin. "Apologies."

Romulus grumbled before continuing on, and though Leila

attempted to follow, Tobias lingered in Her peripheral vision. His hair was the slightest bit tame, and She could actually make out his carved jawline beneath his fading wounds.

"Shepherd. Your question."

Black eyes faded from Leila's mind, replaced with a crystal gaze. Kaleo leaned on his knees, smiling. "What is Your favorite flower? So I can spoil You with them when the time comes."

Cosima hesitated, then matched his grin. "It's funny. I hear everyone decorates with lilies on My birthday, yes? They were My mother's favorite. Lilies are beautiful, of course...but I've always preferred roses. Pink ones."

Leila crossed Her arms, Her glare panning between the two—Kaleo, eternally wretched, and Cosima, who had humored him despite that fact.

The questioning resumed, but Leila had had enough. Cosima filled the role beautifully, carrying herself with a finesse Leila couldn't rival, certainly not with these questions to work with. "What is Your father looking for in Your Champion?" "When would You like us to be wed?" Leila cursed to Herself, Her patience dead and buried. Every so often, Tobias would chuckle from his corner, or he'd fight back a smile, but even that couldn't salvage Her mood. *What in God's name is he laughing at?*

"Now for our final competitor." Romulus turned to the last man. "Artist, ask your question."

Tobias's grin faded. His gaze fell on Cosima, and Leila braced Herself for the idiocy that would surely spill from his lips.

"What is Your name?" he said.

The room went quiet, as did Leila's prickly thoughts. Finally, something real. Something good.

"Cosima." Another smile spread across her painted lips. "My name is Cosima."

"It's a pleasure to meet You, Cosima."

The two stared at one another, their lingering gazes pinching at Leila's gut.

"Your First Impressions have come to an end," Romulus said. "Your questions have been answered. Now it is time for Her Holiness to deliberate. Today's task was more than a simple opportunity. Based on your performance, one man will receive the first reward of the Sovereign's Tournament."

The men murmured amongst one another only for Romulus to bark at them, sending them flinching. "The Savior requires a moment alone. Kneel."

The men dropped to their knees without question, a pitiful sight, then rose per Romulus's bidding. "The results will be presented in the sanctuary." He cocked his head at a nearby portal. "You're dismissed."

One by one, they trudged from the viewing room. Tobias trailed the line of oiled men, glancing once more at the women—at Cosima—before disappearing with the others.

Pippa wrinkled her nose. "Why were they wet?"

Leila leaned back in Her throne, emptying Her lungs. The First Impressions were over, and Her plan had unfolded seamlessly.

From this point forward, Cosima was The Savior.

"A reward," Cosima said. "That means time alone with The Savior, yes?"

"No, it just means time alone with you," Delphi muttered.

Leila sighed. "I suppose then we should deliberate—"

"The Adonis," Cosima declared. "He wins."

Leila wavered. "The Adonis?" She glanced between Her sisters. "Aren't you going to think this through? The Artist certainly asked a superior question."

Cosima let out a laugh. "To hell with the questions. Did you *see* the Adonis?"

"But that horrid line—"

"God, wasn't it awful?" Cosima gave a dismissive flick of her wrist. "He's a dullard, that's for certain. The beauties always are. But You know what they say: For simple pleasures, seek simple minds."

"These men are risking their lives. It's only fair the proper sort are honored justly."

Cosima cocked her head. "Forgive me, I must've misunderstood my role. I assumed since I'm the one accompanying the men—and in turn shielding You from harm—I was to choose the winner of each reward." She smiled, though her gaze was hard. "Please accept my apologies. I meant no offense."

The challenge in her stare wore on Leila's already aggravated nerves, but what truly gave Her pause were the jewels draping Cosima's neck—gems of The Savior, a role Leila depended on.

"So then, oh humble sister of The Savior's court," Romulus said. "Who wins the reward?"

Protests lingered on Leila's tongue, but She swallowed them down. "The Adonis. I suppose."

"Oh, Leila, what a surprise!" Cosima stood from her seat, kissing Leila's cheek. "Thank You, dove. I absolutely must prepare."

She left with Pippa trailing close behind, and Delphi followed, growling under her breath. Only Leila and Romulus remained, glaring at one another through the rippling shield.

Romulus broke the quiet. "Shall I make the announcement?"

Leila ignored his question, Her mind churning. "What of the men?"

"Imbeciles."

"Anything else?"

"Pungent imbeciles."

"What of My assassins?" She said. "What do you know of them?"

"One is large, one is tattooed, and one is covered in many scars."

"Dammit, Rom—"

"You have placed me as the Proctor of this tournament. You have put me down in this rank hole to keep Your charade a secret. I cannot be down here keeping Your secret and up there lending my ear to Your father at the same time."

She clenched Her jaw. "The assassination. I need the date, the location—"

"I do not have those answers."

"Then find someone who does," She spat. "Make yourself useful to Me. You're alive only for the sake of serving My cause."

Red leaked through Romulus's flesh, filling the room. "Yes, Your Holiness."

"Make your announcement."

He walked off with his red cloud, leaving Leila listless and alone.

❧ 7 ❧

THE MARKED ONE

L eila darted through Her chamber, loading Her satchel until it tugged at the seams. Fresh reeds, fortress maps, documents faded with age—anything that stood a chance of furthering Her cause. By the end of the day, She would be one step closer to ruining Her father. She just wasn't sure how.

She threw open Her chamber door only to be met by Asher's plucky voice. "Good day, Your Holiness—"

"For God's sake, My name is *Leila*," She said. "Call Me *Leila*."

He faltered. "Pardon?"

"How many times do I have to tell you My name before you realize it's what I prefer to be called? Or does My preference not at all matter to you?"

"Apologies, Your Holi—" He cleared his throat. "I was trying to be respectful."

"If you wish to respect Me, treat Me as a person of thought and feeling, not as an object to worship. How would you feel if I called you *guard* each day in passing?"

Asher stared back at Her, perplexed. "I... I just..."

"Good day, *Asher*."

With Her chin high, She marched off to Her study. She dropped Her satchel on Her desk and spread out its contents, stopping once She caught sight of the competitors' records.

Tobias.

She plucked his scroll from the stack. *Tobias Kaya. The Artist. Age: 21. Hair: brown. Eyes: black.* The word *REJECTED* was splayed at the bottom with a harsh line drawn through it. Delphi's work, no doubt. She flitted toward a shelf of parchment, snatched up a scroll, and scanned over its list of names. *Titus, Tivadar, Tivon...*

Tobias. Male. Meaning: goodness.

The door flew open, and Delphi tromped inside.

"Well, the dunce of an Adonis is greased up to Cosima's liking. If she returns from her reward covered in oils, we'll know what happened." She plopped onto the couch. "I never would've signed on for this had I known it meant keeping up appearances. Into the labyrinth day after day? The stench is horrendous."

Leila's eyes remained on the scroll.

Goodness.

"Leila?"

She shoved the scroll back onto the shelf. "Did you learn anything? We never discussed your first visit."

"I'm afraid I have little more than gossip. It's clear Neil's compensating for some supreme inadequacy. And two of the men are fucking. I'm certain of it. They wouldn't stop making eyes at one another."

"Nothing of value?" Leila took a seat at Delphi's side. "Any men who could be of aid to us?"

"Perhaps." Delphi sighed. "You were right; most of them are inept. And here they're supposed to be the finest bachelors in all the realm. Which begs the question, is the system flawed, or is the rest of Thessen even worse? Can You imagine?"

"What about the assassins?"

"God, disgusting. Drake is a peculiar one. Refuses to speak. At first I found it unsettling, but after some time in his company I was glad for it. Then there's Antaeus, an idiot who can't seem to shut up. Why is it the imbeciles who always run their mouths? It's as though they want the whole world to know of their stupidity."

"And what of Kaleo?"

Delphi's face dropped. "Have You had a conversation with him?"

"Not really, no."

"Don't."

"Why? Is he that awful?"

Delphi was quiet for a long while. "Mother used to tell me stories of the oddities she witnessed as an herbalist, a midwife. There was one man in particular she said she'd never forget. There was nothing wrong with him—nothing that could be seen with the naked eye, at least. But she said he was the sickest creature she'd ever met. Had a disease of the mind. There's no name for it. She called it a rift. Said there was a hole in him. An empty spot where his feelings were supposed to be."

"You think Kaleo has a rift?"

"I know it."

A tremor rolled down Leila's spine. "What about Tobias?"

"What about him?"

"What was your impression of him?"

Delphi smiled. "Special."

"Details."

"Kind. Intelligent," Delphi said. "One of the few men who treated me as flesh and blood as opposed to a hole for his cock. Certainly no killer, he fears for his life. Most likely convinced he'll die here."

"You did as I asked, yes? Offered assistance?"

"I did." Delphi tilted her head. "Are You looking to recruit him? Make him an ally in our endeavor?"

"What? No, why?"

"You're asking a lot of questions about him," Delphi said. "I'm just trying to understand Your purpose."

"I need information for our plan. It's all very relevant."

Delphi smirked, and Leila's eyes narrowed. "What's that face for?"

"No reason."

Leila shot her a scowl before gazing at Her shelf of scrolls. *Goodness.* Her scowl faded.

"I suppose You have no more need to visit the labyrinth," Delphi said.

"Once more."

Delphi furrowed her brow. "Why? We've gathered all there is to know."

"Hardly. There's still plenty to uncover. We haven't a clue when My assassination is to take place, the location, or the means."

"And You assume Kaleo and the others will, what? Disclose this to You?"

"When I'm down there, I'm healing those men. My light makes them stronger—strong enough to weaken the assassins, perhaps even defeat them." Leila leaned in closer, eyes wide. "Don't you see? Mingling amongst the men works in My favor."

Delphi crossed her arms. "Is that right? And there's no man in particular You wish to *mingle* with?"

"I haven't a clue what you're hinting at, but I don't appreciate your tone."

"Love, I'm all for You mingling with men—"

"It's not like that—"

"But the labyrinth is dangerous. Drake, Antaeus, and Kaleo are dangerous." Delphi took Her hand. "Stay above ground. At least the dangers here are familiar."

A knock at the door sounded, followed by a face peeking in. "Your Holiness?" A servant girl came inside, bowing before handing a package to Leila. "For You."

Leila examined it—a palm-sized box wrapped with a violet ribbon. "What is this?"

"A belated birthday gift," the servant said.

"From who?"

"I'm not certain. It only just arrived. There was no note."

Leila's gut twisted. "Thank you."

Once the servant left the room, Delphi hovered over Leila's shoulder, glaring at the gift. "Don't open it. I don't trust it."

Bracing Herself, Leila shook the package, then unraveled the ribbon.

"God, You never listen to me," Delphi muttered.

Slowly, She opened the box, and both sisters peered inside.

Delphi wrinkled her nose. "It's a ring?"

A thick gold setting with florid carvings, a massive ruby in its center.

This wasn't any ring—Leila had seen it before, could perfectly envision its owner stroking it like a pet.

"It's Qar's," She said.

"Why would Qar send You one of his rings?"

"He wouldn't."

She pulled out the piece of shimmering gold, and the ruby rattled, loose in its setting. She pried the gem from the ring, revealing a hollowed compartment holding a folded strip of parchment—a note boasting Romulus's scrawled handwriting.

Am I useful now?

Conviction surged through Her, fiery and alive. She studied the golden setting and its hidden chamber. Were all his rings like this?

"Qar's the next mark. He'll have answers." Leila ripped up the note. "Or I suppose his precious stones will."

She was already dashing across the chamber before Delphi could respond, dropping the ring into Her pocket and throwing Her cloak around Her shoulders. "You've seen the schedule, yes? Where's Qar at this hour?"

"It's midday. He's training in the southern gardens, same as always."

"Good."

"Leila."

Delphi's sharp tone halted Her, along with her piercing gaze. "Qar is not an old man."

"He's forty-something."

"He's *training*," Delphi maintained. "He'll be armed. And he can fight."

Leila's hand went to Her blade. *Not enough.* She darted to Her desk, reaching beneath its center drawer and unfastening a long piece of sharpened steel.

A sword.

She tucked the weapon into Her belt. "So can I."

"Leila—"

The room disappeared around Her, Her vision awash in green. She stood at the edge of the southernmost forest, far off from the palace and cloaked by the cover of leaves. The clang of steel sounded in the distance.

Qar.

He wove through the nearby garden, poised and at ease, laughing with his instructor amid their playful combat. His royal drape was gone, but his golden-stitched tunic was of the finest make, a beautiful rag for his sweat. And predictably, on each of his fingers was a jeweled ring.

Leila waited. Eventually the two men dropped their swords, exchanging pleasantries before the instructor left. Qar lingered behind, taking a seat on a bench as he polished his sword.

No servants. No onlookers. The time was now.

Leila stepped out of the foliage, Her head bowed and hood low. Qar stared down at his weapon, and She hoped to God he wouldn't notice Her, wouldn't feel Her stalking closer. Sliding Her fingers beneath Her cloak, She gripped the pommel of Her sword.

Qar flinched. "Your Holiness?"

God dammit.

"What a surprise. I do not believe I have ever seen You in the gardens at this time." Smirking, he stood. "Or is it Your intention to be unseen? Are You trying to be discreet with that cloak? It would take considerable draping to stifle Your light."

The sun was blazing, beating down on Leila and setting Her hands aglow. She hid them at Her sides, tempted to curse Her own flesh.

"Your Holiness—"

"I hear you have words for Me," Leila said.

"Oh? Apologies, but I fear You are mistaken."

"I don't think I am."

"Your Holiness..." Qar's voice faded as he followed the path of Her gaze to his hand—and his rings.

"Your stones are striking, I'd like to see them up close." She squared Her shoulders. "Give them to Me."

Qar said nothing, glancing between Leila and his rings.

Leila's eyes narrowed. *"Give them to Me."*

He bolted through the garden.

Leila sprinted after him, eyes trained on the back of his bald head. He zigzagged between manicured trees, traveling farther and farther away, his long stride his sole advantage. Bursting free from the garden, he sped into a nearby vineyard, and Leila gritted Her teeth.

Take Me to him.

The vineyard exploded around Her, Her vision filling with leaves, grapes—and Qar, who staggered to a halt in front of Her. He shot down an adjacent row.

Leila's body filled with fire, and again She appeared in front of him, then beside him. Once more he skidded down a neighboring stretch of vines, and Her vision went white, fading to reveal Qar staring back at Her.

The Senator skidded to a stop. "The holy Queen has tricks." He forced a laugh. "Your magic is greater than Your father knows. He will be displeased."

Leila dropped Her cloak, revealing more of Her glowing flesh—and Her sword. "The rings."

"Come now, You will hurt Yourself—"

She lunged forward, swinging Her sword with a force Qar barely dodged. "Underestimating Me does you no favors."

Qar drew his weapon. "So now it is my turn, Your Holiness? You have come to kill me, like the others?"

"You could make this easier for yourself. Tell Me what you know. I'll see to your end quickly. Or I can sever your fingers one at a time and read your secrets Myself."

"Little girl, You are not as formidable as You believe Yourself to be."

"I've heard that before. Many times. Then suddenly they're choking on blood, and their words just fade away."

A dance began in the vineyard. Qar brandished his weapon theatrically, but Leila was polished. Ready. *You are small.* Her training swept Her thoughts, visions of Talos, the dungeon, and countless wooden wasters. *You are slight.* Qar's sword whipped toward Her, and She wove around it gracefully. *Use Your size to Your advantage. Be lithe. Be agile.*

Be better than them.

The crack of steel against steel echoed in Her ears. Qar staggered backward, colliding with a grapevine, his palpable fear feeding Her fury. She thrust Her weapon forward, again and again.

An ugly *rip* replaced the din of metal against metal.

Qar reached for his gut, clutching his slashed, red-stained tunic. "*Alekbron lajnun,* enough!"

"Hardly," She scoffed. "You're still alive."

"You have made Your point. Now drop Your sword and show Your mercy."

"I didn't come here for *mercy*. I came for your *rings*."

Qar barely evaded Her next jab, wielding his weapon with one hand, gripping his gut with the other. She made contact again, leaving another gash to match the first. They pivoted through the vineyard, painting the grapes red. Not once did Qar's sword mark Leila's body.

"When am I to be killed?" She whipped Her sword.

Qar madly searched for an escape, but Leila didn't waver. "Who else is involved with Brontes?" Another jab. "The guards?" Another. "The servants?"

"God dammit, woman!"

She slammed Her sword against his. "There's been a trickle of funds leaving the vault for some time now. Where is it going?"

"I said, *enough*!"

Qar forced Her off him, fleeing from the vineyard back into the garden. Gripping Her sword, She followed, Her hatred swelling, smothering all traces of Her light. Qar steadied himself on a bench, a pillar, leaving behind bloody handprints, and when he met Her gaze from over his shoulder, She broke into a sprint.

A primal battle between predator and prey waged within the garden. She brandished Her weapon with full force, swinging harder and faster, leaving Qar tattered and torn. He cried out as he nearly toppled into a marble fountain, and before he could gain his bearings, She thrust Her sword, blasting his from his hands.

The steel collapsed to the ground, and Leila pointed Her sword at his chest.

Qar stood like a statue, slack-jawed. "What kind of creature are You?"

"I am your *Queen*."

"You are *damned*. My blood will never wash clean of Your hands." His fists trembled. "You are forever marked. You are a murderer."

She drove Her sword through his gut.

Qar choked, lips sputtering nothingness. Leila launched Her foot forward, kicking him from Her sword and sending him collapsing into the fountain.

The sound of trickling water floated through the air.

You are forever marked.

Blood swirled through the fountain, and the golden rings on Qar's fingers sank beneath the water's surface.

"Shit!"

She dashed toward the fountain, prying each ring from his knuckles. There wasn't time to relish Her victory—She was in the open, and Qar's dead body colored the waters red. Scanning the space, She darted back to the vineyard, plucking Her cloak from the ground before Her vision went white.

The plum walls of Her study formed around Her. Delphi was gone, and Pippa was curled up on the couch, reading a scroll and sounding out the words.

"What are these for?" Pippa asked.

Leila wiped Her sword clean before situating it beneath Her desk drawer. Nearing Pippa's side, She peered at the scroll in her hands: *the Hunter.* "The competitors' records?" She ripped the scroll away. "Where'd you get this?"

"Your desk." Pippa grabbed another slip, pointing to the text. "What's this?"

"Those are measurements of muscles."

"And what's this?"

"That's the measurement of a very particular muscle."

"What kind of—?"

"Pippa, these aren't fables, you shouldn't read these." Leila snatched up the stack before Pippa could rebut, shoving the parchment in Her satchel. A jingle sounded from Her pocket, and She scooped up Qar's rings.

You are a murderer.

"Your Holiness?"

She spun toward the plump man in striking fuchsia drapes standing in Her doorway. "Wembleton..."

"Apologies for the intrusion." He eyed Her over. "Is that a new cloak? It's lovely. Sometimes the best pieces are understated."

Frowning, Leila slipped Qar's rings into Her satchel. "I'm busy."

"Then I'll make my presence brief. I've come to inform You of the results of the challenge."

The tournament. She had forgotten today marked the first challenge—that even more blood had been spilled within the fortress walls.

"On this fine day, a man has fallen in the pursuit of Your hand," Wembleton said. "In a short while I shall announce to the realm that the Poet died a hero in the Sovereign's Tournament. We shall all honor his noble sacrifice."

Leila exhaled. Another man dead. Perhaps She should've ached for him, but this man didn't have black eyes or a mop of wavy hair, and for that She was relieved.

"And it seems another will be joining him in the next life soon enough," Wembleton added.

Leila started. "Another man?"

"Yes. The Artist."

Her gut lurched.

Tobias.

She flung Her satchel over Her shoulder, shoved past Wembleton, and sprinted down the corridor.

The sound of Her rampant breathing echoed in Her ears. All She needed was an empty corridor, the briefest moment of isolation. When the path ahead of Her cleared, the pitter-patter of feet sounded at Her side, and blonde hair bobbed in Her peripheral vision.

"Where are we running?"

"Pippa—"

"I want to come too!"

Groaning, Leila grabbed Pippa's wrist as a blinding light burst around Her.

The stench hit Her first—hot sweat mixed with sour spew, enough to sear Her nostrils. The brick walls of the sanctuary materialized, and She charged ahead, nearly stumbling into a puddle of vomit.

"Boys!" Pippa squealed. "I'm so excited!"

Haggard men were doubled over, clutching their stomachs, while others hurled without shame, cursing whatever had left them so ill. The wall beside Her was open wide, revealing a white room streaked with disarray. In its center lay Hansel's dead body, his face covered in sick.

"Healer girl."

A small group headed Her way, led by a burly man. Orion. The Hunter looked a mess, his long, ashy-brown hair hanging in damp tangles, but Leila was far more concerned with the body slung over his shoulder.

Tobias.

She hurried toward them. "Is he dead?"

"Unconscious." Orion laid him out at Her feet. "Has a pulse, but it's faint."

As Leila knelt beside him, Her throat tightened. Wet curls were plastered to his feverish face, his lips and chin stained with blood. "What happened?"

The Prince marched up to Her side. *Flynn.* "They poisoned our wine, of all things! Ruining one of the finest pleasures man has to enjoy!"

"You're telling me he's poisoned?"

"It was a challenge," Orion said. "They poisoned our drink and tasked us with concocting the antidote."

"An antidote made of frog guts and ox piss." Flynn shoved his hands onto his hips. "Did you hear that? *Ox piss.*"

Orion looked Tobias up and down. "I believe he overdosed on one of the ingredients. Hipnayl? Whatever it's called."

"Fuck the hipnayl, I blame the poison," Flynn said. "He drank like a fish."

Leila frowned. "Well, his friend died."

"I know, that's why I encouraged it."

Leila stiffened. "You encouraged a man in mourning to drink? Excessively?"

"What? It numbs the pain."

Leila growled under Her breath. She planted one palm on Tobias's forehead, the other on his chest, and nausea plowed through Her, nearly sending Her heaving.

"Did I do something wrong?" Flynn said. "He's going to be all right, yes?"

"Does he *look* all right to you?" Leila spat.

Despite the protests of Her gut, Leila weighted Her hands against Tobias. Saliva pooled in Her mouth, but behind the suffering She could feel it—poison snaking through him, an interloper seizing control.

Flynn nudged Her. "Healer girl—"

"Leave." Leila spun toward the men. "All of you."

"But—"

"*Leave.*"

The men hesitated before walking off. Pain stabbed at Leila's fingertips; second by second, Tobias's insides dulled.

He was slipping away.

Pippa popped into Her line of sight. "Is he sleeping?"

"Pippa love, keep the area clear," Leila said. "Make sure no one comes anywhere near this man, do you understand?"

"What for?"

"So he can nap in peace, duckling."

Pippa bounded off, while Leila eyed the men in the distance. *They'll see Me. They'll notice.* Fear nipped at Her insides, but She fought past it, Her voice barely a murmur.

"Slow the toxin. Give him strength."

Heat seared Her palms, Her light galvanized, spilling forth. The poison stirred within Tobias, and the fading of his body sent sweat beading along Her forehead.

"*Strength.* For God's sake, I said *give him strength*."

Power burst through Her hands, setting Her touch aflame. A war waged in Tobias's body—Her holy command battling his frailty.

"He has a fever."

A loud smacking punctuated the voice behind Her. Leila growled. "What do you want, Altair?"

The Physician chomped at an apple, scanning Tobias's body. "It's a side effect of the poison. So you needn't check his temperature, because he's clearly burning up like the rest of us."

Leila yanked Her hand from Tobias's forehead. "Thank you for your astute contribution. Now if you'll excuse me, I'm trying to save a man's life."

"You need ginger tea. Perhaps smelling salts." Dropping his apple, he grabbed Her bag. "If you have any in this bag of yours—"

She snatched Her satchel away. "Don't you *dare* touch my things."

"I've treated many a sour stomach, and the solution is simple. I myself have developed a specialized treatment that works wonders on the gut..."

Altair's words dissolved. Her palm was still pressed to Tobias's chest, taking in his haggard breathing, his tortured stomach, and his slow death.

"...then you remove your finger from the anus, and just like that—"

"You need to go," Leila said. "Now."

"The man needs a proper physician. If only you'd listen to my instruction, I happen to know a great deal—"

Leila ripped Her blade from Her thigh and slammed it into Altair's apple, splitting it in two. Seconds of stunned silence passed, and he cleared his throat. "Well then, I'll be on my way."

Altair vanished, and Leila returned to Her task. No more interruptions. It had to be now. With both hands situated, She was yet again flooded with sickness, suffering—every affliction plaguing Tobias's body. Everything She had to end.

"Slow the toxin. Heed your purpose, and do as I command: Give him strength. Let the antidote fulfill its role." She clenched Her jaw. "Give him some *fucking* strength and peace. That is My will and order."

She dug Her nails into his skin, guiding every ounce of power within Her. His pulse thumped through Her like the blood in Her veins, and with it came a shift—his body answering Her call.

The burn of Her touch died, reduced to its usual warmth. Nausea swirled in Her stomach, but behind it there was no darkness, no death —just a calm heartbeat, a battered body, and an antidote working its way through his system.

"Thank you." She exhaled. "Finally."

She scanned the sanctuary for prying eyes, but the men were oblivious, too caught up in their torture. Hoisting Tobias's head onto Her lap, She brushed his wet curls aside.

"Are you done with him?"

A wreck of a man appeared at Her side with a legion behind him. Leila raised an eyebrow. "Come again?"

"Are you done with him? The rest of us are sick too, you know."

"And why is that any of my concern?"

"You're the Healer."

Right. Dammit. "Fine," She said. "Line up."

One by one the men sat at Her side eager for assistance, and assist them She did—with perfumes and incense, Her sham a Godsend to the stench. The challenge became clearer through their company. Bjorne was certain he hadn't prepared his antidote correctly, while Caesar barely spoke a word, only opening his mouth to spew on more than one occasion. Most of the men left claiming they felt restored, and while they swore of the healing properties of Her sweet-smelling vials, She kept silent of the warmth of Her hands—hands that were once again pressed to Tobias.

Strength and peace.

"Hello, Healer girl."

Kaleo stood beside Her, the last man in line. Leila busied Herself with Her satchel.

He took a seat at Her side, and She sighed.

"Oh, was that a hint for me to leave?" he said. "I've never been all that receptive to subtleties."

"Go."

"I've never been receptive to orders either." His cheeks turned up in a smile, but no amount of charm could fill the emptiness of his gaze.

"You know, I don't think you like me much." His voice was smooth, at ease. "I haven't a clue why. I don't believe I've shared more than a few words with you."

"What can I say? I've a habit of judging vile cocks prematurely."

He laughed. "You're funny. I'll bet that mouth gets you slapped around quite a bit, but I appreciate a nasty little tongue."

"Shouldn't you be off writhing on the floor with the rest of them? Or do you happen to be immune to poison?"

"Not at all, I just didn't drink the wine."

His words halted Her. "You didn't drink the wine?"

"Same as our good Dragon and Giant." He gestured toward the other two assassins. "Never had much of a taste for spirits myself. Drinking is such a foul habit, wouldn't you agree? It seems our Artist learned that the hard way. Though I suppose the Dragon is partly to blame for his situation."

"The Dragon?"

"Oh, you should've seen it. He nearly destroyed the Artist's antidote, and right at the end no less." He chuckled. "It was hysterical, the look on the poor bastard's face. I swear his life flashed before his eyes."

"Drake didn't drink the wine, yet he sabotaged Tobias's antidote."

"All's fair in love and challenges."

Leila stared back at him, repulsed. Turning to Tobias, She pressed Her perfumed hand to his forehead.

"I don't understand why you're working so hard to save him," Kaleo said. "Let him die. Is that not what this tournament is for?"

"Some men deserve the opportunity more than others."

"You think the *Artist* is deserving of The Savior? I mean, he is quite handsome, I'll give you that." His gaze brightened. "Say, you're not fond of him, are you? Keeping him alive for yourself. Is that why you're down here?"

"I'm down here to work, a fact you've thus far ignored."

"Oh, come now, it's human nature to mix work with pleasure. Tell me, once you're done tending to the Artist's tummy, are you going to go back to your bedchamber and think of him? Imagine the feel of his skin, the look of his muscular build? Are you going to touch yourself while visions of his cock dance in your head?"

Leila's jaw tightened. "You can be as abhorrent as you'd like. I'm not leaving until my work is through."

"A woman committed to her job. I admire that. I'm much the same way."

"Oh? You take *shepherding* very seriously?"

"That I do."

Nausea filled Her gut, though She wasn't sure if it was because of the sick man in Her lap or the one at Her side.

"Would you like to know a secret, Healer girl?"

"Not particularly."

"The first time I saw you, I thought for a moment you might be The Savior. You look like a little ghost after all, with that white skin of yours."

Her muscles tensed. "Drake is fair. Did you think he was The Savior as well?"

"Yes, it was a foolish thought. I realized that upon meeting Cosima. She is far more poised than you. Plus those *curves*—the power of purity with a body for sin, the irony."

"Oh indeed. Isn't She the most divine piece of ass you've ever seen?"

Kaleo let out a hearty laugh. "I think I know your story. You're a jealous one, aren't you? The Savior gets all the attention, and meanwhile you're down here sitting in the piss and shit with the rest of us."

"Well done, Shepherd, you've figured me out. I'm utterly green with envy. It's as though you see right through me."

"Well, lamb, don't you worry your little head. When the tournament ends and I win Cosima, know I won't leave you behind. Her tits are enough to leave a man hard for days, but I'd wager your eyes are the most stunning I've ever seen." Kaleo's gaze lit up. "Say, I've got a proposition for you. Come our wedding night, I'll fuck The Savior's tits, as any good man would. Then, once She's sound asleep, I'll slip into your chamber, hold you down nice and tight, then slide deep into your cunt. And while I fuck you hard and for as long as I please, know that I will stare longingly into those beautiful eyes of yours. Doesn't that sound romantic, Healer girl?"

An unsettling chill rolled through Her, but She held firm. "I'll be sure to tell The Savior of our conversation. She'll be absolutely delighted."

Chuckling, Kaleo hopped to his feet. "I imagine not. But it won't matter either way. I think we both know that with Her father's blessing, I'm not going anywhere."

The air evacuated Leila's lungs as he walked off. Her hands were shaking, and She grabbed hold of Tobias to steady them.

Pippa plopped down beside Her. "He's still asleep?"

Leila winced, forcing Kaleo from Her thoughts. "Yes, duckling. He's very sick."

"When will he wake up?"

"I'm not sure. He's had a trying day."

"Have You..." Pippa glanced from side to side. "Have You tried magic?"

Leila frowned. "You know full well not to discuss that here."

"Sorry. I'll think of something else."

Pippa fell silent, while Leila focused on the man in Her lap, the hypnotic rise and fall of his chest.

"Still out, is he? I figured as much."

Leila groaned. Altair was back again, staring at Her with his usual criticism.

"He's doing fine," She said. "Now if you'll excuse us—"

"You really ought to examine that head of his." He took a seat at Her side. "Check for injury."

She clamped down on Her lip. "Altair..."

"Head traumas are serious, and if he hasn't woken yet, he likely never will—"

"Say, I have a brilliant idea. Why don't you leave?"

"And?"

"That's it."

"I've got it!" Pippa beamed with pride. "True love's kiss!"

Leila sighed. "That only works in fables, Pippa."

"I can try!"

"It's not polite to kiss boys while they're unconscious."

Altair shouldered between the two women. "I should take a look at him."

"Altair, I don't need your assistance."

"But I'm a physician."

"And I'm a *healer*."

"You should try Guarana." He pointed his nose to the ceiling. "If you're unfamiliar—"

"I'm familiar, Altair."

"It's an instant jolt to the senses."

"*Altair—*"

"Why don't you move aside and let me take a look at him?"

"Why don't *you* worry about yourself and let *me* do my job?"

A strained, shallow breath. Tobias stared up at Leila from Her lap, his gaze weak, and the tension melted from Her bones.

"See? He's awake." She spun toward Altair. "Now fuck off."

8

THE ARTIST

Leila glared at Altair as he walked off. The day was young, yet
She had already juggled too many burdens to count: a nagging
physician, a soulless assassin, the revival of one man, the death
of another.

You are forever marked. You are a murderer.

"Harsh words."

Tobias's voice rang out from Her lap. She hadn't forgotten he was
lying there, but Her eyes remained on Altair, Her thoughts on Qar's
watery grave.

"He's a pest, that one. Always hovering, forcing his unwanted
guidance." She grumbled under Her breath, "The man just wants to hear
himself talk."

"Maybe he likes you," Tobias said.

"Oh, he definitely doesn't like me."

"Because you accused him of murder?"

"Because I'm better at his job than he is. And I'm a woman. And
shut up."

Leila cringed. She should've held Her tongue. She pressed a hand to
Tobias's forehead, but all that responded was nausea. Pain.

"How are you feeling?"

"Tired," he said. "But alive."

"Alive is good. Time is all you need. Lie here for now. Relax yourself."

"What happened?"

You almost died. I saved your life. "Too much hipnayl. Knocked you right out. Though I suppose you could say you got a nice long nap out of it."

"The challenge... How are the others?"

The Poet's ashen body flashed through Her thoughts. She pulled a rag from Her satchel, busying Herself. "Hansel is dead."

"And everyone else?"

"Many are sick. They'll recover soon enough. A few are already feeling like themselves again." She thought back to the line of men She had treated. "Bjorne—he didn't even prepare the antidote correctly, yet he's perfectly fine. It's as if the man's impervious to injury. Perhaps he'll win simply due to his own resiliency."

Wiping the sweat from his chest, She took in his wretched state. "They're saying this tournament is the most savage yet. That the challenges are to get worse. Sovereign's orders."

"I suspect he's looking for the strongest man for his daughter," Tobias said. "That he wants Her protected, since he couldn't protect Her mother."

Leila clenched Her jaw. "I suspect it's something else entirely."

"Can I kiss him now?" Pippa still sat at Leila's side wearing an impatient grin.

"Pippa, run along," Leila said. "He needs his rest."

Giggling, Pippa darted away, the sweetness spoiled by another wave of sickness. Leila rested Her hand back on Tobias's forehead.

Strength and peace.

"Pippa." Tobias's gaze floated Leila's way. "That's her name?"

"Yes."

"And what is yours?"

"You asked Cosima the same thing yesterday. Is this a theme?"

"Apologies, I didn't realize it was a crime to ask who I'm speaking to."

She forced back a scowl. "Leila."

"Well, it's a pleasure to officially meet you, Leila. I'm—"

"Tobias." His scroll appeared in Her thoughts. She nearly smiled. "Goodness."

"Goodness?"

"That's what your name means. Goodness."

"And what does Leila mean?"

She tensed. "Darkness."

"Your name means *darkness*? Your parents must be horribly depressing."

His words prodded at Her, wounding Her pride. She thought to rebut but was distracted by his nose—inflamed and red, as if he had suffered a blow.

"Is it broken?" he mumbled.

"I don't know, let's see." She pinched the swollen mess only for him to cry out in pain. "Yes, it's broken."

Her self-satisfaction was short-lived, ruined by his pained panting. She plucked a perfume vial from Her satchel. "Here. This will help." Light tickled Her fingers as She dabbed the bridge of his nose. *Ease the pain.*

"You and your potions," he teased.

"Are you going to question my work too?"

"No. I trust you." Grunting, he lifted his arm, curling his hand into a limp fist. Faint scars crisscrossed his knuckles, ones that had been bloody just days ago. "You're good at what you do." He dropped his arm to his side. "It's a shame I didn't meet you sooner."

"And why is that?"

"My sister," he said. "She could've used a healer like you."

"Oh? There are plenty of fine physicians in the realm, I'm sure."

"No one *fine* enough to fix a broken spine. Do you have a potion for that?" His eyes flitted away. "Actually, don't tell me. I don't want to know."

The pair fell silent. Tobias went rigid in Her lap, and Leila's heart sank as blackness wisped from his flesh.

"Is she alive?"

Tobias stared at nothing. "From the waist up."

"She's lucky."

"How do you figure? Because she lived?"

"Because she has you. She has *goodness*. And that is a blessing."

His gaze shot back to Hers, though the bite behind it had disappeared.

Leila looked away. "Of course, the tournament has only just begun. You have plenty of time to prove me wrong—to turn your name to shit."

A laugh escaped him, and Leila started, glancing between his dark cloud and his full grin. "A smile? On *your* face? That's a rare occurrence."

"I smile. Sometimes."

"Ah yes, I remember. Your laughing fit at the First Impressions. You got yourself into trouble."

"*You* got me into trouble."

Leila faltered. "Excuse me?"

"Your faces. While they asked their questions. Your faces were priceless."

"You were laughing at *me*?"

Tobias gazed up at Her, dissolving into another fit. "What's that look for?"

"What look?" She hesitated. "Am I doing it now? The faces?"

"No, it's just, you look surprised."

"I *am* surprised."

"Well, what were you expecting?"

"I was expecting you to be watching Cosima," She said.

His laughter died, a blank stare plastered across his face.

"Is he awake?" Flynn called out from across the sanctuary, startling Leila. She gave him a nod, and he responded with wild cheering.

"He's been asking about you, you know." Leila gestured toward Flynn and his circle of comrades. "Have you made friends?"

Tobias mustered a shrug. "I suppose I have."

Leila took in Flynn's smug smirk, his haughty posture, and the bandages wrapping his chest. "He's a handful. Arrogant too. But he has a charm about him. Sometimes."

"I imagine you could describe all the Lords in that fashion."

She snorted. "Zander? Maybe. But the others? Charming they are *not*."

"Is that so? Not even Beau? He seems to have charmed Cosima."

"And it's a good thing. He would've *never* survived today's challenge."

"Why do you say that?"

"You know why," She scoffed. "The man has shit for brains. He could've taken detailed notes on how to prepare that antidote, and still he would've ended up drinking his own piss instead of the ox's."

Tobias burst into laughter, only to wince. "God, no more. It hurts to laugh."

Leila fought back a stubborn smile. "I won't say another word."

"No, don't do that."

His order halted Her, and his prying stare sent Her cheeks swirling with heat.

"You know, I have a theory about you," he said. "And the rest of the court."

"Oh? And what's that?"

"You're all spies."

"Spies?" Tension shot up Leila's spine. "Is that so?"

"You're gathering information about us. For Cosima."

Her muscles loosened. "And where would you get an idea like that?"

"Delphi," he said matter-of-factly. "She knows everything about everyone. And you seem to have us all memorized already."

"Memorized?"

"You call everyone by name. Hansel, Bjorne, Zander. I haven't a clue who you're speaking of half the time."

"Yes, well, when you're lancing pustules and stitching wounds, you learn a thing or two about the people they're attached to."

"Still, I've spent much more time with these men than you, and I'm forced to rely on their laurels."

Leila grimaced. "I *refuse* to rely on the laurels."

"For what reason?" Tobias said. "Because they're trite? Silly?"

"Because they're dehumanizing."

Leila's voice came out hard, Her latent hatred roused, threatening to bubble over—to break through the composure She'd been fighting to maintain.

"When the first man was killed in the labyrinth, Wembleton announced it to the realm. He said, 'Today, a man has fallen. Let us honor *the Jester,* for he died a *hero* in the Sovereign's Tournament,' and the people cheered." She scowled. "I imagine the reaction would've been quite different if he had told the truth. That *Isaac* was beaten to death. That he was murdered."

Red glinted in Her periphery—one of Qar's rings peeking from Her satchel. She slid Her fingers over its polished stone.

"Wembleton made the same announcement for Fabian, for Milo, for Lucian and Hansel. And the people cheered—for the *Farmer*, and the *Benevolent,* and the *Cetus*, and the *Poet*. Nameless beings, as if they were characters from folklore. Well, I prefer to see you all as you are: *men*. With names, with families..." She glanced at Tobias. "With sisters." She took in the crumbling cracks splintering through the wall. "The masses can remain ignorantly blissful if they please. But I'd rather live my life with my eyes open."

A sting pierced Her palm—Qar's ring dug into Her flesh, wrapped tightly in Her fist. She tossed the jewel into Her satchel and turned to Tobias, only to find him watching Her intently. Her cheeks burned. "Well then, it seems as though I've ruined a perfectly lighthearted conversation."

"You've done no such thing."

"You've become awfully quiet."

"I was listening. Your words are quite comforting."

"Oh?" She let out a nervous laugh. "I speak of death, and you're comforted?"

Tobias studied Her. "It's nice. Knowing I'm not the only one."

"The only one?"

"With my eyes open."

The phrase struck Her like a blow. Her mind raced, questioning his meaning, until She met his gaze—calm. Kind.

"You're right," She said. "We're spying."

"I *knew* it."

There it was again—that enchanting laughter, filling Her up like sweet wine. "I trust you'll keep this between you and I."

"Your secret's safe with me."

Leila reveled in the small wonders of the moment—Tobias's head in Her lap, his steady breathing, and the fluttering of Her insides each time he looked Her way.

Cringing, he groaned. "God, I feel terrible."

"What is it?" Leila planted Her hand on his forehead. "Are you in pain?"

"No, it's just, I'm remembering," he said. "The challenge... All those frogs..."

"You're upset about the frogs?"

"There were so many of them. All beheaded. It was a massacre."

Leila burst into giggles, and Tobias shot Her a mocking frown. "You don't understand. You weren't there."

His frown faltered, giving way to a grin Leila couldn't help but mirror. "Yes, well, if you struggle with the death of *frogs*, I fear you'll find the remainder of this tournament quite hard to endure," She said.

"I suppose I'm not cut out for this competition."

"Maybe you'll surprise yourself. Maybe *goodness* will prevail, yes? Wouldn't that be a nice change?"

Tobias didn't respond, but those large, black eyes were still gazing at Her, muddling Her nerves. She looked away, if only to steady Herself, taking in the air around them. His dark cloud had disappeared, however long ago, She wasn't sure.

He furrowed his brow. "Why are you still here with me? You must have others to tend to."

Her palm burned against his flesh, Her light undulating through him. "They're my potions. I'll use them how I please."

"Well, you'll hear no complaints from me. Your lap is quite comfortable. I could lie here all day if you'd let me." He chuckled. "I'm only teasing."

The heat of Leila's face rivaled that of Her power, as Her thoughts wandered to fantasies She had no business entertaining.

"You're a good person," Tobias said.

"What makes you say that?"

"For helping me forget a little bit. About how much it hurts. That's why you're staying with me, right?"

She nearly smiled—until Qar tore through Her mind.

Murderer.

"You've caught me once again."

"I'm wise to your secrets, Leila. You can't fool me." Tobias stopped short, letting out a yawn that turned into a grimace. "God, yawning hurts too."

"You can sleep if you'd like."

"Unacceptable. If you're stuck with me, then I ought to be as good of company as possible. Mark my words, by the end of this day, I will be your favorite patient."

He poked Her in the ribs, and She relished his touch, however brief.

"I'm sure you're right."

Tiny slips of parchment covered Her bed like wilted petals, an organized mess of smeared ink and water stains. Leila read the crumpled notes as She had a hundred times already—a detailed map of Her demise.

"My wedding night. I'm to be killed on My wedding night."

Delphi stood at Her side, gaze flitting over the notes. "They don't say how."

"I don't think they care about the *how* so long as it's done."

Some of the notes were written with care, others were scribbles about marriage and murder. She had tried to count the different handwriting styles but stopped once She noticed Her father's.

"Over there." She pointed to the corner of the spread. "Those are the plans for the ceremony. Antaeus, Drake, and Kaleo are already prepped for the proceedings. Looks as though they find Kaleo most promising. Probably because he's the most handsome."

"Probably because he's the most heinous," Delphi muttered.

"The job will be taken care of that night, in our marriage bed."

"So strange." Delphi kneaded her chin. "Brontes is to have You killed *after* You're wed. That means the crown is no longer his. Married away."

"I imagine that's the point. It eliminates his motive, removes him from suspicion. None of this works if the people hate their Sovereign."

"Their former Sovereign."

"He'll take the crown back. I'm sure of it. That's his goal, after all— to sit on the throne alone."

Delphi's gaze didn't leave the spread. "It's a flawed plan at best. All this work just to kill You? There has to be an easier way."

"I'm sorry, are you trying to help him or Me?"

"I'm just saying, is he really this obtuse, or are we missing something?"

Leila gestured toward a pile of discarded slips, too stained to be legible. "Perhaps they filled in the missing pieces. They're useless now."

"Well, this is good news," Delphi said. "I mean, as good as it gets given the circumstances. Your assassination is a month away. That means we have the rest of the tournament to uncover Your father's network—"

"And kill them."

"Right. So we strategize, slit a few throats, then off with Your father's head. Simple, really. We can manage."

Still Leila eyed the notes, taking in blips of the vultures' plan. *Win. Marry.*

Murder.

"All right, what's next?" Delphi planted her hands on her hips. "Your assassins? There's a number of ways we can end them. They could fall in the tournament, though I don't see how any of the other men could rival them. But perhaps if they banded together..."

Delphi's words faded behind Leila's overflowing anxieties, enough to drown in. All She needed was a single life-giving breath, and so She lost Herself in simpler thoughts, chuckling as the chaos of Her mind slipped away.

"What are You giggling about?" Delphi's voice tore through Her respite.

"Oh, nothing."

"Tell me."

"It's nothing. Tobias—he said something about the last challenge. All the beheaded frogs—said it was a massacre, and he made this face." She pursed Her lips, attempting to mimic him. "You had to have been there, I can't duplicate it. But you would've laughed, I swear it."

Delphi smirked, and Leila's face dropped. "What?"

"Nothing. I'm just enjoying seeing You giddy over a man."

"Giddy?"

"You heard me."

"I'm hardly giddy. We're friends, is all. Am I not allowed to make friends?"

Delphi raised an eyebrow. "You're friends?"

"Yes! He has a delightful personality."

"And what of his warm skin, his sculpted build, and his dark, mysterious eyes? Are they not delightful as well?"

"Well you're awfully superficial." Leila circled Her bed, picking up the notes. "I hadn't noticed any of that."

"Horse shit. You're a terrible liar," Delphi said. "You should know, I've felt his hair. It's rather soft." She trailed behind Leila, cooing in Her ear. "But his body is *hard*."

"Delphi."

"It's something for You to imagine at night...when Your hands are exploring Your womanhood."

"Delphi!"

"You can pretend Your hands are his!"

"Mark My words, I will end you."

The door flung open, and Cosima barreled inside, flopping onto the bed. "He is divine!"

"He is *not*," Leila spat.

Cosima wrinkled her nose. "Who are You talking about?"

"Who are *you* talking about?"

"The Adonis." Cosima chuckled. "Denser than lead, but my is he a gorgeous creature. Quite skilled with his tongue too."

Leila gasped, while Cosima playfully waved Her away. "Don't be vulgar, we just kissed. Well, he kissed me." She winked. "In various places."

Delphi rolled her eyes, and Cosima shot her a glower. "Do you have the slightest idea how many dream of bedding a god of the Sovereign's Tournament? I've been given the rarest of opportunities. I'm certainly not going to waste it."

"But the *Adonis*?" Delphi snorted. "The man has nothing but air between his ears."

"I'm not particularly concerned about what's between his *ears*."

The two squabbled while Leila retrieved the remaining notes, Her hands filled with parchment—fistfuls of Her death. She cleared Her throat. "Excuse Me."

She wasn't sure if they heard Her, but She left Her chamber anyway, shoving the slips into Her pocket.

Asher greeted Her outside Her door, his expression as stiff as his armor. He bowed. "Leila."

A huddle of men stood farther down the corridor—Kastor, Wembleton, and Brontes, who was glaring right at Her.

"Are You all right?" Asher said.

Leila didn't respond, heading off in the other direction and leaving the guard and Her father behind. It had been a full day since She battled Qar, and unlike Her other marks, she hadn't time to dispose of the body. No doubt he'd been discovered by now, and the thought alone turned the notes in Her pocket to boulders.

Upon reaching Her study, She dumped the parchment into a bowl and set fire to them with Her desk candle. The slightest weight lifted as the slips blackened, but their words were already ingrained in Her mind, as was Her father's stare.

Her cloak and satchel hung over Her chair, beckoning. She gnawed at Her lip, glancing between the notes turning to ash and the invitation in front of Her.

Just once more.

She flung the black fabric around Her shoulders and snatched up the satchel, gathering odds and ends for Her certainly brief and unquestionably final journey underground. Bandages, perfume, soap— soon the bag was too cumbersome, and She stuffed Her pockets instead, filling them with peaches before stopping at the sound of a whimper.

Pippa stood in the doorway, her face streaked with tears.

"Little duckling, come here," Leila cooed. Pippa dove into Her arms, and Leila wrapped Her in a hug. "Everything will be all right."

"I did a bad thing," Pippa cried.

"I'm sure that's not true. You have the purest heart of us all."

"I did!"

"Shh, just breathe." Leila sat on the couch, resting Pippa's head in Her lap. "I was just about to visit the boys in the labyrinth. Would you like to join Me?"

"*No.*" Pippa buried her face in Leila's legs. "I can't go back there. I can't!"

"Pippa... Wait. What do you mean go *back*?"

"Romulus made me."

"What are you talking about?"

Pippa looked up from Leila's lap, red-faced and trembling. "I did a bad thing."

Panic seized Leila, though She feigned calm. "Everything will be all right." Propping a pillow beneath Pippa's head, She slid off the couch. "Rest here for now. I have somewhere important to be."

The room around Her burst into rays of light, then faded into black brick and rank air. She tore into the sanctuary, madly scanning the men —nothing unusual, save for Bjorne sitting off to the side with a cavernous hole in his shoulder.

"My God." Leila hurried his way. "What happened?"

Bjorne shrugged and went back to sipping his water. Leila perfumed Her hand and planted it on the wound, giving him a few pulses of light as She eyed the sanctuary.

Tobias sat in a circle with several others. *Thank God.*

"Healer girl." A meaty hand attached to a tall, blond man snatched Her wrist and dragged Her away. *Caesar.* He stopped Her at the back of the sanctuary, where Beau leaned against the wall, snickering like a child, and the Noble—*Neil*—sat on a wooden bench wearing a churlish scowl. He held his cheek in his bloodied palm, but all She could think of was his perverse lines the day they had met.

"You *have* to see this," Caesar said. "It's absolutely vile."

"Shut up," Neil growled.

"Get ready to spew your guts—"

"I said *shut up*, you stupid fuck!"

Leila glanced between the three Lords. "What is it?"

As Neil lowered his hand, Leila nearly retched. A gash tore across the back of his skull, over his ear, and straight through his cheek, the wound wide enough to expose his glossy gums.

Beau nudged him in the ribs. "Open your mouth so she can really see it."

"Fuck you, it hurts!" Neil barked.

"How did this happen?" Leila said.

"Some brute had his way with him." Caesar propped himself against the wall. "Carved him up like a hog."

"One of the other competitors?"

"God, no." Beau grimaced. "It was an ogre in a leather mask."

A pang pierced Leila's chest. Talos had done this.

"Are you going to fix it?" Neil said.

She shot him a scowl. "Not if you're an ass about it."

"He's an ass about everything," Caesar scoffed.

As the men around Her cursed and bickered, Leila pulled a mending kit from Her satchel, threading the needle. *It's linen. Not flesh. Just linen.* "I take it you had another challenge."

"A *challenge*? It was a bloody nightmare." Neil dropped his hand, allowing Her to come in close. "That *thing* sliced us apart one by one. The Physician was set on fire. And that blonde bitch drugged our food."

Leila stabbed him hard with Her needle, relishing his yelp. "Altair's dead?"

"Burnt to a crisp," Caesar mumbled.

Leila's gut coiled—not for Altair's death, but for the fact that She didn't care at all.

"It's not going to scar, is it?" Neil asked.

"Of course it's going to scar," She said. "There's a hole in your face."

"Thought you were supposed to be good at your job."

"I thought you were supposed to be a worthwhile man. It seems we both have reason to be disappointed."

Beau and Caesar laughed loudly, throwing off Her stitching.

"Bitch," Neil muttered. "Someone needs to show you where you belong."

"I belong in the palace of Thessen." Her eyes shrank into a glare. "You'd be wise to remember that."

"Shepherd!" Caesar called across the sanctuary. "Did you see this?"

Kaleo headed their way, winding Leila into a knot.

"Well, look at that." Kaleo shoved his face into Her work. "That's a fine set of teeth you've got. Dragon, Giant, take a look at this poor bastard." He smiled at Leila. "Hello again, Healer girl. How are we today?"

She leaned in closer, focused on Her stitching, but the task was unbearable with Kaleo, Drake, and Antaeus gathering around Her.

"Be careful!" Neil jerked away. "You're killing me."

"I'm sorry, would you prefer I leave your flesh hanging open?"

Neil cowered beneath the resounding laughter. "You owe me." Leila scoffed, but he continued. "I mean it. You're putting me through this hell. Now you get to make me feel better."

She tied off his stitches while Neil eyed Her like a hungry hound.

"Why must you hide behind this cloak? I'm sure you have a lovely figure."

"My figure is none of your concern," She said.

"Well, if you won't let me have a look..." he wrapped Her in his arms, sliding his hands up Her thighs, "...that means I'll have to feel my way around."

He clamped down on Her ass, and She slapped him straight across his stitches. The sanctuary was in an uproar, but Leila didn't share their amusement, shoving Her supplies into Her satchel and storming off. As She cursed to Herself, heavy footsteps sounded behind Her, and a long shadow stretched over the path ahead.

She knew exactly who this was.

She turned to face Antaeus. He had certainly earned the title of *Giant*—he was the largest man She'd ever seen, even taller than Talos and with none of his softness or grace. But She hadn't yet seen him up close like this—face-to-face, or rather face-to-abdomen. Certainly no woman wanted to marry a man She could never kiss. Except Antaeus wasn't here to marry Leila.

He was here to kill Her.

"Do you need something?" She said.

The Giant didn't respond, his beady gaze hard. Perverse.

"Well?"

"You're here to assist us?" His voice was a low, cold growl.

"I am."

"I could use some assistance."

"I don't see any injuries."

"That's not what I'm talking about."

He came in close, engulfing Her in the stench of his sweat. *Run.* Except maybe this was Her chance.

He threaded his fingers through Her cloak, peering at Her cleavage, and She ripped Herself free. "Don't touch me."

She stomped on his foot and shoved his chest—like ramming Her hands into a brick wall. Still he didn't falter, grabbing Her arm and yanking Her forward. The time was now. She reached for Her blade.

"All right, that's enough!"

Tobias threw himself in front of Her, separating Her from Her mark before collapsing abruptly. As he propped himself up, Antaeus glared at him, tense and ready to strike.

"Hold on." Leila threw Her arms around Tobias, hoisting him to his feet. "I've got you."

He staggered through the sanctuary like a newborn foal; bloody bandages covered one of his legs, rendering it more burden than limb. Steering him, She glanced back at Her missed opportunity. "I was handling myself just fine back there."

"That *fuckery* isn't something you should have to *handle*," he said.

His busted leg gave way again, and Leila tightened Her grip, barely managing to keep him standing. The journey was short, but *God* was he heavy, and She let out a long breath once they dropped alongside his comrades.

"The Artist!" Flynn opened his arms wide. "A hero once again."

"*He's* the hero?" Leila said.

"Don't be embarrassed, everyone needs a hero from time to time."

She grumbled under Her breath, "Speak for yourself, Flynn."

The rest of the circle laughed, a mishmash of men She didn't entirely hate. The Cavalier—Zander—sat at Flynn's side, his emerald eyes beaming. His record was easiest to recall, spilling with flowery praise about wealth and chivalry. Enzo was his antithesis, hard and glaring—or perhaps that's just how his face was, with its small, slate eyes and thin lips. Orion fiddled with the spread of cards, organizing the painted symbols She'd memorized long ago; and then there was the Intellect, his once blank, chestnut stare now harsh and irritable. *Raphael.* She thought to offer him a smile but could've sworn he scowled at Her the moment She caught his gaze.

Sighing, She turned to Tobias. "Let me look at your leg."

"Unnecessary. You owe me nothing," he said.

"I'm not doing this because I *owe* you. I'm doing it because it's my job."

Not bothering to wait for a response, She inspected his injury—sloppy and soggy, tied off at the thigh with canvas torn from the tents. She slid Her fingertips over the mess, taking in blips of throbbing. "May I?"

He nodded, and She stripped the wound, revealing a thick gash oozing blood. "Good God. Tobias, this is quite deep."

"I know. I felt it."

"How have you managed walking?"

He shrugged. "Poorly, as you might've noticed."

"I mean it," She maintained. "This is serious. Completely inopportune. You're going to need your legs tomorrow."

"Don't I need my legs every day?"

"You make jokes? Do you think I'm being playful?" She shook Her head. "I can't believe this. Just another heinous consequence of this vile tournament."

Zander offered a sympathetic smile. "The things we do for a woman, right?"

"You think this is for a *woman?*"

The sonorous voice sent the hair on Leila's arms standing straight. Antaeus hovered over them, a fine, red mist coursing from his pores.

"Is that why you're all here? Risking your hides, all for some pair of glowing tits?" Antaeus spat on the floor. "There are only two prizes to be won here: coin and *glory*. And you waste your time chasing a redheaded whore. Dumb fucks, the lot of you. Fools unfit to be called men. Cocks the size of worms, or have you all got any in the first place?"

"Come on now, we're in the sanctuary," Zander said. "This is hardly the place for altercations."

"Piss off, you little shit. I'm not here for you." Narrowing his eyes, Antaeus turned his attention to Tobias. "I'm here for this one."

Silence fell over the space, but Leila's thoughts screamed for violence.

Tobias flexed, braced for a brawl he was in no position for. "If there's an intention to your visit, get on with it."

"You mind yourself, Artist," Antaeus snarled. "You put a target on your back"—his eyes panned to Leila—"protecting *cunts* like this one."

Her hands acted quicker than Her thoughts, ripping Her blade from its sheath and thrusting it into Antaeus's foot.

"You strike fear into the heart of *no one*." She yanked the blade from his flesh, and his agonized howl rang in Her ears like victory.

"You *bitch*, I'll kill you!"

"*Do it*," She spat. "And watch your precious *glory* fade to nothing, as you're barred from the tournament and executed for the murder of a palace official."

Kill him. Antaeus glowered at Her, fists at his sides ready to strike, but She carried Herself as if Her words held truth, the need within Her growing, raging.

Antaeus limped away, and the other men burst into laughter, singing Leila's praises. Still She glared at the Giant, pretending his red mist was a pool of his blood.

She sheathed Her blade. "Now, where were we?"

Tobias wasn't laughing with the others. He was staring at Her, his lips clamped shut. "That was dangerous, Leila."

"Oh, please."

"I'm serious." He leaned in close. "These men...they don't care if you're of The Savior's court. They haven't any respect."

"Trust me, I'm well aware."

"I'm just saying, it's risky, coming down here with creatures like these."

Protests sat on Her tongue, but She stopped short. His eyes had grown large and pleading, and the vision softened Her.

"You're worried."

He straightened his posture. "Well, someone ought to be. You're clearly not."

Her heart beat faster. *Stop it.* She turned to his leg, assessing the damage.

"Should I be concerned?" he said.

"Normally I'd say yes. But you have a secret weapon."

"And what's that?"

She smirked. "Me, of course."

As She wiped down the gash, fire crackled at Her fingertips, eager and alive. She took a vial at random and doused Her hand, filling the air with vanilla—a sweet-smelling lie—then pressed against the wound, unleashing Her flames.

Slow the bleeding.

Tobias's body clenched. "Must you squeeze it like that?"

"Yes. I must."

Mend the flesh. Heat blazed through Her touch, growing and pulsing before fading away. She dropped Her hand, shaking out Her wrist. The gash was still foul, but at least it had ceased spilling over. She pulled a needle and thread from Her satchel, glancing between it and the wound. *Linens. Soft, clean linens.*

"This isn't going to be pleasant," She said.

"Then we'll distract him with pleasant thoughts." Flynn slung an arm around Zander's shoulders. "Like The Savior."

Leila nearly grimaced, but She kept Her composure, pricking at Tobias's flesh.

"God, *She* is something, isn't She?" Flynn continued.

"Her hair is stunning," Zander added.

"*She* is stunning. Her hair, Her eyes..." Flynn waggled his eyebrows. "Her *other* attributes."

"Flynn, the Healer's present." Raphael gestured toward Leila. "I'm sure she doesn't care to hear us gush about another woman."

Flynn let out a snort. "Oh please, no doubt she's used to it by now."

Leila trained Her eyes on Her work, but their worship pierced Her ears like the needle in Her hand. "Ravishing. A true prize." Harmless praise, yet it turned Her stomach.

"Artist." Flynn cocked his head at Tobias. "Have you nothing to contribute?"

Cringing, She braced Herself.

"Apologies," Tobias said. "I'm a little preoccupied. There's a needle in my leg."

Lelia exhaled. As the others continued their worship, She finished Her stitching, clipping the thread and bandaging Tobias's thigh.

"All done." She tied off the dressing. "No walking, at least until tomorrow."

"If I'm even able to walk tomorrow," Tobias muttered.

"You will. Probably."

A weight dropped in Her stomach. Her job was over. With Her jaw clenched, She loaded up Her satchel.

Tobias's head perked up. "You're leaving?"

"I've finished, haven't I?"

"You should stay." He gestured at the cards. "Play a round with us."

"I'm here to work."

"Do you have anyone else to tend to?"

She shook Her head, and he slid to the side, making room for Her. "Come. Play."

His words rendered Her silent, Her thoughts at odds with one another. *You have matters to tend to. But what's one game of cards? He's a waste of Your time. But he was so kind to invite You, and it's only polite to accept.*

This is Your last visit to the labyrinth. To squander the opportunity would be foolish.

Leila took the spot at Tobias's side, swelling with glee once he smiled.

"It's a memory game." He cocked his head toward the slips of canvas spread over the floor. "You flip a card at random. If the card reveals a symbol, you must match it with another. If the card reveals an all-seeing eye, you solve a riddle."

She glanced sidelong at Raphael, who avoided Her gaze. "I'm familiar."

The competitors busied themselves with their game while Leila opted to observe. A circle of handsome, sweaty men—and She was one of them, no different aside from dainty parts and superior hygiene. She watched as they fought over the symbols, laughed when they hounded Flynn, and delighted in their obscene jokes, ones no guard would dare utter in Her presence. The entire spectacle was foreign—six young men regarding Her so casually, as if She wasn't the slightest bit holy.

The other Lords trudged by, kicking Her satchel, and Tobias flung his arm around Her. "Careful," he barked.

Leila's throat caught, his hand on Her waist heavy and apparent until it slipped away. As Tobias returned to the game, She eyed him over: full brows to match his full lips, a strong nose, and large black eyes—except they weren't black at all, their sable sheen perfectly visible up close.

A burst of laughter pulled Her back to the circle—and to Orion, who was watching Her, smiling. Her face burned. "Excuse me."

She headed off to the water barrels, ladling Herself a helping, then thinking better of it upon inspecting its dusty film. A man appeared at Her side, and She flinched. "Raphael." She pretended to sip from Her contaminated beverage. "Enjoying yourself?"

He scowled. "Did you have to *inflict* him upon me?"

"Inflict who?"

"*Flynn.* Who else? He's been attached to me ever since you made me play that stupid game with him."

She glanced back at the group, where Flynn was throwing a fit, cursing the cards and any man near him. "He seemed scared and alone. Like a lost puppy."

"Well, now that *puppy*'s humping my leg, all thanks to you."

"It can't be that bad," She said.

"It's worse. It's *so* much worse. He's *so annoying.*"

"What about Tobias?" Her heartbeat surged. "He seems nice."

"Oh no. I'm not taking any advice from you. You're a bad judge of character."

"I beg your pardon?"

He trudged off without another word, leaving Her gaping. Shaking off the surprise, She joined the group, flashing Raphael a glower before getting seated.

"I'm telling you, Raph is cheating, the cards are lying, and I've had enough of this duplicity!" Flynn crossed his arms, pouting.

"Why don't we play something else?" Zander's gaze flitted around the circle. "That way everyone's happy."

"Not everyone." Raphael met Leila's glare with his own.

"What about you." Orion nudged Enzo in the ribs. "Any Kovahrian games you can teach us?"

Enzo stroked his square chin. "Yes, yes. Games." His voice came out hard, his accent heavy. Flicking his finger, he gestured toward Leila's hip. "You take blade." She wavered, reluctantly tossing Her blade his way.

"Take hand." He planted his hand on the ground. "Spread fingers." He raised the blade high. "Then slam blade—"

Orion snatched up the weapon, handing it back to Leila. "What about a different game?"

Enzo nodded. "You take blade—"

"Any games without a blade?" Orion said.

"You take fist—"

"What about a game that won't leave one of us inevitably injured?"

Enzo went quiet, his mind turning behind his eyes. "No."

Raphael rolled his eyes. "Artist. It's your turn."

Tobias flipped one of the cards over, revealing a sword, then just as quickly flipped its counterpart. Leila bit Her lip. *He's clever too.*

"All right, as it stands, Tobias, Orion, and myself remain in the game," Raphael recited without an ounce of enthusiasm. "Enzo, Zander, and Flynn are out."

"Seeing as the best among us are out, I'd argue that says more about the game than its players," Flynn declared. "And is the most important game not the tournament itself? How's that going for the lot of you, huh?"

"'Bout the same as it's going for you," Orion said.

"Please, I'm biding my time." Flynn leaned back on his elbows. "Waiting for the perfect opportunity to strike. Besides, I have experience on my side. Plenty of conquests under my belt. No need for details. I'll spare your pride."

"And what about The Savior?" Orion raised a bushy eyebrow. "Are you going to boast when you conquer Her as well?"

"Of course not. How offensive. Her Holiness is in an entirely different class than any other woman. They're not even comparable."

Flynn's words slapped Leila across the cheek. She sat tall, piqued.

"Have some respect." Tobias slugged Flynn's arm. "You're making an ass of yourself."

Flynn turned to Leila. "Please, you live with Her. You must know I'm right."

"I have it on good authority Her Holiness sees no woman as beneath Her."

He waved Her away. "Of course, She's The Savior. She's so good and kind. But just because She sees the world a certain way doesn't make it so."

"I swear, how you ever got a single woman to fuck you is beyond me." Shaking his head, Raphael shuffled the cards. "Your cock must be a mile long to compensate for the moments when you open your mouth."

Flynn winked. "A mile and a half."

"It's average," Leila spat.

The circle silenced, all gazes panning Her way. "Come again?" Zander said.

"His cock. It's average. Not particularly long nor short. Just a regular cock."

Raphael glanced between Leila and Flynn. "How do you...?"

"His records from the pool." She glared at Flynn. "So the mystery of how he manages to get fucked is still at large, because his cock is no more impressive than any other man's."

The group burst into laughter—save for Flynn, who sulked while the others wailed at his expense.

As the men continued their game, pinpricks of pain stung Leila's flesh. The throbbing of Tobias's leg was potent enough to leak through him. She unraveled his dressing, dabbing the wound with perfumes and speaking in whispers.

"Mend the flesh."

"Are you talking to yourself?"

Leila froze. Tobias was staring right at Her.

"What?" She said. "No."

"You most certainly were. I caught you."

"I was not."

He chuckled. "You little liar."

"How *dare* you—"

"Don't be cross with me. I'm not scared of you, or your pointy blade, or your vast knowledge of cocks. You can't intimidate me." Smiling, he nudged Her arm. "There's no reason to be embarrassed. We all talk to ourselves sometimes."

He turned to the game, and Her fear faded behind the beating in Her chest.

Hours slipped by, but Leila stayed at Tobias's side, lending him Her light as discreetly as She could manage. Perhaps She should've left by now, but everything around Her was new, a look into a life She would never live. Besides, this was Her final trip to the labyrinth, Her last chance to hear about Orion's sleep talking, about how Caesar beats his cock each morning. And so She stayed, even as Enzo and Zander gave parting in a dense pink cloud, followed by Flynn, Orion, and Raphael, leaving one man remaining.

"Do I have a fever?"

Tobias's voice carried through the sanctuary, soft and deep. She met his gaze, getting lost for a moment, then eyed Her hand—planted to his forehead, burning with power.

"No." She pulled away. "Apologies, I keep checking. It's a habit, really. I must be driving you mad."

"I don't mind."

Blacks and blues littered his face. Scowling, She cupped his cheek. "God, look at you. Your nose...all bruised, even under your eyes."

"It doesn't feel so bad."

The warmth of Her hand pulsed against his jaw. "Yes, well, you have that secret weapon."

She set Her attention on his thigh, undressing, then inspecting his stitches. Better, but not good enough.

Mend the flesh.

"Oh God, I am an absolute cock," Tobias groaned.

"Why?"

"I've never thanked you." He pointed wildly at his various injuries. "You've tended to my wounds, you stitched my leg, you fixed my nose—"

"It's far from fixed."

"Irrelevant. I should've said something sooner. Know that I normally have much better manners than this."

"Tobias—"

"Thank you. For everything."

Leila rewrapped his thigh, eyes locked on Her work. "You're the only man here who's thanked me. Who's even asked my name. So if you think yourself a cock, understand there are thirteen men here more worthy of that title than you."

"There's still no excuse."

The sanctuary was lifeless, the other men tucked away in their tents. The quiet was nagging, urging Her to utter the words She didn't care to speak.

"It seems everyone has turned in for the night. I should let you get to sleep."

"Oh, I won't be sleeping," Tobias said. "I never do. Not much, at least."

"Why's that?"

"It's hard to relax with these sorts close by. Giants. Dragons. *Shepherds*."

"Yes, I imagine you'd have to sleep with one eye open."

Silence. Leila fussed with Her satchel, biding Her time while the passing seconds pinched at Her.

"You can leave if you'd like," he said. "If you must. But don't think you're doing me any favors because of it."

"Would you prefer if I stayed?"

"Only if you'd prefer it too."

You have matters to tend to—a whisper easy to ignore. "Come." She hopped to Her feet. "We'll go someplace else."

"Of course, since there are so many places to choose from."

"There are more than you'd think."

Shrugging, Tobias stood only to crumple to the floor, defied by his battered leg. "*Shit*."

"Oh right, I forgot." She tugged him upright. "Here. Lean on me."

"But you're so small. I'll crush you."

"Oh, shut up. And I'm not *that* small."

Leila led him through the sanctuary, and after some resistance on his part, deep into the labyrinth, barely tottering on the three legs between them. Squinting, She scanned the walls, searching for those tiny red crowns. *There*. The marker sat in the center of a brick, and She pounded against it, disarming an obstacle with an ease that sent Tobias's eyes wide. Another marker, and the wall split apart, revealing a stone stairwell. They hobbled up the steps, the air shifting from humidity to a cool breeze, and sat at the top, leaning against opposite walls.

Tobias flopped his busted leg over the steps, staring at the latched gate above them. "What is this?"

"One of the many paths to the surface," Leila said. "They're scattered throughout the labyrinth so the Proctor can come and go as he pleases."

"And you, of course."

Leila went rigid, though Tobias didn't seem to notice. He gazed up past the gate, captivated by the blackened sky and the scattered stars.

"It's lovely, isn't it?" She followed his line of sight. "I'm like you, you know. I don't sleep much. It started out for the usual reasons: fear, nightmares. I felt haunted, really. But now... I don't know, perhaps I've adapted. But I rather like the darkness."

Tobias smiled. "Just as your name suggests." He turned once more to the sky, closing his eyes and breathing deeply.

A pang tore through Her. "You can't leave. I'd open it for you—let you run off—but Brontes would track you, and you'd be charged with desertion."

"You'd let me go? Really?"

"I'd let all of you go. If I could. This tournament, it's vile. Just like its creator."

"The Sovereign... You must really hate him."

Vitriol filled Her mouth, but She swallowed it down. She plucked a peach from Her pocket, handing it off to him. "Here. Eat."

"Is it safe?"

She snatched the fruit away and took a bite. "Tastes safe to me." She tossed it back to him.

He tore into the juicy middle as if it was his first meal of the day, while She picked at Her own peach, slowly taking him in. She was right about his eyes—a deep brown, close enough to black to be mistaken. His hair was a wild mess of dark waves and curls, shining at a few ends as if dipped in gold. The moonlight illuminated his rich bronze skin, reflecting off his most pronounced features—his high cheekbones, sharp jaw, and defined form. She traced his broad shoulders with Her gaze, slinking down his chest, counting his muscles—four, five, six on his stomach, not keenly sculpted like Beau or Caesar, but still clear as day.

God, he's handsome.

"You're staring at me," Tobias said.

Shit. Leila straightened. "I'm thinking."

"Thinking what?"

How handsome you are. "That you don't look like an artist."

"I'm no artist."

"Is that so? Your laurel suggests otherwise."

"I'm a laborer. I work in the sugarcane fields." He leaned back against the wall. "I *was* an artist. Almost. I was almost an artist."

"Care to explain?"

Tobias went quiet, twirling his peach in his palm.

"It's all right," She said. "I suppose it's personal—"

"I was an apprentice."

Leila faltered. "Oh? For whom?"

"Petros Elia."

"Petros Elia?" She all but spat. "His work hangs in the palace, you know."

"I know. He's a legend."

She swallowed, feigning casualness despite Her eager thoughts. "I imagine it's very hard to secure an apprenticeship with him."

"It was. I worked under his teaching for, oh, I don't know... Two years? Maybe longer. And then I left."

"Because of your sister?"

He nodded.

A grin sprang across Her cheeks. "Goodness." She poked at his chest. "See? I was right. I usually am—though not when I accused you of murder. Nobody's perfect, I suppose. But usually I get it right."

His soft laughter fueled Her smile. She pulled Her knees into Her chest, hugging them tightly to occupy Her restless hands.

"It's your turn, you know," he said.

"My turn?"

"Tell me a story. I told you mine."

"That's funny, I didn't realize we had worked out an exchange."

"It's only fair."

Leila laughed. "Piss off. You don't care about fairness. You're just prying."

"For sound reason. I can count on one hand what I know of you."

"Oh, please."

Tobias counted along his fingers. "You're a healer. Your name means darkness. You hate the Sovereign. And you're an *acquired taste*. Meanwhile, you know...oh, I don't know, at least a *million* things about me, by my approximation."

Leila chuckled, hoping to God She wasn't blushing.

"You laugh at me," he said. "I'm serious, you know."

"You inquire for no reason. You don't even like me."

"Of course I like you."

"You said you didn't." She raised Her chin. "You called me *vinegar*."

Tobias playfully rolled his eyes. "Well, clearly I've acquired the taste."

Her heart lurched, pounding defiantly. *Stop it.*

"How old are you?"

"Twenty." Her voice came out rushed and eager. "We all are. Except Delphi, she's twenty-two. Just a bit older than you."

"See, you even know my age."

"I know a lot about all the competitors."

"Orion's thirty. A full decade older than The Savior. Strange, yes?"

Leila flicked Her wrist. "Oh, that's nothing. Drake's thirty-five."

"*Thirty-five?*" Tobias gaped. "Isn't that foul? And the Sovereign doesn't mind?"

"Apparently not."

"I imagine Bjorne's the oldest man here."

"Quite the contrary. He's the youngest."

Tobias's expression went blank. "You lie to my face."

"I do not."

"But...he's huge! And hairy!"

"I know! It boggles the mind!"

Their laughter echoed through the stairwell. Tobias finished off his peach, tossing the pit down the steps. "We're supposed to be talking about you, you know."

She didn't bother fighting Her smile. "Is that so? I was hoping you had forgotten."

His attention was both a pleasure and a blazing sun too bright to look at. She plucked another peach from Her cloak, carving it in half to avoid his gaze.

"What of your family?"

Tension shot through Her shoulders. "Complicated. Nonexistent."

"You have no one?"

"I have the court. Pippa, Delphi—"

"And Cosima."

She hesitated. "Yes. They're my sisters."

"But aside from them...you're alone."

"Aside from them?" Brontes floated through Her thoughts. "Very much so."

Her father faded from Her mind, as Tobias was still watching Her, a curious gleam in his gaze. "How long have you lived here?" he asked. "In the fortress."

"My whole life."

"And you've always been in The Savior's court?"

The tension coiled around Her spine. "Court girls are recruited at a very young age. Babies, even. Sometimes." She handed half of the peach his way. "It's considered a great honor to work and live alongside The Savior. They claim the court act as advisors, but we all know the truth."

"And what's that?"

"The court girls are confidants. Friendship, bought and paid for."

"Oh... So, do you even like one another?"

Cosima—her green eyes, her painted lips. Leila forced a slight smile. "I love them all. Sisters, remember?"

Tobias nodded, taking a bite of his peach wedge while She watched him intently. "Now that you've properly interrogated me—"

"I'd hardly call it an interrogation," he countered.

"It's *your* turn. Fair is fair."

Tobias bowed, opening his arms wide. "Then by all means, interrogate me."

Leila tiptoed around Her words. "Today, in the sanctuary...Flynn gushed about Cosima. And you didn't contribute. Not once."

"I was distracted."

"Or were you silent by intention?"

He raised an eyebrow. "What exactly are you asking?"

"I'm just curious what you think of Her."

A slow smirk spread across his lips.

"Why are you looking at me like that?"

"You're a spy," Tobias said. "You think I've forgotten?"

"You believe I'll tell Her of our conversation?"

"Isn't that the entire purpose of spying?"

Her stomach dropped. "What if I promised to keep my lips sealed? To never speak of this to anyone?"

"Then I'd say you're a terrible spy."

"Well, I never said I was any good at it. I did reveal myself to you, didn't I?"

An unbearable eternity passed before he finally spoke. "I contributed nothing, because I had nothing to contribute."

Her heart shot into Her throat. "You're not fond of Cosima?"

"It's nothing like that. I just haven't an opinion."

"None at all?"

He shrugged. "I've hardly spoken to Her. Just a few words."

"She's beautiful."

"Yes, She's beautiful," he said. "But lots of women are beautiful."

"You want more."

"Doesn't everyone?"

"No." Leila chuckled. "For some, beauty is perfectly sufficient."

"Well, perhaps I'm peculiar. A misfit, dangerous to society."

He smiled wide, and She couldn't help but do the same.

"Is that it?" he said. "Has my interrogation come to an end?"

His gentle gaze, his hands casually folded in his lap—everything about him spoke of patience and calm, yet She couldn't escape the memory of his black cloud.

"I have one last question for you."

"You have my undivided attention," he said.

"Are you all right?"

"Well, according to you, I have a hideous bruise on my face. And I did get stabbed in the leg today."

"No, I mean... Milo died only a few days ago."

Color trickled from Tobias's flesh. *Misery*. She'd known it was still there. It had to be.

"I wasn't sure if I should ask," She said. "It didn't seem particularly appropriate, but...I think about it, sometimes."

"And what is it that you think about?"

"Your circumstances. They're utterly *fucked*. I think about how you can't just *be*. How you can't mourn, like most people would. Because you're here."

He stared at the wall, boring holes through it with his gaze. "He dies in my mind every morning, again and again. I watch it happen right in front of me. And when I'm not thinking of him, I'm thinking of how to avoid sharing his fate. And if by some miracle I'm feeling calm, or good, I'm reminded that he's dead. And I feel guilty for my brief contentment. For allowing myself a moment of peace."

Ribbons filled the space between them—except they weren't black at all, but an indigo blue.

Sadness.

"I sound like a madman, I'm sure." He raked his fingers through his hair. "Like a wreck."

"You'd sound like a madman if you were anything but a wreck."

His gaze made its way back to Hers, palpable even behind the indigo. She looked away, dragging Her hand through his streams of sorrow; they separated between Her fingers, dissolving into the night air.

"You're content sometimes?" She said.

"Sometimes."

"When you're with Flynn and the others, I imagine."

"I'm content right now."

His words wrapped around Her, warm against Her skin. Then he yawned, and Her heart sank. The night had to end eventually.

"Ah, and there it is." She tried to mask Her disappointment. "I suppose you're ready to turn in now, yes? Would you like me to walk you back to the sanctuary?"

She tore Her gaze from the stone step. Tobias sat before Her clear as day, not a speck of blue in sight, a hint of a smile resting on his lips.

"In a little while," he said.

9

THE REWARD

The faint light of the rising sun coaxed Leila awake. Stirring, She groaned over Her stiff back, the stone wall a paltry excuse for a pillow. She threw Her cloak over Her shoulders, then stopped short.

Tobias was propped against the opposite wall, eyes shut, chest rising and falling. She watched his rhythmic breathing, hypnotized if only for a moment. The sun was still ascending into the sky, making its way above the latched gate. There wasn't much time.

"Tobias."

He didn't move. She grazed his arm with Her fingertips. "Tobias—"

His eyes shot open, and his hand sprang to life, snatching up Her wrist. Gasping for breath, he faltered. "Oh my God." He released Her. "I'm so sorry."

"It's all right."

"It's not all right. It's completely inappropriate."

"It's fine. You're on guard. And in these conditions, that's a good thing." She glanced overhead. The purple sky was beginning to glow, and soon Her skin would do the same. "Let's get you back to the sanctuary."

They hobbled down the stairs and through the labyrinth. Though Tobias's stride was steadier, Her anxieties piqued each time he stumbled and swayed. Her chest hollowed when the sanctuary appeared, and She turned to go, leaving Tobias to totter toward the tents.

"Leila." He stood in the spot where She had left him, staring back at Her. "Will you be joining us this evening as well?"

Your last visit. You said so. You promised. "I...think so."

He smiled.

"Most likely," She added quickly. "I mean, I'm not sure, but I think so. Yes."

"Good. I was just curious, is all. I'll be seeing you then. Maybe."

She fought back a grin. "Maybe."

"Provided I survive the day."

"Have faith in yourself. You're a better contender than you think."

She scurried off, resisting the urge to skip across the grey stone. For once there was no worry, just wild glee carrying Her from the labyrinth to Her chamber, cradling Her when She flopped into bed, lulling Her as She closed Her eyes.

"Leila."

She opened Her eyes. Sunlight beamed from between the marble pillars, the once-purple sky now bright blue—a few measly hours of sleep gone in an instant. Delphi sat at Her side with her braids knotted at her nape, a beautiful pain in the ass.

"What do you want?" Leila muttered.

"Good morning to You as well. I expected to find You in Your garden blessing our glorious realm."

Leila buried Her face in Her pillow. "I overslept."

"I can see that," Delphi said. "How's Tobias?"

"What makes you think I've seen Tobias?"

"You smell like the labyrinth."

"That bad?"

Delphi fished a satchel from the floor. "You also left Your *healer* supplies right here in plain sight. Aren't we discreet."

"I was tired."

"Tobias wore You out nice and good, I take it."

"Delphi—"

"You've got a lot of stuff in here." Delphi dug through the satchel's contents. "Bandages, a mending kit. Are You going to patch up the tears in their pants?"

"The tears in their flesh."

"Ah." Delphi continued her digging. "Perfumes, creams, an *actual* tonic." She pulled out a grey jar. "Leila, this is clay."

"What? I just grabbed any old thing."

"Even clay? In case one of them needs emergency rejuvenation? There is no torture crueler than dry skin."

Leila waved her away. "Shut up."

"What did You do with Tobias?"

"Nothing. I was working. Remember? We have an assassination to prevent."

"I see. And did You learn anything new about Brontes's plan?"

Leila sank beneath Her covers. "No."

"I'm absolutely shocked." Delphi stood, patting down her dress. "Well, fortunately for You, I'm headed to the labyrinth right now, and there's not a single creature down there who could possibly distract me."

"I wasn't distracted—" Leila stopped short. "Wait, you're going to the labyrinth? Why?"

"To prep Your assassins for their reward. They won the last challenge."

"It was a torture challenge. How is that possible?"

"That's what I aim to figure out." With a wink, Delphi headed for the door.

"Wait." Leila shot upright. "If My assassins won the reward, that means they're meeting with Cosima."

"So?"

"Shouldn't we be worried?"

"What for?" Delphi said. "The Savior isn't to die until Her wedding night."

"But still, what if...?"

"They hurt Cosima?" Delphi rolled her eyes. "How will we ever go on?"

Leila scowled. "You'll be seeing Rom there, yes? Tell him to set up an extra tent in the sanctuary."

Delphi arched an eyebrow.

"It's so we have a place to *work*," Leila said. "Away from the men."

"Mhm."

"Some of them are unruly, and having a safe, quiet space would do us a lot of good..."

Leila hadn't finished before Delphi left Her chamber, letting the door swing shut behind her. Cursing, Leila flopped back onto Her sheets, then smiled as the previous evening replayed in Her mind.

Before She could drift back to sleep, Her usual servants bombarded the chamber, dragging Her to the royal bathhouse and stripping Her down. Light rippled through the pool as the girls babbled, effervescent and unburdened in ways Leila could only dream of.

Nyx dug her sponge deep into Leila's flesh. "You smell like a man."

Faun chuckled. "Maybe She's been rolling around with a man."

"Of course not," Hemera said. "She hasn't seen them since the First Impressions."

"How was it?" Damaris looked up from Leila's foot, lathering between Her toes. "Did anyone strike Your interest?"

Tobias's steadfast stare filled the corners of Her mind. "No."

"She hesitated..." Faun singsonged.

"You'll be seeing them tomorrow, yes?" Damaris said.

"Why would I be seeing them tomorrow?" Leila snapped.

Starting, Damaris glanced between the others. "There's a challenge. You're to be in attendance."

Leila's face burned. "Apologies. It slipped My mind."

"She forgot Her own tournament." Nyx shook her head. "Unbelievable. The gall."

"Give Her time. She's just digging in Her heels." Faun brushed Leila's hair in long strokes. "But sometime soon, She'll soften up. And when one of them finally catches Her eye—"

"One of the men has caught Her eye?" Cecily strolled into the space, a ream of fabric over her arm and her brown curls bouncing against her shoulders. "Which one? I'd be delighted to hear it."

"It's *no one*," Leila grumbled. "They're just speculating."

"No one?" Cecily settled along the pool's edge. "Not even a little?"

"Don't push your luck. She's especially petulant today," Faun said.

"I am *not*—" Leila stopped Herself, tripping over words She couldn't speak. "Oh, never mind..."

The girls around Her shared knowing glances. With a gentle smile, Cecily scooted closer, taking Faun's place and running her fingers through Leila's hair. "It's overwhelming. All these men, the pressure. Poor child, I can't imagine." She wrapped Leila's loose locks into a braid. "But love is such a beautiful thing. I want that for You. When You feel it, deep in Your bones, there is no greater joy."

Cecily's touch soothed Leila's nerves, yet her words, however delicate, were wounding.

"How about this," Cecily said. "You don't have to like the tournament. But maybe You can open Your heart a little bit. Allow room for possibility. Can You do that for me? For the girls?"

A circle of large, prying eyes pierced through Leila. She swallowed the lump in Her throat. "Maybe."

Faun laughed. "You waste your breath."

Cecily peered around Leila's shoulder. "We just want what's best for You."

Leila left the bathhouse sometime after like well-washed rope, Her muscles knotted, Her mind wound. Her bed was just as warm as when She had left, yet nothing about it felt inviting. Schemes pinched at Her, urging Her to wield Her blade, but She had no new leads to work with. All She could do was sit in place, staring at Her wardrobe, Her desk, and the black cloak hanging over Her chair.

One more visit. She'd promised Tobias. Well, perhaps it wasn't a promise, but who's to say he didn't take it as such? She sat up straight. His leg. *What if he didn't survive the day?* But his survival wasn't of Her concern. In fact, She should've been worried about Her own survival, but Tobias's yawning gash was gnawing at Her resolve. One tiny voice would be enough to push Her over the edge.

A grunt sounded outside. The door opened, and Pippa trudged into the chamber, dragging a large, lumpy bag behind her. "Let's go see the boys!"

"If you insist." Leila shot up from Her seat, clasping Her cloak and eyeing Pippa sidelong. "What's all that?"

"Meat! For the boys!"

Pinkish blood trailed from the canvas bag, disappearing beneath the door. "Did you bring this all the way from the kitchen?" Leila said.

"Mhm!"

"Did anyone see you?"

"Lots of people saw me! I've got a big bag of meat!"

Leila cradled Her face. "God..."

"Are we going to see the boys?"

"Yes, just please, not so loud." Leila poked Her head out of the room, wincing at the blood heading clear down the corridor. "Take My hand."

Pippa's fingers threaded between Hers, and with their touch came the white flames of Her light. The latched gate to the labyrinth appeared, and they threw it open, winding through darkened passages and barreling into the sanctuary.

Men of all kinds surrounded Her, but no wavy mop. She scanned the space frantically, passing over blond hair, black curls, a red beard.

There. Tobias stood alone in the labyrinth, and Leila went loose, exhaling. She was slow to register the easel in front of him as well as the other oddities in the sanctuary: Zander's harp, Flynn's waster, the rabbit Orion was skinning by the fire pit.

Cursing rang out. Caesar sat cradling a bloody heap against his chest, while Neil and Beau guffawed beside him. Catching sight of Leila, Caesar flagged Her over. "Healer girl."

Leila trudged toward them, avoiding Neil's gaze. She peered down at the mess in Caesar's possession, only to find that it was his own mangled hand, his flesh hanging in tatters. "What the hell—?"

"It was a pig." Beau snickered. "It was a little, baby pig."

"You shut your mouth!" Caesar spat. "I can still pummel you with one hand!"

"Like you pummeled that pig?" Neil scoffed.

Leila pushed past the absurdity, gingerly taking Caesar's wrist between Her thumb and index finger. He winced, and so did She.

"You can fix this, right?"

Definitely not. She dug through Her satchel. "I...just need the right... tonic..." Her gaze floated up from Her aimless searching to the labyrinth.

To Tobias.

"Healer girl?" Caesar said.

"Found it." She plucked a vial from Her bag, dousing Her palms in perfume the scent of peaches. Gritting Her teeth, She pressed Her palms to Caesar's hand, flattening his loose flesh into place.

He lurched forward. "God *dammit*, it burns!"

"Yes, that happens."

"This will fix it?"

"Oh, absolutely."

Her gaze wandered back to Tobias, who was speaking with Pippa. He let out a chuckle Leila couldn't hear, but Her heart swelled nonetheless.

"How do you expect to complete the challenge with one hand?" Beau said.

Caesar spoke between pained pants. "Hell if I know."

Leila's head perked up. "There's a challenge?"

"We're supposed to prepare a gift for The Savior. I was going to offer up my seed, but apparently it doesn't qualify." Neil laughed at his own joke, then eyed Leila, licking his lips. "More for you then."

The easel. Tobias must be drawing, or painting, or something of the like. One last pulse of light, and Leila released Caesar's soggy paw, wiping Her hands clean and bandaging him up. Tobias was alone now. She charged ahead.

"Healer girl," Neil said. "My stitches are oozing."

"That sounds like a personal problem."

She abandoned the Lords and plunged straight into the labyrinth. The air was especially thick, the walls plastered with scorched wood— remnants of a fire, no doubt another tournament obstacle. Ash flecked from the ceiling, sat in piles on the floor, and covered Tobias's hands, cheeks, and chest in streaks and fingerprints. He studied the easel before him, and when he looked Her way, Her heartbeat surged.

"You're standing," She said.

He smiled. "I am—thanks to my secret weapon."

Bandages peeked through the rip in his harem pants. She cocked Her head their way. "Can I look?"

"By all means."

She crouched beside him, rolling up his pant leg and unwrapping his dressing. His stitches were scabbed and settled, the wound grisly but improved.

"Better?"

"Better." She rewrapped his thigh, then hopped to Her feet. "But still, be careful."

"As you wish."

Beneath the ash, his cheekbones were even sharper, as if the swelling in his face had vanished overnight. "Your nose... It seems to be on the mend as well."

"Is that so?"

"Hardly any sign of bruising," She said. "No new injuries, I take it?"

"It appears I've managed to escape the labyrinth unscathed."

"Then I suppose you don't need my assistance."

Leila nearly cringed, cursing Herself for speaking those words. An infinite quiet lingered, leaving Her to pick at Her cloak.

"How's Caesar holding up?" Tobias said.

She let out a silent breath. "You mean his hand? Ghastly. I'm afraid he won't be stroking his wood for some time, the poor thing."

Tobias chuckled. "You're bad."

Heat flooded Her cheeks, then ebbed soon after. Footsteps echoed through the labyrinth as Drake, Antaeus, and Kaleo appeared from the shadows.

"Pleasant evening, Artist." Kaleo winked at Leila. "Healer girl."

She turned away, unsettled by his presence alone. Tobias watched as they walked off, his muscles flexed. "I take it you had no part in that?"

A clean dressing wrapped Kaleo from hip to shoulder, and a wad of bandages encased Antaeus's foot. *Fucking Diccus.* "I most certainly did not," She said.

"Good. Then they'll heal slowly and poorly."

Tobias softened, the tension in his body easing. She cocked Her head at his easel. "Are you drawing a picture?"

"I'm trying to."

"Am I distracting you?"

"No no, of course not. I'm just having some trouble, is all."

"Trouble?" Her eyes widened. "Can I take a look?"

Tobias nodded, and Leila circled the easel, eager to take in his masterpiece.

Nothing.

The canvas in front of Her was blank, not a single mark to behold.

"Oh, I don't know, Tobias, I think this picture is quite emotive." She took Her chin in Her hand. "It really expresses the vast *emptiness* of the heart in peril, the *bleak void* that is the human experience, or perhaps the *blankness* of the unknown."

"Is that right?" he said. "Well then, it appears my job is done."

"Why haven't you drawn something?"

"I just... I can't think of anything."

"Nothing?"

"Nothing. My mind is a *bleak void*, as you would put it." He frowned. "I haven't created anything in two years. I'm afraid I've lost it."

"Oh, shut up. You haven't lost it."

"How would you know?"

"I just know. I'm very intuitive, and I know lots of things." She studied the canvas, squinting. "You just need some inspiration. Or a muse. Or a good kick in the ass to get you going."

"I need help," he said. "Maybe a drink. But mostly help."

"Well, I haven't done anything artistic since I was a child, which means I'm more than qualified to give you some unsolicited advice on the matter, yes?"

"Consider it solicited. I welcome your pearls of wisdom."

"All right then." Leila's mind pored over every art history lesson She'd ever encountered. "Art is emotion—the visual representation of our deepest thoughts and desires. It should come from within—a place of truth and authenticity, yes?"

"Spoken like a real artist."

"Is that so? Then I'll keep going. I think you just need to tap into your emotions. Good ones, preferably, since this is for Cosima and all." She came in closer. "Dig deep. Find that spark to light your creativity. Tell me, what did you feel when you met Her?"

"Nothing."

"Oh. Well, that won't do. What if you cleared your head? Allowed yourself a moment of meditation? Perhaps it'll unlock the confines of that brain of yours."

Tobias scoffed, "Yes, because our current conditions are ideal for *meditation*."

Leila gnawed at Her lip. She was out of tricks, another blank canvas to match the one beside Her. "I have an idea," She lied. "It's an exercise —helps you center yourself, reminds you of your instincts. I'm sure we can use it to rouse some inspiration. Come on, I'll show you."

She was already circling him before he could object, resting Her hands against his back. Hard. Firm. Standing on Her toes, She poked Her head over his shoulder. "God, you're tall."

"I'm actually not that tall, you're just quite short—"

"Quiet, you. We're focusing." She grabbed hold of his arms—also hard and firm. "Relax yourself."

"I am relaxed," he scoffed.

"No, you're not."

"How would you know if I'm not relaxed?"

"Your muscles," She said, mouth dry. "They're tense."

"Perhaps that's just how my muscles are."

She sighed. "Just do as I say."

"You know, it's that exact tone that'll make a man far from relaxed—"

"*Tobias.*"

"I'm only joking." His arms went loose. "Better?"

"Better. Now close your eyes." She leaned in close, waiting for slow-moving seconds. "Are your eyes closed?"

"Of course they're closed. Can't you see that they're closed?"

"I was looking at the canvas."

"Well, they're closed."

"All right then. Take a deep breath. Still your mind. Focus on nothing but the sound of my voice." Her voice lowered to a whisper. "Right now, we're stimulating your guiding light. We're inviting your inspiration to reveal itself. To come to you. Now tell me, what do you see?"

Bullshit, every last word, but She was touching him, and that made it worth it. Tobias's shoulders rose with a deep inhale, and She held Her breath.

"I see...the backs of my eyelids."

Leila's hands dropped. "Tobias."

"I see black. I see nothing but darkness, because my damn eyes are closed."

She abandoned Her spot behind him, cowering beneath his laughter. "You're impossible. I'm leaving."

"Leila, wait—"

"No, no, you're *clearly* doing well enough on your own."

"No, wait, please." He took Her wrist, halting Her. "Do it again—what you just did. I'll be good this time."

His grin threatened to melt Her, as did his touch. "You're humoring me."

"I'm not."

Her insides danced, but She glared at him anyway, hoping Her scorn was convincing. "Fine." She took Her place behind him. "All right then. Relax yourself."

"Done."

"Close your eyes."

"Done."

"Take a deep breath."

His shoulders rose and sank, and She hopped up to Her toes. "Center yourself. Still your mind. Let the inspiration come to you. Now, tell me...what do you see?"

The quiet between them fueled Her anxious heartbeat, sending it pulsing through Her flesh, strong enough to move Her.

"Tobias? Are you listening?"

He flinched. "Apologies. I am. I promise." His voice softened. "Say it again."

"What do you see?"

Nothing—She was certain of it, but She waited regardless, relishing each small wonder: his warm skin beneath Her palms, his cheek against Hers. Joys that were doomed to end.

"Eyes."

His voice jolted Her. "Really? You see eyes? So it worked?" She hurried around him, met by a disarming smile.

"It worked," he said.

"Oh wow, I'm rather excited." She swatted his arm. "Well, don't just stand there. Get to work. Create a masterpiece."

"You give me too much credit."

"I do no such thing. I have faith in you." She stepped aside, gesturing toward his canvas. "Go on then. I'll let you get to it."

His smile widened, then slipped away.

"Is something wrong?" She said.

He raised his blackened hands. "Apologies. I just realized I probably look rather silly."

Rolling Her eyes, Leila slid Her palms down the labyrinth wall, covering Her fingers in ash. She wiped the mess across Her cheeks like rose tint, then dotted Her nose. "Now we both look silly."

"You're going to walk around the sanctuary like that?" Tobias chuckled.

"Why shouldn't I? No one here notices me anyhow."

"That's not true. I notice you."

His words left Her frozen, but Her face burned hot. Quickly, She headed off.

"Leila," he called out.

She spun around, meeting his gaze.

"Thank you," he said.

A warm caress slinked through Her, unwinding each knot in Her body. "Draw something beautiful. I know you will."

She continued on Her way, determined not to look back, fearing Her grin might reveal Her thoughts. *I notice you.* His words repeated in Her mind, the calm intensity of his voice, the smile in his eyes.

The other men swarmed Her, clutching their wounds, and She soaked them in perfume with a level of pep even She didn't recognize. All the while Her gaze drifted to Tobias, who madly scribbled across his canvas, surely creating a work of art worthy of the gallery. Moving from man to man, She glanced between bloody gashes, Tobias, soggy bandages, Tobias, sticky vials—

Tobias was staring at Her. *Do something.* She stuck out Her tongue, hoping to unleash that infectious laugh. A smile flickered across his lips, but it was gone in an instant, and he returned to his scribbling.

Deflated, She finished Her work. Dragging Pippa from the edge of the fire pit, She made Her way to the stairwell, eyeing the labyrinth over Her shoulder. *Maybe I should say goodbye.* But Tobias was fiercely focused, and She thought better of it. They had wasted enough of the day in the sanctuary.

Her last trip. This time, She meant it.

The sisters retired to their chambers, where Leila collapsed onto Her bed, achy and worn. Another day gone and no progress, but then She recalled Tobias's stare from across the sanctuary, and She allowed Herself a slow, secret grin.

The door swung open, and Her bed bounced as Delphi sat at Her side. "How was the sanctuary?"

"What makes you think I was in the sanctuary?"

Delphi gestured toward Leila's face. The ash. "Oh, hell..." Leila plucked a mirror from Her bedside drawer and dragged Her cloak across Her cheeks, smearing the blackness into grey streaks.

"How's Tobias?"

"Why are you always talking about him? I swear, you're obsessed."

Cosima floated into the chamber, her breasts hoisted high. "There She is. I haven't seen our little Leila all day." She wrinkled her nose. "You're a mess."

"I noticed." Leila dug Her cloak into Her face.

"Oh, stop that, You'll make it worse." Cosima hurried to Leila's desk, grabbing a pitcher of water and a rag. "Here."

Taking a seat at Leila's side, Cosima gently blotted Her cheeks. Leila watched her expectantly, waiting for words that never came. "Well, go on then," She said.

"Go on? About what?"

"Aren't you going to tell us about your reward? With the Beasts?"

Cosima dropped her rag, befuddled.

"What reward?"

❧ 10 ❧

THE GIFT

"They were here," Talos said. "Convening with Brontes. Being treated by Diccus."

Leila slumped in Her seat, eyes locked on the bars of the dungeon cell. Talos sat at Her side on his rickety bench, waiting for a response. *Of course there was no reward.*

She spun toward him. "Did they mention Me? I mean, not *Me* Me. Did they mention a healer? Because in Brontes's mind there is no such woman."

"There was no mention of a healer."

"Are you sure? Because I hurt Antaeus. I stabbed him in the foot."

"A man like Antaeus would never admit to being injured by a woman."

Exhaling, Leila rested Her chin in Her hands. "So, that's it? They just...*convened?*"

"They discussed the terms of their arrangement. They were paid half at the start. All three are expected to make it to the Culmination. Brontes will release two, then crown the final man as Champion."

"Horse shit," Leila said. "He'll let them battle it out and crown the last man standing. You know he only hired three of them to hedge his bets."

"After You're killed, Brontes will provide safe passage from the realm. Tell Your people the assassin fled. Give him asylum in the Outlands."

"Horse shit again. He'll torture him publicly."

"You know Your father well."

Leila picked at Her dress. "Anything else?"

"They discussed their plans for You. Different means of...disposal."

Her insides clenched. "You're sure Brontes doesn't know about Me? No one described The Savior's red hair, or her enormous breasts?"

"He doesn't know. Not yet."

Leila raised an eyebrow. "Do I sense a tone?"

"Your ruse becomes more dangerous each time You venture into the labyrinth. Your intentions are sound. But Your methods are..."

"Careless?"

"Brontes will meet with them again. It is only a matter of time before You are discovered. Especially with Your frequent trips underground."

Leila fidgeted. "I got...distracted. Momentarily. It won't happen again." She sat tall. "It was just one day of rest. I'm allowed that, aren't I?"

The dungeon went silent save for the scuttling of a mouse. Talos remained stoic at Leila's side, and Her eyes bore through him, shrinking into a glare.

"Is there something else, Your Holiness?" he said.

"I heard about the challenge."

"Apologies. I did what I must for You."

"I know." She frowned. "But did you have to carve into his leg so?"

He furrowed his brow. "Your Holiness, with all due respect, You said You didn't care for the men. You thought them all fools."

"I still do! Nothing's changed, not remotely." She folded Her arms. "Couldn't you have at least inflicted more pain on My assassins?"

"It wouldn't have made a difference. They weren't being monitored. There was no way for them to fail."

She sighed. "Brontes rigged the challenge. I suppose that's to be expected."

A war waged inside Her, urging Her to scream. Instead She was a statue, unmoving while Her mind ran amuck.

"Little Light..."

Talos's soft voice soothed Her inner torment, a well-timed comfort. "I have very specific questions about My mother this time," She said. "Is that all right?"

"Yes, Little Light."

"Did you touch Her?" Talos wavered, and Leila quickly added, "No, no, not like *that*, I mean... Did you ever hold Her hand? Touch Her arm in passing?"

"I held Her hand once. Kissed it gently."

"How did it feel?"

"Like an honor and a privilege."

Her gaze drifted, Her thoughts traveling with it. "Did you ever catch Her staring at you from across the room? What did you think it meant?"

"I never caught Her staring. But if I had, I would've thought that perhaps She was fond of me. As I had found myself staring at Her many times. And I was very fond of Her."

Joy filled Her chest, warm and vibrant. She breathed it in, then exhaled, pulling Herself back to reality. "I'm late for the challenge. I have to go."

His shackle jangled, twisting Her stomach into a knot. "I am forever indebted to you," She whispered.

A kiss to his temple, and She burst into light. The grey walls of the labyrinth viewing room surrounded Her, and Her sisters appeared in the distance. Pippa was twirling in circles, while Cosima and Delphi paced.

Cosima's eyes widened. "Where have You been? The presenting of the gifts was to start ages ago."

"Apologies, I was working."

"Leila." Delphi threw a cloak around Her shoulders. "We need to talk."

"It'll have to wait."

"We need to talk *now*—"

Romulus trudged into the room, and upon seeing Leila, his face sank into a scowl. "Your Holiness, how kind of You to finally arrive."

"I was retrieving information from a source—one far more valuable than you."

He gave Her a critical once-over. "I'll bring in the first competitor. They've been waiting for some time. Such delays will greatly disappoint Your father."

"Oh, good. You know how much I love disappointing him."

Romulus left without another word, and Leila snorted. "What an ass."

Delphi grabbed Her hands. "I have good news, and I have bad news."

"Now is hardly the time." Cosima marched up beside them. "The men are on their way, and I'm not at all prepared."

"What is there to possibly prepare for?" Delphi scoffed.

"Have you forgotten? I'm *The Savior*." Cosima flicked her wrist at Leila. "You've been off gallivanting, while I've been here, waiting for Your instruction."

"They're just giving you gifts," Leila said. "That's all."

"Well, do I get to *keep* them?"

Footsteps echoed through the portal. "Shh." Leila took a seat in one of the onyx thrones. "They're coming. Look presentable."

Pippa and Cosima did as instructed, while Delphi remained rooted to her spot, eyes trained on Leila. "I'm going to need You to remain calm."

Cosima gestured to the empty throne. "Will you sit down?"

"Will you stop *interrupting* me?" Delphi snapped.

Romulus emerged with a man at his side. Orion dwarfed the Senator in height and build, his rugged appearance contrasting the white fluff in his hands.

Romulus's nostrils flared. "Apologies. It appears the women aren't yet settled."

Delphi glanced between him, the Hunter, and Leila, her eyes wide. She begrudgingly took a seat.

"Good," Romulus said. "Hunter, it's time for you to present your gift. Please, show us what you've prepared."

One by one, the men filed into the room with a gift for Cosima—a fur muff from Orion, a rose from Kaleo, a rather strange interpretive dance from Bjorne. Leila tolerated the formalities, a nuisance delaying more important ventures. Brontes's dealings were still underway, and there were moves to be made.

"*Leila,*" Delphi whispered.

Caesar strutted from the room, pleased with his display, while Delphi stared a hole through Leila as She had for the entire proceedings. "What?" Leila said.

"There are matters to discuss." Delphi eyed Cosima sidelong. "Privately."

"We're in the middle of a challenge."

"Not to mention requesting *privacy* in the presence of others is in extremely poor taste," Cosima said.

Delphi sighed. "This can't wait."

"Then by all means, share it with the room. Let's all hear it."

"I swear, Cosima, one more word—"

"Ladies, the challenge." Leila's voice cracked. "We'll talk later."

Delphi growled. "No one is listening to me!"

"I'm listening to you." Pippa smiled, taking her hand.

Romulus reappeared with another man, and Leila fought back a grin. Tobias.

Greyish-green fanned from his pores. Nerves. How endearing. *Even the greats doubt themselves.*

"Artist, it's time for you to present your gift," Romulus said. "Please, show us what you've prepared."

Excitement flickered through Leila like starlight. She took Tobias in fully, his drawn face, his clenched hands.

Empty.

Where are his drawings?

"Apologies. It is with great humility and regret that I inform You...I was unable to complete the challenge." Tobias took in a breath. "I have nothing for You."

Leila's jaw went slack, Her starlight snuffed.

Romulus's eyes shrank into slits. "Artist, repeat yourself."

"I have nothing," Tobias said. "No gift."

A groan tore from Leila's throat, and She cradled Her face, wearing his shame as Her own.

"You dare to disrespect The Savior by withdrawing from today's challenge?" Romulus barked.

"It was not without effort. I by no means intended—"

"Silence! This insolence will not be tolerated. Know that the matter will be handled with swift and stern action."

Leila sat up straight.

Brontes.

"I understand." Tobias turned to Cosima, his gaze pleading. "And please believe me when I say I am so, so sorry—"

"Enough!" Romulus ordered. "*Kneel*, Artist."

Tobias did as he was told, while Leila anxiously bounced Her knee. *Swift and stern action.* No, that wouldn't be happening.

"You're dismissed."

Tobias rose and left, not bothering to look back. Seething, Leila turned Her attention to Romulus, a vision of complacency.

"You seem distressed." His voice was smooth, almost pleased. "Are You offended by the Artist's poor display?"

"He will not be punished," She said.

"That is not for You to decide."

"I command you—"

"Your father reviews all tournament challenges, all results and rulings. There is no reality where that man goes undisciplined."

Leila grimaced. "My father doesn't *care* about this tournament—"

"But Your people care, and Brontes caters to their favor. You must know there are systems in place solely for occurrences such as these."

"Systems? What kind of systems?"

"Why do *You* care, Your Holiness?" Romulus cocked his head. "He is but one man. Several have died before him. Where were Your protests then?"

"Don't you dare turn this around on Me—"

"I will do no such thing," he said. "In fact, I'm removing myself from this discussion entirely. The men have waited long enough. I'll bring in the next."

"Romulus, if you even think—"

He left the room, following in Tobias's footsteps. Leila spun toward

Her sisters. "Can you believe him? He just walked out on Me! *I* am *his* master!"

"Well then, I suppose we're starting with the bad news," Delphi mumbled.

"You *knew* about this?" Leila spat.

"I'm sorry, why are we so flustered?" Cosima fiddled with one of her many trinkets. "I'm not sure I'm following the commotion. All this upheaval for...the Artist?"

"Oh, you'll like the Artist," Pippa said. "He's kind, and friendly, and very gracious. And he shares his food, which Faun says is the sign of a generous lover. I'm not certain what that means, but surely he must love an awful lot."

"Can we focus, please?" Leila barked.

They couldn't, as Romulus arrived with Flynn at his side, ready to bestow a gift upon The Savior. Cosima was happy to partake in his swordsmanship lesson, but all Leila could do was stew over Tobias's fate. *Why didn't he draw something?*

All the competitors lined up before Her. The challenge was over, decisions had been made, while Leila fell prey to Her havocked thoughts. Tobias's green mist entered before he did, and his fear did little to quell Her own.

"Your challenge is finished. The Savior has reviewed the gifts presented, and a winner has been chosen." Romulus's gaze swept the men. "The winner of today's challenge is the Prince. Your reward is extended time in The Savior's company. You will be summoned shortly, this afternoon."

Flynn beamed. "And I look forward to it."

"Now, for more pressing matters," Romulus said. "This challenge, unlike some of the others, wasn't designed to have a *loser.* However, in light of recent events, changes have been made. One of you has failed to complete today's challenge, and thus steps have been taken to...*correct* this matter."

Curious whispers filled the room, while nausea heaved in Leila's gut.

"Any man here today must be fiercely devoted to the tournament. Willing to risk his life, to do all that is asked of him for the sole purpose of pleasing our Savior. If this doesn't describe you—if you are unwilling to lay down your life for the woman before you—then you are unfit for the Sovereign's Tournament. You are unworthy."

Romulus's words came out severe—well-rehearsed lies fed straight from Leila's father.

"Right now, I present you with a task. Each of you will have the chance to nominate a single competitor, one whom you believe is unworthy of this tournament." Romulus glared at Tobias. "And we'll start with the Artist, seeing as *he* was the only man unable to complete today's challenge."

Tobias's mossy cloud burst around him, painting the walls in his disgrace.

Romulus instructed him to step forward, his voice coming out in snaps and growls. "Who do you believe is most unworthy of this tournament?"

Tobias's carriage was strong, the churning of his thoughts explicitly clear through his tight jaw, his pensive gaze. He looked straight at Leila.

"The Giant," he said.

Leila's stomach dropped. Antaeus's frame shifted, his teeth gritted— an assassin ready to spill blood.

"And what is your reasoning?" Romulus said.

"He's admitted time and again that he isn't here for The Savior. He's referred to Her in lewd terms, has openly confessed he cares not for Her but for coin and glory exclusively." Tobias's eyes narrowed. "And his contempt extends past words, as he has murdered a man for defending The Savior's honor and assaulted a woman of The Savior's court—"

"You fucking *shit*," Antaeus hissed.

"Silence." Romulus raised a hand. "Artist, you may step back. Giant, since your name has been called, you are next to speak." He waited as Antaeus came forward. "Who do you feel is unworthy of this competition?"

"The Artist," Antaeus spat. "Cunty little shit didn't even complete the challenge. Hasn't the cock to stand beside us men, nor the stones and spine to wear the crown." He glowered at the line of men. "And I dare any one of these fucks behind me to say any other name but his."

Another man stepped forward, then another, though they were a blur in Leila's vision. All She could comprehend was the laurel leaving each of their mouths.

The Artist.

Antaeus stood smugly in line, content in his dominance, and his haughty posture only aggravated Leila's rage. Flynn was called forward, then Orion, and their nominations broke the trend. *"The Giant,"* they said, as did the rest of Tobias's allies, and though She wanted to feel hopeful, it was futile.

There are systems in place.

"Each of you has spoken," Romulus said. "The nominations have been made. Six votes for the Giant, and eight for the Artist. Due to the nature of the information presented, there is only one possible course of action. Tomorrow, in our first public viewing at the fortress arena, the Giant and the Artist will fight to the death."

Loathing ignited within Leila, and She ran from the room.

"Leila, wait!" Delphi's voice echoed behind Her, but Leila didn't stop. A hand seized Her shoulder.

"Leila—"

"Not now." She ripped Herself free.

Delphi grabbed Her wrist. "Come with me." She yanked Leila forward, leading Her toward a speck of light in the distance—torches, water barrels, wooden benches.

"The *sanctuary?*" Leila staggered backward. "No. Absolutely not."

"Just move."

Delphi pulled Her through the sanctuary, shoving Her into one of the tents. A table and chair sat in its center as opposed to the standard cot. This was the tent Leila had requested, though that didn't matter much now.

"He took pity on frogs, Delphi. *Frogs.*" Leila paced as Delphi snatched up a series of scrolls from the tent's corner. "You know how fond I am of animals, but in these conditions, such compassion is a curse. God, right then and there, I should've known he was a dead man. But no, I sat there thinking *he's so sweet. He's so charming.* Yes, what a charming dead man. Dead men are such charmers. And don't you dare say *I told You so,* because I swear to God, I am in no mood—"

"*Look,*" Delphi said.

Four canvas sheets lay on the table—one a scrawled, blackened mess, the others like looking into a mirror.

Portraits.

Leila's throat caught. Intricate charcoal drawings, each in Her likeness. Every strand of hair, the light in Her eyes, even the freckle above Her cheek—all of it was captured with meticulous detail, with attention and care.

She forced Herself to speak. "Who—?"

"Who do You think?"

She tried to breathe, managing little more than a quiet gasp.

Tobias.

Delphi gestured toward the canvas covered in scribbles. "Looks like he got frustrated with himself on this one, but the rest of them... All You."

He drew Me. On the outside Leila stood paralyzed, but Her chest was swimming with life and vitality.

"He's quite talented," Delphi said.

"He's brilliant. This is not apprentice-level work."

"Are You all right?"

"Apologies. I just..." Leila's lips stilled, Her gaze fixed on the drawings.

"Tobias... I'd wager he's very fond of You. Do You feel the same?"

Another breath. Leila tried to center Herself, but everything was muddled and raw. It was both the best and worst feeling—too much and not enough at all.

"Leila?"

"I can't believe he did this." She turned to Her sister. "What does this mean? What if this is just some cruel joke?"

"How could this be a joke?"

"I don't know... What if he's just...just playing with Me?"

"He humiliated himself in front of the court, the Proctor, his entire competition," Delphi said. "And he is to fight to the death tomorrow. You think he'd risk so much just to tug at Your heartstrings?"

The words were of little comfort. Dread picked at Leila's mind, leaving Her doubts bloodied and exposed.

"You're nervous." Delphi spoke in hushed tones. "It's completely natural."

"I'm not nervous," Leila snapped. "I'm just...a little overwhelmed, is all."

"You know You need to speak with him, yes?" Leila nodded, and Delphi's voice darkened. "He's to fight the Giant tomorrow."

"I know."

It was Delphi's turn to be quiet, staring at Leila with a knowing gaze.

"What?"

"It's not my place to make decisions for You," Delphi said. "But if a kind, gentle man were to express such fondness for me—and I were of the disposition to enjoy kind, gentle men—I'd help him with such a perilous endeavor. Use my resources to ensure his win. If I had resources. Like You do."

"I could expose Myself."

Delphi cocked her head at the portraits. "It appears he's already exposed himself a bit, hasn't he?"

Fiddling with the folds of Her dress, Leila turned once again to the drawings.

Delphi gave Her a squeeze. "I'll leave You with Your thoughts."

He drew Me—the only words on Leila's mind as Delphi disappeared, and for an eternity afterward. One portrait detailing Her face, another with a glow cast over Her hair, a third with ash smeared across Her cheeks, and a blackish mess with the word *FUCK* written through its center; She opted to ignore the last one. *Three wonderful portraits.* This was surely something from a dream, or at least one of those erotic scrolls She'd read late at night. She nearly expected the canvas slips to disappear, a vision fabricated by Her fantasies, but they remained before Her. All beautiful. All real.

Delphi was right. She needed to speak to him.

Oh God. I have to speak to him.

Joy morphed into panic. Gnawing at Her lip, She paced the tent, fighting to muster the right words. Noise filtered through the space; the men had arrived, however long ago, She wasn't sure, and their presence wound Her tighter. Wrangling confidence, She practiced.

"Tobias, I had no idea..." She cringed. *Too presumptuous.*

"Tobias, I demand an explanation." *Too forceful.*

"Tobias, if this means what I think it means... God, *does* it mean what I think it means?"

Cursing, She resumed Her pacing. If only Cosima were here. She'd know what to say. Meanwhile time slipped through Her fingers, the floor beneath Her surely wearing away with each step.

"Tobias." *Maybe starting with his name isn't a good idea.* "Good day to you. As you can see, I've come across these stunning portraits." *Beautiful portraits. Lovely portraits?* "I've come across these lovely portraits. Can you tell Me, by chance, what this means?" *Too prying. Needs finesse.* "I was wondering...if I could inquire as to the meaning behind this delightful gift." *No.* "Gesture."

Perfect.

"Good day to you. As you can see, I've come across these lovely portraits. I was wondering if I could inquire as to the meaning behind this delightful gesture."

You're a natural.

The tent flap flew open, and Pippa frolicked inside. "Delphi sent me to check on You." Her gaze flitted to the portraits. "Oh, pretty!"

"Little duckling, if a man were to give you a gift like this, what would you say to him?"

"I'd kiss him," Pippa said.

"Anything else?"

Pippa closed her eyes and puckered her lips.

Leila sighed. "Can you do Me a favor? Could you go fetch the Artist for Me?"

"Are You going to kiss him?"

"No. Well..." She shook Herself. "Can you just fetch him?"

As Pippa darted from the tent, Leila's heart rate climbed. "Good day to you..." She repeated Her words, the slightest bit soothed each time they left Her lips.

The tent rustled, and Tobias stumbled inside, staggering to a halt. His eyes locked with Hers.

The words were gone. She had no words. Where were Her words?

He stared down at the portraits and froze. "Oh God."

Dammit, say something! "Can you explain this?" She choked out.

"How did you get those?"

"Delphi." Her voice cracked. "Did you really think you could just toss them aside and no one would notice?"

Color lifted from his flesh—hideous green spots. "Please, Leila. You can't tell anyone. If this gets out..."

"What is this?"

"I didn't mean—"

"I need to know." She clenched her jaw, Her cheeks flaming. "I need to know what all of this means. Because if this is some...some joke..."

He stepped forward. "Leila—"

"If you blew the whole challenge to taunt me—"

"Leila, please—"

"Because this is serious, and if you can't see that—"

"For God's sake, I tried!" he said. "I tried, I just... I saw you." His voice softened. "I saw you."

Swirls swam through his greenish cloud, permeating his fear with something new.

Pink.

It billowed through the tent in rivers, and when it washed over Her, She swore She could feel his heartbeat, could taste sugar and cinnamon. The ugly green mist was still there, but *God*, there was so much beauty, growing, surging.

All for Her.

She breathed in deeply. "Tobias..."

"You can't tell anyone. You can't tell Cosima."

She trailed Her fingers over the portraits. "Tobias, these—"

"You can't—"

"*These*"—She pointed to the drawings—"are beautiful."

Tobias wavered. "Come again?"

"Absolutely remarkable. The most wonderful portraits I've ever seen. Not solely because they're of me, mind you. I'm certainly biased, but I'm by no means vain. No, they're all, individually, quite stunning. Amazing, really." She plucked up one of the drawings. "This one—it's the stairwell, isn't it? When we sat together in the stairwell. It's so apparent. You can distinctly make out the glow of the moonlight." She grabbed another. "And this one... Well don't just stand there, come look."

She burst through his pink cloud, grabbing his wrist and pulling him toward the table. "This one." She held out his drawing. "The stark contrast between the light and the shadows. You didn't learn that from Petros, did you?"

"It's mine." He cleared his throat. "My own technique."

"I *knew* it. It's different. Poignant, even haunting. Elegant, but dark."

"Your name means darkness."

She gazed up at him, slack jawed. "Is that what that is? Tobias, that's utterly brilliant." Her mind moved quickly, taking Her back to the drawings. "Now *this*—the keen attention to detail. That's from Petros, yes?" Tobias nodded, and She grinned. "I can tell. His influence is unmistakable. But you...*you* are your own creature. An original. It fascinates me, how you can train under someone so closely and still carve your own path. The authenticity—this looks like your art and no one else's." Her face flushed. "I'm sure this is all so trite to you, you probably hear this all the time."

"I don't hear this. Ever."

Leila scoffed. "How is that possible?"

Tobias didn't answer, or perhaps She hadn't waited for a response. She snatched up another drawing. "Look at this one. The smudges. You drew the smudges on my face." Chuckling, She shook Her head. "Tobias, you're so silly."

She turned to the spread again, stopping at the canvas ravaged by scribbles. "It seems you got a bit frustrated with yourself on that one. The mark of a perfectionist. I get frustrated with myself all the time. And *here*." Another portrait, and another flurry of thoughts She couldn't contain. "You even got my freckle. How you noticed it to begin with is beyond me. You miss no detail, do you? I'm rather fond of my freckle, you know. It's the only one I've got. Oh God, I'm rambling, aren't I?"

"No, no—"

"It's the excitement. No one's ever done anything like this for me. It's all just a little..."

She took in an unsteady breath. Each of Her emotions brimmed at the surface, threatening to spill over. It was all too much. Too amazing.

Tobias rested a hand on the small of Her back. "Leila..."

"They're perfect," She said. "The most incredible gifts I've ever received... Well, I suppose I didn't *receive* them, per se. You threw them away. But I'm still counting them as gifts. I get to keep them, right?"

"Of, of course."

"I'll keep them private. In my chamber. No one will know."

He nodded. "Thank you."

She dragged Her fingers over the portraits, passing through his streams of pink. "I do receive gifts on occasion but...nothing like this." She met his gaze. "I can't believe you did this."

Tobias stared at Her, silent. She hadn't noticed how close he was, how his skin against Hers both soothed and awakened Her nerves.

"Leila..." he said softly. "Why did you summon me?"

"I just wanted to thank you."

The tent had filled with color—more pink than Leila had ever seen, enough to get lost in. But that ugly green soup was still there, marring the beauty.

Tobias was fond of Her. He was also terrified.

Leila squared Her shoulders. "And now, I'm going to help you kill Antaeus."

❧ II ❧

THE BLESSING

L eila quickened Her pace through the labyrinth. "Hurry. We haven't much time."

Tobias and Flynn followed far too slowly for Her liking, muttering amongst one another as if the severity of the moment was lost on them. There was a battle to prepare for, an assassin against an artist. A father against a daughter.

She stopped in front of the wall. *Here.* She was sure of it. Hastily, She peeled off the blackened wood, brushing away the pungent soot until the tiny red crown was barely visible. One push of the marker, and the bricks retracted, revealing a stairwell toward the surface above.

"Bloody fuck, will you look at that?"

Flynn's voice faded behind Her. She darted up the stone steps and out of his and Tobias's line of sight.

The training room.

Light engulfed Her, and She stood in a vast palace room made entirely of white marble. Blades, swords, and spears lined the walls, and antiquated helmets and armor sat neatly on shelves. She dashed toward the corner, scooping up wasters, wooden staffs, and a handful of crinkled scrolls.

The stairwell.

The scent of burnt wood invaded Her nostrils. Grey steps extended below Her, and She headed down, meeting an expectant Tobias and a fumbling Flynn in the labyrinth.

"All right. Let's get started." She plopped Her things onto the floor. "Clear the area."

Tobias went to work, while Flynn dawdled at his side, frowning. "You know, neither of you have asked about my time with Cosima."

"Yes, well, we have far more pressing concerns at the moment, as I'm sure you're aware," Leila said.

"Well, it's awfully rude. I feel slighted, really."

"You can tell us all about the feel of Her breasts some other time."

Flynn did a double take. "Wait, I never said I felt Her breasts. I mean, I never said I didn't either. I mean... Wait, what has She told you?"

Groaning, Tobias dropped his armload. "Will you just shut up?"

"I will not. Didn't you two explicitly request my assistance?"

"Yes, and I'm regretting that decision," Leila mumbled.

"And why are you helping him, anyhow? Not that I'm against it. I'm rather fond of the poor bastard, myself. I'm just confused. Does Cosima not like Antaeus?"

"*I* don't like Antaeus. To hell with Cosima." Leila wavered. "No disrespect, of course."

Flynn muttered behind Her, but She ignored him, scanning Her procured parchment. "First order of business: the advantage." She unrolled one of Her scrolls—the weapons inventory. "Judging by history, Antaeus will be selecting both his weapon and yours."

"Fucking hell," Tobias grumbled.

"This could certainly make training precarious, but fortunately for us, Antaeus is a predictable shit. The man fights for glory. He will choose his weapon based on the roar of the crowd. Of course, the crowd doesn't know a thing about fighting, so they will roar for whichever weapon appears the largest—the most gruesome."

"You say this as if it's a good thing," Tobias said.

"Just because a weapon looks fierce doesn't mean it's the wisest decision. A gruesome weapon isn't necessarily swift or maneuverable. But he'll choose it anyway, because he's stupid. And proud, but mostly stupid." She took root at his side, displaying Her scroll. "These are his options. Which do you think he'll choose?"

His eyes panned the painted images, moving from piece to piece before honing in on a long staff with a large, hooked blade. "Good God..."

Leila nodded. "The bardiche. I thought the same. A Kovahrian weapon, hence the grim appearance. Lethal, but certainly a questionable choice for the arena. And since he's picking yours, we should prepare for that as well. Tell me, which weapon looks the most pathetic?"

Frowning, Tobias pointed to the bottom corner of the scroll at a short, plain sword.

"The gladius of Northern Thessen. Still a fine weapon, but compared to the others, it's a flaccid cock." Leila gave a dismissive flick of Her wrist. "It's of no matter. You can kill a man with a gladius all the same."

Flynn wedged between them. "You know a lot about weapons for a woman."

"How observant you are," Leila said. "Next you'll tell me my hair is brown."

"I thought it was black," Flynn muttered to Tobias.

Tobias scowled at him. "It's brown."

Leila sighed. "Second order of business: assessing our opponent's weakness. Antaeus is a professional fighter. He's large, he's strong—"

"None of these sound like weaknesses," Tobias said.

"But that's where it ends. He has build and brute force, and nothing more."

"I do hate to be the withered tit, but isn't brute force really all you need in a fight to the death?" Flynn scoffed.

Leila spared him a glare and turned to Tobias. "*You* are smart. Creative. You can use this against him—turn his stupidity into a tactical disadvantage."

Tobias shook his head. "Apologies, but I'm failing to see how my *creativity* is an asset for tomorrow."

"You'll find opportunities. Take the arena, for example. It'll be adorned in some way. In tournaments past there were glass walls, sinking sand. Once the men fought blindfolded."

"Wonderful," he mumbled.

"It is. For you, at least. A fool will fall victim to the arena, but a cunning man will use it to his benefit. Antaeus knows only how to wield a weapon. He doesn't know how to work the elements in his favor."

"Though I'd argue the weapon-wielding is rather important," Flynn said.

"Which is our final order of business: we practice." Leila sorted through Her things, handing a waster to Tobias. "A gladius for you..." She tossed a staff to Flynn. "A bardiche for you..." She took the final staff. "And a bardiche for me."

Chuckling, Flynn slugged Tobias's arm. "She gets one too. Isn't that precious?"

Leila raised an eyebrow. "Come again?"

"I'm just saying, it's awfully kind of you to want to assist, but perhaps you should let a trained fighter do the honors."

She spun Her staff and slammed it into the pit of Flynn's gut, then once more across his back.

"I'm getting tired of this one." She gestured toward Flynn, who was writhing on the floor. "I don't know how you put up with him all day."

"You can *fight*?" Flynn wheezed, climbing to his feet.

"Of course I can fight! What do you think the slits in my dress are for?"

"To entice men with the subtle glimpse of your milky thighs."

Tobias cradled his face in his hands. "*God...*"

"Ignore him. We haven't time for this." Leila nodded at Tobias. "Go on, take your stance."

"What stance?" Tobias said.

"Your fighting stance."

"There's a stance?"

"Wait..." Flynn furrowed his brow. "You don't know how to fight?"

"Of course not. I'm an artist. Why would I know how to fight?"

"Your tutors never covered the art of swordplay?" Leila said.

"*Tutors?*" Tobias glanced between the two of them. "I live in a village."

"I don't follow." Leila turned to Flynn, befuddled. "Do you follow?"

"Not really. I've never been to a village."

"I *had no tutors*." Tobias leaned in closer, speaking as if to a child. "I live in a *village*. My entire home is smaller than the sanctuary."

"*Seriously?*" Flynn said.

"Never mind that, we must continue." Leila grabbed Tobias by the wrists, pulling him into the center of the tunnel. "*This* is a fighting stance. Your feet..." She kicked his sandals, pushing them apart, "...the same width as your shoulders. Your knees bent. Your body squarely facing your opponent."

She wrested his hips into place, and pink burst from his body like loose sugar. She eyed him sidelong. "Are you going to be able to concentrate?"

His cheeks reddened. "Of course I can concentrate. Why wouldn't I be able to concentrate?"

Nodding, She guided his forearm. "Elbows bent. Your sword— pointed at me." She hesitated. "I suppose that's incorrect. Your opponent is much, much taller than I am." Fuchsia wafted from his flesh as Her fingers traveled up his arm, positioning his sword. "Much better. You'll wield your weapon with one hand. Leave the other free. You never know when you'll need it—to disarm your opponent, or maybe to punch him in the cock. I don't know why you'd punch him in the cock, I just rather enjoy the thought of it."

"Oh, she's brutal," Flynn mumbled.

Leila set Her attention on Tobias's waster. "The gladius holds a set function, but since it's likely your sole aid in this fight, we'll have to improvise—put it to use in a variety of ways. For this endeavor, your weapon will serve three purposes: to block, to cut, and to thrust." She took Tobias's arm, guiding his movements. "You block for protection. If you can deflect or counter, all the better. Dodging Antaeus's moves will be your primary objective, but if you cannot dodge..." She angled his waster in front of his face, "...the gladius is your shield."

Tobias's attention didn't waver, and his steadfast stare made Her stand taller.

"You cut to weaken. A good slash at the tendons goes a long way. And when you swing, you use your whole body." Her hand followed the path of Her words, tracing his form. "Your legs will become tense, the movement will flow up into your gut, you'll feel it in your chest, and then it'll travel through your arm, into the blade."

Her fingers swept up his abdomen, and pink followed Her touch, marking his body with swirls.

"You thrust to kill. You'll carry the intention in your arm and shoulders. A firm, powerful push is all you need." She drove his arm forward. "Thrust. Make contact, and you win the battle."

Tobias stared back at Her, seemingly focused, but the colorful cloud around them said otherwise. She breathed him in, filling Her lungs with sweetness.

"Am I the only one who found that extremely erotic?" Flynn said. "There's something about violence that really gets the blood flowing. Or maybe I'm still worked up from my reward with Cosima—the one *neither* of you has asked about."

The pink dissolved, and Leila cleared Her throat, backing away. "We'll cover the kill later. For now, we practice." She raised Her weapon. "Ready?"

Tobias assumed his stance. "Ready."

With a swift swing of Her staff, She swatted the waster from Tobias's grasp.

"Tobias!"

"What?"

"Hold firm!"

"Apologies. I'm a novice, remember?" He snatched up his waster. "All right. Ready."

She brandished Her staff once again, slapping Tobias in the gut. Coughing, he staggered forward. "*Son of a*—"

"Tobias!"

"What?" he barked. "*You* hit *me*."

"Yes, and you're *supposed* to block it. Or at least hit me back."

"I can't hit you. You're a woman."

"I'm not a woman!" She flailed Her arms. "I'm a stupid, ugly giant!"

"You are most definitely none of those things."

"Attack me!"

"Maybe this is a futile endeavor." Flynn swaggered up between them. "Maybe we should just help the man enjoy his final hours. Find him a woman to fuck." His eyes brightened, and he turned to Leila. "Oh, actually, you could help with that."

Growling, She pinched his nipple and gave it a sharp twist.

"Mother of God, woman!"

"No more from you, do you hear me?" She set Her sights on Tobias. "And *you*. Fight me."

He let out a defeated sigh. "I'll try."

"You'll *try*? What if I appeared more fearsome—mirrored the look of Antaeus?" She spun toward Flynn. "I have an idea. Flynn, over here, we'll make you useful yet."

"Wait, what's that supposed to mean?"

"Quiet, you." She tapped Flynn with Her staff. "Let me sit on your shoulders."

She was climbing onto his back before he could rebut, cursing and wobbling until finally seated atop his shoulders. "How about now?" She kicked Flynn in the ribs, directing his movements. "Together, we're the Giant. Do you see it?"

A laugh sputtered from Tobias's lips.

"Tobias!"

"I must thank you both." He shook his head. "I truly didn't think I'd be capable of laughing today."

"Oh, piss off, we can't possibly look that absurd," Flynn said.

Footsteps echoed behind them. Flynn spun around, nearly throwing Leila off his shoulders as Raphael appeared from the shadows.

"Flynn, where the hell did you—?" He stopped short, staring at Leila and Flynn. Rolling his eyes, he headed off. "Never mind."

Leila sighed, resigned. "All right, put me down."

Flynn lowered Her to the floor, and She took Her place at Tobias's side. "Listen to me: Tomorrow, you face the most dangerous obstacle of your life. So tonight you'll fight us both, for however long it takes, until we're good and bruised."

"I'd rather not be bruised—"

"Shut up, Flynn." She looked Tobias in the eye. "The sole intent of a battle is to eliminate your opponent. And if I'm your opponent, you will *hit me*. I'm giving you permission. No more of this nonsense, all right?"

Gnawing on his lip, Tobias nodded. "All right."

"Good." She resumed Her stance. "We fight."

She trained him with a firm hand, parroting Talos's teachings as best She could. Flynn was eager to showcase his prowess, and so they took turns, then worked together, fighting as a dexterous team against a novice. Each blow She landed reverberated through Her, the welts on Tobias's body like marks on Her conscience. But instead of wincing, She fought harder, trying to harden the man who hurried Her heartbeat.

Lunging forward, She swung Her staff at Tobias's throat. Another sure-hit—except he dodged Her assault, whipping his waster into Her ribs and toppling Her to the floor.

"Oh God." Tobias rushed to Her side. "I'm so sorry."

Pain pulsed through Leila, and She relished it. "Don't be sorry, you're just getting good." She stumbled to Her feet. "Again. But harder."

Hours raced past as they bounded through the tunnel. Ash covered Her dress and filled Her lungs, yet She didn't waver, not even when Her muscles began to ache, when Her stomach growled for sustenance. At some point Flynn retreated to the wall, so Leila fought with the power of two, resolute in Her intention. Tomorrow, Tobias would win. He had to.

"It's time for your final lesson." Taking in a much-needed breath, She tossed Her staff aside. "The kill."

Sweat coated Tobias, yet he stood flexed and ready as She stalked closer.

"Don't rush for the kill. Be patient. Eventually one of you will grow weary. Don't let it be you." She took his waster, rotating it between Her hands. "Antaeus feels at home in the arena. But that means he might become complacent. He'll make mistakes because he thinks he can. Your aim is to prove him wrong." She enunciated each word, hoping to ingrain them in his mind. "Once he falters, you go for the kill. And if you go for the kill, you must commit. You must act quickly."

She eyed the wooden sword, imagining it was steel. "Obviously, there are many ways to kill a man, but given the situation, we're aiming for a degree of certainty, yes? So I would suggest..." She pointed the waster at his neck, "...the throat..." She dragged the tip to his chest, "...the heart..." She stopped it below his navel, "...or deep in the belly."

"You speak as though you have experience," Tobias said.

"I never said I was a saint."

The words left Her mouth before She could stop them. Flynn's eyes went wide, while Tobias's expression became empty, unreadable. She waited for color to flood forth, to give Her some indication of his thoughts, but there was nothing.

"Are you all right?"

Tobias flinched. "Apologies. I was in my head for a moment."

"All right then. Take your stance." Her voice came out meek, cowed by the look in Flynn's eyes.

By the fact that She hadn't seen a speck of pink in hours.

She centered Herself. Now wasn't the time. After tossing Tobias his waster, She snatched Her staff from the floor and leaned in.

"Now fight to kill."

"SO, IT'S SETTLED," BRONTES SAID. "TAXATION IN THE CENTRAL villages will be adjusted to account for military spending. All those in favor?"

Hands shot up, while Leila picked at Her dress. The Senate meeting had dragged on longer than She had anticipated, each passing second one She hadn't to spare.

Counting the raised hands, Brontes scribbled along his scroll. "So it is written. Changes will go into effect come our next rotation. The common folk will be glad to spare their coin for the safety of our realm. Onto the next item: Tariff agreements with the Kovahrians are at a standstill. Kastor proposes—"

"For God's sake, can we hurry this up?" Leila barked.

The room went quiet, all eyes on Her.

"Am I boring You, Daughter?" Brontes's unfeeling voice contradicted his glare. "You're free to leave at any time."

"She's anxious to bless the realm." Phanes chuckled. "Been thinking of nothing else all day, no doubt."

"I imagine our Queen is eager for the theatrics." Wembleton's cheeks were rosy with glee. "Today one of your blessed ones, the Giant, is to battle another in the arena. A Savant, the..." he pulled out a pocket scroll, scanning it over, "...Artist. Are we finally coming around to the tournament? Enjoying the spectacle?"

Leila's lips curled. "Immensely."

"Wonderful. The people will be thrilled to have Her Holiness in attendance."

Leila nearly started. "In attendance?"

"Surely You're attending the battle?"

Nothing. She had no counter, certainly none She could speak aloud.

"Of course She's attending." Romulus's voice broke through the quiet. "That's why She's so impatient to see this meeting end. To watch the battle." He cast a knowing stare Her way. "Isn't that right, Your Holiness?"

Her stomach clenched, but She forced a smile. "For once, I'm in agreement with our little vulture. I'm positively delighted for the bloodshed."

"Splendid!" Wembleton said. "What marvelous news."

Brontes was quiet for a long while. "We can postpone the rest of our meeting. Wembleton, prepare the royal balcony. And when the guards escort us—"

"*Us?*" Leila spat. "You're attending as well?"

"Does this bother You, Daughter?"

She faltered, sitting tall. "I assumed you hadn't any interest in tournament events. You threw such a fit over the prospect of attending the Commencement."

Brontes frowned. "My blessed one is fighting. I aim to show my support."

"Sounds to Me like you don't trust his prowess."

"The people will expect my presence."

"The people will think you a coddling mum."

"Your Highness, with all due respect, the Artist will surely lose," Romulus cut in. "You'd waste your time watching a Savant get slaughtered by one of your greatest fighters? Surely your presence is of value elsewhere."

Brontes said nothing, lips tight and fingers drumming his armrest, while Leila's knee bounced beneath the table. He turned to Wembleton. "You'll report the specifics to me, yes?"

"Of course, Your Highness."

"Who motions to end today's meeting?"

"I do."

"Second."

The men shuffled from their seats, and Leila released a breath.

"Your Holiness." Romulus flipped through several sheets of parchment, not once glancing Her way. "A word about the upcoming challenges."

The others filed from the room, and Leila slumped in Her chair once the door closed behind them. "Make it quick."

Romulus continued his parchment-perusing. "Tournament law dictates The Savior is to choose one of the challenges. I'm here to collect Your decision."

"That's it? This is really about the tournament?"

"You've made me the Proctor. This is me proctoring."

Groaning, She dropped Her head in Her hand. Challenges were the least of Her worries, as inconsequential as Flynn's ramblings about his reward or his rants as he toiled over those canvas cards.

She sat up straight. "Match the Eye."

Romulus's lips pursed. "The card game?"

"A sharp mind is important to Me in a partner."

"It's a card game."

"It is My choice."

"Very well," he said. "How exactly are You going to manage today's battle?"

"Simple. Cosima will take My place on the royal balcony."

"Wembleton will be there."

She stood. "Then I suppose Wembleton will have to die."

She abandoned the Senate room, a wide-eyed Delphi waiting for Her in the neighboring corridor.

"Finally." Exhaling, Delphi kept pace with Leila. "What took so long?"

"There's been a change of plans." Leila glanced across the hallway. "Where's Cosima? The Savior must attend the battle."

"Are You *serious?*" Delphi stopped short. "No. There's no way."

"It's one appearance. She'll do fine."

"And what about Wembleton? The *Master* of *Ceremonies*? Is he supposed to just look the other way?"

"I'll handle him."

"How can You—?"

"I'll *handle him*," Leila spat. "Bring Cosima to My dressing room. Now."

The sisters parted ways in a flurry of panic, meeting soon after in Leila's dressing room. Luxury surrounded them, each jeweled diadem and florid sconce glittering against the sunlight, though only Cosima seemed taken by the opulence. Delphi scowled in the corner, while Leila dressed Cosima in soft green linens.

"I swear, this has to be the most beautiful room in the palace." Cosima spun in a circle, eyeing their accommodations. "How come You've never taken us here?"

"Probably because it's The Savior's dressing room," Delphi said. "For *The Savior*."

"Look at these crowns..." Cosima wandered to the side of the room, half-dressed with her breasts exposed. "You usually wear this one, yes? It's lovely, but I think I prefer this piece. These rubies are divine."

Leila steered her back to the mirror, tying the straps of her dress. "I've spoken with the guards. They've called off your escorts. You're to enter the royal balcony alone—no witnesses from the palace."

"Except Wembleton," Delphi added.

"Right." Leila turned to Cosima, stringing jewels along her wrists. "Don't engage with him if it can be avoided."

"And if it can't?"

"Keep him docile."

"And what of the people?" Cosima studied her reflection as Leila draped her in diamonds. "This is their first time seeing their Queen. Should I address them?"

"Don't say anything," Leila ordered. "Smile, wave, and let Wembleton manage his duties. The quicker we can get through this, the better."

"Are you sure you can handle this?" Delphi gave Cosima a critical once-over. "This is no small task. There are grave risks, yet you seem utterly unfazed."

"I've been posing as Her Holiness for over a week," Cosima said. "I know what I'm doing."

"You're about to face thousands of people—"

"From a great distance. Many of whom won't be able to make out my features, let alone hear my voice."

"No one will hear your voice." Leila's tone became severe. "You won't be speaking."

Cosima gave Her a flick of the wrist. "Of course. But if I can spend hours alone with a man and leave him convinced of my divinity, surely I can maneuver my way around this. Ask the Adonis, the Prince. Are they not worshipping at my feet?"

"It's fine," Leila said. "We were just making sure."

Cosima chuckled. "Speaking of, the Prince is rather impressive. He's no Adonis, but my, what a gorgeous smile. Have You noticed how white his teeth are?"

"I've been a bit busy trying to prevent My death," Leila grumbled.

"He comes from a great deal of power, but he thirsts for more. He didn't say as much, but you can always tell a man's true disposition by his lovemaking."

"Fascinating. Now if we could focus on your appearance—"

"I didn't bed him, if that's what You're thinking," Cosima continued. "But the way he touched me was ravenous. Like he was seeking claim of my body. And when he undressed me, there was no time or care, just an eagerness for flesh. Such men are usually poor lovers—so wrapped up in wanting, they forget to please. Anyhow, there was no point in continuing. I told him we'd save the rest for another time, if he's lucky."

Swallowing profanities, Leila stepped aside. "I think we're done." She threw Cosima's cloak over her shoulders. "Steer clear of the sun. The people will grow suspicious if their Savior doesn't glow."

"I'll be extra careful."

"Promise Me you won't let Wembleton out of your sight."

"You have my word." Cosima smiled. "I won't fail You."

"I mean it. When you exit the balcony, exit with him. He mustn't stray."

Cosima patted Leila's cheek. "You can trust me, sweet Sister."

With one last caress, she turned on her heel and heading for the arena, leaving Leila to stew. How had things gotten so out of control?

"This is a mess," Delphi said.

"I'm taking care of it." Leila paced the floor, only half believing Her own claim. "Cosima will play My part. Brontes isn't attending. I'll dispose of Wembleton."

"And Tobias? Did You help him?"

"I trained him all night."

"You *trained* him?" Delphi spat.

"In the art of the sword."

Delphi's eyes widened. "That's not what I meant by *helping* him! He can't learn to kill an assassin in one evening. He needs Your magic!"

"You'd have Me reveal Myself to him?"

"Of course not. Just bless him discreetly!"

"*Discreetly?*" Leila hissed. "He's to fight in the *arena*. In the *sunlight*. You don't think the glowing handprint might tip him off?"

"God, the handprint." Delphi cursed under her breath. "This whole thing would be a lot easier if You didn't glow."

The blaring of distant trumpets filtered through the space. "The battle's approaching." Leila grabbed Her cloak and satchel. "I have to go."

"But Tobias—"

"If you have a solution, out with it," Leila said. "Otherwise it seems the only other option is to sacrifice My life for his. So what is it?"

Delphi stared back at Her, mouth agape. Leila's heart sank.

"That's what I thought."

She stormed from the room, charging through the palace as Her thoughts spiraled. Once the hallway emptied, She summoned Her light, the white marble around Her replaced with stacked stones, the speckled tiles now hard dirt.

The arena.

She wound Her way through the inner corridor, choking on dust. The muffled cheering of the spectators rang overhead, resonating through the ceiling. She shrank beneath Her cloak and carried on, eyeing wooden door after wooden door, each identical to the last—save for the one enveloped in an olive-green mist.

Tobias's cell.

She stuck Her blade into the door's lock, wrestling it open. Tobias sat on a bench, leaning on his knees. His bronze skin was smooth, free from any hint of soot, and his brown curls spilled over his ears and brow. Leather straps wrapped his chest, iron plates adorned his arms and shoulders, and a green fog rose from his exposed flesh.

"Leila." He burst through the mist, barreling toward Her. "What are you doing here?"

Behind him loomed the barred gate to the arena, the daylight creeping between its slats. She forced a smile, steering clear of the sun's rays. "Seeing you, of course. How are you feeling?"

"Oh, just wonderful. The servant girls got me all clean and presentable. So glad I'll be looking handsome when I die."

"Tobias..."

"And this armor." He gestured toward his leather straps. "It's magnificent, truly, how it exposes all my most vital organs. But thank God my shoulders and forearms are covered. Never mind my heart. Or my gut. Or my *fucking head*."

"Tobias, you're panicking."

"Of course I am. I'm nearly 'bout to piss myself." His expression turned bleak. "I have to fight Antaeus. The Giant. To the *death*."

"And you'll *win*."

"He's a professional killer. He *kills* as a *profession*."

"*Tobias*." She took his chin. "Still your heart. Listen to my words: You're afraid. That's a good thing. Fear is the knowledge of danger. If you know it's there—if you see it—you can conquer it. There is no courage without fear. Do you understand me?"

He swallowed. "I've never killed before. I don't know if I can do it. I don't know if it's in me."

"You'd be surprised what the human will is capable of when it has no other choice."

A wave of applause sounded from beyond the gate, along with an ugly phrase—the Master of Ceremonies. Tobias's gaze drifted.

"Tobias, hear me. Today you'll face an option: Either be good and die, or be dark and live. You're a good man, but you will choose the darkness." Leila crossed Her arms. "And you should. Is it really so bad to rid the world of Antaeus? Not all men deserve the life they've been given."

Tobias's frame was solid, but the grimness of his expression didn't lift.

"Are you feeling any better?" She said.

"Not especially."

"Tobias..."

"God, there are so many people." Staring back at the gate, he raked his fingers through his hair. "All the spectators, the other competitors, the Sovereign—"

"Brontes isn't here."

"He won't be watching? Why not?" Tobias's gaze glassed over. "Oh God, he has me dead and buried already, doesn't he? He doesn't need to watch because he knows I'm going to lose."

"And we'll prove him wrong."

"I can't believe this is happening."

"Calm yourself."

"Be truthful," he barked. "You can't possibly believe I'll win today. I've trained for but a night. Antaeus has fought and killed for years. My chance of survival is slim to none."

Leila's shoulders sank. He was right—the training, the finagling, it was all for nothing. Antaeus had won the moment Her father hired him. Chaos swirled in Her gut, but amid it rang one honest instinct: Tobias was going to die.

Tobias scooped up Her hands. "Leila, if I die today—"

"You won't die," She said.

"I need you to know—"

"You *won't die*—"

"Please, just let me speak. *Please*." He pulled Her close. "If I die, I need you to know I don't regret entering this tournament. I don't even regret the drawings. My only regret is that I didn't take advantage of every opportunity I had to spend my time in your company." His fingers entwined with Hers. "These days have been hellish and miserable, but you...*you* have been my one pleasant memory. And I thank you for that. For making some part of this torment worthwhile and good, if just for a short while.."

Bless him. You have to. Her thoughts unraveled, dissecting each word he had spoken, each plan She had considered and abandoned, while light tickled Her fingertips, begging for release. There had to be something, but all She had were an arsenal of powers She couldn't dare reveal and a satchel of perfumes, soaps—

Clay.

Tobias was still staring back at Her, still holding Her tight. *Don't do it. You'll expose Yourself.* Cursing under Her breath, She dug through Her satchel.

"What are you doing?" he said.

Tonics, bandages. Leila jostled the items aside until She found it—a glass jar filled with bathhouse clay. She poured the grey sludge into Her hands and slapped Her palms against Tobias's chest.

"Leila, what the—?"

"This clay is blessed by The Savior." Heat burst through Her palms. "And now, so are you."

"*What?*"

"With this blessing, you will have the utmost advantage in today's battle." Her power mirrored Her words, obeying Her command. "You will be untouchable. You will walk in the shadows."

"Walk in the *shadows?*"

"Imagine a place in the arena where you'd prefer to be, and it will be so."

"I don't understand."

"Any place at all. See yourself there, and it will be done."

"Leila—"

Wembleton's voice cut Tobias short—"*the Giant*"—and the people roared.

"There isn't much time," Leila said. "Use the blessing. Win the battle."

"But what of Cosima? Will She care?"

"Why would She care?"

"It's Her magic. We're using it without permission."

"Oh, right." Leila wavered, then shrugged. "We'll see, I suppose."

"We'll *see?*"

Give him the gift. Leila ignored his qualms, Her attention split between Her holy bidding and Her desperate plea. *If this clay doesn't stifle My glow, I swear to God...*

"Leila..." Tobias's voice startled Her. She followed his gaze to Her hands—still planted on his pecs.

"Oh God, apologies." Dragging Her palms, She smeared the clay into an X. "There. Looks menacing, doesn't it? Like war paint. Though I imagine it'd look even better in blood."

"Leila—"

"*The Artist!*" Wembleton's voice boomed, chilling Her. "No more talking. They're calling you." She yanked a rag from her satchel and wiped Her palms down. "Use the blessing and *win*." She grabbed his hands, Her heart lurching into Her throat. "Then...you can live your life without regrets."

His silence picked at Her nerves. Then his thumb glided over Her knuckles, back and forth, a calming caress.

A clank sounded, and the gate rose, sending sunlight spilling across the floor.

"I'll be cheering for you. Down here." Leila stepped back into the shadows. "Go on."

His gaze lingered, and he nodded, heading into the arena.

The gate slammed shut behind him, and Leila plowed toward it before stopping short at the edge of the shadows. Sunlight crept between the bars, and She tiptoed around it, nestling Herself within the smallest sliver of darkness while peering out into the arena.

Tall stone walls encircled yellow sand, the blazing heat thick with dust. Leila was familiar with the arena. She had snuck across its grounds twice or twenty times, but She had never seen it like this, its pews overflowing with spectators too rabid to be human. An armored Antaeus stood at the head of the arena, while the other competitors were locked in a barred pew, shaking the rods and squawking with the rest of the animals.

As Tobias marched toward his opponent, Leila's stomach dropped. *The blessing.* She pressed Her face between the slats of the gate, but all She could make out were his back and shoulders. Perhaps on the other end he was glowing, Her light shining straight through the clay. Bile burned Her throat at the thought of it.

Tobias reached the head of the arena, turning to face the royal balcony. Two dried, grey handprints smeared his chest, and neither of them glowed.

"Citizens of Thessen, today you will witness a battle for the ages!"

Wembleton's voice bounced off the walls, turning Leila's hands into white-knuckled fists. He stood in the center of the balcony, draped in sapphire and gold linens and shaded by ruby canopies, another mess for Her to clean up.

"In the pursuit of our Savior and the title of Sovereign, the Giant and the Artist will fight until one man stands as victor and the other is released from this life into the next," he said. "These creatures standing before you are no ordinary men. They are men of the Sovereign's Tournament, the finest of warriors, a caliber above us all. Thus, an ordinary fight is simply unsuitable. Ladies and gentlemen, I reveal to you, the arena!"

The ground vibrated, and dust burst through the arena once, twice, a hundred times. Mirrors tore up from the sand, circling the two fighters.

"Behold the dreaded mirrors." Wembleton waved his arms, no doubt for dramatic flair. "Will our two brave fighters use the arena to their advantage? Or will they find themselves lost? Will they fall victim to their own reflections?"

Two other men appeared in the arena, dressed in simple sable harem pants and sleeveless tunics instead of armor. One was short and skinny with a prominent nose and ashy brown curls, but the other was of Tobias's height and coloring, had the same dark eyes and wavy locks. The similarities were staggering, save for his robust frame, coarse beard, and age, as he was old enough to be Tobias's father.

They stood side by side—by side, by side, as there were hundreds of the same two men throughout the arena.

In each and every mirror.

"The Artist fights with the gladius!"

Tobias clutched his weapon—a plain, short sword—while Antaeus proudly displayed his bardiche just as Leila had predicted. Leila ignored the Giant, Her gaze flitting back and forth between Tobias and the bearded specter looming in the mirrors. *Old enough to be his father.*

Was he Tobias's father?

"Our valiant men are prepared. The battle is just moments away!"

Is his father dead? He never said so. But the resemblance was uncanny, from his angular nose to those high cheekbones. And the small, mousy man next to him? Leila clasped Her hands over Her mouth.

Milo.

"And to my left, I give to you none other than the Artist's mother and sister!"

Tobias's jaw went slack, and all the hope within Leila withered. His family was watching. All of them.

"And for our final guest, and truly the most honorable of all..." Wembleton leaned against the balcony railing, eyes lit with desire. "Citizens, you have waited for this moment. We *all* have waited for this moment. She is the reason we stand here today. She is the very foundation of our great realm."

She was lingering in one of the cells like a servant.

"Ladies and gentlemen, please bow down before Her, The Savior!"

The people sank to their knees, weeping as Cosima sashayed onto the balcony. She lowered the hood of her emerald cloak, allowing her red curls to spill down her décolletage, and adoration poured from the pews like water from an opened floodgate. Wembleton gaped at Cosima, confusion plastered across his face.

"It appears our dear Wembleton is as shocked to see Me as the rest of you. I hope he finds his tongue soon, so he can present what I'm sure will be a legendary battle."

Leila staggered backward. Cosima said that. Cosima was *speaking.* Her sister patted Wembleton's shoulder, appealing to the crowd while Leila's insides boiled. This wasn't part of the plan.

"My Giant, My Artist, know our time together has been cherished, and your courage deeply moves Me." Cosima's words carried throughout the arena. "The two of you may stand as adversaries, but you are united by cause: the noble endeavor of winning My heart. Each morning I wake astonished, wondering how I could be so lucky. To see one of you leave us today will bring Me such sadness, but I take comfort in knowing that through your sacrifice, this realm will be one step closer to crowning its newest Sovereign, and I will be that much closer to finding My husband."

The people roared, while Leila shook with rage.

"Citizens, shall we begin?" Cosima pulled a handkerchief from her pocket. "Allow Me to do the honors." She raised her handkerchief overhead, and Antaeus and Tobias readied themselves. "Good luck, and may the best man win."

As her handkerchief fell, Antaeus hurtled toward Tobias.

Leila flinched at the swing of Antaeus's bardiche as if the assault was aimed at Her. Tobias was still moving, still alive, but his dipping and dodging did little to quell Her fear.

Use the blessing.

Blood sprayed through the arena. Shielding himself, Tobias ducked behind one of the mirrors, his chest marked with a red gash. The men in the reflections gaped in horror, and Leila couldn't help but do the same. *For God's sake, the blessing!*

Tobias bolted across the sand with Antaeus sprinting after him. He zigzagged between the mirrors, a clever maneuver, but Antaeus quickly overtook him, swerving in front of Tobias with his weapon high. Steel clanked against steel, and Leila winced each time the bardiche connected with the gladius, again and again until it swiped Tobias's ribs.

Leila covered Her mouth, muffling Her cry. Antaeus slammed the grip of his bardiche against Tobias's eye, his jaw, while Tobias's ragdoll body whipped back and forth, his sword falling from his hands.

He was a dead man.

Leila stood petrified as Antaeus swung at Tobias's skull.

The blade sliced through wisps of black, but no Tobias. He was gone, a ghost of the arena. A grey cloud erupted paces in front of Leila's cell, taking shape into a tall frame, armored shoulders.

Tobias.

The audience gasped, while Wembleton glanced across the sands, stunned. "It seems the Artist is, um... It appears the Artist has, uh..."

Tobias looked over his shoulder, meeting Leila's gaze and stirring Her heartbeat. She pointed to Her chest, and he stared down at his own, taking in Her handprints.

Her blessing.

Antaeus's voice sounded from across the arena, muddled behind Leila's pulse in Her ears. He plucked Tobias's fallen sword from the sand

—one Giant, two weapons. The sight should've horrified Her, but those clay handprints, however streaked with blood, still marked Tobias's chest. He was armed with something else entirely, and maybe, just maybe he would get out of this arena alive.

Tobias evaporated in front of Her, leaving inky swirls in his wake. A dark cloud appeared at the other end of the arena, and Tobias materialized within its mass as if born from the shadows. Leila sucked in a breath; he stood behind Antaeus, close enough to touch. Quietly, he crept forward, kicking Antaeus in the ass.

Did he just—?

Antaeus whirled, and the fight resumed, a mad Giant with sharpened steel versus Tobias, his wits, and a touch of magic. Just as panic took hold of Her, Tobias grabbed a mirror, smashing it against Antaeus's jaw, then yanked another from the ground and slapped it across the Giant's face. Blood sputtered from Antaeus's lips, and the gladius fell to the sand alongside shards of glass.

With a slide and a swoop, Tobias snatched up the sword, then vanished into another shadow, reappearing below the royal balcony unscathed.

"Could it be?" Wembleton composed himself. "Has the Artist been blessed by The Savior? Has She chosen to share Her divine magic with him?"

Leila cringed at the sound of Her title, though the worry was short-lived. Tobias paced the sands, shouting taunts across the arena, wielding Her magic with skill and ease. He appeared moments later in front of Leila, tossing his sword between his hands, while Her assassin's face was awash with chagrin.

"Can I ask you a question?" he said to Antaeus. "It's relevant, I promise. Tell me, are you stupid because you're an ass, or are you an ass because you're stupid?"

Leila forced back a giggle. Barbs fired back and forth across the sands, stopping once Tobias vanished in an eruption of darkness. When he reemerged, he stood atop the arena wall, staring down at Antaeus ominously.

"It appears our royal father and daughter are at odds with one another," Wembleton crowed. "Today's battle will go down in history, a fight to the death between one man blessed by the Sovereign and one blessed by The Savior. It's the battle of the blessed ones!"

Women swarmed Tobias, running their hands down his body. He ignored them much to Leila's delight, taking a seat on the wall, eyes trained on the Giant like a hawk on a field mouse. His ferocity shook Her, winding a knot of confused emotion in Her gut; She wasn't quite sure if She was excited, or afraid, or aroused. *No, not that. Well, maybe a little.*

Tobias leapt from the wall, and She gasped with the audience when he disappeared, materializing on the arena sands. He circled Antaeus, taunting and marking him, bursting into strings of grey. The people howled, eager for blood, while Leila was transfixed by the shift in Tobias and the sinister look in his eyes.

Steel slashed olive flesh as shadows erupted around the assassin. Tobias had more than learned to maneuver Her blessing—he had mastered it, using the magic to disarm his opponent, to carve him with his short sword, to blind him with sand swept from the ground. Antaeus tottered through the arena, eyes clenched shut and innards seeping from his opened gut. Brontes's man was crumbling, and a fire ignited within Leila, the bloodlust of the audience a fraction of Her own.

Antaeus stumbled and swayed, tripping over his feet. As he tumbled to the ground, Tobias charged toward him, plunging his sword through the Giant's belly.

Rivers of red spilled onto the arena sands. Antaeus went limp, sagging onto Tobias and smothering his much smaller frame. A sweeping relief and booming triumph clashed within Leila's chest.

Her assassin had fallen, and Tobias was still alive.

She sucked in shallow breaths. The men in the mirrors were slumped on one another, exhausted. The older man met Leila's gaze and nodded.

Grunting, Tobias pushed the Giant aside and staggered to his feet.

"The Artist stands as victor!" Wembleton said. "Artist, you live to fight another day in our esteemed tournament. You live to fight for The Savior's heart!" He gestured toward the woman at his side, and Leila's nostrils flared.

Cosima.

"Kneel for The Savior, and if the fates deem you worthy, for your future bride."

Tobias did as instructed, but his gaze travelled to his holding cell—to Leila—and when his stare locked with Hers, She couldn't help but smile.

"Everyone, join me in celebrating the Artist!"

Wembleton. He stood tall in the royal balcony, his eyes perpetually flitting toward the false Savior at his side.

One man down. Another to go.

12

THE COMPLICATION

L eila barreled through the corridor. The audience was still in a frenzy, roaring and stomping, sending flakes sprinkling from the ceiling. Their cheering would easily mask Wembleton's screams.

A silver cloak appeared in a nearby stairwell. "Leila." Delphi ran Her way. "I've been looking everywhere for You. I'm so sorry about Tobias—"

"He's alive," Leila said.

"He is? But how—?"

"I blessed him."

Delphi's face dropped. "He knows?"

"He doesn't." Leila shook Her head. "I'll explain later. Where's Wembleton?"

"I assume he's with Cosima."

"Find them. Bring them to... Do you think the undressing room is empty?"

"Servants will be escorting Tobias there any minute." Delphi pursed her lips, thinking. "The armory."

"Meet Me there."

The two split in separate directions, Delphi toward the balcony,

Leila to the armory. A large wooden door with a heavy knocker shaped like an axe loomed ahead, and She pushed it open, surveying Her conditions. Chest plates, pauldrons, and helmets lined the dusty shelves, the space cramped and cluttered.

No escape. Perfect.

She picked at Her dress and fiddled with Her hair, all the while counting down the seconds. Voices echoed through the hallway, followed by footsteps. Wembleton was nearing. Leila dashed toward the door, pressing Herself against the wall.

"It's just a detour. No need to fret." Cosima floated into the armory first amid a whirl of emerald silk. Delphi followed, and next came Wembleton, staggering to a halt once he caught sight of Leila.

"Your Holiness," he croaked.

Leila gestured toward Delphi. "Seal the door."

Delphi double-bolted the lock and stood in the doorframe. Cosima tucked herself against the back wall, while Leila stood poised and ready before the Senator.

"What is...?" Wembleton glanced between them, paling. "What's going on?"

"Sit down," Leila said.

"Your Holiness—"

She yanked Her blade from its sheath. "Sit. *Down*."

Wembleton froze, then backed into a nearby shelf, taking a seat among a line of helmets. Leila lowered Her weapon slightly, enough for him to make out the sheen of its edge.

"May I ask why You missed the battle?" His voice wavered. "You seemed so excited..."

"I didn't want it to end this way." Leila raised Her blade. "I was hoping you'd be a bit more useful. But plans have changed, and now you know too much—"

"Wait!" Wembleton lurched away. "I can be useful!"

"The time for that has long passed."

"Your father trusts me. I have information."

"You are nothing but a lap dog."

"He says things in my presence!" Sweat beaded along his brow, wetting his hair. "He assumes no one is listening. But I always listen. I hear what he says."

Sighing, Leila pressed Her weapon against his throat. "Goodbye, Senator."

"There's a traitor!"

She froze, Her blade still pointed at the fleshy part of his neck. "Come again?"

"Brontes has a connection beyond the fortress. Someone of significant power and means. Someone who wishes to end The Savior's lineage."

"A tall tale told by a desperate man."

"He's paying him!" he said. "In installments. Once each week, Brontes sends his payment. He's done this for some time now. Your vault steadily shrinks."

Leila hesitated. "The missing funds..."

"I can learn who this traitor is. I can get a name. If only You'd spare my life."

Repugnant green wafted through the space, filtering from Wembleton's pores. She was used to such fear on these occasions, had often sliced through it, adding crimson to the mix. This time, She lowered Her blade.

"How is Brontes in contact with this person? No one leaves the fortress."

"I can find out for You. I swear it."

"There's only one traitor?"

"He has constituents, I'm sure. But if you learn his identity, Your father's plan will crumble."

Leila did nothing, Her blade at Her side.

"Please," Wembleton whimpered. "I'll keep Your secret. I'll aid Your endeavors."

"You can't possibly be considering this," Delphi chimed in.

"We have no new leads," Leila said.

"He's a liar and a coward."

Leila grabbed Wembleton's drapes, pulling him close. "Let Me make this clear: You're alive to serve Me. Stray from My side, and find this blade buried in your gut." She pointed the tip to his stomach. "I will split You nose to navel and strangle you with your entrails, do you understand Me?"

"I am Your loyal servant, now and always."

She pressed the blade deeper, enough to tear through his tunic. "Delphi. Escort the Senator to his chamber. See to it that he stays there for the remainder of the evening."

As She lowered the weapon, Wembleton breathed a sigh of relief, scuttling obediently to Her sister's side. Delphi linked her arm with his, casting a glare Leila's way before leaving the room.

Clearing her throat, Cosima fluffed her dress. "Well, that was rather unprecedented."

"You think I should've killed him?" Leila said.

"Not that, silly. You *blessed* the Artist!" Cosima's eyes widened with intrigue. "Why didn't You tell me?"

"I didn't know I was going to. It was a spur of the moment decision."

"A risky decision, though I'm glad it was made. The display was incredible. That battle will go down in history. My little Leila, writing legends. Why did You do it?"

Leila swallowed. "Antaeus was one of My father's assassins. Naturally it was the perfect opportunity to have him removed."

"A cunning player until the end." Cosima winked. "Well, the Artist owes You significantly. You saved the poor fool's life."

Chuckling, she wafted away, leaving Leila alone in the armory—no body, no cleanup, a position She hadn't expected to find Herself in. Everything seemed out of sorts, a mess within a mess, but She forced the concerns aside. Today was a victory. An assassin had fallen, and Tobias had survived.

Go to him.

Blazing white surrounded Her before fading to black brick. She stood in the center of the labyrinth, the light of the sanctuary shining ahead, laughter echoing off the walls. She brushed out Her locks and ventured forward.

The men were roused in a way She hadn't seen before, wrestling along the floor, guffawing until they couldn't breathe. Most circled the fire pit roasting slabs of meat, their faces clammy and red. Ceramic jugs sat by the fire, and copper chalices littered the space, tipped and spilling with wine.

Drunk as a bunch of skunks.

A giggle bounced across the sanctuary. Pippa waddled through the space, an unwieldy jug in her hands, and she topped off Caesar's chalice, splashing wine over his arm.

"Pippa." Leila rushed to her side, snatching the jug and setting it down. "What are you doing here?"

"I'm feeding the boys!"

"I didn't order you to come down here."

"Of course not. Rom did."

Leila glowered. "You do not take orders from that man. He is not above you."

"He said it was a very important task. The Sovereign ordered wine and meats for all the boys. We're celebrating the Giant's win!"

Tobias sat by the fire pit, his body marked with gashes and bruises, a disheveled mess of a man who left Leila weightless. His allies surrounded him, pestering and prodding while he gnawed ravenously at a goose leg.

He caught Her gaze, and pink billowed from his flesh like organza.

Pippa jutted her head over Leila's shoulder. "What are we looking at?"

Leila swallowed, fighting back a grin. "I have matters to tend to. Will you be all right on your own?" Pippa offered a hasty nod before frolicking away, and Leila's heartbeat surged. She stared at Tobias, allowing Her gaze to speak for Her.

Follow Me.

She wove through the sanctuary and into Her tent, abandoning Her cloak and straightening Her dress—a plum, sleeveless gown, not Her favorite, but the color suited Her skin. Taking in a deep breath, She waited.

Nothing.

What if he wasn't coming?

Busying Herself, She dumped Her satchel's contents onto the table, organizing it into something half-presentable. He was coming. He had to. As the passing seconds nipped at Her nerves, a hesitant voice sounded from outside.

"Leila?"

Tobias. She cleared Her throat. "Come in."

The air shifted, heavier with his presence. She waited for him to speak, trying to predict his sweet nothings. *Leila, finally, we're alone.* But there was only silence, and when She glanced over Her shoulder, his face was twisted with...bewilderment, perhaps?

"Are you all right?"

He shook himself. "Apologies. I just had a very strange encounter, is all."

She turned away. "Well, go on then, close the door. Or the flap. Whatever you call it. I'm not particularly tent savvy."

He headed into the space. "I wanted to thank you. I wouldn't have won without your help. These men, they should be lifting you on their shoulders."

She spun toward him. "You can't tell them."

"I won't. I just need you to know that," he said. "I'm alive because of you."

The tension within Her released. She patted the stool beside Her. "Come. Sit."

As he situated himself, She wetted a rag and brought it to his dirtied chest.

"You don't have to—"

She swatted his hand away, dabbing at the clay. Wipe by wipe, Her mark disappeared, while Tobias remained silent, his eyes faraway.

"You're quiet," She said.

"I'm thinking."

"Of?"

"You've done so much for me. And I fear I can never repay you."

Her mind drifted to his portraits, and She smiled. "You've done things for me."

"Not enough."

"More than you know."

"Still, what you did today, with the blessing..." He studied Her sidelong. "You put yourself at risk, helping me the way you did."

"It was no trouble."

"That isn't true."

"It is."

"You're lying."

The sharpness of his words halted Her.

"How long have you had that clay in your satchel?" He cocked his head at Her bag. "Yet you waited until the last possible second to share it with me, not because you're impartial or uncaring, but because you didn't think it an option. Until you made it one."

"You jump to conclusions."

"Say what you will, but I saw that look in your eye. You've put yourself at risk. Made some kind of grave sacrifice. You don't have to admit it, but know I don't take it for granted."

Panic rose in Her chest, and Her defenses crumbled, turning to rubble at Her feet. "Just, please... You can't tell anyone."

He furrowed his brow. "I won't."

"I had *nothing* to do with it. If people were to find out—"

"You have my word."

"You couldn't possibly understand the danger—"

"You have my *word*," he said. "No one will ever know. I swear it."

Her anxieties ate at Her gut, threatening to consume Her whole. What if She'd made a terrible mistake?

Tobias's face fell. "Do you think I'd betray you? The woman who saved my life?" He took Her hand. "I am not that man."

His thumb glided across Her knuckles, another gentle caress like the one from the holding cell. Her spiking nerves retracted, placated if for a moment.

"Be still." She pulled away from him. "Let's have a look at these marks."

He glanced down at the long gash cutting through his chest. "More stitches?"

"Unnecessary. These wounds are superficial." Grabbing a perfume vial at random, She doused Her hands. "They just need a bit of attention, is all."

"Well, take as much time as you need...or maybe longer."

His voice traveled along Her skin in tremors. Straining to focus, She pressed Her perfumed hand to the gash.

Mend the flesh. Warmth flooded from Her fingertips, and his eyes shrank into lazy slits.

"You must be exhausted." She chuckled. "You'll sleep like a rock tonight."

"Not soon enough. I'm expected to celebrate with everyone else."

"The trials and tribulations of a champion. I'm surprised you're of sound mind. I assumed you'd be drunk with the rest of them."

"God no." He shook his head. "No wine for me. Never again."

"Why's that?"

"I suppose I've lost the taste for it."

"It's not poisoned," She said.

"Still. Once is enough."

Nodding, Leila pressed Her palms against his slashed ribs. "You were quite impressive, you know. Very creative, using the mirrors as you did. And the blessing, of course." She studied him out of the corner of Her eye. "Is it weighing on your conscience, like you had imagined? Killing Antaeus."

"Would you judge me if I said it wasn't?"

"The murderous shit deserved to die. He'll get no pity from me."

A long silence passed before Tobias spoke. "My mother and sister... They were there. Watching."

The battle replayed through Her mind—the blood splattering the sands, the specters in the mirrors—and She closed Her eyes to rid Herself of the visions. "I would've warned you had I known. It was a cruelty I hadn't predicted. To make your family watch and pass it as privilege... God, it's vile."

"I've been consumed. Milo died. I've nearly died. So much has happened." His eyes grew larger. "I don't want them seeing me like this. As a killer."

"You're good, Tobias. They know that. Today changes nothing."

He sank into his seat as if released from a burden. Washing Her hands clean, She thought back to the battle, laughing to Herself.

"What?" Tobias said.

"Nothing."

"Say it."

She bit Her lip. "I just can't believe you kicked him in the ass."

"Are you upset I didn't punch him in the cock as you suggested?" He chuckled. "Perhaps that's why you didn't enjoy the fight. Not nearly enough cock-punching. I'll remember that next time. I wouldn't want to disappoint you again."

She lost Herself in a fit of giggles. "You're bad."

"You just said I was good."

"I take it back. Rotten to the core. That's what you are."

His laughter traveled through Her, making Her stand taller. He was fond of Her. She didn't need his colors to confirm, as She could see it in his gaze, could hear it his voice. She pored over Her perfumes, trying to find Her next useless potion, while his eyes traced Her figure like a soft caress.

She reached toward his bloodied lip, and he jerked away, dodging Her touch.

His eyes widened. "No, Leila, I'm so sorry. It's not you, trust me. It's not you at all." He cradled his face in his hands. "God*dammit*..."

"It's all right." Though Her flaming cheeks said otherwise. "Things are...complicated. But I do have to touch you."

Sighing, he dropped his hands, and Leila tapped Her fingers against his fat lip, filling it with Her blessing.

Ease the pain. Perhaps the embarrassment as well.

"I'm supposed to be here for a specific purpose," he mumbled.

"As am I."

"And I'm finding myself...distracted."

She forced Herself to speak. "As am I."

Quiet wedged between them, and She instantly regretted Her response.

Tobias cleared his throat. "What I said before the battle..."

"Emotions were high. If you didn't mean it—"

"I meant it," he said. "Every word. But truthfully, I fear what would happen if anything were to come of it."

"Yes, well...we share that fear."

Retreating, She distracted Herself with Her perfumes. *This is a mistake.* There were too many variables, and his reservations only fueled

Her own. She wanted to curse Her naivety, to berate Herself for even entertaining the thought. Instead, She squared Her shoulders, bracing Herself for their harsh reality.

"I suppose this means we have a decision to make," She said.

"What's that?"

"Whether we should commit to our original purpose or remain distracted."

Tobias didn't respond.

"You don't have to decide right now," She added. "Take your time. Think it through."

"What about you? This decision isn't mine alone."

"I'll be thinking it through as well."

She pressed Her thumb against his sliced brow, summoning Her light, while Tobias stared back at Her, befuddlement written across his face.

"What's that look for?" She said.

"I don't want to say."

"Well, you have to now." She crossed Her arms and waited, each passing second a knife to Her pride. "Fine. Be silent." She prodded at his eyebrow. "God forbid you answer a simple question."

"This is *shit*," he spat. "I'm losing you before we've even begun. How is that right? *God*, this tournament. How is this fair? We want the *same thing*."

Leila froze, paralyzed by his heated stare, his shallow breathing. *Don't do it*, but She dragged Her fingers through his hair anyway, taking a hesitant look inside. Colors bombarded Her—pinks and oranges, layers upon layers of longing, each one aimed exclusively at Her.

His stare hadn't wavered, except now it was different. Yearning. As he came in closer, Her throat caught.

Is he going to kiss Me?

The tent flap flung open, and Leila jammed Her fingernail into Tobias's brow.

"*Shit*," he hissed.

Leila spun toward their visitor—a drunken Flynn. "Dammit, you can't just barge in here without permission!"

"Apologies," he said.

"Fuck your apologies. You startled me." She pointed to Tobias. "Look, he's bleeding now. It's your fault, you know."

"I was just checking on our champion." Flynn glowered at Tobias. "You're missing your celebration."

"Yes, well, I'm a little occupied, as you can see," Tobias said.

"Will it be much longer?"

"Only if you keep interrupting." Leila crossed Her arms. "Do you think he's sitting here for his own pleasure? That we're just making idle conversation?"

"Well, move it along, you two. Before all the wine is gone."

"*Go*," Leila growled.

Flynn disappeared from the tent—*thank God*—and She snatched up Her rag, dabbing at the blood on Tobias's face.

"You did that on purpose," he mumbled.

"You're welcome."

An unsettling quiet followed, a weight Leila hadn't the patience to manage. *Say something.* "Can I ask you a question?"

"You can ask a hundred if you'd like," he said.

"Have you always known it? That you're an artist?" Tobias nodded, and Leila grinned. "I thought so."

"Just felt right," he said. "Like it was what I ought to be doing all the time. Most people can't understand that."

"That's because most people aren't destined for anything." She wiped down Her perfumes, occupying Her restless hands. "Unless you count banality as destiny. Take Caesar, for example. He's destined to cling to his royal ancestry as a means of entitlement. To inherit his family's fortune, then waste it on wine and brothels. Probably destined to get some unseemly infection too."

His laughter slinked through Her, loosening Her muscles. "It must be hard," She said. "Not being able to do what you're meant for. I imagine it's something like a heartache. Like being torn from someone you love."

"Have you always known you're a healer?"

Light tickled Her fingertips, and She smiled. "Just felt right."

"Then I envy you. For getting to live your life's purpose."

His words brought the reality of Her existence crashing down on Her. "Don't envy me so quickly. We all have our own troubles."

Why is this so difficult? Cosima always made it look easy, could charm a man in her sleep, yet here Leila stood debating duty versus pleasure. Perhaps this wasn't a good idea—a complication She couldn't afford—but once She caught the path of Tobias's fixed gaze, all Her worries shifted into dread.

Her blade. He was staring at it, and visions of their previous evening flitted through Her mind—of secrets She hadn't intended to reveal.

"You're just never going to mention it again," She said.

Tobias looked away. "Mention what?"

"What you said in the labyrinth. When we were training." When Tobias didn't respond, Leila sighed. "I'm not a saint."

His frame stiffened. "You've killed."

"I imagine it bothers you."

"Why would it bother me? I've killed too."

"You make light of the situation? Like it's nothing?"

"I've seen you, Leila. Who you are. You're certainly not to be toyed with, but you're compassionate. And you're kind." His gaze drifted. "If you've killed...then I suppose it's because they left you no choice."

"*They?* You believe it's happened more than once?"

"Am I wrong?"

She sucked in shallow breaths and stared at the floor.

"Moments ago, you were fearful for your life. Speaking of some incredible danger, one you clearly don't feel comfortable sharing with me." He worked his way into Her line of sight. "I may be ignorant to the specifics...but I assume these things are related, yes?"

She nodded.

"Then there's nothing left to be said. I took a life to protect my own. How could I fault you for doing the same?"

"You could fault me if you please. It's human nature to revile."

"You fear I'd judge you?" Tobias leaned in closer. "Look at me."

"It's all right."

"Leila, look at me, please." He waited for Her to comply. "In the holding cell, before the fight...you said I'd choose the darkness." He took her hand, entwining his fingers with Hers. "You were right. I'm choosing darkness."

Her shoulders tightened. "I told you...you should take time to think."

"I've thought enough. Now it's your turn. What's your choice?"

This is a mistake, but that didn't stop Her from reveling in his touch. Cinnamon and sugar—She could taste it each time She breathed him in, and when She pulled free from His hold, swirls of pink sat in his hand. She dragged Her fingers through the palmful of color and up his forearm, tracing spirals in his longing.

"Tobias, you limp cock, hurry the fuck up!" Flynn's voice tore through the tent, and She jerked away.

Tobias cringed. "I should go."

Her heart fired off as he stood from his seat. This wasn't how it was supposed to end. Then their eyes locked, and She could've sworn he hesitated, was leaning in.

"*Artist!*" Flynn spat.

"I'm coming, you stupid shit!" Tobias barked over his shoulder. His cheeks flushed. "Apologies."

He made his way across the tent, Her hopes snuffed until he stopped short. "Leila?" He turned to Her. "Will you be joining us?"

"I wasn't going to..." His face dropped, and She quickly corrected Herself. "But I can. Make my rounds, I mean."

"Well, if during your rounds, you somehow found yourself in my company...it would make the evening worthwhile."

As soon as he left, She cursed aloud. She was terrible at this. And what good did it serve Her anyway? There was a traitor in Her realm and many more in Her own fortress, yet here She stood fretting over the affections of an artist. Tobias was a complication, and She didn't need any more of those in Her life.

But he wanted Her, and She wanted him right back.

She packed Her things and headed into the sanctuary with everyone else. Pippa walked at Her side, slinging an arm around Her waist, and Leila tried to appreciate her playful company. Most of the men circled the fire pit, some fiddling with cards, others lost in their inebriation, while Tobias sat in conspicuous silence.

Flynn turned to greet Her, red-faced and beaming. "Leila!"

Tobias spun around at his side, and pink floated from his flesh, filling the air.

"I see you've finally learned my name," Leila said.

"Of course! I'm a gentleman, after all." Flynn gestured toward the fire pit. "Join us."

Leila wavered, then gave Pippa a squeeze. "Little duckling, can you do Me a favor? Head back to the palace, get a good night's sleep?" Pippa didn't protest, scampering off as Leila approached the circle of men.

"Healer girl, sit next to me!"

"Fuck you, Neil."

The group laughed, save for Tobias, who cast a glare in the Lord's direction. Flynn waved his chalice above their circle. "We're a bit crammed, but you're small. No doubt you can squeeze in somewhere."

Tobias's glare deepened. "Well, go on then, move over. Make room for her."

Frowning, Flynn obeyed, and Leila wasted no time taking a seat, setting Her cloak and satchel aside. She sat shoulder-to-shoulder with the men, Her skin pressed against Flynn.

And Tobias.

"Hope you don't mind the cozy accommodations," Flynn said. "Rubbing shoulders with us scoundrels."

Leila eyed Tobias sidelong. "I'll manage."

The men lost themselves in their chatter, while Tobias leaned back on his hands, the turning of his thoughts explicitly clear.

A complication. But She was the same to him, and he had chosen Her anyway.

The men were caught up in their drunken stupor, ignoring Her entirely. Slowly, She dragged Her fingers along the stone floor, gliding over smooth skin—Tobias's hand. He greeted Her touch with a soft, familiar caress, and She pulled his hand beneath Her cloak pile and threaded Her fingers between his.

Orion chuckled. "Look at that stupid grin."

Tobias bit his lip, failing to conceal his smile. He squeezed Her hand beneath Her cloak.

"It's been a good day."

🐦 13 🐦

THE POEM

Thunder crashed in the distance as rain seeped beneath the black curtain of Leila's chamber. She nestled into Her crimson sheets, the silk like soft fingertips against Her naked flesh. She'd never cared for the rain, but on this night, something about it felt powerful. Something about it excited Her.

Another boom, and Leila shrieked, bolting upright in Her bed. She cursed Her nerves and lit a candle at Her bedside, casting an orange glow across the chamber. Lightning flashed beneath Her garden curtain, followed by a deafening thunderclap, and Her door burst open, revealing a tall, dark figure.

She gasped. "Tobias?"

He stood in the doorframe, muscles glistening with rainwater. The intensity of his gaze sent chills rolling through Her body.

"What are you doing here?" She pulled a sheet over Her bare breasts. "How did you find me?"

"I had to see you." He charged into Her chamber.

"But the labyrinth—"

"Not even the labyrinth could keep me away from you."

Tobias pounced onto Her bed, whipping the hair from his eyes.

Somehow even in his disheveled state he looked ruggedly handsome, smelled of frankincense and cherry blossoms.

"From the moment we met, I knew you were the one." His strong, wet chest heaved with his labored breathing. "I haven't thought of anything else. I can't eat. I can't sleep. All I can do is dream of you."

Leila pressed a hand to Her chest. "Tobias... What are you saying?"

He came in closer, his stare fierce. "I must have you."

The hard bulge of his enormous erection pulled against his saturated pants, begging for release. She ripped the sheet from Her body.

"Take me."

Leila opened Her eyes, blinded by the sting of daylight. No thunder, no rain, and certainly no Tobias. She closed Her eyes, trying to will Herself back to sleep, but it was a lost cause. *Dammit.* Sighing, She allowed Tobias to fill the corners of Her mind, sliding Her fingers between Her legs and relaxing into Her touch.

A knock sounded at the door, and Her hands shot to Her sides. "What?"

The door crept open, and Hylas came inside. "Good morning, Your Holiness." He cowered beneath Her scowl. "Apologies for the intrusion. There's to be a meeting in the Senate room."

Her glare spoke for Her, ushering him from the room. As he walked away, Asher took his place.

"Did you need something?" Leila said.

He closed the door behind him, his lips a straight line. Leila pulled Her lace robe from Her bedframe and threw it on. "I don't recall granting you access to My chamber."

She hopped from the bed, while Asher followed behind Her. "The night before last... You didn't retire to Your chamber for the evening."

"I most certainly did."

"You didn't. Same as a few nights before then. I stood at my post and waited, but You never showed. Yet somehow, in the morning, You left Your chamber as if You had been there the entire time. But You hadn't."

"What an interesting story. Is that all?"

Asher frowned. "I am Your personal guard. It is my duty to know Your whereabouts at all times."

"Sounds to Me like someone isn't very good at their job."

"This is dangerous and unacceptable behavior, and quite frankly unbecoming of a woman of Your station. You've left me no choice but to inform the Sovereign of Your transgressions—"

Leila pounded Her elbow into his nose, sending him collapsing. The blade sat on Her end table, and She snatched it up, pressing it to his throat.

"Tell him and you die."

His eyes shot wide. "Your Holiness—"

"I have worked too hard to have everything ruined by some guard."

"I don't know what You're talking about."

"If you say *anything*, even a single word—"

"I won't speak to him!" he spat. "Just put the blade down."

Her breathing had been reduced to panting, Her hands trembling. The helplessness of Asher's gaze ripped through Her.

"I don't want to kill you," She said.

"I don't want You to kill me either."

The blade shook in Her grasp, digging into Asher's golden flesh. He swallowed. "Leila, please, I just... I don't understand."

There are too many loose ends. Kill him. She dropped Her weapon, heaving him to his feet. "This stays between us. Swear it to Me, as your One True Savior."

"I swear it. Your comings and goings are of no one's concern."

Eyeing him up and down, She grumbled, "Dismissed."

He stumbled from the chamber, glancing back at Her in a daze. She flinched when the door shut, then dressed Herself, Her muscles wound tight.

The large, black door swung behind Her as She made Her way into the Senate room. Wembleton froze midsentence, and the tension within Her threatened to break Her bones.

"Another unscheduled meeting?" She took Her seat, feigning grace and ease. "These have become quite common. What now?"

Brontes flipped through his parchment. "Recent events need to be addressed, namely Qar's responsibilities. According to his records, the Trogolians and the Monarch have accepted their invitations. We're just waiting on word from Kovahr."

"I fear I'm missing something. Where's Qar?" Leila eyed the table.

Someone else was missing. "And Phanes. Why are they not with us today?"

"Phanes is ill. He's retired to his chambers to regain his strength."

"And Qar?"

Brontes stopped his shuffling. "Qar is dead. We found his body in one of the southern gardens, stripped of his rings."

"You mean to tell Me there's a murderer in this palace?" Leila gasped. "I can't fathom it. And thievery, of all motives? The staff is paid fairly."

"It's not a thief."

"Then why would this person have an interest in Qar's jewels? Can you think of another purpose they'd serve?"

Brontes's eye narrowed. "Kastor's in charge of the wedding arrangements." He turned to the Senator in question. "You'll pick up where Qar left off."

"And who's in charge of the investigation into Qar's murder?" Leila said. "Naturally the assailant must be apprehended. I for one am outraged."

Begrudgingly, Brontes flicked a wrist at Erebus. "Assemble a team of guards to investigate Qar's murder." He went back to his parchment flipping. "On to the tournament. Were the wine and meats prepared for the Giant's victory?"

The table fell silent. Leila stared at Wembleton, willing Her eyes to become daggers, and he shrank beneath Her gaze.

Brontes glanced between the others. "Well?"

Red-faced, Wembleton cleared his throat. "Your generous offering was well-received, Your Highness. The men are eternally grateful. But... your Giant was not victorious."

"Come again?"

"The Giant. He did not win the battle."

"That's impossible. It was a fight to the death. If the Giant didn't win, surely he would've perished."

Wembleton swallowed. "The Giant is dead, Your Highness."

A sinister quiet followed—the calm before the storm, as the fury in Brontes's stare warned of thunder.

"He's been *dead* this whole time, and you're just telling me now?" he said.

Wembleton sputtered out his words. "Apologies, Your Highness."

"How did this happen? Who did he fight?"

"Your Highness—"

"*Who* did he *fight*?"

Wembleton's lip quivered. "The Artist, Your Highness."

"The Giant fell against a *Savant*?" Brontes lurched up from his seat. "How could you allow this to happen? You had *one* job. How could you be so *stupid*—?"

"He was blessed!" Wembleton blurted.

Leila bit down on Her tongue, forcing back a wince.

Brontes's voice cracked like a whip through the quiet. "What did you say?"

"The Artist was blessed." Wembleton spoke frantically, stammering. "I don't know how to explain it. He was here one moment, gone the next. He traveled through the arena like a demon, swept away in a black cloud."

"Are you *drunk*?"

"He employed magic, Your Highness." Helplessly, Wembleton glanced Leila's way. "He was blessed by...by The Savior, Your Highness."

The attention in the room shifted. Each man stared at Leila, but She was only concerned with the red cloud lifting from Her father's flesh.

"You blessed the Artist." His voice came out low and even. "Why?"

"I didn't like the Giant," She said. "He was mean to Me."

Brontes spun toward Romulus. "You discouraged me from attending."

"My deepest apologies, Your Highness," the Senator said. "How could I have predicted such an affront?"

"You've seen Her with these men. Has She expressed any fondness for the Artist?"

"He's yet to win a reward. I've only seen but a glance shared between them. Though I admit to being far-removed from matters of the heart. Perhaps that glance meant more to Her than I can imagine. She is a woman, after all. They search for meaning behind the trivial."

Brontes turned to Leila, clutching the table's edge. "Do You know how it looks for The Savior to publicly defy Her father's will?"

"Oops."

He stood in stoic silence, but the red around him became dense, filling the room. She knew what was coming.

"Leave us."

The Senators obeyed Brontes's order, while Leila remained seated and braced.

"My condolences for the Giant," She said. "He will be missed by someone, I'm sure."

Brontes stalked toward Her. "Swept away in a dark cloud. Care to explain?"

He sat on the table's edge, far too close for comfort. Leila kept Her jaw clamped shut.

"No? Do we need a little incentive?"

He grabbed Her throat, forcing Her against Her chair. Her heart pounded hard, calling for action, but She resisted.

"Still nothing?" Releasing Her, he flung open a nearby drawer, pulling out a blade not unlike Her own. Without a moment's hesitation, He carved into Her arm.

Streams of white burst through Her, and She stood at the other end of the room, far from Brontes's reach. She clutched Her bloodied arm, the stinging wound not nearly as painful as Her father's smirk.

"How disappointing," he said. "My Dark One keeps secrets from me."

"You've never shown an interest in My light."

"What of this Artist? Are You fond of him?"

With each step Brontes took forward, Leila took one back. "I told you. I didn't like the Giant."

"Maybe I'll visit the sanctuary. Congratulate the Artist in person."

"I don't particularly care what you do. Are we done here?"

Another step, and Her back hit the wall. Brontes closed the distance between them. "Show me again. Your trick."

"I am not a hired act. I am your Queen."

"Show me."

Gritting Her teeth, She pressed Herself to the wall, fighting to be as far from him as possible. He grabbed Her shoulders, slamming Her against the cool surface.

"Show me Your magic, You filthy fucking—!"

Blazing light surrounded Her, fading to drab, stone walls. She didn't quite know where She was, hadn't chosen any place in particular—just anywhere far from Brontes. *The labyrinth?* Four onyx thrones sat behind Her. This was one of the viewing rooms. The site of the next challenge. Convenient.

She clamped Her hand over Her wounded arm, slowing, then stopping the bleeding. Her breathing wavered, and She grimaced. Brontes shouldn't still scare Her this much.

She wasn't sure how long She stood there before voices sounded from the corridor. Delphi entered first, her arms overflowing with fabric. "Leila, You're early. That's new." She tossed Leila Her cloak. "Are You all right?"

Leila clasped Her cloak at Her neck, covering Her arm as Pippa and Cosima flitted by. "There's a challenge today, yes? At what time?"

"Any moment now." Delphi scanned Her over. "Are You well? You look ill."

"Brontes knows about the blessing."

"And the switch?" Leila shook Her head, and Delphi sighed. "At least there's that."

"Ladies." Romulus's voice reached the room before he did. He entered, his knowing gaze burning through Leila. "Places."

The sisters took their seats, and while Romulus left to retrieve the first competitor, Leila stewed over Her father. "The shadow walking was My advantage. He didn't know...and now he does..."

"Do You regret it?" Delphi said. "Sharing Your blessing?"

"No."

"Then it was worth the sacrifice."

"Does anyone know what the challenge is today?" Cosima fiddled with her beaded bracelet. "What exactly are we watching?"

Footsteps echoed through the room, sending the women to silence. Romulus was the first to arrive, followed by Beau, who swept his golden-brown locks from his face and winked at Cosima.

"Welcome to your fourth challenge," Romulus recited. "This

tournament is designed to test all facets of your character: your physicality, strength of will, loyalty, and soundness of mind. Today, we test the depth of your intentions."

Light beamed from the ceiling, spilling over Beau. He squinted up at the illumination searching for its source, no doubt searing his eyeballs in the process.

"Seated before you is The Savior." Romulus gestured toward the women. "And right here, right now, you will recite for Her a poem."

A poem? From these idiots?

"Describe to us your affection for Her Holiness," the Senator continued. "Speak solely from the heart."

Beau stroked his chin, his lips pursed with fierce concentration.

"Adonis," Romulus said. "Your poem."

"Give me a moment."

Romulus glowered. "Excuse me?"

"I'm trying to think of words that rhyme."

"The poem doesn't have to rhyme."

"Of course it has to rhyme. All poems rhyme," Beau scoffed. "Idiot."

"Adonis—"

"I've got it." Beau grinned at Cosima. "It's a good one. You'll like it." He puffed out his chest. "There once was a handsome Lord, who was long and strong as a sword. He found him a bride, took Her for a ride, and for always, he was adored."

The room fell silent. Beau glanced between the women, waiting for a reaction that never came.

Romulus raised a greying eyebrow. "That's your poem? About Her Holiness?"

"Yes." Beau's face dropped. "Wait, it was supposed to be about Her?"

"You're dismissed."

"You never said so—"

"Dismissed."

The Lord plodded from the room as if he had been slighted, while the women sank into their seats. The next man entered, then the next, each equally bewildered upon learning of their task. *"A poem?"* they'd ask, as if the term was foreign. One by one, they tripped over their words, fumbling for artistry that wasn't there.

Neil shoved his hands into his pockets, speechless for the first time since the tournament had begun. "What is there to say of Cosima? So many things. One look at Her, and the mind is flooded with inspiration. So much to say. So very, very much..."

Flynn came in next. "Oh, Cosima, dearest Cosima. You are...The Savior...and that is good. I would climb mountains just to see Your face. I would swim oceans just to see Your..." his stare lingered on her breasts, then darted up to her eyes, "...face once more."

With each miserable attempt, Leila and Her sisters' impatience grew. Caesar swaggered into the room, his shoulders squared, and Leila nearly laughed at the seriousness of his expression.

"Cosima, beautiful Queen with fair skin, with green eyes," he said. "It is You who keeps our realm mighty, yet it is also You who has left my heart weak. I think of You day after day. What would it be like to kiss those lips? To hold You in my arms?"

His words were strong much like his build, and despite Her misgivings, Leila couldn't help but feel a hint of intrigue.

"I wonder how it would feel to be near You, close enough to whisper in Your ear." His hands mirrored his words. "And I long for the day when I can touch Your face, and when I can hold Your bountiful breasts in my eager hands."

Leila's back shot straight, while Her sisters sat paralyzed, aghast.

"I long to lie with You in our marriage bed," Caesar said. "To be inside You, not as a mere man, but as Your Sovereign. I long to give You my seed so You may carry my child."

He bowed, ignorant to the disgust plastered across Cosima's face. "Wondrous Queen, my heart and my body belong to You."

He marched from the room like a winner, while the sisters sat in disbelief. Delphi broke the silence, inhaling deeply. "Well, that took a turn."

Leila turned to Cosima. "Did he call your breasts *bountiful?*"

"That's the part You noticed?" Cosima spat. "Not the part where he gives me his *seed?* God, men..."

As another man took his place in the viewing room, the sisters grumbled, eager for an end to their torment. Romulus was already halfway through his instructions before Leila dared to take in the fool before Her.

Tobias. He stood within the beaming light set aglow like a god, yet he wore the same blatant confusion as each man before him.

"A poem?" he said.

"One detailing your affection for Her." Romulus's voice came out drained. "Words spoken from the heart, of course."

Leila swallowed a groan. The object of Her affection feigning interest in Her sister—an excellent addition to Her horrid day.

Footsteps sounded behind Her. She glanced over Her shoulder and froze.

Brontes leaned against the wall, his eye trained on Tobias like an arrow. He had threatened to visit, hadn't he? Why hadn't She taken him seriously? Leila turned away, Her throat tight and suffocating. This was it. Her plan would be revealed—and worse, Tobias would be the one to deliver the blow.

"Artist," the Proctor barked. "Your poem."

Tobias shook himself. "Apologies, I was lost in my thoughts."

"Have you found yourself?"

"Yes."

"Then do begin."

Leila stiffened, preparing for Her world to crash down on Her.

"I haven't a way with words or poetry, but perhaps I can tell you, simply, how it is you make me feel." Tobias spoke low and steady, a soothing tone to carry sweet nothings to The Savior—except he wasn't looking at Cosima.

He was looking at Leila.

"Seen and understood. Like I am whole and empty at once. Whole because *you* see me, and empty because...how could I possibly be enough for you? It's as if I've become both large and small. How you possess that sort of power, it's beyond me."

You. He said it many times, and all the while he stared at Leila. Her breath stopped short.

He's talking to Me.

"You pique my curiosity. You fascinate me. Your mind, your words, your nuances, everything. One glance in my direction, and you have my attention. I am captivated, I am...captive." His gaze drifted, climbing the walls. "You terrify me. Because I am not accustomed to being this bold, and unarmed, and stupid—"

Leila giggled into Her hands, Her face swimming with heat. Once again, his eyes were on Her, and his lips turned up into the sweetest grin.

"But I'll be stupid, if it pleases you. I'll be stupid, if it means just a fleeting moment with you." Flecks of color danced around him, creating rainbows within the beaming light. "*You.* Just you." His expression hardened. "You are far more than a taste that I've acquired."

A wave of elation flowed through Her, lifting Her high. This moment was everything, far better than any dream, because it was real. And it was for Her.

"I don't know if any of this constitutes a poem," he said. "But this is how you make me feel."

The room fell quiet, though everything within Leila had become loud—Her racing heartbeat, Her fluttering nerves, Her vitalized thoughts.

Pippa's clapping pulled Leila back to reality. She peered over Her shoulder at Brontes, who still leaned against the wall, glowering. Tobias left the room, and so did he.

Her secret was safe.

"Well then," Leila patted down Her cloak, wrangling composure, "that nearly blew up in our faces, didn't it?"

Cosima stared at the spot where Tobias had stood. "That was the most romantic thing I've ever heard."

Leila's face burned. "It was quite lovely."

"*Lovely?*" Delphi wore a sly grin. "I saw You. You nearly forgot to breathe."

"I felt just as overwhelmed," Cosima said. "I swear I'm beside myself. I can't believe he feels so strongly for me."

Leila did a double take.

For *her?*

"I had no idea." Cosima shook her head. "This whole time he's been standing right in front of me, and I never noticed. I feel so foolish."

"Cosima, I think you're mistaken..." Leila stopped short. "Are you crying?"

Tears filled Cosima's eyes, and she turned away, wiping her cheeks. "Ignore me. How embarrassing. It's just...in all my life, no man has ever spoken of me with such care. I feel as though I'm truly being seen for the first time." She chuckled. "I suppose he and I have that in common. It was a line in his poem, after all."

"Cosima—"

"Thank You. So, so much."

"For what?"

"For affording me this opportunity. If it weren't for You, this would've never happened." She cupped Leila's face. "I am forever indebted to You, sweet Sister."

A pang ripped through Leila—not for Cosima's loving gaze or her tears, but for each misstep she'd made, every bold, audacious request. A chill crept through Leila, the bitter bite of fear latching hold.

Delphi rolled her eyes. "Cosima, the poem was—"

"When does the next man arrive?" Leila spun toward Romulus. "He must be coming soon. I feel as though we've waited forever."

Delphi furrowed her brow. "Leila?"

Another competitor entered the viewing room, sending the women to silence, and for that Leila was grateful. While Garrick sputtered out trite compliments, Leila festered over Tobias and Cosima. The pain in Her chest deepened, tearing Her in opposite directions, and every ounce of glee She had felt was smothered by dread.

The challenge ended, much to everyone's relief—except for Leila. Romulus ushered the men into the viewing room, and when Tobias met Her gaze, She looked away.

"The Savior has deliberated," Romulus said. "A winner has been selected among you, the man who competes with the purest intent."

Leila clenched Her jaw, not at all prepared for the words he would speak.

"The winner of today's challenge is the Artist. Congratulations, your reward awaits you tomorrow in the form of extended time in The Savior's company."

Leila's heart sank into Her stomach, and She left the room.

❧ 14 ❧

THE FIRE

Wembleton snored open-mouthed, cheeks clammy from the morning heat. Leila waited beside his bed, crossing Her arms as She took him in. He looked pitiful up close, with his chin tucked into the rolls of his neck, his white hair plastered to his forehead. A part of Her almost felt sorry for him—a part devoid of reason.

She slapped him across the face.

Wembleton lurched awake, tumbling from his bed in a tangle of sheets. "Your Holiness," he wheezed from the floor. "How'd You get in here?"

"Have you forgotten already?" Leila burst into rays of light, reappearing behind him.

With a yelp, he scooted away from Her, pulling his sheets over his doughy form. "You have wonderful timing. I was planning on visiting You. I have a great deal of information that I think You'll find quite valuable."

"You told My father I blessed the Artist," She said. "You exposed My magic."

"It will never happen again, I swear—"

"You're absolutely right. Because you'll be dead."

She kicked him in his side—like kicking a sack of jelly. He rolled out of his sheets and into the wall, clambering to his feet in time to spy the blade in Her hand.

"I implore You to reconsider." He pressed himself to the wall—large, pink, and naked, his belly hanging over the spot where his genitals likely sat, and for that Leila was grateful. She dragged Her blade over the curve of his stomach.

"Nose to navel. That's what I said, yes?" She stopped the sharpened tip above his groin. "You have three seconds to convince Me to spare your life."

"Your Holiness—"

"Three..." Blood beaded at the end of Her weapon. "Two..."

"News from the traitor arrives today!"

She steadied Her hand. "Explain."

"The traitor. Outside the fortress." He panted through the pain. "Your father has been in contact with them. Word arrives today."

"What kind of word?"

"I'm not certain."

"How will his word arrive?"

Wembleton sputtered out the name. "Ph-Phanes. Your father sent him to deliver payment. He returns today. And he never returns empty-handed."

"How is this possible? No one leaves the fortress."

"Brontes has made it so."

"He'll have information? He'll know who the traitor is?"

Wembleton nodded. "He should be arriving any moment now. Through the Garden of Megaera."

Leila dissolved in a surge of light, leaving Wembleton behind.

After digging through drawers and wrangling supplies, Leila stood in the watchtower staring out at the fortress. The rising sun beat down on Her, blazing through the black cloak over Her shoulders. She was used to heat in all forms, but today it was stifling.

"So, this is it?" Delphi slumped against the sill. "We just wait?"

The tall gates to the outside world stood far in the distance, and it wouldn't be long before a tiny speck of a man came marching through them. "Until Phanes returns," Leila said.

"Then I suppose we have time to discuss Your lapse in judgment yesterday."

Leila stiffened. "We're tracking a man complicit in My murder."

"Cosima's with Tobias at this very moment. A reward he won for a poem he recited for You. And You allowed it to happen."

"What was I to do?"

"You could start by telling her the truth. You owe her nothing."

"I know that."

"Then why?" Delphi said. "Why put Yourself in this stupid situation?"

"Because I don't trust her!" Leila gripped the sill, fighting to calm Herself. "You saw her at the First Impressions. Boasting of her light. Performing tricks. She uses her fictitious title to worm her way into bed with these men. She makes spectacular speeches in the arena."

"She made a speech?"

"*Yes.* An eloquent speech, no doubt rehearsed. She is drunk with power."

Delphi furrowed her brow. "What are You saying?"

Leila's voice came out meek. "I'm not trying to provoke any...hasty decisions."

"You think she'd use her position against You?"

"Do you?"

Delphi's silence ate at Her.

"You think I'm mad," Leila muttered.

"You're wise to be skeptical. But Cosima? A traitor?" Delphi snorted. "I don't think she has it in her. Though she may have Tobias in her right about now."

Her laughter was a dagger to Leila's chest. At that moment, Tobias was alone with Cosima, his reward for his *pure intent.* It was the one worry She had managed to repress, yet Her sister had resurrected it amid a flurry of giggles.

Delphi eyed Her over. "Please, You know I'm teasing. You can't possibly think she'd have any sway with him."

The tiniest movement fluttered far below—a pinprick of a man flitting through the garden, heading for the palace. Leila cocked Her head his way. "Look."

Delphi squinted. "That can't be Phanes. How did he get in?"

Leila glanced between the gates locked tight and the tiny man skittering through the garden—another unanswered question. "Fucking Brontes..."

The Garden of Megaera. The heat within Her turned searing, and soft grass crunched underfoot.

Marble statues on raised pedestals loomed on either side of Her, each with an ivory finish and outspread wings. The collection of Saviors was both beautiful and haunting, a graveyard filled with angels instead of tombs. The pinprick of a man was now strong and robust, strolling through the grass yards ahead. A navy cloak draped him, concealing all but his self-assured swagger.

Phanes. Even from behind, She was sure of it.

A limp satchel hung over his shoulder. She nearly thought it empty until he clutched it, making certain its contents were safe. She followed a careful distance, timing Her steps with his as Her hand crept down to Her blade. Second by second She came closer, until She could hear the jangling of his gold chains. The hollow-eyed statues were the only spectators in sight. This was going to be easy.

Phanes glanced over his shoulder, meeting Her gaze, and broke into a sprint.

Leila plowed after him, but Her stride was no match for his.

Closer.

She exploded into flaming light, clearing a stretch of the garden, but not enough. Once more She disappeared, closing the gap between Her and the Senator. His navy cloak was right in front of Her, and She lunged forward, tackling him to the ground.

The two rolled through the grass, a mess of fabric and legs, until Phanes elbowed Her in the ribs, breaking free of Her hold. As She staggered to Her feet with Her blade drawn, he was already waiting for Her, his own dagger in hand.

"Who's the traitor?" Leila pivoted. "Your source outside these walls. Who are they?"

"Your father knows everything," Phanes said. "You realize this, yes?"

"Answer My question."

"You killed Qar. The others before him. It's an ambitious plan, though quite basic. I'm disappointed. I always took You for a strategic—"

Leila swung Her blade, grazing his tunic. He swerved away, steadying himself before resuming his stance.

"Gelanor and Toma were old men." His breathing was even, unfazed. "You've overstepped Your capabilities this time, I'm afraid."

Clenching Her fists, She disintegrated into white-hot rays, reappearing on his back. She wrapped Her arms and legs around him as he thrashed, slamming Her blade deep into muscle.

A howl tore from his throat as they collapsed. Perhaps the blow was fatal—perhaps he'd fall limp beneath Her—but still he flapped and squawked like a wounded duck. Her blade was wedged in his shoulder. *Dammit.* She yanked the steel from his flesh.

"Guards!" he barked.

Footsteps pounded behind Her. Two armored guards fresh off their morning watch charged toward them, one with a sword in hand, the other carrying a torch.

Phanes struggled beneath Her. "Help me!"

Hands grabbed Her shoulders, hoisting Her from the Senator with ease. Her hood fell, exposing Her disheveled hair and glowing skin, and the guards gasped.

"Your Holiness?" The guard brought his torch in closer as if to get a better look.

She strained against their grasps. "Stand back!"

"The Queen's gone mad!" Clutching his bloodied shoulder, Phanes staggered to his feet. "She's lost Her mind!"

"Let go of Me!" She spat.

"I found Her here, idolizing the statues. Worshipping the mad Savior. She's lost Her senses, just as Megaera had. I fear it's genetic."

"He's lying! He's trying to kill Me!"

"Do you hear Her?" Phanes's eyes grew large. "I knew She was troubled, but I never expected such lunacy."

Profanities filled Leila's mouth. She dug Her heels into the grass, fighting for freedom. "Unhand Me! That's an order!"

The guards looked Her over, then turned to Phanes. "Apologies, Senator. We'll take Her to His Highness."

"That's for the best," Phanes said.

"Don't you dare!" She thrashed as the guards dragged Her away. "He's trying to kill Me!"

"Be safe, men." A grin crept across Phanes's lips. "Blessed be The Savior."

Rage bellowed through Her, and She closed Her eyes, allowing Her light to swallow Her up.

The hands around Her disappeared. Instead She loomed behind one of the guards who stared slack-jawed at the spot where Leila once stood. Whipping Her arm around him, She swiped Her blade across his throat.

The guard fell to his knees, clutching at the spewing gash. His counterpart gaped as She barreled toward him, then dropped his torch, attempting to flee.

"I don't want to do this," She said. "But you've left Me no choice."

"Your Holiness—"

She slammed the sharpened steel into his eye, knocking his helmet off center. He wobbled in place as She yanked the blade from his skull, blood spurting from the ragged socket before his legs gave way.

She spun around. Phanes was already running off across the garden, and he disappeared behind thick, black smoke.

The grass was on fire.

Flames bled from the guard's fallen torch, slithering across the ground like serpents. There wasn't time for this. Someone would see, and Phanes was—

Where was he?

Fire nipped at Leila's heels, and She stumbled away, scanning the garden. Phanes was nowhere to be found, and with no other options, She bolted down the path he had taken. Skidding to a halt, She glanced frantically between the manicured trees, the marble statues. Green and white stretched endlessly ahead, while waves of orange roared behind Her.

Navy fluttered in the distance—the hem of the Senator's cloak as he darted behind a statue.

Take Me to him.

She sprinted, blinded by light once, twice, each surge of power bringing Her closer. Phanes zigzagged between the marble figures, and

She trained Her eyes on his cloak, fighting to ignore the raging heat. One last burst of light, and She was behind him, slamming him face-first into the ground.

They scrambled in a pile, Leila fighting to subdue him while fishing for Her blade. He flipped Her over effortlessly, pinning Her beneath his heavy frame.

"You're making this very difficult." His voice came out in grunts. "We've been given explicit instructions not to kill You yet. But I *will* hurt You if I must."

He shoved the side of Her face into the dirt. Heat filled Her nostrils, and orange flickered in Her periphery, the flames inching toward Her face. She writhed beneath him, but he tightened his grip, pressing his pelvis into Hers. The fire spread closer, threatening to singe Her dress, Her hair. She bit into Phanes's finger.

Crying out, he cradled his hand while the taste of salt and metal coated Her lips. She kneed him in the groin and wriggled out of the fire's reach.

"Who's the traitor?" She straddled him, swatting his flailing arms. "Who's Brontes working with?"

He punched Her in the gut, forcing the air from Her lungs. Another solid blow, and She crumpled at his side, more pained by Her show of weakness than Her throbbing stomach. A hand clamped over Her mouth, and a sick smile spread across Phanes's face, perhaps because he was on top of Her, or because of his fleeting power. Whatever it was, She loathed it—his grin, his touch, his existence.

"God, I wish I could kill You." He dug his fingers into Her cheeks, forcing all his weight against Her. "All this would be over by now if I could just—"

Kill him. Phanes disappeared behind white rays, the light within Her lifting Her high. When Her vision returned, She stood paces behind the Senator, staring down at him. He started, baffled by the emptiness beneath him.

"What the—?"

She plunged Her blade into the back of his neck.

His garbled choking coalesced with the crackling fire. She dug Her weapon in deeper before pulling it free, wiping it off on Her cloak as Phanes dropped to the ground.

Blazing orange stretched far ahead, lapping at the statue pedestals. Countless marble faces stared down at Her, their gazes lifeless, their arms open wide. A familiar ivory figure lingered a short distance away.

"Forgive Me, Mother."

A condemning quiet hung in the air, followed by distant shouting. Guards were headed Her way, barely visible through the rising flames. She dug through Phanes's pockets—empty—then snatched up his satchel and summoned Her light.

Canvas tents surrounded Her, along with black brick walls. She hadn't given Her light specific instructions, just to take Her someplace comfortable, someplace safe. *But the sanctuary, of all places?*

Voices bounced off the walls. The men were already present, resting after whatever horrors they had endured. Leila wove between the tents, nestling into a darkened corner and digging through the procured satchel. An empty coin purse, a slip of parchment folded in half, and a long, glittering string of topaz.

A necklace?

"Leila."

Deep brown eyes connected with Hers. Tobias was headed Her way, and Her throat went dry as he drew near.

"Tobias." She stuffed the necklace into Phanes's satchel. "You're back."

"I wanted to speak with you." He took Her arm, guiding Her behind one of the tents. "Cosima... She knows you gave me Her blessing."

The reward. It had left Her thoughts, but now it weighed heavily in Her mind and in Her chest. "Yes, I imagine She does."

"But She insisted She wouldn't tell the Sovereign. Said you were Her sister—that She would never wish to harm you."

"That sounds like Cosima," She said.

"You need to know, I didn't tell Her it was you. She just...*knew*. I don't know how, but She did. Believe me when I tell you, I said nothing."

A familiar scent permeated the air, overpowering the musty stench of the sanctuary.

Cosima's rose perfume.

Saliva pooled in Leila's mouth. "I believe you."

"Good." He exhaled. "I was worried."

The rose scent surrounded them, pungent enough to make Her sick. Cosima's perfume was all over Tobias—as were her hands, her body, her lips. *He was quite skilled with his tongue. The way he touched me was ravenous.* Cosima's words echoed in Leila's skull, another torture She didn't need, certainly not while Tobias stared at Her with that penetrating gaze—a gaze She adored. A gaze She hated.

"Well, your concern is much appreciated." She turned away, fumbling with Phanes's satchel. "Is that all?"

Tobias faltered. "Pardon?"

"Is there anything else I can do for you?"

"What do you mean?"

"Are you hurt?" She said. "Did you injure yourself on the way back from your reward? Do you need my assistance in any way?"

Tobias furrowed his brow. "Well, no, I'm fine, I just thought—"

"You thought what?"

"You and I, we usually...talk."

Anger rose through Leila's chest. They *used* to talk. Not anymore.

"Tobias, I'm the Healer. I'm here to *heal*. Not to give *you* my undivided attention."

Tobias hesitated. "Leila, I'm confused. Do you want me to leave you alone?"

"If you haven't anything further to discuss, then yes, I would like that very much, actually."

His face dropped. Long seconds passed before he stepped aside.

"All right," he muttered.

She swerved around him, fighting to get as far away as possible. A stabbing pain pierced Her chest—resentment, hurt, emotions She was ashamed to feel. This was for the best, even if it wounded Her.

Forcing Tobias from Her thoughts, Leila focused on the satchel. She scooted aside the necklace and empty coin purse, plucking up the folded parchment—a note written in a foreign tongue. *Kovahrian?*

"Healer girl."

She had nearly forgotten where She was. The nearby men were

marked with deep scratches as if having fought off an army of cats, and a massive pit sat in the floor at the head of the sanctuary—an endless abyss as grim as Her mood. Shoving the note into Her satchel, She trudged toward one of the men. No bandages, no perfumes; She groaned, rolling Her eyes and catching Tobias in Her periphery. He sat with his comrades playing their card game. *Her* card game. *He doesn't even care.*

Moving from man to man, She cleaned their wounds with canvas scraps and water from the leaking barrels, all the while stewing over the foreign note. *Definitely Kovahrian.* But She was familiar with their language, and these words were obscure to Her. Finding Phanes was supposed to answer Her questions, not create more of them.

"Healer girl!" Neil dragged Her from Her station, pulling Her toward his usual group. Beau sat alongside the pit, while Caesar kicked pebbles into the nothingness. Catching Her gaze, he bared his sinewy back—lined with the same scratches as every other man—and She went to work washing his wounds, Her mind still on the parchment.

Neil pinched Her hip, hovering close. "You're awfully quiet today."

"Does she usually talk much?" Beau said. "I hadn't noticed."

"Are you sad?" Neil nuzzled against Her neck. "Is it because you missed me?"

Leila elbowed him in the gut, sending Beau and Caesar bursting into laughter. Gritting Her teeth, She tended to Caesar's wounds simply to occupy Her hands. The lingering warmth of Neil's cheek against Hers reminded Her of Phanes's hands on Her face, Brontes's grip on Her throat...

"Someone's in a sour mood." Neil stumbled away, pretending Her jab hadn't hurt. "Probably hasn't had a good romp in some time."

"Or ever," Caesar scoffed.

"You think she's pure?" Beau eyed Her over. "I suppose she looks it. You can tell with ladies. They wear it right on their faces."

"Is that so? Are you *actually* pure?" Grinning, Neil slid his hands around Her waist. "I can fix that for you."

Leila pulled away, Her jaw tight. Phanes wasn't in the forefront of Her mind any longer—it was the all-consuming fire that had ravaged the garden. She could've sworn the flames had followed Her into the sanctuary, had made a home inside Her.

"Healer girl, when are you going to give us a peek beneath your cloak?"

Neil lifted the hem of Her cloak with his foot, and She yanked it away. "Just as soon as you stop being such a worthless ass."

"She's a bit bitchy, isn't she?" Beau said.

"Nonsense, she's simply a good judge of character." Caesar chuckled.

"Lies. She's playing." Neil spoke into Leila's ear. "You like me, don't you? Tell them you like me."

His lips brushed against Her flesh, and She recoiled. "I'd like you much better if you'd finally shut your mouth."

The surrounding Lords laughed, fueling Neil's resolve. "Healer girl, now you're just being cold. And I'd much prefer you warm...and wet."

His hands moved quickly, sliding beneath Her cloak and grabbing Her breasts. Leila tore free from his assault and spun toward him, not bothering to restrain the inferno within Her. "Touch me one more time, and I swear it will be the last thing you do."

Neil glanced between his friends. "Did you hear her? Healer girl, was that a threat..." he dragged his fingers down Her neck, circling Her breast, "...or a *dare?*"

Leila shoved his chest, sending him plummeting into the pit.

His screams echoed from the abyss, a song that slowed the racing of Her heartbeat. The ghost of his hands on Her skin faded as soon as his cries disappeared.

Exhaling, She swung Phanes's satchel over Her shoulder. The sanctuary had gone silent, each man now staring at Her.

"What?" She said. "He wasn't going to win anyway."

She left the sanctuary, untroubled for the first time all day.

15
THE GAME

Leila dragged Her finger over the parchment, tracing each curve of the Kovahrian letters. Deciphering this note was of the utmost importance—a fact She had reminded Herself of a thousand times, yet Her thoughts were on Tobias, Cosima, and what they most certainly did together. She saw him undressing her, his face buried between her legs, the visions like needles lancing Her eyes.

Groaning, She snatched up the note, the necklace, and Phanes's empty coin purse, shoving them into Her pockets and leaving Her chamber.

Asher stood at Her door, flushing at the sight of Her. He opened his mouth to speak but wavered, offering a nod instead. Clearing Her throat, Leila walked on.

Cosima was headed down the corridor. *Oh, for God's sake.* No doubt she'd have words about her reward, stories Leila had no interest in enduring. She turned on Her heel, bounding in the opposite direction.

Safely out of sight, Leila hurried up the grand staircase where a vast window displayed the palace courtyard. Servants in straw hats made their way past the marble fountain toward the fortress gardens, some with baskets hoisted onto their hips, others carrying contraptions Leila couldn't place, no doubt for manual labor.

Brontes stopped at Her side, an understated crown on his head to match the gold stitching of his drape. He stared out the window, and She tried to mirror his casualness despite the stiffness of Her muscles.

"Where's everyone headed?" She said. Brontes snorted, and She straightened. "Your Holiness asked a question."

"There was a fire. Servants were called to clear the mess."

"A fire?" She shrugged. "The weather *has* been particularly dry."

"How was Your reward with Your friend?"

"Pardon?"

"The Artist," he said. "What did you do together? Or are the details too intimate to share?"

Leila scowled. "He's not My friend."

"He and I had a very revealing conversation the other day. I understand now why You're drawn to him. He's arrogant, like You. Dares to mock those who stand above him. Of course my daughter favors a smart mouth."

"I'm so sorry he hurt your feelings."

Leaning against the window, he came in closer. "Three bodies were found in the fire. Senator Phanes was among them. You wouldn't know anything about that, my little Dark One, would You?"

"Isn't that how fire works? It kills those who get too close."

Brontes's eye narrowed, and Leila made sure to give parting before his silence ended. "Send My sympathies to Phanes's family. Or did he not have any? I suppose no one will miss him, then."

She flitted off, glad to be rid of Her father's gaze. Taking to Her study, She gathered Her cloak and satchel before disappearing to the labyrinth. Today marked another challenge, and though She wasn't sure of its nature, it had to be better than spending another second with Brontes.

The darkened tunnel led to one of the many viewing rooms, though this one was different from the others. Beyond the four onyx thrones and invisible shield was a large, oddly constructed table, its surface a mess of metal rods and springs with evenly dispersed tiles sitting atop them.

Blonde tangles burst into Leila's line of sight. "You're here!" Pippa said. "You're just in time. We're playing a game!"

Leila gestured toward the table. "What is...?" Her voice trailed off—the ceramic tiles were laid out in a perfect square like canvas cards. "Oh. Match the Eye."

"Finally, She reveals Herself!" Cosima fluttered to Leila's side. "I haven't seen You in days, it feels like. My little bird, floating off with the breeze. I absolutely must tell You of the last reward. You will be *astounded*."

Leila's gut heaved. Footsteps echoed from the adjacent portal, and Romulus entered the room.

"Not now, Cosima, the challenge is beginning." Taking Her seat, Leila flicked Her wrist at Romulus. "Go on. Bring them in."

Romulus gave Her a sideways glance before obeying. Waiting for Cosima and Pippa to lose themselves in conversation, Delphi claimed the throne at Leila's side and spoke out of the corner of her mouth. "I met with the men today."

"Is that so?"

"One seemed especially dejected. Would You like to guess who?"

Leila rolled Her eyes. She knew what was coming.

"His face." Delphi sighed. "It was heartbreaking, truly. Like a pouting puppy dog. And those eyes. Have You seen them when they're sad? I swear they grow larger."

"Stop it."

"I will not."

"I'm ordering you to."

"Oh, fuck Your orders," Delphi said. "I am Your sister, Your advisor, and Your friend. And I will tell You when You're being foolish."

"So, get on with it."

"You're being foolish."

"Good. Now it's done."

Silence, save for the prattling of Pippa and Cosima. Leila was glad for the moment of peace, until Delphi turned to Her, sticking out her bottom lip.

"Why are you looking at Me like that?" Leila said.

"This is what he looked like." Delphi fluttered her lashes. "I'm sure I'm not doing him justice. I don't have the eyes."

"God, I swear..."

The men filed into the room, each wearing a befuddled expression as they took their place around the table. Leila nearly smiled at the conspicuous absence of Neil—until She spotted Tobias.

"Welcome to your fifth challenge," Romulus droned. "The twelve of you have proven yourselves stronger and truer than those who have fallen. We have tested your brawn, your valor, and your heart, and you have shown yourselves worthy enough to continue on in the pursuit of our Savior's hand. Still, there is one facet of your being we have yet to test: your mind."

Light spewed from the ceramic tiles like geysers, fading to reveal symbols in black ink. Most of the men stared at the painted swords, hearts, and chalices in confusion, while looks of realization swept the faces of a few. Raphael. Zander.

Tobias.

"Before you is a game," Romulus said. "One that tests the soundness of your mind. Each tile holds a symbol. Learn their place on this table, and pray your memory serves you well, for these symbols will disappear in three, two, one, zero."

Another surge of light, and the symbols faded from the tile surfaces.

As Romulus rambled off the game's instructions, Delphi leaned toward Leila. "This was Your choice? Match the Eye?"

"What?" Leila said. "I chose at random."

"You *randomly* chose the exact game Tobias plays each day in the sanctuary? One he can easily survive without strain or harm?"

"You jump to conclusions."

"For each correct match you give, you will continue on in this challenge," Romulus said. "But answer incorrectly, and the consequence will be...unpleasant."

A snap echoed off the walls, and a spring-loaded mallet shot up from beneath one of the ceramic tiles, smashing it.

Leila sat tall, pretending Her gut wasn't churning. "See?"

Romulus called the men one by one to take their turn, starting with Raphael, who played with ease, then Drake, who was surprisingly adept as well. Leila lost interest in the challenge, drawn to more important matters. Her satchel sat on the floor beside Her, and She nudged it with

Her heel, giving Her a glimpse of topaz—one gem for each question She desperately needed answers to.

"Brontes knows about Phanes," She whispered.

Delphi scoffed. "Everyone knows about Phanes."

"I couldn't get him to talk, but I did retrieve his things. They're... puzzling at best. We have much to discuss."

"We most certainly do. At a later time."

"What do you mean?"

Delphi cocked Her head at the table, where Flynn was taking his turn. "There's a challenge at hand."

"Since when do you care about the tournament?"

"Artist," Romulus announced. "Your move."

Delphi offered Leila a knowing glance, which Leila returned with an eye roll. "I don't care how he performs."

Turning away, She fought to ignore both Her sister and the game, though She couldn't help but watch Tobias out of the corner of Her eye. He stared at the tiles, his lips pursed in the most adorable manner. *Hideous. His lips are hideous.*

He placed his hand on a tile, revealing a painted eye.

"You've drawn a riddle," Romulus said.

A riddle? Tobias was good at this game, could've passed his round easily. But the worry came and went. Tobias wasn't Her concern anymore. No, She hadn't a single care for him. As Romulus recited an inane riddle, Leila leaned back in Her seat, casual as ever.

"Grown in the darkness, this beauty shines bright with pale light," Romulus read from a scroll. "Though it is not the light of The Savior, She keeps it close to Her heart, Her hair, Her dress."

Pearls. They weren't Leila's favorite, but Cosima wore them often, even at that very moment. No doubt Tobias would breeze past such a silly task—not that it mattered to Her.

A snap echoed off the walls, followed by a throaty "Fuck!" Tobias's hand was planted on a now broken tile, his fingers caught beneath a heavy mallet.

"He lost?" Leila spun toward Delphi. "How could he lose?"

Delphi cracked a smile. "Good boy."

"What?"

"Nothing."

Tobias cradled his broken fingers against his chest, sucking in shallow breaths through his teeth. *Idiot.* Groaning, Leila slapped Her palm to Her forehead.

"Artist, you are the first man to answer in error and the loser of this challenge. For that, you must be punished." Romulus pointed a knobby finger at the portal. "Your penalty is solitude in the sanctuary. Go now, and spend your time contemplating the deep disappointment you've bestowed upon our Savior."

Tobias left the room, shrunken and wounded, and Leila could've sworn She saw that puppy dog Delphi had described.

～

"Here's what we have."

Leila's voice echoed through the viewing room, now vacant save for Her and Delphi. She dumped Phanes's things onto the floor. "The missing funds." She plucked up the empty coin purse. "Wembleton said Phanes was tasked to deliver payment. I assume that's what this is for. But I can't wrap My head around this..." She flipped the slip of parchment between Her fingers, "...and certainly not that." She cocked Her head at the string of jewels.

Delphi swept up the necklace from the floor. "A wedding present?"

"Some present. These are the palest topaz I've ever seen." She bit into a peach. "Maybe it's some kind of message. Maybe the traitor is a woman."

"Why would a woman send Brontes her jewels?"

"Let's not worry about the necklace." Leila snatched the jewelry from Delphi's grasp, replacing it with the note. "Can you read Kovahrian?"

"Naturally. Can't You?"

"Of course. Well, mostly. I've never seen these words. It's like another language entirely. Maybe an ancient dialect?"

"We're wasting time. We can't answer these questions on our own."

Leila ignored her, finishing off Her peach as She paced the viewing room floor. "Do you think the Kovahrians are aiding My assassination? I don't understand. We've always been peaceful with them."

"We'll worry about this later. When we have the proper resources."

"Enzo. He's Kovahrian. Do you think he has ulterior motives? He's certainly not here for The Savior. His tryst with Zander has made that clear."

"I will visit the records. Search for a translation." Delphi shoved Leila's satchel into Her arms. "You need to go to the sanctuary."

"Why are you rushing Me?"

"Tobias is waiting for You."

Leila scoffed. "That man is none of My concern."

"He spoke of You in the poetry challenge," Delphi said. "You know it."

"I also know Cosima has the most enviable breasts in the fortress."

"Does Tobias strike You as the type to fall prey to breasts?"

"He strikes Me as a man. So, yes."

"He confessed his feelings for You. In public. In front of Your father."

"Cosima's father." The words stung Leila's lips. "She's The Savior, after all. I'm just Her sister."

Undeterred, Delphi planted her hands on her hips. "Go to him. *Please.* Or are You going to let him compete tomorrow with broken fingers?"

Leila tried to appear unfazed, but the thought of Tobias's mangled hand plucked at Her worries. Glaring at Delphi, She headed off through the portal.

The darkened tunnel opened up to the labyrinth, and with each step She took, Her stomach lurched. She fidgeted with Her cloak, Her dress —*oh God, what am I wearing?*—then scowled at the midnight blue fabric. She always looked pale in blue. Why had She chosen blue? She shook Herself. She had no need to impress Tobias.

Neil's grave appeared with the sanctuary waiting behind it, and She stomped on the tiny crown marker, sending stepping stones floating up from the pit. She made Her way across, trying Her best not to look at Tobias, who sat cross-legged on the floor, staring a hole through Her. They were the only people there, yet somehow the air felt thick, even more so when She took a seat at his side, when She unfastened Her cloak, and when his gaze swept Her figure.

She smacked his arm.

Tobias recoiled. "What the—?"

"What is wrong with you?" She spat. "Has your brain turned to dust?"

"Leila—"

"You play that game every day. Every. Day. And here you are, the first man out. I can't believe it!"

A smile crept across his lips. "I know. It was a poor move."

"A *stupid* move."

"Yes, stupid. Completely. The correct answer was clearly the pearls. And to think, it was just three tiles to the right."

Leila straightened. "You knew the answer?"

"Naturally," he said. "Or did you really think my brain had turned to dust?"

"Did you lose on *purpose?*"

"Perhaps."

"Tobias!" She smacked his arm again. "Why?"

"Well, you didn't seem too thrilled when I won the last challenge."

"You lost for *me?*"

"What else was I to do? You wanted nothing to do with me after my time with Cosima." He raised an eyebrow. "Tell me, are you still utterly repulsed by my presence?"

Cosima. The name on his tongue sent those horrid visions crashing through Leila's mind. "It's not that. It's just...I *know* what happens during rewards. With Cosima."

"Maybe you don't."

"We're sisters. We talk. Frequently."

"Did you talk about my time with Her?"

His lips on her neck, her breasts. Leila could see it all. "No."

"Good," he said. "Then you can hear it from me."

"I don't want to hear it."

"Leila—"

"I *don't* want to hear it." She scowled. "You *will* respect my wishes."

Tobias opened his mouth to speak, then stopped short, frowning. "Fine. But you're making a mistake."

Shooting him a glare, She plucked his hand from his lap. His first three fingers looked perfectly fine, while the two at the end were like crooked red sausages. "God, look at you. You're an artist, and you broke your fingers. On your right hand, no less."

"It's a good thing I'm left-handed, then."

A sly grin spread across his cheeks. He had planned this, and that single fact made Her heart beat faster. She wished it wouldn't.

"Please don't let my sacrifice be in vain," he said.

"And what exactly do you expect from me in return for your *sacrifice?*"

"Just your company."

Damn Her heartbeat; it was pounding hard, certainly loud enough for Tobias to make out. "Here, let me take a look at your fingers." She tossed him a rag. "And while I'm at it, wipe yourself down—with your good hand. You look like you belong in a damn brothel."

His laughter rolled through Her in chills. Even covered in those perverse oils, he was handsome, his unruly brown waves like a wreath atop his head, his carved form only slightly blemished by tournament scars, his sable eyes large and kind.

He bedded Your sister. None of this was remotely fair.

While he de-oiled, She took his mangled hand. *This has to be quick.* She raised Her free hand overhead, snapping Her fingers. "Tobias."

His gaze flitted Her way. "Hm?"

She popped his finger into place, the ugly crack of his bones reverberating through Her.

"*Shit!*"

"Apologies," She said. "I know it hurts, but the pain will subside in a moment." She snapped Her fingers again. "Over here."

"What?"

Another crack, and his little finger was perfectly straight, though his face was contorted with pain.

"God*dammit—*"

"All done. The worst is over."

She coated Her hand in Her favorite perfumes and rubbed his

swollen fingers. *Mend the breaks. Ease the pain.* Once Her light subdued, She bandaged his injury, mentally cursing Herself for treating him with such care.

"So tell me, Tobias..." She eyed him sidelong, "...why are you here?"

"That's a silly question. I'm here because I lost the challenge."

"No, I mean, why are you *here*—in this tournament? You're obviously not here to be the Champion. If you were, you'd be with Cosima right now, and your fingers wouldn't be pointing in opposite directions."

Tobias looked away. She thought back to the conversations they'd shared—stories of his life. His family.

"Your sister."

"Her care is expensive," he said.

The fight in the arena entered Her mind, particularly the men in the mirrors. "And what of your parents?"

"My father's dead," he confirmed. "Killed in the accident that crippled my sister. My mother cares for her all day. I started laboring, trying to support them both." He stared down at his lap. "It's not enough. She is wrought with challenges. With suffering."

"What's her name?"

"Naomi."

"Is she older or younger?"

The shame in his face lifted, revealing a smile. "We're twins."

"Twins?" She cocked Her head. "Do you look alike?"

"Identical. My female equivalent."

"And what else? Is she an artist like you?"

He laughed. "*God* no. She's terrible. Her efforts, like a child's scribbles. No, she was to be a metalsmith."

"A metalsmith? Really?"

"I know. It's a bit unprecedented, but she does what she pleases." His smile widened. "I think you'd like her."

"I bet you're right," Leila said. "She's clearly an individual, not unlike yourself. I'm sure it's one of the many traits that bind you two together. And one of the countless reasons why you'd sacrifice yourself just for her."

His gaze drifted, climbing the walls. "You think I'm a fraud. That I dishonor The Savior. Play a part for personal gain."

"Actually, I think you just might be the only man here for valid purpose. You're here for the sake of love, aren't you? It's just not the love of The Savior."

"Well, don't tell that to Flynn. He certainly thinks he's here for love."

"God, Flynn, what an ass." Leila leaned back on Her hands. "He doesn't *love* The Savior. You can't love a person you don't know. He's infatuated with Her—or the idea of Her, at least. But love? Definitely not."

Chuckling, Tobias nudged Her shoulder. "It's your turn. You heard of my sister. Tell me about yours."

"But you've met them."

"Still, I'm curious to hear your take on them."

Delight prickled beneath Her skin. "Well, I'm closest with Delphi. True sisters, not just in title, but in heart. I'm sure you've gathered that already. Pippa—she's darling, isn't she? My little duckling, following me wherever I go. And Cosima..."

Her gut wound tight. She had forgotten.

"What of Cosima?" Tobias said.

Leila clenched Her jaw. "She drifts away from me. Every day, She's a bit further. And I don't know how to fix it."

"I imagine I'm not helping the matter."

His lips on Cosima's, his hands on her body. The visions were a self-inflicted torture, one Leila had the power to end, if only She'd muster the words.

"I suppose you can tell me about it," She said. "Your reward. With Cosima."

"Are you certain?"

"You'd have me change my mind?"

He cleared his throat. "Well, I'll have you know, it wasn't eventful. She called me *Artist* the entire time, as if She couldn't be bothered to learn my name."

"I know how that feels," Leila grumbled.

"We discussed the tournament at some length—or rather She did, and I listened. And then She talked about Her divine light. Did the most uncomfortable thing: She put Her hand on my chest and asked if I could *feel* Her light."

Leila's jaw went slack. "She did *not*."

"Oh, but She did."

Obscenities filled Her mouth, but She swallowed them down. *First grand speeches, now this?*

"Then after all that mess..." Tobias continued, "...She offered me a kiss."

His words hit Her with force. Perhaps She should've felt relieved. After all, it was just a kiss. But that did little to stop the sinking of Her stomach.

"Well, I suppose it was inevitable," She said. "You're quite handsome, plus you delivered that beautiful poem. It's only natural She'd want to kiss you. And in your position, how could you possibly refuse?"

"I didn't kiss Her."

Leila flinched. "*What?*"

"I didn't kiss Her. Just blabbered some nonsense about being shy. I don't know, I don't even remember. It was all so uncomfortable."

"You jilted Cosima."

He shrugged. "I suppose I did."

"Why?"

"I think you know why."

Nothing. She had no response, just quiet disbelief. Finally, She found Her voice. "That...was incredibly stupid."

"Yes, well, *I'm* incredibly stupid." Laughing, Tobias raised his bandaged hand. "I think that's been made quite obvious by my decisions as of late."

"You really didn't kiss Her?"

"I didn't kiss Her." He leaned in closer, his gaze penetrating. "Leila... have my intentions not been clear?"

Her gut caved in on itself. "I suppose I owe you an apology."

"Nonsense. I'd just prefer that, in the future, you come to me with your worries instead of stewing by yourself."

"I'm not very good at this."

"I wouldn't be so sure," he said. "I did break my fingers for you. Seems as though you're doing something right."

A disarming smile swept his face, and Her burdens lifted. She scooted closer to him, hugging Her knees tight. "Tell me a story."

"A story?"

"Yes. A good one." Her eyes widened. "Tell me of your first love."

"I've never been in love."

"Well then, tell me of another first. Your first kiss."

He scoffed. "Oh God, so you're looking for a horror story."

"It was that bad?"

"Worse."

"Who was she?"

"Stheno." His nostrils flared. "Milo's sister."

"You kissed your best friend's *sister*?"

"Don't judge me so quickly, she started it. Was fond of me for years, and let me tell you, the feeling was *not* mutual."

"You didn't care for her."

"She's a cock!" he said. "Mean-spirited. A bully, really. But I always caught her staring at me in that lecherous way. Made my stomach turn, to be frank. Then one day... God, I was, I don't know, maybe ten at the time? She was thirteen—turning into a woman already, and not a decent one. Anyway, I was on my way to see Milo, and Stheno—she grabbed me from behind, pinned me to the wall, and *bam*. She kissed me. With tongue and everything." He grimaced. "It was disgusting."

"The miscreant!" Leila gasped. "She *pinned* you to the wall?"

"She was very large for her age. Quite muscular too. Sometimes I wondered if Milo envied that about her."

"I don't think I like her. Not at all."

Tobias eyed Leila over. "Your turn. What of your first love?"

Shit. She hadn't thought this through. Sighing, She flopped onto the floor, staring at the bricks overhead. "I've never loved a man. Not romantically, at least. It's not as though there are many options in the fortress. Plenty of beautiful young women and dirty old men, but suitable bachelors? Those are a rare breed. Just guards, maybe the occasional page, but nothing more."

"And what of these guards? They never caught your attention?"

"It wouldn't matter if they did. No man looks my way. Not like that, at least."

A snort-laugh sounded above Her. Leila lifted Her head. "What's so funny?"

"You're lying to me." He raised an eyebrow. "Have you not seen yourself?"

Heat rose up Her neck. "Yes, well, I've been told I can be intimidating."

Tobias lay down beside Her, flustering Her nerves. "Intimidating? Well, I suppose I can see it. You're confident, intelligent, not to mention very beautiful. It's a formidable combination. It's certainly easier on the ego to pursue a lesser woman."

"If that's true, why are you here?"

"I don't care about my ego, and I don't want a lesser woman."

"Does that mean I don't intimidate you?" She said.

"Well, now that I'm thinking about it, I suppose you do. But that's a good thing, yes? The best pursuits in life are challenging. That's how you know they're worth it."

Everything within Her was vibrant, beaming. She traced Her fingers down his arm, taking a daring peek inside. Fuchsia connected with Her touch, floating from his flesh, and She drew shapes across his forearm, turning his passion into art.

"You give me chills," he whispered.

She spoke against his ear. "Good."

He turned toward Her, his eyes on Her eyes, then Her lips.

He's going to kiss Me.

He leaned in, a slow-moving second that lasted a lifetime. Her first kiss.

Leila bolted upright. She had no idea what She was doing, would surely muck it all up the moment their lips touched, and that worry latched on tight, taking control. She mentally cursed Herself, until She caught Tobias staring at Her, the grin on his face enough to lessen the embarrassment.

"So tell me," She said. "What are your plans for the future?"

"What future? I'm stuck in this tournament. Most likely to die."

"Stop it."

He shrugged. "It's true. My future has been determined for me. Even before this tournament, my fate was sealed. I was to labor each day until the end of time so my mother and sister would be taken care of." Sitting upright, Tobias stared down at his palms. "My life has become a series of...necessary sacrifices. Just one after the next. I don't resent it...but it would be nice to keep something for myself. Something that couldn't be taken away. To have—"

"One good thing," Leila finished. "That would be wonderful."

"Sounds like you know what I'm talking about."

"I know exactly what you're talking about."

His gaze became too much to bear, and She turned away, studying the ends of Her hair. "So, is that how you see your future? Just a succession of bad things?"

"Naturally. I'll either die here or marry Cosima, which isn't exactly a superior outcome. To marry Someone I don't care for, Someone I've barely spoken to."

"You could be speaking to Her right now."

"But I'd rather be speaking to you."

A pang shot through Her. "I'm sorry." She leaned against his shoulder. "For making assumptions about you. I do that a lot. I really shouldn't, but I'm so used to disappointment."

"Leila, it's long been forgotten."

"I'm feeling guilty."

"Well, that's unfortunate, because I'm feeling incredible—here, with you."

She bit Her lip to keep from giggling, then snatched up his bandaged hand. "I still can't believe it. You broke your fingers for me. You're either extremely romantic or a madman."

"Perhaps both?"

"Something we can agree on."

She tasted it first—a cinnamon sweetness on Her tongue—then pink wafted from his flesh, circling them in tendrils and ribbons. Tobias held Her hand gently, as if it were precious, and She relaxed into him as he nuzzled against Her hair.

Kiss Me.

She turned away, taking a seat across from him.

She wanted to. But She couldn't.

Tobias offered a soft smile. "So, what about your future? What are your plans once all the bloodshed has ended?"

"Would you believe me if I told you that this tournament has made a real mess of my future as well?"

"That doesn't surprise me," he said. "In fact, I'm starting to think that's the true purpose of this tournament—to destroy the lives of everyone associated with it. Except for Cosima. She seems to be enjoying Herself."

Cosima. Leila forced Her sister from Her mind. "Well, I hate this tournament and everything that comes with it. I hate the Sovereign, I hate the labyrinth, I hate the challenges and the entire purpose of this ruse. I want no part in it. Yet it appears I have no choice."

Tobias's gaze drifted to the wall, as if Her words weighed on him. She scooted closer. "I have an idea. A game."

"I don't know about that." He held up his bandaged hand. "I've already played one game today, and it ended quite painfully for me."

"We can pretend. The tournament doesn't exist. All is well in your home and in this fortress. Tell me, what would you do then? If not for the tournament, what would you do?"

Tobias chuckled. "All right. If not for the tournament, I'd go back to Petros. Be an artist again. I'd only come to the fortress if I were commissioned."

"You would be too. You're very talented."

His smile widened. "Your turn."

"If not for the tournament, I'd leave."

"Leave?"

"The palace," She said. "Not permanently. But I'd just...leave. Sometimes. See what's out there, past the fortress."

"You can't do that now?"

Leila shook Her head.

Frowning, Tobias continued. "If not for the tournament, I'd marry who I wanted, when I wanted to, because I wanted to. Not someone I *won.* Someone who bores me."

"She bores you?"

"*God,* yes." He faltered. "No offense. I know She's your friend. Or sister. Your sister-friend. This is confusing. God, what a mess."

Leila giggled, more pleased than She cared to admit. "If not for the tournament, I'd live freely. Make the decisions I want to make without questioning the cost or risk. Without fear."

"Is Cosima controlling?"

She hesitated before shaking Her head.

Tobias furrowed his brow. "The Sovereign."

She nodded.

Tobias cleared his throat. "If not for the tournament, I'd die an old man. In my sleep, surrounded by my children and grandchildren and great-grandchildren."

"That could still happen."

"Unlikely."

Leila gave his arm a playful smack. "If not for the tournament, I'd heal people. In the realm. Put my skills to proper use."

Instantly Her mind was filled with dreams: a life without walls, without Her father. She thought of using Her light beyond the fortress, of fulfilling Her duty. All of it seemed like fantasies—but then again so did this moment, and it was real.

"If not for the tournament..." Tobias said, "...I'd ask to kiss you."

"I'd say yes."

Leila turned to stone. She had spoken without thinking, the words tumbling free of their own bidding.

Tobias stared at Her, wide-eyed. "You didn't say the first part."

"And you still haven't kissed me."

Silence hovered in the air, dense and tangible. *You don't know what You're doing.* But perhaps that didn't matter.

An eternity passed before Tobias closed the distance between them, his fingers threading through Her hair. She gasped at his touch, torn between his potent gaze, his mouth. He took Her chin, guiding Her closer, then pressed his lips to Hers.

It only lasted for a moment—a single delicate kiss.

She wanted more.

Tobias cupped Her cheeks. "Leila, you're shaking."

He was right. She tried and failed to still Herself. "It's just...I'm realizing...this makes things quite complicated."

"This doesn't have to go any further. We can stop right now. Pretend it never happened."

Her nerves spiked. "Is that what you want?" He shook his head, and She let out a breath. "It's not what I want, either."

He gazed back at Her for a second longer, then gently kissed Her bottom lip. Again. Goose bumps trailed his fingertips as they slid down the back of Her neck. She wasn't sure how he did it—how each touch of his hands and his mouth managed to be soft and powerful at the same time.

Tobias came in deeper, his kiss long and yearning. She didn't need to see his colors any longer. They traveled straight through Her, tasting like sugar and fire.

The next kiss was Her doing; She was hungry for it, his lips everything She needed, yet not enough. Emboldened, She glided Her fingers up his sculpted stomach, taking in blips of his passion. He grabbed Her hand, and as he pressed it to his chest, color exploded behind Her eyelids. Her palm burned, Her senses overflowing with want and heat and a beautiful ache—with everything he felt for Her. His arms wrapped around Her, bringing Her close, and She welcomed the warmth of his body and the echo of his heartbeat.

Footsteps. Leila pulled away, glancing at the tunnel behind them. "The first group is coming. I have to go."

Tobias tugged Her close, tucking a loose strand of hair behind Her ear. "I wish you could stay."

"Is that so?"

"The moment was too fleeting."

He kissed Her hard, and She melted into his embrace, soaking him in. Composing Herself, She threw Her cloak and satchel over Her shoulder. "We'll see if you still feel this way tomorrow."

"You think I won't?"

"I think men can be fickle in matters such as these." She gave him a peck on the lips. "I have to go."

Every impulse within Her rebelled, but She hopped to Her feet anyway, heading across the stone steps and into the labyrinth.

"Leila," Tobias called out. "I'm not fickle. I'll still feel this way tomorrow. Nothing will change."

She smiled. "I hope so."

She continued down the labyrinth, turning into one of the hidden portals as the other men's voices bounced off the brick. Grinning, She leaned against the stairwell wall. *Nothing will change.*

God help Her, She believed him.

❧ 16 ❧

THE INTELLECT

"He's a cock gobbler. I'm sure of it."

Cosima flopped onto the bed, while Leila and the rest of Her sisters sat in a circle around her. It was only a matter of time before Cosima blabbered about her reward with Tobias, and when the moment finally came, the story burst free from her like water from an opened floodgate.

"I gave him every opportunity, welcomed him straight into my arms. I even explicitly *asked* for a kiss. And still nothing." She flung her hands overhead. "This man hasn't an interest in women. He should be barred from the tournament, because whatever his motivation, I assure you—"

"For God's sake, he likes *Leila*," Delphi groaned. "His poem was for *Leila*."

Cosima sat up straight. "Are you certain?"

"Of course! He was staring at Her the entire time."

"You're sure?" Cosima turned to Leila. "Sister..."

Leila shrank beneath her gaze. "There was a line in the poem. *A taste that he's acquired.* It's from a conversation we shared the day we first met."

Cosima's lips parted. "Why didn't You tell me?"

"You were so excited. I didn't know how."

"Well, do You return his affection?"

Heat swirled through Leila's cheeks. She stared down at Her lap.

"Oh, I know that look," Cosima said. "That's the look of a woman enraptured by a man. You little minx, You're fond of him, aren't You?"

Leila started. "You're not upset with Me?"

"Precious dove, of course not! This is wonderful news. We can take down Your father *and* find You a husband."

"That's a premature assumption."

"And he's so well-suited for You." Cosima squeezed Leila's hand. "Little Leila and the Artist. I'll stay away from him from now on. How does that sound?"

Cosima's smile was wide, but her gaze was empty, and Leila could've sworn her eye twitched at the corner.

"You're sure you're not angry?"

Cosima scoffed. "He's not exactly my type. Now, the Adonis—*he's* my type." She chuckled. "Just be careful, dove. You might be waiting forever for a kiss."

Leila's face burned. "Excuse Me. There's a Senate meeting shortly." She darted from the chamber as memories of the previous day sent tremors rolling through Her.

"Leila."

Delphi's voice rang out behind Her, and Leila spun around, wrangling composure. "Yes? Did you need something?"

Smirking, Delphi took root at Her side. "Something happened."

"What happened? Nothing happened."

"You kissed him."

"I didn't—" Glancing down the corridor, Leila lowered Her voice. "I didn't kiss him. *He* kissed *Me.* And I accepted. That's all."

"You're allowed to be excited, You know."

"Have you found a translation for the note?"

"Dodging the details, are we?"

"Delphi—"

"No translation yet," Delphi said. "Did you know the Kovahrians have hundreds of dialects? One for royals, another for the eldest royals, another for military codes—"

"Let Me try." Leila waited as Delphi handed the note over, then shoved it into Her pocket. "I have to go."

She rushed down the hall, losing Herself in thoughts of Tobias's touch.

"Was it at least good?" Delphi called out.

This time, Leila couldn't stifle Her grin.

The black door to the Senate room appeared before Her, and She opened it wide. Only five men were seated at the round table: Romulus, Wembleton, Erebus, Kastor, and Brontes. It shouldn't have surprised Her, but the emptiness was loud and triumphant.

"Let's be quick, shall we?" She took a seat, folding Her hands on the table. "There's a challenge in a short while, and I mustn't be late."

Brontes didn't look Her way. "Who calls this meeting?"

"I do."

"Second."

"First matter of discussion," Brontes said. "Any word from the royals?"

"All have confirmed attendance for the finale of the tournament." Kastor flipped through a few parchment notes. "Trogolia, Ethyua, and Kovahr."

Kovahr. Questions flooded Leila's mouth, but She kept Her lips clamped shut, waiting for answers or information—*something*—that never came.

"Second matter..." Brontes unclasped a ring from his belt, tossing it onto the table with a clank. "Erebus. Your keys."

Ten or more keys of varying design hung from the ring, splayed out in a pile. "What are these for?" Leila said.

"I am the Vault Keeper, Your Holiness." Erebus gave a slight bow. "Have You forgotten?"

He drew the keys from the table—one piece of weathered steel after the next, save for a single key with a perfectly polished finish as if it never saw age or wear.

"I didn't realize the vault required so many keys," Leila said.

"Now that Phanes's and Qar's bodies have been discovered, it's logical to assume the others met a similar end by the same party."

Brontes's one eye narrowed. "Someone with sinister intentions, no doubt."

"I'm amazed by your bravery. If someone were picking off every person of My station, I would be trembling in fear."

"We seek comfort in our aid to Your reign, Your Holiness," Kastor added.

"Given the circumstances, we thought it best to have the most sensitive items guarded by Erebus, the most acclaimed soldier not only at this table, but in the whole of Thessen." Brontes glowered. "Any fool who crosses him will no doubt meet a slow and excruciating end."

"Do You agree, Your Holiness?" Erebus said. "Am I capable?"

His deep-set gaze pierced through Her, but She forced a sneer. "No need to seek My approval. Have confidence. I'm sure your sword work is adequate."

Erebus clipped the ring to his belt without breaking their gaze. It was Leila who finally looked away, eyeing the keys a moment longer—a bridge She'd cross another day—but that single silver key held Her attention, so luminous She could've sworn it glowed.

The room around Leila faded into the background of Her mind, making way for much more pleasant thoughts. She recounted the warmth of Tobias's lips, the thrilling juxtaposition of his hard body and soft caress. As each moment played over and over in Her mind, She sank into Her seat, contented.

"Your Holiness?"

Leila started. Kastor was staring at Her from across the table.

"I said, no objections, Your Holiness?" he repeated.

Brontes huffed. "You're in rare form today."

Leila frowned. "And what form is that?"

"Silent."

"Would You prefer to sit these meetings out, Your Holiness?" Kastor said. "This isn't the first time your attention has strayed. Perhaps You're overworked?"

"The tournament has been occupying much of Her time," Wembleton cut in. "We've been keeping Her very busy with the dramatics." Hesitating, he bowed to Brontes. "Your Shepherd continues to outperform the others, naturally."

"And what of the Artist?" Brontes said. "How is he performing?"

Tension shot down Leila's spine. "You mean the loser of yesterday's challenge? Poorly, if that wasn't indication enough."

"You must be disappointed."

"I haven't thought much of it, to be frank."

Brontes gestured toward Romulus and Wembleton. "Keep me abreast of the Artist's performance. If he's the man my daughter favors, we must pay him special attention." He met Leila's gaze. "Does this please You?"

"It makes no difference to Me. As I've told you, I have no interest in him."

He held Her gaze for an eternity longer. Perhaps if he was the smiling sort, he'd be doing that as well, smug over his upper hand. No doubt he thought he could unnerve Her with a single mention of Tobias. And he was right.

"Who calls to end this meeting?" he said.

"I do."

"Second."

As the men filed off, Leila perked Her head up. "Romulus. You have news of today's challenge, yes?"

Nodding, he watched with beady eyes as the others left the room. He closed the door behind them, judgment plastered across his face. "Distracted?"

Leila dug through Her pocket, tossing the Kovahrian note his way. "Translate this."

After a glance, he handed the parchment back to Her. "I cannot."

"You dare to defy Me?"

"I dare to admit I cannot read Kovahrian."

"Who can?"

He shrugged. "Perhaps Erebus, though asking for his assistance isn't exactly an option."

"Who is the powerful figure Brontes has aligned himself with outside the fortress?"

"I spend my days in the labyrinth per Your orders. Proctoring challenges. Keeping Your secret. I have no knowledge of this person."

"Then *who does*?"

"Perhaps Your new pet Wembleton can help You," he said. "But I cannot."

Leila shot up from Her seat. "Have you forgotten where you stand, Proctor? This is not a partnership. You killed My mother, you work for Me, and you *will* learn your place, is that understood?"

Romulus stood in stoic silence. Red fanned through his robes, circling them like a mist of bitter saffron.

Leila cocked Her head at the door. "You're dismissed."

He left without a word, leaving behind flecks of red that stung Her nostrils. With Her chin high, She abandoned the Senate room, gathering Her cloak and satchel before heading to the labyrinth. The stairwell She traveled plunged deeper than the others, leading far underground, perhaps straight to hell. She thought She had seen every passage of the labyrinth, but not this one, and that troubled Her.

The steps underfoot ended, bringing Her to a narrow tunnel, a portal, then a room—no, a cavern, vast and wide. The walls stretched far above Her, ending at a ceiling stories high, and paces ahead lay a ravine filled with water as black as the surrounding bricks.

Four onyx thrones stood ahead where Her sisters were already seated. Delphi peered around her chair at Leila, who promptly sat at her side.

"What is this place?"

Delphi swallowed. "I don't know."

A familiar invisible shield ebbed before them, and beyond it, satchels littered the stone floor. "What are the men to do?"

"I think they're going for a swim," Delphi said.

Sighing, Leila slumped in Her throne. Pippa sang a blissful tune, while Cosima sat in silence, eyes on the blackish water.

Leila leaned toward her. "Sister, are you all right?"

Cosima flinched, then smiled. "Of course, dove."

Her lips flattened, and again there was stillness. The temptation to touch her—to take in a color, peer into her mind—ate at Leila. She reached toward her.

An eruption of brick resounded high above. Leila and Her sisters jumped as the colossal wall ahead of them became a looming cliff, the uppermost portion of it crumbling away. Tiny men darted toward the cliff's edge, peering down at the ravine and the women below.

The challenge was beginning.

Romulus appeared beside the men, an hourglass in his arms. He gestured toward the water, and though Leila usually opted to ignore his words, this time She fought to take in their echo. *"At the bottom... Keys to The Savior's heart... Collect as many as possible."* Her eyes scoured the cliff, searching for Tobias.

A man forced his way to the front, throwing himself off the edge. Leila winced when he crashed into the water, then again with the next man, and soon bodies rained down into the ravine like corpses into a mass grave. A few heads popped up above the surface, sucking in breaths before plunging below, leaving the waters still.

The silence plucked at Leila's nerves like talons at frayed harp strings. *Keys to The Savior's heart. Collect as many as possible.* But there had to be more to it. There always was.

Water burst from the ravine as a man shot above the surface— Caesar, his eyes wide and skin pale. Another explosion, and Zander appeared at his side, followed by Beau, madly paddling toward Leila. She grabbed Her chair, pressing Herself against its back, nearly forgetting the invisible barrier before Her. Another man bobbed to the surface—Tobias, hair plastered to his face as he threw himself onto the floor.

"What the fuck is down there?" Caesar spat.

"Something touched me." Beau scooted far from the ravine edge. "Did you see it? What is it?"

Tobias stood upright, whipping his wet locks aside. "They're creatures."

What? Leila's eyes penetrated the water, but there was only darkness.

Zander's lips parted. "Creatures?"

"Monsters," Tobias said. "Eels or something. But with teeth."

"How do you know this?" Beau asked.

Tobias glanced between the men. "You can't see them?"

"See what?" Caesar wrung out his pant leg. "It's black as shit down there. There's nothing but darkness and...and glowing *dots*."

"They're Guardians."

Romulus's voice shook Leila. She hadn't noticed his arrival, but there he stood beyond the invisible barrier, the hourglass in his grasp.

"The keys to our Savior's heart are kept well protected," he said. "Beware the Guardians, and swim with caution."

Caesar glowered. "How the hell do we *swim with caution* if we *can't see?*"

"You waste time. The sands are shifting. Compete, or forfeit and suffer the consequences."

Cursing, the men plodded toward the ravine's edge. Romulus barked at them to retrieve their satchels, which they reluctantly slung over their shoulders before disappearing into the water.

Leila glared at Romulus. "Guardians?"

"Your father deemed them so."

"And how exactly did My father bring these *Guardians* to the fortress?" When the Senator shrugged, Leila scoffed under Her breath. "Useless." She turned to Delphi. "Monstrous eels with teeth. Have you heard of such a creature?"

"Only in tales of the Outlands," Delphi said.

"Those are just stories."

"Your great grandmothers exist in stories, yet they were very much alive."

Sickness swirled within Leila. A man bobbed to the surface of the black water to suck in a breath, then another, but neither were Tobias, and the slow-passing seconds wound Her throat into a knot. What of these creatures? Why hadn't Tobias shown?

"It's only been a short while," Delphi whispered as if privy to Her thoughts. "He's fine."

A man burst above the water, and Leila nearly jumped until She made out his black hair. *Just Flynn.* He swam toward the ravine edge and spilled onto the floor, the heaving of his chest more angry than depleted. Another man tore from the water.

Tobias. *Finally*.

"What the *hell*, Tobias?" Flynn spat.

Tobias planted his hands on his knees, steadying his breathing. "What?"

"What do you mean *what*? You're glowing!"

His words pummeled Leila in the gut. Glowing.

How?

Several men pulled themselves from the water. "He's glowing?" Beau said.

"Are you *blessed?*" Flynn hissed.

Tobias stood wide-eyed as the men circled him, though his confusion was surely a fraction of Her own. *I didn't bless him. This can't be. I didn't...* And then memories bombarded Her: Tobias's lips against Hers, Her hand pressed to his chest, his vivid colors, that blazing heat...

Oh, no. No, no, no...

Tobias scanned the room, stopping at Leila. A blow plowed through Her gut.

He knows.

Her ruse was over, ruined by a kiss.

"Cosima..." His gaze panned down the line of women. "She touched my chest."

Cosima sat still, poised in ways Leila could never manage. Was Tobias lying? She racked Her mind for explanations, until his words from the other day tumbled into Her thoughts.

She put Her hand on my chest and asked if I could feel Her light.

Caesar flung his arms into the air. "Fucking hell, She blessed him again!"

"And you said *nothing?*" Flynn snapped.

"I didn't know," Tobias said.

"He lies." Beau puffed out his chest, failing to appear fearsome. "How could he not know?"

Tobias flashed him a glare. "Even if I did, why would I need to inform any of you?"

"Good God, look at all your keys!" Flynn squealed.

"Proctor, the challenge is flawed." Caesar marched toward Romulus, leaving puddles in his wake. "The Artist has a tactical advantage!"

Kaleo's hearty laugh brought the circle to silence. He sat along the ravine's edge kicking at the water, watching the spectacle for God knows how long.

Caesar stomped forward, his brawny arms crossed. "You think this is funny?"

Kaleo's laughter spiked higher. "It's hilarious. All your bitching and moaning over our blessed Artist. Completely shortsighted, the lot of you."

"Shortsighted my ass," Caesar said. "You may not give a shit, but the rest of us aim to win."

Shaking his head, Kaleo smiled at Tobias. "Enjoy your swim, Artist. Look out for monsters beneath the surface. Hard to hide from them when you're glowing, yes?"

He dove into the water before Tobias could respond.

"Continue," Romulus ordered.

The men disappeared into the ravine, while Leila bounced Her knee, analyzing the entire mess only to come up empty-handed.

Delphi leaned in close. "You didn't tell me You blessed him."

"I didn't know," Leila said.

"How can You not know You've blessed someone?"

"I don't know! This has never happened before."

"Well, when did You touch his chest?"

Leila shot her a glare. "When do you *think*?"

Delphi's eyes widened. "*Oh*." She smiled. "*Very* interesting."

"I must've been caught up in the moment. I think. I don't know..."

"Must've been quite the kiss."

"Not now," Leila spat.

She swallowed a growl. Had Her power expanded? It had done so before, grown much like Her own body and mind. Or perhaps She had always had this power and never the means to express it. *The ancient scrolls.* Maybe they listed instances such as this with past Saviors. But She had read of Her grandmothers hundreds of times already, back when She sought to understand Her light—to learn the lessons Her mother was supposed to teach Her. No, there was never a mention of an *accidental blessing.* She sank into Her chair. Her light was the one thing in Her control, and now even it mystified Her.

The water stirred. Ripples turned into sputters and splashes, and a sodden head shot above the surface, sucking in a rasping breath.

Tobias.

Just as quickly as he had appeared, he was gone, replaced with Kaleo. The assassin writhed and jerked, eyes boring through the blackness beneath him, and he clamped his teeth before dropping down into the water.

The surface gushed and bubbled, but the men remained unseen.

Was Kaleo *drowning* him?

Leila spun toward Romulus. "Do something!"

He ignored Her; She should've predicted as much, but logic had fallen by the wayside. Tobias was right in front of Her, yet She could do nothing. The water stilled, and the beginnings of a scream formed in Her throat.

Tobias erupted from the surface, lunging toward the ravine's edge. He threw himself onto the stone floor, flopping flat on his back as he hacked and wheezed. Leila jumped from Her seat but stopped short; the air rippled in front of Her, and so She watched helplessly as he stumbled to his feet.

Kaleo vaulted to the floor, wiping the hair from his eyes. Barbs rang from his tongue, and Tobias charged at him, slamming his fist into the Beast's jaw.

Leila flinched as Kaleo whipped to the side, the first hint of weakness She'd seen in him. A second later he was on the floor, and Tobias was on top of him, pummeling his face as though it were a target. The beating ended, and Tobias gripped Kaleo's throat, the veins in his arms bulging as he strangled the life from the creature beneath him.

Her second assassin was about to die.

"Enough!" Romulus barked.

Leila gaped at him, aghast, while Orion and Flynn pried Tobias from his mark. *Traitors. Every last one of them.*

Grinning, Kaleo clambered to his feet. "Artist, you're stronger than I recall last. I'm proud of you, really. They grow up so quickly—"

"*Fuck* you," Tobias spat.

"*Silence*," Romulus said. "No more speaking. *No* more altercations." He pointed at the water. "Now dive."

"I'm not going back in there—"

"*Dive.*" Romulus's eyes locked onto the limp satchel on Tobias's shoulder. "The challenge is nearly finished, and it seems as though you've fallen behind."

Defeated, Tobias hurled himself into the water. While the others followed, Leila seethed, waiting less-than-patiently for the men to disappear.

As the waters stilled, She cast a glare at Romulus. "You conspire against Me."

"I conceal Your charade."

"Another assassin was nearly killed—"

"And what do You think Your father would say when he heard his man died at our feet and no one intervened?" he said. "You think he wouldn't grow suspicious?"

"I don't *care* about his suspicions, the entire point—"

A horn blasted through the space—from where, She hadn't a clue. "The challenge is over." Romulus gestured toward the pile of sand at the bottom of his hourglass. "You'd be wise to compose Yourself before the men emerge."

Leila cursed him, feigning some shoddy semblance of poise. One by one, the men popped up from the water, their faces drawn, lumpy satchels hanging from their shoulders. Perhaps their burden was over for now, but Leila had several hoisted upon Her this day alone, and the weight of Her circumstances was heavier than ever.

Tobias exploded from the surface with Raphael at his side, and the water around them morphed from black to red.

Leila stood from Her seat. Blood followed the two men as they swam through the ravine, even as their bodies tumbled onto the floor with a wet slap. Tobias's skin was unmarred, but large punctures wrapped Raphael's ribs, steadily streaming.

Tobias planted his hands on the wound. "He's badly injured. We need the Healer now."

Leila darted forward, then skidded to a halt. The shield wavered in front of Her, keeping Her at bay. *Shadow walk.* But She couldn't.

She turned to Romulus. "Lower the wall."

"Such action is unpermitted."

"*I'm* permitting it. Lower the wall *now*."

"He's losing blood." Red painted Tobias's fingers. "We need to act quickly."

"We will count the keys." Romulus spoke with slow apathy. "You will return to the sanctuary, and then the Healer will assist the competitors."

"For God's sake, we don't have that sort of time!" Tobias spat.

"Romulus, let me tend to him," Leila said.

"The challenge will continue as planned."

"You bastard, I *command* you—"

"The only commands I obey are those of The Savior." Romulus's gaze panned to Cosima, and *dear God*, Leila could've sworn he bowed. "If She wills it, it will be done."

Hatred pumped through Leila's veins. She turned to Her sister. "Cosima...*make* him lower the wall."

Cosima cocked her head, silent. Leila gritted Her teeth. "Cosima—"

"Be mindful of your tone, Sister." Cosima's words came out sharp. "I am The Savior. You cannot force My hand. We will continue the challenge as planned."

Leila's jaw went slack. "*Cosima*—"

"Her decision is made," Romulus said. "Artist, unhand the Intellect."

"He'll bleed to death!" Tobias barked.

Raphael's weak voice sounded from Tobias's lap. "It's all right."

"It's not *fucking* all right!"

Leila's nails dug into Her palms. "Proctor, you *will* lower the wall, or I swear to God, I'll kill you myself—"

"Sit down."

"Do as I *say*—"

"Learn your place, *Healer*," Romulus snapped. "Sit *down*."

The Senator's glare bore through Her, equal parts warning and dare, and the blood on the floor was soon matched by his growing red mist. *Do something.* But all She could do was take a seat, Her pride marred.

Romulus turned to Tobias. "*Unhand him.*"

Raphael grabbed Tobias's wrist, mumbling something—perhaps his last words, another death on Leila's shoulders.

As Tobias and a barely functioning Raphael took their places in the line of men, Romulus continued his proctoring. "The counting will commence. Each of you will present your keys, and we will determine who has triumphed and who has floundered."

"Get on with it," Leila said.

"The three men with the most keys will win today's challenge—"

"Faster."

He cast Her a sideways glance. "And while these three men partake in their reward, the remainder of you will be confined to the sanctuary."

"Cosima, he's stalling intentionally to spite me."

"Proctor," Cosima called out. "Count the keys. Quickly, please."

Perhaps *quickly* was a foreign term to him, as he made his way down the line at a glacial pace, plucking key after key from each satchel as he counted the competitors' spoils. Fifteen for Beau. Twenty for Garrick. All the while red trickled from Raphael's wounds, his knees shaking beneath his narrow frame. A stab pierced Leila's gut. *You could've shadow walked past the wall.* But She had a ruse to maintain, a realm to protect. That was surely worth more than one man's life.

Raphael collapsed, and every trace of Her resolve evaporated.

"*Hurry*," She cried.

A few of the men helped Raphael to his feet, while Romulus continued his count, unmoved. Unable to bear the sight any longer, Leila stared instead at Cosima, who held her chin high, self-satisfaction twisting her lips.

Leila's sister. A miserable bitch.

"The keys have been counted," Romulus said. "The Cavalier, the Regal, and the Shepherd win the reward of extended time in The Savior's company. You will see your reward tomorrow. Until then, seek comfort in the sanctuary. You're dismissed."

Leila tore from Her seat, flying through the portal, up the endless flight of stairs, and into the sanctuary. The men hadn't yet arrived, and while She gasped for breath, Pippa trotted to Her side.

"I'll help," she said. "Sisters help sisters."

Men flooded the portal across from Her, spilling into the sanctuary. Pippa clapped her hands, squealing something; Leila hadn't a clue what, as She was too busy scouring the horde, searching for brown skin dripping with blood.

A red-streaked Orion and Flynn appeared from the darkness with Raphael held limply between them, and Leila shoved through the mob, grabbing Orion by the wrist and leading them to Her tent. She bolted through the flap and dragged the table aside, clearing a spot on the floor. As Orion and Flynn laid Raphael flat, light crackled at Her fingertips. If She was going to this, it had to be now.

Flynn hovered, hands on his hips. "What if we—?"

"Clear the tent." Leila dropped down at Raphael's side. "I need space."

Orion leaned forward. "Is there anything—?"

"Just go."

"We could—"

"*Clear the tent*," Leila spat. "*Now*."

Orion and Flynn wavered, mumbling something before plodding out. She was alone—just Raphael, his leaking ribs, and his eyes rolling into the back of his skull.

"Raphael." She shook him. "Are you with me?"

Nothing. His jaw hung low, and Her hands were already smeared red. Heat pooled in Her palms.

"Mend the flesh." She pressed down on his ribs. "Slow the bleeding."

Her touch burned like wild flames, hot enough to melt through him. Normally She relished the pain, but not in this moment. Raphael was fading in front of Her.

"Mend the flesh. Hear My command. Slow the bleeding so he may live."

She dug in Her nails, repeating the words again and again. How long had it been? Had She missed Her chance? *No.* This had to work. Bodies were already piling up around Her, and She didn't need another.

"Please," She whispered. "Just do this one thing for Me."

The heat of Her touch died, and Her heart lurched. He was gone. Her frame went limp, and blackness splintered through Her insides, filling Her up with despair.

But then his chest rose and fell beneath Her fingertips, and She lifted Her trembling palms, revealing the half-circle of cavernous punctures—dry.

Exhaling, She leaned back on Her hands. "Thank you." She gasped for air, Her lungs haggard and strained. Had She breathed at all this entire time?

A rustling sounded behind Her, followed by a soft voice. "I'm here to help."

"Pippa, guard the tent," Leila said. "See to it that no one enters. This man will be in My care for some time."

Another rustle, and Pippa was gone, no doubt taking post with the resolve of a soldier. Finally composed, Leila rummaged through Her satchel for the proper tools. "All right then. Let's get you fixed up."

"Thank You."

Leila froze. Raphael's weak, chestnut gaze was pointed right at Her.

"Your Holiness."

❧ 17 ❧

THE SLAP

Leila stormed down the corridor. Anger had been building within Her for a full day, festering without any means of release. She wasn't waiting any longer.

She thrust the door open and charged ahead. Cosima stood at the far end of her chamber, flipping through multi-colored reams of silk. "Dove, what a pleasant—"

Leila slapped her across the face, sending her stumbling. "How dare you defy Me?"

"Sister, please—"

"You may play the part, but never forget your station. *I* am The Savior. You do not get to wager a man's life for your own pride and pleasure. Do you understand? Your crown is a *lie*."

Cosima's lips trembled. "Apologies. But You overstepped—"

"I overstepped *nothing*—"

"They think You're a healer, but You behaved as a queen. I sought to bring reality to the ruse."

Heaving breaths filled Leila's lungs. She hadn't realized Her hands were balled into fists, that Her powerful frame betrayed Her small stature—or that Her sister cowered before Her, tears streaking her cheeks.

"I sacrifice myself for You, Sister," Cosima said. "Have You forgotten?"

Leila's gut pulled in opposite directions. Clenching Her jaw, She left the room.

Shame nipped at Her insides, a punishment She surely didn't deserve. She headed down the corridor into a second chamber, where Delphi lay across her sheets wrapped in a sheer blue robe, Nyx nestled at her side. Delphi dragged her fingertips up the curve of Nyx's hip, then stopped, eyes on Leila. "Now's a bad time."

Leila cocked Her head at the door. "Leave us, Nyx."

Nyx bowed before darting from the room, while Delphi gaped at Leila. "You're a real bitch, You know that? I understand Your plate is full, but I'm allowed my own life." She plucked a long, braided belt from her sheets. "Look, she left this behind. Now You've given me a chore. Or perhaps You've given me an invitation. Maybe I should thank You."

"Raphael knows," Leila said. "Who I am. He knows."

"And how exactly did that happen?"

"I blessed him."

Delphi rolled her eyes. "And You were being *so* discreet."

"He was *dying*."

Sighing, Delphi tightened her robe. "All right then. What now?"

"I don't know." Leila took a seat at her side. "Everything is *so wrong*."

"Not everything. One of Your assassins is dead. Only four Senators remain, two of whom aid Your endeavors."

"They aid Me? The men who exposed My shadow walking to My father and saved My assassin from death? What fine assistance." Growling, She snatched the note from Her pocket. "We still haven't a clue what this note says, or the purpose of those stupid jewels. And now it seems I can't control My light."

"Perhaps Your power has expanded. Untethered by a kiss."

"No," Leila said. "I refuse to believe that."

"Why?"

"Because it's trite. *Untethered by a kiss.* Do you hear yourself? No, the kiss was just a coincidence. Or a participant. But it didn't *untether* anything."

"Well, that's another good thing to add to Your list, yes? A lovely man who kisses You." Delphi flopped onto her sheets, eyeing Nyx's belt. "And *I* have a lovely woman who kisses me."

"You have many women who kiss you."

"She's beautiful, isn't she? I think I like her a bit more than the others. I think she might be the one."

Leila scoffed. "You can't have just one."

Delphi winked before directing her attention back to the braided leather, humming as she wove it between her fingers.

Leila hopped from the bed. "I'll leave you to your lecherous thoughts. Thank you for being absolutely useless."

"Thank *You* for ruining my fun. They'd be lecherous *acts* if You hadn't come along."

Leila waved Her sister away before taking leave, returning to Her chamber. Pressing Her back to Her golden door, She drew in a long breath. *Not everything is wrong.* She tried to believe Delphi, but it was hard when even the light coursing through Her had betrayed Her trust. She stared at Her glowing palms as if they could provide clarity, and when they didn't, She turned to Her mirrored wardrobe, eyes fixed on Her mothers, particularly the one with the pale blue eyes.

"Say, Mother, on the off chance You decide to speak today, I have a question. Did Your light ever...act of its own accord? Pour into another person without You knowing?" She gazed at the ceiling, wrangling the right words. "Did You ever bless someone without intending it, without thinking or uttering a word? Say, in the middle of a very...involved exchange. Intense, even. Hypothetically speaking, of course."

Her mother's lips parted, but She didn't speak.

"Nothing?" Leila said. "Because I'm stuck here. There are no other Saviors around. No one to guide Me."

Silence. Leila scowled. "Fine."

She stomped to Her desk, rummaging through scrolls and trinkets. The crystal rose Cosima had given Her glittered in Her periphery, and She pushed it away with a huff. Her healer's satchel sat in a pile, bombarding Her with thoughts of the last challenge, with Raphael's blood on Her hands, his knowing gaze. He had fallen unconscious shortly after their exchange, leaving Her with no answers—something She'd have to rectify on this day. She shoved Her satchel aside.

Steel scattered from its opening.

Keys.

She plucked one from Her desk—long and thin with a heart-shaped grip. The keys from the challenge. How had they gotten there? She dug through Her things, stopping at the sight of a message scrawled along the fabric of the satchel itself.

Nothing's changed.

Tobias had done this.

Her heart raced—so many keys, certainly enough to have won the challenge with—and a smile played at Her lips. Another reward thrown away, and he had done it for Her.

"Which one is he?"

The voice startled Leila. Faun stood in Her doorway, her tattooed arms folded.

"Pardon?" Leila said.

"You're floating. You have been for a while now. Carried by clouds, I'm certain."

"You're silly."

"Don't try to pretend otherwise. We know You sneak into the labyrinth."

Leila's panic must have been written across Her face, because Faun laughed in response. "Calm Yourself. We won't tell Your father. Heaven forbid he learns his daughter is off gallivanting with all the men."

"I'm not *gallivanting.*"

"I know that. You're not the type. Which means there's one man in particular who's caught Your attention, and I want to know who."

Damaris popped her head in. "What's going on here?"

"I'm just asking Leila who She's been sneaking off with," Faun said.

Hemera barreled into the chamber. "Oh, tell me too! I'm dying to know!"

The girls surrounded Leila, prodding and cooing while ushering Her to the royal bathhouse. She had a reward to prepare for—one Cosima would be attending in Her stead—but Leila sat in silence, enduring the prattling servants as they lathered Her in sweet-smelling soaps. At some point Nyx joined the madness, flushing beneath Leila's gaze, though Leila was more concerned with the questions being thrown Her way.

"All right then," Faun said. "This man of Yours—"

"I don't *have* a man," Leila maintained.

Damaris shook her head. "She's never going to tell us."

"Is it the Adonis?" Hemera came in close, clutching a rag. "Please say it's the Adonis. You would have the most beautiful baby."

"It's no one."

Nyx scoffed, "It must be him. He's an *Adonis*."

"He's also as dumb as a bag of stones." Leila pointed Her nose to the ceiling. "I can barely tolerate him."

"Oh, that's unfortunate," Damaris said. "All beauty and no brains."

"What about the Regal?"

Groaning, Leila splashed at Hemera. "No!"

"The Prince?" Hemera continued. "Is it at least one of the Lords?"

"Of course it's not one of the Lords." Faun chuckled, brushing out Leila's hair. "Leila has a fine palate. She can't be satisfied off appearances alone. And She certainly doesn't need the coin."

Hemera's eyes grew large. "What about the Intellect? He's smart, yes? It's in his laurel. Or the Brave. Such courage!"

"Ladies, there is no man—"

"It's the Artist," Damaris blurted. "She loves art. It has to be the Artist, right?"

The girls stared at Leila, waiting, while She sank into the water, trying and failing to muster a response. The servants burst into squeals.

"I knew it!" Damaris clapped her hands.

"How was he not our first guess?" Faun said. "She falls weak at the sight of a painting, just imagine Her reaction to a *painter*."

"Has he painted anything for You?" Hemera sat on the pool's edge, her duties abandoned. "Please tell me he has."

The charcoal drawings filled Leila's thoughts, fueling Her heartbeat, and She could've sworn the girls heard it pounding when their squealing resumed.

Hemera scooped up Leila's hands. "Is he handsome?"

"I wouldn't know. I have no interest—"

"He's very handsome." Delphi's voice echoed off the walls as she walked into the bathhouse, her sheer robe replaced with a teal dress. "Lean but strong, with large, emotive eyes. And his hair is lovely too."

Leila frowned. "Thank you, but your opinions aren't required—"

"Have you fucked?"

"Hemera!"

"I'm just curious!" Hemera giggled, tawny hands clasped beneath her chin. "He's a creative. Perhaps he's creative in *other* ways as well."

"Well, we haven't fucked. Tell Me, who would want to fuck in the labyrinth? It's filthy down there. God, these questions..."

"Have you kissed?" Faun said.

Leila opened Her mouth to speak but fell short, groaning once another swell of shrieking nonsense resounded around Her.

Damaris buffed Leila's nails, a grin on her round cheeks. "Do You think he's the one?"

"What?" Leila wrinkled Her nose. "I don't know. It's been but a week or two."

"He's a cut above the rest," Delphi said. "A kind soul. You'd all really like him. He'd make a fine and fair Sovereign. And he is utterly enamored by Leila."

"Aren't they all?" Damaris asked. "They're competing for Her."

"The others are fools. The Artist is a man deserving of The Savior." Delphi smiled. "And he wants Her. Badly."

The girls around Her were clapping and squawking yet again, fueling Leila's chagrin. "You're all making Me feel very embarrassed."

Faun blew a raspberry and waved Her away, continuing to lather Her up and polish Her down until Her skin glowed without the help of Her light.

The questions continued, leaving Leila to count the hours until Her grooming was over. Each girl paid extra close attention to their work, tying braids around the back of Her crown and laying them over Her freshly combed locks. "It opens up Your face. I'm sure the Artist adores Your eyes." They draped Her in the finest silks and sparkling sapphires, layering not one, not three, but five bangles on Her wrists. "The Artist will love it." At some point Delphi left to prep the challenge winners, and Leila bid the servants farewell, disappearing into Her chamber. She stared at Herself in the mirror, admiring the ornaments before stripping them away.

Tan leather sandals and a flowing periwinkle dress were all that remained of the servants' work. She gathered Her satchel and summoned Her light.

The sanctuary.

Tents loomed ahead, a flurry of male voices in the distance. She stood against the back wall of the sanctuary, out of sight, but not for long. She had matters to address.

She charged ahead, winding past the stretch of canvas before reaching the men. No injuries, no blood, no challenge at all, as Brontes had deemed it so. *"Too many competitors dead, and too soon,"* Romulus had said. *"The tournament must last thirty days, and at this rate, there won't be anyone left at the end."* And so a day of rest was granted—such generosity from the merciful Sovereign, so he could resume their slaughter a day later.

She stopped short. Tobias stood at the water barrel, gazing Her way. Her heart hammered in Her throat, but She swallowed it down.

"Raphael," She said. "Come. Let's look at your stitches."

Raphael waited at Tobias's side, his eyes boring through Her. He mumbled something before following Her through the sanctuary, his clomping steps keeping pace with Hers until they slipped into Her tent.

They stood across from one another, braced as if for battle. Leila cocked Her head at the stool. "Well, go on then. Sit down."

"You're actually going to look at my stitches?"

"I said I was, didn't I?"

Reluctantly, Raphael took a seat, cringing as he shifted his weight. Leila unwrapped his bandages in delicate strokes, revealing the massive wound and the black thread piecing it together. His muscles tightened as She pressed Her palm to the bite, but all She could think of was the look in his eyes the night prior and the words that had left his lips.

Your Holiness.

"No potions?" Raphael said. "Or, wait... *Are* they potions?"

She dug through Her satchel, tossing him a random vial. "Smell this."

He uncapped, then sniffed the vial. "Smells like vanilla." His eyes widened. "Have You been slathering us in *perfume?*"

"Not just perfume. Sometimes it's water."

He muttered something under his breath; Leila didn't know what, didn't care. She pressed Her hand to his ribs, contemplating Her next move.

"Are You doing what You did yesterday?" he said.

"No. That was a blessing."

"And what's this?"

"I'm touching you, clearly."

Raphael was visibly confused, and Leila sighed. "Light pours from Me regardless of My bidding. Touching you is healing enough. Yesterday, however, required reinforcement."

Raphael said nothing—still. She tried to focus on Her light, to will him to speak through the sheer power of Her silence, but the tension ate at Her.

"So tell Me, Raphael... Now that you know who I am, what do you plan to do with this information?"

"That depends on what You're willing to do for me."

Leila grimaced, and Raphael mirrored the sentiment. "God no, not *that*," he said. "I'm not a savage."

"Yet still, you threaten Me."

"It's not a threat. Just an agreement."

"That suits *you* exclusively."

"It's clear You mean to conceal Your true title," he said. "I haven't a clue why, and frankly, I don't care. But I'm willing to keep this secret for You, however long You require."

Leila raised an eyebrow. "Provided...?"

Coming in closer, Raphael lowered his voice. "Provided You get me out of this Godforsaken tournament."

Leila leaned back against the wooden table, cursing under Her breath. "You have no idea the hardship you're placing upon Me."

"Then call us even. I did, after all, enter this tournament for You. In theory."

"I'm in a very dangerous position—"

"And I'm not?"

Stupid, selfish man. Or perhaps he wasn't. Perhaps She would do the same in his position, or worse. But that didn't matter now. She had Her own assassination to prevent. She didn't need another burden.

"I think I'm being quite agreeable," Raphael said. "I'm not asking

You to choose me as Your Champion. I'm not threatening to reveal Your true self to the others—"

"That's *exactly* what you're doing—"

"I'm only asking that You *release me*." His gaze turned desperate. "Please, Leila. Or Your Holiness. Should I call You—?"

"Shut up." Leila gnawed at Her lip, Her thoughts swirling. *Kill him.* God, why was that always the first solution to spring up?

"You won't say a word?" She squared Her shoulders. "Swear it to Me, as your One True Savior."

"I swear it. Provided You release me, no one will know who You are."

Protests lingered on Her tongue, but She forced past them. "Fine."

Raphael faltered. "So, I'm released?"

"Not now, you idiot. There are formalities. Two men are to be honorably released from the tournament. I'll see to it you're one of them."

"Sooner rather than later, yes?"

"I agreed to your game," She said. "Don't push Me. I don't take kindly to it."

Raphael let out a long breath. "Well then, now that that's out of the way, I suppose we can speak more freely. I'll be honest, a part of me is relieved. Cosima plays the role well, but You on the throne makes some sense."

Leila scowled. "You're too kind."

"I just mean You seem a capable queen. It's a good thing." He tried to lean on his knees, then cringed, opting to sit up straight instead. "What I can't believe is that Tobias figured it out before I did. The man is smarter than the others, but still..."

"He knows?" Leila snapped.

"Doesn't he? Why else would You keep blessing him?"

Heat flooded Leila's cheeks. She turned away, fiddling with Her satchel while Raphael's penetrating stare burrowed through the back of Her skull.

"Oh my God," he said. "The two of you? *Together?*"

"Not another word, I swear."

"That's why he's always disappearing, isn't it? I just assumed he went off to beat his meat. Then again, no one takes *that* long to beat their meat." He waggled his eyebrows. "Unless someone else is doing it for them."

"I am *not* beating his meat. Tobias is a true gentleman, and *you* are a filthy degenerate."

Leila picked at the ends of Her hair. *Dammit*. First the servant girls, now Raphael. Each day, Her life was a bit more complicated.

Raphael cleared his throat. "So the two of you are...involved...but he doesn't know You're The Savior?"

"And I aim to keep it that way. For now." She took in his judgmental gaze and set Her jaw. "It's a matter of safety."

"Well, I don't understand how that can be so. And I don't understand why You visit the sanctuary so frequently."

"I thought You didn't care about what I do or why I do it."

"I'm just saying, if You're so keen on hiding Yourself, why come down here at all? To bless us?"

"Of course not," She said. "Blessings are for special circumstances. Like a man bleeding to death."

"Or Tobias, whatever his circumstances are."

Her eyes shrank into a glare. "Interesting. A man of loose morals wanting the same treatment as a man who is just and good."

"I'm trying to survive. Surely You can understand."

She did understand—too well, actually—but Her contempt remained all the same. "I've finished." She cocked Her head at the tent flap. "Go on then. And—"

"Not a word. I know." Wincing, he stood. "I'll be waiting for news of my release."

Leila's eyes traced the second half of his bite as he hobbled toward the opening. "Raphael."

He turned, meeting Her gaze.

"Don't make Me regret saving your life," She said.

"I'm pleased to hear You don't already. I assumed You did."

He disappeared, taking none of the tension with him. Leila turned away, resting Her hands on the table as She sucked in a strained breath. Another mess. She didn't bother going through them all; there were far too many at this point, and Her schemes were buckling from the sheer weight of each mishap.

Footsteps sounded behind Her, and She snatched up Her blade and spun around.

Tobias—eyes wide and hands high. She dropped Her weapon. "Tobias..."

"Apologies, I didn't mean to startle you."

"You're awfully bold..." She slid Her blade into its sheath, "...charging in here without warning."

"It's difficult, you know... Being so close to you, but not being able to so much as look in your direction. Not being able to touch you."

A full breath filled Her lungs. Pink and yellow dusted the air around Tobias, painting the tent, and the tension within Her faded away.

"We're alone now," She said.

Tobias glanced over his shoulder. "But they're just outside."

"Where's your boldness now?"

A grin bloomed across his face, and between that and the keys in Her satchel, Leila allowed Herself to forget Raphael, Her father, and the rest of Her burdens. *Everything is so wrong.*

But not this.

THE MESSAGE

Tobias's hands slid up from Her waist, settling on Her cheeks. Leila wrapped Her arms around him; a few days ago She would've felt bold doing so, but somehow it had become natural, easy. The noise of the sanctuary was muffled, the tent around them a hidden refuge of their own making. His gaze danced across Her, taking Her in.

"What?" She said.

"Nothing." He threaded his fingers through Her loose locks. "I like your hair."

The braids. She had forgotten about them. "Oh God, that. The servant girls, they held me hostage. Tried to do something different. You can ignore it."

He drew Her in close. "I will do no such thing."

His stubble tickled Her chin as he kissed Her, rendering Her fluid and weak—a welcome release. Each day She stood on Her own. How wonderful it was to lean on someone, if only for a while.

A rustling sounded, and She tore Her lips from his, eyes locking on the tent flap.

Nothing happened.

Tobias sighed. "This probably isn't the smartest idea."

"Right. We could be discovered at any moment."

Her stare remained, waiting for some headache to reveal itself. But then Tobias was taking Her chin, was bringing Her closer, and suddenly his lips were pressed to Hers.

"Tobias."

"What?"

"I thought this wasn't the smartest idea."

"It isn't." He spoke between short, sweet pecks. "It's very, *very* stupid. But I'm still going to kiss you."

Lost in a fit of giggles, Leila buried Her face into Tobias's neck, only for him to guide Her lips back to his. "You know, you should've never allowed me to kiss you in the first place," he said. "I fear I've become insatiable."

"I don't mind."

She dragged Her fingers through his curls, and soon after he was kissing Her, lingering on Her bottom lip as if it were a wedge of candy. His touch was firm and tender, and despite the eagerness of his gaze, his hands never once strayed from Her back, Her hair. Something about his arms around Her felt like safety—the antithesis of every other facet of Her life.

Tension shot down Her spine. She was thinking about it—Her father, Cosima, the terrors She battled each day. Why did Her troubles have to plague Her even in moments such as these?

"Is something wrong?" Tobias said.

She shook Herself. "I was just thinking...about the challenge yesterday."

"Oh God, what a mess that was. Fucking Flynn running off at the mouth, all because of that blessing. I hadn't a clue She did that, for the record."

Her cheeks burned. "Trust me, no one was more surprised by that than I was."

"I don't even want to think of Her. The Savior, willing to let a man die in front of Her. It disgusts me. *She* disgusts me."

His words pierced Her to the bone, a blow She hadn't seen coming. She composed Herself. "The entire challenge was horrific. Did Kaleo try to *drown* you?"

"He did."

"Are you all right?"

"Better than all right." He took Her hands. "What about you?"

"What about me?"

"The way the Proctor spoke to you, it was appalling. You didn't deserve that."

Leila rolled Her eyes. "Yes, well, the Proctor has a personal problem with me that goes back quite some time."

"Then I have a personal problem with him," Tobias said.

"Haven't you made enough enemies because of me?"

"What do you mean?"

Leila raised an eyebrow. "I heard about your little visit with Brontes."

"Oh. That."

"And I heard you were very, *very* bad."

"The man's a cock," Tobias said. "A deplorable, one-eyed shit. I don't like him at all."

"Still, I must insist you tread lightly. Don't alert his attention, not any more than you have. Than I have." She cradled Her forehead. "God, this is all my fault."

"Your fault? Because of the clay? The blessing?"

"I've put a target on your back."

Tobias scoffed. "I'd rather be targeted than dead."

"Still..."

"Leila, you saved my life. For that, I am eternally grateful." He took Her face in his hands. "The Sovereign can scowl at me all he pleases—"

"He can do more than scowl."

"Then I'll handle his offenses as they come."

"Tobias, you don't understand," She said. "The man's dangerous."

She clenched Her jaw, fighting to still Herself. So much had changed since the start of the tournament. Her life wasn't the only one at risk.

"Leila, if something's troubling you, you can tell me," Tobias said.

"Just promise me you'll be careful. Promise me you'll stay away from him. That you'll avoid his line of sight."

"If it gives you peace, then I'll do it."

She exhaled. "Thank you."

Her worries didn't lift. A part of Her wondered if She should tell him more—until his words echoed between Her ears.

She disgusts me.

Tobias's fingertips traveled up and down Her back, a soft caress. Resting Her head against his shoulder, She mirrored his touch, sweeping his chest with spiraling strokes. She waited for color to swirl from his skin, but nothing happened.

"What are you thinking?" She whispered.

"I'm wondering how long I can get away with being here before people notice I'm gone."

"Not long, I imagine. You've become rather popular."

"Know I'd stay here all day if I could." He shook his head. "God, I can't believe that's even an option. *A day of rest.* I don't know why the Sovereign suddenly deems us worthy of kindness."

"It's a formality of the tournament, not a kindness. Don't allow yourself to be fooled. Brontes knows nothing of that word."

Tobias grabbed Her hand, stopping Her invisible artwork. "Whatever it is, I'll take advantage of it, and spend my time with you."

Her heart throbbed, and reprieve only came once his lips found their way to Hers. Each kiss was a drop of wine, and She was content to stand there pressed against him until She drank the chalice down.

A man barged into the tent, skidding to an abrupt halt.

Tobias spun toward the intruder. "Enzo..."

The Kovahrian glanced between them, while Leila stood frozen, nails digging into Tobias. This is what happened when She allowed Herself to be happy—to forget.

"I seen nothing." Enzo shrugged, calm, even chipper. "You two were having the conversation, nothing more. I go." He turned on his heel only to stop short. "I stand outside. If someone want in, I direct elsewhere. You can finish the talking amongst together, eh?"

He was gone seconds later, but Leila remained paralyzed, eyes trained on the spot where he once stood.

"Oh my God." Tobias exhaled. "I swear I stopped breathing. Mother of shit..."

"That shouldn't have happened," Leila said. "We need to be more careful."

"You're right. God, that could've gone horribly wrong."

Her insides whirled, roused into a panic. "We should go after him."

"No, it's all right. We can trust him."

"You're sure?"

"He owes me."

She only barely heard him, Her thoughts howling for action—for Enzo's blood on Her hands, another mouth silenced. But a soft touch broke through the spell, as Tobias glided his fingers through Her hair.

"Well then, I suppose we ought to finish our conversation, yes?" he said.

Enzo's footsteps crunched as he paced in front of the tent, standing guard as promised. Perhaps forgetting wasn't the worst thing She could do. Perhaps a little recklessness was exactly what She needed. She stood on Her toes and kissed Tobias, leaving Enzo a burden for another day.

KASTOR'S VOICE FADED INTO THE BACK OF LEILA'S MIND AS HE rambled off whatever was on the parchment in front of him. Another Senate meeting, another string of formalities, more amendments and decrees She'd have no power to influence. Instead, She reveled in the memory of Tobias's lips and their easy conversation shared in whispers and giggles. A grin threatened to streak Her face, but She forced it back.

"All those in favor of additional military recruitment?" Kastor said.

The men around Leila raised their hands, while Hers remained folded in Her lap—as if Her opinion made any difference.

Brontes counted the votes. "Erebus, begin the process tomorrow. See to it that our forces are doubled." He scribbled on his scroll. "What of the tournament?"

Wembleton jolted upright. "As it stands, twelve men remain. Four Beasts—may the Giant find eternal peace in the next life. Two Stalwarts —a surprise, they typically fare rather well. Four Lords, as it appears one went missing between challenges. And two Savants."

"I thought the Intellect was dead," Brontes said.

"It seems he's made a full recovery."

Brontes frowned. "The people. What of their word?"

"Your Shepherd and Dragon continue to garner favor among nobility. The lords of Thessen trust the approval of their Sovereign."

"And the commoners?"

Wembleton's gaze shied away. "It appears they favor the Artist."

Leila fixed a blank expression on Her face, but Her fingernails dug into the meat of Her palms.

Brontes's eye narrowed. "Why?"

"M-mostly due to his performance as of late, particularly in the battle against the Giant." Wembleton's face reddened as he read over his scroll. "They're calling him the Giant Slayer. And the Keeper of Kin. And the Man with the Purest Intent...among other things."

Brontes shifted his attention to Leila, his one eye boring into Hers.

"Is there something on My face?" She said.

Brontes's stare lingered for an unbearable second before darting away. "This is hardly surprising. Common folk will surely favor a common man. The tide will shift upon his inevitable death." He gestured toward Erebus. "Give Her the order."

Erebus tore a slip of parchment from his belt and tossed it Her way. Apprehensive, She unfolded it, taking in the weathered ink: *The Savior's Choice*, followed by wordy instructions.

"Tomorrow marks the halfway point of the tournament," Erebus said. "A man is to be honorably released. You will choose him."

"The Shepherd." She pushed the slip aside. "Next topic."

Kastor scratched his beard, his brow creased. "Apologies, Your Holiness, but a man with the Sovereign's blessing cannot be removed at this point in time."

"Says who?"

"Says the law."

He passed another slip Her way—clean and unbent at the edges, still chalky to touch. A tournament regulation She had never heard of until this moment, written with such detail, as if the matter was of grave importance. She slid Her finger through the ink, creating a long, black smudge across the page. Fresh.

"Think wisely while making Your choice," Brontes said. "You could squander this power, or You could use it to spare the life of a man who will most certainly meet a slow and deserving end otherwise."

Her blood simmered within Her veins. Tobias was Brontes's mark. This was all the confirmation She needed.

"I'll have My answer by tonight."

A knock sounded at the door, and a servant girl hesitantly came in. "Your Holiness, it's time for Your fitting."

"Can't we postpone—?"

"That won't be necessary," Kastor said. "Matters of The Savior are of the utmost importance. Your care is our greatest concern." He slid his hand across the table, stopping just shy of Her fingertips. "We can cover the rest another time."

"Who calls to end this meeting?" Brontes grumbled.

"I do."

"Second."

The Senators filed from the room, but Leila wasn't finished yet. Stopping beside the doorway, She waited as each man passed until only one remained. She slammed the door shut, sealing him in.

Silence filled the space between them. Romulus stood in calm acceptance, while visions of the last challenge ravaged Leila's mind—of Raphael bleeding out in Tobias's arms and the mess that followed soon after.

"I have news regarding the day's events." Romulus folded his hands, speaking evenly. "The men are to navigate the labyrinth. There is one particularly lethal obstacle along their route, but their odds of encountering it are as low as can be hoped for. I realize this information isn't suited to Your endeavors, but I thought You might find it agreeable given Your recent interest in...certain competitors."

Leila allowed Her glare to speak for Her.

"I crossed a line the other day," he said. "My intention was to help maintain Your façade."

"Your intention was to rebuild Your shattered pride by breaking mine. Do I appear broken to you?"

"I see now the error in my ways."

She was quiet for a moment longer. "Do you remember Anker, former page to the Sovereign? He's the one who first told Me Brontes's plans were in motion, though he did so quite reluctantly. He was so loyal to Brontes. Saw him as a father. I thought that strange, given how Brontes treats his kin."

She plucked Her blade from its sheath, trailing Her fingers along its edge. "I tried to be reasonable, coax the details from him gently—a stab here and there—but he refused. So I cut off his toes one by one, then his fingers, until finally he gave to Me what I required." She met Romulus's gaze. "I don't pride Myself on these tactics, but steps must be taken to handle those who disobey."

Romulus's stare didn't waver. She came in closer, Her weapon on display.

"I know how deeply you despise Me," She said. "But I am the only thing keeping you from death. If any part of you values your life, then you'd be wise to remember that."

"It will never happen again."

He waited for Her order before leaving in haste. Shaking off the unpleasant chill of Her own words, Leila abandoned the Senate room and the fetid animosity that came with it.

She reached Her dressing room, pacing the tiled floor to pass the time. No Cecily—clearly Her fitting wasn't ready, and the Senate meeting had been cut short for no reason at all. Why that bothered Her, She hadn't a clue, but the meeting had left Her tightly wound, stirring up worries She wished She could forget.

The door opened. Just Delphi.

"You don't mind if I join You, yes? I've been bored all day." Delphi took a seat on a floral couch, dragging her fingers over its gold stitching. "Cosima was right about this room. It's a feast for the eyes. So much *pink*. You should bring us here more often."

"Enzo knows," Leila said.

Delphi sat up straight. "That You're The Savior?"

"About Me and Tobias."

Slumping, Delphi rolled her eyes. "And?"

"What do you mean? This is a huge complication! Tobias and I are committing treason!"

"Except you're not." Delphi toyed with a ruby diadem. "Because You're The Savior."

"But Enzo doesn't know that. He could have Tobias condemned."

"And You could reverse the punishment."

"And reveal the switch in the process?"

"Oh," Delphi said. "I suppose that is a bit complicated."

Sighing, Leila resumed Her pacing. "Tobias says we can trust him. But...I don't know..."

"Of course You don't. You don't trust anyone."

"I'm glad My troubles amuse you."

"Sister, if I wet myself over every misfortune, I'd have no pretty dresses left to wear." Delphi kicked her legs onto the couch's armrest. "Brontes is down one assassin and many constituents. We're progressing, troubles or none."

The door opened, and two servants glided into the space: Cecily, her fluffy curls bouncing atop her shoulders, and Mousumi, dour per usual.

"Apologies. I hope You haven't been waiting long." Cecily nestled up beside Leila, pulling yarn from her pocket and wrapping Her waist. "Just measurements today. Mousumi requires some details as well."

The servant keeper whipped out a scroll and scanned it over. "Tomorrow, Your suitors will join us in the palace—"

"Suitors?" Leila said.

"The competitors of Your father's tournament. They're leaving the labyrinth tomorrow."

Leila stammered, "Apologies. I suppose I never saw them as...suitors."

"Child, they're here to marry You." Cecily chuckled, looking up from her measurements. "Of course they're Your suitors. Fine ones, I'm sure."

"Their accommodations are being prepared," Mousumi continued. "Two to three to a room, depending on the numbers."

"Have you chosen their chambers?" Leila said.

Mousumi scanned her scroll. "The Dragon is paired with the Shepherd. The Prince with the Hunter. The Artist with the Intellect—"

"Switch them."

Mousumi faltered. "Come again?"

"The Artist can stay with the Hunter. Place the Intellect with the Prince."

The room fell silent as Cecily and Mousumi glanced between one another, perplexed.

"What a kind gesture." Delphi smiled. "The Prince and the Intellect have become fast friends."

Cecily nodded, and Mousumi turned to her scroll. "It's custom for The Savior to bestow a gift to each suitor. Have You any preferences?"

Colors swirled through Leila's thoughts—paints of all shades, endless slips of canvas, all for Tobias. "I'll give it some thought."

Cecily crouched at Leila's feet, measuring Her hem. "If You ask me, these men have already received the greatest of gifts—Your care and affection. I think the Kovahrians say it best: *Neit podratscha bijshespo a chellak vras, uhvük, ie stüktsapul.* No gift is more precious than a person's time, ear, and beating heart."

Leila's head perked up. "You speak Kovahrian?"

"My father was a soldier. He's taught me many lessons from his travels."

The weight in Leila's pocket became heavier—Phanes's note, still a mystery. "What about the various Kovahrian dialects?"

"I know a few, yes. Why do You ask?"

Hesitating, Leila turned to Delphi, who stared back at Her with an eager gaze.

"Is something wrong?" Cecily said.

Leila fished the note from Her pocket. "Could you by chance tell Me what this says?"

Cecily took the note and read it over. Her eyes widened. "Where did You get this? Who gave this to You?"

"What does it say?"

"It's unspeakable. I can't."

"Please, just tell Me—"

Mousumi snatched the slip from Cecily's grasp and read it aloud. "Death to The Savior, Her line, and all who bathe in Her feeble light. May Thessen waste away beneath the rotting corpse of their Queen."

Leila faltered. "*You* can read that?"

"It's wartongue," Mousumi said matter-of-factly. "All Kovahrians can read it."

"*You're* Kovahrian?" Delphi eyed Mousumi from the couch, studying her tawny skin, her black hair—a far cry from the pale standard in the north.

Mousumi's nostrils flared. "My father was Ethyuan."

"We need to alert the guards," Cecily said. "Mousumi, fetch Erebus—"

"No." Leila snatched up the note. "That won't be necessary."

"Child, this is clearly a threat."

"Nonsense," Delphi added. "It's certainly little more than a cruel joke."

"How can you be sure? These are blasphemous words. There's nothing funny about them."

"The note was slipped beneath My chamber door," Leila lied. "I recognize the handwriting. One of My servants—we had an argument the other day. She's lashing out."

Mousumi's voice came out flat. "Shall I have her punished, Your Holiness?"

"That won't be necessary. I'll handle her." Leila turned to Cecily. "I appreciate your concern, but I assure you, there's nothing to fear. I'll get this straightened away. Now, in fact." Pocketing the note, She grabbed Delphi. "We'll be on our way. Thank you for your service."

The sisters barreled from the dressing room arm-in-arm, waiting a safe distance before speaking. "Did you hear that?" Leila whispered.

"I most certainly did."

"*Death to The Savior.* Written in wartongue, whatever that is." Leila shook Her head. "Kovahr is plotting against Me. After so many years as allies, they rebel, the pasty bastards."

"Your father's source... He must be from the north as well."

"What exactly is their play? They want Brontes to take My crown— for what purpose? How does it benefit them? And who knows what other aid they provide? Perhaps weapons, coin, spies—"

Leila stopped hard, sending Delphi staggering to a halt along with Her. "Oh My God." Her chest tightened.

"Enzo."

LEILA DRAGGED HER BLADE ACROSS THE SMOOTH STONE, ITS EDGE glinting against the candlelight. The sun had long since set, and thus

Her time would soon belong to the labyrinth. She sat in Her chamber, Her satchel packed, Her weapon sharpened. Strapping it to Her thigh, She sucked in a breath, preparing for what was to come. Tonight's visit wasn't for Tobias.

It was for Enzo.

We can trust him. Tobias's voice rang in Her skull, words She wanted to believe but couldn't. A part of Her envied his naivety, wished She could have such faith in people, but that instinct had died long ago. She pulled the note from Her pocket, scanning over the thick black letters before crumpling it.

As She clasped Her cloak around Her neck, a knock sounded. "Come in."

Metal plates clanked behind Her. She glanced over Her shoulder. "Asher. Did you need something?"

Crossing his arms, he leaned against the door. "I know why You're sneaking around. You're seeing someone. A man."

"Yes, I am."

He wavered. "You are?" He opened his mouth to speak. "But..."

Leila raised Her eyebrows. "But?"

"You're the..."

"I'm the...?"

"Are You mocking me?"

"How astute of you to notice."

He frowned. "You can't sneak off with a man in the middle of the night."

"And why can't I?"

"You're The Savior."

"I'm The Savior, and thus I cannot do as I please?" She said. "Speak to whomever I want? Make My own decisions?"

"You can do all those things."

"Then what exactly is your meaning?"

His frown deepened. "You are a gift from God Itself. You are held to a higher standard."

"You judge Me." Leila looped Her satchel over Her shoulder. "For spending My time with a man."

"This behavior is beneath You."

"Tell Me then, what would you have Me do? Sit alone in My chamber, waiting for some stranger to claim Me as his wife? Is that what you'd do? Would you wait your entire life passively until someone was chosen for you?" She let out a laugh. "We both know you wouldn't. You couldn't even wait a full day to stick your cock inside My sister. But I am The Savior, and thus I must wait. Unbelievable. You must think so little of Me to deny Me of the basic freedoms you readily enjoy."

"Leila—"

She burst into rays of light. The black bricks of the labyrinth appeared around Her, and She charged forward, resolved. Tobias's voice still echoed between Her ears, claims She had to push aside. He knew nothing of the world She lived in.

Movement flickered in the distance, followed by voices.

"What the fuck is going on?" a man shouted.

She hurried Herself, first jogging, then running until the sanctuary opened up before Her. The men were clustered beyond the fire pit, all eyes on Caesar as he struggled against the wall, pinned by four men— and in the direct center, leading the onslaught, was Tobias.

"Healer girl!" Caesar barked.

Tobias's head spun toward Leila, but the rest of him didn't move— not his forearm, which was jammed against Caesar's throat, nor his opposite shoulder buried in the Lord's chest.

"Healer girl, stop them!" Caesar writhed, failing to break free. "You have to make them stop!"

Embers floated through the air, a black and red mist emanating from one man. Enzo seethed at the end of the horde, muscles flexed as rage spilled from him like magma. Nearby, Zander lay on the floor, his body limp, his neck twisted.

Another dead man.

Enzo was barely contained where he stood, his colors filling the sanctuary with hatred—for Caesar.

"Healer girl, they're trying to *kill me*," Caesar said. "Make them *stop*."

Clarity hit Her in an instant—the dead man on the floor, his paramour's fury, and even Tobias, not nearly as naive as She had assumed.

She met Caesar's gaze. "I don't know what you're talking about. I haven't seen anything."

"You bitch!" Caesar's voice climbed higher. "You stupid bitch!"

She tossed Her blade to the floor. "Oh look, it appears I've dropped something. How careless of me." Her eyes narrowed. "I'm such a *stupid bitch*."

Enzo scooped up the weapon and headed straight for Caesar, taking his fiery rage with him.

"No." Caesar's face paled. "No, no no no..."

Enzo stopped in front of his mark, waiting. Without a word, Tobias exposed Caesar's throat before nodding at the Beast—an unspoken command.

"No!" Caesar howled. "Dog, stop! Get away! GET THE FUCK AWAY!"

Enzo dug the blade into his throat, turning his screams into gurgling. Blood rained down the Lord's chest, while Leila and the others watched on.

THE KOVAHRIAN

eila lay flat on Her back, staring up at Her chamber ceiling. A glimmer of sunlight peeked beneath Her curtains, slowly lifting the dark of night. Morning was approaching, though She wished it wouldn't. Whatever it took to prolong this decision.

"So then, who are You sending home?"

Delphi's feet wiggled near Leila's shoulder. They lay parallel to one another in Leila's bed, hands folded on their stomachs.

"Raphael knows I'm The Savior," Leila said. "I promised to release him from the tournament in return for his silence. Now's the perfect opportunity."

"And then there's Enzo. A Kovahrian spy aiding in Your assassination."

"We don't know that for certain."

"We found a note penned in Kovahrian *wartongue* calling for Your death, while a northern soldier, personal guard to the Kovahrian Queen no less, is a competitor of Your father's tournament." The scorn in Delphi's words stung. "Of course he's a spy. Or worse."

"So...you think I should release Enzo."

"I know You should. And I think You do too." Delphi flicked her wrist. "You can handle Raphael. Have him released the next time around. It's not ideal, but one man's a snitch, the other's a spy. Which is worse?"

Leila sank into Her sheets. "And what about Tobias?"

Delphi shot upright. "You want to release *Tobias?*"

"I want him to live."

"He is *thriving*. He is emerging a leader, does well in challenges—"

"He's barely cheated death on more than one occasion. At what point does his luck run out?"

"It isn't luck," Delphi said. "You and I both know this."

Leila wilted. "What happens when I'm unable to protect him?"

"He grows stronger with Your influence. Each day, he is more powerful than the last, and that's because of You and Your light. He has proven himself a worthy ally, has killed one of Your father's men, was willing to kill again the other night."

"You'd have Me use him in a battle he knows nothing about?"

"I'd have You defeat Your father and find happiness."

Leila looked away. It didn't matter how much logic Delphi preached. Her insides still twisted, separating Her in two.

"I know You want Tobias safe," Delphi said. "But he is capable. Isn't there a part of You that longs for him to be Your Champion?"

"He hates it here," Leila muttered.

"But he cherishes his time with You. Have You seen the look in his eyes when he says Your name? I know You have."

"It's a selfish choice."

"Or is it?" Delphi said. "Because I do believe if he knew You were The Savior, he wouldn't be so keen on leaving. I do believe he'd fight for You."

The weight on Leila's chest nearly lifted, until Tobias's voice rang in Her ears.

She disgusts me.

Delphi flopped down onto the bed. "Well if You're not going to send home Enzo, at least let it be Raphael. God, to throw away Your one move on Tobias—"

"I'm *thinking*," Leila spat. "*I'm* the one with My life on the line, yet you dictate My actions as if you have anything to lose."

The chamber fell silent, the sisters stiff at one another's side.

"Brontes killed my mother." Delphi's voice was hard and level. "I have a stake in these plans just as You do. Or have You forgotten?"

"Apologies. I spoke carelessly."

Delphi was quiet for a while before sighing. "So then, what's Your choice? Is it Raphael, Enzo, or Tobias?"

"If Enzo is in fact a spy...he has to go."

"I agree."

Leila didn't move, Her mind overwrought as She clung to the folds of Her dress.

"Is there something else?" Delphi said.

"You'll think I'm silly."

"I think that quite often but love You all the same."

Leila bit Her lip. "He was wrecked by Zander's death. I pity him." Propping Herself upright, She met Delphi's gaze. "Is that bad?"

"Your time with Tobias has made You soft."

Leila scoffed, swatting Her sister.

"It's a good thing." Delphi cracked a smile. "It suits You."

"It's ridiculous. I know he could very well be abetting My end...but he was so broken..."

A knock sounded, and Hylas entered with a bow. "Your Holiness. It's time."

Leila's eyes darted toward Her floor, now covered in light. Daybreak. As Hylas departed, Delphi hopped from the bed. "I'll go fetch Cosima."

"No. I want it to be Me this time."

"But Your cover..."

Leila threw Her cloak around Her shoulders. "I need answers."

She left Her chamber in a whirl of black fabric, heading past the courtyard down the long path to the labyrinth. Shadow walking wasn't an option; the palace staff was waiting to see Her walk through the gardens, off to deliver a harsh blow to a man who would surely lament his fate. None of this resonated with Leila. Release from the tournament was more gift than burden.

Upon reaching the latch, She abandoned Her escorts, plunging underground alone. The sanctuary was eerily quiet, the men fast asleep. Hope swelled within Her, and She crept toward a familiar tent, Her hand on Her blade, until rustling sounded inside along with low voices.

Of course Her assassins were awake. Growling, She sheathed Her weapon, finding the original tent She had come for and tiptoeing inside.

Tobias lay belly-first in his cot, his strong back rising and falling. She watched him for a moment, Her impulses writhing, urging Her to go to him. She turned to the cot at the other side of the tent.

"Enzo." She shook his meaty shoulder. "It's time to wake up."

He roused effortlessly, looking Her way.

"Follow me," She whispered.

She led him through the portal, traveling a winding stretch before reaching a small grey room. Enzo appeared behind Her, glancing over the walls.

"Come in, please," Leila said.

He did as told, standing a comfortable distance away from Her, arms behind his back. Every facet of his being was that of a soldier, from his sturdy carriage to his muscular build, but the blackish blue cloud encircling him spoke of deeper wounds he wasn't inclined to share.

"Do you know why you've been summoned?" Leila said.

Enzo's accent came out stiff and broken. "A challenge?"

"No. There's no challenge."

Confusion filled his gaze. Leila took a step back, resting Her hand on a brick. "There's something I need to show you."

She pressed down on the red crown, and the wall at Her side caved in, each brick collapsing onto the next until a staircase to the surface was created. Sunlight poured through the opening, and She stepped into the white rays.

Vacant awe swept Enzo's face. Leila stood in silence, waiting as he took in Her glow, his beady eyes larger than She'd ever seen.

"You... You are the holy Queen."

Leila nodded. "I am The Savior of Thessen."

"And the other?"

"Merely playing a part."

Enzo swayed from side to side, then abruptly came to life, kneeling.

"Oh no, that isn't necessary, please stand," She said.

He did as instructed. "They say You glow. I did not believe..." He scanned Her over. "It is like sunlight on fresh snowfall."

"Do you need a moment?"

Enzo shook himself. "'Pologies, I...I did not believe. But now..."

He never finished. Leila swallowed the knot in Her throat. "Zander was one of the kindest men I've ever had the pleasure of knowing. My heart breaks for his cruel death...and for your suffering."

"He was good man. True comrade. But...I do not understand..."

"I know of your affection for one another."

His eyes widened.

"It's all right," Leila said. "I'm not upset. I'm just sad he's gone. I'm sad for you as well." She choked over Her words. "I feel responsible. He died in My tournament. I couldn't stop it."

"It is not Your fault. You were not there."

There it was again—the steadfast soldier, all trace of emotion gone in an instant, save for his dark colors streaming through the air.

"There's no need to be stoic with Me. I have lost before. I won't judge." Leila inched toward him. "May I?"

Enzo eyed Her glowing hand, nodding before She rested it on his chest.

Anguish plowed through Her, sending tears welling in Her eyes. "I'm so sorry. I wish I could fix it."

"I wish I could fix it too."

She kept Her hand in place, enduring the hurt. This was a pain She knew well, yet it still cut so deeply.

Enzo's face dropped. "No, don't cry."

She wiped Her cheeks. "Apologies. It's not My place. It's just, there are so many things I can heal...yet I can't heal this. But I want to so, so badly."

He glanced down at Her hand. "You feel?"

As She nodded, his eyes glistened over. He pulled Her hand from his chest, freeing Her from his torment. "You are strong and good." He nestled Her hand in his. "Heart of true queen."

Her stomach lurched. "There's another reason I've come to speak to you. I've heard things...about Kovahr. And I have reason to believe that perhaps You didn't join this tournament to seek My hand. Is there something I should know?"

He didn't answer, though the shift in his gaze told Her everything. Her heart sank. "Enzo..."

He dropped to his knee, bowing. "*Hanzipo*, please forgive, I obey orders. I do what I must for my realm."

"You were commanded to come here. To spy."

"It is as You say."

Leila looked away, swallowing the bitter taste of his words. "I don't understand. Why do your people seek to harm Me?"

"Harm? No no, that is not the way."

"Then why spy? What purpose does it serve?"

"My Queen does not say."

When Leila didn't respond, Enzo stood. "She is good. I come to observe and report." He planted Her hand on his chest. "Can You feel? I speak truth."

She cringed as pain rushed through Her in torrents. "I...want to believe you."

"Feel. You will see."

"It doesn't exactly work like that—"

"She rules with honor. Her word is true."

Leila nearly scoffed. People made the same claims about Brontes. She pulled away.

"As The Savior of Thessen, I am awarded one act of power in this tournament: the ability to release a single man with his life intact." She displayed the stairwell. "I release you. You are free from this cruelty."

"But—"

"Mourn the loss of your love in the comfort of your homeland. Know you will forever be held in My highest regards."

He stared back at Her for a long while before bowing and heading for the stairwell. "The Artist," he said. "He is good man. He will protect You."

Leila's voice wavered. "I'm trying to protect him."

"You are good for each other then."

He continued on his ascent, and Leila sealed the wall once he disappeared, encasing the room in darkness. Some semblance of calm should've claimed Her, but the nagging of Her mind continued, as did the restlessness of Her gut.

∾

Sleep came easily. She hadn't expected it, given Her tumultuous thoughts, but after a night of emotional labor, She had drifted away as soon as She met Her pillow.

"Hold Her down."

Leila's eyes shot open. Armored guards hovered over Her—ten, maybe more. One on each side took hold of Her arms, pinning Her to the bed.

"What is—?" Leila thrashed beneath Her sheets. "Let go of Me!"

"Keep Her still."

Brontes appeared within the pack. Two more guards held Her ankles, while Her father pulled a dagger from his belt.

"No!" She kicked Her legs. "Stop him!"

A guard yanked Her arm, pushing it flat as Brontes dug his dagger into Her flesh. Pain sliced through Her, and She screamed. *Shadow walk,* but Her mind was too havocked to command.

Brontes pointed a vial to the wound, collecting a trail of blood. "It's done."

The guards released Her, following Brontes from the room. Breathless, Leila sat up as they retreated. Asher stood dumbstruck in the doorway, glancing between the disappearing line of soldiers and Leila.

Wrapping a sheet around Her body, She charged ahead.

"I'm sorry," Asher said. "The Sovereign ordered... I couldn't stop—"

She slammed the door in his face.

Pressing Her back to the golden surface, She fought to both catch Her breath and wrangle Her dignity. The wound stung, trickling red onto Her white sheet.

Brontes had Her blood.

She bandaged Her arm and dressed, bolting to Her sisters' chambers and forcing them from their beds. The women headed to the eastern end of the palace, plowing into the scroll room, a crowded space with cream walls and endless shelves filled with weathered parchment. She stopped in front of the far left corner, where each record from every tournament past was stored, and dumped the scrolls onto the floor.

"Begin," She ordered.

The women took root around the pile, scanning each scroll before tossing it aside. Cosima sighed. "What exactly are we looking for?"

"The blood of The Savior." Leila's eyes panned the parchment in front of Her. "The labyrinth depends on the blood of Saviors past. It can't function without it. But the men are being released today, so we need to know how the blood is used above ground."

"Tell me again why we're doing this?" Cosima said.

"It's for Tobias."

"Who?"

"The Artist," Pippa chimed in.

"Brontes vowed that if I didn't release Tobias, he'd have him killed. And now it's happening..." Leila's gut lurched. "God, I'm going to be sick."

"Yes, I understand all that, but how does this benefit Your cause at all?"

"It doesn't." Delphi didn't bother looking Cosima's way, reading over a slip of parchment. "We're saving Tobias. Now get to work."

"Leila, please don't tell me You ripped us all out of bed just so we can save the Artist. I know You're fond of him, but You do realize there are other men—"

"I am searching for the answer," Leila spat. "You can either help, or you can leave. But I refuse to listen to you prattle on for another moment."

Rolling her eyes, Cosima grabbed a scroll.

Leila skimmed infinite streams of text, Her brow wet with sweat. Time wasn't on Her side; the sun was high in the sky, and there were still hundreds of scrolls to go through—tales of violence, heroism, and not a single mention of The Savior's blood on palace grounds. "We have to find it. I won't allow—"

"Calm Yourself," Delphi said. "We'll see it through."

"I found it!" Pippa held up her parchment, then faltered. "Wait. Never mind. I'll keep looking."

Leila glanced out the window. "When are they to be released?"

"I would've assumed it happened long ago," Cosima said. "We very well could be wasting our efforts."

"We have time." Delphi shot her a glare. "Keep going."

"I found it!" Pippa wrinkled her nose. "No, wait. That's someone else's blood. There's a lot of blood in these scrolls."

"You know who else is handsome? The Regal." Cosima nudged Leila's shoulder. "Why don't You play with him instead?"

"He's dead," Delphi said.

"Since when?"

"I found it!" Pippa squealed.

Leila sighed, digging through the pile. "That's nice."

"It's the garden of Meg...aera." Pippa shoved the scroll in front of Leila. "See?"

A single word cried out to Her: *blood*. She read over the text.

For when The Savior marked the statues with Her blood, She gave to them a power bestowed by God, and each man who gazed into their eyes or touched their marble figures saw an end most gruesome and vile. Such was the legacy of Megaera and Her deadly garden.

"Oh My God." Leila snatched the slip from Pippa's hands. "You found it."

"I said I did."

Tears brimmed in Leila's eyes. "Little duckling, thank you. Thank you so much." She threw Her arms around her.

"Did I help?"

"You saved a man's life today. Do you know that?" She cupped Pippa's face. "You're a hero."

"I don't want to be a hero. I want to be a sorceress."

"Sorceresses can be heroes too."

"Oh, good!"

"I have to go." Leila kissed Pippa's cheek. "Thank you." She squeezed Delphi's hand. "You too."

"What about me?" Cosima huffed.

Leila burst into blazing heat, Her sisters dissolving behind Her. Black brick and brown canvas stretched far ahead; She had been far too hasty, shadow walking straight to the sanctuary, but the men were off by the fire pit talking amongst one another, and it seemed no one had noticed Her at all. She tiptoed toward the voices, peering past a tent. The men had formed clusters, their bodies adorned in leather straps and shining armor, and in the middle of the mess stood Tobias.

"Did you hear about Enzo?" he said.

"I know." Flynn shook his head. "Poor bastard, he's missing the best part."

Leila cleared Her throat, once more a bit louder, and Tobias glanced over his shoulder, meeting Her gaze. His eyes widened, and he slipped away from the others.

"Leila..." He joined Her behind the tent, checking for prying gazes. "I take it you're not supposed to be here."

"Not exactly. Keep your voice low."

"About last night—"

"You needn't explain yourself," She said. "Fuck Caesar. May he rot in the ground for all eternity."

Tobias exhaled. "Enzo... He was honorably released."

Her chest pulled taut. "I know."

"He was released by *The Savior*. That means She has some semblance of power in this tournament. And maybe I could appeal to Her, could help Her see reason, and you and I—"

"She can only release one man. Just one. And She chose Enzo."

Tobias's shoulders dropped, and the disappointment in his eyes unleashed every ounce of guilt within Her. "Tobias..."

"It's all right. It was wishful thinking. Nothing more."

She took his hands. "I don't have much time. Listen carefully, all right?"

"Always."

"You'll be leaving the labyrinth and entering the Garden of Megaera. It's filled with statues, each in the likeness of a past Savior. Absolutely stunning, flawless faces immortalized for all eternity." She tightened Her grip. "You mustn't look at them. Any of them."

"Pardon?"

"Don't look at them. Don't *touch* them. Make your way through the garden, and do so quickly."

"You sound worried."

"I am."

Tobias furrowed his brow, perplexed concern streaking his face.

"I'll be waiting for you." Her voice trembled. "In the palace."

"I'll see you there."

"Promise me. Promise you'll see me there."

He leaned closer, his voice strong and even. "I swear it."

"I have to go."

Taking Her chin, he left Her with a kiss. "Go."

Every part of Her wanted to stay, but She did as She was told, weaving between the tents before summoning Her light. The black bricks turned to grey, and the heat of daylight spilled over Her. The watchtower was empty per usual, and She had counted on that. Its perch had the perfect view of the Garden of Megaera.

A summer breeze carried the sound of distant cheering; tiny bodies speckled the fortress walls, waving banners Leila couldn't make out. She ducked, shielding Her glow with the tower sill only to realize how silly that was. The people weren't looking Her way. They were there for the same reason as Her—to see the men emerge from the labyrinth.

Far off on the fortress grounds, a tuft of grass caved in, creating a crater—an exit. As the men trickled out, the spectators' cheering grew louder, as did the noise of Leila's thoughts. Wembleton's voice echoed in the distance while She analyzed the men, trying to make out one speck from the next. *There*. Brown hair. She was certain it was Tobias. Now all he had to do was get through the garden.

The garden. She'd traveled its grounds countless times, even played there as a child, but now it felt ominous. The destruction from Her encounter with Phanes had long been cleared, the grass lush and green. Marble statues lined the pathway, each Savior dressed in a flowing gown and adorned in feathered wings. So many statues. Too many.

A lump lodged in Her throat. The men were heading off, their slow pace a sharp poker to Her patience. Tobias was keeping his head down —or was he? It seemed as though he was, but then nearly all the others looked the same, save for Beau, who flitted through the garden like a child. In fact the entire journey was monotonous, hardly the spectacle the onlookers likely anticipated. Maybe they'd get through without issue. Leila squinted, straining to see. The men *were* staring at the ground—even Her assassins.

Brontes had told them. *Of course he did.*

Movement flitted in Her peripheral vision, though She couldn't place it. The men continued on their lackluster stroll, while Beau fluttered between them, gazing up at the statues without care. Then it happened again, and Her blood ran cold.

A statue turned its head, watching the men as they passed.

One by one the Saviors observed them, until every statue they passed was looking their way. Beau hopped onto a marble pedestal, and Leila clasped a hand over Her mouth.

The statue beside him came to life, burying its teeth in his neck.

His scream ripped through the air. The statue spat out the remains of his throat, crimson streaking its face. As Beau toppled to the ground, the other men spun in place.

"Don't!" Leila shouted, but it was useless.

Tobias's voice cut through the quiet.

"Run!"

The men dashed through the garden, unleashing an onslaught. The statues had been roused to life, some stepping down from their pedestals and trailing the men, others beating their wings and soaring into the sky. Leila kept Her eyes on Tobias, willing him through Her thoughts to keep moving.

He skidded to a stop as a statue landed in front of him.

Tobias and the others wove between the marble figures, their heads down and movements calculated. Saviors congregated nearby, touching him, and goose bumps traveled across Leila's skin as if She too could feel their fingertips. *Don't look at them.* The order repeated in Her mind, and it seemed to do the trick, as the journey continued with little disarray— until Flynn gazed up at a statue, frozen.

Tobias yanked the Lord from the statue's clutches, bolting through the grass as chaos ensued. The palace wasn't much further, and when Tobias shot up the courtyard steps, Leila's heart raced. He was so close. He was going to make it. But the courtyard was dense with horrid statues and howling men, and it was nearly impossible to make out anything amid the madness. White stone streaked with blood, tan flesh marred with gashes. Where was Tobias? She had lost him in the shuffle, and when She finally spotted him, Her breath caught.

He was pinned to a pillar, a statue looming before him.

He strained away as the creature dragged its face against his neck. The courtyard lay just beneath the watchtower, and Leila could see everything—Tobias's cringe, the familiarity of the statue's face. Bile rose in Leila's throat.

Her mother.

Tobias darted around the pillar, and Leila tried to shake Her horror, tracking his movements. The other competitors were gone, and he wove through the horde, tottering over fountain edges, zigzagging between grasping white hands. He was nimble, resilient, and a part of Her recognized the thriving competitor Delphi had described—a man who could be Champion, if only he'd reach the palace.

He catapulted up the front steps and disappeared from sight.

Leila's heart stopped. The tower sill blocked Her view of the palace entrance, but when the slamming of its double doors rang through the air, the tension within Her released.

Tobias had made it.

A deathly silence stretched across the grounds. The statues trudged back to their pedestals, leaving dirt, blood, and destruction in their wake. Beau's corpse lay in the distance, the lone fatality, while the other men were tucked away within the palace walls. Leila took in an unsteady breath. Tobias was safe.

And so were Her assassins.

❧ 20 ❧

THE WELCOMING

The hum of voices filtered through Leila's bedchamber, the palace so roused not even Her thick golden door could block the noise. She sat at Her desk, staring at the crumpled parchment. Kovahr's threat. There was little point in reading it again. She had Her answers.

The door swung open, and dancing feet pitter-pattered across the floor. "There's a party tonight!" Pippa spun in circles. "I'm going to wear pink. Or powder blue. Or maybe lavender."

Delphi came up to Leila's side, wrapping her arms around Her shoulders. "Today's the big day. Well, one of them. There are so many big days lately."

The Welcoming was approaching, a grand event honoring the men of the tournament, one of the palace's most anticipated traditions. But while the servants buzzed with excitement, all Leila felt was dread. On that night, She would dine and dance with the palace hands—everyone who worshipped Her as their One True Savior—along with the exact eight men who knew nothing of Her title. And She needed it to stay that way.

"We're going to have to be...careful," She said.

Delphi nodded. "I agree."

"I want you, Cosima, and Pippa to attend My dressing, so we can prepare."

"Sounds reasonable."

The softness of Delphi's voice did little to calm Her. She scanned the note for the hundredth time.

"I imagine something else is on Your mind?" Delphi said.

"The assassins are in My home." Leila clenched Her jaw. "I want them dead."

A knock sounded, and a zaftig girl came into the room, bowing. "Your Holiness. It's time for Your bath."

Shoving the parchment into the desk drawer, Leila eyed the girl over —a servant She didn't recognize. "Is Faun already there? She usually retrieves Me."

"Apologies. Your servants are required elsewhere today."

"There must be a mistake."

"The competitors of Your father's tournament are being prepared for the Welcoming," the girl said. "Your servants offered their assistance. I believe they were eager to meet one suitor in particular. A crowd favorite."

Leila's gut turned. Her servants were with Tobias. What if they revealed Her?

The girl paled. "Have I upset You? Your Holiness, forgive me, I didn't mean—"

"It's all right. Let's tend to My bath."

The hours passed with painstaking slowness, as Leila sat flexed and on edge in the warm pool, deadened to the soft hands and sweet smells. The unknown servants worked in silence, a relief, though She wouldn't have engaged regardless. Tonight was no celebration for Her; the Welcoming was a battlefield riddled with traps, and She'd have to maneuver it with caution.

It's just one evening. But how could She keep Her assassins in the dark in a room full of people who bowed to Her?

Properly bathed, She retreated to Her dressing room. Delphi, Pippa, and Cosima were already lounging on the couches, conspicuously quiet. As Leila changed into a sheer violet robe, Cecily and Mousumi arrived, nearly starting at the sight of all four sisters waiting expectantly.

Cecily's stunned expression morphed into an awkward smile. "Isn't this a pleasant surprise? Having the royal court present for Her Holiness's dressing."

"It's odd," Mousumi said.

Leila stood tall. "They've played an integral part in this tournament. I'm indebted to them. I'd like them to be made just as beautiful as Me. The finest silks and jewels."

Cecily chuckled. "Child, they're of *Your* court. They already wear the finest silks and jewels."

"As fine as your Queen's?"

Cecily shrank beneath Leila's challenge. "Well, the more the merrier, I say." She gave the court a nod before beginning her measurements. "It seems I have many to dress today. I'm draping Your suitors, in fact. The fabric is exquisite, hand-stitched and the blackest black I've ever seen. Eight warrior drapes for eight tried and true warriors."

"You're draping all of them?" Leila said.

"Oh dear, no. Nessa has half, and I have the others. Let's see, I've been assigned the Brave, the Shepherd, the Dragon, and the Artist."

Tobias floated through Leila's mind, and a hint of Her dread thawed.

"You take precedence, of course." Cecily brought several strings of jewels to Leila's throat. "That reminds me, weren't You to give them gifts? What did You decide upon?"

"Garrick got a sword with a golden pommel." Pippa plucked a cylindrical bottle of perfume from one of the tables, brandishing it in the air. "The weapon of a mighty hero."

"Paying tribute to their laurels? Let me guess, a bow for the Hunter, jewels for the Prince, an easel for the Artist..."

"Paints and brushes too, of course," Leila said before She could stop Herself.

Cecily smiled. "What about the Sovereign's blessed ones? The Dragon and the Shepherd? I can't imagine gifts that would match—"

"Nothing," Leila said.

"Pardon?"

"I gave them nothing."

The palace fitter stared back at Her, slack jawed.

"I told Her it was highly inappropriate," Mousumi grumbled.

"Enough of this nonsense, let's get our Leila dressed up." Cosima hopped up from the rose couch, fluttering toward one of the racks. "I've been dying to see Her gown. She has the most beautiful collection."

Cecily's eyes lit up. "I have the perfect piece in mind."

She joined Cosima, flipping through an entire rainbow before plucking one gown from the others: deep scarlet, a color only suitable for a queen. Leila's blood ran cold as Cecily headed Her way, the gown in hand.

"It's much more extravagant than Your usual tastes, but given the circumstances—"

"I'd like to wear the black one," Leila blurted.

Cecily halted. "But You always wear red for these occasions. An event such as this demands a royal color."

"I'm feeling daring. This is My preference for the night."

"But black—"

"Is the warrior's color. The very color the competitors will be wearing. I aim to honor them."

"A sign of solidarity," Delphi said. "Your suitors will be pleased."

Cecily frowned. "With all due respect, I imagine most of them are unfamiliar with the color's meaning."

Delphi raised an eyebrow. "You belittle The Savior's kind gesture?"

"Oh, it's a *gesture* in more ways than one. This gown is utterly explicit." Cosima grabbed the dress in question, a mischievous grin on her face. "Look at this neckline. Leaves nothing to the imagination, that's for certain."

Leila laughed. "Cosima!"

"You know I'm right. And who could blame You?" She pressed the dress to her figure, sashaying through the room. "Who wouldn't want to look seductive for eight valiant suitors? No doubt the men will beg for more once they've laid eyes on Her." She swirled toward the servants. "Of course She chose this piece. Don't pretend you can't relate. We all can."

"I can't," Mousumi muttered.

Cecily cleared her throat. "Apologies, it just occurred to me that if I'm to dress all four of you, I'll need a much larger wardrobe. Excuse me."

She left in a hurry, likely escaping the turn in conversation, and for that Leila was grateful.

"There are formalities to cover before tonight's festivities." Unamused, Mousumi pulled a scroll from her pocket and scanned it over. "The event will begin with entertainment, followed by dancing and feasting. Your sisters will enter first, then Your suitors, and finally Yourself."

"Bring My sisters out at My side," Leila said.

Mousumi met Leila's gaze. "Your suitors, *then* You...*and* Your sisters?"

"Yes. All together."

The servant keeper's lips twisted in disapproval.

"I don't want a big fuss, is all," Leila mumbled.

"The Welcoming is to honor the competitors of the Sovereign's Tournament." Delphi made her way to Leila's side. "Surely Her Holiness isn't trying to upstage their glory."

"Exactly. I want them to feel like the kings they so rightly are." Leila's eyes widened. "In fact, I'd rather not wear a crown tonight."

Mousumi recoiled. "Your Holiness—"

"A fine idea." Cosima joined her sisters, standing with them in a line. "I couldn't agree more."

Not to be left out, Pippa marched into formation with them. Leila was glad for her presence, stronger with Her court at Her side. "I'd also like My throne removed."

"Your *throne?*" Mousumi groused.

"I'd like to sit on equal ground with My sisters. They've served as such fine council. The least I can do is show My appreciation."

"Oh Leila, how very thoughtful." Cosima swerved in front of Her, taking Her hands. "I swear, we'll remember this night for the rest of our lives."

Mousumi sighed. "Your Holiness, that throne weighs—"

"If that's the last of this, why don't you see to its removal," Leila said.

"But—"

"Your Savior commands it," Delphi ordered.

Mousumi scanned the line of soldiers, her annoyance written across her face. "Yes, Your Holiness."

With much less grace than Cecily, she left the room. Exhaling, Leila slumped into an armchair. The Welcoming hadn't begun yet, and already She was exhausted.

"How long do You expect to keep this up?" Delphi said. "We won't always be here to fawn over Your wondrous decision-making."

"It worked for now." Leila massaged Her temples. "That's what matters."

"And what about the next time, and the next?"

"Oh, relax." Cosima spoke over her shoulder, flipping through Leila's gowns. "There's a party tonight."

Leila's nerves hadn't time to lift, as Cecily returned with more servants and even more gowns. The room filled with noise and color as the palace staff decorated each sister with crystals and creams. Leila eyed Her reflection as Her visage transformed—soft pink for Her lips and cheeks, jeweled sandals lacing up Her calves. After much arguing, Cecily convinced Her to abandon Her blade for the evening, and in its place She was showered in jewels. Black garnets lay in tiers across Her neck, in a belt at Her waist, and a glittering headpiece atop Her hair.

"There." Cecily tied off the last stitch. "I believe we're finished."

Leila beamed. Cosima was right—the gown was a coquettish delight, its neckline plunging nearly to Her navel, Her back bare and legs peeking through long slits. There was a boldness to the look—a power She had never known, certainly not in Her other gowns.

Once properly ornamented, the sisters left for the parlor, sipping wine and making final preparations. Pippa, dressed in dusty pink with rose quartz braided into her bun, snuck a peek into the atrium, where four onyx thrones waited for the sisters much like the ones in the labyrinth. Leila let out a sigh of relief. Perhaps tonight would run smoothly, though that seemed a whole lot like wishful thinking. She downed Her wine and refilled Her chalice.

A hand rested on Her shoulder. "Calm Yourself."

Delphi. It was as though she could see straight through Her. "This needs to work," Leila said.

"Our thrones are identical. We're entering together. And there isn't a speck of red among us. We're dressed as equals." Delphi eyed Cosima, garbed in teal and embellished with peacock feathers—on her neck, across her crown, in the layers of her dress. Delphi's nostrils flared. "Well, almost."

"I suppose it's a good thing. She's The Savior, after all. Perhaps she *should* look—"

"Ostentatious?"

Anxiety rolled in Leila's gut. She sucked Her wine down, grabbing the pitcher for a third pour only for Delphi to yank it from Her hands. "I imagine You're at least somewhat excited to see the men." Delphi gestured toward the atrium. "Or rather one man in particular."

"There are too many complications to entertain such thoughts."

"He looks handsome. Your servants did a fine job. Even cut his hair—"

"They *cut his hair?*" Leila spat. "Why would they do that?"

"Ladies." Wembleton peeked into the parlor. "It's nearly time. Places."

Once the Senator left, Leila turned to Her sister. "His hair was perfect as it was. *Perfect.*"

"Leila." Delphi cupped Her face. "Breathe."

Chagrin burned Her cheeks. "God, look at you." Leila sighed, eyeing Delphi up and down—her sky-blue gown tied at the neck, her armlets and circlet in gleaming gold. "You may not know it, but each day you're more beautiful than the last."

"I know it." Delphi smirked. "And *You*. I swear, You look positively sinful. Nothing about this number says pure. Tobias is going to blow his load right in his pants."

Leila burst into laughter. "Delphi! My God!"

"He's going to dream naughty dreams about stripping this dress right off You."

"Do You really think he'll like it?"

"He will die. His feet will lift from the floor, and he will float up to the heavens above."

Voices filtered through the parlor; the Welcoming was beginning, and Leila wasn't sure if it was nerves or excitement parading through Her stomach.

"Are You ready?" Delphi said.

She wasn't, though Wembleton's voice carried from the atrium regardless.

"Ladies and gentlemen, please stand in attention for Her Holiness and Her court."

The parlor doors opened, and Leila's heart pounded as She dragged Her feet past the armored guards, the burgundy curtains. The palace hands stared at Her, but with Her sisters at Her sides, perhaps it wasn't so obvious. Perhaps they could be staring at any one of them. The dining table was gone, the ebony floor open wide, and far across at the other end of the atrium sat eight suitors' thrones with a line of men standing at attention before them.

Tobias.

Breathing fell by the wayside. No more tournament rags; he wore harem pants in black linen, a perfect match to the golden-stitched drape wrapped across his bare chest and thrice around his arm. His flesh shined against the candlelight, polished and smooth, as if it had turned to actual bronze overnight. His hair delighted Her in ways She hadn't anticipated, shorter on the sides but still long on top, his dark curls spilling over his brow. Whatever hint of boyhood he previously possessed had been washed or snipped away, as a man stood before Her, broad and striking. She shouldn't stare, not so openly, but She wasn't the only one. He was staring back at Her, wide-eyed and wanting.

"Kneel."

Tobias dropped to his knee, as did the seven other competitors whom She had forgotten entirely. She took a seat in Her throne, and when Wembleton ordered the men to rise, Tobias's eyes went straight to Her.

Music filled the space, and dancing girls pranced across the floor in gowns of yellow and fuchsia, with purple ribbons streaming from their wrists. Once they departed, fire-breathers took their place, shooting bursts of orange across the atrium like dragons. The guests laughed, gasped, and drank, save for Tobias; his eyes belonged to Leila, fierce and unwavering, and She cooled Herself with a feathered fan to keep contained.

Cosima sat at Her side, shielding her knowing smile with her fan.

"My beautiful sister, I believe the Artist is undressing You with his eyes."

Leila's throat caught. "What do I do?"

"Has he been a good boy? Treating You the way You long to be treated?" She nudged Leila. "Then reward him. Go on, give the hound a treat."

Leila hesitated, then threaded Her leg through the slit of Her gown, crossing it over Her lap as seductively as She could manage.

"Good girl," Cosima said.

"I don't look silly?"

"God, no. You're a natural. Look at him stir."

Tobias's chest rose with a deep breath, and his hungry stare sent a tremor rolling through Her. "This is exhilarating."

Cosima winked. "We'll make You a siren yet."

Couples dispersed through the space, dancing to the music and blocking Tobias from view. As if lifted from a fog, the atrium became clear again—the staff in their colorful linens, the blazing candles, the roses decorating each marble column.

"Roses?" Leila lurched back in Her seat. Where were Her lilies?

Cosima chuckled. "No need to fret, dove. I had them brought in."

"But the lilies—"

"The men believe roses are The Savior's favorite flower. Lilies wouldn't make sense. The façade, remember?"

Leila stared at Her sister, hurt in a way She couldn't articulate. Her mother's favorite flower...gone.

Cosima met Her blank gaze with a smile. "I told You I'd help in any way I can. Assisting You has brought me such joy. And doesn't the atrium look beautiful?"

Leila turned away, festering in Her indignant thoughts. Before She could lose Herself to Her ire, Delphi hopped up from her throne, gesturing toward the throng of people. "Ask someone to dance."

Leila let out a snort, sinking deeper into Her seat.

"They're *Your* suitors," Delphi maintained. "It's expected."

She wove through the crowd before Leila could rebut, heading straight for the line of men. Leila noticed it then—an unsettling gaze, reawakening Her anxieties. Muttering Her parting, She maneuvered past the dancing bodies until the man in question was right in front of Her.

"Raphael," She said.

He scowled. "Leila."

"Care to dance?"

It would be an honor. Those were the words he was supposed to speak, but he simply took Her hand, his hold light as if he couldn't bear Her touch. They situated themselves among the dancers, taking in the melody of the harps and double flutes. The Amantos was underway, Leila's favorite dance. He pressed his palm to Hers and led Her through the steps.

"An interesting thing happened the other day," he said. "The Savior was to release a man from the tournament, and She chose Enzo. Isn't that odd?"

She glanced between the nearby dancers. "Keep your voice down."

"We had a deal."

"We still do. Nothing's changed."

"You're right about that—nothing's changed. Because I'm *still in this tournament.*"

"My hands were tied," She said. "It had to be Enzo, for reasons of life and death."

"*My* reasons are life and death. I'd like to *live* and not *die* in this tournament."

"I will have you released. On My crown, I swear it." She met his glare with Her own. "But if you say anything to anyone, I will leave you to rot within these walls, do you understand?"

He sighed. "I'm trusting You."

"Lovely. I don't trust you in the slightest."

Raphael shifted them into their second position, entwining his fingers with Hers. "So why Enzo?" he asked. "He wasn't the most social fellow, but I somewhat liked him. At least more than the others."

"I'm sorry, are you under the impression that we're friends?"

"I don't see why we can't be."

She snorted. "And here you're supposed to be the smart one."

"Is that why You placed me with Flynn?"

"Come again?"

"Our chambers. I'm rooming with Flynn. I'm told it was *The Savior's* decision." His lips flattened. "You could've placed me with Tobias."

"Except I couldn't, could I?"

"Why not?" His face dropped. "Oh, I see. You're afraid I'll expose You to him."

"Isn't that exactly what you've threatened to do? *Expose* Me?"

Raphael pulled Her into their third hold, bringing his stiff arm around Her waist. As he rambled on, Her gaze swept the room, searching for escape, maybe a kind soul to free Her from his company.

Tobias. He and Delphi had joined the line of dancers, talking and laughing like old friends. Up close, the smoothness of his skin was even more apparent, and the hard lines of his muscles begged to be touched. She had never thought much of royal drapes, but on Tobias the look shined, as if he alone deserved such a fine garb. *I wonder what he'd look like in a diadem. A crown.* A wave of heat rolled through Her.

I wonder what he'd look like naked.

"For God's sake, have You heard a word I'm saying?"

Her eyes shot back to Raphael. "You mean your insufferable whining? Unfortunately."

He glanced sidelong at Tobias. "The two of you are about as discreet as a giant cock flopping about the room."

"You think people have noticed?" Leila went rigid, shrinking beneath the stares that were apparently pointed Her way.

"The men are too busy scrambling for Cosima's attention to notice where Your gaze lies. Your secret's safe."

"You're just saying that."

"I never *just say* anything."

He pulled Her into their final hold, his frame stiff as a board, though perhaps a bit gentler. "The execution has been rather masterful," he said. "For the switch, I mean. I feared the whole charade would be revealed tonight, but even in a room full of people who *clearly* know Your title, Your suitors remain fooled. I don't know how You managed it —or why, for that matter—but I'd be lying if I said I wasn't impressed."

Leila gave him an incredulous glance. "Did you just say something kind?"

"It's not unlike me."

342

"It most certainly is."

A smile graced his lips—the first She'd ever seen on the man—and dimples dove into his cheeks. The look suited him far better than his usual scowl.

Their time together ended, the dance demanding a partner switch. Breaking their hold, Raphael bowed. "We'll speak soon, yes?"

She nodded, then drifted down the line of dancers, stopping before Her new partner.

Tobias.

A ring of the brightest pink encircled him. Perhaps it had been there the entire time and She hadn't noticed, too enchanted by his lips, his eyes—by *him*. She held out Her hand. "Dance with me?"

He bowed. "It would be an honor."

He led their dance with strength and grace—or at least She assumed he did, as She was busy counting the curls along his forehead, relishing the heat of his palm against Hers. An eternity passed before She caught his gaze dancing over Her figure, drinking Her up, and the parched look on his face made Her stand taller.

Tobias took in Her knowing gaze and laughed. "What?"

"You're very, *very* bad."

"Have you found fault with me already? We've only just begun to dance."

"Earlier, while we were seated," She said. "If you stare at *me* instead of the dancing girls, you'll draw attention to yourself."

"What dancing girls?"

"Very funny."

"You're in no position to criticize. I caught you staring when you came in."

Heat flooded Leila's cheeks, and She fought back a grin.

"What?" Tobias's laughter rose. "What's that look for?"

"You look very handsome."

A smile blossomed on his lips. "Is that so?"

"Like a king. An honorable one. The drape suits you."

"Look at you, all red in the face."

"Don't tease me."

"You look stunning, Leila. The only woman in the room as far as

I'm concerned." He waved Her away. "But that's nothing new. In fact, I'm rather bored of you being so beautiful all the time. I wish you'd surprise me. Grow a hunchback, maybe spoil your teeth. Keep me on my toes."

"You're in awfully high spirits."

"I'm clean, I'm fed, and I'm with you. I'm especially excited about one of those things in particular."

Another grin threatened to streak Her face, and She bit Her lip to tame it. Seamlessly, he shifted them into their second position, his calloused fingers threading between Hers. She cursed the placement of his hands, wishing they were tight around Her waist, crawling up Her back, or weaving through Her hair.

"Look at the lovebirds." Tobias cocked his head toward Orion, who danced with a wide-eyed Pippa a few rows away.

"Isn't that precious?" Leila watched them spin in circles, contented. "Orion's so kind. I swear to you, this is probably the happiest moment of her life."

"Does Pippa like him?"

"Pippa likes everyone. She sees the world in rainbows. She is good and pure and thus assumes everyone else is the same." She turned to Tobias. "I envy that sometimes. I wish I thought the world was beautiful."

"If everything looks good and pure, then nothing's truly beautiful. The ugliness is what makes beauty so distinct."

"How poetic."

"I'm a master poet, didn't you know?" He shrugged. "I wrote a poem for a girl once. There was a bit of confusion involved. I'd rather not talk about it."

Leila chuckled. "Oh, stop it."

Tobias's smile lingered. "They're Petros's words. About the ugliness. He said life was ugly, and it was our job to find the beauty in it. Cast a light on it. Remind people that it's there."

Leila's breathing hitched as he brought his lips near Her ear. "I don't think the world is beautiful," he whispered. "But you are."

Threading his arm around Her, he pulled Her into their third hold, his hard form against Her both a pleasure and a tease. Everything was wonderful, perfect even—until She recalled the people nearby, no doubt watching with eager gazes.

"What now?" Tobias said.

Leila eyed the fellow dancers, skeptical of everyone within Her line of sight. "I have to watch myself when I'm with you. You make me feel as though we're alone."

"If only."

"I'm afraid we're being conspicuous."

"How so?"

"It's all the smiling," She said.

"Oh?" He scoffed. "We're too happy? Are we supposed to be miserable? I can do that."

His face fell into an unconvincing frown, sending Leila into a fit of laughter. "Tobias, you fool."

"God, Leila, when will this night be over? I'm dying here. Absolutely loathing your company."

Her giggles died. Brontes stood across the room staring at them. She'd forgotten him entirely, but now he was the eyesore of the atrium, circled by the remaining members of his dwindling Senate.

Tobias furrowed his brow. "Is something wrong?"

"Brontes is watching us."

Tobias said something, but Leila had lost all focus. She knew that look in Her father's eye—one of violence. Was it for Her, or Tobias?

"Leila." Tobias dipped his head into Her line of sight. "It's all right. He can't hurt you."

"Yes, he can."

"He'll have to hurt me first. Badly."

He gave Her a spin before bringing Her into their final hold, and She eased against him, relishing the safety of his arms. Brontes was surely still watching, but in that moment, with Tobias close, She felt secure.

"Who are those men skulking around him?" Tobias said.

Leila shot a scowl at the horde of politicians. "The vultures."

"Vultures?"

"His Senate." Her eyes shrank into a glare. "Vile. All of them."

"Well, they seem to have stolen his attention. Lucky for us. We're alone in a room full of people yet again."

The line shifted on either side of them; the dancers were changing partners. "Not for long." Leila's stomach sank. "Time to switch."

Tobias met Her frown with his own, then stopped short, his gaze bright. Without warning, he lurched into Her, tromping over Her feet and sending them tottering out of line.

"Tobias!"

"Apologies." He straightened his drape, failing to conceal a grin. "My God, how clumsy of me."

She laughed into Her hands. "You're bad."

"Be kind, I only just learned these steps today." He turned to the dancers waiting nearby. "Ignore us, we're a mess. It's her fault, really."

"Tobias!"

"You tripped me!" He flashed an apologetic glance at the onlookers. "She tripped me. Please, carry on. Go around us. Hopefully she'll get it right this time."

Exchanging a few awkward stares, the dancers paired up and delved into their steps. Leila fought to uphold some semblance of sternness, but Her amusement crept through in giggles. "You're an ass."

"Dance with me."

"That's my line."

"I couldn't wait any longer."

As She took his hand, he spun Her in a circle, falling into their steps with ease.

"You're good at this." Leila raised an eyebrow. "Aside from that utterly unconvincing stumble of yours."

"*Your* stumble. Don't try to pin it on me. That's bad form."

"Did you really just learn today?"

"I did. In the bathhouse. Ask Delphi, she was there." He faltered. "On second thought, don't ask her."

"Do you like it?" She asked. "Dancing. It's fun, yes?"

"It has its benefits."

"Its benefits?"

"If the only way I can hold you tonight is by dancing with you, then I'll do it."

Another spin, and he pulled Her into their second hold, clasping Her hand tight.

"You never told me, you know," She said.

"Told you what?"

"How your first day was, here in the palace."

"Mostly uncomfortable. *Very* embarrassing."

"*Poor* Tobias."

"We received a considerable number of warnings regarding our time here," he said. "No wandering eyes. No unsound intentions. The punishment for such behavior will be determined by our kind and merciful Sovereign."

The light within Leila dulled. "I see."

Silence wedged between them. Was he having second thoughts? Before the worry could overtake Her, Tobias leaned in close, lowering his voice to a whisper.

"When can I see you again?"

She wavered. "Pardon?"

"*Can* I see you?" He glanced from side to side, searching for prying eyes. "I imagine things will be different now that I'm here in the palace, but—"

"It'll be different. But better."

"Better?"

"Easier."

His eyes brightened. "When can I see you? Just the two of us."

"Soon."

"Tonight?" Leila shook Her head, and he sighed. "Not soon enough, then."

Leila held back Her laughter, more pleased with his eagerness than She cared to reveal. Again his arm slinked around Her waist, except this time his hold was tight and yearning, their bodies pressed together in a way that seemed intimate, even indecent. She wanted to stay in that position forever.

Red swept Her vision. Brontes was still lurking with his Senators, watching from afar.

"Leila?"

She flinched, stirred by Tobias's voice. "Apologies."

"Captivated by the Sovereign and his flock of birds?" he asked.

"I didn't know they were coming. I assumed..." She clenched Her jaw, Her thoughts turning to violence. "Only they could ruin a night such as this."

"But you're safe for now, yes?"

"Safe? Of course, why?"

"Your blade is conspicuously missing."

Leila started. "Eyeing my legs, are we?"

"How could I resist?"

She forced a laugh, though it was hardly convincing. She had forgotten about the ruse, had allowed it to slip away with the music. What else had Tobias noticed while She was being careless?

"Servants said the leather didn't exactly complement my dress," She said.

Tobias didn't respond, his gaze traveling the walls as if he were deep in thought.

"Tobias..."

"You don't have to tell me your secrets," he said. "I've only known you a short while. I understand if you don't trust me."

"It's not that I don't trust you. It's just...things are—"

"Dangerous?"

Immeasurably. I am to die. Her lips parted, but the words never came.

Tobias smiled. "Now's not the time. We're celebrating, and you look absolutely incredible. But one day, if you'd care to tell me your secrets, or at least what I'd have to do to be worthy of them, know that I'm here. And I'm very good at keeping my mouth shut."

Her heartbeat calmed as He rested Her hand over his chest for their final hold. She dropped Her head against his neck, taking in his rhythmic pulse and savoring the scent of cinnamon and firewood along his flesh.

He sighed. "It's nearly time to switch."

"Yes. And this time, we have to." Her heart sank. "Know that I don't want to."

His lips brushed against Her ear, his voice a warm whisper. "I wish I could kiss you right now."

A deep, resounding heat filled Her to the brim, and when Tobias pulled away, his black drape was yet again encircled in pink.

"I'll be seeing you," he said.

She nodded. "Soon."

She hurried away, praying he wouldn't see Her silly grin. God, the way he made Her feel wasn't fair.

She needed more of it.

"Your Holiness."

A new partner waited before Her, dressed in a fine plum tunic with silver stitching, his long, black waves tied back and brown eyes beaming.

"Hylas..." Her gut churned. Had any of the competitors heard him?

"Did I startle You, Your Holiness?"

She cleared Her throat. "No, it's just...I didn't know you liked to dance."

"Everyone likes to dance."

Leila's gaze flitted across the room, connecting with a pair of beady eyes. Romulus stood at the edge of the atrium, free of Brontes and his constituents, his hard stare a wordless command.

"Your Holiness?" Hylas said. "Apologies for my flippancy, I meant no offense."

"Excuse Me. There's somewhere I must be."

She abandoned the dance floor, snatching up a chalice of wine and heading Romulus's way with an air of forced casualness. He walked down a neighboring corridor, and Leila eyed the atrium one last time before following his lead.

Romulus's footsteps echoed through the hall—empty. Perfect. She quickened Her pace, matching his gait. "You have words for Me? I thought you no longer had the means."

Long purple robes with golden seams covered him, but even beneath the rich fabric She could see his shoulders tense. "There was nothing to proctor today, nor the day before, and thus I had time to show my service to You," he said.

"Then by all means, enlighten Me."

"Kastor is Your next mark."

"For what reason?" She asked.

"It appears Phanes had several unique responsibilities. And now that he's been *relieved* of his position, the task falls to Kastor."

A lump lodged in Her throat. "Kastor is to leave the fortress? To speak with the Kovahrian traitor?"

"Your father was vague on the details. I don't know of the task. But he's to complete it tomorrow."

"Tomorrow? Where? At what hour?"

"They didn't say."

Leila sighed. "So Kastor is to do *something, somewhere,* at *some time.* Wonderful." Growling, She took Her leave.

"Your Holiness." Romulus remained rooted where he stood, his gaze lit with severity. When he spoke next, his voice chilled Her. "From the moment day breaks, do not let that man out of Your sight."

✿ 21 ✿

THE DRESSING ROOM

Light pulsed from Leila's flesh, pouring into the ground beneath Her. The swampy blackness reached up with eager claws, much closer to the surface than it should've been. She hadn't blessed the land in days.

"I'm sorry. I've been busy with other matters. Important ones. Ones that will allow Me to bless you for years to come." She rolled Her eyes. "Why am I talking to grass? God."

She sent one more surge of power before hopping to Her feet, heading into Her chamber, and throwing on a simple pink dress. Sickness or none, She had far more pressing concerns. Day had already broken, and Kastor was Her mark—for what reason, She hadn't a clue.

As She bounded through Her doorway, an unwelcome pair of honey brown eyes met Her. She growled, shouldering past Asher.

"Leila, wait," he said.

She turned to face him, arms crossed and foot tapping against the floor.

"The other day, I..." He cleared his throat. "What His Highness did to You... It shouldn't have happened. And I want You to know, I have Your back."

351

"Is that so? Did you have it when I was pinned to My bed, screaming? When I was assaulted? Humiliated?"

"It was a momentary hesitation. I assure You, You can count on me."

"And when exactly have you proven that to be true?"

Asher stared at Her, slack jawed and stupid. She continued down the corridor.

"It's the Artist, isn't it?" he called out. "The man You spend Your time with each night."

Leila fell silent, meeting his gaze.

"The two of you were dancing at the Welcoming," he said. "I've never seen You smile like that. Not once."

Warmth swirled in Her cheeks, and She walked off before he could see the rosy flush.

The palace opened up around Her, and for once She was starkly aware of its enormity—the light pouring through the stained-glass windows, the eyes following Her. *The competitors lurk within these very walls, and here You are waltzing down corridor after corridor, glowing like the sun in the sky.* She kept to the shadows, forcing Her thoughts to Kastor, who was hopefully far from wherever the competitors had congregated. She had memorized his schedule with little confidence he'd keep it, certainly not if he was to do Brontes's bidding. As suspected, She reached the scroll room, and Kastor was nowhere to be found. *Off somewhere being duplicitous, no doubt.*

A pair of servants rounded the corner. "Leila!" Faun flagged Her over, laughing with Nessa. "Would You like to join us in the entryway? Your suitors are training for the Reverence as we speak. We plan to feast our eyes on the display."

"Especially since we aren't permitted to attend tomorrow," Nessa said. "It's a bit rude, I think. I've so been looking forward to it. They wear golden armor, You know."

The entryway. At least Leila knew where to avoid. "I'm actually needed elsewhere. Do you happen to know where I can find the Senate?"

"What Senate? It's so scant these days." Faun bit back a chuckle. "Apologies, that was in poor taste. I'm not sure about Wembleton or

Romulus, but Erebus is likely prepping the soldiers for the Reverence, and Kastor I'm sure is in the kitchen."

"The kitchen?"

"He's *always* in the kitchen." Nessa sighed. "Precious, isn't it? What I wouldn't give to be the cooking staff on days when he visits."

Befuddled, Leila shoved Her questions aside. "These windows. It's rather bright in here, yes? See to it they're covered."

Faun wrinkled her brow. "It's the middle of the day."

"Yes, and everywhere I turn, I'm..." Leila gestured at Her own beaming skin, "...like this."

Nessa and Faun stared back at Her in confusion.

"My suitors are present," Leila said. "I don't want to pose as a distraction."

Faun let out a knowing laugh. "She doesn't want them to faint. Bless You, Leila, for shielding their pride. We'll take care of the windows."

The servants began tugging the curtains shut, and Leila resumed Her quest. What business did a Senator have in the kitchen? The hair on Her arms stood straight as worst-case scenarios bombarded Her thoughts.

Laughter bounced off the walls, and the warm scent of baked goods filled the air. The kitchen was a short distance away, and Leila kept Her steps light, willing each to be quieter than the last. The rounded arch of the doorway appeared ahead, and She shielded Herself with its stone frame, peering inside.

The kitchen staff bustled through the space, rolling dough and tending to the fire. All of them wore the same cheeky grin, their eyes on the handsome man in their company. Kastor's long, black hair was tucked behind his ear, his hands sticky as he molded mounds of dough into balls the perfect size for sweet rolls.

He was helping them cook?

Leila blinked once, twice, but still Kastor rolled each pastry, placing them on a silver pan. She focused on his nimble hands, searching for hidden vials or herbs to sneak amid the ingredients, but there were none. Instead, he dotted a servant on the nose with his doughy finger, then snapped a rag at another's bum and sent her squealing. The staff chased him through the kitchen, playful and delighted.

What in God's name...?

Mousumi entered through the back way, sending the servants into obedient formation with a chastising glance. Kastor bowed, squeezing one of the girls' arms affectionately before heading for the exit—for Leila. She hurried away, positioning Herself behind a pillar as he gave parting.

The Senator headed through the palace, and Leila stalked behind him, maintaining a cautious distance. His first stop: the scroll room, just as his schedule had suggested. *Keeping up appearances, no doubt.* She waited behind the doorframe as he flipped through parchment, scribbled notes, dictated orders to the keepers. Next he visited the soldiers' keep, collecting figures for Erebus, and afterward he broke his fast in the garden, eating the exact sweet rolls he had assisted in baking hours prior. One by one, he completed his scheduled tasks, and he did so with a smile, with *please* and *thank you* rolling off his tongue. Nothing about his behavior was crooked. He was charming, even kind.

Kastor stopped in the middle of a corridor to marvel over a child, crouching low to play with him while his servant mother beamed. A smile flickered across Leila's lips, but She stifled it at once. Romulus had made Kastor's deceit clear, yet nothing had happened. Had Romulus sent Her on a fruitless task? Was he the one deceiving Her?

Kastor continued through the palace, and She followed.

The entryway appeared, stopping Leila in Her tracks. The competitors stood in the distance, clumped into groups with wooden staffs at their sides. Tobias led his group, twirling the staff between his hands, and Leila lost Herself in his fluid movements.

Focus. She tore Her stare from Tobias as Kastor disappeared beyond the entryway. *Dammit.* Clenching Her jaw, She dashed down a neighboring hallway, dodging the competitors in a roundabout fashion before following Kastor's path.

Staggering to a halt, She glanced across the darkened corridor. The Senator was gone. Her nerves spiked. A doorway stood to Her left, and She peered inside. Nothing. Another, and it was as vacant as the last.

She'd lost him.

Cursing, She dragged Her feet. *Unbelievable.* The defeat was not only ill-timed but embarrassing. Soon She reached Her dressing room and trudged inside, mentally berating Herself as She slammed the door behind Her.

Kastor sat in the chair in front of Her.

"Senator." Leila stiffened. "What are you doing here? These are private chambers."

"Apologies, Your Holiness. But I figured if You were seeking my attention, I ought to be a gentleman and offer You my willing ear."

"What would make you think I seek your attention?"

"You've been following me all day."

His words plowed through Her gut. "You're mistaken."

"Apologies, but I don't believe I am."

She stood like a statue, petrified. Casually, Kastor plucked a pitcher from the end table at his side, gesturing toward the chair across from him. "Please, these are Your chambers. Have a seat. Would You like some wine?"

Leila wavered, Her mind a blank canvas. She took the seat across from him, Her hands locked in Her lap.

"Your Holiness, You seem uncomfortable," Kastor said.

"You're in My dressing chamber without express permission."

"But Leila—may I call You Leila?" He handed Her a chalice of wine, and when She didn't budge, he sipped it himself. "I saw You today. Watching. Hiding in the shadows. I simply aimed to end our little game."

"What *game*?"

"There's no need to be coy. Your pursuit today made Your intentions clear." His hazel eyes never once broke their hold of Her. "Initially I thought it wrong to indulge, but...I suppose I can't help myself."

She stared back at him in confusion, then started. "Oh My God. Senator, you've *completely* misjudged the situation."

"I've seen the way You stare at me during meetings. So boldly too, right in front of Your father. I'd be lying if I said my gaze hadn't lingered as well. Though You know that already, don't You? That's why You're here."

"Your ego has blinded you," She said. "You are far too old for My tastes."

"I am not much older than You are."

"Ten years."

A bashful smile swept his face. "Thirteen. You flatter me." He leaned in closer. "Does not every woman long for a man of experience? Certainly a woman of superior wisdom such as Yourself."

Leila dug Her fingers into Her thighs, gripping the blade beneath Her dress. "I have suitors within these walls."

"They're not Your suitors. Well, perhaps the Artist is, but I took that for a tryst. The most desired woman in the realm choosing an *artist*? I always thought You a ruler who values power."

"What do *you* know of power?"

"I am the only Senator in Your father's cabinet of common birth. I escaped my meager circumstances, climbed my way from noble house to noble court, until finally I earned the title of the second youngest Senator to ever sit alongside the royal family. I *am* power."

His words came out strong—too strong, as She nearly bent beneath them. Nothing about this was as She had predicted, and She found Herself second-guessing each assumption She had made, doubting Her instincts.

"I've entertained this conversation far too long," She said. "Please leave. I want nothing to do with you."

"Then what other reason is there for Your presence? Why follow me from room to room, watching with such fire in Your eyes?" Kastor scooted onto the edge of his seat, closer to Leila than he'd ever been before. "Tell me Your reasons. Otherwise I will take Your heavy breathing as wanting. The same way that I want You."

Her heart hammered. *I followed you so I could learn your secrets. So I could kill you.*

"These are private chambers, Your Holiness. We can do whatever we please." He placed his hands on Her knees, running them up Her thighs, through the slits of Her dress. "My deepest desire is to serve You."

Leila slapped him across the face. "Don't touch Me, you fucking pig!"

Stroking his jaw, Kastor chuckled. "You're not interested. Understandable. I suppose if You're not trying to fuck me, that means You're trying to kill me."

Every faculty within Leila came to a halt. She grabbed the sheath on

Her thigh.

Empty.

Kastor raised Her blade, wiggling it between his fingers. "I'm not going to hurt You, but I do need to take You to Your father."

She lunged forward, tackling him and his chair to the floor.

They crashed into the hard surface, fumbling free from the limbs of the chair. Kastor was on top of Her before She could gain Her bearings, a wall of muscle crushing Her against the tile, Her blade still wedged in his grip.

"Be *reasonable*." He blew the hair from his face. "I'm not here to hurt You. Just keep still."

She struggled beneath him, heedless of the sharp steel nicking Her flesh. The man didn't give, so She thrust Her knee into his groin, sending him slack. Wriggling free, She grabbed Her blade right as Kastor snatched up Her wrist. Her arm flailed, the blade waving wildly as they fought for control. Grunting, he shoved Her into an end table, and as She toppled back with the wooden limbs, the blade flew from Her grasp.

Her back hit the floor, and once again Kastor was on top of Her. "Be still!" He seized Her wrists, pinning Her down. "You're only making this worse for You!"

She thrashed Her legs, desperate to inflict pain. Nothing. She sank Her teeth into his forearm.

Kastor cried out, loosening his grip enough for Her to grab hold of something—the end table, now in pieces. She lifted one of its legs high and slammed it down on Kastor, again, beating him until it snapped in half. He shielded himself, taking blow after blow before grabbing what remained of the table leg and tossing it aside.

Kastor punched Her in the jaw, sending Her sprawling to the floor. Thundering pain exploded through Her cheek, and She lurched backward, dragged by Her ankle across the tile. The blade—it was paces away, and She slammed Her heel into his face. As Kastor fell, She scrambled toward Her weapon, closer and closer—

A hand grasped Her leg, yanking Her back, then suddenly both his hands were on Her, flipping Her over. He was on top of Her again, blood dripping from his nostrils.

"It doesn't have to be like this," he growled. "Just stay *still*."

Do something. Her blade was out of reach, and Kastor was slamming Her against the floor, hard enough to rattle Her bones, to shake the table at Her side.

The table.

She reached overhead, clawing at everything above Her—Kastor's face, the table's edge. He swatted Her away, but that didn't stop Her from patting down the wooden surface. Her fingers dug into something silky—a table runner—and She gave a hard yank, sending gold raining down upon them.

Kastor flopped onto his ass, shielding his head from the onslaught of ornaments. Free of his grip, Leila scanned the sea of gold surrounding Her—and the crown sitting close by, a circle of pointed spikes.

A weapon.

Snatching it up, She threw Herself toward Kastor.

His eyes shot wide. "Leila—"

She smacked the crown against his jaw, landing him flat on his back. Blood burst from his lips, and She straddled his waist, taking aim again, spikes down.

She slammed it into his face. Crimson pumped from his cratered flesh, his breathing morphing into ragged, wet hics. Another blow. Another. Her hands dripped red, and the body beneath Her fell limp, his beautiful face now a pulpy mass of flesh.

Leila fell back onto Her palms, sucking air into Her strained lungs. Her favorite crown clattered at Her side, its spikes painted red with the Senator's blood. It had never been this close before. She had allowed the man to disarm Her. Worse, She hadn't a single answer, not even a hint of information. Another Senator was dead, and She had nothing to gain from it.

She looked to Kastor, moving quickly from his unrecognizable face to his body. There had to be something. Her trembling hands flew across him, unraveling his drape, fiddling with his tunic. No hidden pouches, no rings with loose settings. She plunged Her hands into his pant pockets, grabbing fistfuls of something hard.

Jeweled necklaces.

Her necklaces.

22

THE JEWELS

"He stole Your jewelry?"

"He stole My jewelry!"

Leila sat on the watchtower sill, clutching Her procured necklaces as if they might once again disappear. Delphi stood with Her arms crossed, the morning sun illuminating the golden undertones of Her skin. She snatched one of the strands of jewels and examined it. "There was a necklace among Phanes's things. Was that Yours as well?"

"*God* no," Leila said. "It was a terrible piece."

"Why would Brontes need jewelry?"

"Maybe he's selling them."

"Is all the coin in the vault somehow insufficient?" Delphi said.

"Maybe it's a message? Some kind of signal?"

"Maybe Brontes just wants to feel pretty." Delphi held the necklace against her décolletage, waggling her eyebrows.

"What if they're gifts?"

"For who?"

"An ally." Leila's stomach lurched. "The Queen of Kovahr."

"Plausible. But that doesn't explain why he's having jewelry brought *into* the fortress versus the other way around."

"She's coming for the tournament. All the neighboring royals are."

The hum of distant cheering carried through the air. Far beyond the fortress, a celebration was underway—the Reverence, a ceremony glorifying the tournament bloodshed. Thousands of citizens lined up to watch the competitors march, and roar, or do whatever it was they were doing. But the spike in the noise told Her a specific man had been introduced—the people's favorite.

Delphi leaned over Leila's shoulder, cooing into Her ear. "Look how majestic he is."

Tobias. Excitement rolled through Her. "He's hardly visible."

The cheering peaked higher, inarguably female, and Delphi sighed. "Can You imagine all the tits he must be seeing? Lucky bastard."

"Tits?" Leila said. "Why?"

"Have You no understanding of the Reverence? Tobias is favored."

"What does that have to do with tits? You're telling Me those women are just standing out in the open in the nude? Of all the vulgar things..."

Delphi chuckled. "I hate to inform You, but I'd wager nearly every woman and man in Thessen now lusts for Your precious love." She gave Leila a pinch. "Don't You fret. I'm sure the only tits he longs to see are Yours, insane as that may be."

Leila kept Her eyes on the spectacle, though She wasn't sure what for, as it was little more than a mass of specks. Suddenly the sea of bodies parted as a pinprick of a man barged into the crowd. *It could be any one of them.* But that didn't stop Her from gripping the sill as guards tore after him, and Her throat caught as a laurel was chanted.

"Artist. Artist."

She held Her breath, and the guards fell back as Tobias returned toward the Reverence grounds, the people cheering in triumph.

Leila exhaled. "Thank God."

"Thank God?" Delphi wrinkled her nose. "For what?"

Leila's shoulders curled as She shied away from Delphi's gaze.

"You thought he was escaping."

"I didn't want him to get hurt, is all," Leila said.

Delphi rested a hand on Her shoulder. "I want him to stay as well. It's all right to admit the depth of Your feelings."

A flush crept up Leila's face, but Her tension eased beneath Her sister's touch.

"This is exactly why You should tell him, You know," Delphi said.

"Tell him what?"

"That You're The Savior."

Leila spun toward her. "*What?*"

"Why are You surprised? Were You going to allow him to be blind forever?"

"No, it's just..." Faltering, Leila fiddled with the lining of Her gown. "I've honestly never thought about it."

"Not once?"

"I've been a bit preoccupied, Delphi."

"Well, it's clear your connection runs beneath the surface. And if You care to include him in Your future, he'll have to know who You really are."

"Yes, of course." Leila nodded, though Her stomach swirled.

Delphi raised an eyebrow. "But...?"

"But nothing. I'll tell him tonight. Look at you, making a fuss for no reason."

Clearing Her throat, She hopped from the sill and hurried down the stairwell, abandoning Her sister before she could figure Her out. The day was young, and with no news from Romulus, Talos, or any other source, She was left to Her own devices—staring at Her necklaces while pondering Kastor's intentions, researching the upcoming tournament challenges, and dwelling over Her new, unexpected task.

You should tell him.

Day turned into night, and eventually the nerves in Leila's gut were coupled with glee. The tournament didn't resume until tomorrow, which meant She had the entire evening at Her disposal—an evening She could spend with Tobias.

She found him wandering the palace halls snacking on a peach while eyeing the marble busts. She hadn't yet grown accustomed to his new appearance—clean and clothed, his hard form dressed in simple black harem pants and a matching shirt, sleeveless with a cowl hood much like what the guards wore off duty. As his eyes traced the walls, She walked his way, passing him with a whisper.

"Follow Me."

Footsteps sounded behind Her. She couldn't suppress Her grin, nor the hammering of Her heartbeat, as She wove through the palace, floating high within Tobias's gaze. Bounding up the grand staircase, She stole a glance over Her shoulder. He still followed, and the yearning in his eyes sent Her soaring. The doorway to the watchtower appeared, and She darted up the steps before reaching the top.

The blistering sun had long since set, replaced with blackness and glittering stars. Leila settled in Her usual spot, combing Her fingers through Her hair until it hung just right over Her shoulder, fussing with Her dress so it lay neatly against the sill. Anxious seconds passed before Tobias joined Her, his eyes locking with Hers.

"Should you really be sitting there on the edge like that?" he said.

Leila scoffed. "Oh, please."

"I'm serious. Seems dangerous..."

Rolling Her eyes, She flailed, feigning a fall. "Oh no, Tobias, rescue me!"

"Stop it!" Tobias raced toward Her. "You make me nervous."

Chuckling, She resituated Herself, acutely aware of Tobias's gaze tracing Her figure. His hand dipped into his pocket, pulling out a rose. "For you."

Leila cradled the gift in Her hands, smiling—until Cosima intruded into Her thoughts.

"What?" Tobias said. "Is something wrong?"

"No, it's lovely."

"Say it."

She hesitated. "Usually the palace is filled with lilies. But now it's filled with roses... I just really loved the lilies."

"Is that so? Well then, let's get rid of this." Tobias snatched the rose and flung it over the tower's edge.

"Tobias!"

"What?"

"You threw away my gift!"

He shrugged. "It was a terrible gift."

"It was not!"

"I'll get you lilies."

"You can't." She wilted. "They're all gone."

"I'll find a way." Tobias eyed the dusty walls, taking in their surroundings. "What is this place?"

"The old watchtower." She said. "For times of battle. Of course there hasn't been a war in centuries. We have no use for it now. I just come here when I want to be alone."

"Then why did you bring me here?"

"I want to be alone with you."

Tobias's smile spread through Her, too potent to look at. Instead She stared at the realm, studying the curves of the hillsides, the cottages painted blue by the night sky. "It's beautiful, isn't it? This is all I've ever seen of the realm. Makes me feel free, being up here. It's as if I've left the fortress for a moment. Almost."

Fingertips slid down Her spine, and She relaxed into Tobias's touch.

"You see that hill, right over there?" He pointed at a cluster of cottages far in the distance. "That's my village."

Leila leaned forward, peering through the darkness. "Is it really?"

"I live at the very top. I'll bet you can see my cottage from here. At night, Milo and I would sit by the edge and stare down into the fortress. Have a drink. Admire the palace from afar. On Savior's Day, he spent the entire time trying to convince me to enter the tournament."

"Savior's Day?"

"The Savior's birthday," Tobias said. "What do you call it?"

"Just..." *My birthday.* "Her birthday."

"I suppose that makes sense."

She cleared Her throat. "Well, on *Savior's Day*, I was up here staring out at the realm. Dreading the tournament to come."

Leila's gaze drifted back to the green fields and thatched roofs—to the realm She'd never once stepped foot in—but with Tobias standing at Her side, the longing She usually felt had dulled, replaced with comfort and ease.

"How often did you do that?" She threaded an arm around his waist, nestling against his chest. "Look down at the palace."

"All the time."

"How funny. To think we've been staring at one another for so many years and never knew it."

Fine slips of pink spread from his flesh, disappearing into the night. She smiled, though Her joy was fleeting. A stretch of forest lingered in Her peripheral vision, souring Her mood.

"Down there." She cocked Her head at the mass of trees. "Do you see those darkened woods? That's the site of tomorrow's challenge."

"Do you know what's in store?"

"Just that it's dangerous," She said. "Not that I would've expected anything less from Brontes."

Tobias's face dropped. "Oh God, I nearly forgot..."

"What?"

"The Sovereign. He spoke with me at the Welcoming."

Leila's nerves spiked. "What did he say?"

"He told me to stay away from his daughter. That I wasn't what She needed. And when I tried to defuse the situation, he mentioned you." Tobias's eyes widened. "I think he knows."

She emptied Her lungs. Of course Brontes knew. He had known for ages.

"Tobias..."

"He knows about us," he said. "He knows I don't care for Cosima—"

"Brontes has more important concerns. I assure you, your cares and passions are the furthest thing from his mind."

"That's all well and good, but what about you?"

"I've been handling Brontes since I was a child," She maintained. "I can certainly handle him now."

"Leila—"

"Listen to me." She took his hands. "Rid yourself of these worries. Just please...stay *away* from him."

Tobias stared at Her, silent for a long while before releasing a breath. "God, that family is mad. The Sovereign and The fucking Savior. I swear I loathe them more and more each day."

Pain shot through Her like an arrow to Her confidence. *You brought him here to tell him.* Except it wasn't that simple, not when his words were dripping with scorn, the air around him flickering with red. *He's speaking of Cosima.* But his anger was for the tournament, and those men hadn't died for Her sister.

They had died for Leila.

"Apologies if I've burdened you." Tobias leaned in closer, making his way into Her line of sight. "It's just...it made me nervous when he said your name."

"Why?"

"*Why?* What do you mean *why?* Leila, you are precious to me. I don't want anything happening to you."

A fraction of Her discomfort melted. She forced a smile. "You know, I watched you. During the Reverence."

"Is that right? From up here on your little perch?"

"Mhm."

"Well then, did you enjoy it? Us big, strong men, pounding our chests like gorillas, smearing blood on our bodies like loons."

Leila chuckled. "Oh yes, it was all *very* arousing."

"It's a shame you were so far away," he said. "You had to be *right there* to appreciate the manliness. You missed it all, really."

"Well, go on then. Why don't you show me that mighty roar?"

"No!"

"Fine, what about that pounding thing."

Tobias hesitated, then pounded his chest only to explode into laughter.

Leila gasped. "Oh my, *Tobias*, that was so mighty! You have me absolutely trembling. Is this the part where I show you my tits?"

"I mean, if you insist, I won't stop you."

Leila swatted his arm, giggling childishly.

"I don't think I'm a pound-my-chest sort of man," he said.

"No, I don't think so either. But I like the sort of man you are just fine."

His laughter subsided, though his grin remained intact, a little too perfect to bear. She looked away. "Thank you."

"For what?"

"For coming back," She said.

"What do you mean?"

"When you went out into the crowd, I thought for a moment you might be...trying to escape."

"Escape?" Tobias scoffed. "You think I'd leave you here?"

His gentle smile burned through Her, a wonderful ache. A bandage wrapped his palm—a byproduct of the Reverence—and She scowled. "Let me look at your hand." She plucked it up, unraveling the dressing. "So stupid. What was the point of this? Such mindless cruelty for the sake of entertainment. Poor thing. I'll fix it."

"But you don't have your potions."

"I can still make it better."

She set the bandage aside, revealing a thick scab straight through his flesh. Wembleton had spoken of this ritual as if it were glorious—*"The men carve a line into their palms, spilling their blood on the sands of the realm they give their life for"*—but all Leila saw was needless pain. She dropped a soft kiss in his palm. "Better?"

"Not quite," Tobias said. "Once more for good measure."

She gave his palm another kiss. "How about now?"

"Ah, yes. That made all the difference. I'm cured."

Pink and yellow encircled him, and She glided Her fingertips up his forearm, tracing letters through his colors.

Goodness.

"You know what else hurts?" Tobias said.

Leila's gaze darted to his. "I swear to God, if you point to your cock..."

"My lips! I was trying to be romantic, you know. You've ruined it."

She grabbed the cowl of his shirt and kissed him hard, laughing against his mouth. "Don't be harsh with me, I'm a respectable lady."

"And a difficult one too. You're making it hard for me to court you properly."

She faltered. "You're courting me?"

"*Yes*, Leila. How was that not clear?"

"Well, you never said so."

"It doesn't exactly work like that. You don't *say*, 'I'm courting you.' You hold her close, you kiss her, you tell her how fond you are of her. Or in my case, you draw her pictures, then hide them away. You recite poems that land you on a reward with another woman. You give her a rose and then toss it off the side of a tower."

Her cheeks ached from laughing, and She pressed Her lips to his. "Don't stop."

"Kissing you?"

"*Courting* me," She said. "I'll never tire of it."

Streams of yellow, pink, and orange cascaded through the night air, a sunset of affection and joy—of everything She roused within the man before Her. *You should tell him.* And She would.

Another day.

~

"THEY WERE HERE AGAIN?"

Talos nodded. "Yes, Your Holiness."

Leila sank into Her seat. The dungeon was dim and dreary, the morning heat turning the air rank. She took in a deep breath, the scent of tart herbs stinging Her nostrils. "When?"

"The day Your suitors were welcomed into the palace. And nearly each day since."

"And no mention of—?"

"The assassins have not once mentioned a healer," Talos said.

"Or a redheaded Savior?"

"No, Your Holiness."

Leila's shoulders loosened. "Any mention of Kovahr?"

Talos shook his head. "They mostly discuss the challenges. Brontes gives them special means."

"Cheating bastard." Huffing, Leila crossed Her arms. "I suppose we know who will be winning today's challenge."

"Your father didn't instruct them to excel today. He had other expectations for them."

"What kind of expectations?"

Talos didn't answer, his eyes drifting away. "The competitors are in the palace, Your Holiness. Your identity won't remain secret for much longer."

"All the drapes are closed. I haven't glowed in days."

"Your staff know You are The One True Savior."

"I keep to Myself," Leila said. "Spend My time in My chambers while the men are about. I'm down here with you right now. No one will find Me here."

Talos met Her stare with a knowing gaze, and She sighed. "I know.

367

But what choice do I have? Tell Me, is there any other way?"

Silence. A suggestion would've been nice, but at least Her point was proven.

"Can I ask you a question?"

"Yes, Your Holiness," he said.

"What would you do if you cared for someone a great deal, but they didn't know something very important about you? Would you tell them?"

Talos shifted, his discomfort not so easily hidden. "I suppose I would."

"What if they might not like it? And if you do tell them, and they don't like it, the consequences could be very dire."

His eyes narrowed in thought. "My father used to say the bond of brotherhood can be shattered by a single act of dishonesty. I imagine the same can be said for relationships of all kinds. But Your safety is imperative above all else, for the good of Your realm. You must do what is right for You."

"That's entirely unhelpful."

Her thoughts swarmed within Her skull. She had lost sleep the night before stewing over Tobias's abhorrence for The Savior. She certainly couldn't fault him for mourning the loss of his comrades, but that was hardly the end of Her worries. If Tobias didn't accept Her title, what would he do? Would he tell Her father of Her ruse? Would he expose Her? *No, he wouldn't. He's not that kind of man.* But deception was all She knew of men. Was Tobias an outlier, or was She fooling Herself?

Talos's low voice filled the space. "The body You brought last time... It appeared as though there was a struggle."

"I handled Myself just fine. He was dead, wasn't he?"

"These men are very dangerous."

"Which is exactly why I'm taking care of them."

His critical gaze pierced through Her. "I'll be careful," She said. "I promise." Her nerves stirred. "You didn't have trouble with the... disposal...did you?"

"No, Your Holiness."

He never told Her what he did with the bodies—hadn't wanted to burden Her, She assumed. *Perhaps he buried them, fed them to the pigs, or burned them.* The speculation was little more than a distraction from more potent concerns.

"I fear I'm becoming him," She said. "Each day I look in the mirror, wondering if this is when it'll sneak up on Me. That I'll stare at My reflection, and all trace of Myself is gone. All that remains is My father."

"Just because You carry his blood does not mean You've inherited his heart."

"We both kill people."

"Everyone who crosses paths with Brontes becomes a killer," Talos said. "It is his legacy. His Senators align with him, and thus they must kill. I am his warden, and thus I must kill. You are his mark...and so You must kill."

His words offered little comfort, and She shook away the tension. "Enough of this. How about more pleasant conversation. My mother... Was She a lush? Spare no details. I'm a grown woman after all, I can handle it."

The trap door rattled. "Diccus," Talos whispered.

With a kiss to his temple, Leila summoned Her light, reappearing in Her chamber. Golden rays crawled up the marble steps from Her garden —the only speck of sunlight within the palace, at least if Her servants had heeded Her warning. A part of Her wanted to wait until nightfall before showing Her face, but hiding was beneath Her, and there was work to be done. She'd worry about Tobias another day.

She crept from Her chamber only to meet Asher's wide-eyed stare. As he opened his mouth to speak, She swerved down the corridor, heading as far from him as possible.

"Your Holiness." The pitter-patter of feet echoed behind Her, and soon a servant appeared at Her side. "Have You been locked in Your chamber all morning?"

A growl bubbled in Leila's throat. "It appears that way."

The servant—Eos—shoved a scroll into Leila's grasp. "I hate to intrude, but Mousumi has asked that You approve Your schedule for the day."

"For what purpose? I approved it yesterday."

"It seems You missed Your bath. And all Your other morning activities, actually."

Leila sighed. "Apologies. I had a meeting."

"I thought You were in Your chamber all morning?"

"Leila." Faun fluttered up beside them. "I was wondering when You'd show. You missed Your bath. I came to fetch You, but You weren't in Your chamber."

"Nonsense, She's been in Her chamber all morning," Eos said.

Leila kept Her eyes on the scroll, Her patience waning. "I'll have My bath tonight."

"It's awfully dark." Eos glanced across the corridor. "Why are all the drapes closed?"

"I like it like this," Leila said.

"Really? I find it a bit unnerving."

"You heard Her." Faun gave Leila a wink. "She likes it like this."

"But surely I can open the drapes if—"

Shouts echoed off the walls. The entryway loomed ahead, its golden doors open wide, and sunlight spilled across the tiled floor like boiling pitch. A horde of men stood amid the rays, and Tobias was among them, staring right at Her.

Leila staggered back into the shadows. The competitors had returned from their challenge, and one of them was gripping a servant's arm, his face flaming red.

"What's going on?" Leila said.

The man spun toward Her. *Garrick.* She'd hardly noticed him the entire tournament, but now She couldn't escape his heated gaze.

"*You.*" He rushed toward her. "Bring me the Sovereign. I need to speak with him immediately."

"He's tending to other matters," She said.

"This can't wait. It has to be now."

"*What* has to be now?"

"I'm quitting the tournament."

She looked back at Her servants, who stood in slack-jawed bewilderment. "Come again?"

"I'm *quitting*," he spat. "I need to get out of this fortress."

"You can't just quit the Sovereign's Tournament."

"I've worked hard and true these past nineteen days," he said. "Now my life is in jeopardy."

"Were you not aware that was a byproduct of this endeavor?"

"I've served The Savior's army." His breathing became heavy. "I've paid my dues. The Sovereign knows this, and he *will* release me."

A laugh caught in Leila's throat. "It isn't that simple—"

"*Listen*, woman, you tell the Sovereign, and you tell him now, I *quit*."

Her servants gasped, but the shock was lost on Garrick, who stormed off to his chamber. The other competitors lingered, a mere fog in Leila's periphery, but Tobias broke through the haze, stopping at Her side.

"Can he do that?" he whispered. "Just quit?"

She shook Her head. "No."

"Then what's going to happen?"

"I have no idea."

The commotion materialized: the competitors' perplexed stares, Her servants' hushed voices, and the daylight streaking the floor paces ahead.

"Leila, are you all right?" Tobias said.

"Yes, I just..." She wrangled composure. "Apologies, I have to go."

She rounded the entryway, keeping to the shadows before disappearing into a hallway. Garrick was quitting, a nuisance She hadn't the time nor care for. Perhaps it was a good thing, would distract Brontes with bureaucracy. Soon Garrick had left Her mind entirely, and by the time She reached Her study, Her intentions were yet again sound.

Leila took a seat at Her desk, rifling through Her drawer before grabbing a fistful of jewelry. *Gifts for the Kovahrian Queen.* Why else would Phanes smuggle them into the palace? Why would Brontes instruct Kastor to steal more?

A knock sounded at the door, and a servant poked her head in. "Pardon the intrusion. One of Your suitors has requested to see You."

Tobias. Leila straightened Her dress. "Bring him in. Discreetly, please."

The servant bowed before departing, and not long after, a man made his way into the study—long and lean, with brown skin and short, black hair.

Leila frowned. "Ugh. It's you."

"Who were You expecting?" Raphael stopped short. "Oh. Right."

371

With a snort, Leila went back to Her jewels, ignoring Raphael.

"You saw what happened?" he said.

"Of course I saw. He was yelling in My face, wasn't he?"

"What are You going to do about it?"

"Nothing. It's beyond My control and none of My concern. Why is he quitting anyway?"

Raphael shrugged. "Drake threatened to kill him."

"A threat of death? In the Sovereign's Tournament? Unheard of."

"Well, the threat came right after Drake gutted Bjorne, so it left an impression."

Leila tensed. "Bjorne's dead, I take it."

"Unless he can somehow function with his insides on the outside."

She waited for the gloom to wane before meeting Raphael's gaze. He still stood by the doorway, anxious and fidgety.

"Is that why you're here?" She said. "To discuss Bjorne's demise?"

"You promised me an out."

She sighed. "God, this again."

"Things have gotten more...complicated. With this challenge in particular."

"Are you scared Drake might kill you as well?"

"I'm scared *anyone* might kill me, but that's not the point. My place here is getting more precarious by the day. You're supposed to find a solution."

"I'm *supposed to find a solution*." She scowled. "What delicate wording for the position you've put Me in."

Raphael went rigid, as if Her words were a slap to the cheek. "The Sovereign's Choice. I have to be released at the Sovereign's Choice."

"You know about the Sovereign's Choice?"

"I'm a keeper at the Thessian Archives. Of course I know. I know the full tournament history."

Leila cast him a sidelong glare. Raphael was right; Brontes was allowed to release one man from the bloodshed. It was a tournament tradition—a challenge of sorts, though to Leila, it was merely a means for placating the male ego. With each tournament, the Sovereign chose one suitor he felt unworthy of his daughter's love. Men like Raphael. Men like Talos.

"Well, I was planning for you to be released then, anyhow." Leila waved Raphael away. "There was no need to barge in like this."

"So, You've asked him?"

"Asked who?"

"Your father," Raphael said. "I'm assuming You've asked him to release me."

"I can't ask him."

"Then how are You going to make this happen?"

"I have other means."

"But—"

"I have *other means*," She growled.

Raphael hardly seemed convinced. He ambled into the room, leaning onto the chair in front of him. "When's the Sovereign's Choice?"

"Perhaps a week from now," She said.

"Dammit. That's too far off."

"Gives us plenty of time to influence Brontes's decision—"

"I don't see why You can't ask—"

"Do you want release or not?" Her eyes narrowed. "If you're to leave this tournament, you will do so by My terms."

Raphael exhaled. "All right. Fine. Thank You."

Finally. She waited for him to leave, but he stayed put, his eyes tracing the walls. "So, this is Your study?" he said.

She clenched Her jaw. "It is."

"And do You often study...jewels?"

She shoved the necklaces aside. "They're gifts for the Kovahrian Queen."

"I see." He pursed his lips. "A rather inappropriate gift, if I do say so myself."

"Inappropriate how?"

"She's the Queen of Kovahr. What need does she have for jewels?"

"I pity your future wife. Your understanding of women is supremely lacking."

"She's *Kovahrian*," he said. "They place no value on jewels outside matters of trade. They prefer metals. Steel and silver. Armor and accolades. Has Your father not taught You this?"

Leila sat up straight. "You're telling Me not even a queen would wear these?"

"Certainly no queen from the north. You know, The Savior is supposed to be made aware of neighboring customs in preparation for Her reign."

Leila ignored the slight, twirling the glittering strands between Her fingers. "Then who would they be for?"

"You just said they were for—"

"I know what I said. I'm not speaking to you."

"Then who were You—?"

"Did you need anything else?"

Raphael glowered. "No."

Leila went back to Her jewels, but She could still feel Raphael in front of Her, hovering as if he had something to say.

"You know, the rest of my day is free," he said. "I could help You with...well, whatever it is You're stewing over."

Her muscles loosened. She could certainly use the help, as all She had were Talos, Delphi, and Her own two hands. Perhaps Raphael could do some good. He was the Intellect, after all.

He was also threatening to reveal Her secret.

Raphael nodded, as if he could read Her churning thoughts. "Right. You don't trust me. I'd forgotten." He wavered. "I know it's my fault. I'm sorry for that." He headed for the door, then stopped short. "If I can offer a suggestion—"

"That's highly inappropriate—"

"Keep an eye on Your father. I don't know how Tobias has gotten so deep under his skin, or maybe he'd just prefer You marry a more accomplished warrior..."

Leila went rigid. "What about Tobias?"

"Kaleo and Drake. They weren't looking to kill Bjorne. Or Garrick for that matter." He hoisted the door open. "Tobias was their mark, as ordered by the Sovereign. We heard them discuss it clear as day."

Sickness spread through Leila as Raphael left Her with his parting words.

"Your father wants Tobias dead."

❧ 23 ❧

THE HEARING

Leila's footsteps echoed off the palace walls, Her shoulders low, chin high. Perhaps Her poise would mask the strain on Her face and the circles under Her eyes. She hadn't slept most of the night, not with Raphael's words plaguing Her thoughts.

Brontes plans to kill Tobias.

She had known this of course, for days really, but She had hoped he'd moved past this nonsense, was back to plotting Her death instead. She cursed Her foolishness. Brontes never left a plan unfinished or a man unmaimed.

The Senate room appeared ahead, and She readied Herself. As She shoved the door open, a mess of male voices bombarded Her, deep in conversation. "Did you start without Me again—?"

The sentence died in Her throat. Erebus, Romulus, Wembleton, and Brontes waited in their usual seats—and across from Her, sitting in silence, were an old man with clouded eyes and a wiry beard; and a young man with long, black hair and anxiety written across his freckled face.

"What is this?" Leila said.

Brontes's drapes were finer than usual, stitched with intricate black thread, and a golden crown sat amid his dark curls. *Why is he wearing a crown to a Senate meeting?* He cocked his head at the two new faces. "You're familiar with Diccus, the palace apothecary, and Hylas, my former page."

"Why are they here?"

"They're the new members of my Senate."

His words hit Her hard. She took Her seat. "Where's Kastor?"

Brontes glowered. "Since most of the Senators have disappeared, positions need to be filled. Diccus and Hylas were thrilled to hear of their promotion. The Senate will be as it was shortly."

"You didn't answer My—"

"The Brave." He turned to the others. "Are we in agreement?"

"We're not in agreement. I've only just arrived."

"The Brave has asked to be released from the tournament." Romulus nodded at Leila. "We were discussing the proper course of action."

"Your perspective is always welcome," Wembleton added.

Garrick. Leila shrugged. "Let him go. He's an ass. If he wants to leave, he can leave."

"Not an option," Brontes said. "The Brave must die."

"And why's that?"

Diccus's shrill voice sounded from across the table. "Every man who's conceded throughout the history of the Sovereign's Tournament has faced execution. If Your father pardons him, he'll be seen as weak. Or worse, a blasphemer."

"Or maybe he'll be seen as merciful." Leila flashed a scowl at the supposed Senator. "That's how mercy works, after all."

"The decision is made." Brontes shuffled through slips of parchment. "The Brave dies today."

"Then what exactly was the point of this meeting? To perpetuate the façade that I have a modicum of authority? I'm fully aware that I don't. There's no need to pretend."

An awkward silence lingered, leaving Diccus to fiddle with his gnarled thumbs and Hylas to shift in his seat.

"Your Highness, may I suggest calling the issue to a vote?" Romulus gestured toward the two uncomfortable faces. "So our newest Senators can see how the law is upheld."

"Who votes to execute the Brave?" Brontes said.

One by one, the Senators raised their hands—save for Hylas, his eyes flitting between the others. Brontes glared at the former page, his gaze sharp enough to draw blood, and Hylas raised a meek hand.

Brontes turned to Leila. "More than enough to make the call, though I do hope You feel included."

Frowning, Leila pushed the loss aside. There were more important concerns to consider, as Raphael still buzzed in Her thoughts. She had to get him out of the palace, not only for his sake, but Her sanity as well.

"Will Garrick's absence have any bearing on future challenges?" She said.

"Tomorrow's will be canceled." Brontes scribbled along a parchment sheet. "All others shall resume as promised."

"What about the Sovereign's Choice?"

Brontes raised an eyebrow. "What *about* the Sovereign's Choice?"

"I'm just wondering if you've given it any thought."

"You're wondering if I plan to send Your Artist home."

Leila lurched back in Her seat. "That hadn't at all crossed My mind."

"We haven't the time for this." Brontes waved Her away. "Who motions to end this meeting?"

"Why haven't we the time? It's still the morn."

"The hearing." Erebus's deep voice filled the room. "It begins shortly."

"What hearing?"

"The Brave is to plead his case in the arena, before the citizens of Your great realm," Romulus said.

"But you've already made your decision. What's the point if you're just going to kill him?"

"Your Holiness, as much as we'd love to hear Your thoughts, Your people have already arrived." Wembleton smiled, though his voice wavered. "We mustn't keep them waiting."

"They're here?" Leila started. "Right now?"

"Yes, Your Holiness."

"So now these events are planned without even notifying Me?"

"Enough." Brontes pushed his pile of parchment aside. "Who ends this meeting?"

"I do," Erebus said.

"Second," Diccus eagerly added.

Brontes stood, cocking his head at Leila. "What are You waiting for? Up."

Leila's eyes widened. "Me?"

"The hearing. Our escorts are waiting."

"*I'm* to attend the hearing? For what purpose?"

"To support the Sovereign's decision," Wembleton said.

"But I don't support the Sovereign's decision."

"Your Highness, with all due respect, won't The Savior's presence pose as a distraction?" Romulus added. "After all, this is *your* ruling. The people must feel your greatness."

"The people need to see a united front," Brontes grumbled.

"Are you certain—?"

"*A united front!*"

A knot wound in Leila's throat. A public hearing. In broad daylight. All these weeks of keeping Her title concealed, for what? For one coward to ruin it all?

"No." She dug Her nails into Her chair. "I won't watch a man plead his case only to die."

Brontes clenched his jaw. "We are not doing this. You're going to the hearing."

"The law forbids you from forcing My hand. You have no legal right—"

"*I* am the law."

She spun toward the others. "Wembleton, tell him!"

"I'm warning You, I haven't the patience," Brontes said.

She kept Her eyes on the portly Senator. "*Tell him.*"

Wembleton didn't speak, his downcast stare boring through the table. Before Leila could react, two brawny hands grabbed Her, yanking Her from Her seat.

Leila collapsed, fighting against Her father's grasp. "Let go of Me!"

Hylas shot up from his seat. "Your Highness, please, you can't—"

Brontes kicked open the door, and Leila's body lurched across the floor. He dragged Her thrashing and shrieking from the Senate room through the heart of the palace, while sandaled feet marched at Her sides—guards escorting them along their way, deadened to The Savior's screams. Servants lined up to gawk, and Delphi darted toward the scene only to be stopped by a drawn spear. Leila fought to channel Her light, but still Her spine scraped along the tiles, Her mind too overwrought to function.

Brontes held the power, and now everyone knew it.

He dropped Leila's arms, letting them crack against the floor. She scrambled onto Her knees, tears streaming down Her cheeks. Sunlight washed over Her; She sat at the entryway of Her palace staring out at the courtyard.

"Are You ready to behave?" He lowered his voice. "Or would You like me to release my frustrations on someone else? Perhaps a foulmouthed Artist?"

His words were a knife to Her pride, but She stood, allowing the blade to plunge deeper. He snatched up Her arm and led Her down the steps and through the fortress, digging his claws in deep enough to bruise. Men walked in formation around Her—the guards, perhaps others, She didn't know, didn't care. Her skin was glowing.

Soon the people—and the competitors—would know who She really was.

Bile sat in Her throat as She filed up the steps of the arena. The royal balcony appeared, a vast space lined in marble pillars with gold molding, with trays of meats, cheese, and wine, but Her eyes went straight to the ruby canopy blocking the unforgiving sun.

Thank God.

Her father shoved Her, sending Her teetering onto the balcony. The arena lay ahead, its yellow sands, its brick walls, and the countless pews brimming with thousands upon thousands of howling spectators.

Her hands trembled. She had never seen so many people before, and God, the *noise*. Gasping for air, She pressed Her back to the wall.

"Take a seat."

Brontes waited in the stairwell with his guards. Glowering, he gestured toward the two golden thrones before Her.

One for the Sovereign, and another for The Savior.

"Take a seat."

Delphi shouldered past him, shooting up the balcony steps. "Leila."

She took Her hands. "I hadn't time to grab our cloaks. I'm sorry. I'm so sorry."

A few stray tears escaped Leila's eyes. "Everyone's here."

"So are we." Delphi gestured behind her—Pippa and Cosima had joined them—and lowered her voice. "We stand as one. No one will know Your title."

"The Savior could be any one of us," Cosima whispered.

The women lined up alongside Leila, taking root against the wall. Pippa leaned forward, eyeing Leila. "Why is Your face red?"

"Leila, God dammit," Brontes spat.

"She chooses to stand with Her sisters for comfort." Delphi shot him a glare. "We're about to witness an execution. You know how sensitive women can be to the sight of blood. It betrays our delicate nature."

Brontes let out a huff but said nothing. A clank sounded, and one of the arena gates opened, sending the audience into a frenzy. Guards poured through the portal, lining the sands with their spears pointed up to the sky, and six men adorned in golden armor followed—the competitors.

Except for Garrick.

They stood in formation, the sun casting a brilliant sheen across their golden shoulder plates. For once Leila didn't search for Tobias, too lost in the havoc of Her thoughts. *So many people.* Each breath came out sharp, Her ribs crushed by the grip of the audience. Did they know who She was? Could they tell?

Wembleton burst onto the balcony. "Citizens of Thessen, please join me in welcoming your Sovereign!"

A wave of applause washed over Leila. Brontes marched toward his throne, not bothering to look Her way as he took his seat. "Bring him out."

Another gate opened, and Garrick emerged, unleashing vitriol from the pews.

Was this truly Her realm? A horde of bloodthirsty animals?

"The hearing begins now," Wembleton said.

The arena went quiet, all eyes on the royal balcony.

On Her.

Brontes. They're staring at Brontes. She clutched Her dress, fighting to keep Herself still.

"Who stands before me?" Brontes said.

Garrick bowed his head. "The Brave, Your Highness."

"And what is your purpose here?"

"I am requesting permission to leave the Sovereign's Tournament."

Venom erupted from the audience, but Brontes silenced them with a raised hand. "The Brave appeals to leave the Sovereign's Tournament. You see the irony here, yes?"

"It is not without just reason, Your Highness."

"My daughter... She was distraught this morning. Even now, She refuses to sit in Her throne, hangs in the back like a common servant. You've deeply offended Her."

A blaze crackled in Leila's chest. As Garrick spoke, Cosima's hand wriggled into Hers, giving a comforting squeeze. Surely the people thought Brontes spoke of her. They had to.

"Do you know how many tournaments this realm has held?" Brontes said.

Garrick hesitated. "No, Your Highness."

"Neither do I. It's a tradition that's lasted centuries. Ingrained in our very culture—a part of who we are as Thessians. This tournament isn't just for my daughter, it's for the people. You've failed them."

There was no greater failure to Thessen than Brontes himself.

"Do you know how many men have quit the Sovereign's Tournament?"

"No, Your Highness," Garrick said.

"Three. In its entire history. Do you know what happened to those three men?" Brontes didn't wait for a response. "Executed. On the spot. One was hung. Another beheaded. Another was dragged for miles through the heart of the realm. They say the streets were red with blood for weeks. Rain was especially scarce that season."

He leaned back in his throne, too comfortable for Leila's tastes. "But today, before the people, I grant you a hearing. You are the Brave, a man of The Savior's army, and such a man wouldn't withdraw from the mightiest of endeavors without good cause. So after much deliberation, I feel it's only right to hear your case."

"That's because you're kind and merciful, Your Highness."

"Speak," Brontes ordered. "Tell me your reasons. Why do you choose to abandon my daughter?"

Garrick launched into his defense, well-rehearsed and brimming with lies. "I am meant to wear a helmet, not a crown." Leila stopped listening, distracted by Her churning thoughts. What was the point of this hearing in the first place? How could this possibly benefit Brontes in any way?

"Your aim is to serve the realm at your greatest capacity," Brontes said. "As a soldier."

"Yes, Your Highness." Garrick exhaled. "As the leader of Her army, you of all people can understand the importance of my service."

Brontes sat in silence, strumming his fingers against the armrest of his throne. "It's very noble of you to sacrifice the crown to return to a life of service."

"It's a sacrifice I'm willing to make for the good of Thessen." Garrick's shoulders drooped. "And to be honest, I don't think your daughter will miss my presence. I've yet to win any time alone in Her company. I by no means attempt to speak for Her, but I don't believe She favors me."

"And who do you think She favors?"

"Your blessed ones, of course. The Shepherd and the Dragon."

Leila's gaze shot toward the competitors in their golden armor. Her assassins stood tall, the sight simmering Her blood.

Garrick choked out his next words. "And possibly the Artist as well."

"*ARTIST. ARTIST.*" The pews were roused and alive, shouting Tobias's laurel ravenously. Despite Her better judgment, She looked for Tobias within the line, only to find him staring at Her—or was he? It was so hard to tell from such a distance, and if She couldn't make out the path of his gaze, certainly the people couldn't either.

"So, Brave," Brontes said, "you leave this tournament, not as an affront to my daughter, but to return to your rightful position in Her army. You see that She doesn't favor you, and you believe you're of better service as a soldier than as Champion. Is this correct?"

"Yes, Your Highness."

"Sound reasons."

None of this made sense. Brontes hadn't the time nor the patience to toy with men. Why was Garrick still living?

"You mentioned my blessed ones earlier." Brontes gestured toward the line of competitors. "They stand behind you, you know."

Garrick didn't answer, so Brontes continued. "The Dragon. Do you fear him?"

"Pardon?"

"Are you *afraid* of the Dragon, *Brave?*"

Garrick squared his shoulders. "I fear no one, Your Highness."

"He's killed two men in this tournament. One of those kills occurred just the other day. He's fought diligently for the crown and for my daughter. You know this, yet still you don't fear him. Is that right?"

"Yes, Your Highness."

"Then why is it you demanded to leave this tournament just after the Dragon put an end to the Bear?" Brontes spat. "After he challenged *you*, publicly? Why did so many report to me that after he called your name, you came running to the palace like a little bitch?"

The pews stirred, as did Leila's nerves.

"Lies, Your Highness," Garrick said. "All lies."

"*You* lie, *Brave*. You leave to protect your hide, not for the service and glory of Thessen."

"Your Highness—"

"I gave the Dragon my blessing for a reason. Because I knew he was capable of exposing *cowards* like you." Brontes stared out at the pews, his chin high. "People of Thessen, I am a hard and stern Sovereign, but I am not without warmth."

Leila started. *What did he say?*

"To these men, I have offered shelter. Council. Camaraderie." Brontes glared down at the competitors. "I welcome you into my home. Treat you as royal guests. As *sons*. Yet still, I am betrayed."

The pounding of Her heart turned explosive, rattling Her bones.

"As for my daughter?" Brontes said. "She is my world, just as Her mother was before Her. Her mother, slaughtered in the street. Killed by a man with no regard for Her rule. You all know what I do to those who cross me. Who cross The Savior. That traitor was tortured for your approval. I carved his blasphemous tongue from the back of his throat myself. For The Savior. For *Thessen*."

The audience overflowed with rage, and Leila felt it too—for Her father, the falsehoods on his tongue, and the ease with which he spoke them.

"Now my daughter stands before you of age, free to select a husband, and it is my duty to ensure Her choice is fit for this throne. Throughout this tournament, challenge after challenge, I have stood beside Her, not for my own pleasure, but for Her aid exclusively." He pointed out at the competitors violently, as if his hand were a blade. "These men have witnessed our affection, can attest to our unshakable bond, for we are united not just as Rulers of Thessen, but by the love that only a father and daughter can share."

Gripping his armrests, he seethed with an anger that almost appeared real. "My daughter is a woman forced to grow without a mother. I am all She has. I ended the man who took Her mother. Do you think for a second I would allow *anyone* to cross Her?"

Leila clamped down on Her lip, counting the seconds until Garrick lay dead. Surely this was worse than any execution—listening to Her father speak of a love that never existed.

Garrick paled. "Y-Your Highness, please—"

"Enough!" Brontes spat. "You've lied to me. I can overlook that. But I cannot overlook the pain you've caused my daughter. Her heart breaks because of you. Inconsolable, because of you. Weak, even in this moment. Because of *you*."

"I'm so sorry—"

"Look at my daughter. You vowed to die for Her. And today, you honor that vow." Brontes gazed out at the back of the arena. "Guards!"

Three men in silver surrounded Garrick, holding him still before slamming a spear through the small of his back. Blood poured onto the sands, painting the ground red as Garrick collapsed in a heap. All of it was a meaningless blur to Leila; She stared up at the waves of people chanting a horrid word.

"CYCLOPS."

The title echoed off the arena walls—Her father's laurel from his time in the Sovereign's Tournament.

"A warning to the men who stand before me," Brontes said. "Challenge me, and I promise your fate will make the Brave's look like mercy."

"*CYCLOPS. CYCLOPS.*" The people roared with adoration, and Leila's heart splintered beneath the weight of their praise. They loved Brontes, a doting father willing to kill for his daughter. A man who would never harm The Savior, and if some horror were to befall Her, surely he would have had nothing to do with it. It was all so convincing.

Leila didn't bother halting Her tears. This hearing had nothing to do with Garrick. It was about Brontes, his honor and piousness. In a few days, Leila would die within the walls of Her own home, and no one would suspect the Sovereign.

❧ 24 ❧

THE GARDEN

Garrick's corpse hung above the fortress gate. Soldiers must've spent hours securing him, a hideous warning for anyone on the other side. The news of Garrick's resting place had spread throughout the palace, but Leila had to see it for Herself. All She could make out was his ashen back, his strung arms, and the yawning entry-wound of his fatal blow. Thank God he was too far up to smell.

Delphi shook her head. "I swear, Your father wants to take us back to the Age of Darkness."

Guards stood at attention beside the wall, though Leila paid them no mind. Her eyes bore through the body—Her father's legacy.

Death.

"Come." She turned away. "We do it now."

The sisters walked back to the palace in silence. Yesterday's humiliation was fresh in Leila's mind, Her bones quaking with untapped rage. Someone would pay for the affront.

They headed down the secluded corridor, stopping at a familiar door. "Do You think he's in there?" Delphi said.

"It's barely sunup. He likely hasn't even risen yet."

"I'm coming in with You."

"Absolutely not. You stay here and watch."

Delphi crossed her arms. "Who are You to dictate my actions?"

"I'm The Savior."

"You're a dumb bitch is what You are."

A servant rounded the corner, starting at the sight of the sisters. Bowing her head, she cooed a pleasantry before walking off.

"She saw us." Leila turned to Delphi. "What if she tells someone?"

"She won't."

"How do you know?"

Delphi smirked, and her wink sent Leila's eyes rolling. "God..."

The door swung open, revealing a rotund Senator. "Your Holiness?"

Leila grabbed Wembleton's drape, shoving him into his bedchamber while Delphi slammed the door behind them. Grasping his face, She pinned him to the wall, his oily flesh squishing beneath Her fingers. How could such a large man be so weak?

"Your Holiness, please—"

"You had one chance," Leila said. "One opportunity to prove your allegiance to Me. And you failed."

"I'm so sorry—"

"My father dragged Me through the palace. Demeaned Me in *My* home. Thrust Me on display before *My* people. And you did *nothing*."

"It wasn't my fault. It happened so fast—"

"Well I promise you this"—Leila unsheathed Her blade, pressing it against the Senator's belly—"what you're about to endure will be *very* slow."

"Someone moves against You!"

"Save your begging, I already know of the Kovahrians."

"In the palace!" Wembleton winced. "Someone moves against You within the palace. Outside the Senate. Someone in Your access, close to You in some way."

Leila faltered. *Close to Me?* She spun toward Delphi. "It can't be Pippa." Her eyes widened. "Cosima."

"If it were Cosima, Brontes would've learned of our ruse long ago," Delphi said.

"There's no one else."

"Except for Your lovely servant girls who dote on You day after day, well within Your *access*."

Leila's gut sank. Hundreds of faces passed through Her mind, along with white dresses, bowed heads. "Oh My God... There are so many of them..."

"I'm the only one who knows of this informant," Wembleton croaked. "There was another—"

"Who?"

"K-Kastor is dead, Your Holiness."

She swallowed the curse words in Her throat. Someone was betraying Her, and Her only link to them was the waste of a man before Her.

"I don't know who this traitor is, but I can find out for You," Wembleton said. "Brontes is speaking with them through secret means —through packages and...and gifts—"

Leila's back shot straight. "The necklaces."

She dissolved within a surge of light, materializing in Her study and snatching up the string of jewels. Power burst through Her as She reappeared in the Senator's chamber, where Wembleton was still clambering against the wall.

"Give this to Brontes." She thrust the necklace his way. "Fabricate whatever story you need, just make sure he has it. And once he does, you will discover this traitor. Follow him, beat it out of him, I don't care. This is My order, and you *will* obey."

He took the jewelry in his trembling hands. "Of course. I won't fail You."

"You're a lucky man, Senator. No other has crossed Me as you have and lived to speak of it." She brought Her blade to his throat. "You'll remember that, yes?"

His larynx bobbed against the sharpened tip. As he opened his mouth to speak, Leila took Delphi's hand and disappeared amid beaming white.

The heat of Her body faded, leaving the two women in Leila's darkened study. Leila plodded through the chamber, Her sister's gaze tracing Her every move.

"Do *not* chastise Me for sparing him," Leila said. "We have nothing else. This is our only lead—"

"I know."

The defeat in Delphi's voice stung. Sitting at Her desk, Leila rested Her head in Her hands. *Another traitor.* One on the outside of Her palace and one within, not to mention the guards, the Senate, Her own father. Her lungs throbbed, urging Her to scream. This traitor...did She know them? Did She trust them?

"This is good news," She lied. "We know the purpose of the jewels. Wembleton will find the source. Maybe this is the last of Brontes's network. We can finally be free of him."

Delphi nodded. "The traitor... Do you think they're linked with the Kovahrians?"

"I can't think of any other reason he'd need them." Leila faltered. "*Her.*"

"Who do You think she is?"

"This palace employs hundreds of servants. She could be any one of them."

A knot coiled in Her stomach. Deception had become a familiar ache, but it pained Her all the same.

"So what next?" Delphi took a seat opposite Leila. "Maybe take out one of the new Senators? Poor Hylas, he's a bit of a daisy, isn't he? I'd hate to see him go."

"We wait for Wembleton's findings. You watch the servants. Look for suspicious behavior." Leila stiffened. "I'll see Tobias. Tell him the truth."

"You haven't told him? You said You were going to days ago."

"Yes, well, he made it difficult."

"How? Was his tongue too far down Your throat?"

Leila cowered beneath Delphi's cheeky laughter. "He said some things and...I lost My nerve."

"What could he have possibly said?"

"I swear I loathe The Savior more and more each day."

Groaning, Delphi leaned back in her seat. "God, men. Always choking on their own foot." She raised an eyebrow. "You know he wasn't speaking of You."

"He said *The Savior*. Is that not who I am?"

A knock sounded, and Mousumi barged inside without preamble.

"Your Holiness. The ally royals will be arriving in a few days' time. There are matters to discuss. May I?"

At Leila's nod, Mousumi rattled off instructions from a scroll that nearly grazed the floor. Though Leila occasionally responded, Her thoughts belonged to greater troubles, Her gaze tracing the servant keeper before Her. Long white dress. Brown leather sandals. A woman in the same garb was lurking in this palace.

A traitor.

The thought picked at Leila well past Her meeting with Mousumi. Come the evening, it sat heavily on Her shoulders, enough to ruin Her appetite. She pushed Her nearly full dinner plate aside, Her belly lined with little more than wine, and gazed past the steps of Her bedchamber into Her lush garden. The flowers reflected the glow of the moonlight, a beautiful distraction, and for once Her worries loosened their hold.

A woman called from the other side of Her door before making her way into the chamber. Damaris walked to Leila's bedside, collecting Her dishes. "Not hungry, I take it?"

Leila nearly smiled, but stopped short. White dress. Leather sandals.

"Too much on My mind, I suppose."

"You've been taking Your dinner in Your bed for several days now. Is something troubling You?"

Leila cast a skeptical gaze the servant's way. "I'm just seeking some time alone. There's so much commotion in the palace."

"Because of the tournament. I understand."

She headed for the door, while Leila's mind was yet again occupied, this time with more pleasant thoughts. Large brown eyes. Deep brown curls.

"Damaris? Can you do Me a favor? Summon the Artist. I'd like to see him."

The servant's plump cheeks flushed, and a grin spread across her face.

"To My study," Leila said. "For conversation. It's rather urgent, I won't bore you with the details."

Damaris bowed before taking leave, and Leila flopped back onto Her bed. Perhaps that was a mistake. Could She trust Damaris? Before

Her mind could drift into dark corners, She picked Herself up, straightening Her peach-colored dress and combing Her hair.

Tonight, She'd tell Tobias the truth.

He was already waiting in Her study by the time She arrived. For a moment, She lingered by the doorway, taking in the width of his shoulders, the firmness of his ass. Swallowing a giggle, She tiptoed behind him, planting Her hands over his eyes.

"*Leila.*" His voice flowed through Her, more intoxicating than the dinner wine.

"Actually it's Flynn," She said. "I've been mad for you since the moment we met, I just didn't know how to tell you."

He let out a laugh. "You scared me half to death, you know. I thought I was about to get my stones chopped off, or something else equally vile."

"Is there anything equally vile to having your stones chopped off?"

"Oh hell, I don't know," he said. "Why are you covering my eyes?"

"I have a surprise for you."

"Is that right?"

"You have to close your eyes."

"What for?" he scoffed. "You're covering them."

Light tickled Her fingertips. "It's a dual precaution."

"This must be *some* surprise."

"Are your eyes closed?"

"Of course, Leila." He chuckled. "I'm at your service."

They staggered through the study laughing and teasing one another, heading straight toward a wall. *The garden.* Heat surged from Her palms through his body, enveloping them in Her power and giving way to a cool breeze. They had materialized at the edge of Her bedchamber, color splayed out before them like a rainbow beneath the night sky. She ushered him down the short steps and far along the grassy pathway, stopping once flowers and life surrounded them from all angles.

"All right." She dropped Her hands. "Open your eyes."

Tobias sucked in a breath. The anticipation plucked at Her nerves, so She made Her way into his line of sight. "What do you think? It's beautiful, isn't it?"

He didn't stare at the garden—he stared at Her, his cheeks pulled up into a grin. "I've never seen anything like it."

Blushing, She turned to Her hydrangeas. "This is my *favorite* place in the fortress."

"Do you come here often?"

"Every day. Do you like it?"

"I do."

Tobias was beaming, but not for long. His gaze flitted across the garden, no doubt searching for prying eyes.

"No one can see us," Leila said. "We're alone."

"You're sure?"

"I've been naked out here before."

Tobias's gaze darted back toward Her. "*Naked?*"

"Completely."

A cheeky smirk sprang to his lips. "Lies. I'll believe it when I see it."

Laughing, She batted his arm before heading off through the garden, stopping at a familiar stretch of grass. She unstrapped the sheath from Her thigh, flinging it aside before dropping to the ground.

Strength and peace. The garden rejoiced in response, showering Her in life.

"What are you doing?" Tobias said.

Leila nestled deeper into the grass. "This is my spot."

"Well then, where's my spot?"

"I don't know. Pick one."

As Tobias lay down beside Her, a smile bloomed across Her face. "A wise decision."

She stared at the stars above, but Her mind was on the power around Her—the light radiating from Her body, the blackness reaching up toward the surface. The syrupy strings shriveled beneath Her, and She relished its submission, the one semblance of control She had these days.

Tobias's arm wrapped around Her waist, and Her heartbeat surged when he rested his cheek against Her neck. "You're encroaching on my spot," She said.

"My spot is with you."

Pinpricks of the brightest fuchsia rose from his body, fading into the night. Leila pressed Her hand to his chest, and color pulsed within him, traveling up Her arm, down Her stomach, and between Her legs.

"What are you thinking about?" She said.

"I'm imagining you lying out here. Naked."

Leila burst out laughing, and Tobias flashed Her a playful scowl. "What?"

"You dog."

"I'm an honest man. Don't deprive me of my imagination."

She smacked his chest, and his glare morphed into feigned outrage. "Leila!"

"Stop that."

"This is the single most glorious vision I've had since the start of this tournament. You'd deny me that? Cruel. Just cruel."

Color wafted from his flesh, orange and yellow as vibrant as the surrounding flowers. Leila traced Her fingers through the beautiful haze, writing words in his affection.

Mine.

"I wish I could live in the night with you." Tobias nuzzled closer. "Just sleep through the challenges and wake up to this."

"Perhaps one day. Once the tournament is over."

"You think so?"

Leila pulled away. "You don't?"

"I try not to think about it. I fear the tournament will end in my death or my marriage to Cosima. I'm not certain which one is worse."

"Oh, I don't know," She said. "I think we might be able to work something out. If we put our heads together."

"You do, do you? How do you figure?"

"I can be very tenacious with the proper motivation."

He chuckled. "That I can believe."

His breath warmed Leila's throat, beckoning Her to come closer, to taste his lips. Instead She went rigid, staring at the darkness above.

There was a purpose to this visit.

"Tobias..." She breathed in. "I brought you here...to tell you something."

"Oh? What is it?" He hoisted himself onto his elbows, staring down at Her. "Leila?"

"Apologies. I'm nervous," She said.

"You don't have to be nervous."

She strayed from his gaze. "I fear once I say what needs to be said, you'll regret a great deal...particularly your decision to be with me."

"No. You're wrong."

"Tobias—"

"Hear me, Leila." He fought his way into Her line of sight. "You have secrets. I'm not blind to it. But secrets or none, you're the woman who saved my life. The woman I long to be with day after day." His fingers threaded through Hers, gripping tight. "This is the path I've chosen. And each day that passes, I thank God I didn't choose The Savior. That I chose you instead."

A stab ripped through Her, stopping Her heart.

Tobias settling in the grass at Her side. "Now, say what you need to say."

No. She couldn't. Everything within Her pleaded for silence, but She forced Herself to speak.

"At the Welcoming... You remember those men hovering around Brontes? His Senators?"

"The vultures?" Tobias said.

"Yes, them. Well...that flock used to be much larger. It's been shrinking as of late. Because..."

"You've killed them."

The air evacuated Her lungs. A part of Her was grateful he had spoken for Her, but that didn't eliminate the silence between them, nor the impenetrable tension.

"Yes," She said.

Tobias didn't respond, and Her thoughts spun frantically. "I tried everything," She stammered. "There was no other way. I would never... I mean, I wouldn't even *think* it if it weren't absolutely necessary—"

"You don't have to justify yourself to me. I know you." He looked Her in the eyes. "My only question is...why?"

This was it. All She had to do was reveal Her title.

I didn't choose The Savior. I chose you instead.

Tobias faltered. "Leila—"

"It's complicated." She turned Her head away.

"I don't doubt that, but I'm willing to listen."

But he wasn't. As much as She wished it were true, as much as She wanted to believe him, She couldn't. Not when all his colors had disappeared.

"You'll know everything," She said. "Once it's taken care of... Once all is said and done—"

"And what if that day never comes? Killing Senators? That's no petty offense. What if you're discovered?"

"I won't be."

"You don't know that." His voice came out hard. "What you're doing, it's incredibly dangerous—"

"It's just as dangerous if I do nothing. More so, even."

"But—"

"I've told you what I can," She spat. "And when the task is complete, I'll explain the rest. It's for the best."

She winced. She had spoken too harshly—too much like a queen—but Tobias remained stoic, his eyes on the moon.

"All right," he said. "I trust you."

Leila's insides shrank. She didn't deserve his trust, certainly not after such cowardice.

A tentative hand reached for Hers. "I'm still here," Tobias whispered.

Calm enveloped Her, releasing Her burdens, if only slightly. *This is the superior path. He'll understand once all is said and done.* She was sure of so few decisions these days, but this one felt sound. Tobias was the only pure, good thing in Her life. She brought Her cheek to his, allowing him to wrap his arms around Her.

"Well then, I suppose since you've told me a secret, it's only fair I do the same," he said. "Let's see... Back when I was sixteen, Naomi was seeing this smith in our village. Alex. A pathetic cock."

Leila smirked. "I can see where this is headed."

"It only lasted a few weeks. Maybe longer. Then she finds out he'd been fucking the potter's daughter the entire time."

"A pathetic cock indeed."

"Naomi was devastated. I was livid, naturally. Swore I'd go straight to his home and beat his ass." Tobias scoffed. "I don't know what I was talking about. I'd never beaten anyone's ass before, not really. But Naomi insisted I keep my distance. She was appalled by the whole idea of it."

"Did you do it anyway?"

"Of course not. She's my sister, I respected her wishes... For the most part."

Leila raised an eyebrow. "What did you do?"

Tobias shied away from Her gaze. "Well, I passed Alex's cottage every day on my way to town. And I had a clear view of his window..."

"And?"

"God, I can't believe I'm telling you this."

"Say it."

He cleared his throat. "His washbasin was right there on the sill. So...I pissed in it."

Leila couldn't suppress Her laughter, while Tobias continued, grinning. "He didn't seem to notice. Saw him washing himself later that evening without a care in the world."

"He was washing himself *in your piss?*"

"Indeed he was. And it was oddly satisfying. So the next day, I pissed in his basin again."

Leila gasped. "Tobias!"

"And then the next day. And then every day for the next two weeks."

"You're bad."

"It became my morning routine. Get up, grab a bite, piss in Alex's basin. Then one day, he figured it out. Came to my cottage and punched me in the eye."

"Then what?"

He shrugged. "Well, that was that. Though I did watch my step for a while. And checked my own basin daily, just in case. Naomi thought the whole thing was hilarious, and that's really all that matters."

Leila buried Her face into the cowl of Tobias's shirt, drowning in giggles.

"Your turn." He wrapped an arm around Her, pulling Her close. "Tell me a secret. And it better be good."

"You already know about the watchtower. That was a secret."

"Unacceptable. I told you a piss secret."

"Well, I've never pissed in anyone's washbasin. I've been stuck here in the fortress not having much fun at all."

"There has to be *something*."

A thought came to Her. "All right. There is something. It's not much of a secret, but I think you'll like it."

"I'm all ears."

"You can't judge me."

"Never."

Leila bit Her lip. "You remember that one challenge with the keys?"

"Unfortunately."

"Raphael nearly died," She said. "The whole thing was deplorable. Well, I spent all night tending to Raph, trying to keep him alive. And once it was all over, I was just so upset. With the Proctor. *Especially* with Cosima. So, the next time I saw Her...I slapped Her."

Tobias gaped at Her. "You *slapped* Cosima?"

"Right in the mouth."

"Oh my God!" He rolled onto his back in laughter. "You're a madwoman!"

"It was liberating."

"What did She do?"

"She cried. I felt awful. It was wrong of me."

"I don't know about that. It sounds more than fair to me." He eyed Her with a mischievous gaze. "And to be honest, I don't think I've ever been more attracted to you."

Self-satisfaction surged within Her. "Your turn." She glided Her fingers through his locks. "Tell me a secret."

Tobias wavered. "I dream about you most nights."

"Is that so? What kind of dreams?"

"Sometimes it's just you and me together, like this. Other times we're more...involved."

Fire pulsed through Her veins, Her heartbeat echoing in Her ears.

"Apologies if that makes you uncomfortable," he said.

"I don't mind."

Tobias met Her gaze. "Your turn."

Leila summoned every ounce of courage within Her. "I dream of you most nights as well."

The sky overhead morphed from black to wild pink. Leila reveled in the sight, while Tobias's fingertips swept Her figure from Her ribs down to Her hip.

"Are you ticklish?" he asked.

"No. Are you?"

His silence was all the answer She needed. She launched Her hand into his armpit.

"Leila, you bastard!"

His cries fueled Her, and She tickled without remorse while he floundered beneath Her onslaught. "You betray me! Stop!" But She continued, the two of them rolling through the grass, laughing in one another's arms. Escaping Her torture, Tobias latched onto Her wrists, pinning Her to the ground.

Leila's lungs ached, Her giggles dying in breathless spurts. "I surrender."

Tobias's smile consumed Her vision. He lay on top of Her, stifling Her with his weight, but something about it felt freeing and good.

His eyes strayed from Hers, tracing Her form.

"What?" She said.

"You're so beautiful."

"So are you."

Tobias chuckled. "*I'm* beautiful?"

Leila nodded, basking in his heat. He pressed his mouth to Hers, and the sugary taste of his kiss bombarded Her senses, filling Her to the brim.

She ran Her hands up his back, then through his hair, drawing him in. He lingered against Her lips before moving to Her cheek, down toward Her collarbone, leaving breathy kisses that seeped into Her veins. His tongue drew fluid circles on Her neck, eliciting wave after wave of pleasure that forced a moan from Her throat.

Don't stop.

His mouth latched onto the curve of Her neck, loosening Her senses. He nipped at the soft flesh, and the pulsing between Her thighs turned fervent, desperate. Wrapping Her legs around him, She pressed him against Her, his hard cock digging into Her pelvis.

She wanted it.

She wanted him.

Leila ripped his shirt over his head, running Her hands down his sculpted stomach. Tobias's breathing turned fast and heavy, and a second later his hips were circling against Hers, pressing his manhood between Her legs. *He wants Me.* It was vibrating through him, calling for Her to pull him closer, deeper. She pinned Her legs against his back, willing the thin layers of fabric between them to disappear.

I chose You instead.

Leila's eyes shot open. This couldn't happen. Not like this.

Tobias still writhed against Her, and She led his hand up Her thigh, stopping it at the slit of Her dress.

"This is where I draw the line," She said.

Tobias froze, his gaze darting between Her eyes, Her leg. Long seconds of silence passed before he took Her hand in his. "And where do you draw the line on me?"

He pulled Her palm down the hard planes of his chest, and Her breath caught once Her fingertips reached his waistband.

"Here."

Tobias nodded. "All right."

"Things are complicated enough as it is." Leila's nerves stirred. "I just—"

"Leila, I require no explanation. The lines are drawn. And if they change in any direction, I hope you'll show me as unequivocally as you have just now."

"It's not that I don't want to. Or that I don't think about it."

Tobias's eyes lit up. "You think about it?"

"Maybe."

"Are you blushing?"

She turned Her head. "Don't tease me."

His laughter loosened the tension within Her. When She dared a glance his way, he was waiting at Her side, a smile on his face as his fingers danced through Her hair.

"I hope I haven't ruined the moment," She said.

Tobias snorted. "Of course not. Do you think I'm stupid? That I assume you exist simply for my pleasure? I'm perfectly content with holding you and kissing you for the entire night, so long as that's what you want as well."

"Well then, you should know I really, *really* want you to kiss me right now."

"Where?"

"I get to choose?" Tobias nodded, and Leila pointed to the sweet spot at the base of Her throat. "Here."

His full lips grazed Her skin, leaving a long kiss that sent tremors rolling through Her. His gaze locked onto Hers, and She teased Her fingertips down Her décolletage. "Here."

His kiss only fueled Her temptation, Her mind wandering to places it didn't belong. She tapped Her lips. "And here."

She nearly lost Herself in his captivating smile before his mouth was once again pressed to Hers. His body sank into Her, but this time he moved gracefully, gentle in a way that spoke volumes, a tenderness She'd never known.

"Tobias?"

His eyes flitted to Hers. "Yes?"

"Nothing..." She shook Her head. "Well, no, it's not nothing. I just think you're the most wonderful man I've ever known. I wanted to tell you that. That's all."

Another grin lit his face, and when he kissed Her, She could've sworn She'd become weightless, free of every hardship that bound Her to the fortress.

Safe for the first time in years.

❦ 25 ❦

THE SERVANTS

Kisses trailed Leila's neck as flecks of yellow and pink floated above Her like fireflies. Her garden used to be the most beautiful sight She'd ever seen, but not anymore. That title now belonged to Tobias's colors painting the night.

"You've certainly found your favorite spot," She said.

"You seem to like it."

"I hate it."

His head perked up. "You hate it?"

"Because I like it."

Chuckling, Tobias resumed his worship, nipping at Her skin.

"You have me so conflicted," She said. "On the one hand, I want you to stop, because you're making it hard to behave. On the other, I want you to keep going, because it feels fantastic. Like your lips are traveling through my entire body."

"How about I continue, and if at any point you *misbehave*, I'll politely remind you of your manners."

Leila raised an eyebrow. "You will, will you?"

Tobias laughed. "Don't look at me like that. If anything happens between us, I want you to remember the moment with excitement, not regret."

"You should know, as soon as things...uncomplicate themselves...I won't regret anything with you. Not at all."

He smiled against Her ear. "Does that mean you want me?"

She answered with Her touch, drawing fluid strokes down his chest, circling his stomach before teasing the line of his waistband. Swallowing a groan, Tobias flopped back onto the grass, his hands folded on his lap as he hummed to himself.

"What are you doing?" Leila said.

"I'm distracting myself from all of this." He waved a hand at Her. "All of...you."

Leila laughed, while Tobias clamped his eyes shut. "Don't mind me, I'm a respectable man not without self-control. I can keep it together. I..." he let out a breath, "...can keep it together."

"Oh, please."

"Don't *oh please* me," he said. "You started it all."

"I didn't, actually. You told me about your dreams."

"Right." Tobias sighed. "Dammit."

As he resumed his humming, Leila let out a snort. "Tobias, it's only me."

"Don't pretend for a second I'm the first person to find you utterly tempting."

"I've told you. Men find me—"

"Intimidating, yes, I know. But trust me, all these *intimidated* men go off to beat their meat the moment you leave the room."

Leila could hardly suppress Her giggles, Her hands planted over Her mouth.

"I'm serious! You're gorgeous. You're so, *so* gorgeous." He rolled on top of Her, pressing Her into the grass. "You're amazing."

His kiss was passionate and raw. Leila responded in kind, raking Her fingers through his hair.

"I'm the luckiest man," he whispered.

"Why?"

"I get to be with you." He donned a cocksure grin. "But apparently no one else has ever tried, which certainly makes me smarter than the others. I might be the smartest man alive, actually."

"Don't flatter yourself."

"I'll flatter myself if I please, thank you very much," he said.

"Well, I think I'm the smart one here." Leila braced Herself, treading dangerously outside Her realm of comfort. "I don't know if you've realized, but a large number of eligible bachelors recently entered the fortress."

"I'm vaguely aware, yes."

"I took them as fools. Might've referred to them as *idiots* on a few occasions."

"You're very astute, Leila. We are all idiots."

"Not all of you." She swirled Her fingertips along his chest. "As much as I despise this tournament, I seem to have found the goodness in it all."

The night sky disappeared, blanketed by a sunset of joy bleeding straight from Tobias. He brought his lips to Hers, the smile in his kiss apparent, a spot of happiness that belonged solely to Her.

"We don't have to leave anytime soon, do we?" he asked. Leila shook Her head, and his smile widened. "Good."

Her eyes closed with his slow kiss, an indulgence She would relish for however long the night would allow.

LEILA'S EYES FLICKED OPEN. THE SKY WAS STILL AWASH IN BLACK, THE grass fluttering against Her ears. Tobias lay at Her side, propped up on his elbow as he watched Her.

"Tobias... Did I fall asleep?"

"You did." His voice came out deep and melodic. "You were so beautiful. A goddess of the night."

She luxuriated in his palpable stare before eyeing him over: strong shoulders, a chiseled stomach, powerful thighs.

He was nude.

"Your clothes." She sucked in a breath. "Where did they—?"

"The same place your dress disappeared to, I imagine."

Leila looked down at Herself and froze. The whole of Her womanhood was on display, not a shred of Her pale flesh covered. "Oh God."

"Shh." He pulled Her close, running a hand down Her cheek. "It's all right. You are breathtaking. You are mine."

Leila relaxed in his embrace. Their clothes must've blown away with the evening breeze. *Perfectly logical.* He pressed his mouth to Hers, and a pulsing heat sank deep into Her belly, leaving Her yearning and wet.

"Let me make love to you." Tobias spoke between kisses, cupping Her breasts. "Let me please you, again and again."

"But we can't—"

"Why? What's stopping you?"

His gaze was overwhelming, two pools of the darkest chocolate deep enough to drown in. Why was She waiting? She racked Her mind but couldn't remember.

"Nothing," She said. "Nothing at all."

Tobias licked his lips, pushing Her to the ground with a force She craved. Seconds later he was on top of Her, spreading Her legs wide, caressing Her face, pulling Her hair; how he managed to be all over Her at once, She hadn't a clue. Pressing his cock against Her, he brought his lips to Her ear.

"Can I?"

"Please." She trembled. "I want you."

One swift thrust, and Leila moaned, pleasure spilling through Her in waves. Tobias undulated in strong, broad strokes, and She followed the movement of his hips, edging to the brink of climax.

"Come here." He rolled back onto the grass and pulled Her on top of him. "I want to see you. All of you."

She rode him with a confidence well beyond Her prowess, as if fucking Tobias was innate within Her, a gift She'd always known. He gripped hard at Her ass, his longing everything She'd ever wanted, nearly as gratifying as his thickness between Her legs. She panted his name, teasing Her breasts as She prepared to spill over.

Heat poured down Her shoulders—a blazing light.

The sun had risen, casting Her celestial skin aglow.

Tobias's eyes widened. "Get off me!"

He shoved Her aside, collapsing Her to the grass. She scrambled to right Herself. "Tobias—"

"Don't come any closer."

Leila's gut hollowed. The heat of the sun lost its power, as the look of abject loathing on Tobias's face sent Her blood cold.

"To think I ever felt any affection for You..." He snarled. "God, it disgusts me. *You* disgust me."

"You don't know what you're saying."

"Is that right? Who then controls my tongue? Answer me this."

Tears streamed down Her cheeks as She gaped at Tobias, a man She no longer recognized. He grabbed Her arms, lurching Her forward.

"What are you doing?" She shrieked.

The chill of Her veins turned to ice. Tobias was gone. Her father loomed before Her, spittle flying as he roared.

"Kill The Savior!"

Leila's eyes shot open. Her cheek was buried in the prickly grass, the air still and silent. Tobias lay across from Her, eyes closed in peaceful slumber. A sigh of relief escaped Her as She took in the rise and fall of his shoulders, the gleaming bronze of his skin, the way the golden tips of his hair shined in the sunlight.

It was daytime.

She was glowing.

Panic gripped Her lungs. Slowly, She shifted upright, flinching with each movement Tobias made. She snatched up his shirt and Her blade before resting a hand on his shoulder.

To his chamber.

Fire burst through Her, and the grass beneath them morphed into a bed, the garden an empty wall brightened by the morning sun.

His chamber was illuminated.

Dammit.

She held Her breath, willing Herself to be silent. Tobias was still asleep, curled atop his bed as if he had always been there. She could make this work. As gracefully as possible, She placed Tobias's shirt at his side and turned to leave.

Another bed sat at the opposite side of the room, and in its center was Orion. He polished the arrowheads in his lap, eyes on Leila.

"Your Holiness." He nodded.

Cursing, She summoned Her light and disappeared from the chamber.

Leila collapsed onto Her bed, cradling Her face in Her hands. *Orion knows.* She kicked at the sheets and pounded Her fists into the mattress, ending Her fit with a huff. *What if he threatens You? Puts You in a corner, like Raphael?* Rolling onto Her stomach, She screamed into Her pillow.

Another man to manage.

Gathering Herself, She changed Her dress and secured Her blade before charging through the palace. It didn't take long to plan Her next move, though each passing second felt like an hour She didn't have. One servant led Her to another, who led Her to Mousumi, who informed Her that Orion, along with Kaleo and Flynn, would soon be heading to a reward with *The Savior*. "I see You've forgotten," the servant keeper said with scorn, but Leila hadn't time to find an excuse. She prepped Cosima for the formality, and then She waited.

One by one, the men left their chambers: first Flynn, then Kaleo, and finally Orion, heading down the corridor in a line. Leila glanced over the walls—no open windows, not a single trace of sunlight—then followed the competitors, catching up to the burly woodsman. As She opened Her mouth to speak, Orion broke the silence.

"I won't tell anyone." His voice came out low and even. "Your secret's safe."

Leila nearly started. "Have you known for long?"

"Known what? That You're with Tobias, or that You're The Savior?"

She hesitated. Flynn and Kaleo were far ahead, out of earshot, but She whispered regardless. "Both, I suppose."

"Tobias says Your name in his sleep sometimes."

"He does?" Leila said. "In a good way?"

"In a *very* good way." Orion furrowed his brow. "I didn't know You were The Savior until You...appeared in our room? In a cloud of smoke, it looked like. Very theatrical."

"You're not mad? About the ruse?"

Orion shrugged. "Haven't thought much about it, to be honest."

"The reasons are complicated."

"I imagine so."

"I'm in a world of danger," Leila said.

"This is a dangerous place."

"You're so understanding."

Another shrug. "Life is only complicated if you make it so."

"Sometimes complications aren't a choice."

Orion cracked a smile. "Tobias is a good man. The best among us. You've chosen wisely. Though I wouldn't expect any less of Her Holiness."

Leila's shoulders curled. "Please, don't tell him who I am. That I'm The Savior."

"He doesn't know?"

Leila shook Her head, and some semblance of realization crossed Orion's face. "That explains a lot," he mumbled.

"I need to be the one to tell him. Eventually. It has to come from Me."

"It means he loves You, You know." Orion stopped in the hallway, eyes locked on Her. "He doesn't know Your title, yet he calls Your name in his sleep. He longs for You, and in his eyes, he blasphemes for You. He loves You for who You are, in Your soul."

His words shook Her. She hadn't considered it before, too distracted by schemes and death, but now the thought rang loud between Her ears.

He loves You. Maybe She loved him back.

"You care for him a great deal," She said.

"We've become close."

"Thank you, then. For protecting him."

"It seems as though You've been doing a much better job of that than I have."

His lighthearted wink relaxed Her. Then Her gaze journeyed past him altogether, focusing onto the wall behind him—and the mirror hanging in a golden frame, carrying a reflection She didn't recognize. A woman with deep copper skin, long black hair as straight as an arrow, and a sharpness in her cheekbones that contrasted the warmth of her dark eyes. Eyes that were on Orion.

"Healer girl? Are You all right?" Orion wrinkled his crooked nose. "Did I just call You *Healer girl?* Old habit, I suppose."

Leila stared back at the woman in the mirror. She held a baby in her arms—a little boy of her likeness, save for the light brown of his eyes.

Leila met Orion's gaze.

Light brown.

"I'm sorry."

"For what?" he said.

"She's at peace. As is your son. They're together. And they're so, so happy."

His demeanor shifted, somehow heavy and light in an instant. "Thank You."

She waited for color to spill from his body, but the air around them remained stagnant, almost eerily so. Had She ever seen Orion's colors before? Had he always been surrounded by such...nothingness?

"Right then." Orion cleared his throat. "I suppose I should be off to see... Who is she, anyhow?"

"Just Cosima."

"Then I'm off to see *just* Cosima."

"Orion—"

"I know," he said. "She's The Savior, and You're *just* Leila."

Before he could begin his trek, he stopped short, looking back at Her. A smirk spread across his lips.

"What?" Leila said.

He pointed to his throat. "Love bite."

Leila studied Her reflection in the mirror. Two deep purple bruises decorated the curve of Her neck, and She gasped, pulling Her hair over the marks while Orion headed off for his reward, chuckling.

Leila left in the opposite direction, shaking away the embarrassment. Orion was handled. For once, something had gone Her way. As She tore down the corridor, Wembleton waddled from a far-off room, stopping once he caught sight of Her. Fear spilled from his pores in a green mist, and She couldn't help but smile to Herself. He should be afraid of Her. He disappeared down an adjacent path.

The plum walls of Her study surrounded Her, and She took a seat at Her desk, plucking a hand mirror from Her drawer and eyeing the spots on Her neck. The door flung open, and She shoved Her mirror aside, situating Her hair over Her shoulder as Delphi walked into the room.

"*You* weren't in Your chamber this morning." Delphi carried a bowl of fresh strawberries, speaking between nibbles.

"I was occupied," Leila said.

"Meeting with Wembleton? He's been scarce today as well."

"It wasn't anything like that. Trivial matters, really. How's your day?"

Delphi came in closer, staring hard at Leila, her eyes shrinking into slits. She flipped Leila's hair from Her shoulder, revealing the purple marks. "You little liar, You got fucked!"

"I did not!" Leila spat.

"You most certainly did, and You weren't even going to tell me!"

"I didn't *get fucked*." Scowling, Leila pulled Her hair into place. "That's why I didn't say anything. There's nothing to tell."

"*That* doesn't look like nothing."

"You're being silly. It was a brief visit. Completely inconsequential."

"Cosima isn't here." Delphi took a seat across from Her, a sly smile on her face. "No one's going to use this against You. And I *know* You want to share."

A flurry swirled in Leila's chest, and She struggled to contain a fast-forming grin. "Oh My God, it was incredible. We were kissing."

"I gathered as much. In multiple places, even."

"He was lying on top of Me. Writhing himself against Me. He was..." Glancing at the closed door, She lowered Her voice. "He was *hard as a rock*. The whole thing was so arousing, it was all I could do to keep My clothes on."

"Then why did You?"

"What do you mean?"

"If You want to fuck him, *fuck him*. He clearly wants to fuck You too, if he's writhing his cock against You." Delphi bit a strawberry off at the stem. "You're a grown woman. You can do what You please. *Whom* You please."

Leila slumped in Her seat. "I can't. He thinks I'm the Healer."

"*Still?*"

"We're in pursuit of a *traitor*. That's our priority, need I remind you." Her nightmare rippled through Her mind. "I'll tell Tobias once the dust settles. It's better like this. That way the job is done, and he can see all the good that comes of it."

Delphi crossed her arms. "Mhm."

"I can't take things any further... Not until he knows who I am. It wouldn't be right."

"So tell him the truth." Delphi popped another strawberry into her mouth, smiling with bulging cheeks. "Then fuck him."

"I'm not going to tell him just so we can make love."

"Consider it an added incentive. And *make love*? Really, Leila?"

"I was trying to be tactful."

Delphi chuckled. "Once You finally scrounge up Your courage, You must tell me the intimate details. I want to hear all about how the Artist fucks."

The door swung open, revealing four familiar servants. "How the Artist fucks?" Hemera bounded inside, the others following. "Did You fuck the Artist?"

Leila rolled Her eyes. "*No*, I did *not* fuck the Artist."

"Are You sure?"

"Of course I'm sure. How could I not be sure of who I have and haven't fucked?"

Nyx frowned. "But Damaris said You summoned him last night." Damaris elbowed her in the ribs, and Nyx flashed her a glare. "What? You did."

"We had a lovely conversation," Leila said. "I showed him one of our gardens, he told Me a delightful story about a man in his village by the name of Alex—"

"God, how dull," Nyx groaned.

"Nothing happened?" Damaris said. "I thought for certain You would've—"

"Ridden his manhood with a fiery passion!" Hemera squealed.

Damaris's cheeks reddened. "I'm just saying, You were so beautiful together at the Welcoming."

"Did You *at least* tickle his berries?" Hemera said.

"Oh, leave Her alone." Faun stood at Leila's side, wrapping an arm around Her shoulders. "This is *Her* romance. Let Her move at Her own pace."

Leila raised Her chin. "Thank you."

"But seriously, when You *do* fuck him, we require specifics." Faun crouched low, her gaze lit with intrigue. "We already know all about his gorgeous figure and top-notch cock, so You can get straight into performance."

"Ladies, The Savior would like some privacy," Delphi said. "You're dismissed."

"But—"

"Dismissed."

Frowning, the four servants trudged from the study, shutting the door behind them. Leila remained stiff in Her chair, their words still buzzing in Her ears. "I don't want them knowing the intricacies of My personal life."

"Well, they're gone now. And on a positive note, *apparently* Your Artist has a top-notch cock." Delphi waggled her eyebrows. "Won't that be fun?"

Leila bit Her lip, Her servants' faces dancing through Her thoughts.

"You think one of them might be the traitor?" Delphi said.

"Yes." Leila shook Herself. "No. I don't know. What do you think?"

"They seem to adore you. Nyx and Hemera especially. They sing Your praises behind closed doors all the time."

"Even Nyx? But she's so testy."

"She's much more agreeable under the proper circumstance."

Leila sighed. "I can't be too careful. Until Wembleton finds the source, it's too great a risk."

"When do You think he'll have news?"

"Soon. If he knows what's good for him."

The topic dissolved as the two sisters pored over lists of the palace staff, marking all potential traitors, crossing off those who didn't fit. Chione was barely thirteen years of age—certainly not experienced enough for politics—and Elin had expressed contempt for the Sovereign between sweet nothings in Delphi's bed. By the time they were finished, nearly a third of the names were struck. Leila would've felt pleased had Her four favorite servants not been among the many remaining.

"What now?" Leila muttered, staring at the names.

"Kill Your father?"

"Delphi—"

"There's nothing to be done. Not now, at least." Delphi lounged back in her seat. "We wait for Wembleton's word. Find the traitor. And assuming they're the last of Brontes's network—"

"*Then* we kill My father."

Together, the sisters smiled.

A soft knock sounded at the door, followed by a tentative face poking into the room. Damaris came inside with a tray of sweet rolls. "Thought you might prefer to eat in Your study." She arranged their place settings. "I assumed You wouldn't want to be disturbed."

Leila nodded. "That was very kind of you."

Damaris bowed, then waited, her eyes cast downward.

"Is there anything else?" Leila said.

"My deepest apologies. I shouldn't have told the other girls about your meeting with the Artist. I understand if You don't trust me any longer."

A stab of guilt pierced Leila—except maybe that's what Damaris wanted. This sweet, unassuming servant. A traitor.

Apprehensively, Leila took the girl's hand. Colors swam from her touch—soft blues and periwinkles, sadness and guilt wrapped in a blanket of embarrassment. Nothing about Damaris felt calculating or cruel.

"I know how you can make it up to Me. Summon the Artist. I'd like to see him."

Damaris's face flushed. "For another delightful conversation?"

"Of course," Delphi said. "I'm here, after all. What else could possibly go on?"

With a bow, Damaris left the room, failing to mask her excitement. As the door closed behind her, Delphi flashed Leila a smug smirk.

"What?" Leila scoffed. "You said it yourself, there's nothing left to be done today."

Chuckling, Delphi stood. "I'll leave You to Your *riveting conversation.*"

She headed to the door, staggering backward as it swung wide open. Cosima plowed into the study with a red-faced Pippa trailing behind her.

Delphi stumbled out of the way. "Good God, Cosima—"

"What are you doing here?" Leila said. "Is the reward over already?"

Cosima rushed to Her side, panting. "He's coming."

"Who's coming?"

"Brontes."

"He's so angry." Pippa's lip quivered, her cheeks wet with tears.

Leila stood from Her seat. "What's going on?"

Cosima's eyes were wide, her skin ashen. "Your father knows about the switch."

A boulder dropped in the pit of Leila's stomach.

"He's going to hurt me." Pippa's breathing turned into gasps, her shoulders trembling. "I didn't do anything wrong. I didn't—"

"Shh." Leila pulled her close. "Little duckling, everything will be all right."

"What do we do?" Cosima said.

The door flew open, crashing against the wall. Red mist seeped through the room, and a beast of a man stood within its mass.

The study fell quiet. Cosima plastered on a strained smile, though her gaze was bleak. "Your Highness. What an unexpected surprise."

Brontes was still for a long while before coming forward, his steps slow and heavy. Cosima headed for the door, closing it gently, while Pippa cowered behind Leila. Raising Her chin, Leila tried to appear stoic, yet everything within Her was withering away.

He knew.

"You have something to tell me," Brontes said.

Delphi and Cosima took their place at Leila's sides, a wall Her father could easily plow through. Leila swallowed, his red rage burning Her throat. "Is that so?"

"Say it. Say You've been lying to Your staff, Your people, and Your Sovereign for weeks."

"I don't know what you're talking about."

"*Say it!*"

Leila flinched. Seconds of nothingness crept by, and Brontes snatched up Cosima's wrist. She yelped as he yanked her into his hold. "What did—?"

"We switched places," Leila blurted. "Cosima's been posing as The Savior. I'm her sister."

Brontes froze, his eye on Leila while Cosima struggled in his grasp. "So it's true." He released Her sister, sending her tottering. "I knew it was. But I needed to hear it from You. I needed to hear it from Your *filthy mouth*."

Pippa trembled against Leila's back, or perhaps Leila was the one shaking, Her strength slipping away. "Who told you?"

"*That's* what You have to say?"

"I don't see why you're so—"

"What the *hell* do You think You're doing?" he barked.

"Your Highness, this outburst isn't becoming for a man of your station," Delphi said.

"Lower your voice," Leila growled.

A vein bulged from Brontes's forehead. "You dare to give me orders?"

"It's best not to attract attention." Cosima raised her hands as if to placate. "People will wonder—"

"I can't believe this." Brontes paced the floor. "The *entire time?*"

"There's no need for hostility," Cosima said. "No one meant any harm—"

"Save the excuses, I know exactly who's at fault here." He stopped suddenly, his glare set on Leila.

Her heart pounded against Her rib cage. "I made My feelings clear."

"I won't stand for this. You've made a mockery of this tournament. And what, You were down there? *Healing* them?"

How does he know this? "Seemed only fair considering how much you've tortured them."

"Oh, don't You play that game with me, You little shit," he snapped. "This has *nothing* to do with those men. *Nothing.*"

A tremor rolled through Her. She took in a breath, cringing when it wavered.

"This ends now." He came in closer, grinding his teeth. "That is an order."

Leila steadied Herself. "No."

"It ends now!"

"You can control the tournament, but you cannot control how we choose to participate—"

"Dammit, You selfish *bitch*—"

His hand flew high, and Leila winced, bracing Herself for the hurt.

"Excuse me!" a man shouted.

Her eyes shot open. Brontes's hand had frozen in the air, and Tobias stood in the doorway, his shoulders squared.

"Apologies, I think I'm lost." Tobias's voice was firm and challenging. "Which way is the atrium again?"

Leila choked. She had summoned him. How much had he heard?

Another stiff smile spread across Cosima's lips. "Just down the corridor and to the right, dove."

Tobias nodded. "Thank You."

Silence. Brontes dropped his hand, but otherwise no one moved, the two men staring at one another.

"You heard Her." Brontes cocked his head at the doorway. "Atrium's on the right."

"Is something going on here?"

"None of your concern," Brontes said. Tobias's feet remained rooted, and Brontes's voice turned into a growl. "*Go*, Artist."

"I'd rather stay."

"*Leave.*"

Tobias stared at Leila for a long while before turning to Cosima. "Your Holiness, are You all right? You look uncomfortable."

Leila nearly whimpered in relief. He didn't know—at least not everything.

"I'm fine, Artist," Cosima said. "You're so kind to ask. My father was actually just leaving." She looked to Brontes. "Isn't that right?"

The fire in Brontes's expression turned to unbridled fury. He opened his mouth, ready to erupt—to destroy everything Leila had worked for.

A flicker of something crossed his gaze—something Leila didn't trust—and his lips flattened. He thrust his finger at Cosima. "You and I will exchange words."

Leila's stomach dropped. "But—"

"But *nothing*."

He stormed from the study, knocking into Tobias as he disappeared.

The red lingered, floating through the air before dissolving away. Brontes and his rage were gone. *Just like that?*

Why?

Cosima cleared her throat. "Well then, I should be off now."

She hurried from the room, cooing some nonsense to Tobias before rushing off. Pippa was next to leave, darting away as if fearful for her life, while Delphi lingered at Leila's side.

"We'll figure this out. We always do." She gestured toward Tobias, lowering her voice to a whisper. "I'll leave you two alone."

Leila barely felt her pull away. *Brontes knows.* She held Her face in Her hands, fighting to steady Her breathing. How could everything have gone so wrong so quickly?

"Leila... Are you all right?"

Tobias was waiting at Her side, his gaze probing.

"How much of that did you hear?" She said.

"How much did I hear? Leila, the Sovereign was going to *hit* you."

Her body ached for his comfort, but She kept still, kneading Her temples. "God... I have to go—"

"Wait. I've tried not to press the issue, but you need to tell me what's going on."

"Tobias—"

"What's happening?" he maintained. "You've said you're in danger. That the Sovereign's mad, that you're putting an end to his Senators. And now *this?* I have all these pieces, and none of them fit together. *Help me* put them together."

His words pierced through Her, ripe with pain. She shook Her head. "I can't."

"You *can.*"

"You don't understand. Everything has become infinitely worse, and I don't have time for this." Her thoughts turned feverish. "I have to... I have to fix this—"

His shoulders dropped. "Leila—"

"I'm sorry, I have to go."

"Leila, please—"

She hurried past him, charging down the corridor. Now wasn't the time. She had to make this right. Her first task was simple: kill the sniveling shit who had betrayed Her. She knew exactly who that man was.

Wembleton.

She ran through the palace, fire raging in Her lungs. Where had She seen him last? She climbed staircases and barged into rooms, while the blade on Her thigh called to Her, begging to carve through treacherous flesh. She wouldn't think twice this time. She headed down another corridor, and Her heart lurched.

Wembleton rounded the corner.

His gaze met Hers, and green snaked from his skin—the fetid fear of a traitor. Gritting Her teeth, Leila grabbed Her blade.

The clinking of metal plates and the marching of footsteps echoed off the walls. Guards came around the corner, their spears high as they followed the Senator.

Leila lowered Her weapon.

What is this?

The guards surrounded Wembleton, ushering him through the hallway, past Leila altogether. A soldier glanced Her way and nodded. "Your Holiness."

Wembleton's terrified stare didn't stray from Hers, his green cloud dense. He and his legion disappeared from sight, leaving Leila alone in the corridor, shaking with rage.

Brontes had paid for Wembleton's knowledge with muscle and steel.

Her breathing turned rampant. Were the guards always to accompany him? She wanted to scream, but She clamped Her jaw tight, charging down the corridor. If She couldn't kill Wembleton, She'd do something else. *What else? There's nothing to be done.* Still She moved, racking Her mind for a step forward, for some semblance of a plan. She had Her sisters, had Talos, had— Her eyes widened, and She dashed down an empty hallway.

To his chamber.

White-hot power burst within Her, and the blinding light gave way to brown walls, an emerald rug.

"Romulus," She said. "Something's happened..."

She halted. Romulus sat in a chair in the center of his chamber, his limp body tied down with rope, the front of his tunic saturated with blood.

His throat sliced open.

417

26

THE STORM

Romulus was dead.

Leila lay in Her bed, eyes on Her ceiling as his bloodstained robes plagued Her thoughts. She had long been buried in rotting corpses, but this one haunted Her, a ghost far more ominous than the ones in Her mirrors.

A knock sounded. Asher entered, and Leila gripped Her sheets as two armored guards joined him.

"What do you want?" She barked.

"They're here to escort You to Your Senate meeting," Asher said.

She loosened Her hold. Escorted by guards? And why a meeting? Given yesterday's revelation, She had assumed formalities were the least of Her father's concerns. Apprehensive, She followed the guards from Her chamber.

The servants stopped their work, staring pointedly as She and the soldiers trod by. News of Her ruse had spread past the Senate through the entire fortress, and within less than a day, everyone was aware of Her duplicity. She held Her head high, carrying Herself with the composure required of Her station, but everything within Her shrank beneath the piercing gazes.

The black door to the Senate room loomed ahead. Nodding, the guards ushered Her into the space, and when She caught sight of the five faces around the table, She tensed. An onslaught was sure to come.

"Your Holiness," Diccus said.

Frowning, Leila took Her seat. "Were the escorts necessary?"

Brontes ignored Her, shuffling his parchment. "Who calls this meeting?"

"I do."

"Second."

The quiet was stifling. Wembleton sat across from Leila avoiding Her gaze, though his reddened face offered Her some satisfaction. Hylas was seated at his side, his knee bobbing so fiercely he nearly shook the table.

"First line of discussion," Brontes said. "Sugar trade with Trogolia. Any word on the tariff negotiations?"

Leila sat up straight. *Sugar trade?*

"Trogolia agreed to your terms, Your Highness." Hylas choked out the words. "The mills will be notified shortly."

Brontes grunted through further questions—quotas, arbitrations, legalese tedious enough to lull a man to sleep. But Leila was wide awake, eyes darting between Her father, enraged just the day prior, and his former page, shaking in his seat as if he might wet himself at any moment.

"Next item." Brontes scribbled along his scroll. "The royals are to arrive on which day?"

"Pardon Me," Leila said. "I just…"

Brontes's gaze lifted from his parchment. "You just what?"

"Is this really what we're discussing today? Trade agreements?"

"Today's matters were listed in the agenda. What were You expecting?"

Leila scanned the table, searching the faces. Erebus and Diccus stared back at Her, while Wembleton and Hylas gazed into their laps.

Erebus's low voice tore through the room. "She thought we would discuss the switch, Your Highness."

"Right." Brontes's eye shrank into a glare. "The lie You've told to the entire realm."

"You seemed very angry about it the other day," Leila said.

"I'm still angry."

"His Highness sought council with the Senate," Diccus chirped. "After much discussion, we've agreed to keep Your title hidden, per Your request."

Leila started. "Come again?"

"It's what You want, yes?" Brontes growled. "To keep the competitors and Your realm in the dark? We're granting Your wish."

"Yes, but...why?"

Diccus smiled, revealing a mouthful of rotted teeth. "For the honor and glory of Her Holiness. Is that not enough reason?"

"For the lot of you? No, it isn't."

"Would You like us to change our minds?" Brontes said.

A knot wound in Leila's throat. "We can continue with the meeting."

Brontes let out a snort. "The neighboring realms?"

"They arrive in three days' time, Your Highness," Hylas said.

"Erebus." Brontes turned to the armored Senator. "The vault."

"The flow of coin is steady. Your payments have been sent in full. The vault will be in proper standing within the next few days." He toyed with the ring at his hip, passing each key between his thick fingers. A glint of silver caught the light, and Leila's eyes narrowed, boring through the steel wedged in the Senator's grasp.

"And the tournament?" Brontes said.

Wembleton coughed, stirring to life. "The competitors are to meet with...Cosima...in two days' time. The day prior to the Sovereign's Choice, it seems."

His gaze flitted between Brontes and his own lap, not once daring to venture Leila's way. Still She fixed Her stare on him, willing him to feel Her hatred.

Wembleton cleared his throat. "On the subject, I by no means intend to pressure you, Your Highness, but we will be needing your choice shortly."

"The Sovereign's Choice." Brontes leaned back in his seat, cracking his knuckles. "Who will I be sending home? Such a difficult decision."

Tobias. Leila gripped Her armrests.

Wembleton curled into himself. "I beg your pardon, Your Highness, but I am legally required to remind you...The Savior is to grant one competitor immunity from dismissal."

The tension in Leila's muscles dissipated, as did the smugness on Brontes's face. "A simple court girl has been parading as Her Holiness for the duration of this tournament," he said. "Should we bestow the privilege onto her?"

"You blaspheme Me?" Leila snapped.

"The ruse was Your decision. You blasphemed Yourself."

"How I choose to present Myself is My own concern. Regardless, *I* am The Savior, and thus *I* will choose which man is immune."

The table silenced, each man staring Her way. Wembleton squeaked out a response. "Your choice then, Y-Your Holiness?"

"The Artist. He stays."

"You've sentenced him to death," Brontes said. "When the time comes, his blood will be on Your hands."

Red fanned from his pores, filling the room with hatred.

"And your choice, Your Highness?" A whimper escaped Wembleton's lips. "Who will be dismissed from the tournament?"

"I'll think about it."

Raphael's face swept Leila's mind. Opportunity hovered in the air before Her, waiting for Her to snatch it up.

"If I may offer some pearls of wisdom," She said, "the Shepherd is far too fanciful for the crown. And those scars? Can you imagine the looks he'd receive?"

"My blessed ones will remain in the tournament," Brontes spat.

"Well then, if the decision were Mine—"

"It isn't."

"I'd send home the Prince."

Brontes faltered. "The Prince?"

"Did you see how he carried himself at the Welcoming? So cocksure, as if he'd already won the crown. I don't believe he respects you much at all."

"Since when do You care whether or not I'm respected?"

She shrugged. "I'm just saying. He seems the obvious choice. Or perhaps the Hunter. He's a kind man, but I question his intentions. I believe he pines for another."

"And not the Intellect? Why is that?"

"The Intellect? Which one is he again?" Leila flicked Her wrist. "Oh yes, the tall one. I'd nearly forgotten about him. He hasn't left much of an impression."

Brontes barely smirked. "I'm sure."

A smile nearly formed across Leila's cheeks, but She resisted. Brontes looked pleased with himself, as if he'd stumbled upon a secret, and that was exactly what She wanted—the tiniest victory.

Wembleton's nervous gaze flitted Leila's way before retreating to Her father. "If there isn't anything further, perhaps we can end things here, Your Highness? There's a challenge shortly. Archery, I believe. My presence is required."

Brontes nodded. "Yes. Mine as well."

"Yours?" Leila said. "For what purpose?"

"I'm the new Proctor. Or did You not get the message?"

Romulus's limp, haggard corpse. Leila forced back a shudder.

"Who ends this meeting?" Brontes barked.

"I do."

"Second."

The men filed from the room; Hylas raced through the doorway, and Leila cursed under Her breath as the guards grouped into formation, nestling Wembleton within their mass. *Never mind him.* She had more pressing concerns.

Brontes.

She left the Senate room, scanning the surrounding space for a speck of crimson. There—Brontes was already rounding a far-off corridor. She took the path he had traveled, watching him ignore the greetings of his servants, his head held high and drape proudly displayed as if he was worthy of it. She stopped at the base of the grand staircase, Her eyes not once leaving his person. He stood at the top, staring out the window at the courtyard below, wasting more of Her precious time.

A chortle bounced off the walls as a redhead passed by.

"Cosima," Leila said.

Cosima's eyes locked onto Leila, widening. "Leila. What a pleasant surprise."

"How are you?" Leila rushed to her side, eyeing her up and down. "Are you all right?"

"What do You mean?"

"Did he hurt you?"

"Dove, I'm fine."

Leila sighed. "Apologies, it's just...Brontes said he'd share words with you...and I know how ugly his temper can be."

"Look at me." Cosima stepped back, arms open. "Not a scratch. I'm perfectly well."

"What did he say?"

"Pardon?"

"When you met?" Leila lowered Her voice. "Did he say anything?"

"Nothing of note," Cosima said. "Just gave me a stern lecture. You know how fatherly types are."

"No. I don't."

Cosima smiled. "It's so kind of You to worry. My sweet sister, always fussing about. It was merely a scolding. I said my piece, he said his. I won't bore You with the details, they wouldn't serve You, I'm sure." She squeezed Leila's hands. "I must be off, but it was so good seeing You."

Cosima left in a hurry, floating away as if carried by a breeze, while Leila watched with Her hands wound tight. A stern lecture.

A lie—and not even a good one.

Dread bubbled in Leila's gut. She checked the window—Brontes was gone—and changed Her course, winding through corridors until She reached Her darkened study. Exhaling, She plopped down at Her desk. No more Romulus. No more Wembleton. Her father and the whole of Her staff knew of the switch. Her plan had been upended.

Stop it. Now wasn't the time to dwell over losses.

I have My sisters. Cosima slinked through Her thoughts, and She glowered. She'd deal with her later.

I have Talos. Shackled in a dungeon for twenty years.

I have Tobias. No, She wouldn't include him. He was in enough danger already.

To hell with allies. She'd thwart Brontes on Her own. The traitor within the palace walls—She'd find them Herself.

But what if there is no traitor, and Wembleton was biding his time? And why in God's name are they keeping My title a secret?

"Your Holiness?"

Leila jumped. Cecily stood in the doorway, her head cocked and hands clasped in front of her. "Apologies, I didn't mean to startle You."

"What are you doing here? These are private chambers."

Cecily's brow furrowed. "You've summoned me here many times before."

"I didn't summon you today."

"You missed Your fitting for tomorrow's banquet."

Heat flooded Leila's cheeks. "Right. That..."

"Mousumi said You've missed several appointments lately." Cecily closed the door behind her. "She was going to speak with You, but given the recent revelation, I offered to come instead. Save You the trouble. You know how she can be."

Leila said nothing, Her shoulders rigid. No one was beyond Her suspicion.

Cecily fished a roll of yarn from her pocket. "May I?"

Leila nodded, stiffening once Cecily reached Her side. The fitter worked in silence, circling Leila's bust and waist, while Leila festered in the awkward tension.

"I take it the entire staff knows?" She said.

"They were informed to keep up appearances. There are strict orders not to disclose Your true title to the competitors, per Your bidding."

Per Your bidding. Leila pursed Her lips. "I imagine you think I'm mad."

"You are Her Holiness, The Savior of Thessen. It is not my place to question Your decisions."

Leila remained tense, eyeing the woman sidelong as if she might draw a blade from her pocket.

"Pardon my intrusion," Cecily said, "but if the competitors don't know of Your title...I take it that includes the Artist as well?"

"It's a private matter."

"Child, I understand—"

"You don't," Leila snapped. Cecily's lips parted, and Leila's insides clenched. "Apologies."

"No, You're right. I *want* to understand, is all." Cecily swept Leila's hair over shoulder. "I know You have Your sisters, but...if You ever need a willing ear..."

"Are we finished?"

Cecily sighed. "Yes, Your Holiness." She gathered her things, then gave Leila a squeeze. "Better days are coming. I promise."

Warmth bled from Cecily's touch, a dreamy blend of orange and yellow—tenderness and affection, potent enough to thaw even the iciest of exteriors. Nodding, the fitter took leave, while guilt stirred in Leila's gut. *I'm just being cautious.* But the words did little to ease Her mind.

Pushing past Her self-reproach, She whipped out a reed, inked its tip, and procured a fresh slip of parchment. She had work to do.

She scrawled Her notes, heedless of the passing time, intent on making sense of Her mission. Her ruse was ruined, and Brontes was up to something—what, She hadn't a clue—but that didn't mean She was defenseless. She listed everything She was certain of.

Two assassins. One dead. She beamed, recalling Tobias skewering Antaeus in the stomach.

Assassination on My wedding night.

Brontes reclaims the crown after My—She grimaced—*husband is executed.*

Two Senators remain. No, *four Senators.* Poor Hylas. She wouldn't enjoy killing him at all.

An outside source. Kovahrian. The Queen? She'd sent a spy to the tournament after all, and was arriving shortly. Leila would have to watch her closely.

An inside traitor. Receiving jewels from Brontes. Likely a woman.

She bit the inside of Her mouth. *Link between Kovahr and the traitor?* She underlined the phrase, racking Her brain for something that never came.

Find the traitor. What else could She do?

She'd follow Brontes.

Now.

The door burst open, and Leila shoved Her parchment into a drawer and flew from Her seat. Delphi was already leaving, barking "Handle him" over her shoulder. She slammed the door, leaving behind a man.

Tobias.

His muscles were flexed, his hands balled into fists. Leila eyed him over—his rigid stance, his shallow breathing. "What happened?"

"Orion's dead."

An archery challenge. Orion was the greatest archer of them all.

"But how—?"

"It was Kaleo," he said. "It's *always* Kaleo."

Leila wilted. "Oh, Tobias..."

"I'm fine."

She reached for his hand. "Tobias—"

"Don't."

He ripped away from Her, and black tendrils tumbled from his flesh, stretching toward Her like the sickness beneath the soil. It'd been so long since his misery had appeared, but now it was alive again, refueled.

"I won't touch you, if that's what you want." She took a hesitant step forward. "But I know you, and forgive me, but I don't think you mean what you say." She came in closer, and his despair washed over Her, nearly forcing the air from Her lungs. "Tobias..."

Nothing. His face flushed red, his jaw locked tight as if to keep himself contained.

"You carry so much pain." She slid Her fingertips up his arm, taking in his torment. "Enough to crush any other man, but not you. You're always strong. Always being the man you need to be—the man everyone else needs you to be. But you don't need to be that man right now."

The blackness was everywhere, a night sky filling the chamber. He stood firm, avoiding Her gaze.

"That pain you carry? It'll weaken you. Day by day, it wears you down." She took his hand, threading Her fingers between his. "Release your burdens. Pour yourself out to me. If I can be nothing else, let me be your refuge."

Tears brimmed in his eyes, his lips still and silent. He shook his head.

"Tobias, hear me." She came in as close as he would allow. "There is no tournament. Not here in this room. You don't have to be strong. You don't have to be proud. You can be weak. You're with me. Do you think I won't protect you?" She searched his gaze. "Tobias..."

Silence—and then his tears broke free, releasing an explosion of black and blue. He cradled his face in his hands, but his colors already painted the walls, a crashing sea threatening to swallow him up.

Leila wrapped him in Her arms, immersing Herself in his torture, and Her heart throbbed as if it too were breaking. She led him to Her rose couch, pulling him into Her embrace, and as he sobbed on Her shoulder, She clung to him, fighting to absorb his hurt.

"I can't." His voice came out thick and rasping. "I can't keep watching my friends die."

Leila's chest ached. "I'm so sorry."

"I can't do it. I couldn't save Milo. I couldn't save Orion—"

"Their deaths are not your burden to bear."

"It's my fault," he said. "Kaleo was aiming for me. It was *my* end. Orion...he threw himself in front of me. He's dead, and it's my fault."

"Tobias—"

"It's my fault. I killed him."

"He made a choice," Leila maintained. "He acted with purpose—to let you live. Don't you dare for a second wear his decision as your own. He wouldn't want that."

She squeezed him tighter, though Her thoughts drifted back to the Senate meeting—to Her father's threats.

His blood will be on Your hands.

"I *hate* this tournament." Tobias's hands raked up Her back. "I *hate* the Sovereign. I *hate* The *fucking* Savior."

Leila cringed. "Tobias..."

"My friends *died* for Her. She's The Savior, and She does *nothing*."

"It's beyond Her control—"

"Dammit, just let me hate Her," he spat. "*Please. I need to hate Her. The Sovereign. All of it. I need to."

Pain surged within Leila, but She said nothing.

"Everything is fucked, and I can't fix it," he said. "The people I care for...they're dead. And if they're not dead, they're suffering." He shook his head. "My sister will never walk again. She'll never be happy again. I try, but no matter what I do, I can't fix it."

"You do more than you know."

His hand sifted through Her hair, tugging Her close. "I will never have you."

Leila faltered. "Tobias?"

He stared at the floor. "The way I feel about you... Each day, I fall harder. And all it does is put you in greater danger."

"That's not true."

"Don't lie to me."

"Tobias, look at me." She took his face in Her hands, willing him to meet Her gaze. "My life is complicated. I've fought for everything I have, it's all I've known. But when I'm with you, I feel safe and seen for the first time since I can remember. Do you hear me? You are a *blessing*."

His gaze was penetrating, his lashes slick and eyes spiderwebbed red. Sighing, he rested his head against Hers, and She glided Her fingers up the nape of his neck, stroking back and forth.

"Leila?"

"Yes?"

"Is the Proctor dead?"

She froze. "Yes."

Long seconds passed, the silence screaming in Her ears.

"Did you kill him?" Tobias asked. "I won't judge, but I need to know—"

"I didn't kill him. I hated the man...but I needed him alive."

"Then who was it?"

Thunder rumbled within Her. "Brontes."

Tobias took in a slow, wavering breath. "You weren't supposed to be in the labyrinth. You weren't supposed to be healing us."

"No. I wasn't."

"Why'd you do it?"

"It started out for specific reasons." She stiffened, forcing out the words. "Then my reasons...changed."

Tobias sank into Her arms. The harsh shades of his misery had been reduced to a bruise, patches of black and blue floating in the air.

"Has the storm cleared?" She whispered. He nodded. "How are you feeling?"

"Like shit," he grumbled.

"Tobias, my darling..." Leila went rigid. Was that too forward? Too soon? "Apologies," She murmured.

"Why?" His head perked up. "I like how it sounds—being yours. Say it again."

She hesitated. "My darling."

He pressed his lips to Hers, kissing Her hard before taking Her face in his hands. "You. Are. *Everything.* Do you understand? Whatever happens to me, I need you to know that. Tell me you understand."

"I understand."

His breathing was haggard, his face raw and red. As She wiped the tears from his cheeks, his gaze flitted away. "This is embarrassing," he muttered.

"Why? You cry, and thus you're human? I've seen you bleed. I already knew you were human. It was no secret."

"What you said before—it's a lie. I'm not strong. I feel myself breaking."

"Enough." Leila threaded Her fingers between his. "You are the strongest man I've ever known. And you're kind. And you're good. You are bruised by this tournament, but you are not broken."

"I don't know how much more of this I can take. Another blow, another burden, and God, I think I'll lose it. I can't take anymore. I can't."

Leila's throat tightened. This tournament, Tobias's suffering—it was all for Her. Whether directly or not, She carried the blame.

Tobias scowled. "Stop it."

"What?"

"Whatever you're doing. The guilt is etched across your face. Whatever the worry, abandon it."

She chewed Her lip. "Is there something that soothes you? Something to make it better? Anything—"

"You."

The word loosened every knot in Her body. "Then know that you have me."

As She sifted Her hand through his curls, he closed his eyes, his chest rising with a long, deep breath. "Can we stay here for a while?" he whispered.

Brontes. She was to follow him tonight. Then Tobias snaked his arms around Her waist, and the misery in the air shrank ever so slightly.

"For as long as you'd like, my darling."

THE GALLERY

"The entire wall, Your Holiness?"

"The whole thing."

"Empty?"

"Yes." Leila flicked Her wrist at the opposite end of the room. "Move them over there. Make the space."

The servants bowed before bustling through the gallery, peppering the gold and marble with their white linen dresses. Leila had spent all morning following Brontes, and when that proved fruitless, She moved on to more immediate tasks. For now, that meant the gallery, Her favorite room in the palace, one She used to frequent before the tournament began. Funny, She hadn't realized how much She missed it: the prized jewels in glass cabinets, the polished statues, the pottery, busts, and ancient coins. All of it was captivating, even if She'd already seen each piece a hundred times. But Leila didn't come for the trinkets. She came for the paintings.

"You're certain You want them moved?" A stocky servant waddled Leila's way, a large framed portrait hoisted onto her back. "Won't it look...imbalanced?"

"It is My will and order."

"Perhaps a few guards can help us?"

"No," Leila snapped. Containing Herself, She forced a smile. "Apologies, I believe they're with Erebus at the moment."

"All of them?"

"Leila?" Damaris walked into the space with Raphael at her side. "You summoned him?"

A hush fell over the gallery, the servants staring at the Intellect in confusion. No doubt they had expected the Artist. Leila hooked Raphael's arm. "Walk and talk?"

She dragged him off before he could refuse. Heading down the corridor, She nodded at passing staff only for them to look away.

"Everyone's been acting strange lately," Raphael said. "Did something happen?"

Leila scanned the space, searching. "You could say that."

"It's as though someone died. Well, someone *did* die, but even before then..." His eyes widened. "Oh my God, did someone *else* die?"

"Romulus."

"Who?"

"The Proctor. He's dead." Her shoulders tightened. "That's why everyone's so grim. No other reason."

"How's Tobias?"

Leila turned toward him. "Pardon?"

"After Orion's passing. I imagine he took it very hard."

"He did."

Raphael chewed his lip. "Is there anything I can do?"

"Can you resurrect a man?"

"Can *You* resurrect a man? I mean, You're The—"

"I can't bring the dead to life, Raph."

"It was worth asking. Why did You summon me anyhow?"

Leila's eyes flitted across the palace, locking onto a single man. Her feet slammed to a halt at the base of the grand staircase. "I've summoned you for this." She took Raphael's hands. "Right here."

Raphael glanced between Her face, Her hands, then Her face again. "You're not going to kiss me, are You?"

"No," She said. "We're going to stand here, gazing into one another's eyes."

"I...don't follow."

"Just gaze into my eyes, Raph."

"But—"

"Smile, while you're at it."

Raphael forced a strained smile, his dimples Her only consolation. She glanced sidelong at the top of the staircase, where Brontes stood looking out the window.

"Say something funny," She whispered.

"What?"

Leila laughed theatrically, throwing Her head back. Another glimpse, and Brontes was staring at them, his one eye narrowed. *Victory.* Holding Her grin, She rested a palm on Raphael's cheek, ignoring the clamminess of his skin. Raphael forced a few hoarse chuckles, but it didn't matter; Brontes gave the pair one last look before stalking off.

Sighing, Leila dropped Her hands. "Congratulations. You're free of the Sovereign's Tournament."

"What?" Raphael watched Brontes disappear. "Right now?"

"Not now. But in two days' time, you will be the Sovereign's choice."

"Because of this?" he said. "I don't see how—"

"Brontes doesn't want any man in My favor to win the tournament. So long as we are seen together in any sort of affectionate manner, you will be free."

Raphael released a long breath, leaning onto his knees as if rid of a massive weight. "I take it You've given Tobias immunity? I imagine he'd be Brontes's first choice otherwise."

"You're free, Raph. Isn't that what you wanted?"

He hesitated. "Yes. Thank You. I just... Thank You."

Tense and fidgeting, he studied the place by the window where Brontes once stood. Leila crossed Her arms. "What?"

"Why does Your father not want You to marry a man of Your choosing? All we did was stand here, holding hands, and that's enough to have me freed."

Servants and staff passed, whispering. Leila faltered. "You should go."

"Is something...wrong...between You and the Sovereign?"

"I've hidden My identity for the entirety of this tournament, and you're now just asking Me this? After threatening to reveal My truth?"

"Well, I've been concerned with my own wellbeing."

Heat rose through Leila's veins. "There's a banquet soon. I must prepare."

"Leila, You can tell me—"

"*Go.* That is an order."

Raphael opened his mouth but didn't speak. His eyes flitted over the passing servants and their piercing gazes, as if he was piecing a fraction of the puzzle together.

"I wish You luck in Your endeavors," he said. "I wish... I suppose it doesn't matter."

He trudged off, regret trailing in his wake.

At some point servants hauled Her away, preparing Her in near-silence before the banquet began. The atrium was sparkling, each golden place setting impeccably polished, reflecting the candlelight like blinking stars. It would've looked grand had it not been for the sour faces surrounding the dining table, each one either pointed down at their lap or at Leila, judging Her.

She sat at the end of the table with Her sisters like always, but this time the competitors were seated among them, and Cosima sat in Leila's throne. Mousumi hadn't questioned the request. Instead, She had bowed and taken her order, though the scorn was clear in her pursed lips. Cosima was ornamented like a queen, a crown on her head and a much-too-eager smile plastered across her face.

Grey wafted through the air like smoke. Tobias sat at Leila's side, handsome in his black drape, but his vacant gaze spoke volumes. Leila wasn't the only one struggling through the day. Beneath the table, She slid Her hand into his, squeezing until the cloud around him shrank in size.

Wembleton stood, his guards at attention behind him, and raised his chalice. "Esteemed staff of the palace of Thessen, thank you for joining us for this fine banquet. In just a few days, we will welcome our royal guests from beyond our glorious realm, and so it gives your Sovereign the greatest pleasure to share this feast with you." He gestured toward the end of the table, hands trembling once his gaze met Leila's. "Before you sit Her Holiness, Her court, and Her final five competitors. Tonight we honor them and their dedication to the Sovereign's Tournament. May the best man win."

A few people nodded, while others cleared their throats. The tension was consuming, and Leila prayed for something to pull focus away from Her lies.

Tobias lurched up from his seat, staggering as all heads turned his way. For a second his cloud evaporated, his cheeks bright pink.

"Apologies," he muttered, slinking back into his seat.

Confusion festered within Leila before She plunged Her hand into his, its resting place for most of the evening. Eager to be rid of the stares, She ate quickly, then slipped away, excitement fluttering in Her chest.

Rounding the table, She leaned toward one of Her servants. "A moment of your time?"

Damaris's head popped up from her dinner plate, and she followed Leila out of the atrium. "How can I assist You?"

"The Artist. Once the feast is over, summon him for Me."

"Yes, Your Holiness. To Your study again?"

Leila shook Her head. "The gallery."

She paced amid the artwork for far too long, restless energy rattling Her bones. When footsteps echoed down the corridor, She yanked the door open, pulling Tobias close and throwing Herself into his kiss. The past few days had been a battlefield, war-torn and ugly, but Tobias's smile—the first She'd seen all day—was beautiful.

Locking the gallery door, She took his hand. "Come."

She led him through the space while his eyes climbed the walls. "What is this?" he asked.

"The gallery. Filled with the finest pieces in Thessen. Wonderful, isn't it? Here, let me show you." She stopped in front of a large, greyish painting. "This is—"

"*The Wretched*, by Alena Tantas," he said.

"Of course you know. I should've guessed."

"She was one of my favorites when I was younger. I liked the dark works." He gestured toward a far more colorful piece of a lovers' embrace. "And this is—"

"*The Devoted,* by Demetrius Shaya. A depiction of him with his wife."

Leila reveled in his impressed smirk before taking in the work around them. A glass case filled with crystal animals of Northern Thessen stood against the wall, and in its translucent reflection was a man with long hair, a full beard, and a yellow-wrapped bundle in his arms. *Orion.* He caught Leila's gaze and smiled, giving Her a glimpse of his armload—a raven-haired baby, fast asleep.

"What are you looking at?"

Tobias stared at Her as if he'd been speaking the entire time.

"Hm?" Leila said. "Oh, nothing. Come, over here."

She dragged him through the room, stopping once they'd reached the newest edition to the gallery. *Mother.* She hadn't seen this piece since Her birthday. Tobias's eyes canvased each spot of color, each dab and stroke.

"This is Petros's work," he said.

"A true apprentice. You recognized his mark straightaway."

"I recognize it because I assisted."

Leila spun toward him. "You did?" She pointed to the piece. "This is your work?"

"Just parts."

"Which parts?"

"Not many." He shrugged. "The trees, the flowers, the village, the sky..."

"So everything, essentially."

"Everything but The Savior." He came in closer, eyes locked on the painted woman. "He said he had a specific vision—that he needed to see it through in full. God, he had been working on this for years. I had no idea this was for the palace."

"Petros didn't tell you?"

"He never told me where any of our pieces went. Said it would spoil my mind, that I should work with heart and purpose regardless of where the painting was headed. I just never thought I'd see one...here. Then again, I never thought I'd be here in the first place."

Leila took in the awe of his gaze. *Her favorite.* Both the painting and the man.

"When did this arrive?" he asked.

"Not even a month ago."

"Savior's Day?"

She faltered. "It was a birthday gift."

"Well, that's unfortunate. A gift for Cosima..."

A sting lanced through Her. "When I first saw it...it took my breath away."

"Then I take comfort in that, knowing you enjoy it." A true smile spread across his face, though it melted soon after. "Leila, there's something I need to tell you. I fear it'll ruin the moment, but it wouldn't be right not to mention it."

"What is it?"

"There's only six days left in this tournament...and I've been told that I'm favored."

"So I've heard." Leila chuckled. "The *Giant Slayer*. The *Keeper of Kin*."

His gaze drifted. "What if this favor includes The Savior?"

"Oh, I wouldn't concern yourself with that."

"I hadn't planned to, but then we had that banquet, and Cosima grabbed my leg beneath the table."

Leila whipped toward him, nearly toppling over. "She did *what*?"

"She grabbed my leg," he said. "My thigh. She squeezed it."

"You're certain."

"I nearly choked on my damn food."

Panic took hold of Her. "What kind of squeeze? Like a friendship squeeze? Maybe it was a friendship squeeze."

"She was a hair shy of my balls."

It couldn't be. Cosima hadn't an interest in Tobias. She had made that clear.

Tobias's face dropped. "I'm not trying to upset you."

"I just don't understand. I don't see why She would..." The words died in Leila's throat. Cosima had been behaving strangely for days. What exactly had changed?

Brontes.

"So...She doesn't favor me?" Tobias said. "She's never said anything?"

"No," Leila barely whispered.

THE SAVIOR'S SISTER

"Then maybe it was nothing. A fleeting impulse, gone in an instant." Tobias took a step closer. "I don't want Her. I just had to tell you..."

"I know. I'm glad you did. Thank you." Leila forced the worries aside. She had brought Tobias here for a reason. Cosima wasn't going to sour that. "I nearly forgot. I have a surprise for you."

"Another?"

Grabbing his wrists, She pulled him through the gallery, stopping in front of Her grand creation: an empty wall.

"Right here." She planted Her hands on Her hips. "What do you think?"

Tobias furrowed his brow. "It's a wall."

"Yes. For you."

"You got me a wall?"

"For your paintings," She said. "It's the best spot in the room, wouldn't you agree? I moved some of the pieces so your art can be the focal point for all to see. Your sketches are in my chamber. I'm keeping them to myself. But anything else—any future pieces—they can go right here. And everyone in the palace can admire them whenever they please."

"You did this for me?"

"Of course. Well, it's mostly for me, to be honest. So I can stare at your art all the time. It's a selfish endeavor, truly—"

Tobias pulled Her close and kissed Her hard. Speckles of orange and pink poured from his touch, flowing through Her like sugar and honey. *Happiness*. She had done that.

As their lips parted, he spoke against Her cheek. "Thank you."

"It's just a wall."

"For everything. For all you've done for me. I feel like an ass. I have nothing to give to you in return."

She waved him away. "Oh, that's all right. I have plenty of walls already."

"Then tell me, what do you want? Whatever it is, I'll do it."

"Stay alive."

He chuckled. "I'll try my best. I think I'm managing all right thus far."

"Fill the wall. So I have something beautiful to admire."

"Of course. What else?"

Her throat caught. "Be good to me."

A cheeky grin spread across his face. "Leila, are you not the most demanding woman I've ever met? God, these requests." He basked in Her laughter, kissing Her bottom lip. "I'll be good to you, my darling."

She sank into his arms. "I want to show you something."

"There's more?"

She was already pulling him across the space, winding between statues. "The wall of scrolls. Poems, epics, all legendary." Compartments descended from the ceiling to the floor, and She snatched up a single piece from one of them. "Are you familiar with the work of Karti?"

"Of course," Tobias said. "Who isn't?"

"This is 'The Warrior's Chant.'"

"That's one of his greatest pieces."

Leila smiled. "It's my favorite."

"Well, you're lucky to have a copy. They're hard to come by."

"Copy?" Leila snorted. "This is the original."

Tobias's eyes shot wide. "You lie."

"I do no such thing. Care to look?"

"Are you *joking*? I can't touch it! My filthy peasant hands. No, I'm unworthy."

"Go on," She said. "You know you want to."

"You're mad. I can't."

Leila tossed the scroll into his grasp, and he gaped at Her, gobsmacked. "Leila! What if I dropped it?"

"It's parchment. It's not going to shatter. Go on, open it."

He cast Her a critical look, then slowly, gently unrolled the scroll. "Oh my God."

"Isn't it glorious?"

"This is the original." His eyes panned the text. "This is the bloody fucking original."

"I said that already, you know."

"There are scribbles in the margin and everything. Look, he misspelled *sanguinary*."

"You like it?" She asked.

"*Like* it? People would *kill* to see this." He raised an eyebrow. "Are you going to get into trouble?"

"For what?"

"I don't know. For fiddling with palace property."

Leila's lips flattened. "Tobias, this is mine."

"This is *yours*?"

"I get gifts sometimes."

"Gifts like *this*?"

She nodded, giggling into Her hands. "Do you want to see more?"

His eager gaze spoke volumes, and She scoured the scrolls, snatching up famed pieces, historic lore. Once the stack of parchment was nearly too much to manage, She dropped it to the floor.

"You're making a mess!" Tobias laughed.

"Oh, hush up, I know where they go." She took a seat in front of the pile, patting the spot at Her side. "Come. Sit."

Tobias obeyed, while She displayed each prized piece. "This is 'The Hero's Escape.' And this is 'Reclaiming the Crown'—"

"*No*." He snatched the parchment from Her hands. "Original?"

"Not original, but penned in her very own ink."

"Original enough." He locked onto another slip. "Oh my God, is this the *Epic of Ethyua*? Fucking hell, this was my favorite growing up. Had it memorized—I still do, I'm certain." Laughing, he read over the text. "This is madness."

He fawned over each poem and fable—pieces Leila had dissected since childhood, but never with this passion, this love. She took in a long breath, holding it in Her chest—clean and pure. Tobias's cloud was gone. No darkness. No misery.

Tobias's gaze strayed from the epics to Her, tracing Her jaw. Without a word, he tugged Her onto his lap and kissed Her.

"What was that for?" She said.

"I know what you're doing. Thank you."

"I just hate to see you sad."

He nuzzled against Her cheek. "You make it difficult to remain sad for long."

Her gut twisted. "I won't be seeing you tomorrow. You're to spend the day with Cosima. All five of you."

"Well then, if I don't get to see you, I suppose we'll have to make the evening count, yes?"

His words sent chills rolling through Her, and then his lips did the same. He took Her face in his hands, and She could've sworn his gaze penetrated past Her flesh, a balm against every bruise and scar, the bloodshed, the lies.

He cleared his throat. "All right then, back to the epics."

Chuckling, Leila swatted him on the arm, nestling into his lap as they scoured the pieces together.

~

"He's not doing anything," Delphi said.

"Quiet," Leila muttered.

"It's been hours."

"*Quiet.*"

The two sisters lay on their bellies, peering between the balusters of the second story. The passing servants stared at them, their brows twisted in confusion. Perhaps Leila should've been more discreet, but She wasn't hiding from Her staff—She was hiding from Brontes standing in the entryway below.

He'd been speaking with that guard for ages, going over slips and scrolls—trivial matters reserved for Senators, though there were considerably fewer of them as of late. She narrowed Her eyes, trying to bore through him, to read his mind. Maybe She'd discover the traitor that way, since all Her other attempts had failed.

A servant snorted as she walked by, eyeing the sisters as if they'd sprouted horns. With a huff, Delphi stood upright. "This is ridiculous. You're a queen, yet You have us sneaking around like roaches."

"You're not taking this seriously at all."

"Because nothing has happened," Delphi said. "Your father's broken his fast, he visited his study, he's looked out the damn window—"

Leila clambered to Her feet. "This sort of work takes *time*."

"Wembleton is a worm. He was exploiting Your paranoia for his own gain."

"You think I'm *paranoid?*"

"There is no traitor. Not within these walls. We've been following Your father all day, and nothing."

Leila shook Her head. "I can't accept that."

Sighing, Delphi straightened her dress. "I'm leaving."

"But I need you—"

"You *need* to take care of the Senators." Delphi lowered her voice. "We've done what we can. Your father and the Kovahrian Queen are in league. It's clear as day. End this now so we can get on with our lives."

She flipped her braids over her shoulder and headed off, leaving Leila rattled. Growling, She stared down at Her father. *Do something, you worthless sack of—*

Laughter echoed off the walls. Cosima waltzed down the entryway, her suitors—*Leila's* suitors—trailing behind her. The men of the tournament were to spend the day touring the palace with The Savior Herself, though only Flynn appeared interested, the others trudging along in the most lackluster fashion. Leila nearly reveled in their distaste until Cosima and Brontes locked eyes, nodding at one another before Cosima disappeared with her gaggle down the corridor.

Brontes headed in the opposite direction, and Leila flew through the hallway, keeping the man in sight.

As She followed Her father, Her confidence withered. Brontes's activities were innocuous, and Leila found Herself wondering what kind of ruler had nothing to do but wander and talk. *You wander. You talk.* But that was different; She'd been stripped of Her power. Meanwhile Brontes spent an eternity with Erebus, sharing military stats of little importance; then discussed the arrival of the royals with Wembleton, who remained shielded by his legion of guards. No secret meetings, no traitors, at least none Leila wasn't already aware of.

Brontes made his way up the grand staircase straight toward Leila, and She darted behind a column, peering around it. Her father stopped by the window at the top of the steps, leaning against its frame while staring out at the courtyard. Again.

Delphi was right. This was useless.

Brontes plodded off, but this time, Leila didn't follow. She sank to the floor, grumbling to Herself. Five days—that was all that remained of the tournament, all She had left to uncover Her father's network. She had wasted Her time following him from room to room, watching him scribble across scrolls, converse with Senators, and God, how often did he have to look out that window?

The window.

Leila bolted upright, racing to the window in question. Was the courtyard really that interesting? She pressed Her hands to the glass, searching the view. Nothing about the courtyard was unfamiliar or different, so She studied the window itself, its glass and panes. Nothing. Desperation clawed at Her as She dragged her fingers along the frame— cool, polished metal. Then something rough.

Parchment.

The frayed corner barely stuck out from behind the pane. Pulling the parchment slip free, She unfolded it with trembling hands.

Plans have changed. Meet soon. Wait for my word.

A bitter blend of anger and validation spun within Her. Her shaking turned violent as She stuffed the note back into its hiding place.

Someone—*the traitor*—was waiting for this note. And She would be waiting for them.

She rushed down the corridor, leaning against a nearby pillar, hoping the mass of marble would shield Her. As She waited, Her eyes danced between the hallway, the window, Her nails, the window, the ends of Her hair, the window. Each time a servant or guard walked by, She stiffened, waiting for them to pause at the window, to run their hand along its pane. Nothing. Restless energy flurried within Her, but She held firm, eyes trained on the spot where Her father's note was tucked away.

"Your Holiness."

She spun toward the voice—a woman, eyes narrowed, lips in a straight line. "Yes, Mousumi." Leila exhaled. "Make haste."

Mousumi's gaze strayed. "Why are You waiting here, staring at the windowpane?"

"I'm not staring at the windowpane, I'm...admiring the courtyard."

"You've been here a long while."

Leila scowled. "Have you been watching Me this entire time?"

"Your presence is quite evident, if You weren't yet aware."

Leila's scowl deepened. A throng of servants hurried around the corner, catching up to Mousumi as if she'd left them behind.

"Your Holiness," Mousumi raised an eyebrow, "a word while You...do whatever it is You're doing."

"I haven't the time."

"The royals arrive tomorrow. I am under order by the Sovereign to make relevant arrangements with You regarding their stay. To shirk Your duties would be highly inappropriate."

The servants behind Mousumi whipped out scrolls and reeds, their eyes wide and eager. Leila swallowed Her protests. "Fine. Walk with Me."

The servants kept pace at Her side, their eyes on their parchment while Hers actively searched. *Delphi.* If She couldn't wait for the traitor, She could at least find Her sister, could have her keep watch instead. Mousumi dove into her instructions, rambling about guest quarters and banquets, none of which held Leila's attention. Soon they reached the atrium, and Leila stopped in Her tracks. Cosima and a handful of the competitors sat at the dining table drinking wine and picking at fruit— save for Drake and Kaleo, who stood off with Brontes, whispering in the shadows.

"Your Holiness?"

Leila cast a critical look Mousumi's way, and the servant keeper returned it with vigor. "Apologies, *Leila.* Your guests are expected to arrive at staggered intervals, but once they're comfortably accommodated, Your father and sister will greet them with a proper welcoming—"

"My sister?" Leila lowered Her voice. "I didn't realize we were keeping My title from the neighboring royals as well."

"We are simply honoring Your request."

Dread turned in Her gut. She glanced across the atrium where Her father once stood, but he was gone.

Her breath caught. Tobias was staring at Her, and Her heart beat faster.

"Provided You're comfortable with these orders, all You'll have to do is avoid drawing attention to Yourself. Which seems to be Your preference." Mousumi rolled up her scroll, and the other servants followed suit. "Do these terms suit You, Leila?"

"Yes, thank you."

Mousumi started to bow, then faltered, offering Leila a nod instead. Eager to be free, Leila hurried away, adamant in Her purpose. *Find Delphi.*

She threw open the doors to the gallery, giving it a quick once-over. *Dammit.* She had hoped She'd find Her sister picking over the scrolls as she often did, but all that awaited was silence. Leila nearly frowned, but Her eyes landed on that empty wall, and She smiled instead.

The doors shut behind Her, and She turned around.

Drake stood paces away.

A chill rolled through Her. Had She ever spoken to the man? He hadn't seemed to notice Her before, but now She couldn't escape his beady gaze.

"You're lost," Leila said. "Cosima's in the atrium."

Drake didn't move. Tensing, Leila stood tall. "Cosima isn't—"

"I'm not looking for Cosima." His voice shocked Her, low and gravely. He took a step forward. "I'm looking for The Savior."

Ice spiked through Leila's veins. She grabbed the sheath on Her thigh, but not soon enough. Drake lunged at Her, moving with a grace and speed that contradicted his bulky frame. She dodged, but his hands connected with Her, grabbing Her shoulders and driving Her backward.

Her spine cracked against the wall, sending Her crumpling. She scrambled for Her blade, thrusting it forward only for Drake to snatch up Her wrists and throw Her against a table. Glass shattered beneath Her, and Her stomach lurched when Her blade fell to the floor.

Before She could cry out, Drake grabbed Her throat, wrenching Her from the table and pounding Her against the wall. Aches pulsed through Her, muted compared to the pull of Her lungs. Shadow walking was impossible, not when She couldn't channel Her light, couldn't even breathe. She clawed at his grip, Her mouth open wide as She fought for air that never came.

Shards of ceramic burst over Drake's head, and he staggered away, dropping Leila to the floor. She gasped for breath, black speckling Her vision, Her ears ringing with chaos—fists slamming into hard flesh, bodies crashing into walls. It wasn't until red splattered Her dress that the madness took form; Drake's mouth was stained with blood, and across from him stood Tobias, lit with rage.

He swung at Drake once, twice. The Dragon wove between his assaults, then latched onto Tobias's throat.

"Stop it!" Leila bolted to Her feet. *Do something.* But She had nothing —no maneuvers, not even a weapon.

Tobias launched his knee into Drake's gut, breaking his hold. He slid to the floor, plucking up something from the strewn glass—Leila's blade. With one quick blast, he swung the knife at the Dragon, slicing the assassin's ear from his temple.

Drake's scream ripped through the gallery, his ear tumbling to the floor with a piteous splat. Tobias passed the blade from hand to hand, preparing to make his next kill.

Faun burst into the room. "What the—?" She glanced over the shards and blood. "What's going on? I heard screaming."

Drake stood firm, as if he weren't clinging to his own earless head. Tobias stared at Leila, willing Her to say something, but there was nothing. She was frozen.

"Should I alert the Sovereign?"

Faun's words stirred Leila. "No, no, everything's fine."

"Everything's *not* fine," Tobias said.

"Everything's *fine*. The Dragon was just leaving."

Leila glared at Drake, forcing back a shudder once his sinister gaze met Hers. Growling, Drake plucked his ear from the floor and trudged from the gallery.

Leila turned to Faun. "Not a word to the Sovereign."

"Leila..."

"Promise Me."

Faun's frown spoke for her, and Leila hardened Her tone. "*Promise Me.*"

Faun glanced to Tobias, as if she was awaiting his rebuttal, then sighed. "I'll fetch Damaris. We'll take care of the mess."

As she left the room, Tobias came to life. "My God, are you all right?"

He took root at Leila's side, pulling Her close. She knew it was happening, yet She could hardly feel it, his touch a whisper, Her skin cold and numb.

"Leila?"

"I'm all right," She said.

"Are you sure?"

"I'm fine." She broke free from his hold. "You should go."

"*Go?*" He scanned Her over. "Leila, you're bleeding."

Pain cut through the numbness—the sting of Her shoulder, the ache of Her throat. She had tasted blood before, but never like this. Never this close.

"It's all right," She said. "Go back to Cosima."

"Are you mad? I'm not leaving you like this."

"Tobias, just go."

"Like hell."

He scooped Her from the floor, gathering Her in his arms.

"Tobias! What are you doing?"

"I'm taking care of you whether you like it or not."

He barreled from the gallery with Leila tucked in his embrace. She hadn't a clue where they were headed, though the wonder drowned beneath the screaming of Her thoughts. The heat of Drake's hands was fresh on Her throat, and everything within Her longed to claw at Her flesh, to rub it clean until no trace of him remained. Instead She clung to Tobias, unmoving save for Her firing heartbeat.

She wasn't in his arms any longer. She sat on a rose couch while Tobias probed through desk drawers. Her study. When had they arrived in the first place?

"What are you doing?"

"I'm looking for your potions," he said.

"Tobias..."

"You're bleeding. I'm taking care of you."

Sighing, She urged Herself to move, plucking a few vials and a rag from a nearby shelf—left behind by servants, no doubt—and taking Her place on the couch. Tobias sat behind Her, studying the vials as She handed them off.

"What is this?"

"Water," She mumbled. "And mint soap."

"Leila, this isn't—"

"It's fine."

The throbbing of Her shoulder cut through the numbness—the

injury, She assumed. She pulled the straps of Her dress down Her arms, exposing Her from neck to navel. Perhaps at another time this would've felt bold, but not now. There was only cold. Pain.

Tobias spoke against Her cheek. "Tell me if I'm hurting you, all right, darling?"

He lingered close, waiting for a response that never came. Gently, he wetted Her shoulder—sharp, stinging. It must've been the glass. She tried to focus on each pang and wipe, but Her mind was wrapped up in far more grueling tortures.

Back in the gallery, She had nearly died. She had been helpless.

"You're quiet," Tobias said.

Leila forced Herself to speak. "I'm thinking."

"About what?"

"I've gotten you involved in such a mess."

"I believe I did it to myself."

She shook Her head. "You didn't."

"I entered the tournament." His voice came out firm. "I drew those pictures of you. I asked to kiss you. I did it, Leila. Me."

I'm only alive because of him. How could She protect Tobias if She couldn't protect Herself?

"I'd do it all again, you know," he said. "I have no regrets."

"It's so stupid. I could hardly defend myself."

"I don't understand."

"I've trained for this." She choked over the words. "I've trained for years. And then the time comes, and...I'm a fool. Disarmed in seconds. I failed."

"Drake is a mercenary, easily three times your size. There was nothing you could do."

"I was pathetic."

"You can't possibly blame yourself for what happened." Tobias waited in strained silence. "Leila, speak to me."

The pain dulled to a steady ache. Tobias had stopped cleaning Her shoulder. A part of Her yearned for the soothing power of his touch, though it wouldn't do much good now. This wound cut too deep.

"Have you finished?" She whispered.

"Yes."

447

Disappointment laced his words. Still She said nothing, sliding Her straps into place. She wasn't empty any longer; something was filling Her up, turning Her veins from ice to fire, blackening Her from the inside. She had felt this before as a child. So many years had passed, and She was still lost.

"I know you don't want to hear this," Tobias said, "but you need to tell someone what happened."

Leila's chest clenched. "Tobias..."

"Something has to be done. Drake needs to be removed from the palace—"

"Just stop."

"I'm begging you, you have to tell Cosima—"

"Cosima is *nothing*," She spat. "She is *useless*."

Tobias hesitated. "And Brontes... He isn't an option?"

A pang shot through Her, the sharpest blow of them all. "God, I don't even want to hear his name. Please, don't ever speak it again."

"Do you think he had something to do with this?"

"I *know* he did."

The blackness within Her erupted. She balled Her hands into fists, fighting for composure, but Her hatred poured forth in tears, rolled through Her body in trembles and shakes.

"I am so *sick* of feeling powerless. Of having no control." She gritted Her teeth. "This is my home. I should feel *free*. I should feel *safe*. This is my *fucking home*, and yet I am a *prisoner*."

Tobias grabbed Her arms and pressed his lips to Her neck. "Leila darling, breathe. Come to me. Let me hold you."

She turned toward him, nestling into his lap. Incapable. Weak.

His fingers swept through Her hair, his voice gentle against Her skin. "Right now, you are free. Right now, you are safe."

"I've made so many mistakes." Her throat thickened with sobs. "Everything I've worked for...it's crumbling around me. And all I can do is watch."

"Whatever your troubles, know they're not yours alone. Tell me what to do, and I'll do it. If you need me to pick up the pieces. If you need me to stand by your side as you watch it all crumble. Whatever it is, I'll do it. I'm your man."

"I don't deserve your kindness."

"Leila, that is the single dumbest thing I've ever heard you say."

She buried Her face into his chest. *You are free. You are safe.* Because of him.

"You are everything. You remember?" he said. "For as long as I'm living, I'll take care of you. Even in the next life, I'll find a way. I'll take care of you always."

"I haven't a clue what I'm going to do now."

"Then do nothing at all. Just stay here with me."

She obeyed without protest, clinging to him, snug against his chest. At some point Her body stilled, and Her tears stopped streaming, but Tobias stayed put, cooing into Her ear until he fell asleep in Her arms. Still, Leila remained awake, and though the rage within Her had cooled, the havoc of Her mind remained.

She was supposed to be killed on Her wedding night.

Plans have changed.

"Tobias?"

He didn't answer. Blinking past tears, She whispered, "I'm The Savior."

His chest rose and fell in a steady rhythm. Peace. If only it were so easy to tell him the truth while he was awake.

"I'm afraid you'll hate Me when you find out." She gripped his shirt for stability. "I'm afraid you'll hate Me just as My father does."

She nuzzled beneath his chin, while Tobias was fast asleep, a blessing She was never granted.

✣ 28 ✣

THE LIE

Fingertips grazed Leila's shoulder. The wound was barely tender, stiff and scabbed. A body filled with healing light had its benefits, even if it had put Her in danger in the first place.

Delphi sighed. "I should've been there. This would've never happened."

Leila readjusted the straps of Her dress, staring out at the light pouring over Her garden steps. She and Her sister had been bundled up on Her bed all morning. At some point they'd have to leave, but the palace wasn't safe for Her now—not that it ever had been in the first place.

"Brontes's note said the plan had changed." Leila turned to Her sister. "I was supposed to die on My wedding night. This attack... It was far too early."

"You think that's what he meant?" Delphi said. "The change of plans?"

"There's no other explanation."

"Why go through the trouble of orchestrating this tournament specifically for Your assassination, then toss it all aside days from completion?"

Leila hadn't an answer for that, Her ignorance a knife to Her pride.

"We have to find the traitor. He mentioned a meeting place. We'll track it down."

"We have to keep You *safe*." Delphi took Leila's hands. "Our timeline has changed. Beware the assassins, the Senators. Any one of them could be a threat."

"And the Queen of Kovahr. She arrives today."

A knock sounded, and Asher made his way inside. "Apologies. You've been spending a great deal of time in private chambers. The staff is worried."

"Tell them I'm occupied," Leila said.

"People are talking."

A weight dropped in Leila's gut. She dragged Herself from Her bed, and Delphi took Her arm as they left the room.

Eyes followed them as they walked hand in hand, headed to nowhere in particular. She was used to the staring, but this was different. This was condemning.

"Have You tried shadow walking recently?" Delphi whispered.

Leila scoffed. "I shadow walk all the time."

"No, I mean...have You tried walking beyond the wall?"

"Past the fortress? You know I can't."

"But have You tried *lately*?"

Leila met Her sister's gaze. "You want Me to escape."

"It might be necessary."

"I am a queen. This is *My* palace."

"Brontes tried to have You killed yesterday, and he almost succeeded." Delphi's face dropped. "We're losing this battle."

The severity of her words stopped Leila in Her tracks. "I can't do it. I'm not capable. I've tried many, many times. I can't."

Delphi said nothing, her silence wounding. Leila swallowed hard. "Our only option is to defeat him from the inside. Otherwise, I'm dead."

A feeble smile flickered across Delphi's lips. "We'll figure it out. We always do." She scanned the hallway, and her tension faded, revealing a cheeky smirk.

"What?" Leila said.

Delphi cocked her head at a nearby door. "This is Tobias's chamber."

Leila's heartbeat quickened. "It's daytime."

"It's a good thing I don't glow, then."

"Delphi—"

She disappeared into Tobias's chamber before Leila could finish, shutting the door behind her. What was she thinking? Nerves pricked at Leila, and She watched the passing servants, searching for scrutiny that didn't exist.

Delphi re-emerged, a mischievous grin on her face. "You should go in there."

Leila sighed. "Delphi, I can't."

"He's shirtless. My, those rippling muscles—"

"He was shirtless for half the—"

"The drapes are closed," Delphi said. "Not a speck of sunlight to be seen."

Leila hesitated. "You swear?"

"Have I ever told a lie?"

Leila's gaze darted between Tobias's chamber and Her sister. Holding Her breath, She knocked at the door.

Tobias's muffled voice sounded. "Come in."

Winking, Delphi glided off, while Leila peeked into the chamber. Two beds—one empty, the other a mess of tangled sheets with an easel propped in front of it.

Tobias's head popped up above the easel, his face dotted with pink and yellow paint. "Leila. What are you doing here?"

Shadows blanketed the space from wall to wall. Exhaling, Leila made Her way inside. "I thought you might be lonely with Orion gone."

"How are you?"

"I'm all right."

He frowned. "You've said that before."

"I am. I promise." Her cheeks warmed. "I wanted to thank you. For being so kind the other night."

"There's no need to thank me. I'm your man. Whatever you need."

His easel boasted a large strip of canvas—a mystery She was more than intrigued to uncover.

"Are you painting?"

"I am." He patted the spot at his side. "Join me?"

Leila hopped onto the bed and took in the painting. Her heart lodged into Her throat. "Lilies?"

"I promised you lilies. And I also promised to fill the wall."

"This is for me?"

"Of course. Who else would it be for?"

Large white petals curled at the tips, vibrant spots and stripes in fierce magenta. Stargazer lilies, and so meticulously captured. All the times they had stared at the night sky together—perhaps there was a connection? She clasped Her hands beneath Her chin, beaming brighter than the light within Her.

"It's so beautiful." Her lips parted as She grasped for coherent words to speak. "I don't even know what to say, I'm so excited."

"It's nearly finished."

"Then it's mine?"

Tobias nodded, and She took his face in Her hands, kissing him. "Thank you. I love it so much."

Tobias laughed. "Let me look at your shoulder."

"Oh, it's fine."

"Don't you brush me off like that, show me."

"Listen to you, spouting orders like your words hold title."

"Shoulder," he said. "Now."

Leila smiled. "As you wish, *Your Highness*." She pulled Her strap low while Tobias eyed the injury. "Better?"

"Much better." He resituated Her dress. "I think I might've missed my calling. Perhaps I should be a healer as well."

"I much prefer you as an artist. That way I get gifts. And I must say, you look awfully adorable covered in all those spots and smudges."

The colors of Her lilies caked his hands and streaked his chest, a playful blend of sweet and inviting. "How adorable?" he said. "Show me."

A part of Her wanted to tempt and tease, but She kissed him anyway, lured by his cocksure grin. Tobias came in hard, deepening the kiss, and Leila chuckled. "You're in a fine mood this morning."

"It's all your fault. I never get to see you this early. You look stunning, you know."

She reveled in his gaze before nodding at the painting. "You don't mind if I watch you work?"

"Not at all. Do you want to try?"

He handed Her something—a paintbrush.

"Try?" Leila straightened. "You mean paint something?"

"Sure."

"Oh no, I couldn't possibly…"

"Of course you can. I'll show you." He folded Her fingers around the brush. "Soft strokes. See? Like that."

She cringed as the bristles pressed against the canvas. "Like that?"

"Perfect. You're a natural."

"You lie. I'll ruin it."

"No you won't." He sat tall, coming in closer. "And if you do, I'll fix it. You forget, you're sitting with a master."

"Oh, so you're a master now?"

"Indeed I am."

Leila let out a laugh. "Loon."

"That's no way to speak to a master."

She waved him away before staring long and hard at the painting as if it might somehow calm Her nerves. Tobias's arm snaked around Her waist, his chin propped along the curve of Her neck as he breathed Her in.

"Am I doing this right?" Leila said.

"Absolutely."

"Are you even looking at the canvas?"

"Mhm." He buried his face in Her hair. "Yes. Completely."

"You know, I'm trying to learn."

"And you're doing wonderfully. A star pupil."

Surrendering to his touch, Leila dropped Her brush and leaned into his chest. He nipped at Her neck, and She swallowed the beginnings of a moan. "Don't kiss me there, you know it makes me weak."

"That isn't much of a deterrent."

She chuckled. "You fool."

His lips traveled up Her flesh, then froze. "Do you really want me to stop? I will. Just say the word."

Her gaze strayed, traveling down to his mouth. She shook Her head.

Leila flopped back onto the bed, giggling as Tobias climbed on top of Her. His carved figure, his smile, the paint smudged across his skin—all of it pulled Her in, begging to be touched. She slid Her fingers down the planes of his chest, while he latched onto Her hips, his hard cock digging into Her thigh. Her throat tightened, and Her hands worked of their own bidding, latching onto his bulge.

Tobias flinched, and She broke Her hold. "Apologies." Her face burned. "Oh my God, was that horribly presumptuous of me?"

Tobias stared at Her, wide-eyed and silent. A second later, he dove forward, kissing Her roughly and thrusting Her hand back onto his cock.

You said You wouldn't. Not yet. The thought was there, a nagging fly in the back of Her mind, but that didn't stop Her from stroking his manhood over the thin layer of linen. Desire swirled in Her belly, Her heart beating wildly. They were alone. Now was the perfect time, and God, She wanted him. She grabbed his waistband, ready to set him free, to unleash his beast, to behold his cock for the first time.

He has no idea who You are.

"Tobias." She stopped short. "Wait."

Tobias looked down at Her, panting. "What's wrong?"

I'm The Savior. The words sat on Her tongue, ready. *Say it.*

Footsteps sounded outside.

"Someone's coming," She said.

They bolted upright, situating their clothes as the footfalls grew louder. Leila flicked Tobias's temple.

"*Ow*—" He winced.

The door swung open as Leila grabbed Tobias's head, examining it. "I don't know what you're moaning about, you look perfectly fine to me." She turned to the intruder—only Flynn. "Oh, hello. Don't mind me, I was just leaving."

She left in a hurry, fighting to stifle Her grin until She was safely out of sight. The thrill of the moment still danced within Her as She headed through the palace, and soon She couldn't control the smile spreading across Her face.

She peeled around the corner, then came to a halt. Kaleo leaned against the wall paces away, a half-eaten apple in hand. Chuckling, he eyed Her up and down.

"Clever little thing, aren't You?"

He knew. Of course he did; Brontes naturally told him. She nearly reached for Her injured shoulder but stopped Herself, turning the way She had come and escaping Kaleo's line of sight.

Nyx retrieved Her from Her idle wandering, ushering Her to the royal bathhouse while chastising Her for the paint on Her dress. Leila half-listened, thankful for the silence Her other servants offered. Damaris and Hemera wore looks of discomfort, while Faun pursed Her lips, visibly perturbed.

"All done." Faun's voice was hard as she tied Leila's dress into place. "You're to meet the rest of Your court in the throne room. The challenge will begin shortly."

"Challenge?" Leila said. "What challenge?"

"Today's the Sovereign's Choice."

The clanking of metal plates echoed off the walls, and a line of guards appeared at the entrance of the bathhouse.

"And there they are," Faun mumbled. "Your trusted escorts."

"Make way." Asher shoved to the front of the line, his golden locks peeking from his crested helmet. "I am Her Holiness's personal guard. I will see Her there." He nodded at Leila. "Come. I'll stay by Your side."

Dumbfounded, Leila glanced between the embittered Faun and beckoning Asher, then hesitantly joined him.

The group traveled in strained silence through the palace, drawing more unwanted attention. Asher placed a hand on the small of Her back, his touch piquing Her nerves.

He spoke out of the corner of his mouth. "Don't worry, Leila. I'll protect You."

"Protect Me from what?" She said.

"I've fought diligently to uphold Your honor. No one will believe the rumors. No one with any sense, at least."

"What rumors?"

The throne room appeared—ancient and worn, the floor uneven stone, the pews faded wood. It hadn't been renovated, let alone used, in decades, an outdated convention for monarchs with too much ego to spare. Monarchs like Brontes, who sat in the golden throne at the head of the room.

Leila's throne.

Her throne was fashioned like the rays of the sun, a symbol of Her divine light sullied by Her father's ass. His one eye locked onto Her, and he gestured lazily at the side of the room. "Over there. With Your sisters."

Delphi, Pippa, and Cosima were seated in the back of the pews, and Leila took root at Delphi's side. Palace hands trickled into the room, filling the empty seats, and as the drone of voices filled the air, Leila whispered with Her sisters.

"What's going on?"

Delphi sat rigid. "The Sovereign's Choice."

"I know that, but..." Leila looked out at the accumulating people. "All this? An audience?"

"He's drunk with power," Delphi muttered.

"And we're here in the back row. Not even Cosima joins him at the head?"

Cosima scoffed. "Don't be silly, it's the Sovereign's Choice. Why would The Savior join him?"

"That's Your throne." Pippa wrinkled her nose. "Why is he sitting there?"

"It's a formality, dove," Cosima said.

Pippa turned to Leila. "He stole Your throne."

"Nonsense. The Sovereign's Choice is an important challenge. He's simply exercising his part in the manner. We're back here to aide Leila's façade."

Leila looked Cosima in the eye. "You defend him?"

"You asked what was going on. I'm answering Your question." Cosima's voice was soft, but her gaze had turned cold.

Heads turned as the competitors arrived, lining up before the Sovereign. Tobias's eyes flitted Leila's way, and She eased into Her seat. He had immunity from dismissal. For once, She had little to worry over.

The pounding of footsteps sounded, and Wembleton and his guards appeared, marching up to the throne. Anxious sweat coated the Senator's face as he spoke. "Ladies and gentlemen, welcome to the ninth challenge of the Sovereign's Tournament. This is the Sovereign's Choice. None of you will be competing today. This is a challenge unlike the others. In fact, it began the moment you entered this tournament—the challenge of impressing our esteemed Sovereign."

Leila snorted, sinking into Her seat.

"Dragon, Shepherd, Prince, Artist, Intellect," Wembleton continued, "as the final five men of this tournament, your laurels will be regarded with honor for all eternity. But only four of you will remain in the palace to compete for The Savior's affection. One of you will be released today, the man who is least fit to wear the crown as deemed by the Sovereign himself."

Wembleton cleared his throat. "Per tradition, The Savior is not without say in the Sovereign's Choice." His voice cracked. "It is within Her power to select one man to be free from release. The man exempt from the Sovereign's Choice as dictated by our One True Savior is the Artist."

Leila exhaled. At least one thing had gone according to plan. Her eyes locked onto Raphael. *Please, Brontes. You've failed Me so many times. Don't fail Me now.*

"And now for the decision," Wembleton said. "The second man to be honorably released from the Sovereign's Tournament, the man least fit to wear the crown, is the Intellect."

Raphael evacuated his lungs, and Leila did the same. She should've been happy, but a twinge pulled in Her chest. If only She could escape this mess as well.

"Intellect, you will be escorted off the fortress grounds immediately." Wembleton fussed with his drapes, preparing to leave. "With that said, the Sovereign's Choice has come to a close—"

"I have a question," Tobias said.

All eyes flicked his way. His shoulders were squared, his stance hardened.

Wembleton furrowed his brow. "Pardon?"

"I said I have a question."

"Well, yes, but—"

"The Shepherd and the Dragon," Tobias continued. "Why are they staying?"

"The Sovereign has determined—"

"I'm not asking you." Tobias turned to Brontes. "I'm asking him."

Leila's heartbeat quickened. What was the purpose of this? The challenge was over. Tobias had been saved. But now Her father was staring at him, wrath alive in his gaze.

"Choose your words wisely, Artist," he growled.

"You send home a good man today." Tobias stepped forward. "Yet a man who marks his kills on his arms and another who preys on women get to stay. Why?"

"I'm not obligated to explain my decisions to you."

"And have you no obligation to your daughter? Or would you prefer She marry a murderer? Is that simply your taste? Did you just pick out the most heinous killers in this tournament and give them your blessing?"

Brontes's eye shrank into a slit. "You will learn your place, Artist. You stand below me for a reason."

Fear gnawed at Leila's gut. *Stand down, Tobias. You will get yourself killed.*

"The Shepherd and the Dragon are not fit to rule alongside your daughter," Tobias said. "They're rabid dogs that need to be put down."

"And tell me, who is better fit for the throne in your humble opinion? A laborer? One without a father? Who keeps the company of cripples?"

"You have no care for your daughter. No care for your staff. You put their lives at risk each day. You let murderers share their home." Tobias's lips curled into a snarl. "You're a liar and a coward."

"And you're a fool who can't see what's right in front of him. You speak as if your words matter, but you are blind, and you are stupid, and your common blood reeks of pity and shit. You're worthless—a little boy playing a man's game. You're in over your head. And your only ally lies to your face."

Leila's stomach dropped. She waited for Tobias to look Her way, for the realization to hit him, but he remained unyielding.

"I wanted to send you home today," Brontes said. "But for whatever reason, my daughter, the daft cunt, She saved you. So here we are, stuck with one another yet again. But now...now I'm growing fond of this decision. Because at least I still have the pleasure of watching you die."

His words carved at Leila, piercing to the bone. He leaned forward in Her throne. "You *will* die here, Artist. You will."

The quiet that followed was thick and stifling. Brontes flicked his wrist toward the guards. "The challenge is over. Send the Intellect on his way."

Hushed voices filled the space. Raphael glanced at Leila, the only thanks he could offer, then vanished soon after, ushered by the very guards who had retrieved Her in the first place. A sinking feeling took root within Her—for Tobias's bizarre display; for the freedom Raphael was so easily granted, yet She was denied; for the entire quandary of Her existence.

Leila and Her sisters gave parting, dispersing with the rest of the staff. Cosima walked ahead at a brisk pace, and Leila hastened Her stride, scowling.

"Cosima."

She whirled around. "Yes, dove?"

"We haven't shared words in some time."

"Is that so?" Cosima pursed her lips, seemingly deep in thought. "Oh my, You're absolutely right. I've been so busy aiding Your plans, the days have slipped by and I hadn't noticed."

Leila hardened Herself. "We can speak now."

"Dove, I wish we could. I have a terrible headache, and if I don't lay down, I fear I'll grow faint."

"We can speak while you lay down." Leila crossed Her arms. "I can heal your ache. You know this well."

"Nonsense, I'd hate to steal You away for such trivial matters. I promise I'll be fine."

"Cosima—"

"Another day, dove." She continued on her way, blowing a kiss over her shoulder. "Love You."

Delphi and Pippa sauntered up to Leila's sides, watching as their fourth sister faded from view. Fire crackled in Leila's chest. "She's hiding something."

"She can't be the traitor," Delphi said. "She would've told Brontes of the switch long ago."

"Then what's the explanation?"

Delphi said nothing. Grimacing, Leila turned on Her heel and walked off.

The three women traveled through the palace in aimless circles, Delphi and Leila fighting to make sense of their plans while Pippa nodded along. *Why is Brontes keeping the ruse a secret?* That was but one question they needed answers to, along with his and the traitor's meeting place. "We'll start there." Leila said the words with confidence, though Her insides shrank, desperate for a guiding light.

"And King Jaco? When does he arrive?"

"Tonight, I assume."

Brontes's voice halted Her. The entryway lay ahead, where servants hoisted leather trunks onto their shoulders, and fair-skinned soldiers in heavy furs stood beside ebony guards in sapphire plates. Brontes stood in the center of it all—alongside Cosima, a glittering circlet atop her head, her supposed ailment long forgotten. Smiling, She greeted two visitors: a slender man with deep brown skin dressed in white robes with copious jewels; and a woman with pale skin, silver armor, and a brown braid hanging down her back.

The Monarch of Ethyua and the Queen of Kovahr.

"No need to bother with the banquet," Brontes said. "Servants will show you to your chambers. Rest for the evening."

"Oh no, that will not do." The Monarch's accent was smooth and melodic. "I came to experience your tournament. I will miss nothing, let me assure you."

"Tonight is merely a formality. There will be plenty more events."

"Ones far grander than this." Cosima's eyes sparkled. "The true theatrics begin tomorrow."

"Ah, yes. The challenge." The Monarch grinned, flashing white teeth. "Tell me, will they really fight to the death?"

"With their bare hands," Brontes said.

Cosima chuckled with the royals, petting the Monarch's hand as if they stood as equals, while Leila simmered in the shadows.

A head turned Her way—the Kovahrian Queen, her small eyes clear from a distance. Cocking her chin, she studied Leila and smirked.

"Leila," Delphi said. "Let's go."

The disquiet in Leila's stomach twisted, a rag wrung at opposite ends. At some point Cecily prepared Her for the banquet, though not as liberally as usual, and Leila took Her seat at the head of the atrium table among Her court and Her competitors. Cosima sat in the center, carrying herself with the poise of a ruler, but what truly unsettled Leila was the memory of the Queen's gaze.

Leila shook Herself. The challenge tomorrow—that was a problem She could address now. *A fight to the death*. She slinked Her hand beneath the table, reaching past Her lap to Tobias. His fingers entwined with Hers, and Her resolve burned brighter.

She couldn't save Herself tonight, but She could save him.

She abandoned the banquet before it was over, pulling Damaris aside. "Fetch the Artist." She'd make the evening worthwhile yet. After a trip to the scroll room, She retreated to Her study, dumping the parchment onto Her desk. A fight to the death, and with their bare hands. This challenge was reminiscent of the ancient tournaments when the rulers were especially savage. Was there a loophole then? A blessing, or immunity?

The door creaked open, but She kept Her eyes on Her scrolls. "Tobias, come. I've learned of your next challenge. It's very dangerous, and there isn't much time to prepare, so it's best we get started now."

"For what purpose?" he asked. "So I can be one step closer to winning Cosima? To marrying your sister?"

She stopped in Her tracks. Tobias's face was drawn, but what truly struck Her were the fine wisps of black trailing in his wake.

"Is something wrong?"

"I just don't understand why you're helping me." His voice was low and bleak. "Why you're doing any of this, really."

She set Her scroll aside. "You know why."

He wasn't looking at Her, not directly. She came in closer. "Tobias..."

He yanked away from Her, swift and shocking. Leila gaped at him. "Tobias, what's going on?"

"You must know what we're doing is pointless. That there's no happy ending for us."

"That's not true."

"Then you're a fool."

Leila's eyes widened. *"Tobias—"*

"Flynn knows," he said.

"What?"

"Flynn knows about us. And he's threatened to tell The Savior if we don't end things at once."

Leila's shoulders slumped. Tobias stood before Her a miserable mess, and for nothing. *How do I tell him?*

"Did you hear me?" he said. "Flynn *knows*. He could end us both."

"He won't. I assure you, everything's under control."

"Is that right?" Tobias laughed, though it sounded hateful. He paced the room. "I put my hands on him. I promised to *kill him* if any harm came to you. I was *this close* to strangling the life from him. You may have your end of things under control, but I...I am *far* beyond that."

The cloud around him turned dark and dense, and Leila's nerves eddied. "Tobias, please try to relax."

"How can I *relax?*" he spat. "Am I supposed to be comforted by the thought of your death? Or the thought of mine? Is this all supposed to amuse me?"

"Of course not. Why would you say that?"

"Look at you! You're hard as stone. You act as if this doesn't matter."

"Because it *doesn't.*"

He stopped pacing, eyes wide. She had spoken carelessly. Breathing in deeply, She wrangled composure. "Flynn knows. It's a complication—"

"A *complication?*" he said. "Do you hear yourself?"

"There have been delays, but we still have time to make it right. There are moves left to be made, maneuvers yet to be considered—"

"What are you even talking about?"

"Brontes is formidable, but we can still stay one step ahead of him," She maintained. "He's gaining ground. I won't deny that. But I'm not without resources. I knew of the garden, of Garrick's execution, even today, with Raphael's release—"

Tobias flinched. "You knew?"

"Pardon?"

"That Raphael was going home today. You knew. For how long?"

Something had shifted in his voice—coarse and stern—and in his gaze, which bore through Her, an onyx knife.

A new color lifted from his flesh.

Red.

"I..." Leila stammered. "I'm not entirely sure."

"But you knew before the Sovereign's Choice. And you didn't tell me?"

"There are more important things—"

"More important than release?" he hissed. "Than being free of this madness? Than a life with you as opposed to watching men die around me, waiting my turn."

"Tobias—"

"Do you know how badly I wanted to be released today?" He curled his hands, red spilling between his fingers like blood. "Not so I could see my mother or sister, but so I could spend the rest of my days with *you*. God, and to think I barked at the Sovereign, hoping by some miracle he'd throw my ass out of this damn tournament."

Leila faltered. "Is that what that was about?"

"Why else would I humiliate myself? Not to mention put my life in jeopardy. I'm surprised he didn't kill me himself."

"He wouldn't."

"Is that so?" he scoffed. "Yet he sics Drake on you like a damn hound."

"He wouldn't just *kill you*. It's not part of his plan."

"His plan? What *plan*?" He flung his arms into the air. "This is what I mean. My life hangs in the balance, and I'm lost. All these schemes, and I haven't a clue. You knew Raphael was leaving. What else do you know? What are you hiding?"

The red was consuming, blanketing the room. *He doesn't know who You are.* She had told Herself it was better this way, that She was protecting him—all lies. Tobias was breaking before Her, collapsing beneath his troubles. She could've lifted them, but She didn't.

She took in a trembling breath. "I can explain—"

"Brontes was telling the truth, wasn't he? I'm in over my head. And you're lying to me."

"Tobias—"

"You're lying to me, aren't you?"

Leila opened Her mouth to speak. *Tell him.* But there was only silence, and the despair that crossed Tobias's face was enough to wound Her.

"God, see?" Wincing, he shook his head. "You can't even say it."

"I'm not lying to you." Her voice wavered. "I mean, there are things I haven't told you—"

"Enough. I can't take it."

"I'll tell you everything," She said. "Right now. Whatever you want to know."

"I don't want to know. Not anymore."

"Just let me speak, I promise I'll—"

"*Enough!*" His bellow crashed through Her, echoing in Her bones. "You're a liar. You leave me hanging, and I let you, because I..." His eyes clenched shut. "Because I'm stupid. I'm just a pawn in some game you're playing with the Sovereign."

"That isn't true." Tears came of their own bidding, streaking Her cheeks. "I've done nothing but try to protect us. I promise, I'll tell you everything right now. I swear it."

"It's too late. Flynn knows. The damage is done."

"It's not. It's not done." With a deep breath, She came in closer. "Tobias, things aren't as they seem. I'm—"

"Stop it."

"I'm trying to—"

"I said stop."

"Tobias, please let me speak—"

"For God's sake, why?" he barked. "So you can lie to me again and again? I am done being toyed with. I am done being used and bartered and *played*."

"That's not what's happening. You know how I feel for you. You know what we have—"

"What we have is a mistake. *You* are nothing more than a *mistake*."

His words rammed Her in the chest, pounded Her in the jaw; She felt them everywhere, a resounding pain. The sobs died in Her lungs, leaving Her still. The man She adored wasn't standing before Her any longer. That mass of red and those wicked remarks were too familiar. Too much like Her father.

The red thinned, revealing Tobias's shamed stare. "Leila, I didn't mean that."

"Oh no, you meant it," She said.

His eyes glistened over. Clearing his throat, he took a tentative step forward. "I'm here for Cosima whether I like it or not. What I want and how I feel...it doesn't matter. We have to end things. I couldn't bear it if something happened to you. We have to end things, because I have no choice."

"Is that all?"

"I'm just trying to do the right thing."

"Is that *all*, Tobias?"

The red was gone. It had disappeared so quickly, though the room remained thick and heated. The fire belonged to Leila now. She would make this man burn.

"Leila, can you just... Can you say something? Can you speak to me?"

"Speak to you?" She said. "Why? So I can lie again and again?"

"Leila, I didn't mean—"

"You didn't mean it?" She spat. "Were you lying? No, you wouldn't dare. Now if I'm to understand you correctly, we're done, yes?"

"Yes."

Another blow, but this time She was ready. She held Her chin high. "Well then, I suppose this is the part where I tell you to go fuck yourself."

"Leila—"

"Go." She cocked Her head at the door. "You're dismissed."

"I just had to—"

"Leave."

"Leila, I'm—"

"*Get out!*"

She hadn't intended to scream—to reveal Her wounds. Tobias stared at Her, his eyes wide and wet, and another cloud encircled him—black, again. God, She wished She could revel in the sight. It shouldn't have pained Her as much as it did.

Nodding, he and his misery left the room.

Leila sucked in a breath. Her body shook, the air in Her lungs insufficient, as if something was smothering Her from within. Tears came in a violent rush, shaming Her. She had known betrayal, deceit, and death. Why did *this,* of all things, hurt so badly?

Barely contained, She summoned Her light. The warmth of Her power came and went, but She kept Her gaze on the floor, leaving Her with brown panels and a familiar laugh.

"Is that right?" Delphi cooed. "Well, I happen to find these curves quite worthy of admiration."

A giggle sounded, followed by a squeak.

"Leila?" Delphi said. "Good God, what did I tell You about—?" Her voice stopped short. "Oh no. Nyx, sweet beauty, let's continue another time, yes?"

The servant fluttered off, closing the door behind her. Only then did Leila look Delphi's way, the vision of Her sister clouded by tears.

"What happened?"

"He left Me." Leila's voice broke. "He said it's over. He wants nothing to do with Me."

Delphi's face dropped. "Come here."

Leila ran to the bed, throwing Herself into Delphi's arms. Between sobs and shudders, She choked out what She could of the story, demeaned by Her emotions. She was stronger than this, yet with a few words, Tobias had torn Her to shreds.

"I should've told him." Leila buried Her head in Delphi's lap, gripping at her dress. "I tried to, but it was too late. He was *so* angry. He looked just like Brontes."

"He is not Your father." Delphi ran her fingers through Leila's hair. "He feels betrayed. He's hurting."

"I should've told him sooner. I just thought..." The words died in Her throat. "Please don't say *I told You so,* I can't right now, I—"

"I would never say that."

Another caress. Leila tried to revel in the comfort, but the tears never ceased.

"This will right itself," Delphi said.

"It won't."

"Relationships are complicated."

Leila scoffed. "Is that right? I hadn't noticed."

Brontes. She saw him again, a ghost forever haunting Her. The vision was a clawed hand ripping apart whatever shreds of Her remained. She clenched Her eyes shut, fighting to free Herself of his visage, but there he stayed.

"What is it about Me...that makes Me so hard to love?"

"I love You," Delphi said.

The ache in Her chest lifted enough for Her to take in a breath.

"Tobias does too." Delphi pushed Leila's hair behind Her ear. "You know this."

"He hates Me."

"He loves You, just as You love him."

Leila shook Her head. "I don't love him."

Of all the lies She'd ever told, She wished the most that this one was true.

29

THE KEYS

Leila stared out the window. Brontes's window.

A crystal fountain, manicured trees, marble benches reflecting the morning sunlight. Nothing unusual. She slid Her hand down the golden pane. No parchment. The traitor must've taken it. *Dammit.* She'd check again later.

Voices sounded behind Her—servants whispering about the Viewing. The tournament competitors were to be presented to the visiting royals in a short while. Tobias would be among them. Of course he would be.

You are nothing more than a mistake.

A pang lanced through Her, reopening the still-fresh wound. She headed down the stairs.

"Leila."

A servant appeared beside the courtyard window, arms crossed and eyes narrowed.

"Faun?" Leila retraced Her steps. "A bath so soon? I thought we had plenty of time—"

"What the hell is going on?" Faun spat.

"Excuse Me?"

"We knew You didn't favor the tournament, but to hide Your title from Your realm? To let the men believe they fight for Your sister?"

A brick landed in Leila's gut. "It's complicated."

"Apparently so. Half the staff saw You kicking and screaming while the Sovereign dragged You to the hearing. Then You cut off the Dragon's ear, all because he sought Your attention."

"What did you—?"

"And last night You're heard crying for hours." Faun lowered her voice. "Do You realize what people are saying?"

"I did *not* cut off Drake's ear—"

"They're calling you Megaera. They're saying You're the new mad Savior."

The air evacuated Leila's lungs. Mad. That's what Her staff thought of Her.

"I don't want to believe it," Faun said. "But armed guards are escorting You through Your own palace for the safety of Your staff."

Leila opened Her mouth to speak, only to stop short. *There's a traitor within these walls.* Could She even trust Faun? "I said, it's complicated."

Faun came in closer. "Reveal Yourself to these men. End the rumors once and for all."

"Why do you care so much about My decisions? They have no effect on you."

"At least explain to me this insanity," Faun said. "Why the lies? Leila, we worry for You. I'm trying to understand as Your friend—"

"We are *not* friends."

Faun froze, taken aback. "I see. Excuse my tone then, Your Holiness. Good day."

She bowed before leaving, and her silence ate at Leila, another burden She hadn't need for. Leila steadied Herself. She was right to be skeptical. She was right to be vexed.

A lump lodged in Her throat, but She swallowed it and carried on.

∿

"I'M LOSING."

Leila sat on the carved sill of Talos's cell, knees pulled into Her chest. Talos waited on the bench beside Her, gazing out at the dungeon. She liked it like that. She didn't want anyone to look at Her, certain Her shame was written across Her face.

"There is time left, Your Holiness," Talos said.

"The tournament ends in three days." She shook Her head. "That doesn't even matter. Brontes's plan has changed. I could die at any moment. Have you heard anything?"

"With the assassins in the palace, they have plenty of places to meet in secret. They don't need the dungeon any longer."

Leila didn't respond, staring at the bars ahead.

"Are You giving up?"

"I can't give up," She said. "If I give up, I die. And if I die, the realm dies with Me."

"What move would You like to make next?"

"I don't know."

"How can I aid You?"

"I don't know. I don't know anything, I..." She hung Her head. There wasn't a point in pretending. She was neck-deep in shit and sinking. Even Tobias had abandoned Her.

"Would You like to hear stories of Your mother, Little Light?"

"No."

Cold air wafted through the cell. Was it ever cold anywhere in Thessen? She tightened Her hold around Her legs, resting Her cheek on Her knees.

"Did She love you?" She whispered.

Talos was quiet for a while. "No, Little Light. She loved the Sterling. A Lord."

"Dumb bitch."

"She was free to love whomever She pleased."

Leila sighed. "Sometimes I think about what it would be like...if you were My father, instead of Brontes."

Talos said nothing.

"Everything would be so different," She said. "My mother would still be alive. There'd be no Senate, no schemes. I can't even imagine a life like that." She scooted closer to him, threading Her hand into his boulder of a fist. "If you were My father, would you have made Me follow the tournament?"

"It's tradition."

"You were kidnapped, tortured, and locked away because of this tradition."

His brow creased, his thoughts visibly turning. "You are The Savior. If You were not fond of the tournament...I suppose You could've swayed my opinion." He eyed Her over. "Is the Artist well?"

"I don't care how the Artist fares."

"He's fallen out of Your favor?"

Tears pricked Her eyes. "It seems I've fallen out of his."

"Dumb bitch."

Talos sat stiff and uncomfortable, but the smile in his eyes coaxed one across Her lips, Her tears brimming at the surface.

Rumbling. The wall beyond the cell shook, dust spilling from between the stacked stones.

"What is that?" Leila said.

Talos sat tall. "I don't know."

Another spray of dirt, and the stones retracted from one another like a mouth opening wide. A man trudged from the hidden portal, a torch in hand and a silver breastplate across his chest.

Erebus.

He fumbled with his ring of keys before stopping before the cell. His deep-set eyes locked with Leila's, a second that lasted an eternity, and he bolted back through the portal.

Leila leapt from the sill, sliding between the cell bars and sprinting into the darkness. A tunnel stretched out before Her, pitch black save for the bobbing light of Erebus's torch. *Shadow walk*, but She'd never been here before, hadn't known of its existence in the first place.

A tunnel beneath the palace, another mystery to solve.

The sound of Her feet slapping against dirt bounced off the walls. The torch shone farther and farther away, so She forced Herself forward, wrangling every ounce of strength and speed. *What will You do once You reach him?* Erebus was a warrior, the one Senator She couldn't kill. But he had seen Her in the dungeon. He would tell Her father. She ran faster.

The light of the torch clattered to the floor. Leila caught up to it—

abandoned at a crossroads, the tunnel splitting in two directions. She fought to silence Her breathing, listening for the echo of Erebus's footsteps. *To the right.* She followed.

Darkness blinded Her journey. She tripped once, tumbling to the dirt, then righted Herself. Finally, a glow in the distance—another portal. The pounding of Her heart turned to thunder, and She dashed through the opening.

Leila slid to a stop. Grey stone floor, plaster walls. This was the southern wing of the palace, but what concerned Her were the guards accumulating around the portal. One stared at Her, perplexed.

"Your Holiness, what is...?"

Erebus walked at a brisk pace far ahead. She shouldered past the mob. "Excuse Me."

She left them to their questions, following in Erebus's footsteps. *Faster.* He rounded a corner, and Her heart lurched. Holding Her breath, She half-walked, half-jogged, looking back at the guards as She disappeared down the adjacent corridor.

Leila launched into a sprint. The passage was empty, and Erebus was far ahead, his body propelled like a spear. *He can't tell Brontes.* She channeled Her power, heat rising within Her as She burst into light once, twice, farther and farther down the corridor until Erebus was right in front of Her.

Take Me to him.

She dissolved amid wisps of fire, reappearing with a slap against his back, toppling him. Without a hint of exertion, he rolled from beneath Her, flinging Her into the wall. Pain spiked through Her, but there wasn't time for weakness. She staggered to Her feet, shooting around the corner Erebus had taken.

The corridor was vacant. She searched the walls for hidden portals, peeked inside doorways, but there was nothing. She swallowed a cry, desperation fueling Her footsteps as She bolted into the throne room.

A fist rammed into Her gut, crumpling Her to the floor.

Leila gasped for air, consumed by the throbbing ache. A kick to the ribs, and She cringed, grasping at the floor as She fought past the suffering. Staggering to Her feet, She drew Her blade and thrust it forward, but the sharpened steel froze, caught in Erebus's grasp. Blood trickled between his fingers, and he yanked the blade from Her grip, tossing it aside.

Leila stumbled. Erebus stood unfazed before Her, his body the only weapon he needed. He lunged for Her, but She burst into nothingness, reappearing behind him. Another attempt, but She dissolved away, materializing beside Her throne.

The Senator stared at Her, unblinking. She could play this game all day, but She didn't need escape—She needed him dead. Her eyes flitted to Her discarded blade, and She channeled Her light, appearing at its side. She swiped up the weapon only for Erebus to grab Her wrists, tweaking and wrenching until the blade clattered to Her feet. She writhed within his grasp to no avail, and he threw Her to the floor.

Low on options, Leila propped Herself onto Her hands and knees, then swayed upright. "You can't kill Me."

"I can kill You if I please," he said.

"You defy My father's will."

"On the contrary, I honor it."

He hurtled toward Her, snatching up Her wrists again and throwing Her off Her feet. She slid along the tile, and soon Erebus was on top of Her, pinning Her down. Panicked, She slashed at his face, their arms a snarl of raking claws. Fingers dug into Her flesh, but She didn't relent, fighting like mad until he wrested Her hands to Her sides.

"This end was of Your choosing." He straddled Her chest, crushing Her ribs. "Stupid girl. Hiding Your title from Your realm. You can disappear today, and no one beyond this fortress will know."

The plan has changed. She tried to scream, but he grabbed Her throat and squeezed.

"Your father thanks You for the convenience of Your decision-making," he said. "Silencing the staff will be tiresome, but worthwhile."

Leila kicked Her legs, but Erebus only dug in harder. His face was a mask of nothingness—no effort, no care—while Her lungs burned in anguish. This was it. She had failed. Darkness splintered into Her vision, bringing Her closer to death.

Her body jerked forward, and Erebus released Her throat, sending Her smacking down against the floor. She filled Her lungs and gripped Her chest, half-expecting it to be gone—that She was a ghost, Her tangible body done away with. But She was real, alive, and Erebus was now high above Her, dangling from two scarred hands attached to a massive frame.

Talos.

He wrapped one arm around Erebus's neck, the other around his chest, turning the Senator's face from olive to red. As Erebus wheezed, Talos snapped the man's neck with a fierce twist.

Erebus tumbled to the floor. Leila sat trembling, eyes locked on the corpse at Her feet—the man who'd nearly ended Her life.

"I will dispose of him, Your Holiness."

Talos's words barely registered. Erebus was sprawled on his belly, head pointed to the side at an unnatural angle. His deep-set eyes were wide with horror, his final moments forever etched across his face.

"Breathe," Talos said.

Leila sucked in a breath. Her gaze flitted up and down Her friend, stopping at his ankle—raw and red.

Free.

"Your shackle."

Talos fished a handful of steel from his pocket. "He dropped these."

The keys clinked in his meaty palm, worn and rusted, save for a single flash of bright silver—a key so lustrous, it glowed.

"That's... That's the one."

The enchanted key. Talos nodded, then pulled Her to Her feet. Pain sliced through Her, an afterthought.

"You're free now." Her voice wavered. "Leave this place."

Talos stared at Her in silence. He folded the keys into Her palm.

"What are you doing?" She said.

"Go to Your vault, Your Holiness. Collect Your coin."

"Where will you go?"

"To my cell."

Her heart seized. "Talos, no."

"I live to serve The One True Savior. Until You are free, I am not."

"I order you—"

"Set Yourself free, Little Light. I will aide in any manner You require."

Her throat became thick, Her hands outstretched before Her. She had to say something, racking Her mind for words She couldn't piece together.

"Go to Your vault." He placed Her blade in Her hands. "You know where to find me."

Tears slid down Her cheeks, but She forced Herself to move. Looking over Her shoulder, She met Talos's gaze once more before staggering into the corridor.

Breathe. She took in short gasps, fighting to ignore the terror quaking through Her. Sheathing Her blade, She pocketed the keys and charged ahead.

Her knees wobbled, nearly tripping Her along Her journey. Blood painted Her dress, Her arms marked with scratches, Her lungs heaving despite Her efforts. She summoned Her light, and Her power took hold, bringing Her to the giant, steel slab.

The vault. *Her* vault.

She fumbled for the keys, nearly dropping them once or twice. Three locks and so many keys. She tried each one, Her heart sputtering with every failed attempt. The fifth key snapped into place, then turned, and a squeal vibrated in Her mouth. Another attempt, and this one clicked into place on the first try. One more to go. She went through key after key, sweat beading along Her forehead. The seventh key lurched forward, then turned, stopping with a clank. She forced open the door.

The overwhelming darkness hit Her, and nausea foamed in Her gut. Before Her stood the vault. Her vault.

Empty.

🕷 30 🕷

THE RAGE

Grow.

Warm light spilled from Her body into the grass below, but She was cold. Her power had become inconsequential, the darkness beneath the soil barely registering in Her mind. She eyed the patch of grass beside Her—Tobias's spot.

My spot is with you.

Tears crept down Her cheek, bleeding into the soil below.

A droplet splattered on Her forehead. *Shit.* She knew what was coming. *Never cry outdoors.* Grey clouds swept the sky, and rain poured forth, spattering Her and Her garden.

Hopping to Her feet, She darted into Her chamber and drew the curtain shut. As She changed into something dry, a knock sounded at Her door.

"Your Holiness, Your sister would like—"

The door swung open, and Delphi shouldered past Asher, wrapping Leila in a fierce hug.

Leila pulled away. "What was that for?"

"It's raining."

Heat flooded Her cheeks. "I'm so embarrassed."

"Don't be." Delphi gave Her a squeeze. "Everything will be all right. We'll figure it out."

Arms linked, Delphi led Leila from Her chamber, traveling through the palace in what was hardly a casual stroll. They had spoken of Erebus, of the empty vault, the hidden tunnel, and Brontes's ever-changing plans. *"No one beyond these walls knows I'm The Savior. I can die at any moment. It affords him more time to execute his schemes."* A chill crawled down Her spine. She had done this to Herself.

Delphi tightened Her hold on Leila. She could serve as Her guard all she liked, but at some point, Leila would be vulnerable.

"I met with Nessa last evening," Delphi said. "She claimed Astrea has been strange lately. Moody and cross. Perhaps she's the traitor. I've also been keeping an eye on the Queen all morning. Nothing of note to mention. Broke her fast, kept mostly with her soldiers. Pretty in the proper lighting."

Mousumi came down the corridor, a scroll in hand per usual. "Delphinium." Her eyes flitted to Leila, and she scowled. "*Leila.* A word about today's schedule?"

"Proceed."

"Your royal guests will be in attendance at tonight's feast. We have reserved seats for them nearest the Sovereign. Is this suitable to You?"

"Yes." Leila tensed. "Did any of them ask to sit closer to Me?"

Mousumi's nostrils flared. "No." She eyed her scroll. "The feast will honor the winner of today's challenge. The unexpected weather makes the conditions precarious, but the Senate has agreed to continue the challenge as planned."

"The Senate?" Leila said. "When did they make this decision?"

"Moments ago, Your—" Mousumi stopped herself and sighed. "*Leila.* I've only just come from the Senate room."

"They're meeting? Right now?"

"Yes."

Leila swerved around the servant keeper, abandoning both her and Delphi.

"Leila?"

She ignored Her sister's calls, Her blood boiling. Servants gawked as She passed, no doubt whispering about the *mad Savior*, but Leila was transfixed on the Senate door ahead and the two guards standing on either side of it.

One of the guards faltered. "Your Holiness—"

She thrust the door open, and the voices within faded. Four men stared at Her—Wembleton, surrounded by his legion; Diccus, fiddling with his beard; Hylas, his face drawn; and Brontes, the most miserable bastard of them all.

"What a surprise." Brontes's voice came out flat. "As You can see, we're presently occupied."

Leila clenched Her jaw. "Holding meetings without Me. I thought the depth of your treachery couldn't sink any lower, but it seems I underestimated you."

Hylas glanced across the table with anxious eyes. "If Her Holiness would like, I can recapitulate the points—"

"You've chosen to forsake Your crown," Brontes said.

"I've forsaken *nothing*."

"Participating in political matters would only serve to reveal Your true title." Brontes glowered. "We wouldn't want that, would we?"

Wembleton cleared his throat. "Your time is precious, Your Holiness. Senate meetings are trivial compared to—"

"Yes, you've said this before. My vast array of duties, my mornings spent blessing the realm."

Snorting, Brontes shook his head. Leila opened Her mouth, but the words lodged in Her throat, leaving Her to digest what he hadn't spoken.

"You don't believe it," She said. "That I heal the land."

The other Senators looked to Brontes, who remained aloof. "Your magic tricks are charming," he said. "But the land has been fertile for centuries."

"Because of My line." Leila pointed at the window. "You see the sun out there, roasting us alive each day? Have you noticed how seldom it rains?"

"It's raining today."

"Do you not understand what sort of climate that produces? Desert sand for miles. *I* keep the land fruitful. *I* turn the realm green. My light does that, as did the light of every Savior before Me. Or have you forgotten where we came from? Thessen was a *wasteland*." Her nails dug into the meat of Her palms. "A plague lurks beneath our feet. I alone keep it at bay. You act as though you're invincible. Will you feel so strong once boils cover your body? Once your shit turns black and your piss to blood?"

Brontes's gaze glassed over, his fingers tapping the table. There was nothing She could say. His mind had been made up long ago.

"You're all going to die when I'm gone."

She turned on Her heel, leaving the way She had come.

RAIN WATER POOLED ALONG THE MARBLE SURFACE, SEEPING THROUGH the hem of Her dress. Leila sat on the steps of Her garden staring at the storm, knees tucked into Her chest. Still no response from the traitor at Brontes's window, and She couldn't stand the whispers of Her staff. *Mad.* This time She had heard someone say the word aloud. Retreating to Her bedchamber was the only way to preserve Her sanity.

Someone hammered at Her door, but She ignored it, content to watch the rainfall. The golden slab opened, and Asher spoke from behind Her.

"Leila. Your escorts are waiting."

A growl bubbled in Her throat. The challenge would soon be underway, which meant She'd have to see Brontes and Cosima.

And Tobias.

Begrudgingly, She left with Her armed patrol.

The trek through the palace was short but humiliating. They stopped at the entryway, where Delphi, Pippa, and Cosima were waiting.

"Leila, my dove!" Cosima beamed. "We thought You'd never show. How are You?"

Leila said nothing, glaring without a hint of subtly. Cosima cleared her throat. "Well then, shall we be off? The others are already on their way."

Leila shouldered past Her sister, charging down the palace steps and into the rain. Guards marched behind Her, hoisting a canopy overhead that took the brunt of the downpour. Her sisters reached Her sides, walking in silence across the muddy lawn toward the site of the challenge. The tournament had left Leila's mind given recent events, and now that it had returned, dread resurfaced in Her gut.

A fight to the death.

One of the northern gardens appeared, marble benches and olive trees bordering a plot of grass. She used to play on these grounds as a child, hosted picnics with Her sisters, watched for shapes in the clouds. Now the sky was grey, the grass sodden, and a line of royals stood beneath a canopy much like Her own. The Ethyuan Monarch wore a customary white gown, a heavy gold collar hanging from his throat, the blue paint around his eyes smudged from the rain. Beside Brontes stood a fat pasty man in layers of navy and a young girl with a horrid scowl and hair painted pink—Trogolian royals, the least palatable of the bunch. Then there was the Kovahrian Queen, her cloak lined in silver furs, her eyes on Leila.

Tobias stood like a soldier at the end of the plot, as drenched as the other competitors. She knew they were present, could see them scattered around the grass, but Tobias took Her focus, staring at Her intently. The rainwater did wonderful things for his shirtless physique, which was completely unfair. Her eyes shrank into slits, lit with a hatred She wished was real.

A sneer flickered in Leila's peripheral vision. Drake growled something at Tobias, who responded in kind, their voices muffled by the rain. A bandage wrapped the assassin's skull with a reddish-brown patch resting over his ear, and Leila fought back a shudder.

Wet sandals squelched in the mud as Wembleton waded through the garden. His white tunic was slick against his skin, revealing far too much of his pinkish flesh. He took his place in the center of the garden.

"Ladies and gentlemen, royals of Thessen and afar, welcome to the tenth challenge of the Sovereign's Tournament. Today will determine who goes on to compete in the Culmination. Four of you stand before me, but only three will leave here alive."

Leila's eyes went to Tobias, then flitted away. *Don't.* His fate was no longer Her concern. Perhaps if She repeated the sentiment, She would soon believe it.

"Your task today is as simple as it is mighty," Wembleton said. "Today you will fight to the death using only the hands at your sides and your God-given strength. And for the man who falls, know that while you may not stand as Champion, your efforts and valor—"

"Get on with it," Brontes rasped.

Wembleton's face fell. "Right." He joined the royals, struggling to poke his head beneath their canopy. "Gentlemen, ready yourselves."

Leila's heart rate spiked as Tobias took a running stance. Kaleo, Drake, and Flynn—they were his opposition. Two assassins, and a man who had betrayed him.

Delphi leaned close to Her. "You've blessed him, yes?"

"What?" Leila said. "No. How could I?"

"Steady..." Wembleton barked.

"Then what's the plan?" Delphi hissed.

"There is no plan."

"How's he going to survive then?"

Leila swallowed. "I don't know."

Wembleton dropped his arms. "Begin."

All four men sprinted to the center of the garden, crashing into one another like battering rams.

Leila flinched. A pile of thrashing arms and sopping bodies wrestled with Tobias in the middle, his hands around Kaleo's throat. Perhaps Her worries were unfounded, and the battle would be over soon. Then Drake and Flynn yanked Tobias backward, and Leila's hopes died when Kaleo struck him in the jaw.

Again.

Sickness swam in Her stomach. *Tobias is going to die.* Blood streaked his face, and She dug Her nails into Her palms. The man She loved would meet his end, and She could do nothing but watch.

Tobias broke free, pounding his fist into Drake's stomach, against Flynn's jaw. His three opponents banded together, toppling him to the ground, and mud caked their flailing forms, rendering them indistinguishable from one another. Panic lanced through Leila, and She stood on Her toes as if it would somehow help Her differentiate one slick brown limb from another. Nothing—until a man burst free from the pile, gasping for breath as the rain pelted him. Tobias staggered to his feet, his chest heaving, color snaking from his body.

Pippa darted behind Leila, hiding from the carnage, while Leila remained rooted, transfixed. "Oh My God..."

"What?" Delphi whispered.

Red. It flowed from him in rivers, tinting the raindrops, collecting in puddles. She had never seen rage like this, like blood coursing from hidden wounds. Tobias slammed Kaleo against a pillar, and his rage followed him, leaving reddened streams in his wake. This was no man before Her. He had become something different. Something primal.

Drake slammed Tobias to the ground and stomped on his head, digging Tobias's face into the mud—red. Tobias yanked the Dragon's ankle, breaking his footing, then stumbled to his feet, painted from head-to-toe in wrath. Roused and feral, Tobias jabbed Flynn in the jaw, then kicked him to the mud. Even when he lost his ground, he gained it soon after, head-butting Kaleo and crawling on top of him, battering the assassin's face until Leila could no longer tell which crimson streaks were rage or blood. Her stomach twisted. Tobias was going to win, but at what cost?

Drake grabbed Tobias's shoulder, tugging him free from Kaleo, and Leila winced, predicting what was to come. Tobias pummeled the man, making a mess of his face, and when those soggy bandages drooped from Drake's head, Tobias wrenched his sewn ear free from its stitches. The Dragon cried out, and only then did Leila see the others; Kaleo and Flynn waited off at the side of the plot, the realization of the turning tide alive in their gaze. Then there was Tobias, his eyes panning from man to man, selecting his kill.

A roar spilled from his throat as he charged toward Drake, striking him in the mouth. Grabbing the Dragon by the ponytail, he smashed his face into a marble bench, sending blood shooting across the white. A crack cut through the madness as Tobias stomped on Drake's arm, bone jutting from his flesh. Suddenly Drake was on the ground, and Tobias was on top of him, strangling the life from his opponent—Leila's assassin. *Don't watch*, but Her stare never wavered. Another roar, and red erupted around him, leaving nothing untainted.

Drake's thrashing stilled. Tobias gave another squeeze, then released, pointing his face to the sky as he steadied his breathing.

Silence, save for the rainfall. The red retreated, swirling back to where it came from, making a home in Tobias's chest. Shocked faces waited in the wings: Flynn, Kaleo, many of the royals, the sisters at Leila's side. The Kovahrian Queen said something Leila couldn't distinguish, too consumed by Her havocked thoughts.

Another assassin was dead. The man who had nearly ended Her life. Tobias had done this for Her.

As he rose from the body, Wembleton waddled through the garden, raising Tobias's hand into the air. "The Artist..." His voice cracked. "The Artist stands as victor."

"You didn't bless him," Delphi said. "You're sure."

Leila let out a shallow breath. "Yes."

Tobias met Her gaze, and Her chest ached. *He killed Your assassin. Brought You that much closer to defeating Your father.* The words brought little comfort, as the look in Tobias's eyes was hollow.

The tournament was destroying him, and there was nothing She could do but watch.

❧ 31 ❧

THE LIGHT

"Ladies and gentlemen, esteemed guests. In two days, this tournament will come to a close."

Brontes's voice carried through the atrium. The glittering candlelight cast a sheen across the fruits and meats, the only opposition to the shadow looming over the feast. Applause sounded, but it was stilted. This was not a joyous occasion.

"Tonight we celebrate the final three competitors." Brontes stood at the end of the dining table, his lips a straight line. "The Shepherd, the Prince, and the Artist."

Tobias sat beside Leila, a brittle shell. They were commemorating him on this night, the winner of the day's challenge, the noble and valiant *Dragon Slayer*. Leila should've been pleased to have one less assassin, but Tobias's black cloud was potent, leaving an ashy taste in Her mouth. Perhaps if She could see Her own colors, they would look just as despaired.

"As a token for your bravery, you will spend tomorrow with Her Holiness," Brontes continued. "My daughter, and for one of you, your future bride. Shepherd, Prince, you will share the day with Her. Artist, as a reward for your victory, you will share the evening with Her. Do have a *wonderful* time."

Leila fought back a wince. An evening with Cosima.

"Come the following day, the three of you will battle in the Culmination, and only one man will remain: The Savior's Champion. May the best man win."

As the staff raised their chalices, Brontes glared at Tobias. "And may all those unworthy drown in their own blood and piss."

Enough. All of this was unfair—to Tobias, to Herself. She should speak to him. She should make things right.

Her stomach dropped. A hand had latched onto Tobias's thigh, stroking close enough to his nethers to force bile into Her throat. Cosima dug into his flesh as if he were her property, and though Leila waited for Tobias to move or flinch, he did nothing.

Something delicate shattered within Her. She rose from Her seat and left the table.

Tears pricked Her eyes as She abandoned the atrium. Tobias had made his intentions clear. How could She have possibly thought to sway him?

Footsteps echoed behind Her. A gown adorned with a steel breastplate, two long braids hanging down to her waist. The Kovahrian Queen was following Her.

"Girl," the Queen said.

Leila hastened Her stride. "*Girl.*" But She pressed on, Her shoulders tight.

"Your Holiness."

The words sent Leila to a halt. Slowly, She turned as the Kovahrian Queen walked toward Her.

"Ah, yes. She responds to Her title." The Queen flagged Leila over. "A word."

Leila trudged her way, resenting her pull. Stopping in front of the Queen, She eyed her over, taking in the intricate armor on her chest, the furs lining her shoulders, the freckles splattering her crow's feet and nose.

"You're The Savior, yes?" The Queen spoke curtly, her accent rough and clipped. "The real one."

"What brought you to this conclusion?"

"You are Your father's daughter. Plus, that woman with the crown—she is no queen."

"Or perhaps Enzo told you."

The Queen went quiet, her brown eyes squinted. "What is Your name?"

"Leila."

"Leila. Pretty. Why do You hide Yourself?"

Leila said nothing, and the Queen cocked her head. "You don't trust me."

"If I trusted anyone, I wouldn't be hiding Myself in the first place."

"You fear for Your life?"

"Among other things."

"This palace is a dangerous place for You." Her voice came out a shade softer, though her stare remained unreadable. "How unfortunate. The home of a queen, no home at all. You are smart then—taking measures. Whatever they are. You don't have to tell me. But smart woman, yes. How does Your father feel about this?"

"I don't particularly care how he feels."

"You don't like him. Neither do I. Unpleasant man, very rude. I don't know if You are as him. So far, I enjoy You more." She tapped Leila's hand. "Don't worry, Your Holiness. I keep Your secret."

The tension didn't dissipate. Leila tried to mirror the Queen's stance, hoping She appeared formidable, that perhaps the woman feared Her. *She should.*

"You have a question for me?" the Queen said. "I see it in Your eyes."

"You entered a spy into My father's tournament. Why?"

"You take Your measures. I take mine."

"That's an awfully vague response."

"Your Holiness, we do not trust each other. You have made that clear."

Leila fought back a scowl, though the Queen seemed unfazed.

"I have a question." The Queen clasped her hands together. "Tobias. Why do You break his heart?"

"Excuse Me?"

"I am Queen of warriors. I know rage of man who lost great love." She shrugged. "He also stares at You very much."

"They all believe Cosima is The Savior. Perhaps he was staring at her. Perhaps she's the cause of his rage."

The Queen laughed freely, squeezing Leila's arm a little too hard. "You're funny. I think I like You. But tell me why. Why do You break his heart?"

Leila dug Her nails into Her palms. "*He* broke *Mine*."

"Why?"

"It's complicated."

"Much in this palace is complicated, it seems."

Cosima's hand on Tobias's thigh—the vision tumbled through Leila's thoughts, stirring the wave of emotion She had fought past moments ago. *No.* Not in front of this woman. She could not, would not appear weak.

"Go to Your Artist," the Queen said. "Give him his love again. Save him from his rage. It will destroy him. I know. I have seen."

"You sent spies into My home. Forgive Me if I'm skeptical of your advice."

The Queen paused, her head once again cocked. "You have much rage too. I did not think I would like this tournament, but so far, it is *very* interesting."

Without proper parting, she headed off, her cloak dragging behind her. How she managed to stay comfortable under so many layers, Leila hadn't a clue. She watched the woman fade from view, then carried on.

Leila cursed under Her breath. The Queen was an issue. She should've requested, no, *demanded* information. *Stop it.* Degrading Herself would get Her nowhere. Erebus was dead—a triumph. Drake as well, another victory to Her name.

Cosima's hand on Tobias's thigh. Her chest pulled tight, a pain She couldn't shake.

The door to Her chamber stood in the distance with Asher waiting beside it. His head perked up. "Turning in already? Isn't the feast still underway?"

"I have no reason to stay," She said.

"Poor company, I take it?"

"The worst." She grabbed the door handle. "Good night, Asher."

"Leila."

What? The word caught in Her throat, as She was suddenly trapped in Asher's arms. His lips slammed into Hers, a rough kiss that tasted of yearning long repressed. His fingers dug into Her hips with a possessive grip, while his tongue invaded Her mouth, wet and prying. He pulled away breathless.

"I know You are to wed the Champion," he said. "But I also know You have no intention of following through with this. The Artist has left Your favor, and I've been wanting to kiss You for some time now." He took Her chin, bringing Her closer. "The Artist is a fool. You should reserve Your affection for a man who knows better."

Leila stared at him, digesting each strange sensation—his breath on Her face, his armor digging into Her ribs. She pressed Her hands to his breastplate. "Did you know, the moment I first saw you, I was taken aback by how handsome you are."

He smiled. "Is that so?"

"I thought you very well might've been the most beautiful creature I'd ever seen. And when you came to make My acquaintance, I swear, I felt as though My heart would burst free from My chest."

As Asher leaned in for another kiss, She turned Her cheek. "Such a shame all those feelings vanished once you fucked My sister."

Asher's gaze became wide, confused, then aghast.

"Step aside, please," Leila said.

A long silence passed, the man before Her—engulfing Her—processing Her demand. He dropped his arms and backed away, smaller than he'd been before, as if obeying Her will had cut him off at the knees. She retreated into Her chamber.

Leila took a seat on the edge of Her bed, Asher's intrusion still fresh on Her lips. She wiped Her mouth to be free of him, yet still She felt caged, the walls around Her sinking in. Cosima's hand on Tobias's thigh. *Dammit*, She didn't need this. She closed Her eyes, imagining Her version of freedom, allowing the vision to take Her away.

An evening breeze dampened by rainfall swept the hair from Her neck, carrying the stale scent of dust and rubble. The watchtower. She opened Her eyes, ready to feast Her gaze on the rolling hills.

Her view was blocked by a narrow frame, a mane of black hair. A man stood ahead staring out at the realm, his shoulders rising and falling with a deep breath.

He stepped onto the watchtower sill.

"Hylas?"

The Senator stumbled, flailing as he regained his balance. "Dear God, You scared me. I mean, pardon my language, Leila. I mean—"

"Were you going to jump?"

Hylas hopped down from the sill. "No. I was...looking for something." His eyes widened. "Oh God, is it blasphemous to lie to The Savior? *Shit*, my language!"

"What the hell were you thinking?"

"I... I just..." His lip wobbled, and tears tracked down his freckled face.

"Oh no, please don't cry."

She took his trembling hands, grateful that She, for once, wasn't the one crumbling. The Senator felt delicate in Her hold like weathered parchment, and She kept Her touch gentle, guiding him to the stone bench where he sat and wept.

"I came to the palace with such hopes and dreams," he said. "My father always said to serve The Savior was the utmost honor, and when the opportunity came, I seized it most enthusiastically. But this? This is not what I'd anticipated."

"This fortress is a prison. I understand."

"No, You *don't* understand. The Sovereign, he wants me to...to... I can't even say the words—"

"He wants to kill Me."

Hylas started. "You know?"

"Why do you think I hate him so much?"

"That does make sense..."

Sniffling, he wiped his face dry, while Leila eyed the empty sill. "So... that's why you were going to jump? Because of the assassination?"

"You are the holy gift of Thessen. I cannot... I *will* not—"

"Shh, it's all right. Breathe."

His chest heaved. "I don't care about the coin, or the power. I won't be complicit in his schemes. They are heinous, and unthinkable, and... and *ungodly*. But I can't leave the fortress. I've tried, but there's no escape. And if I defy Brontes, he'll torture me, then kill me. So either way, no matter what I do, I die. At least this way, it's on my terms."

A twinge pulled in Leila's stomach. "Do you want to die?"

"No." His shoulders drooped. "I had plans, Your Holiness—"

"Leila's fine."

"My mother came here seeking asylum during the Ethyuan civil wars. She had nothing, yet was welcomed warmly. Made a home and a family. I wanted to do great things for the realm. I just assumed everything would be much simpler. Seems silly now."

"It's a beautiful dream."

They sat in silence, their eyes on the night sky. Quiet tears ran down Hylas's cheeks.

"What will You do?" he whispered.

Leila slumped against the wall behind Her. "I'm trying to stop Brontes. Unlike you, I can't throw myself from a tower. If I die—"

"The realm dies." Hylas shook his head. "The Sovereign's plan will destroy Thessen. It's stupid... It's so, so stupid..."

"Yes, well, he's not *that* stupid. I'm not sure I can win this."

"You can. You *will*." He turned toward Her. "Leila, You are The Savior, Her Holiness, God's sacred gift to—"

"I know My title, Hylas."

"If anyone can defeat him, it's You. I have the utmost faith."

"You're a loyalist. You *have* to have faith."

"I've seen you in the Senate meetings," he said. "You're a beast! And I mean that as a compliment. Your fire is inextinguishable."

She stared at Her lap, fiddling with the folds of Her dress. "Thank you. But it's felt quite extinguished as of late."

"I can only imagine Your sorrow. Betrayed by Your father. Makes my troubles sound pathetic."

"We all have burdens. It seems ours are intertwined."

Sadness swaddled them both. Straightening his tunic, Hylas stood. "I know my place. I am not a brave man. But I can't spend my life abetting treachery. So I will see my end as a coward—"

"You're no coward." Leila leapt to Her feet. "It takes the bravest of men to challenge My father. I know very few who've had the stomach for it."

"The Artist?"

His words stabbed through Her. She took his hands. "Help Me. I need friends within these walls. I need you."

Resolve washed across his face. "What do You need me to do?"

"Remain in Brontes's Senate. Go along with his plans. Whenever you hear anything of note, tell Me. We can meet here, in the watch tower."

"I can do that."

"There's a traitor within the palace."

"Yes, I know," Hylas said. "Diccus, Wembleton, and the Shepherd. Erebus was among them, but he's missing—"

"No, no. Not them." Leila wavered. "Well, yes them. But there's someone else. A woman. Have you heard anything about her? About anyone at all?"

"No, not yet."

"They exchange messages. Slip them beneath the pane of the grand staircase window. I need to know their meeting place. Can you help Me find it?"

"I will do my absolute best, for the glory of Thessen and service to our One True—"

"Leila's fine."

He offered a slight smile. "Apologies, I felt inspired."

Leila met his smile with Her own. "I should go." Her eyes traced the sill. "Promise Me you won't—"

"I won't," Hylas said. "You can trust me. I won't let You down."

She'd heard those words before, and rarely had they been true. As She retreated to Her chamber, She prayed for this moment to be the exception.

～

"I LOVE YOU."

Leila rose with Tobias's full breath, Her cheek pressed to his chest. She dragged Her fingers down his naked form, losing Herself to the rhythm of his heartbeat.

He rested a kiss on the top of Her head. "I love You too."

"Never leave Me. Please, never—"

"I'll never leave You."

Leila propped Herself upright. They lay in Her bed, sunshine illuminating Her skin, but Tobias didn't waver. He stared straight into Her gleaming gaze, unblinking and calm.

"You promise?" She whispered.

"I promise."

"Do you mean it? Do you swear? Every man before you has wronged Me. I can't take another heartache. I can't."

His eyes bore into Hers, but he didn't speak.

"Tobias?"

Nothing. He was frozen, a statue. She took his face in Her hands. His cheeks were cold.

"Tobias, what's—?"

He was gone, his imprint fresh in Her sheets. She turned to the rest of the room, and the walls changed to speckled cream, the moldings rich wood. This wasn't Her chamber any longer. A large bed in teal throws heaved with passionate lovemaking, and a familiar voice moaned within the mound.

"Tobias?"

Leila didn't want to move, but Her feet brought Her closer, stopping beside the bed. Tobias undulated like ocean waves, while Cosima lay beneath him, her legs around his waist, her head tipped back in ecstasy.

"Tobias..." Leila's throat tightened. "Why?"

Cosima stared back at Her, grinning and lurching with each thrust.

"I'm The Savior." She let out a derisive laugh. "*I'm The Savior!*"

Leila shot upright, gasping. Daylight flickered beneath Her velvet curtains. Still fighting for breath, She cradled Her head, trying to massage the images from Her mind, though they refused to release Her. Cursing, She jumped free from Her sheets, dressing before leaving Her chamber.

Leila let out an *oof*, colliding into a cushy bosom. Delphi grabbed Her shoulders, stabilizing Her. "Calm Yourself. I've never seen You in such a hurry."

"Apologies." Leila glanced sidelong at Asher, who watched them with a surly frown. She took Delphi's arm. "Come."

As they veered away, Delphi peered over her shoulder at the guard. "What climbed up his bum?"

"Asher kissed Me."

Delphi chuckled. "Oh, really?"

"I haven't a clue what provoked it. I've been nothing but mean to him."

"Well, that explains it. Men love a bitch."

"Are you calling Me a bitch?" Leila said.

"It's not a bad thing. Bitches make history. How'd he take the rejection?"

"What makes you think I rejected him? I'm not tied to anyone. I'm free as a bird."

Delphi rolled her eyes. "Please. You're too much woman for that sack of meat. What would you two discuss? What fond memories do you share? Besides, You love Tobias. And judging by that gift he left, he's clearly hopelessly in love with You."

"What gift?"

Delphi cocked her head at a door in the distance—the entrance to the gallery. Reluctantly, Leila made Her way inside.

Servants huddled in a circle, chirping amongst one another by the empty wall. Tobias's wall. A head popped up, then bowed as Leila approached, causing the others to do the same.

"Your Holiness. Apologies, it's just..."

A parchment sheet, curled at the corners, was propped against the wall.

Tobias's Lilies.

Leila's breathing hitched. Dazzling color contrasted by fierce shadows, a mix of light and darkness. The piece was complete. Remarkable. And waiting in the gallery.

I promised to fill the wall.

"Hang it," Leila said. "Frame it, and hang it."

Her heart thundered as the servants worked. At some point Delphi pulled Her away, but not before She spied Her lilies hung for all to see.

"Do You want to see him?" Delphi linked their arms, leading Leila through the palace. "I imagine after the night he had he's reeling in his own spew, but we could arrange a visit. I could speak with him."

A gift from Tobias. A storm bellowed within Leila, inundating Her with feelings She wasn't ready to face. What about the other night? There was too much to decipher, and Her overworked gut couldn't handle it all.

The grand staircase loomed ahead of them, and standing at the top, staring out the courtyard window, was Brontes.

"Leila?" Delphi said.

He leaned against the sill gazing at nothing, a well-rehearsed lie. Seconds later, he turned down the corridor, his loose drape flapping at his side.

Leila bounded up the steps, running Her fingers along the windowpane, digging, searching—there. Parchment. Delphi appeared at Her side as Leila snatched up the note and read it over.

The time draws near. Await my package.

"Package?" Leila brought the slip closer to Her face. "What package?"

Delphi yanked the note from Leila's grasp, stuffing it back beneath the pane. "To *hell* with the package. '*The time draws near.*' That's *You*, Leila. Your death."

"But this can lead us to the traitor."

"We need to get You hidden." Delphi took Leila's arm, hoisting Her down the hallway. "You're not safe—"

"We *need* to get to work. Once we find the traitor, we reveal Brontes's network. This is how we *win*. We act now, or never."

Delphi gnawed the inside of her cheek. "Fine. We work."

Leila's gaze traveled the length of the staircase, Her mind swirling. There were so many loose ends, so much confusion to sort through. *Focus.* The Senators—Wembleton and Diccus. They were useless. The assassin—Kaleo. Too dangerous. She'd keep Her distance.

"Find Hylas." Leila turned to Her sister. "Tell him of the note."

"*Hylas?*" Delphi said. "Are You mad?"

"He's on our side."

"He's a bloody *Senator*."

"We spoke last night. He's a loyalist. He'll help us."

"You're certain?"

"No, but time is running out, and we haven't many options." Her thoughts built on top of one another, piecing themselves together. "Tell him to follow the Queen of Kovahr. Be discreet. Search for clues. You'll wait here. Watch the window. I'll follow Brontes. See if he leads Me to the package."

"*We'll* follow Brontes. I'm not leaving Your side."

"Wait for the traitor. She has to retrieve the note eventually." Leila took her hands. "Please. I need this to work."

Delphi stared at Her, exasperated. Her features softened, and a hint of a smile, albeit forced, crept across her lips. "I hate You for this."

Leila kissed Her sister's cheek before darting away, scouring the corridors for that sickening red drape. A familiar sour face appeared ahead.

"Mousumi."

The servant keeper looked up from her scroll and scowled. "Yes, Leila?"

"What's the itinerary for the day?"

"There is none. For You, at least." She flipped through various sheets. "You're to begin Your monthly blood in a few days' time, but other than that—"

"What of the tournament? Of My father?"

Mousumi raised a clean, black eyebrow. "Today is a day of reward. The Shepherd and Prince are spending their time with Your sister, *Her Holiness,* as we speak. The Artist is to spend the evening with her."

A weight dropped in Leila's stomach. "And My father?"

"Off the records."

"Why?"

"You're permitted Your days of rest. So is he."

Mousumi bowed before marching off. Leila continued on, keeping a brisk pace.

There. The red drape. She picked up the folds of Her dress and followed.

A century training in the armory, an eternity in the Senate room with the visiting royals. Leila waited behind a pillar, willing the black door to open, or become translucent, or maybe set aflame with the royals inside. She tried to appear calm, snacking on a peach or five, and when Her stomach was full She sat on the floor, glaring at the door without discretion. Hylas joined Her, waiting for the Kovahrian Queen as he'd been assigned, but his endless fidgeting made the seconds drag.

"What about the other side?" he said. "We can watch through the window."

"Rather conspicuous, don't you think?"

He sighed. "Apologies. I'm new to this."

The door taunted Leila, unmoving. Growling, She hopped up.

"Where are You going?"

She didn't answer, charging through the palace, past the entryway, winding through halls until a tall, dark door stood before Her.

Brontes's bedchamber.

Was it empty? It had to be, as Brontes was in the Senate room. *But what if?* Apprehensive, She took the handle and pushed.

Locked. *Obviously.*

She glanced over Her shoulder, checking for prying eyes and finding none. *Brontes's bedchamber.* Power poured through Her, filling Her vision with white light.

A four-poster bed covered in burgundy throws with copper stitching. A stately wardrobe no doubt filled with tunics never worn. A gleaming mirror and rug the color of wheat. Brontes's chamber was similar to Leila's, albeit smaller and lacking in gold—facts that delighted Her. She had visited many times in the past but found it fruitless. Perhaps Brontes was smart enough to know better.

Maybe not anymore.

She dug through drawers, beneath the mattress, making sure to leave every inspected piece as She'd found it. Nothing—just drapes, sandals, documents of little importance, trinkets that appeared sexual in nature. She swung open his wardrobe—tunics, as She had expected—then flipped through the linen and silk.

A glass vial fell to the floor, rolling toward Her. Sapphire liquid.

Elixir of purgar.

She picked up the vial, inspecting it. Another example of science blended with the magic of Her ancestors. In Her palm was a substance as potent as Her touch. Her mother, and Her mother's mother, and likely their mothers before them had all lent their blood to this concoction. Leila had done so less-than-willingly a time or two. "*The purest of all medicinal remedies.*" Diccus had said that once.

Why did Brontes need this?

Leila pushed through the wardrobe, trying to find the purgar's hiding place. A pair of harem pants jingled, and She fished through its pocket, pulling out a handful of vials.

The click of a lock sounded. Someone was coming. Leila threw Herself into the wardrobe, nestling behind the tunics and closing the doors shut. Footsteps shuffled into the space, and through the slim crevice between the wardrobe doors, Leila spied a hunched, grey figure.

Diccus.

He was heading toward Her.

Leila summoned Her light, and Her belly was suddenly pressed against cool tile. She lay beneath Brontes's bed staring at Diccus's ashy heels and leather sandals. Against Her better judgment, She poked Her head out.

The apothecary juggled several blue vials, dropping them into the very pocket She had searched.

But why?

Diccus pivoted toward Her, and Leila dissolved away.

She materialized at the end of the neighboring hallway, struggling to catch Her breath. A short time later, Diccus hobbled from Her father's bedchamber, scooting off without paying Her any mind.

Elixir of purgar. It didn't make sense.

Defeated, She glanced out the nearby window. The sun had set, a few final shimmers peering over the fortress wall.

The day was over, and nothing had come of it.

She trudged through room after room, kicking at the nothingness in front of Her. Perhaps She could continue following Her father, though the Senate room was empty, and She hadn't a clue where he'd disappeared to. Servants whispered as they passed, prattling about the Culmination, where Tobias, Flynn, and Kaleo would battle to the death until only the Champion remained.

The tournament would end tomorrow.

She reached the royal parlor, stopping at the sound of laughter. The doors to the atrium stood ajar, and beyond them Cosima sat at the dining table, lost in a fit of giggles as She gave parting to Flynn and Kaleo, squeezing the latter's arm.

Leila's sister, petting and playing with Her assassin.

"I see I am not the only one with spies."

The Kovahrian Queen took root beside the doorway, stony and aloof. Leila mirrored her stoicism. "I haven't a clue what you're talking about."

"Your friend. Tall. Skinny. Black hair. He tried his best."

"I don't know such a man."

The Queen snorted, then gazed out at the atrium. "Who are we watching? Your warriors, or the bitch?"

She may be in league with Brontes, but She's right about one thing.

"I would ask if it bothers You, seeing her with Your suitors. But Tobias is not among them, so I imagine You care little." The Queen gestured toward Flynn. "That one—he is useless. A plaything, no value." She turned her attention to Kaleo. "That one is a killer."

"What do you want, Your Majesty?"

"I want what is best for my realm."

"Our realms are supposed to be at peace."

"Supposed to." The Queen's eyes shrank. "What an appropriate phrase."

Tension prickled beneath Leila's skin.

"Oh look." The Queen's voice came out cold. "Your father is here."

She turned away without another word, leaving Leila to Her spying. Kaleo and Flynn had left, and Cosima and Brontes stood toward the back wall, his hand on the small of her back, intimate in a way he'd never been with Leila. He spoke in hushed tones as Cosima nodded along, and Leila's blood ran hot, threatening to melt the skin from Her bones.

As Brontes left the atrium, Leila thrust the doors open, plowing inside.

Cosima jumped. "Leila! What a—"

"Why?" Leila charged forward. "Tell Me *why?*"

"I..." Cosima cleared her throat. "I don't understand—"

"I can't control My birthright. I can't change My skin. My light. They are burdens I didn't ask for. Why can't you love Me anyway? Why must you covet what I have? You are beautiful, powerful, wealthy. Why is that not enough? Why must I be miserable for you to find happiness?"

Servants had stopped working, watching the two of them. Cosima glanced from side to side. "I don't know what You're—"

"Have I not been good to you? Have I not loved you as My sister?"

"Leila—"

"You said you didn't care for him." Leila clenched Her jaw. "You said he wasn't your taste. Is he your taste now? Have you changed your mind?"

Cosima laughed. "Is this about the Artist?"

"You can have any man you want. He is the *only one* I want. *Why?* Tell Me *why?*"

"Dove, calm Yourself—"

"What did you discuss with Brontes?"

Cosima started. "Pardon?"

"*What* did you discuss with *Brontes?*" Leila gritted Her teeth. "Answer Me."

"People are staring."

"You spoke in private chambers. I want to know what he said. Tell Me *now*."

Silence. Cosima stared back at Her, dumbfounded, then erupted into tears. "My dear sister, why must You treat me this way? All I long to do is serve the highest power." She cradled her cheeks. "I'm so overwhelmed. Is it hot in here? I'm growing faint. Help me, someone, please!"

She stumbled backward, and two servants sprang forward, catching her.

"I love You, Sister. You know that, yes?" Her face was sopping, Her voice even and calm. "I'm just frail, is all. I need comfort and care." She flicked Her wrist at the servants. "To my chamber, please."

They ushered her off, leaving Leila where She stood, a seething cauldron ready to spill.

"One day those tears will be real," Leila called out. "I promise you this."

Cosima gazed back at Her for too long as the servants escorted her away.

The space fell silent, Cosima's horrid laugh and ugly tears flooding Leila's mind.

Her sister. A traitor.

Leila left the atrium, Her muscles tight. Night had fallen, another blow to Her already ruined pride. The day had come and gone, and She had nothing to show for it. Her bedchamber door stood ahead.

"Leila," Asher began. "About yesterday—"

She threw Her door open and slammed it behind Her, sinking to the floor. It was over. She hadn't found the package. She hadn't revealed Brontes's network. There were too many traitors to choose from, and Her sister was one of them.

"Leila?" Delphi's voice was muffled by the door. She hadn't knocked; perhaps Asher had warned her. "Leila, are You—?"

"I want to be alone."

"Leila—"

"Please."

Silence. Leila leaned Her head against the door. "Did the traitor ever come?"

"No. She didn't."

Another loss.

"Are You sure You don't want company?" Delphi said. "I can braid Your hair. We can talk about frivolous things. You'll forget they're together in no time."

Leila cringed. Tobias was on his reward with Cosima. It had slipped Her mind entirely.

"Just go." She choked back tears. "I mean it, just... I'm fine. I want to be alone."

Another stretch of quiet. "All right."

Delphi walked off—at least Leila assumed so, as the air had become heavier. Scrounging up what remained of Her dignity, She peeled Herself from the floor, plodding through Her chamber as if heading to Her demise. She loosened Her dress, letting it drop to Her feet, then untied Her sandals, unclasped Her jewels. She stared at Her naked self in Her wardrobe mirrors.

Her mothers were there.

"I'm sorry for failing you."

Their gazes were ripe with pity. It was pathetic.

She fished through Her wardrobe, pulling on one of Her robes. Black lace, a favorite. Cinching it at the waist, She walked to Her desk and shuffled through Her drawers. The necklace. The Kovahrian note. Was there something else to be done? Another angle She hadn't considered? She racked Her mind as time escaped Her, flipping through clues and tools as if Her death weren't mere moments away. Qar's rings. Erebus's keys to Her empty vault.

Light glinted in Her periphery—the glass rose at the corner of Her desk, a gift from Cosima. So much had changed in thirty days.

Muffled shouting cut through the air, loud and heated.

"I need to see Leila."

"No one's permitted in this room."

Someone was at Her door. Leila headed its way.

"If you don't leave, I'll be forced to remove you—"

"Goddammit, just let me pass!"

Leila threw the door open. "What's going on...?" She froze. "Tobias?"

He stood before Her as if plucked from a dream, his cheeks red, his bare chest heaving. He exhaled. "Leila."

As he plowed into Her chamber, Asher gathered his spear and attempted to follow. "He can't just—"

"Oh, shut up." Leila slammed the door, leaving him to his post.

Tobias waited in the center of Her chamber, hands on his knees as he caught his breath. He turned to face Her.

Large eyes, dark and disarming. God, why did he have to look at Her like that?

"What are you doing here?" She said.

"I had to see you."

"Why?"

"You know why." He took a cautious step forward. "Because what happened the other day was wrong. Because I made a mistake."

"I thought I was the mistake."

The tiniest wince flickered across his face. "I'm so sorry. I should've never said that. I don't know what came over me. I should've never—"

"But you did. You said it."

He swallowed. "I regretted it instantly."

She couldn't take his gaze any longer. She hurried through Her chamber, past Tobias altogether, and anchored Herself beside Her desk. "Aren't you supposed to be with Cosima right now?"

"I left Her," he said. "To see you."

"You should go back."

"I can't, Leila. I can't go back to Her chamber."

Every muscle within Her went taut. "Her *chamber*?"

Tobias's face fell. "Yes."

Tears prodded at Her, but She resisted. It didn't matter what they did together. It wasn't Her concern. She held Her breath, Her only means of self-control.

"I left to be with you," Tobias continued. "So I could make things right. I was only there for a moment—"

"A quick performer, are we?"

"What?" He furrowed his brow. "No, you don't understand—"

"Oh, I understand completely."

"That's not what happened."

"It's awfully audacious of you," She said. "Coming here after you've fucked Cosima."

"I didn't fuck Cosima! Dammit, you have to listen to me!"

"Why? You didn't listen to me the last time we spoke."

"I know." His shoulders slumped. "I'm *so* sorry."

Her heart lodged into Her throat. "I want you to leave." She cocked Her head at the door. "Go."

"I'm not leaving."

"Fine, then I'll just pretend you're not here." She turned toward Her desk as Her tears fought for control. *Stop it.* The crystal rose taunted Her.

Precious dove, I'd do anything for You.

"I didn't fuck Cosima. I *hate* Cosima." Tobias's voice softened. "But I did kiss Her."

Leila's eyes clenched shut, Her nails digging into the woodgrain of Her desk.

"I didn't want to." His words piled on top of one another. "You need to believe me, I didn't want to. When I kiss Her, I feel a sickness. A loathing for myself. For betraying you."

"You can kiss whomever you like. I have no claim on you."

"And that's the next thought in my mind: that I'm not yours. And that realization—that understanding—it breaks my bones. It *kills* me." He came in closer. "I swear, I'm not lying to you. She cornered me, wouldn't take no for an answer."

Leila went rigid. *What?*

"And when I rejected Her advances, She accused me of straying," he continued. "Said She'd speak to Brontes—"

Leila spun toward him. "Brontes?"

"She said my behavior was suspect." His expression turned bleak, his skin wan. "That She'd find this *other woman* and do something about her. I feared She'd find out about you. That you'd be punished, or killed—"

"Dammit, She already knows."

Tobias froze. "She knows?"

"She's known this whole time. She *fucking* knows."

He stared at Her, lips parted. "Then...why did She proposition me?"

"Because She's a traitorous bitch!"

Leila snatched up the crystal rose and launched it at the far wall. Shards sprayed across the floor, and She could've sworn She saw Herself in each and every one of them, broken and discarded.

"God, how did it all go so wrong?" She surrendered to Her tears, caving into Herself. "This tournament. I've lost my sister. I've lost you."

"You haven't lost me. I'm right here."

"I *trusted* you," She spat. "Made sacrifices for you. Took risks that left me vulnerable. And you repay me with contempt. I trusted you, and you *crushed* me."

"I'm so sorry."

A sob escaped Her, and Tobias's arms swept around Her waist, pulling Her close. "No, no," he whispered. "Please don't cry."

"Don't touch me." She tore free from him.

His eyes welled. "Tell me how to fix this. Tell me how, and I'll do it. Do you need me to beg?" He dropped to his knees. "I'll beg, Leila. I'll beg."

"Tobias—"

"I need you." He took Her hands. "I let doubt and fear cloud my instincts, but I see things clearly now. And I see you. I've always seen you."

Black and blue tore from his flesh, a vision of heartache. She closed Her eyes, freeing Herself from his pain only to wallow in Her own.

"Leila, I've racked my brain and come up with nothing," he said. "There is no answer—no outcome that leads me to you. Yet still, I can't marry Cosima. I choose you. Even if it's impossible, it's the choice I'm making. And I will reap whatever consequence it brings. But I can't be with Cosima. I can only be with you."

She couldn't fight Her tears, the wall within washed away. Every impulse urged Her to scoop him up, to love him, but She remained still.

Tobias deflated. "God, this is it. I've literally ruined everything."

"No," Leila choked out. "This is my fault."

"It's not."

"It *is*."

"I'm a fool." He stared up at Her, defenseless. "I've made so many stupid decisions, and I'm willing to pay whatever price comes from them. But I'm not willing to lose you."

"Tobias, you don't know what you're talking about."

"You're *wrong*. You need to know, I decided to end us due to fear and coercion. I thought I was endangering you. It was never what I wanted. You are *all* I've wanted."

She shook Her head. "God, there's so much you don't know. And I fear your reaction when you discover it."

"You have me regardless. No matter what is said and done, you have me." He pressed Her hand to his chest, his heart thumping against Her palm. "It's yours. *I'm* yours. And all that's left is for you to be mine."

Fire bombarded Her touch, bright and blazing. *Holy light.* No, this was different—strong enough to blind Her, an amalgamation of every color, all within Tobias. It bled from his chest, building with each beat of his heart, then seeped through Her veins, filling the empty places within Her. She was warm. Whole.

Loved.

"Please, Leila." His voice wavered. "Say you'll be mine. Please."

The light surged through him, its message singular.

He loves Me.

"I'll be yours," She said.

Tobias choked. "You will?"

"I will."

He leapt to his feet, wrapping Her in his arms. A wonderful ache pulsed in Her chest, and She became free in his embrace.

"I'll earn your forgiveness," he said. "I'll never be so stupid again, I swear it." He wiped Her cheeks. "Leila, please don't cry."

"Oh, shut up, you're crying too."

"But I deserve it. This trouble is all my doing, I have no one to blame but myself."

"That's not true," She said. "I should've been frank with you. I should've told you everything weeks ago, the moment you entered the palace."

"No, stop it."

"I'm so sorry—"

"Leila, hear me. You are my greatest gift—the one beacon of light in this hellish place." He grabbed Her hand, bringing it to his chest. "You are mine. And you should apologize for nothing."

Pearlescent light—Tobias's love. She threw Her arms around his neck and kissed him, drinking up his adoration and giving him all of Hers in return.

"I want to hear everything," he said. "Whatever you have to say. I'll listen intently. I won't say a word." He took Her face in his hands. "Are we all right?"

She gave a hasty nod. "Yes, darling..."

Her words disappeared within a kiss, their bodies melding into one another. Everything She'd wanted was at Her fingertips—Tobias's soft touch, his deep voice, the colors beating through him. Tremors rolled within Her, quickening Her pulse.

She had his love. Now all She wanted was him.

Taking his hand, She guided him along the seam of Her robe, down to the knotted belt at Her waist. She loosened it, and the robe swayed open, an invitation.

Tobias's eyes panned down Her exposed flesh, then widened. "Oh my God, you're naked."

"Not quite." She forced the words out. "But I could be..."

Tobias stared at Her, stunned. Her breathing hitched.

His lips plowed into Hers, a shock of a kiss that nearly threw Her backward. He wanted Her; it oozed from his hands raking up Her back, from his labored breathing, from the hard bulge digging into Her groin. She pulled him to the bed, groping and stumbling until they collapsed onto the sheets.

Tobias sank into Her, grinding against Her body, a wicked temptation. With a quick tug, She yanked his pants down and latched onto his ass—firm and tight, just as She had imagined. He wriggled and writhed, freeing himself from the confines of his clothing, and She took in his carved form, his bronze skin fading a shade or two at his waistline.

His cock.

A gasp swelled in Her throat. It was staring right at Her. Long, smooth.

Spectacular.

She kissed him hard, ravenous in a way She'd never known before. *I saw his cock.* It filled the corners of Her mind, igniting Her fantasies, leaving Her burning up and wet. With a grab and a roll, Tobias flipped Her on top of him, ripping Her robe free and tossing it aside. *So strong. So bold.* His palpable gaze swept Her naked body.

"Oh my God, you're so beautiful." His eyes lit up. "Oh my God, you're perfect."

His hands followed the path of his gaze, tracing Her hips, massaging Her breasts. Delicate waves fluttered within Her at each nip and caress, rippling beneath Her skin. His mouth moved from Her breasts to Her neck, and the pleasure surged in heavy pulses, a beating drum between Her legs. She grabbed hold of his cock, giving long, firm strokes. *Like polishing silver* Faun once said, and She must've been right, as Tobias groaned into Leila's ear, gripping tight at Her ass. His hands and lips molded Her like clay, an artist through and through. She craved more.

Tobias broke free from their kiss. "Leila, I need you to know, all I want is you. I don't want The Savior. I've never wanted The Savior. I just want you. I..."

The fire within Her died.

She hadn't told him.

"Leila?" Tobias said.

He doesn't know. Her heartbeat reignited, lit with something ugly. Fearful.

Tobias's eyes widened. "No no no, wait, what happened?"

Her tears erupted. She rolled off him, cowering beneath a sheet.

"Was it something I said?" He hovered close. "If it's what I said, I take it back."

"God, you don't understand."

"You're right, I don't understand. I'm very, very confused."

She spoke between sobs. "You have me utterly terrified."

"No, that's not what I wanted. Please, I hate to see you cry."

I don't want The Savior. The words replayed in Her mind, along with the taunts of Her father. She winced, forcing past the torment. "Nothing's changed. We've made up, but the problem's still there. Nothing's fixed."

"Then we'll fix it," he said. "How do we fix it?"

"I have to tell you everything."

"All right then, tell me."

I'm The Savior. She burst into tears.

"Leila!"

"Everything will change, and you'll never forgive me," She cried.

"Why would you say that?"

"I haven't been forthcoming with you..."

"About what?" His face dropped. "Oh my God, are you betrothed?"

"No, it's bigger than that."

"*Bigger?* Are you *married?*"

"Tobias, *no.*"

"Is there someone else?" he said. "Please tell me there's no one else. I'd die."

"There's no one else. There's only you."

"Then tell me what it is." He waited, his gaze probing. "Does it have to do with Brontes?"

She nodded. Her power had shriveled away, and She buried Her face into Her pillow.

"Leila darling, don't turn away from me." Tobias scooped Her up into his embrace. "You don't have to say anything right now."

"But I need to. Before anything else happens between us, I need to. It wouldn't be right."

"Then nothing has to happen. I'll wait for as long as you need."

She met his gaze. "You're not leaving?"

Tobias shook his head. "I want to know everything, but I won't force you. You'll tell me when you're good and ready. And until then, I'll be right here."

His fingers slid through Her hair, a soft caress that stilled Her heartbeat. This beautiful man—everything She wanted, everything She was at risk to lose. She rested Her head against his chest, immersing Herself in his refracting light.

I'm The Savior.

This time, She would get it right.

❧ 32 ☙

THE PACKAGE

S oft lips brushed Her shoulder. Again, at Her nape. Each kiss climbed higher, coaxing Her awake.

The song of birds rang from Her garden. It was morning time, though Her chamber was cloaked in shadows, the curtains shut tight. An arm looped around Her waist, and the lips continued their march up Her neck.

Tobias. Her love.

"I was sleeping, you know," She said.

"Oh good, you're awake."

She rolled onto Her back, and there he was, beaming. Disheveled curls spilled down his brow, his jaw dotted with fresh stubble. His eyes drifted from Hers, slinking lower as pink wisped from his skin.

Leila laughed. "You're staring at my breasts."

His gaze flitted back to Hers. "Lies, you're staring at mine. Don't you dare treat me like a piece of meat. I will not stand for it."

Chuckling, She shoved him down into the sheets, resting Her head in its spot on his chest. His heart beat against Her ear.

Mine.

"You smell like peaches," he said.

"You smell like wine."

"Well, that makes sense. I've been drowning in the stuff since I lost you."

She gave him a squeeze. "It's a good thing you've found me again, then."

The happiest sunset lifted from his flesh—streams of orange, yellow, and pink. Her fingers danced across his stomach, creating colorful loops. "What are you thinking?"

"I'm thinking this, right here, is the single greatest moment of my life," he said. "And I never want to leave your bed."

"Is that because my breasts are pressed up against you?"

"No, but I do like that a lot."

"Cosima's are bigger."

"Don't compare yourself to Her." He recoiled. "God, I don't even want to think about Her."

"Did She really say those things? About Brontes and the *other woman*?"

"She did. Among other things." He stared at the wall, his jaw set. "When I told Her not to touch me, She mocked me in response, like I was miles beneath Her."

"You're not beneath Her. You're a good man."

His face dropped. "I'm sorry I kissed Her."

"Don't," She said. "You were protecting me. You should've never been put in that situation to begin with." Guilt stirred within Her, and She picked at Her fingernails. "I'm so sorry for what She did to you. She's become someone I don't recognize. My sister... Gone."

Tobias pulled Her closer, tearing Her from Her ugly thoughts. "I'll never hurt you again. I'll be good to you for the rest of my life, however short it may be."

"Short?"

"I left Cosima's bed for yours. I'm fairly certain that's not a forgivable offense." He sighed. "It doesn't matter. I mean it does, but...I tried doing what I was supposed to do. It turned my stomach." He looked Her in the eyes. "This is the only decision I can live with. Whatever happens because of it, it doesn't matter. This is what's right for me."

"You're not going to die," Leila said. "I won't let that happen."

"That's very kind of you, darling, but between my *transgressions* and the Culmination today, I find that hard to believe."

"Your transgressions will be ignored. And you're not going to compete. Kaleo and Flynn will fight alone, and you'll remain safe and sound."

"How do you know this?"

Leila went rigid. No more dodging. No more lies. The time was now.

"Does this have something to do with what you need to tell me?" he said.

I don't want The Savior. His words were an echo in the back of Her mind, but She pushed past the noise. "I believe you and I have some matters to discuss."

Tobias leapt into action, wrangling pillows and propping himself upright, a child ready for story time. Leila situated Herself between his legs, and a stiff bulge dug into Her stomach.

Hello, you.

Tobias furrowed his brow. "What?"

"You're hard."

"You're beautiful. And naked."

Warmth flooded Her face, and She couldn't fight Her laughter.

"What now?"

"I'd never seen one before," She said. "A cock."

"Really? Is that right? You've killed a man, but you've never seen a cock. I swear, you baffle me. Well, I hope I didn't disappoint— aesthetically speaking, that is, since we've yet to put it to work."

She giggled relentlessly, hiding Her face in Her hands.

"I suppose I have a confession of my own." Tobias looked away. "I've never... I mean I've done *things*...but I've never—"

"Fucked?"

"You're so blunt," he said.

"But you're so handsome."

"And you're beautiful. What's your excuse?"

She gestured around the room. "I've been here, locked away in the fortress."

"Well then, I suppose that's my excuse as well." A cheeky grin spread across his lips. "You've been here, locked away in the fortress."

Pride beamed through Her, making Her sit taller. "Well, this is all wonderful news. We can be terrible at it together. I'll feel much more comfortable knowing you're just as clueless as me."

The bulge against Her stomach pulsed. Was that a thing cocks did? Shifting Her weight, She lifted the sheet, admiring the polished bronze in Tobias's lap.

Majestic.

"Leila!"

She dropped the sheet. "What? I only got the briefest look last night."

"You degenerate." He laughed.

"It's fascinating. How do you even walk with all that flopping around? Seems rather cumbersome."

"You're supposed to be telling me something."

"Oh, right." She tucked his piece away. "God, you must think I'm mad."

His laughter softened, leaving behind a radiant smile. "There's something I need to tell you."

"I'm going first. You've said enough already. No talking over me, do you understand?"

"As you wish."

She took in a long, deep breath. "Well, for starters...you're not dying today."

"That's a good opening. I hope this conversation continues on this trajectory."

"And you won't be participating in the Culmination. You're staying here."

"The good news continues."

Her heart thudded. "Additionally...I'm not betrothed. Nor am I married. But that is expected of me in the near future."

"And I imagine laborers aren't the sort of suitors the palace is looking for."

Leila scowled. "You're supposed to let me speak."

"Apologies, you have me anxious."

She faltered, his words sinking into Her mind. "You'd want to marry me?"

"Of course," he said. "Isn't that the entire purpose of courting someone? To eventually marry? I mean, perhaps not today or tomorrow, but in my wildest fantasies I had imagined it would come to that."

"In your wildest fantasies, you married me."

"Well, we did other things too."

She charged at him like a battalion, Her lips on his. *This perfect man. Too perfect?* Frowning, She pulled back. "You're not just saying this because I'm naked, are you?"

"Put your clothes on, I'll say it again. Though I'll admit, I prefer you like this."

Another kiss. Her insides dissolved into a fit of contradictions, finding strength in his arms and weakness in the thought of them pulling away.

"Please don't be wonderful if you don't mean it..." She said. "If you're just going to take it back."

"Leila, I'm baring my soul to you. Laying out all my cards." He swept Her hands up in his. "I want you. No matter what you say, I'm yours. And this story—I want to hear it, truly—but all I really care about is whether or not it ends with us together. If it ends with this"—he tightened his hold on Her—"every day. Now finish your story."

His prismatic light surged through his touch, pulsing into Her palm. Her breathing stilled. "All right."

She gave him one more kiss, slow and smooth, as if it might be their last. The words sat on Her tongue.

I'm The Savior. This time, She was ready.

A fist hammered against the door. "It's me," Delphi said.

Tobias grabbed Leila's hips. "Tell her to go away."

"Come in!"

"Leila, that's the opposite of *go away.*"

The door opened, and Delphi strutted inside. "Good morning, Leila." She smirked. "*Good morning,* Tobias. I see our lost puppy dog has found his way home."

"This isn't the best time," he said.

"I can see that, but unfortunately I must interrupt." Delphi's gaze landed on Leila, severe in a way that wound Her muscles tight. "The package is arriving."

Leila's back shot straight. "The package? Now?"

"In minutes, if that."

The fire within Her ignited. She'd finally have Her answers.

But I haven't told him.

"Tobias..." Leila cringed. "I'm so sorry..."

Tobias furrowed his brow. "Wait, why?"

"She has to go," Delphi said.

"No, she can't. She was in the middle of telling me something very important."

Delphi's eyes widened. "You *still* haven't told him?"

"I was trying to, but he keeps interrupting." Groaning, Leila hopped from the bed, scampering across the room to Her mirrored wardrobe. Her mothers were conspicuously absent, *thank God*, but someone else stood in the reflection—a small, mousy man with a headful of curls and eyes like saucers.

Milo.

His gaze latched onto Leila's breasts, discretion thrown to the wind. Flashing Milo a glare, She yanked the wardrobe open, fishing through Her dresses.

"How can a package be of any importance?" Tobias called out behind Her.

"It is. Trust me."

"But it's just a package..."

"Tobias, *this* package requires her attention far more than *your* package," Delphi said.

He grumbled under his breath as Leila situated Her dress. "I'll be back shortly." She headed to his side. "Until then, you stay right here."

"He can't," Delphi said from the doorway. "You've forgotten the Culmination."

"He's not participating. He's *staying here*." Leila turned to Tobias. "Do you understand me?"

Tobias sighed. "Leila..."

"I'm only leaving because I absolutely must. I promise I'll return, and I'll tell you everything. Every detail. On my life, I swear it." Her gaze became pleading. "You'll stay put, yes?"

His shoulders sagged, but he nodded. "All right."

"I'll have Pippa bring you breakfast," Delphi said.

"But don't open the door for anyone else." Leila's voice came out stern. "The guard will remain on duty, and I'll return as soon as I'm able."

She offered a peck only for him to draw Her close, deepening the kiss. He whispered against Her lips, "*Stay.*"

Passion surged in Her belly, the warm pleasure of the other night alive in Her memory. *The package.* She pulled away. "I'll be back soon."

She leapt from the bed and shot straight for the door, certain She'd lose Her resolve if She looked his way. Delphi and Tobias shared a few barbs, and the sisters left, Leila wincing as Her door slammed behind Her.

A grimace waited for them. Asher wore his shattered ego for all to see, scowling at Leila as if She'd slighted him.

"Are you on duty for the rest of the day?" She said.

"I am."

"Good. Do not leave this spot." She pointed to Her chamber. "No one goes in there, is that understood?"

"Except Pippa." Delphi nudged Leila in the ribs. "Breakfast, remember?"

Asher said nothing, pouting like a petulant child.

"Is that understood, Asher?"

"Yes, *Your Holiness.*"

Delphi dragged Leila away before She could rebut, though there wasn't a need; so long as Asher kept watch, he could be as bitter as he pleased. As they rounded the corner, Delphi chuckled. "You dirty dog. You two finally fucked?"

"We didn't," Leila said.

"It certainly looked like you did."

"I didn't want to. Well, I *did* want to, but not until I told him the truth."

"I see. So the plan was to tell him You're The Savior, *then* fuck?"

"Essentially."

Delphi nodded. "A wise maneuver. Tell him while You're good and naked. The elixir goes down much smoother with a heaping dose of sugar."

A smile overtook Leila's face, and Delphi laughed. "What?"

"I saw his cock."

"Was it everything You've ever dreamed of?"

"It's big."

"Is it now?" Delphi shrugged. "Then again, You are a bit small. I imagine everything looks big to You."

Leila swatted her arm. "Where are we going anyhow?"

"To fetch the package."

"I thought the package was arriving?"

"Hush. He'll explain."

"Who's *he*?"

Delphi didn't answer, pushing Leila through a doorway. Sparkling gems, golden crowns, and perfume bottles. Hylas stood in the center of Leila's dressing chamber, fidgeting with his tunic, eyes climbing the walls. He faltered, then bowed.

"What is...?" Leila said. "What's going on?"

"It's me." Hylas swallowed. "I'm to deliver the package."

"Where? To whom?"

"To the Sovereign. I'm to bring it to his chamber so he can give it to...whomever else. I imagine he's hiding his source."

Leila sighed. Could nothing be straightforward? "So, what is it then? What's the package?"

"That's the issue. You see, I have to...procure it."

"Procure it?"

"He's requested jewels. A necklace or bracelet. Apparently he used to have a supplier, but his means have since been compromised, so...I'm to find something for him however I see fit."

The jewelry. Of course. She walked over to a table, snatching up a necklace. Wait—this was one of Her favorites. She grabbed another, shoving it against Hylas's chest. "Here."

"You're sure? They're Yours."

"I'm not exactly lacking in jewels."

He scanned the surrounding pieces as if to validate Her claim. A wavering breath filled his lungs, and he trembled as he exhaled.

"It'll be all right," Leila said. "Bring him the necklace. I'll follow."

"And then?"

"And then we catch the bitch." Delphi leaned against the wall, smirking.

Hylas didn't seem to appreciate her flippancy, gripping the necklace like a lifeline. Leila cocked Her head at the door. "Go on."

"I thought You were following?"

"From a distance. No one can see us together, Hylas."

"Right." He shook himself. "Apologies, I'm learning."

Leila forced a smile, gesturing for the door. He slipped away from the dressing room in a dense green cloud, and Leila and Delphi shared a knowing glance before following.

It wasn't hard to track Hylas, as spots of terror trailed him like breadcrumbs. The sisters walked in silence, aloof on the outside, a storm of nerves within. They stopped at the corridor to Brontes's chamber, hiding behind the adjacent corner. Hylas already stood at the door, his green cloud filling the hallway. Two knocks, and then he waited.

The door hinges creaked.

"Your Highness," Hylas croaked. "The package, as requested."

Brontes grunted, the necklace jingling as it passed from Senator to Sovereign.

"Is there anything else I can—?"

The door slammed shut, followed by a heavy exhale. Hylas tumbled around the corner, nearly colliding into Leila and Delphi.

"Heavens." He staggered to a halt. "Didn't know you were here yet."

"He took the necklace?" Leila said.

Hylas nodded. "What now?"

Leila peered around the corner; the door was still shut, Her father tucked away doing God knows what. Servants came down the corridor, and Leila ducked, shielding Herself. "I have to go inside."

"What?" Hylas said. "How?"

"I can't stay out here. It's too conspicuous. What if the traitor is meeting him at his chamber? She'll see Me and run."

Delphi crossed her arms. "And if Brontes discovers You in his bedchamber?"

"He won't. I promise."

The servants walked past, starting, then bowing at Leila before heading off. She was too visible.

"Your job is done." Leila offered Hylas what She hoped was a comforting smile. "Continue with your day as if nothing is amiss. If you hear anything of note, find us." She turned to Delphi. "Wait out here... somewhere. Find a place to hide. I don't know."

"How very specific."

There wasn't time to argue. Kissing Delphi's cheek, She summoned Her light.

Brontes's chamber.

White rays gave way to blackness, the space around Her cramped with linen. She was hunched in Brontes's wardrobe, wedged between his harem pants and unworn tunics. She pressed Her ear to the wardrobe door. Silence. Cringing, She pushed the slightest bit on the wooden slabs, allowing the doors to part.

A rug. A bed. Brontes was out of view, perhaps scrawling some nonsense at his desk or doing something repugnant She'd rather not see. *Or maybe he's gone.* Memories of the hidden tunnel bombarded Her thoughts, but She shook them aside. He was there. He had to be.

The quiet picked at Her for too long before a knock sounded at the door.

The traitor.

"What?" Brontes shouted.

The door crept open. "Your Highness. A word?"

Leila's throat swelled shut.

She knew that voice.

"Be brief," Brontes said. "I have a meeting."

A silk gown glided into view. Leila's chest burned, a blaze powerful enough to match the woman's fiery red hair.

Cosima.

It can't be. Leila knew Cosima had turned, but *the* secret traitor? *It doesn't make sense.* Why didn't she inform Brontes of the switch from the beginning, long before Wembleton had done so?

Cosima went rigid. "Your Highness, I...wasn't able to fulfill your request."

A chair slid across the floor. "Repeat yourself," Brontes said.

"The Artist. I wasn't able to sway him."

"You didn't fuck him, is what you mean."

Leila winced.

"He was disagreeable, to say the least."

"So pin him down!" Brontes spat. "Sit on his cock and ride it wet. Cover his mouth if you have to! God, stupid woman."

"I tried, Your Highness, truly. I was *very* forceful."

"Not forceful enough."

Cosima staggered backward as Brontes stomped into view, while Leila's hands shook at Her sides, fueled with rage.

"He pushed me aside. Threw me, really, like a madman." Cosima watched Brontes pace. "I can try again—"

"The opportunity's gone. Today's the Culmination." He massaged his beard. "*God dammit.* How many times has She blessed him before?"

"Just once," Cosima lied.

"You're certain?"

"Absolutely."

"Where did he go after tossing you aside?"

Cosima's gaze drifted to the floor, while pride beamed within Leila. *He went to see Me.*

Brontes read Cosima's expression and scowled. "Shit."

"The Shepherd is strong. He can take down the Artist, blessing or none."

"I trusted you to separate them. Challenge after challenge, Her light keeps him alive."

The rage within Leila crackled and spat. So long as Tobias was Hers, he stood in the way of Brontes's plan.

"He dies today, in the Culmination." Cosima spoke with assurance, Her chin high. "The Shepherd will see to it. You've chosen well."

Brontes didn't answer, pacing in and out of view.

"I'm still at your service, Your Highness," Cosima said. "Provided our agreement stands—"

"Our agreement was clear: the Artist in return for a crown. You had one task to complete. *One.* And you failed."

His words quaked within Leila's bones. *The Artist in return for a crown.* Did Cosima truly believe Brontes would allow her to rule at his side? How could she be so foolish? So *desperate?*

The quiet became thick. For a second Leila thought Brontes might kill Cosima, pull out a blade and slash her throat. Perhaps Leila wouldn't mind if he did. Instead, Her sister raised a suggestive eyebrow. "I'm perfectly capable of any other task you may require. You know this well, Your Highness."

Her fingers danced down her décolletage to her breasts, and Leila's stomach lurched as Brontes's one good eye followed their path. *Please don't.* Brontes lunged forward, grabbing a fistful of Cosima's hair. He shoved her face-first onto the bed, then pulled up her dress, exposing parts Leila never hoped to see. He fumbled with his pants and thrust into Cosima, pounding hard and quick.

Leila stumbled backward, falling into the tunics. Cosima's forced moans and Brontes's grunts assaulted Her, and She clamped Her hands over Her ears, trying and failing to block out the horror. Bile rose up Her throat, threatening to spill. *Get out.* But no package had been exchanged, and thus She had to wait, Her eyes closed and teeth gritted as Her father plowed into Her sister again and again.

A guttural groan, and the chamber went quiet. Leila dared to open Her eyes as Brontes walked out of view, Cosima still flat on the bed, adjusting her dress. After smoothing down her hair, she gave a cordial parting Brontes didn't return, leaving the room with the utmost casualness. Some time later, Brontes followed suit, snatching up Leila's necklace before disappearing.

Leila threw open the wardrobe doors, crumpling to the floor and unleashing the contents of Her stomach. Wiping the back of Her hand against Her lips, She clambered to Her feet, willing Her gut to still as She stumbled out the door.

Delphi appeared from behind a marble statue, a self-satisfied smirk on her face, though it dropped the instant She caught Leila's gaze.

"They *fucked,*" Leila choked. "They fucking *fucked.*"

"Cosima's the traitor?"

"No." Leila shook Herself. "I mean yes, but not the one we're looking for."

"What?"

"The package wasn't for her. He must've recruited her after discovering the switch. There's someone else. He's meeting them now." She glanced down the hallway. "Where did he go? Show Me."

Delphi led the way, the two sisters dashing through the palace until a flash of red appeared in the distance. Brontes was far ahead, and they tried to keep it that way, hoping to remain unnoticed. Her throat burned, Her heart pounding with enough force to erupt from Her flesh, but everything within Her came to a halt as Her father reached the dismal southern wing of the palace.

The hidden tunnel. That must be where he was headed.

Leila came to a stop at the end of the hallway, urging Delphi to do the same. Peering around the corner, She spied the far-off wall—the exact one that had split apart per Erebus's command.

The one Brontes stood before at that very moment.

Glancing over his shoulder, he pressed his hand against the surface, and the plaster opened up like a toothy mouth. He vanished into the darkness, the wall swallowing him whole.

"*Shit*," Delphi hissed.

They hurried toward the wall, studying it. *Where did he push?* Leila's eyes landed on a familiar marker—a tiny red crown. How many of these were scattered throughout the palace?

Holding Her breath, She pressed down on the marker, and again the wall folded away, reopening the portal. A glowing speck glittered in the distance, growing farther and farther away. Leila turned to Delphi. "Stay here."

"Oh, to hell with You."

Shouldering past, Delphi marched through the portal, and Leila hurried after. A rumbling sounded, and the wall pieced itself together, sealing them in.

Darkness covered them. Leila felt Her way through the blackness, latching onto Delphi's hand and squeezing.

They ran ahead, charging into the darkness while Leila trained Her eyes on the faraway orb. Step by step, the light became larger, and they slowed their pace to a brisk walk. The back of Brontes's head materialized, the torch in his hand painting shadows across the floor. Leila and Delphi timed their pace with his.

One step. Two.

Brontes came to a halt, and the sisters did the same, far enough behind to remain hidden. He stood at a crossroads—the same fork Leila had met when chasing Erebus—and waited, eyes trained on one of the faraway paths.

Footsteps sounded, and a light bobbed into view. Brontes dropped his torch into a receptacle and held out the necklace—Leila's necklace, its gems twinkling in the fire's glow.

"For you," he said.

A woman chuckled, the sound a pail of ice water to Leila's face. The glow grew brighter, morphing into the flames of a torch, illuminating a hand, an arm. Piece by piece, the woman emerged, first her fluffy hair, then her white dress. Leila's stomach caved in.

Not her.

❦ 33 ❦

THE CULMINATION

Leila pressed Herself against the tunnel wall, Her stomach rolling. When Delphi squeezed Her hand, Leila half-expected Her bones to collapse, crumbling into dust. She hadn't anticipated feeling like this—weak and weathered, the sheer sight of the traitor enough to beat Her down. Still, Leila couldn't look away from her.

From Cecily.

Dropping her torch into its receptacle, Cecily scanned the necklace in Brontes hands. "This looks familiar."

"I thought you'd like it."

"You took this from your daughter."

"All that belongs to Her will soon belong to you." He strung the jewels around her throat. "How does it feel?"

She fanned her fingers over the piece. "As though it's finally come home."

Leila flinched when Brontes kissed her, his mouth firm and unyielding, as if the woman were a roasted boar to devour. Cecily wore a smile Leila had seen many times before—soft and radiant, except now it felt sinister.

"Your father," Brontes said. "Were you able to correspond with him? What's his word?"

"Everything's perfect." Cecily threaded her arms around his neck. "As soon as you make the call, they march."

"Good. I have to go."

"Oh, but stay a while. We so rarely get time alone together."

"There will be plenty of time once we're wed."

Leila's breath caught. *Wed?*

"Spare me but a moment, darling?" Cecily took his hand, stopping him as he pulled away. "For the contentment of your future bride and father-in-law?"

Darling. That was *Leila's* and *Tobias's* word. Brontes wavered, then trudged back into the fitter's embrace, planting her with another far-too-aggressive kiss. *They're to marry. How is that possible?* Perhaps he loved her—except he stood rigid in her arms, impassive and cold, while Cecily beamed brighter than the torchlight, oozing tenderness and warmth.

A weight dropped in Leila's gut. The affection shining through Cecily days ago wasn't for Her.

It was for Brontes.

"Your message said the time is near." Cecily played with Brontes's drape. "Tell me more?"

"I've given the Shepherd his orders. She dies today."

Delphi's nails dug into Leila's hand.

"Today?" Cecily frowned. "But the Culmination is moments away. The tournament will be over, the Champion selected—"

"What's your point?"

"The original plan was seamless. The wedding is already arranged. We can host it tomorrow, even. She would be out of your hair by the evening."

"She can be out of my hair tonight," Brontes said.

"It's careless."

"She hid Her title. She dies, and no one knows—"

"Except for your staff." Cecily came in closer, her tone reprimanding. "Do you know how many servants dote on Her? There are too many traitors to your cause within these walls."

"So we kill them."

"You plan to wipe out your staff?" Cecily sighed. "It would be far too suspicious. Imagine if the Dragon had been successful. The headache that would've caused. You can't make hundreds of people vanish. Not to mention, you'd still have to do away with Cosima—*two* Saviors to manage instead of one. Darling, we've discussed this—"

Brontes snatched up her wrist, yanking her into his chest. "You defy my will?"

"No, darling—"

"*Your Highness.* You think we stand on level ground?"

"I will soon be your Queen."

"Today is not that day."

Cecily stared at him without fear. *Foolish.*

"Apologies, I simply long to see you rise to power where you belong. Everything I do is in aid to you. Brontes, Your Highness—"

"Your *Majesty.*"

Cecily hesitated. "I look forward to the day when I can greet you with such a title. Once you've taken your rightful seat as king."

Brontes scowled before releasing her, sending her tottering through the dirt. She steadied herself, her composure intact, her face a mask of adoration. Perhaps Leila would've pitied the woman if She didn't hate her.

"I can see your wheels turning." A smile sprang to Cecily's lips. "Tell me. I'm certain it's brilliant."

Brontes stroked his beard. "We'll keep Her contained. Once the Shepherd becomes Champion, we'll have them wed. Tomorrow, most likely. She dies, and we proceed as discussed."

"A fine plan. My darling is so wise."

Delphi snorted, and Leila could practically feel her rolling her eyes.

"I have to go." Brontes grabbed Cecily by the jaw, forcing another kiss onto her mouth. "I have a meeting with the Shepherd."

"Of course. I love you."

Brontes didn't return the sentiment, snatching up his torch. Leila wrangled Her light, certain Brontes would head their way, but instead he took a different path—toward the dungeon, if She recalled the route correctly.

The tunnels fell quiet, save for the crackling of the burning flame.

Cecily watched Brontes fade away, then plucked her torch from its receptacle.

This was Leila's moment.

Holding Her breath, Leila took a step forward. Another. Her sandal crunched against the dirt floor, and something beneath it snapped.

Cecily stopped in her tracks. Glancing over her shoulder, she swept her torch back and forth, casting a light over the depths behind her.

Illuminating Leila and Delphi.

Cecily bolted down the tunnel, her torch clattering to the floor. Leila sprinted after her, plunging headfirst into the all-encompassing black with only Cecily's footfalls to guide Her. She clawed at the nothingness, raking through empty air, dank heat. Hair. She grabbed a handful and yanked, collapsing Cecily and tumbling with her.

Pain pulsed through Her—nails scratching, knees lurching, or at least She assumed so, Her vision awash in black. She fumbled with the sheath on Her thigh, snatching up Her knife and slamming it into the darkness. A cry rang out, but the thrashing continued, until Cecily wriggled free from Leila's grasp.

Orange firelight burst through the tunnel, and a fist plowed into Cecily's face, toppling her to the floor.

Delphi hovered over Leila, Cecily's torch in one hand as she shook out her opposite wrist. She gestured at the palace fitter. "Go on. Secure her."

Leila sprang to action, dragging Cecily across the floor and propping her against the wall. Her head flopped over—unconscious—which gave Leila a modicum of time to strategize. *Secure her.* How? She tugged at the slit of Her dress, ripping the fabric into one, two, three strips, and wove them into a hasty braid. After wrapping Cecily's wrists and ankles, Leila slumped her against the wall. Blood saturated her shoulder, the mark of Leila's blade steadily seeping.

Rousing her took longer than Leila had the patience for. Finally Cecily's eyes fluttered, and Leila snapped Her fingers, then slapped her cheeks. "Are you awake?"

Cecily nodded, and Leila stood. "You're going to tell Me everything."

Cecily's lazy gaze panned to Leila. "And why is that?"

"There's a blade in Her hand, if you haven't noticed," Delphi spat. "What do you think it's for? Picking Her teeth?"

Leila tensed. "Delphi..."

"Don't *Delphi* me. She's a traitor. Been prancing around for God knows how many years, and the whole time she was trying to get You killed!"

Cecily sat unfazed, her hair disheveled, her dress twisted, wet, and red. A small part of Leila ached at the sight—a part She left to die. This woman wasn't the one She'd known.

"I have nothing but time. My sister and I are happy to stand here while you rot." Leila eyed the blood creeping down Cecily's chest. "Starvation or sepsis. I wonder which will get you first."

Snorting, Cecily looked away.

"Is something funny?"

"You don't have much time. Not really, at least."

Crouching low, Leila drew Her blade. "Well then, I suppose I ought to get to work straight away."

Cecily's jaw tightened. "Do Your worst. I'll never betray my king."

Leila met Delphi's gaze, a silent confirmation that failed to still Her nerves. This would be a first in many ways: the first time She'd do something so vile in front of anyone, much less someone She loved. The first time Her victim was a friend.

Not a friend. Never truly a friend.

Leila grabbed Cecily's foot, wrenching it while the woman jerked back and forth. Delphi wrapped the fitter's legs in her arms, stilling her, and with a deep breath, Leila positioned Her blade.

Toes popped free, tumbling across the dirt like pebbles. Cecily's screams ripped through the tunnel; perhaps someone would hear them, but no portal opened, not even when she called Brontes by name. The women were alone in the darkness, one holding a torch overhead, another sawing away one, two, three toes. Blood painted the dirt, but Leila deadened Herself to Her work, Her mind sinking into numbness.

"Wait."

Cecily's eyes were clenched shut, her chest rising in short spurts.

"Change of heart?" Delphi said. "That didn't take long."

Leila stood, towering over Her captive. "Start from the beginning. When did you align yourself with Brontes?"

"Child—"

"*Don't* call Me that."

Cecily's gaze flitted over her discarded toes before meeting Leila's. "The stars aligned us. We were meant to be."

Delphi rolled her eyes. "Oh my God..."

"Elaborate," Leila said.

"His family estate was near to mine. We grew up alongside one another, the blood of the military coursing through our veins. He never said anything, but we knew our union was inevitable. Two powerful families joining as one."

"You knew him before he became Sovereign?"

"He chose the path that would lead him to greatness. I can't fault him for that."

Leila kept Her voice even, hiding Her incredulity. "You left a life of nobility...to become a servant?"

"I left a life of nobility to claim what is mine."

"And what's that?"

"My husband." Cecily's jaw became wooden. "And my crown."

"What makes you think Brontes will give you a crown after killing Me for Mine? He wants the glory. He wants to rule alone."

"He can have his glory with me at his side," Cecily said. "I have no intention of undermining his rule."

"You know he's promised Cosima the same thing."

Cecily scoffed. "Young girls will believe even the silliest lies. She'll be disposed of when the time comes."

"They're fucking. I saw it Myself. Right before he met with you, he bedded My sister."

Cecily's expression wavered, a flicker of weakness in her gaze. "A man behaving as men do. We all make difficult decisions in the pursuit of our destinies."

"God, some women." Delphi paced the tunnel. "Who falls for this?"

"So, that's it?" Leila crouched in front of Her prisoner. "The death, the deceit. It's all to make Brontes king?"

Cecily looked Her in the eyes, an unnerving stare. Sweat dampened her brow, and blood crept down her breast, but she didn't speak.

"Brontes is already Thessen's Ruler," Leila said. "He's the Sovereign."

Chuckling, Cecily looked away.

Delphi's glare bore through the servant. "Say something!"

"There's a plague beneath our soil. My light keeps Thessen alive." Leila's heart raced, Her impatience climbing. "You kill Me, and you die. Brontes doesn't believe, but surely you must know this."

"Child, there are other sources of light. You are not required."

Sapphire filled the corners of Leila's mind—the vials of elixir hidden in Brontes's wardrobe. Her light, however watered-down, in medicinal form.

"There's not enough purgar for the whole realm."

"But there's enough for a husband and wife," Cecily said.

The realization sucked the air from Leila's lungs. She had been wrong about Her father. He was prepared for mass destruction.

"Brontes believes, he just doesn't care," She whispered.

"Sacrifices must be made for good to prevail."

"Sacrifices?" Delphi came forward. "You mean countless innocent people?"

"People die each day, lost to the wind." Cecily words came out light and melodic. "But men like Your father—they are remembered. Immortalized in the archives. And I will be by his side, living in the comfort he provides to me."

"Or you'll be dead," Delphi scoffed. "Brontes has a habit of killing his wives, after all."

"You would ruin the realm," Leila said, "lay waste to millions of people, all because of your unrequited love?"

"It's not unrequited," Cecily spat. "He loves me, and we will be together."

"God, I can hardly tolerate this. Just kill her."

Leila sighed. "Delphi—"

"She's delusional. Useless to us." Delphi resumed her pacing. "There is nothing I despise more than a woman who betrays her own for a worthless cock."

"Go to the arena," Leila said.

Delphi came to a stop. "Excuse me?"

"The Culmination begins any moment now, if it hasn't already. Observe and report back to Me."

"I'm not leaving You here—"

"I need someone watching Brontes. And I need to know if Kaleo wins." Leila stood, turning to Delphi. "Tomorrow's My wedding."

Delphi gaped at Leila for a long while before succumbing to Her will, casting Cecily a glare as she handed off the torch and trudged off. A pinprick of light appeared in the distance—the portal opening and closing as Delphi made her way to safety—and only then did Leila return to Her task.

"He doesn't love you." Leila met Her captive's gaze. "I know you know this."

Cecily remained hunched against the wall, her hair a sodden mess, her foot stained with blood. "He gives me what I need."

"And you're content with that? *What you need.* Sounds an awful lot like a dog settling for scraps."

"You know nothing of the world, child. Nothing of powerful men—"

"Oh, I know of powerful men. Far better than you do, it seems. And if I'd settled for My father's scraps, I'd be dead. Just as you will be soon enough, either by My hand or his."

Cecily smirked. "It's endearing, how You fancy Your Artist the exception."

Leila tightened Her grip on Her blade. "You never answered My question. Why does Brontes fight for a crown he already wears? He took My power long ago. Is it really all about the title? The worship?"

"I did care for You." Cecily cocked her head. "All these years. I've grown very fond of You."

"You conspired to have Me killed."

"That doesn't mean—"

"It means everything."

"I thought I mattered more to You than this. At least more than..." her eyes danced over her battered form, "...throwing me into the dirt, dismantling me piece by piece."

"Answer My question."

"There was a part of me that saw You as family, in a way. I'm to marry Your father, after all—"

Leila slashed Cecily across her cheek, sending her crying out. "What is Brontes's goal? Why seek to rule a realm knowing he'll inevitably destroy it? I won't ask again."

Blood tracked down Cecily's neck. She cringed. "Thessen doesn't matter."

"Then why would he—?"

"Thessen is the beginning."

The beginning? Leila's eyes narrowed. "Tell Me about Kovahr."

Cecily kicked Leila in the shins, then again in the gut, sending Her crumpling face-first to the floor. Her blade. She'd dropped it. Leila scrambled, hands fanning through the dirt, but Cecily snatched the weapon up and hobbled into the darkness.

Once Her breathing normalized, Leila grabbed the torch and ran after her. How had Cecily gotten free? Perhaps she'd loosened the ropes while Leila's back was turned. How far could she run with only seven toes? None of that mattered. Cecily had traveled these tunnels before. She had Leila's weapon.

She had the advantage.

Leila slid to a stop, squinting through the darkness. A crossroads. Holding Her breath, She strained to listen, ignoring the ache of Her muscles. Footsteps—to the left. She sprinted down the pathway, hoping it wouldn't fail Her.

The pull of Her lungs burned deeper, reducing Her breathing to gasps. How long had She been running? It was hard to tell with nothing but blackness to guide Her, but the throbbing of Her legs told Her She was wasting time. She staggered to a halt. Another crossroads. Tunnels spiderwebbed beneath the palace, too many to count. Where did they lead? Leila bounded down a tunnel at random.

Light appeared in the distance, igniting Her hope only to snuff it in an instant. A blazing torch sat in a receptacle, illuminating grey, stacked stones.

A wall.

A dead-end. Well, not exactly, as this wall almost certainly opened up to a wing of the palace, or some part of the fortress, or perhaps the pits of hell. But still, no Cecily.

I lost Her. No, that wasn't an option. She had to be somewhere in these tunnels. She couldn't have gotten far in her condition.

Leila grabbed the torch, heading down the path She had taken. Her throat rubbed raw, and Her nerves screamed, but She kept Herself steady, Her eyes straight ahead. Nothing, not for the entire stretch, until that familiar crossroads appeared. Four separate tunnels. She swept Her torch back and forth, hoping to get a glimpse of a white dress, of curly hair. The first tunnel was empty, as was the second, the third—save for a red patch along the dirt floor.

Fresh blood. Leila swallowed and followed.

Cecily's blood tracked down one tunnel, another, and all the while Leila's heartbeat surged behind Her ears. The red became thicker—puddles and mangled footprints. Her wounds were getting worse. She'd have to stop at some point.

The footprints ended.

Silence. The torch's glow faded paces ahead, the rest of the path cloaked in darkness. Cecily had to be there somewhere, watching, waiting. *Charge*, but Cecily was armed. With little options, Leila braced Herself.

"Cecily?"

The servant leapt from the shadows, Leila's blade held high. She pounded Leila against the wall, the torch falling to the floor while the two women fought against the stone surface. Cecily swiped the blade in a frenzy, but Leila latched onto her arms, keeping the weapon at bay. Grunting, She pushed Cecily off Her, sending her collapsing beneath her marred foot. Cecily lunged forward, slashing at Leila's legs, then grabbed Leila's ankle and toppled Her to the dirt.

The women rolled barely out of the torch's light, leaving Leila with shadows of movement, the occasional glint of Her blade. A blow to Her gut sent Her gasping, and a second later Cecily was on top of Her, straddling Her waist. Blood covered her chest, yet she fought with unrelenting desperation.

With a shrill cry, Cecily thrust the blade at Leila's throat, but Leila caught her wrist, struggling for control. Her arms ached, and the weapon inched closer, grazing Her skin. Gritting Her teeth, Leila forced Cecily back farther, prying at her fingers. Rage roared within Her, and She twisted the blade around, swiping it across Cecily's face.

Howling, Cecily dropped the blade and stumbled backward, allowing Leila to stagger to Her feet. Blood dripped down Cecily's chin, Her top lip split open, torn up around her nose. She slammed Leila against the wall, a fraction of the woman she was before, her weakness clear in her strained face, her loose grip. Leila lunged forward, ramming Cecily into the opposite wall again and again. Cecily didn't bother to hide her suffering, wailing with each attempt. Another thrust, and Leila kicked something against the floor.

Her blade.

As Cecily recoiled, Leila ducked low, snatching up Her weapon. Cecily lunged at Her, and Leila drove the blade into the woman's gut.

Cecily froze, her eyes wide. She drooped in Leila's arms, limp as Leila pinned her to the dirt. Leila pointed the blade at her neck, though it didn't matter. Cecily had lost the battle, and she knew it.

"You can't." Cecily laughed, her teeth stained pink. "We're family."

Leila fumbled for Her torch, illuminating Her captive. Blood blossomed across Cecily's stomach, spreading through her dress. She didn't have much time.

"Tell Me about Kovahr," Leila barked. "Tell Me now."

"To hell with Kovahr."

"You've aligned with them. Tell Me the plan."

Cecily's breathing became thick, her gaze glassy. *Think.* What had Cecily told Her already? What could She work with?

"Your father." Leila's pulse quickened. "He's a man of the military—"

"He *is* the military."

"Explain."

Cecily coughed, then hardened herself, glaring at Leila.

"I understand," Leila said. "You won't tell Me because you know I'll kill him. You know he's weak—"

"He is anything *but* weak," Cecily spat. "He trains the finest. Brontes sought no one but *him*."

"Your father trains soldiers." Leila faltered. "For Kovahr?"

"For the purse."

Leila went rigid. The empty vault.

Her coin had paid for mercenary soldiers.

Her disbelief must have been plastered across Her face, because Cecily chuckled in response. "Glory doesn't come for free."

"Brontes doesn't need sellswords. Thessen has an army." Leila waited for a response, then pressed Her blade deeper against Cecily's throat. "Tell me about Kovahr."

"Kovahr dies first," Cecily murmured.

"Kovahr is your ally, I saw the note—"

"I knew it would work. I knew the people would see and believe." A crimson smile spread across her face. "My father... He's such a learned man. Knows all the dialects. I could never hope to achieve his greatness."

Leila lurched backward. "Your father wrote the note."

"To place beside Your corpse."

Sickness plowed through Leila's gut. "Brontes is framing Kovahr for My murder?"

"My darling will wage war against the north, then every other realm in his way. He will make the world his own. Everyone will bow before their king."

The churning of Leila's insides turned violent. The planning, the tournament, each intricate maneuver—it all made sense. This wasn't about Thessen, or even Leila. Her death would be a spectacle—the beginnings of a war. Brontes would conquer the other realms.

Brontes would colonize.

"I love him, You know." Cecily was barely lucid, her voice slurred. "He's a flawed man, but they all are."

"You don't love My father. You would've never spoken if that were so."

"It doesn't matter. Brontes has an army, and You have nothing but Your black shadow and Your precious light."

Cecily's delirious laughter ate at Leila, prodding at Her mounting rage. Leila dug Her blade into Cecily's throat, blood spurting as the soft flesh split apart.

"Goodbye, Cecily."

Cecily's mouth hung open, gaping like a caught fish—marred and coated in crimson, a mess of a corpse mangled by Leila's hand.

Leila's knees wobbled as She stood. She had imagined this moment differently—the fight of Her life, Her ultimate triumph. Instead She was exhausted and launched headfirst into a war.

She wiped Her blade dry. *What now? I could kill Brontes.* But what about Cecily's father? She didn't know how to track him. *I should warn the Kovahrian Queen.* But she was surely at the Culmination alongside Brontes at that very moment.

Tobias. She was going to tell him the truth. She had promised.

Her hands trembled, but still She closed Her eyes, summoning Her light.

My bedchamber.

Birds warbled in the distance. She had arrived, but She refused to open Her eyes, afraid of what would happen next. *Tell him while You're good and naked.* But She was worn and haggard, Her dress streaked with the blood of a woman She'd murdered. Not only that, the story She'd have to tell had become so much darker.

I'm The Savior.

My father is going to kill Me.

To start a war.

To colonize and kill.

With a deep breath, She opened Her eyes.

Her chamber was peaceful, the drapes parted, welcoming the sunlight. The bed was empty, its sheets tossed to the side.

"Tobias?" She searched through the space. "Tobias, I'm back." Only birds answered Her. He must've been in the garden.

She headed its way, then stopped short. *My light.* She dug through Her wardrobe, snatching up Her black cloak and throwing the hood overhead. Calling his name, She headed into the garden, winding past trees, craning to find a headful of brown curls. She walked past roses and hydrangeas, even visited their spot along the grass, but Tobias was nowhere to be found.

"Asher!" She shot up Her garden steps. "Asher, where did he—?"

As She thrust Her door open, the words died in Her throat. Asher lay on the floor, eyes wide, neck twisted.

Dead.

A weight dropped in Her stomach. *Where the hell is Tobias?*

She launched Herself through the palace, running down hallways, screaming his name. Servants gawked at the new mad Savior, but their judgment didn't stop Her. Rational thought had fallen by the wayside, and panic took over, fueling Her limbs, sending Her voice climbing higher.

"Tobias?"

"Leila!" Delphi shot around a corner, sweat slick across her brow.

"Delphi?" Leila glanced across the palace, still searching. "You're supposed to be at—"

"The Culmination," Delphi panted. "Something's happened."

"I can't find—"

"It's Tobias. He's at the Culmination."

Leila froze.

"He's *competing*." Delphi sucked in a breath. "It's bad, Leila. It's really bad—"

Leila burst into light, turning the world around Her from marble to stone. She ran through the inner corridor of the arena, barbs and jeers resounding through the air, the rattling pews sending dust bursting from the ceiling. Elbowing past guards, She bounded up the stairs, faster, until She reached the top. Two golden thrones, servants with pitchers of wine, and liberally decorated guests, all shielded from the sun by a canopy.

The royal balcony.

"Tobias!" She threw Herself into the throng of people, pushing aside the Monarch of Ethyua and a shrieking Trogolian. "Tobias?"

The arena opened up before Her. Spectators howled, but Her eyes went straight to the sand—to Kaleo's head lying a considerable distance from the rest of his body.

To Tobias on his knees, the tip of Flynn's sword pointed at his throat.

Her final assassin was dead, and Tobias was about to join him.

Tobias's eyes latched onto Her. "Leila!"

He turned to Flynn, barking orders that faded into the back of Her mind. Glowing handprints marched up his skin, another blessing She hadn't intended, though that was the least of Her concerns. Blood covered him, slashing his ribs, crisscrossing his chest. The worst of it was his back, painted red from his nape to his waist as gashes upon gashes tore through his flesh.

"Get rid of her!" Brontes spat.

Leila spun around, bearing Her blade as guards swarmed Her. "Any closer and I gut you. You know I will."

Cosima rose from her throne—*Leila's* throne—and approached. "Leila—"

Leila recoiled, Her blade readied. "Don't touch Me, you vile *bitch*."

The pews gasped, but Leila didn't falter, glaring at Her sister—a traitor.

"Leila..." Tobias's voice awakened Her from Her spell. She turned to the arena, Her gut twisting. So much blood.

"Tobias," She said. "Oh My God..."

"There is no darkness when you're near. You are the light. You are everything." His chest rose and fell. "I love you, Leila. So much. I love you."

Disarray ensued around Her, a vague obscurity in Her peripheral vision. She reveled in Tobias's penetrating gaze, the rawness of his words, the glowing handprints across his body. Her handprints. Her man.

Tobias nodded at Flynn, who positioned his sword, ready to kill.

Leila gripped the balcony sill. "Wait!"

"*Do it!*" Brontes called out.

Clenching Her jaw, She summoned Her power. "*Stop!*"

A fire roared beneath Her flesh. Her body erupted with light, then became whole again, the rays of the sun beating against Her back, the gasps of the audience echoing in Her ears. Sand crunched underfoot, and a sweaty, armored man stood paces away, a sword in his hands.

She was in the arena.

Flynn tottered backward. "What the...?"

Leila charged at him. "You drop your sword, or I swear to God—"

"How did—?"

"As your Savior, I command you, *drop* your *sword*."

She threw back Her hood, and Flynn's eyes shot wide, the sword falling from his grip. Shrieks spilled from the stands, followed by the thumping of fainting bodies, but Leila held firm. There was no use hiding any longer.

"Leila?" Tobias said.

She spun toward him. "Tobias."

He stood paces away, staring at Her quizzically. Then he lurched backward as if struck by a bolt of lightning.

By the force of Her glow.

Leila pressed Her hands to Her mouth. "Oh, shit."

He fell like a tree cut down at the roots, his back slapping against the ground.

Silence loomed over the arena. Tobias didn't move, didn't stir.

"Tobias?" Leila rushed to his side. "Tobias."

She shook his shoulders, patted his cheeks. Nothing. Pulling his head onto Her lap, She scanned him over—so much blood, on his face, his chest.

"Tobias, wake up." Tears pricked Her eyes. "Darling, please." She planted Her hand to his chest, Her power flooding forth. "I love you too. I love you, just wake up."

A heartbeat thumped against Her palm. *Thank God.* Exhaling, She stared up at the sky, wrangling what little composure She could manage.

The hum of voices filtered into her consciousness. She'd forgotten about the arena, but the stillness had turned deafening.

Rows upon rows of Thessians gawked at Her, beholding The One True Savior.

Panic skittered beneath Her skin. So many people, more than She'd ever seen in Her lifetime. Flynn pivoted through the sand, his face twitching between shock and confusion as if he were trying to decipher how he felt. The royal balcony boasted an array of bewildered expressions, save for the Kovahrian Queen, who appeared entertained, even smug. Then there were Brontes and Cosima, who glanced across the pews, nervous.

Afraid.

The voices grew louder, a rumbling of murmurs, then shouting. They pointed ahead, the path of their ire leading straight to Cosima.

"Who is she?" Outrage spilled from the pews. *"Fraud!"* Brontes raised

his hands, trying to subdue the masses, and when that didn't work, he glared at Leila.

"Seize Her!"

The arena gates clanked open, and guards spilled forth, their spears drawn. Leila latched onto Tobias.

Away.

The noise vanished, and a bedchamber appeared around Her—Delphi's. She couldn't think of any other place to go, as Her own chamber had been compromised. Was She safe anywhere? Was She endangering Her sister?

Her fingers slipped, wet with Tobias's blood. How much time did he have? Tobias's head rolled in Her lap, and every visible inch of him was gritty and red.

Grunting, She linked Her arms with his and heaved, but only his torso lifted. Another hoist, and She dragged him across the floor, collapsing beside him. Blood streaked Her arms. *You're making it worse.* Her tears came out in sobs, and She clung to Tobias, desperate to keep him close—to keep him alive.

The door flew open. "Delphi, where the hell is—?" Faun staggered to a halt. "Leila?"

Several others followed, plowing into Faun's back. "Leila's here?" Hemera tumbled inside. "Oh my God, we've been looking—"

Nyx's gaze landed on Tobias, then widened. "What happened?"

"Oh God, the Artist," Damaris said.

Leila pulled Tobias against Her chest. "Stand back!"

One last servant joined them—Mousumi. "What's going on?" she asked.

Leila said nothing, Her eyes darting between the women. Cecily had betrayed Her. Perhaps they had as well.

"You're looking at us as though You're afraid of us," Hemera said.

Faun took a step forward. "Leila?"

"I..." Leila swallowed a sob. "I don't know who I can trust."

Hemera's face dropped. "We're here to serve You."

"We love You," Damaris said.

Leila didn't speak, Her arms trembling around Tobias.

Mousumi turned to the others, her face its usual brand of apathy.

"Hemera, fetch supplies. Rags, a mending kit, balms from the apothecary closet, a fresh pitcher, and a clean dress. Nyx—find Delphi. Alert her to Her Holiness's whereabouts. When you return, knock twice in rapid succession, then state your name. Is that understood?" She cocked her head at the door. "Go. Swiftly."

As the twins departed, Mousumi continued down the line. "Damaris —lock the door. No one is to enter without two knocks and a name, are we clear?" Damaris did as told, returning to Faun's side and standing at attention. Mousumi gestured toward Tobias. "Carry him to the bed, both of you. Roll him on his side. His back requires treatment. Stabilize him with a pillow or two." Mousumi met Leila's gaze. "We'll clean him up. Then You can heal him."

Faun and Damaris scooped Tobias from Leila's hold, rousing the panic within Her. "Please don't hurt him—"

"No one's going to hurt him," Mousumi said. "You are The One True Savior. We're here to serve. You may not trust us, but we'll prove ourselves faithful yet."

Two quick knocks sounded, followed by a muffled voice. "It's Hemera."

Mousumi opened the door just enough for Hemera to slide inside, a lumpy satchel over her shoulder, a pitcher and basin in her hands. "Cleaning supplies to the bed," Mousumi barked. "Balms and mending kit on the desk."

"And the dress?"

"To Her Holiness. She's filthy." Mousumi turned to Damaris and Faun. "Wash him gently. He's wounded."

"We can see that," Faun muttered.

Hemera appeared at Leila's side, smiling. "Let's get You out of these rags."

Leila stood loose and malleable as Hemera unclasped Her cloak and threaded the dress from Her shoulders. A wet rag dragged across Her dirtied flesh, but Leila could barely feel it, Her eyes on Tobias. Blood and sand disappeared from his body wipe by wipe, revealing the depth of his injures—long slices along his ribs, countless lashes across his back. The unmistakable marks of torture.

Brontes had done this.

"Once he's clean, balm the wounds. Damaris, take the task," Mousumi said. "Faun—you're skilled with the needle? Stitch the gashes closed."

Faun faltered. "I've never sewn wounds before."

"It's no different than clothing, except it's skin." Mousumi's eyes flitted between Leila and Hemera, and she frowned. "Hemera, tend to Her. She's shaking. See to it that She's soothed."

Arms wrapped around Leila, though they were a whisper against Her skin, as was Her new, clean dress, Her combed hair.

"It'll be all right," Hemera cooed. "We'll take good care of him. You'll see."

Leila convulsed, choking over Her tears. "Everything's so wrong."

"But You always make it right. Give it time. All will be well shortly. It's what You do. It's Your birthright."

"I don't think I can fix this."

"What's going on?" Hemera said.

Leila met the servant's gaze. "You really don't know?"

"You've been troubled for years—it's plain to see—but beyond that we're lost."

The room grew quiet. Damaris and Faun still worked, but they eyed Leila sidelong, as did Mousumi, each woman awaiting an answer.

Leila took in a wavering breath. "My father... He plans to have Me killed. To take My crown as his own, then wage war on our allies."

A string of gasps. "Leila, my God..." Faun covered her mouth, and even Mousumi's blank stare garnered a hint of concern.

"All his men, his guards, everyone," Leila said. "They're aligned to him. Even Cosima... She *chose* him. I have nothing."

"You have us." Mousumi cocked her head at the bed. "You have him."

Leila's eyes shot to Tobias—and the women around him rubbing balms in his wounds, cleaning the grit from his flesh. Her tears stopped falling.

Hemera followed the path of Her gaze. "Is he Your Champion?"

"I don't know. I ended the Culmination before it could be determined."

"Do You love him?"

The pang in Leila's chest tore deeper. "So much."

"Then he's Your Champion. You choose Your man, not Your father, nor his tournament."

Leila rested Her head against Hemera's, watching the others work.

"He's quite handsome," Hemera said. "I mean, not right now, in this state. I'm just saying, I bathed him. I saw *everything*."

Leila raised an eyebrow, and Hemera cleared her throat. "This might not be the right time."

Two quick knocks and a soft voice. Mousumi opened the door, and Delphi ran in with Nyx trailing behind her.

"Leila." Delphi threw her arms around Her. "Are You all right?"

The story flooded free from Leila—Cecily's revelations, the war—but the words didn't carry quite as much weight as they had before, not with Her sister at Her side, Her servants hard at work, and Tobias getting stitched nearby.

Brontes has an army. But so did She, in a way.

The servants retreated from the bed, giving Leila a proper view of Tobias—clean and treated, the havoc of the tournament stripped away.

"We can't stay here. It'll alert attention." Mousumi turned to the other servants. "We'll disperse. Continue our regular duties. Ladies, is there any blood on our clothing?" Her eyes narrowed. "Damaris, to the washroom. Change yourself. The rest of us, we haven't a clue what happened, is that right? We're here to serve. And if the Sovereign asks us to find Leila, we will search far and wide—we will ransack the entire palace—except for these chambers. Understood?"

"Yes, Mousumi," the servants said in unison.

"Practice with me now. Show me your oblivious faces." Shock and confusion swept their gazes, and Mousumi nodded. "Good. You're dismissed."

Before the servants could scamper off, Leila corralled them, lending each one Her shadow walking before sending them out. Faun lingered for a while longer, adjusting her dress to conceal the glow of Leila's mark. She gestured toward the bed. "He's ready for You."

Their conversation from days prior filled Leila's thoughts, cutting through Her like a knife. "I'm sorry. I'm so, so sorry."

"Don't—"

"We're friends, right?" She took Faun's hands. "I'm so sorry."

"We're friends." Faun smiled. "I understand."

She gave Leila's hands a squeeze before parting. Mousumi eyed Tobias over as if inspecting the others' labor, nodding in approval. "He's weak now, but You'll make him strong. He'll wake shortly."

"I can never thank you enough for your kindness."

Mousumi responded with her usual blank stare. "Right."

She disappeared behind the others, leaving Leila with Her sister. Delphi rubbed Her shoulder, watching Tobias as he slept. "I can stay here. Keep You company."

"No," Leila said. "Find Pippa. Make sure she's all right. Steer clear of Brontes."

"You're sure?"

"He saw My light. I have to speak with him alone."

Delphi didn't move. "You know he can't stay here. Brontes will—"

"Kill him." Leila's heart sank. "We'll help him escape."

"I'll gather supplies."

After her own blessing, Delphi left as the others had, the chamber still and quiet. Leila took a seat beside Tobias, who lay propped on his side, his eyes closed. Black-and-blues dotted his flesh, his upper lip split and swollen. She pressed Her palm to his chest.

"Strength and peace. Ease the pain. Mend the flesh."

She wasn't sure how long She sat there with Her light pouring forth, but eventually Tobias's bruises yellowed, and the color returned to his cheeks. She couldn't help but eye the door or flinch at every noise from outside, but still no one knocked or bothered Her in any manner. The servants must've been doing their job, and the thought alone loosened the strain within Her.

"Strength and peace. Ease the pain. Mend the flesh." The burn of Her power seared Her palm, and memories of the arena consumed Her. Tobias's face as he beheld Her glow. The light knocking him from his feet.

He wasn't supposed to find out like this. She took in a deep breath, exhaling Her command. "Make him as he once was."

Stirring. Two dark eyes stared up at Her, cradled beneath heavy lids.

"Tobias..." Leila braced Herself. "You're awake."

❧ 34 ❧

THE PROMISE

The silence was agonizing. Tobias stared at Leila, an unblinking gaze as palpable as a kick to the gut. *Why is he looking at Me like that?* Then the heat of the sun reminded Her—She was glowing.

She should've closed the drapes.

Tobias's eyes traced down Her figure to his own, stopping at the beaming handprint in the center of his chest.

"It'll go away in time," Leila said. "Once it's finished serving its purpose."

The confusion didn't leave his face. He scanned the walls, the window, while Leila sat at his side, resisting the urge to fidget.

"Where are we?" he asked.

"Delphi's chamber. We're safe for now. Most of the guards are still at the Culmination—trying to pacify the crowds, apparently."

He rubbed his head. "Did I—?"

"Faint? Yes, you did." Her words piled on top of one another. "Don't be embarrassed, it happens quite a lot. It's this damn light. Such a burden. I can't exactly change My skin. And I'm certainly not going to cover up. It's hot as hell most seasons."

He squinted. "You're The Savior."

"I was going to tell you. Just before I left. I was going to tell you."

I hate You. I want nothing to do with You. Every possible reaction ran through Her mind, but Tobias remained quiet, and somehow that seemed worse than the alternative. Wincing, he pushed himself upright.

"Careful—" Leila reached toward him, only for him to stop Her short. Retreating, She played with the folds of Her dress.

"You're not a healer," he said.

"Of course I'm a healer. It's in My touch, see?" She dragged Her fingertip down his chest, drawing a line of light across his skin. "All that I touch becomes new again. Stronger. It's My birthright. My duty to this realm."

"And all Your potions?"

"Water. Clay. Perfumes from the bathhouse. Some of it had medicinal qualities I'm sure, but most of it did little more than alleviate the smell."

Still no reaction. His words were even, his gaze unreadable.

"What of Cosima?"

The name drove through Leila's gut. "A woman of My court. An ideal replacement. She certainly looks the part, doesn't she? That porcelain skin, and those eyes. And most importantly, she was happy to play along. To be spoiled with attention. Too happy, it turns out."

Sifting his hand through his hair, Tobias gazed off at the window. If only he could say something, could love Her, or leave Her, but all he offered was bloody, rotten nothingness.

"The signs were there," he said. "I should've known."

Leila shrugged. "Signs are easy to ignore if you don't know to look for them."

"You must think I'm an idiot."

"Tobias…"

"God, You and the Sovereign even have the same hair."

"Stop it, please."

Sighing, he dropped his hands. "So, what happens now?"

"I'm not sure, to be honest. I don't know who won the tournament. It was either you or Flynn. Either way, I believe I'm promised to be married, except I don't know to whom. I might be promised to two men, even. What a scandal."

She forced a laugh that was little more than a squeak, while Tobias kept quiet and stoic.

"Tobias?"

Color lifted from his flesh, sending Her heart plummeting.

Red.

"Tobias..."

"You lied to me," he muttered.

"I never lied to you. Not really. I just...withheld the truth. But what I said to you—our conversations—it was all true. All real."

"Call it what You will, You lied to me. You did. You know it."

She cowered. "It was not without reason."

He met Her gaze, his stare sharp and jagged. "This tournament... It was all for You. You said You hated it."

"I do." She sat taller. "I'm the Ruler of this realm, yet I can't choose My own husband. No, I'm *assigned* one, a man I hardly know aside from a few brief interactions, *rewards* for all the killing. And it's *tradition*? Do you understand how absurd it all sounds? Men died—"

"For *You*, Leila. They died for You."

She shrank beneath his voice. "I know."

Red filled the room like blood fanning across the walls. Her heart raced. "It's not what I wanted. I fought to have it all called off, but Brontes—"

"Milo... He died for You. Zander... *Orion*." Tobias cringed. "My God..."

Tears filled Leila's eyes. "I'm so sorry."

"And they didn't know," he said. "*I* didn't know. The woman we were fighting for was with us the whole time."

"Tobias..."

"You could've told me at *any* moment, but You didn't. You let me remain a fool. And for what purpose?"

"Tobias—"

"Was it all part of Your plan?" His eyes glossed over. "You trick twenty men into thinking they're competing for Cosima, and all the while You, what? Observe? Manipulate?"

Leila faltered. "No, you have it all backwards."

"You said Your family was nonexistent."

"My mother was murdered when I was still in Her belly."

"Your father is living," he said.

"Brontes is no father to Me."

"Cosima propositioned me." He set his jaw. "Was that of Your doing?"

"*God*, no." She recoiled. "How could you think I'd be capable of such cruelty?"

"I don't know what to think. I clearly don't know You."

"You *do* know Me—"

"You play with my emotions." Tears fell from his eyes, but he squared his shoulders, straightening himself. "Did You think this was a game? It wasn't a game to me. I've fallen in *love* with You. It kept me up at night, thinking of what would happen to us if we were caught. It's the only reason I ended things. And it was for nothing? Do You understand? I'm in *love* with You."

"I'm so sorry." She bit Her lip. "Believe Me when I say, I never meant to hurt you."

"Then why? This whole façade, and for what?"

"I was protecting myself—"

He scoffed, "Right, from love and heartbreak, shielding Your poor heart—"

"I was protecting My *life*." Her voice came out booming, a thunderclap that stilled the room. She leaned in closer. "Brontes is trying to kill Me. My *father* is trying to *kill Me*."

The red dissipated. There was only Tobias, his slack jaw, his bewilderment.

"I..." He rested his head in his hands. "I don't understand."

"Did it not strike you as strange that he blesses the three most heinous killers in this tournament? That he pits them against *you*, My ally? This tournament was never about marriage. Brontes was grooming My assassin—getting him into this fortress so he could *win* Me, then *marry* Me, then *kill* Me."

Tobias didn't move, didn't say a word. Leila crossed Her arms. "Are you going to let Me speak now?"

He nodded.

"Yes, I disguised Myself. Yes, I lied to you. Because I needed to study My assassins. And I needed to dismantle Brontes's plan before it… came to fruition."

"The Sovereign is trying to kill You," he said.

"In the same vein in which he killed My mother."

"Wait. But he was devastated when She passed."

"Devastated?" Leila scoffed. "Is that what everyone believes? Well, perhaps that isn't completely inaccurate. He *was* devastated about one thing—the fact that I survived. I was never supposed to be born."

"No, wait." Tobias shook his head. "The man who killed Your mother…the Sovereign had him tortured. He cut out—"

"His tongue. How convenient the poor man was unable to speak of his innocence."

"I don't understand. If the Sovereign is to have You killed, why not just kill him Yourself?"

Leila rolled Her eyes. "Oh, what a brilliant idea. I never considered that. You have truly opened My eyes."

"Leila—"

"It is so much more complicated than that. It is more complicated than you could possibly imagine."

Her breathing had become heavy, Her words dripping with hate. Meanwhile Tobias sat in silence, his gaze yet again pointed at the wall.

"If you long for it, I'll tell you everything." Leila's voice softened, devoid of assurance. "Answer every question you throw My way. But I need you to know, unequivocally: I never intended for this to happen. I never intended to hurt or deceive you. This tournament was about preserving My life and My crown. It was never about a Champion to Me." She toyed with Her dress. "I didn't intend to find you. To love you, like I do."

His eyes flitted back to Hers. "You love me?"

"Of course I love you. I exposed Myself to the whole arena just so I could save you. Because I'm madly and hopelessly in love with you. What a pain in the ass it is too. Made a real mess of My plans, I'll have you know. God, *do I love you*, as if you don't already know. How could you possibly not know?"

Tobias stared at Her vacantly. It was too late.

She'd lost him.

"If you don't feel the same way for Me any longer, I understand." She shook Herself, wrangling strength. "No, you know what? I don't understand. I may not be perfect, but I am smart, and I am compassionate, and I happen to think My hair is quite lovely and rather soft. And, you know, I helped you an awful lot during this tournament. I risked My *life* for you, nearly exposed Myself on multiple occasions, not because it served any purpose to My endeavor, but because I care deeply for you." Her eyes welled. "Because I love you. And if you let one silly lie—hardly a lie, a *fib*—ruin all we've shared, well then, you're just as mad as they come—"

Lips pressed against Hers—Tobias's lips, a kiss out of nowhere, silencing the madness of Her thoughts. She froze while his hands snaked up Her back, and when he pulled Her close, She melted into his familiar embrace.

"You're not upset with Me any longer?"

"No," Tobias whispered. "I'm not upset."

"You were so angry just moments ago."

"Feelings change. You were angry with me last night."

"You were an ass."

He chuckled. "I was an ass. You were The Savior in disguise. Call it even?"

Her emotions flooded over, spilling down Her cheeks. Tobias tightened his hold on Her. "You're shaking."

"You had Me so worried. I nearly thought I'd lost you."

"I'm stupid, but I'm not *that* stupid."

Leila choked out a laugh, while Tobias wiped Her tears away, his gaze once again penetrating. He was staring at Her light.

"It's distracting," Leila said. "I can get the shades."

"No." He cupped Her cheeks. "If this is who You are, then I want to see You."

"If you start treating Me like some untouchable being…"

"I'm touching You right now, aren't I?" He cocked his head. "You said it Yourself, I know You. The light is a mere detail. Trivial, really."

"It's hardly trivial. I'm the Ruler of the realm."

"I imagine it changes a few circumstances, but it certainly has no bearing on how I feel about You." He smiled. "Or maybe that's a lie.

Perhaps I love You more now. Because the more fully I see You, the more I love You."

Her tears defied Her, and She burrowed into the curve of his neck.

"Why are You crying?"

"I just didn't think you'd be so kind," She said.

"I love You. No matter what shape or form You come in." He brought Her face to his. "If You're the Healer, then I love a healer. If You're a goat, then I love a goat." Leila giggled, and his smile widened. "If You're The Savior...then I love The Savior."

The tension within Her dissolved, a heavy breath held for far too long finally released. She was weightless, would surely float away had it not been for the strength of Tobias's arms.

I love The Savior. She'd heard those words before, but for the first time, someone meant it. Someone She loved back.

He threaded his fingers through Her hair. "You could've told me. I would've kept Your secret."

"I wanted to," She said. "But..."

"But what?"

Scowling, She mimicked his voice. "I can't stand The Savior. I *loathe* The Savior. Please, let me *hate The Savior—*"

"*Cosima.* I thought The Savior was *Cosima.*"

"Yes, but you still said My name. That you hated Me. I hadn't a clue how you'd react. And any negative response... If you turned against Me—"

"I would never—"

"I'd be dead," Leila said. "You understand why I feared the risk. And of course, the moment you find out, you're enraged. And I can't blame you. This tournament, all of your suffering—it was because of Me. I'm not blind to that. Seventeen men entered for Me, and thirteen of them were slaughtered by My father's bidding. You think that doesn't wear on Me?"

Tobias wavered. "Twelve men. You killed Neil Yourself."

"Oh. Right. And then there was Caesar, but we both know he had it coming."

Tobias burst into laughter, and Leila frowned. "Tobias, this is a very serious matter."

"It's ridiculous. This whole thing, it's just...so tangled." His shoulders drooped. "And You had it all on Your shoulders. Alone."

"I had Delphi."

Tobias's frown didn't lift. Taking Her face in his hands, he kissed Her. "No more secrets. Promise me."

"I promise. There's still so much to tell you, but I swear you'll hear it all." She raised Her hand, Her light flickering as She wiggled Her fingers. "This, however, was the most vital point. And the whole assassination detail, of course."

Tobias's gaze strayed, visibly consumed. "What's that look for?" Leila said.

"I just can't understand why anyone would want to hurt You."

"Power is very seductive. And I happen to have a lot of it."

He nodded only to wince. Stitches, bruises—She saw them again, standing at attention. "God, look at you..."

"I'm fine," he said.

Her hand danced through his hair, his curls looping around Her fingers. "I'm so sorry for what My father's done to you. You're kind, and you're brave, and you're *so* good. The greatest man I've ever known... And My father chooses to torture you."

"You saved me."

Leila's throat caught. "I love you so much."

He kissed Her again, and light beamed behind Her eyelids, refracting from blinding white to pink and yellow—his love.

Tobias spoke against Her mouth. "I hope this dress isn't one of Your favorites."

"Why?" Leila straightened Herself. "Oh God, you're not going to rip it off Me, are you? Because now's hardly the time."

"Actually, I'm bleeding on it."

Red trickled from the stitches along his ribs. "Oh, darling. Be still. This might sting." She patted the wound with a bedsheet, then pressed Her hand to it. Power pulsed from Her touch, until suddenly Tobias's lips were yet again pressed to Hers.

"Tobias, I'm trying to bless you."

"And I'm trying to kiss You. We can multitask."

Snaking Her arms around his neck, She lost Herself in his vibrant colors. So much in Her life was wrong, but this, right here, was right.

Delphi burst into the chamber without so much as a knock, juggling satchels and linen throws. "Oh good, you're not tearing each other apart." She dropped the items onto the bed. "Look at that. You got blood all over my sheets."

"Apologies," Tobias scoffed. "The Sovereign had me the slightest bit tortured prior to today's Culmination."

"A likely excuse." She turned to Leila. "There's a horse waiting out back. Help me gather everything."

Leila's stomach dropped. Tobias had to leave. Feigning a smile, She gave him a kiss. "You stay here."

She took root at Delphi's side, sorting through the trove. Herbs. Blankets. Blades. Tobias would need all of it. She stuffed the satchel, while Tobias watched with his brow furrowed. "What's going on?" he asked. "What are you doing?"

"Preparing."

"For what?"

"Brontes," Delphi said. "And the shitstorm he's about to usher in."

Tobias straightened. "But wait... Kaleo, Drake, Antaeus—all the assassins—they're dead. It's over."

Leila sighed. "It's not as simple as that."

"How is that the simple part?"

A shirt. He'd need that too. She tossed it his way. "Now's not the time."

"Of course it's the time. You said You'd tell me everything."

"Sweet puppy dog, it's a *very* long story," Delphi added.

Scowling, Tobias dressed himself. "You're the Ruler of the realm. Brontes is beneath You. Surely You have the means to stop this *shitstorm*, whatever it is."

"Except I don't," Leila said. "Brontes made sure of that."

"But You're The Savior."

"And I've been made prisoner for it, with no domain of My own realm. I'm The Savior, yet I have no control. Just My light. Nothing else."

"But it doesn't make sense," Tobias said. "Thessen is prosperous thanks only to The Savior's reign. It's for the good of the people."

Leila snorted. "Yes, well, when you act exclusively for your own self-interest, the good of the people becomes irrelevant."

"What if the realm falls apart? What if You're gone, and everything reverts to the hell it once was?"

Delphi stopped her sorting and let out a condescending laugh. "Love, do you think men like Brontes care for the greater good? Whatever lies beyond this fortress is meaningless so long as he owns it all."

"Then we'll kill him." Tobias's voice came out hard. "*I'll* kill him."

"You assume he works alone?" Leila said. "If he dies, I lose all hope of finding his network."

"God, I have so many questions..."

"I know. And I meant what I said, I'll spare no detail." Leila hoisted Tobias's satchel up and took a seat at his side. "But not right now. Now you're in danger. And now you must leave."

"Wait, *I* must leave?" Tobias gaped at Her. "You make it sound as though You're not coming with me."

"I'm not."

"Leila!"

She shoved the satchel his way. "This should be everything you'll need."

"No, Leila. I'm not leaving without You."

"My father plans to rip Thessen out from under Me," She said. "I can't let that happen. I have to stay here."

"Stay here and *die?*"

"You don't understand—"

"You said just moments ago Brontes left You with nothing." Tossing the satchel aside, he took Her hands. "But You still have me. If You come with me, I can protect You."

"It's not your job to protect Me."

"You've helped me throughout this entire tournament. Please, let me help You now. *Please.*"

Say yes. An impulse She had to fight against. Desperate, Tobias turned to Her sister. "Delphi, reason with Her."

Delphi exhaled. "He's right."

Tobias faltered. "Oh wow, I wasn't expecting that."

"Are you *mad*?" Leila spat.

"Brontes has us in a corner," Delphi said. "There's nothing You can do from here."

"I can't just abandon My people."

"You're not abandoning them, You're saving their Queen. And in doing so, You save them from destruction."

"Delphi—"

"They will suffer under his rule," she maintained. "Thessen turns to dust if You stay here. You know this."

Protests bombarded Leila's thoughts, but She resisted.

Delphi was right.

"Leave with him." Delphi cocked her head at Tobias. "Save Yourself. Then once You're able, You can reclaim what is rightfully Yours."

"You forget, this fortress is My prison," Leila said. "I can't leave."

"Yes, You can. You can shadow walk."

Tobias glanced between them. "Shadow walk?"

"You know," Delphi said. "She's here one moment, then suddenly, poof?"

"For the thousandth time, I can't shadow walk to places I've never been before," Leila groaned. "I've never left the fortress."

"But *he* has."

Leila froze, staring at Tobias. She hadn't considered it before, too hellbent on taking down Her father, but now the solution was blatantly clear.

Tobias was Her escape.

"Give him the gift," Delphi said. "He'll take You out of here."

Tobias's eyes widened with understanding. "Wherever You need to go, I'll take You. We can figure out a way to defeat Brontes together."

Freedom. Leila had dreamt of it for so long, but never did it look quite like this. *Running for My life.*

She spun toward Delphi. "Are you coming with us?"

"Later. You'll come back for me."

"*Delphi*—"

"There are people in this palace who are loyal to You. I can't leave them to be slaughtered." Delphi shrugged. "I'll round 'em up. We'll join You shortly."

Leila tried to find the words, but they escaped Her. Delphi crossed her arms. "You know full well I won't let that worthless shit lay a hand on me."

Absolutely not. She'd drag Delphi kicking and screaming if She had to. Then the faces of Her servants filled Her mind, along with dear Pippa, sweet Hylas. What would become of them?

"The watchtower." Leila's voice came out meek. "We'll meet there."

Delphi rifled through Her pile of supplies, snatching up a second satchel. "For You." She tossed it at Leila. "And I lied, there's two horses waiting."

"You sneaky bitch." Leila let out a laugh muffled by fresh tears. She lunged at Her sister and hugged her tight, memorizing the feel of her skin, the warmth of her embrace. The journey ahead suddenly reeked of betrayal, Her resolve splintering as the seconds crept closer to their parting. With a shallow breath, She pulled away from Delphi and into Tobias's arms, his hold the only thing keeping Her standing.

"We'll see you soon," he said.

"Keep Her safe." Delphi's voice wavered, an uncharacteristic weakness in her words. "She's the only family I have left."

He leaned into Leila, whispering against Her hair. "It's all right."

"This wasn't supposed to happen," She murmured.

"Everything will be fine. You are the strongest person I know, and I'll be by Your side through it all, no matter the obstacle. You remember —You are everything."

Leila wiped Her tears. "Where are we going? I don't know My way around, I don't...I don't even know My own realm."

"I know my way around. That's what I'm here for, darling." Tobias glanced between the two sisters. "We'll go to the Krios woods. They stretch for hundreds of miles. If we keep moving, Brontes will struggle to find us."

The Krios what? Judging by the emptiness of Delphi's gaze, she didn't know either. Leila nodded. "All right."

Delphi cocked her head at the door. "You should go now."

No more tears. Leila stifled their flow, feigning as much strength as she could. She slid Her hand up Tobias's chest, summoning the comforting heat of Her light.

"To the woods?" he said.

Not without My sister. The words sat on Her tongue, begging to be spoken.

My sister.

"Wait." Leila met his gaze. "We have to make a stop first."

A SHACK. THAT'S WHAT STOOD BEFORE HER, WITH FLAKING PLASTER walls and a dry, thatched roof. Tobias had called it a cottage, but they had always looked quainter from Her watchtower. Up close, everything was so small.

This is how My people live.

The mutterings of passersby nipped at Her, and She tugged at Her hood, hiding Her face. Tobias had already disappeared inside, but She'd insisted on waiting. *"For politeness's sake."* She'd promised not to lie anymore, but this one was innocent. She fiddled with Her dress, staring at the wooden door in front of Her.

What was She so afraid of?

"Leila." Tobias's muffled voice sounded from within the shack. *Cottage.* "You can come in."

She headed inside.

A crooked table, a fire, a rocking chair. This was the smallest room Leila had ever seen, and it was a home. A woman with grey-streaked hair darted between the cupboards, packing leeks and potatoes into a satchel, while Tobias crouched by a younger woman of his likeness— same bronze skin, same dark eyes. Naomi, his sister. Leila would've smiled had it not been for the sunlight pouring through the window, illuminating the space.

Holding Her breath, She lowered Her hood.

Naomi gasped. Leila wove through the cramped cottage, stopping as She reached Tobias's side. His sister was sitting on a lumpy pillow in a wooden frame—a bed, most likely—her legs tucked to the side, her feet feeble and grey.

"It's an old injury," Tobias said. "I don't know if anything can be done. But she suffers a great deal, and the pain is—"

"Something can be done. Perhaps not a cure. But something." Leila turned Her attention to Naomi. "Your back... Can you show Me?"

Naomi said nothing, her eyes lit with the same vacant awe Leila had seen a hundred times before. *At least she didn't faint.* Tobias swatted his sister's arm, and she came to life, lowering the straps of her dress and turning her spine Leila's way.

Tobias rested a hand on Leila's shoulder. "Do You need me?"

"Go." Leila gestured toward the other woman. "Help your mother."

He did as told, leaving Leila with the bared back before Her. She pressed Her palm to its curve.

Pain crackled against Her touch, bursting like lightning, and She yanked away. Cursing Herself, She slowly, hesitantly placed Her hand back into position, wincing as fire lashed through Her flesh.

"I know this is a stupid question." Naomi's voice was soft and sweet like a ripened peach. "You're glowing, and it's plain as day, but...are You The Savior?"

"Yes," Leila said. "I'm The Savior."

"And not the other one. The redhead."

Leila frowned. "No."

"Who is she?"

"She's no one."

"Well then, The Savior wields a blade and calls *no one* a vile bitch. That's my kind of queen."

Naomi's smile was warm, so very much like her brother's, but it waned soon after. "Do You know where we're going?" she asked.

"I honestly don't. Some forest, I believe."

"But why?"

Leila tensed, watching as Tobias darted in and out of the cottage. "It's best if we tell you together. The story is rather complicated."

Another bolt to the palm. Agony splintered through Naomi, a spider's web of burning rivulets cascading down her spine. A latticework of suffering.

"I don't have to walk," Naomi said.

"Pardon?"

"I don't have to walk. If it isn't possible, I'll manage. I've accepted my circumstances, and I will live my life as fully as I can without a moment's self-pity." Her eyes welled. "But if You could do something for the pain...I would be eternally grateful."

Her legs. Leila had forgotten about them entirely, consumed by the torture rippling down Naomi's back. They lay curled beneath her, ashen. Perhaps Leila couldn't help with that. But the pain was fresh and alive. She could work with it.

"I don't want false hope..." Naomi said.

"I'll do everything I can." Leila took her hands. "You have My word."

"Leila?" Tobias stood by the doorway, a barrow at his feet. "It's time to go."

They loaded what they could onto the two horses, latching the barrow to one of the saddles like a cart. Villagers had emerged from their homes, and Leila shrank beneath their stares.

After knotting the final rope, Tobias turned to Leila, pointing toward his shirt and the blessing beneath it. "How exactly does this work?"

"Imagine the place we are to travel. See us there, and it will be so." She looped the horses' reins around his arm. "Hold on. We can't leave anyone behind."

He scooped Naomi up against his chest, while Leila threaded Her arm around his waist, gesturing for his mother to do the same. Her heartbeat throbbed behind Her ears, and She closed Her eyes, stilling Herself.

"They're here!"

A horse charged up the main road—three horses, ten, each carrying an armored soldier.

Brontes had targeted Tobias's home.

"Shit," Tobias hissed.

His mother paled. "What's going on?"

"Everyone keep calm." Tobias looked Leila in the eyes. "Are You ready?"

She squeezed him tighter. "Do it."

"Seize them!" a soldier shouted.

Crested helmets and drawn spears rushed closer. Burying Her head against Tobias's shoulder, Leila breathed in his colors, tasting sugar and cinnamon.

She wasn't afraid.

"Hold on!"

Tobias's words bellowed through Her, the soldiers paces away. Heat flooded Her chest, branching through Her body in streams, and the world around Her disappeared behind a blinding light.

ABOUT THE AUTHOR

Jenna Moreci is a bestselling author of dark fantasy and science fiction, as well as a YouTube sensation with hundreds of thousands of subscribers. *The Savior's Champion*, her first novel in *The Savior's Series,* was voted one of the Best Books of All Time by Book Depository.

Born and raised in Silicon Valley, Jenna spends her free time laughing until her face hurts with her goofball fiancé and snuggling with her tiny dog.

www.JennaMoreci.com

youtube.com/jennamoreci

instagram.com/jennamoreci

twitter.com/jennamoreci

facebook.com/authorjennamoreci